– Acknowledgments –

A big, huge thanks to everyone who contributed to making this happen. Anita and Jeremy Walker, Amanda Bentley, Karyn Tulloch, Ben and Tracey Kreplins, Kate and Tim Brand, and Karen Weaver for donating to the editing process.

Ulyssa Kernohan, Kate Brand, Michelle Jennings, Anita Walker, Amanda Bentley and Cindy Glover for being my unofficial editors and reading countless versions of the unfinished manuscript(s)! So much love for you.

Ben Kreplins, Gregg Huntly and Paul Kappes for braving the chick-lit genre and vetting my man-voice.

Gillian Burnside, Jo Toyne, Jen Craig, Vicky Harris and Sophie Scotton for being my test subjects at various states of manuscript disarray. Your feedback was integral.

To the rest of my family and friends who have helped and supported me in immeasurable ways, this book wouldn't have been possible without any of you.

— Dedications —

For my favourite person in the world ever… *Tyler*, you are my greatest achievement. Thank you for being the gorgeous little soul that you are. You have kept me real (oh boy sooo real), and even though it's been tough at times, your cheeky smile has never failed to light up my heart. Don't ever let anyone break your spirit or dim your light because you are perfect just as you are. You are destined to be a great man my love and I am so unbelievably proud to call you my son.

I love you to the moon and back.
xx

To my other favourite person in the world, the most unwaveringly supportive and caring human who I know. Mum, there are no words to express my gratitude for your resolute belief in me. You've always had my back and through those hard times, you have been there to help without question. Parenting is bloody hard work, but you've made it look easy, and through your example, you have molded me into the mother, and the person, that I am today.

Love you
xx

And to the people who came into my life to teach me some challenging lessons, thank you for making me stronger.

Contact N.J. Ewing

Website: www.brandartisans.com.au/njewing
Facebook: www.facebook.com/N.J.Ewing Author
Instagram: www.instagram.com/njewingauthor/

Sales and Distribution enquiries to Brand Artisans Australia
Email: info@brandartisans.com.au

STORIES
from the
CITY

N.J. EWING

- *Prologue* -

Let me guess... you're here for the love story right?
Well, of course you are. Why else would you pick up a romance novel?
The whole point of chick-lit is to be transported into a fantasy world of passion,
desire and fairytale endings.

The thing is... that's not exactly how this story goes.

I hate to be the bearer of bad news, but if there's one disclaimer I need to make
from the outset, it's that this book is gritty and raw and definitely not your average
love story. It delves into heavy topics with potentially triggering moments that you
can't avoid, much like real life.

Although this story is fiction, a lot of it has been taken from real world experience so
if you're looking for a polite, watered down version of graphic events... this ain't the
series for you.

There will eventually be a happily-ever-after for some of our characters, but not
just yet. I promise there's an epic romance on the horizon, but before I can let you
revel in the dizzying heights of true love, we must first wade through the bog of
eternal despair. Because that's where this story really begins.

R.C. xx
(Your mystery narrator)

The beginning...

- ASHLEY GRANGER -

"What the fuck Ashley?!" Dominic bellowed from the other side of the locked bathroom door, as it wobbled relentlessly beneath the weight of his pounding fists.

The chaos inside my house was a vast contrast to the beauty and stillness of the crisp Autumn morning outside. It was 5a.m. and the sun had begun to rise peacefully over the Thames, while I sat cowering on the toilet seat of our guest bathroom, in a bloodied, teary mess.

I took a deep breath and stood up to face the mirror. My tired, blurry eyes needed a moment to focus, so I squinted through the blood and tears. When I finally caught sight of my own reflection, I recoiled at the sickening image staring back at me. My lip was split open; my left eye had swollen up like a grapefruit; my cheek was rapidly turning a dark shade of puce; and a thick strand of my bottle-black hair was plastered to my thin eyebrow with gooey, red blood.

With a feather-light touch, I ran my shaky fingers over my damaged cheekbone. Dominic's brutality was nothing unusual, but he'd never punched me in the face before. I wiped the blood from my cracked lip, and winced in pain. How had my life gotten so out of control?

Leaning over the counter, I stared at my reflection and peeled away the sticky strand of bloodied hair with disgust. Strangely, I wasn't disgusted at the blood, but rather at my hair colour. I hated it black, but Dom wouldn't let me change it back to my natural blonde because he thought it made me look trashy.

I ran a face cloth under the cold water and my hands shook uncontrollably as the adrenalin, and the drugs, began to wear off. I'd popped some top-quality ecstasy earlier that evening, but Dom's ferocious outburst had sobered me up way too abruptly. I pressed the wet flannel against my eye and grimmaced from the sting. What a mess I was. No matter how many excuses I made for myself, I'd known Dom was dangerous from the beginning.

The first time I'd met him, he'd reminded me of a less civilised version of a pre-Khaleesi Khal Drogo, yet I'd been so blindly in love with him that I'd disregarded all the obvious signs that he was a bad guy. I'd looked past his tough exterior and convinced myself that underneath the big hairy beard and the chest full of tatts, there was a gentle giant... but there wasn't. He'd always been a monster.

As if picking up my thoughts, the monster banged hard on the door, causing my entire body to jolt with fear. If it hadn't been for the class A's running through my system, I probably would have completely fallen apart. This was my life and there was no way out of it. I knew I needed to leave him, but I was too petrified to try again after what he'd done to me the first time, so chemical courage was my only salvation.

"You can't hide in the bathroom every time we have an argument Princess," he yelled irately. That was a point on which we would always disagree. Locking myself in the bathroom had been a fairly successful tactic thus far. In fact, I'd barricaded myself in the guest bathroom so many times that I kept an emergency kit in the cupboard. My stash consisted of all the essentials one might need in the face of physical danger: a first aid kit, toiletries, a bottle of high-quality vodka, a credit card, a £50 bank note, and an 8 ball of cocaine.

I glanced over at the little locked cupboard that guarded my secret stash. Oblivion was calling. As I reached towards the handle, the pounding stopped. I paused and listened, suspecting that there would be more to come.

Just as expected, Dominic's gravelly tones echoed loudly through the cold, marbled bathroom once again. "You know hiding is only gonna make things worse Ashley," he drawled with the deep voice that I'd once found irresistibly sexy. I didn't respond. There was no point. My words weren't going to make a difference. Ashley!" he bellowed, recommencing his thumping. "You fuck'n bitches are all the same. You all run away when things get a little bit hard. Fuck'n gutless cunts..."

I rolled my eyes in disgust. It always came back to the same thing with Dominic: 'All women are cunts'. Bleugh, I hated that word, but he'd used it so often that I was almost becoming immune to it.

"Come out of there Ashley," Dom roared with venom. "Grow the fuck up and deal with this like an adult."

I did my best to ignore the subsequent stream of obscenities that spewed forth, but my brain was emerging from its cozy drug-induced haze, which made zoning him out infinitely more difficult. I unlocked the cabinet and grabbed out my emergency Grey Goose, dabbing some onto my split lip, before taking a massive swig straight from the bottle. The searing warmth of the vodka momentarily distracted me from my overwhelming pain, so I took another huge gulp and then scrambled through the drawer for my cocaine.

I was aiming for complete obliteration. I needed to numb myself completely so that I didn't have to face the depressing reality of my life with Dominic Doyle. The man had me trapped. Staying was dangerous but running would get me killed.

"Please baby, come out," Dom called calmly, "I didn't mean it, I'm so sorry. You know I'd never deliberately hurt you. It's just that it makes me crazy when I see you flirting with other men." It almost sounded as if he believed his own bullshit, but I knew better than that. Blocking out his voice, I racked up a fat line on the bench top, rolling the bank note as best I could with trembling fingers. "Come on Princess," Dom ordered, but I offered no response. "He's my fucking client Ashley. How the fuck do you think that made me look?" he raged, as he recommenced banging on the door. "You can't feel-up my client and expect me not to get angry Princess."

It was the one and only time that Dominic had ever been even remotely justified in his violent jealousy, however I refused to feel guilty about it. I had indeed been attracted to the tall blonde stranger, but it wouldn't have made a difference if I hadn't. I still would have copped a beating the same way I always did. At least this time I'd had a moment of fun for my trouble.

"For fuck's sake Princess, what the fuck else do you want me to say?! Just get the fuck out here and deal with this like a grown-up."

I ignored Dom and carefully snorted up my magic white line, inhaling deeply as I waited for the coke to hit my brain and dull the pain of my shitty existence.

"Come on baby. You're being silly. I'm the one who should be upset here," Dom said with muffled condescension. "I'm sorry I hit you babe, but you really embarrassed me tonight. I love you so much, it kills me baby."

I sighed heavily and took another long swig of the vodka. The so-called apologies had begun which meant the worst of his temper had subsided. It was time for me to relent. If I stayed in the bathroom any longer I'd make things worse for myself.

I stashed away my drugs and mopped up the crumbs of cocaine with my finger, rubbing the last of it into my gums so as not to waste any. I needed all the help I could get because, despite the emerging daylight, the night was far from over.

I glimpsed my reflection in the mirror again. The purple in my cheek was beginning to turn black. It was emphasising the green in my eyes, but I doubted I'd be starting any fashion trends. Knowing there wasn't much I could do for it besides an ice pack, I tidied myself up as best I could, and cautiously opened the door.

"That's better," Dom said, ignoring my new black-eyed look. "Come here baby," he smirked with arrogant triumph, then grabbed my arm and pulled me towards him. I fought against my revulsion and allowed myself to be encased in a possessive hug that sent chills down my spine. I knew what was coming next and I regretted not snorting a couple more lines whilst I'd had the opportunity. At least the vodka was starting to kick in, so with any luck I'd be drunk enough for sex with Dominic to be bearable.

"I'm sorry if I scared you Princess, but you can't flirt with my clients. It makes me look like a twat," Dom told me, as he kissed my neck. A wave of nausea swept over me. I had become so repulsed by him that most of the time I actually preferred the arguments to the making up. Unfortunately for me, we rarely had one without the other. It was as if the violence was an aphrodisiac for Dom, and although it made me sick to my stomach, I had long since learned not to fight the inevitable. The more I resisted, the more traumatic and painful it was, so it was better to comply.

Dominic peeled my bloodied shirt over my head, and my stomach lurched at the lecherous look in his eyes. My bruised and battered body was his masterpiece, and he wasn't afraid to admire it. He discarded his own shirt, and the dead eyes of the skull tattoo on his chest stared menacingly at me. I hated that fucking tattoo. In fact, I hated everything about Dominic. Even the sight of his well developed six-pack did nothing to stir my interest anymore. There had once been a time when I'd found Dominic sexy, but after discovering who he really was, his vile nature far outweighed any of his favourable attributes.

Dom ran his hands across my ribs, lingering over the jagged scar he'd created a few years earlier. He smirked unashamedly at the squiggly line that represented his ownership over me. He was proud of that scar. It was a visual reminder of what he'd done to me when I'd tried to leave, and he knew it had been enough to scare me into staying.

"It's time for you to make it up to me Princess," he informed me arrogantly. Dom took one last smug glance at my scar and then threw me over his shoulder, carrying me into the bedroom like a sack of potatoes.

He plopped me unceremoniously, onto the king-sized bed and stripped off my remaining clothes. My stomach churned at the thought of having him inside me, so I scrambled to my knees and quickly got to work on his zipper.

"I know a perfect way to make it up to you," I purred as provocatively as possible. I was hoping like hell that I could avoid actual sex by distracting him with one of my well-perfected blow jobs.

"Not tonight Princess, it's going to take a lot more than that this time," he said, shaking his head as he pushed me away and flipped me onto all fours.

Knowing that it was pointless to fight, I gritted my teeth in sickening trepidation, as I waited for him to begin his deed. Without hesitation, Dominic shoved himself straight into me, and I sank my damaged face into the pillow, wincing in pain as my black eye pressed against the fabric. I wasn't sure which pain was worse, so I gripped tightly to the sheets and tried hard to mentally vacate my body, while Dom pounded back and forth.

In an effort to make his grinding vaguely tolerable, I shut my eyes and let my mind wander to more pleasant thoughts of his sexy client from earlier that evening. Something about the blue-eyed man had sparked an unexpected desire in me. After years of being completely detached from my physical body, the intensity of my attraction had caught me off-guard.

Admittedly the effects of the ecstasy had probably contributed towards awakening my libido, but the mysterious blonde man had re-ignited a spark inside me that had been long since extinguished.

Replaying my brief interlude with the gorgeous stranger helped ease the pain, and I was able to fool myself into believing that I was a willing participant in what was happening.

My body may have belonged to Dominic, but my mind was my own and, even though it was hidden under a thick fog of drugs and alcohol, at least I knew he would never get control of it.

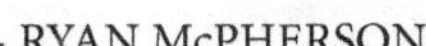

- RYAN McPHERSON -

The neon Mareechi's logo was glowing like a warning beacon above Ashley's empty desk. It was 9:45 on a Monday morning and she still hadn't shown up at work. It was so unlike her to be late, especially when we had a project meeting starting in fifteen minutes. On a normal day, Ash would have been sitting at her desk at least an hour earlier than anyone else.

I picked up my phone to text her again. She hadn't responded to my first five texts, so a sixth one probably wouldn't make a lot of difference, but I couldn't sit and do nothing. Just as I began tapping out yet another text, my phone beeped with an incoming message.

'Can you meet me outside?' It was from Ash. Thank God she was okay. Her request struck me as bizarre, but knowing Ash, she had a good reason for it.

'Sure. I'm on my way,' I replied, and bounded into the warehouse-style reception area. I nodded at the receptionist as I headed straight past her and through the brightly branded front door.

Outside, the brushed-steel security gate slid open and my heart pounded in my chest at the sight of Ashley standing uneasily on the other side of the road. She looked exhausted but she was still gorgeous. Ash was too skinny for my liking but with her catlike beauty and tall lanky frame she could have passed for a supermodel, especially at that moment as she leaned against a signpost wearing ridiculously over-sized, black sunglasses.

"Ash!" I called, waving eagerly. Why did I always act like such a plonker around her? I could only imagine what my parents would say if they knew I fancied a white girl. They'd probably cut off my trust fund just to make a point. Although, Ashley's parents were wealthy enough that mine possibly would have made an exception for her.

I crossed the road, trying my hardest to look cool and nonchalant.

"Hey," she mumbled, shifting self-consciously on her feet as I met her on the other side of the busy street. Up close I could see that she was pale and, if it was even possible, more gaunt than usual.

I shoved my hands into my pockets to prevent myself from wrapping her up in a bear hug. "What's with the cloak and dagger entrance? Our project meeting starts at ten."

"I know," Ash said, as she raked her shaky hands through her disheveled black hair. She looked like she hadn't slept in days. I cocked my head as I scrutinised her from head to toe.

"Everything okay?"

"Yeah fine," she lied with a stiff nod, before gingerly removing her humongous shades.

"Holy shit," I blurted, stepping back reflexively as I caught sight of the massive black eye she was sporting. She winced and squinted towards her feet. It was hard to tell whether it was embarrassment or a response to the bright sunlight assaulting her bloodshot eyes. Probably both.

"Yeah, I had a big weekend," she mumbled with a shrug.

"Ash," I said breathlessly, "what happened?"

"You know me Ryza. Always partying too hard." Her tone was light, but there was something about her demeanor that belied her words. "I took too many drugs and shit got crazy," she concluded flippantly.

I studied her closely. Although her explanation was plausible, it didn't sit right. She did have a tendency to party pretty hard, but every bone in my body told me there was something more to her story.

I chose not to press her on it, and instead took her face in my hands to investigate her shiner more closely. I bit down on the inside of my cheek when I realised how easy it would be to kiss her from that position. With her chin tilted upwards, her mouth was so close to mine that if I'd leaned slightly forwards our lips would have been touching. Nothing good would ever come from me kissing Dominic Doyle's girlfriend, so I forcefully shifted my focus back to her wound. I wasn't an expert at black eyes, but it didn't look like it had occurred accidentally.

"It's pretty bad," I told her pointlessly, as I stood with my dark hands cupped gently around her porcelain face. We were yin and yang.

"Yeah I know," Ash agreed. "How am I going to show my face in there?" She stared up at me with her big green eyes and all I wanted to do was hug her and kiss her and tell her that everything was going to be okay. That was, until I looked up and saw the hulk-like frame of Dominic Doyle striding menacingly towards us. The guy was like an angry, white version of that bloke who played Aqua-Man.

"How about you take your black hands off my girlfriend McPherson."

Ash jumped away from me instantly. "Dom!" she blurted in panic. "What are you doing here?"

"I came by to make sure you're okay baby," he told her with a creepy grin, before turning back to me. "She had quite a weekend," he said, squeezing Ash possessively around the shoulders.

Ash cringed slightly but forced a smile to her face.

"Yeah I can see that," I answered, wishing that I had the guts to punch the prick in the face. "I was just taking a look at her eye. She's got herself a pretty good shiner there."

"I keep telling her she needs to tone down her partying."

"I think you're probably right Dom." I nodded stiffly, not wanting to antagonize him. Dominic was always looking for an excuse to rumble. The three of us stood in silence for a moment and the tension was tangible. I looked between Dom and Ashley, as the predator eyed me suspiciously.

"McPherson...hmmm..." he mused, "that's a strange name for an African isn't it?"

I sniggered with a mixture of nerves and disgust. My obscenely privileged upbringing had provided me with many skills, however the art of physical combat was not one of them. If Dom wanted a dance-battle I could happily oblige, but there was no way I'd walk away from a fist fight with the guy.

"I'm English actually," I told him calmly, "born and raised in South London in fact...but yes, I do have Scottish heritage, hence the Celtic surname."

"A Scottish African from England. Interesting", he said patronizingly. Dominic Doyle wasn't the first arsehole to belittle me for my colour and he wouldn't be the last. I was pretty good at letting racism roll off my back, but it bothered me immensely that this particular arsehole was sleeping with the woman I loved.

"We'd better get inside Ash," I said with a forced smile, "our meeting is about to start."

"Yeah," she agreed, and Dominic reluctantly released her from his claw-hold.

"I don't want you to be late," he said in an eerily perky tone. "Good luck babe. Probably best to tell them you got hit in the face with a football or something huh?"

"Yeah," she agreed with a tight smile, "maybe I'll keep the sunnies on for a little while."

Dom nodded with approval. "Good idea."

"Bye Dom," I said, purposefully dragging Ashley back to our side of the road. Dominic stood and watched us like a hawk as we escaped to the safety of our huge, designer-graffitied office building. Once we were on the secure side of the steel gates, I peered through the silver slats. Dom was still loitering on the other side of the road, staring after us, but he hadn't followed. I let out a sigh of relief, feeling like we'd made a narrow escape. I caught Ashley's eye and she appeared to be thinking the same thing. "Come on, let's get inside," I said, gently taking her hand.

She nodded and wrapped her fingers around mine, but her eyes were still trained on her hulk of a boyfriend lurking beyond the Marcheechi walls. I swiped us in through the main door and turned back to Ash, catching her in the act of subtly brushing a tear from underneath her huge glasses.

"Everything okay?" I asked casually.

"Yeah," she breathed, "I just needed to see a friendly face."
I nodded silently, feeling suffocated with the weight of my concern for her. There was obviously more to her black eye than she was letting on, but I had no idea how to get it out of her.

"We'd better get to the boardroom," I said, ushering her through the brightly coloured hallway. We huried through the industrial style building as subtly as possible. I drew to a halt a few feet from the boardroom door, spinning on my heel to carefully remove the sunnies from Ashley's face. I folded up the glasses and handed them back to her. "It looks worse with the shades."
Another tear ran down her cheek.

"Thanks Ryza," she whispered as I gently wiped the tear away with my thumb.

"Just go with the football story my love." I couldn't believe that I was actually agreeing with Dominic, but a football in the face was definitely the most palatable explanation.

"Okay," she nodded meekly. Ash closed her eyes and took a deep breath to compose herself.

"I worry about you, you know?" I admitted, as I studied her face. "You're so self-destructive."

"I know," Ash replied, avoiding eye contact.

"How about we go grab a coffee after this? Then we can have a proper chat."

"Yeah that sounds good," she agreed.

"Have you eaten today?" I asked, trying not to sound like her mother.

"You know I don't eat breakfast," Ash snapped defensively.

"You don't eat any meals as far as I can tell." Apparently I had become the food police. She rolled her eyes like a teenager.

"Here we go again," she groaned melodramatically. For a moment I had the distinct urge to shake her by the shoulders to wake her up to herself, but instead I rubbed my own face with frustration.

"I wish you would take better care of yourself," I muttered through my hands.

"You always say that," she said. I sighed heavily and dropped my hands from my face. Ash was scrutinizing me intently with that cute scrunchy-nosed look of hers. "Why do you worry about me so much?" she asked curiously.

"Because I care about you Ash. You're such an amazing person but you don't seem to realise it. Why do you punish yourself so badly?"

She dropped her gaze, "I don't know."

Our quiet moment was interrupted by Pamela, the CEO's highly-strung Personal Assistant, who appeared out of nowhere flapping like a headless chicken.

"There you are!" she cried in a fluster, herding us towards the boardroom. "They've been looking everywhere for you two. Neil is waiting to see the McEwan pitch concepts."

Ashley's hand automatically flew up to her damaged face in a panic.

"Oh my God, I didn't know Neil was going to be here! Since when has my work been of interest to the CEO?"

Pamela sighed impatiently as if Ashley was a misbehaved toddler.

"This is the most important pitch of the year Ashley. Neil wants to make sure it's up to task. The McEwan Racing account is worth 3 million pounds a year, so we can't afford to lose it to Artemis Advertising."

"Holy shit," Ash breathed, looking to me for reassurance.

"It will be fine," I told her confidently. "The concepts are good, no… they're great. You've totally nailed it Ash, we've got nothing to worry about, I promise."

- KAT TAILOR -

I gazed vacantly at my computer screen as reality turned on its head. I couldn't speak. My breath was caught somewhere between my chest and my throat. It couldn't be true. Was Xavier Brownlough really getting married?

"Kit-Kat? Are you okay?" my sister Rosie asked gently from the other end of the phone.

"Not really," I squeaked, forcing the words out. How could I be okay when my heart was shattering into a million pieces? It had been a decade since I'd last seen Xavi, but he was the love of my life and I wasn't ready to let him go yet. While we'd both been unmarried there had been a slight chance that somehow things might work out between us, but now...

"I'm sorry kiddo," she said, softening her tone. "I thought it would be better if you heard it from me."

"Yeah, it was," I assured her, trying my hardest not to cry at work. There was only one day to go until our huge pitch presentation, so my team was relying on me to keep it together. My boss Gareth would never let me hear the end of it if we lost the McEwan pitch to Mareechi Media.

"If it makes you feel better, her name is Agatha," Rosie blurted randomly.

"Why would that make me feel better?!" I asked, with a weird laugh-cry.

"Because it's a horrible name. She must be fat with a name like that," Rosie said with a chuckle, sounding like a disturbing Dr Seuss rhyme.

"Rosie that's not funny," I scolded her, as I resisted a smirk. I wouldn't have admitted it out loud, but it did actually make me feel a little better.

"I'm not trying to be funny. I know women Kat, and Agatha is a fat girl name," she paused as if she was telepathically sensing the tears welling in my eyes. "I'm so sorry honey. I honestly thought you and Xavi were going to end up together."

"Yeah, so did I," I whispered quietly. It was shitty news and awful timing, but I couldn't let this get to me. I had too much work to do.

I glanced around the office and noticed that whilst everyone else was working hard on our pitch, my Junior Designer was busy flirting with our resident man-whore, Nathan Stone. Nathan was our Client Director and a long-term feature at Artemis Advertising. He was a good guy at heart and although I understood why he was the way he was, it still didn't change the fact that he was a player.

"Are the pitch designs still on track for the end of the day Beck?" I called authoritatively, causing my older sister to giggle down the phone line.

"Ooh you sound so professional and grown-up," she teased from her end, while Becky peered up at me sheepishly.

"Nearly done Kat," Beck replied, glancing back to Nathan with a blush.

"Great," I said with an approving nod. "Nathan, have you prepped your half of the presentation?"

"Isn't Nathan the hot slutty one?" asked my lesbian sister, uncharacteristically enthusiastic about the hotness of a man.

"No doubt on the latter," I said eying the office playboy, who raised a mocking eyebrow at me.

"I'm good to go Tails. How's your half coming along?" he drawled with a tone that was intended to remind me that I was not his superior.

"I'm done," I told him flatly, unwilling to buy into his flirtatious power-play.

"They say the best way to get over someone is to get under someone else," Rosie informed me mischievously. I rolled my eyes. Rosie had never been the best source of dating wisdom.

"Thanks Dr Tailor, I'll take that under advisement," I said, before turning my attention back to Nathan, as he rose from Becky's desk with a cocky grin. He swaggered his tall, lanky frame in my direction and I gulped involuntarily as I noticed the determined look in his eyes. A thick chunk of my curly hair flopped into my face and broke our eye contact.

"It's a legitimate and proven solution," Rosie argued pointlessly in the background as I pushed away my unruly curls.

"I have to go," I told her abruptly, hanging up the phone so I could pin my wayward hair off my face. As I fussed with my disobedient curl, Nathan turned and shot a wink back at Becky.

"See you tonight sexy," he told her over his shoulder. Becky giggled like a brainless bimbo.

"Okay," she twittered like a baby bird. I fake gagged, and rolled my eyes again. Becky Wheeler was normally an incredibly intelligent woman, but when it came to Nathan Stone she seemed to completely lose her mind.

The man-whore arrogantly plonked his rear-end onto my desk. "Do you always have to suck the fun out of things Tails?"
I pushed his uninvited butt off my table.

"Do you always have to distract my team Stone?"

"It's not my fault they get distracted by me." He leisurely pulled up a chair and threw his leg over the back of it so he was straddling the damn thing. "I didn't choose to be so charming and handsome."

I glanced up at him mockingly, "and modest too."

"What can I say? I'm a complete package," he grinned, draping himself nonchalantly over the backwards seat.

"Err, no…you're a complete tool," I retorted with a smile, and then turned my attention back to my computer screen, in an attempt to pretend that he wasn't there. Nathan seemed to interpret my disinterest as some sort of challenge, and he rolled his chair right up to mine so that our heads were only inches apart. I looked up at him with trepidation.

"What are you doing?" I asked, tilting my face away from his.

"I thought we should run through the pitch," he answered, flashing me his baby blues. "If we're presenting it together, then we should really rehearse it right?" If he was attempting to charm me, it wasn't going to work. No matter how many sparkly white smiles he shot in my direction, there was nothing on Gods' Great Earth that would ever convince me Nathan Stone was anything more than a womaniser.

"I suppose so," I agreed with a resigned sigh. "We might as well set up in the meeting room and do it properly then." I quickly rose from my chair to put some distance between our bodies.

"Any excuse to get me alone huh?" Nathan teased, jumping up from the chair like an obedient puppy.

"Oh please," I laughed, swallowing back a little bit of vomit at the thought of having sex with Nathan Stone. I could only imagine how many venereal diseases the man was carrying. "I swear to God Nathan, you're the most egotistical man I've ever met."

"Don't hate the player Tails," he grinned, before patting me condescendingly on the top of my head. He did that a lot. With at least one foot of vertical distance between us, he had an unfair advantage.

"Well at least you're self-aware enough to realise that you're a player," I retorted, swatting his hand away from my hair, which was only barely holding in place with the one measly bobby-pin I'd found in my desk draw.
Nathan darted into the meeting room ahead of me.

"Come on Tails, why don't you just admit that you're jealous."

"Jealous of what?" I asked in confusion, closing the door behind us.

"Of Becky Wheeler."
I snorted and raised a disdainful eyebrow in his direction.

"Why on earth would I be jealous of Becky Wheeler?"

"Because you want a piece of the Stoner action," he said with a confident shrug.

"Oh good God," I mumbled impatiently. "Nathan, I can sincerely promise you that I do *not* want a piece of the Stoner action."

"Yeah right." He laughed with wild amusement, as if it was inconceivable that a woman wouldn't want him. I watched him, straight-faced, as he ran his hands through his long, blonde, mop of hair, and then struck a pose like a male model, casually tucking one hand into his trouser pocket. I shook my head with a smile, feeling slightly sympathetic that he genuinely believed his own hype.

"I hate to burst your bubble tiger, but you're not my type," I told him bluntly.

Nathan looked stunned. "How could I not be your type?"

"Wow, you certainly don't have any self-esteem issues do you Stoner?"

"It's never been a problem, no," he replied, shoving his other hand into the vacant pocket.

"Should we get started then?" I asked chirpily, changing the subject in an effort to move things along.
Nathan scratched the back of his head with dismay.

"You're serious, aren't you?" he asked in apparent bewilderment.

"Yes, I am. I don't want to be in here with you for too long or people will start talking," I said steering his attention towards the projector screen.

"No, I mean about me not being your type."

"Oh, for crying out loud." The man was relentless. "Of course I'm serious. Why would I lie about that?"

"I don't know," he answered in mystification. I could see that he was actually struggling to process the information. "So what type of guy do you go for then?"

"Well I don't do blondes for a start. Blonde boys are always trouble," I said, buying into his stupid discussion.

"So what about Peterson then? He's blonde and you've shagged him."

"I haven't shagged Beau!" I said appalled.

"Oh come on Tails, you two are always all over each other."

"We are not!"

"Yes you are," he disagreed with a wink. "So if you haven't already shagged then you both want to. Why don't you just get it over with and fuck him."

"Okay, for one thing," I said indignantly, waving my pointer finger in Nathan's face, "Beau and I are just friends, and secondly... he's gay."
Nath snorted with amusement.

"That guy ain't gay Tails," he said in a fake American accent, imitating Beau's L.A. twang.

"He's my best friend Nathan, I think I'm in a better position to know his sexual orientation than you are."

"And which position is that exactly? Doggy?"

I rolled my eyes for the fiftieth time. "You're disgusting."

"That's fair," he agreed with a proud grin, "but it doesn't mean I'm wrong. In fact, I'd bet my ball-sack, that Beau Peterson is trying to get into your pants."

"Oh my god Nathan, believe it or not, there are guys out there who know there's more to life than getting laid."
Nathan cackled uproariously as if I'd just made the funniest joke in the world.

"Oh come on Tails, there's not a man alive who thinks there's more to life than getting laid."

I shook my head in dismay. "You're a lost cause. Speaking of which, what's going on with you and Becky?"

Nathan shrugged and took a seat. "Nothing."

"That didn't look like nothing."

"It's just harmless fun. We haven't even shagged yet." I couldn't help but facepalm. It was hard to believe he was for real sometimes. "What?" he asked indignantly.

I sighed exhaustedly. "You have much to learn young Jedi."

Nath grabbed my arm excitedly. "Wait…you know Star Wars?"

"Of course I know Star Wars."

"Tails, I have the perfect man for you."

"Fabulous," I retorted dryly. "I'm sure he'll be a keeper."

- NATHAN STONE -

After enduring an entire fortnight of the ball-breaking, sex-depriving activity we humans otherwise refer to as 'dating', I had finally charmed my way into Becky Wheeler's bedroom. Admittedly my success wasn't due to charm alone; it had also taken a hundred quid's worth of London's finest cocktails, but I was there none-the-less. I perched uncomfortably on Becky's flouncy, white bed and straightened up the self-help book that was sitting crookedly on her bedside table. '*The Power of Love: Healing your Relationship with Yourself.*'

"Pfft," I muttered under my breath, "what a load of bollocks." I casually swiped my floppy fringe out of my face as I waited impatiently for her to join me in the bedroom. I was trying to be cool, but I was desperate. Two weeks of celibacy had already done most of the hard work (pun intended), so I was as antsy as fuck.

After what felt like hours, the door creaked open and Becky finally returned from the bathroom.

"Get over here gorgeous," I joked, barely able to control my enthusiasm.

"Shhh…" she whispered drunkenly, closing the bedroom door behind her, "…you'll wake my flatmate."

"That's okay, she'd be welcome to join us," I said with a shrug and a mischievous wink. I hadn't met Becky's flat-mate yet, but apparently she was Brazilian, so it was highly likely that she was smoking hot and up for fun.

"You're so naughty Nathan Stone," Becky giggled, but she seemed determined to drag the moment out. It was worse than Chinese water torture.

"If you come over here I'll show you exactly how naughty I can be," I said, hoping for the sake of my balls, that she'd get the hint.

"Nathan!" Becky exclaimed with false modesty. "You just cut straight to the chase, don't you?" I groaned inwardly at her prudish façade. She wanted me, and I wanted her, so why the fuck was she playing coy?

Needing desperately to expedite the situation, I stood up from the bed and closed the gap between us with one big stride. She was a good foot shorter than me, so our close proximity only served to highlight our height difference.

"Don't pretend to be shy Miss Wheeler. I know you want me."

"You're pretty confident, aren't you?" she said with a slight slur.

"I know what I want," I pulled her body tightly against mine to emphasise my point, "…and right now, all I want is you."
Becky wrapped her arms around my waist with a love-sick smile.

"Oh my," she swooned. That was confirmation enough for me, so with one swift movement, I lifted her off the floor and clamped my mouth firmly over hers, afraid that she'd sober up and change her mind.

I felt Becky's mojito-drenched tongue explore mine as she fumbled with my shirt buttons. I made an attempt to unzip her dress, but in the process, I tripped over one of her discarded stilettos and tumbled to the bed, with Becky in my arms and my pants around my ankles. I landed ungracefully on top of her, and despite my frustration I couldn't hold back a laugh.

"At least now I've got you where I want you," I joked, finally managing to extricate the woman from her skin-tight dress. She giggled again and flicked off the lamp, while I threw her dress across the room.

I began licking my way down her body and her giggles soon turned into moans. I'd spent many years perfecting the fine art of cunnilingus, so I knew my well-honed skills would dissolve any last shred of self-control that she might have been clinging on to. I let my tongue work its magic, while Becky wriggled in pleasure beneath my touch.

I added some fancy finger work, and she let out a loud moan … but then there was silence. Maybe she was breathless with pleasure? I increased my efforts but when she still hadn't made a sound or a movement minutes later, I ceased my licking.

"Beck is that okay?" I asked, wondering whether the cocktails had hampered my usually stellar, oral performance. There was no answer. "Becky?"

I strained to glimpse her face in the dim light and, as much as I would have liked to think of myself as Superman, my lack of x-ray vision made it hard to see anything. I joined Becky at the top of the bed to see what was going on.

"What the fuck?!" I couldn't believe it. She was passed out cold. "No fucking way," I muttered, as my body screamed at me in desperation. Two weeks of ball-breaking work were seconds away from paying off, and she'd bloody fallen asleep. "For fuck's sake," I sighed with frustration. My balls were so tight they felt like they were about to implode.

I pulled the cover over her and rolled off the bed. Sex was off the cards, so it was time for me to make my exit. I quietly searched for my discarded clothes in the dark, and after fifteen minutes of crawling around on the floor naked, I finally located my pants. Superman I most definitely was not. Wearing nothing but my jocks and socks, I snuck silently out of Becky's bedroom, carrying the rest of my belongings.

"I guess we'll have to wait a bit longer buddy," I told my straining cock as I carefully shut the bedroom door behind me.

With great disappointment, I began to dress myself but stopped dead in my tracks when I looked up to see Becky's hot flatmate standing at the fridge in a vest top and teeny tiny pyjama shorts. My eyes slid involuntarily down to the little slivers of naked bum-cheeks that were poking out from beneath her shorts, and I was hit with a strong urge to bite into them.

With the excruciatingly painful boner that I was already sporting, I was worried that the mere sight of the woman was going to cause me some permanent damage.

The foxy flat-mate glanced curiously over her shoulder at me as I stood outside Becky's bedroom door, half naked and horny as hell. Her eyes dropped down to my crotch and she raised a pencil thin eyebrow at the sight of my massive hard-on. A sneaky smile crossed her plump lips, before she pointedly returned the jug of cold water to the fridge and strutted her way over to me.

"No need to wait," she purred into my ear, as she ran a finger up the front of my G-Stars. "I could help you with this."

My cock jumped enthusiastically in agreement to her offer, as the pouch on my boxers strained heavily under the force of my ridiculous erection. I held the Brazilian's gaze. Was this a trap or was she legit?

As if answering my unvoiced question, the hottie gave my package a motivational squeeze. That was all the encouragement I needed, and without another word, I let the sexy seductress lead me to her bedroom. She flicked the light on, clicked the door shut and pushed me down onto her bed without preamble. She couldn't have been more different to Becky if she'd tried. With no further ado, the girl stripped off her teeny tiny pyjamas and kindly freed me of my pants.

Her big brown eyes flashed with lust at the sight of my rock-solid cock, and before I'd even seen her move, she'd rolled a condom onto it and jumped on top of me. She proceeded to fuck me so ferociously that I was seeing stars. Within minutes, my body heaved with elated relief as two weeks' worth of sexual frustration erupted from me forcefully. I was too far gone to care whether the girl got her rocks off but conveniently for her, the force of my super cum-shot pushed the girl over the edge. It hadn't been the way I'd expected to break my two-week drought, but at least the job was done. Hopefully all the ground-work I'd put in with Becky would still pay off too.

The Brazilian climbed off me abruptly and I groaned with a mixture of pleasure and pain as she peeled off the condom.

"All better?" she asked with a wink, tossing the used rubber into the bin.

"Much better," I agreed, tiredly pulling on my pants.

"Good."

We straightened ourselves up, and I headed for the door.

"Thanks for that," I said, stopping to give her a friendly peck on the cheek.

"My pleasure," she said with a wink as I opened the bedroom door to see Becky standing in the lounge room holding my wallet and keys.

"Becky!" I blurted in shock. When had she woken up? Had she heard everything? Why the fuck hadn't I thought to grab my other stuff off the coffee table?

"Well that didn't take long," she retorted with venom.

"Look babe-" My sentence was cut short, as my wallet hit me square in the face. It stung like a mother fucker, but I was impressed by her perfect aim.

"Don't speak Nathan. Just get out." Becky threw my keys at me with slightly less precision and they hit my leg before falling to the floor with a loud clatter.

"I'm sorry," I apologised as I scooped up my belongings in a fluster.

"No, *I'm* sorry," Becky snapped. "I'm sorry that I ever met you Nathan Stone."

Stories from the City: Part 1

Sticks & Stones

- *Chapter 1* -

FIVE YEARS LATER

- NATHAN STONE -

It was the morning of my thirty-sixth birthday and I was awoken by the sharp trill of my alarm clock at six a.m, as had been my daily routine for nearly two decades. Geez, two decades. I was getting old. Anyway… my point being that the day started like any other… except that this day was far from normal.

I stretched contentedly across my cushy king-sized bed and let out a loud, satisfied yawn. The night before had been the best birthday celebration I'd had in a long time; just me, a hot red-head and a night of frenzied fucking. The fact that I'd only needed to catch an elevator home, had made my pre-birthday session with Stacy, the saucy solicitor from upstairs, even more gratifying. I rolled languidly out of bed with a pleasing feeling that my body had been well used.

Bare-arsed, I strutted to the window to let in the early morning light.

"Yep…this is the life," I said, enjoying the feel of the emerging sunlight on my face. A ginger flash flew towards my window, making me recoil in shock, as it landed on the narrow sill. "Shit," I swore, laughing as I realised it was just the stray cat that had been hanging around the building lately. "Morning Fleabag. How the fuck did you get all the way up here?" I asked the mangy-looking thing, as it stared blankly at me through the thick glass.

I pressed my forehead against the window and peered outside to see how the hell it had made it all the way up to the sixth floor from its usual spot on the doorstep.

"Oh, the tree," I said, answering my own question as I saw the solid branch of the massive oak tree, curving towards the balustrade of my lounge room balcony. "Clever cat."

The cat stood on the other side of the window eyeballing me so intently that I suddenly felt weird about being naked. I threw on my bathrobe and scooped up my dad's old guitar. Ignoring my onlooker, I quickly ran my hands over the intricate, hand-painted patterns before strumming a few chords of the happy birthday song to myself.

Someone knocked loudly on my front door and, as I jumped in surprise for the second time that morning, my hand slipped over the frets, causing them to screech their disapproval.

"Who the fuck…?" I asked the cat. My building was like Fort Knox, so no-one could have gotten up here without me buzzing them in. I carefully tucked my beloved guitar back into its stand, and wandered out to the front door as the knocking recommenced.

"Rise and shine tiger," a sexy voice purred from the other side of the door.

Oh shit. It was Stacy. Maybe there was one small flaw to my in-house shagging plan after all. The woman was smoking hot, but if I'd wanted to see her this morning, I would have stayed at her place last night. I opened the door with slight trepidation.

"Stacy," I greeted her with a cautious smile.

"Oh," she exclaimed, glancing down at my insufficiently fastened robe, "or perhaps just shine."

"Oops!" I hastily pulled my bathrobe closed. "Lucky you weren't old Mrs Pritchard from down the hall. That would have been a greeting she'd never forget."

"It might have been the highlight of her life," Stacy teased with a wink.

"Or she might have had a heart attack." Quite frankly the latter was the more realistic outcome. I was pretty sure the old bird hadn't set her eyes on a dick for at least half a century.

"I'm sure you would have found a way to revive her."

"Err... I do have standards thanks," I replied, feeling queasy at the thought of giving old Mrs Pritchard mouth-to-mouth.

"Of course you do," Stacy agreed as she ran a well-manicured hand over her tightly fastened bun. It was hard to tell if she was being sarcastic. I rubbed my head awkwardly.

"So what can I do for you at this hour... well, besides the peep show?"

"You left this at my place," she explained, holding out my gold Rolex. "I thought I should get it back to you before you left for your trip."

"Oh, thanks," I buckled the expensive watch back onto my wrist. I was surprised that Stacy was capable of such a thoughtful act. "I would have been lost without my lucky watch."

Stacy waved her hand in dismissal of my sentimentality, "I know, it was your Dad's old watch, blah blah blah. It's mostly because I've got a friend coming around tonight and I didn't want him to find another man's watch on my nightstand."

"Oh. Right. Of course," I nodded, feeling strangely perturbed by the rejection.

"I had fun last night," she said, changing the subject abruptly.

"Me too. We should do it again some time."

"Absolutely," she answered with a wink. "Anyway I have to get to work."

"Yeah me too, thanks for bringing the watch back."

"Not a problem sexy," she replied, sauntering to the lifts. "Good luck with your big meeting."

"Thanks." I closed the door behind her and grinned with excitement. It was time to get this auspicious day under way. It had been seventeen years since I'd started working at Artemis and back then I had been a fresh-faced grad student not quite in my twenties. Now, I was thirty-six, and about to land a client who would mark the culmination of all my hard work over those seventeen years. I couldn't have asked for a better birthday present.

I shrugged into my gym gear, grabbed my packed suitcase and hustled my arse down to the gym for my weights session with Ritchie.

"Morning Gina!" I greeted the receptionist cheerfully.

"Morning babe," she said with a warm smile, "Happy birthday!"

"Shhh… I'm keeping it on the down-low."

"Ah okay," she nodded knowingly. "Mid-life crisis moment?"

"Jesus Gina, I'm only thirty-six!"

"That's mid-life Nathan."

I gripped my chest playfully. "Why don't you just stab me in the heart while you're at it?"

"And deprive the world of the illustrious Nathan Stone?"

"Well you've got a point there," I agreed with a wink. She grinned and nodded towards my small suitcase.

"Another business trip?"

"Yeah," I replied, swiping my membership tag. "Would you mind stashing this behind the desk?" I asked, wheeling my suitcase around.

"Of course babe," she said, taking my case. "So where are you off to this time then?"

"Paris."

"Ooh la la," she joked, as I made my way into the noisy gym. "See you on the way out."

At the cardio equipment I spotted a cute little brunette torturing a rather hefty bloke on a treadmill. Whilst I was mid-perve, the girl looked up from her training session, and glared at me coldly. Oh bollocks. I'd shagged her a few years back. Her name was Candy. Or… Cindy? Yeah, definitely Cindy. Fuck. When did she start working at my gym?

"Nathan Stone," she sneered from across the room. I had a vague recollection of being less than chivalrous after our athletic sex-session all those years ago.

"Umm… hi," I answered tripping over a rowing machine in an attempt to avoid walking too close to her. "Oops! Shit," I muttered in embarrassment as I regained my balance. Cindy shook her head in disgust, and viciously increased the speed on her client's treadmill. The poor guy was paying the price for my ancient crime. I edged towards the safety of the weights room, feeling the daggers from my disgruntled one-night stand. I took one last glance back at her and then made a cowardly retreat behind the frosted glass wall. Thankfully Ritchie Carlton, one of my best mates, was at the bench-press already. Ritchie was six feet and five inches of solid Australian muscle. I'd never been classified as short on any scale, but I always felt like a midget standing next to Ritch. His bulky rugby frame far outweighed my more footy-esque stature, so those two inches might as well have been five.

"Here's the birthday boy," he bellowed in his usual over-enthusiastic manner.

"Shh," I said as I peered out to the gym to make sure Cindy hadn't followed me. "I'm trying to keep it on the down-low mate."

"Mid-life crisis?" he asked sympathetically.

"Jesus, I'm not mid-life yet, why does everyone keep saying that?" I asked, casting another look over my shoulder.

"You okay mate? You look a bit pale," Ritchie asked, setting up the bench press for me. I caught sight of my reflection in the mirror. He was right, I did look a bit pale...but mostly good. I ran my hands through my long hair and tied it into a man-bun before turning my full attention back to my obnoxious best mate.

"Actually I need your help with a little problem."

"Mate, I'm not checking your dick for herpes again," he teased, causing several guys to snigger and glance up from their weights. My face flared red and I shrugged as if I had no idea what Ritchie was talking about.

"That was one-time Ritch," I hissed irately, "and it turned out to be an allergic reaction."

Ritchie chuckled sadistically.

"Yeah and who would have known that glow-in-the-dark frangers would irritate your dick like that huh?"

"Fuck off cunt," I snapped childishly, protectively adjusting my package at the reminder of the humiliating moment. He'd told me not to get those damn novelty condoms but I hadn't listened. "You swore you'd never mention it again."

"Okay, okay," he relented with a laugh. "So what's the problem this time then?"

I slid onto the bench and took the opportunity to peer quickly out at my hot little hater. "Did you see the cute brunette trainer out there?"

"Yeah I did, she's pretty fit," Ritchie agreed, following my gaze.

"Well she's that Cindy bird I shagged that time, and she's not best pleased with me."

"Only you Stoner," he said, shaking his head as he handed me the bar. "So what am I meant to do about it?"he asked unsympathetically.

"I don't know, distract her when we leave or something. Just help me get out of here without having to deal with her," I pleaded with a grunt, as I bench-pressed my weights.

"Don't you think you should face it like a man?"

"What do you mean?" I asked, pushing the heavy load upwards again.

"Err...I mean, maybe you should talk to her. Or even apologise for running out on her," he answered over-exaggeratedly, as if I were an imbecile. I plonked my bar in the holds.

"Why would I want to do that?!" Honestly, some dumb shit went through that guy's head sometimes.

"Because if you sneak out today, you'll have a worse situation on your hands next time."

"You the fucking Dalai Lama now?" I retorted. He rolled his eyes and stared me down with a warning look.

"Stoner..."

"Ritchie," I imitated as we switched places. He sighed in resignation as he adjusted his position on the bench.

"You're a worry mate."

"So, does that mean you'll distract her?" I asked hopefully.

"Fine," he reluctantly agreed. Anyone would have thought I'd asked him to murder her or something.

"Thanks buddy, I owe you one."

"Stoner, you owe me so many I stopped keeping count years ago."

"That's probably true," I agreed, spotting his bar.

"You ready for your big meeting with Delfontaine?"

"I don't know," I said, feeling strangely nervous about meeting the famed French millionaire. "The presentation is done, but it needs tweaking."

"You'll be right mate," Ritchie grunted, heaving his insanely heavy weights up and down, "and if not, just do what you do best and fuck her."

- KAT McPHERSON -

Our alarm sounded loudly, but I was already awake. I hadn't slept a full night since I'd hit my third trimester because the little blob inside me was determined to torture me beyond recognition. I still had three months to go before I was an actual real-life mum, but I was already in an epic state of sleep deprivation.

I quickly clicked off the alarm as my husband stirred under the blanket beside me. At least one of us was getting some sleep.

"Morning babe," he mumbled burying his face further into the plush pillow, causing the duvet to slip down and reveal one of his scrumptious shoulders. The white of the cover made his dark skin look even more chocolatey than usual, and the sight of it instantly lit a fire in the pit of my belly. Oh, how I loved those broad shoulders of his. I lightly kissed his bare skin.

"Morning," I whispered as I let my hand slide under the covers along his smooth, bare flesh.

"Mmmm…" he muttered as I trailed my fingers down the length of his body, and then stopped at his semi-erect penis. I knew it wouldn't take long to get him up to full-mast, so I began rubbing and massaging as best I could with a bump protruding between our bodies. "What a nice wake-up call. What's this in aid of? It's not my birthday," he said, muffled by the pillow.

"No, it's Nathan's," I answered simply, too preoccupied with his hardening cock to elaborate on my response.

"I'm getting a hand-job because it's Nathan's birthday?" he joked, finally un-burying his head.

I ceased my efforts. "Nathan's birthday is our anniversary Ryan."

"Nice try but it's only April. Our Anniversary is in July."

"Our wedding anniversary is in July," I agreed, "but we met each other three years ago at Nathan's party."

"Wow, you're right." Ryan replied, rolling over to face me, "and you're still as beautiful as you were that night Mrs McPherson."

"Aww," I said, losing myself in his big brown eyes, "and you're still a charmer Mr McPherson."

He grinned cheekily, "Does that mean I still get that hand-job?"

"You're getting more than just a hand-job… you're getting laid."

"Excellent! Nathan should have birthdays more often," he chuckled, pulling my face to his for a passionate kiss. I savoured the feel of his tongue against mine, and I heard myself let out a little moan as my whole body ignited with desire. Ryan smiled with satisfaction. "God you're sexy."

"Even with the bump?" I asked, needing reassurance that I was still desirable, despite my frumpy state.

"Especially with the bump," he assured me, emphasising his point by using his thumb to massage my over-excited clit. My breath caught in my throat.

"Oh," I gasped, my heart thudding rapidly in my chest. Ryan's eyes flashed with excitement. He knew exactly what he was doing to me. He let his fingers roam, and the warmth between my thighs spread through my entire body. I could feel fireworks beginning to gather in the pit of my over-sized belly so Ryan rolled me gently onto my other side. It was the easiest way with my huge stomach.

"You're sexier than ever," he whispered into my ear as he entered me carefully from behind. I moaned with pleasure as he filled the small amount of space that was unoccupied by the child.

Even though the angle wasn't perfect, the feel of Ryan's long, hard penis inside me was enough to push me close to orgasm. I pressed my bottom hard against his pelvis and ground myself against him, luxuriating in the sensation. The one good thing about pregnancy was that sex was amazing. In addition to the horny hormones rampaging through my body, having a belly full of baby also made the rest of my lady-bits a lot more sensitive. I was already teetering on the edge of ecstasy, so when Ryan reached around and let his fingers explore between my thighs again, I immediately shuddered with pleasure.

"Oh my gohhhhhd…" I gasped breathlessly as my body shook and writhed of its own accord. Ryan paused and held his position, but I didn't want the sensation to subside. "…keep going." I begged, feeling like a junkie desperate for another hit of smack.

Ryan recommenced his movements and the fireworks continued exploding in my brain. I wanted to jump on top of him, but the logistics of such a feat would no doubt kill the moment of passion. I felt his penis begin to twitch and I knew he was about to cum so I arched my hips to guide him deeper. I was completely filled with him, yet I needed more. We were both making noises like wild beasts and, as he hit a magical spot somewhere deep inside me, our moans turned to howls. I could feel his fluid gushing into me and it only added to the force of my already intense orgasm.

"Holy shit," Ryan puffed, "I've never seen you go like that before."

"Yeah I know. Pregnancy definitely has its perks," I giggled as his retreating penis tickled my thigh.

"So it wasn't anything to do with my amazing skills then?"

"It was a combination," I said, inelegantly rolling over to face him.

"Can you believe we only have three months to go?" he said rubbing my belly.

"No, it's going very quickly."

"Has Gaz found anyone to cover your maternity leave yet?"

"Nope, but he's got an interview today, so fingers crossed."

"Really? So you're not freaking out about this then?" he asked disbelievingly.

"Not at all," I lied. The truth was, I was totally freaking out. I mean, what if this person came in and fucked up all my hard work. Or worse yet… what if they were totally amazing?

"You're such a liar," Ryan teased.

"Okay, so I'm a bit worried," I conceded. "What if they're better than me and Gaz doesn't want me back?"

"That will never happen."

"What makes you so sure of that?"

"Because you're the best Creative Director in London," he replied, kissing me on the forehead.

"You always know the right thing to say." I felt my whole body relax at his confidence in me.

"That's because I'm your husband, and I know you better than you know yourself."

I smiled and stared into his beautiful brown eyes, "I love you."

"I love you too," he said kissing me gently on the lips, "which is why I think you should start your maternity leave as soon as Gaz finds someone."

"No. I'm not stopping until I'm about to pop," I half-joked.

"Honey, you need to rest up. That little frame of yours is under a lot of pressure."

"I'm fine Ryan. Besides, we need all the money we can get."

Ryan sighed disapprovingly. "Every extra cent counts, but I don't want you pushing yourself too hard."

"I'd rather go as long as I can, so we've got the mortgage covered for a bit longer."

"Just let me worry about that stuff. You're doing enough work cooking up our baby."

"Ugh. I'll be glad when she's out and I can have my body back again. I feel like an incontinent whale," I joked, rubbing my huge belly.

"Well you look beautiful," he said, placing his hand on top of mine.

"There's that charm again," I said running my fingers through his curly hair.

"Well I am your Prince Charming after all," he teased. "I have to play my part."

I grinned and nudged him playfully, finding myself lost in his big brown eyes.

"Did you ever imagine three years ago that we'd be here now?" I asked dotingly.

"Having hot sex you mean?" he teased, grinning like an idiot. "Absolutely. You didn't have me fooled with your girl-next-door looks."

"No, you plonker," I said, slapping his arm playfully. "You know what I mean. Did you think we'd end up getting married and having a child? I certainly didn't."

"No, of course you didn't. You were only using me for my body," he grinned. "Little did you know that you'd never get rid of me. Mwahahahaha." Ryan threw his head back with a pretend evil laugh.

"Or maybe it was part of my plan all along," I teased with a wink. "Maybe you fell right into my trap."

"Well I hadn't thought of that," he agreed with a smile, casting his eyes down to my belly.

He leaned down to gently kiss the bump.

"Hey baby," he whispered, "you have a very clever mummy."

- RYAN McPHERSON -

With my head resting against Kat's belly I felt a huge rush of love for both her and the little girl she was growing inside there. I still couldn't believe that I was going to be a dad. Hopefully I'd do a better job than my own father.

"I might not always get things right, but I promise that I'll be the best daddy I can be," I told our nameless baby. "I love your mummy very much, and I love you too... Maddie?" I suggested, testing out another name.

"Nope, I'm not a fan of Maddie," Kat asserted firmly.

The baby kicked against my face.

"Oh my god, she just kicked!" I squealed like an excited ten-year old girl.

"Yeah I felt it."

"I guess she doesn't like Maddie either." I placed my palm where my head had been and looked up at Kat, who was more beautiful than ever. "I can't believe we're going to be parents."

"I know, right?"

I crawled to my knees to kiss her, "I love you."

"I love you too."

"You know you had me at hello," I joked, remembering our flirtatious first-meeting by the sparkling turquoise pool of Shoreditch House. Kat had captured my attention immediately with her joyful laugh, wild auburn hair and big hazel eyes.

"I'm sure anyone with two legs could have had you that night given the amount of coke you'd snorted in the bathroom with Nathan."

"No way," I disagreed, wrapping my arm around her shoulder. "Cocaine makes me fussier my love, and you were the hottest woman in the place. It was just good luck for me that Nathan was on a mission to hook us up."

Kat snuggled into my chest.

"Yeah, I guess we do owe him that much don't we?"

"I owe him everything," I said, gently rubbing her beautiful bump as I looked into her eyes.

She groaned, "Oh no."

"What? Are you okay? Is it the baby?"

"No. It's just that you're being so sweet it's making me horny all over again."

I laughed loudly, "Well that's a relief."

"For you maybe," she joked, "but it's the opposite of relief for me."

"It's a problem that can be easily fixed," I said, running my hand towards her bare thigh.

"Nice thought babe, but we'll be late for work," she said rolling ungracefully out of our queen-size bed.

"What if I offered my services as a sex-slave for the evening? Would that make you feel better?"

"I don't know, I do have a hectic sex-slave schedule tonight, but I'll see if I can squeeze you in somewhere," she teased, giving me a quick kiss before she waddled off to the bathroom for a shower. I sighed contentedly and leaned back against the bedhead feeling satisfied.

"What about Lindy?" I called after her.

"Ugh, no, definitely not Lindy," her disgusted reply echoed from the bathroom.

"What's wrong with Lindy?"

"Lindy's an airhead name."

"Seriously?!" I asked with a laugh. "My favourite nanny was called Lindy."

"You've just made my point for me Ryan. We're not naming our daughter after one of your childhood nannies."

"Why not?"

"Because it just feels weird," she answered honestly.

The sound of the shower filled the room. Kat had always felt envious of my aristocratic upbringing, which was poetic because I was secretly jealous of her relatively humble one. Although her mother had caused a lot of stress and scandal in their family, Kat had had a relatively nice childhood, complete with a sibling, as well as parents who actually parented. My parents, on the other hand, had been barely present and on the odd occasion when they were around they'd been cold, distant and unaffectionate. The only reason they'd had a child was to carry on the McPherson line and, if it hadn't been for my Grandfather threatening to cut them off from the family fortune, they wouldn't have had a child at all.

Soon I'd have to make a decision whether or not to allow them to be grandparents themselves. I wanted to believe that they'd make up for all the mistakes they'd made with me, but deep down I knew that our baby would be better off without them.

- ASHLEY GRANGER -

It was a bright, shiny Monday morning, and I hoped that the early summer sunshine was a sign of good luck for my job interview. Wrapped in my damp towel, I scrutinised myself in the full-length mirror. I was still getting used to my new look and sometimes it felt like I was staring at a stranger. Most people would have lost weight after spending three years practicing yoga in Bali, but not me. I'd gained about thirty pounds and was shapelier than I'd ever been in my life. If truth be told, I preferred my curvy figure to my previously gaunt one, but I wasn't convinced that the rest of London would agree; especially in conjunction with the bleached blonde hairdo I was now modeling.

My freshly dyed hair looked slightly less dramatic wet, but it was still undoubtedly white. What on earth had I been thinking letting the hairdresser talk me into ash blonde? Who did I think I was, Daenerys Stormborn? Thankfully, three years in the tropics had also gifted me with a caramel tan, otherwise I would have looked more like Brienne of Tarth than The Mother of Dragons. Although realistically, with my height, I probably wasn't far off being a Brienne look-alike.

I bit my lip as I studied my reflection. Was I totally out of place in the city now? Would this look cut-it for one of London's biggest ad agencies? I had no idea. I was so out of sync with British fashion. It had only been a month since I'd moved back to London from my Indonesian hideaway and, amazingly, my life was beginning to resemble something that other people might refer to as 'normal'. I had a regular yoga teaching gig at one of the gyms; I'd moved into my own flat; I'd made a couple of friends; and Dominic Doyle was locked-away behind bars where he belonged. The nightmare of my decade with Dom was finally behind me and, if I got this job, then I'd legitimately be able to consider myself part of the real world again. I knew I was placing too much emphasis on this interview, but it felt like a pivotal moment for my new life and I couldn't under-play that fact.

Swallowing against my rising nerves, I opened my wardrobe and felt a rush of awe as I pulled out the stunning new dress that I'd bought on credit specifically for the occasion. I ran my hand down the soft fawn-coloured fabric. I wasn't normally one for labels, but it was hard not to be impressed by the immaculately designed garment. I'd never owned anything quite so perfect and I was almost too scared to wear it.

In addition to my unaffordable dress, I'd also purchased an extortionately expensive, vegan-friendly handbag; a pair of stilettos; an array of matching jewelry and a whole kit of organic, ethical make-up. Needless to say, I was determined to make a good first impression for this interview without compromising my cruelty-free principles.

I carefully zipped myself into the beautiful dress and, as I rifled around my box of essential oils for my smell of the day, I caught a glimpse of the pink stuffed rabbit that was shoved to the back of my wardrobe. My heart gave a little twinge. That rabbit was the only remaining evidence of a life long-gone. I had no idea why I'd unpacked it; I shouldn't have even kept the damn thing. I pulled it out of the cupboard and tossed it into the rubbish bin. I didn't want the reminder anymore. That rabbit was a symbol of everything that Dom had stolen from me. It was like a morbid replacement for the baby I'd lost.

I snorted in disgust. 'Lost' wasn't exactly the most accurate description of what had happened to my daughter. 'Lost' made it sound like I'd misplaced her, but the reality was much darker than that. My unborn child had been violently beaten to death inside my body before she'd even seen the light of day. Beaten to death by her own father. There were no words to adequately describe my feeling of loss. Only a mother would ever understand the pain of losing a baby. A mother... which I was not. My first experience of motherhood had been stolen from me, and I had never had the chance to meet my beautiful little Mia.

I pushed my feelings down deep and moved the bin out of sight as if it would stop the sadness. But nothing would ever stop the sadness. I swallowed back hot tears. It was my own fault. I should have left Dom the second that I'd seen that test result. Why the fuck had I stayed?

I heard a beep from the depths of the aforementioned handbag, and fished out my brand-new smart-phone which, thanks to a clever package deal, had been the least expensive purchase I'd made for the sake of this interview.

'Good luck with the interview babes. You've totally got this. Kesh xx' Kesha worked as an instuctor at the gym I taught yoga and she was the only real friend I'd made since moving back home. The feisty brunette and become my biggest supporter over the previous few months, and had relentlessly encouraged me to apply for the job at Artemis. I'd told her a tiny bit about my history and she seemed to have taken it upon herself to be my own personal life coach.

'Thanks Kesh. I'll keep you posted. xx' I sent my response and stared at the recent calls list in my phone. My finger hovered over my Mum's name. Should I tell my parents about the interview? How would they feel about the fact that I was planning to go back to agency life? They'd probably flip out. If it was up to them, I'd still be living under their roof, wrapped in cotton wool.

No. There was no point in telling them until I actually had a job offer. Or maybe after I'd already started? I needed to do this, and I needed to stay focused and calm. This interview was the most exciting opportunity in my career to-date, and I had to give it the best shot I could.

I scrolled down my contacts list and dialed Jan Irving instead. Jan was the psychologist who had been assigned to me when I was in the hospital recovering from Dom's attack. If truth be told, I hadn't been particularly fond of her back then. She had this annoying habit of pointing out issues that I was more comfortable ignoring. I thought back to the day I'd first met Jan.

"Ash love, this is Doctor Irving," Mum said introducing the petite blonde woman standing next to her. With her cropped suede boots and her funky, chunky jewelry, Doctor Irving looked way too trendy to be a psychologist. The well-dressed doctor smiled kindly as she approached the bed.

"Hi Ashley. You can call me Jan," she said, as my parents began edging towards the door. "Your mother tells me you're feeling a little dejected?"

"We'll give you two some privacy," said my mother as the two of them snuck out into the hallway. I stared silently at Jan. What exactly was she expecting me to say?

"Do you want to tell me about what happened?" she asked gently, as she pulled up a chair.

"Not really."

"Okay," Jan nodded patiently and settled back into her chair as if preparing herself to be there for a while. "I'll just sit here and you can talk if you want to."

I knew Jan wasn't going to go away, but I was too scared to talk about the attack. If I talked about it, then it would be real and I wanted to forget it ever happened. But that was stupid. It did happen and whether I talked about it or not, nothing would ever change that. I sighed, deciding it would be better to talk and get it over and done with.

"I'd been ill for a few weeks," I said quietly, giving in to the pain as I cast my mind back to the day of Dom's attack. Jan nodded but remained silent. "It got so bad I had to take a few days off work," I paused. "I never take time off work." Work had always been my sanctuary. It was the one piece of 'normal' in amongst my insane world of abuse and violence. It was also the one part of my life that Dom hadn't managed to infiltrate, and being sick at home, had meant that I'd been constantly under Dom's scrutiny.

"I decided to go to the doctors so I could get back to work," I told Jan, intentionally omitting all Dom related information, "and that's when I found out I was pregnant."

"I take it the pregnancy wasn't planned then?" Jan asked gently. I shook my head slightly as a lump rose in my throat. Although I was grief-stricken at losing the baby, there was a small part of me that had felt relieved. A baby would have tied me to Dom forever. If we had shared a child, my life would never have been my own. Guilt engulfed me at the thought that this tragedy had actually been a narrow escape from a life of hell. "Ashley, it's okay to have mixed feelings about this," said Jan comfortingly as she read me like a book.

I squeezed my eyes shut and shook my head, trying to fight the tears but it was a hopeless battle. Ten years of suppressed pain began exploding out of me with astonishing intensity. It was all too much to handle and my grief, my guilt, my shame and my anger all hit me in relentless, violent waves. I was in excruciating pain both physically and emotionally, but I had absolutely no control over the loud, heavy sobs that were escaping, unpermitted, from the depths of my soul.

As time went on I'd grown to appreciate Jan's head-shrinky ways and also her willingness to call me out on my bullshit. Even though I was no longer her client, she still liked me to check-in whenever I encountered any major life events, and this interview certainly counted as a major life event for me.

"Ah the lovely Ms Granger," Jan answered cheerfully. Jan was the only person I knew who could be chirpy at that time of the morning. "How are you sweetheart?"

"Hey Jan, I'm really well thanks," I replied, splashing nearly half a bottle of my Serenity oil onto my wrists to curb my anxiety. "How are you?"

"You know me, I'm great as always," Jan said while I quickly dabbed the dripping liquid onto my neck. "It's good to hear from you Ashley. How are you settling back into London life?"

"Surprisingly well actually… which is kind of why I'm calling you," I told her, feeling a sense of calm wash over me as I inhaled the comforting lavender and vanilla scent emanating from my pulse points. "I've got a job interview today."

"That's fantastic!" she said. "For yoga or design?"

"Design."

"Ashley that's brilliant," Jan said. "How are you feeling about it?"

"Nervous. And excited..." I studied myself in the mirror. I looked acceptable. "...but mostly nervous."

"Nervous isn't a bad thing. It means that you're pushing your comfort zone," she told me reassuringly. "So what's your biggest concern about it?"

"That they're going to laugh me out of the interview. I've been out of the industry for three years, how am I going to explain that?"

"You just tell them you took some time off to live abroad. Anyone with common sense would understand that. It means you're a well-balanced individual."

I snorted with amusement. "Or that I'm a total train wreck."

"Don't project your own perception of yourself onto other people Ashley. You may feel like your life is a train wreck, but that's not the reality of it. You're one of the strongest, most resilient people I know, and you've worked hard on yourself these past few years so don't undermine that. I work with corporate CEOs who are less together than you are, so I think it's about time you gave yourself some credit for how far you've come."

"Thanks Jan. I hope you're right." What if she was wrong?

"Of course I'm right," she said with a smile in her voice. "Now go in there and show them how amazing you are. You've got this Ashley. I know you do."

"Yeah. I've totally got this," I agreed, half believing myself.

"I'm so proud that you're reclaiming your life sweetheart."

'Reclaiming my life'. I liked the sound of that.

My nerves hit full-force as I climbed into the back of the waiting black cab. I quickly dabbed on some more of my lavender oil to keep myself calm.

"Where to luv?" asked the taxi driver.

"Marylebone Road please," I answered with a polite smile, carefully placing my leather portfolio on the bench seat next to me. After the painstaking hours I'd spent meticulously laying out my designs, it was possibly the most valuable item I owned... with the exception of my new outfit.

"No problem," the cabbie replied, slowly pulling out into the bustling London traffic while I rifled around my bag for my good luck charm. I needed it today more than ever. I extracted the black leather box that housed my special Mont Blanc and flipped open the box to admire the exquisite gold pen. It had been a 30th birthday gift from my father and it was such a work of art that I'd never actually used it for writing. Today, that would change. After three years of solitary confinement, the pen was finally going to fulfill its life purpose.

I popped the box back into my bag and rolled the pen in my hand, re-reading the inscription on the back. '*My Dearest Ashley...the world is yours. PB*'. My mind flashed back to the day my dad had given me the pen.

In all the times I had thought about how I would celebrate my thirtieth birthday, lying incapacitated in a hospital bed had never been on my list of possible scenarios.

"Happy birthday cupcake," Dad said as he kissed me on the forehead and handed me a present.

"Doesn't feel very happy," I answered solemnly, as I reached up to take the gift from him. It was a rectangular box, neatly wrapped in gold paper with a massive white ribbon around it. Very professional and most definitely not personally wrapped by my father.

I winced as one of my ribs twinged in pain at the movement. Even with the heavy-duty pain-killers they were running through my IV, I was in a world of hurt, and I was severely lacking the ability to find birthday cheer given the circumstances.

"Oh love," Mum cooed comfortingly, as she popped her own multi-coloured birthday gift down on the dresser, alongside a bunch of yellow and pink gerberas. I knew she was trying to brighten the place up, but all the cheery colours were only serving to fuel my depression.

Mum stroked my hair, planted a soft kiss on my cheek and gently cuddled me as best she could amongst all the tubes and casts. My right leg was broken, my left wrist was fractured in several places, I was covered head to toe in bruises. I was unable to laugh, sneeze, cough or breathe heavily because of my four cracked ribs, yet strangely all of those injuries paled in comparison to the grief that haunted me over the loss of my unborn child.

"Open my present pumpkin," prompted Dad excitedly, as Mum reluctantly relinquished her position at my bedside. "It's a little something special for your 30th just from me," he announced proudly.

"Your father insisted on getting you a present of his own this year," Mum explained, rolling her eyes good-naturedly. Obviously there had been some sort of 'discussion' surrounding the additional, unapproved present that Dad had purchased.

"Oh. Thanks Papa Bear," I said, rewarding him with a half-hearted smile. I slowly untied the ribbon and tore off the thick gold paper to reveal a white cardboard box with Mont Blanc stenciled on the front in bold black writing. It didn't take a genius to figure out what was inside. I opened the cardboard packaging, slid out the black leather box and flipped open the lid to reveal the most exquisite gold pen that I had ever seen. "Wow Dad," I breathed in admiration, "this is gorgeous."

"That's not all, turn it over," he instructed, bouncing like an excited child. There was an inscription on the back. A tear rolled down my bruised cheek as I read it. How exactly did my father think the world was mine, when my world was in complete tatters? I had nothing. No money, no house, no car, no job…no baby. I failed to see how the world was anything close to being mine.

"Whereabouts are you off to then?" The driver asked chirpily.

"Artemis Advertising," I exhaled in one long breath, as I returned to the present. I still hadn't quite processed the fact that I had been invited to meet with the CEO of London's largest advertising agency.

"That's quite a fancy firm isn't it?" he asked, making casual conversation.

"Yeah it is."

"Do you work there?"

"Not yet," I answered, fidgeting with the pen. "I'm going in for an interview."

"Ah, that's grand," he said with an understanding nod. "So what's the job you're going for?"

"Creative Director."

"Sounds important."

"Well, I used to be," I chuckled. "I've been out of the game for a while so I'm hoping they don't laugh me out of the interview."

"Just go in there believing that the job is yours," instructed my impromptu life coach. "So what was it that took you out of the workforce? Travel or baby?"

My hand shifted instinctively to my stomach and an unauthorised tear sprang from the corner of my eye. "Umm… both I guess."

"Sorry love, I didn't mean to pry, I just thought because you had time off…"

"No, it's fine." I hastily wiped away another rogue tear before it ruined my make-up.

"I'm sorry."

"Honestly it's fine," I repeated, fumbling around my handbag for my compact. The sweet old driver left me to my thoughts, while I glanced dubiously at my reflection. My bright blonde hair shone in the sunlight. Maybe it wasn't a total disaster, or maybe it was. It was hard to tell. I patted down my fringe and stared intently at my reflection. "The job is yours," I told myself quietly as I began to re-apply my eye liner, "so don't fuck it up."
The truth was, I was perfectly suited to the job. In fact, I'd done so much extra study whilst I was in Bali that I was actually over-qualified for the position… so why did I doubt myself? Probably because my decade with Dominic Doyle had eroded any self-confidence I'd once had. How had I stayed with him for so long? Why had I waited until he nearly killed me to leave?

"We're here love," the driver called before I'd even realised the cab had stopped.

"Oh r-right," I stuttered. I hastily shoved everything back into my purse and passed him the fare with a shaky hand. "Thanks," I said, grabbing my portfolio off the seat. I closed the cab door behind me and the heavy folder slipped out of my grasp. "Oh shit!" I grappled to save the folder, but in the process, I dropped my bag. Both of my prized possessions landed on the dusty curb with a loud clatter and the contents of my expensive handbag scattered all over the footpath. It was not an encouraging omen.

"Fantastic," I mumbled, clambering around the dirty pavement in my brand-new dress, trying to salvage my belongings. "So fucking clumsy." I'd grabbed a few of the loose items, before I heard the cab driver climb out of his taxi.

"You need a hand love?" he asked, as a pair of well-polished leather shoes appeared in front of me. If a cabbie could afford shoes like that then I was definitely in the wrong profession.
One of my tampons floated in front of my face.

"Here, I caught your lipstick trying to make an escape," joked the owner of the flashy shoes in a smooth deep voice. I blushed with embarrassment and peered up in mortification at the owner of the expensive shoes.

"Oh my god," I blurted accidentally. Standing in front of me was the most divine specimen of a human male I had ever seen in my life. He was Thor. A well-groomed version of the Norse god mind you, but with his blonde hair and chiseled features, there was a definite Thor-ness about him. The gorgeous, tall stranger knelt down next to me and my stomach flipped at the waft of his spicy after-shave. "Thor- err…thanks…" I stuttered, blushing as he handed back my tampon with a kind smile. I giggled nervously embarrassed by my Freudian slip.

"Are you alright love?" the driver asked from behind Thor. I quickly shoved the tampon back into my bag.

"Umm, yes thanks." I gave him a 'thumbs up', unable to tear my eyes away from the luscious man kneeling in front of me.

"Okay," he said with what sounded like amusement, and from the corner of my eye I saw him climb back into his cab.

"Nice handbag," said Thor as he flashed me a confident smile. My heart skipped a beat. There was something distinctly familiar about his sparkly blue eyes, but I couldn't put my finger on it.

"Thanks." My voice was barely a whisper. Our eyes locked, and I felt that same flash of recognition. Thor leaned forward to grab the tube of mascara that was rolling past his knee and I could feel the warmth of his minty breath against my skin. It sent a rush of desire through my body and my eyes instinctively flicked to his mouth.

'Ashley Jane Granger, do not even think about kissing the beautiful stranger,' my mother's disembodied voice scolded me from somewhere in the depths of my logical brain. I bit my lip to avoid the temptation and when the man handed over my runaway mascara, a tiny spark of electricity crackled between our hands. We both laughed as the static sparked, but neither of us moved.

"Looks like we made sparks," he joked with a sexy wink that took my breath away. I stared at him speechless, unable to form a response. "Well, I think we got all of it," Thor added with a smile, still gripping tightly to his end of my mascara wand.

"Yeah," I replied stupidly, catching a glimpse of the time on his vintage gold Rolex. I was about to be late for the most important meeting of my life. "Oh my god, I have to go!" I yanked the mascara from his grasp and scooped up the rest of my belongings.

"Oh, okay," he nodded in confusion, clearly taken aback by my sudden retreat.

"Sorry, it's just that I'm running late," I explained, jumping hastily to my feet. I brushed the dirt off my bare knees, thankful that my expensive new dress was unsoiled. "Thanks again."

"No problem," Thor said, standing up. He was even more impressive at full height. "Do you work around here?" he asked, sliding his hand casually into his pocket as if he was settling in for a chat.

"Umm… err…" I stuttered, glancing between the beautiful stranger and my possible future workplace. Come on Granger. Focus woman. Don't blow this interview for a hot stranger. My eyes landed on the Artemis building. My decision was made. I looked back at Thor and shook my head with a grin.

"Not yet." I smiled at the beautiful man, then turned and ran towards Artemis Advertising, nearly bumping into a skinny guy who strode out of the building wearing a huge black Stetson.

"Oh, sorry," I said, noticing that the man was wielding some sort of sporting equipment. I stopped and stared at him agape for a moment. Cowboy hats certainly weren't a common sight in London, let alone when combined with a net stick thing.

"Oh excusez-moi," the quirky man said with a grin, tilting his hat as he walked on. I laughed in shock and looked back at Thor, waving a hand in gratitude before I quickly bolted through the big glass doors.

Thor might possibly have been the man of my dreams, but the job of my dreams was within my grasp and I wasn't going to risk that for anyone. Not even an astonishingly handsome stranger.

- NATHAN STONE -

I watched silently, as the green-eyed goddess made a hasty retreat. She was the most stunning woman I'd ever met, and she was as impressive from behind as she was front-on. Despite the fact that I was enjoying the view as she ran away, I was also silently devastated about her abrupt exit. In three minutes and barely ten words, the woman had completely blown me away. Besides having the most sensational rack I'd ever seen in my life, she was the first female in history to walk away from me without leaving so much as a phone number. Was I losing my touch?

"Good luck in Paris," called my eccentric French Creative Director, as he waved a lacrosse stick in greeting. I waved back, unsurprised by his peculiar choice of accessories.

"Thanks Francesco. Anything you want me to bring back?"

"Oui," he said with a nod, "Sandrine Delfontaine."

I laughed. "I'll do my best."

"Are you getting in mate?" the cab driver shouted through the window.

"Umm…yeah," I said as I gave Francesco another quick wave and threw my wheelie-case into the back of the cab. "Kings Cross St Pancras please."

"Right you are."

I reached over to close the door, and something on the ground outside caught my eye. It was a pen. A very nice pen. A gold Mont Blanc to be exact. It was the sort of pen that one would not be happy about losing. I scooped up the pen and checked my watch in one seamless move. 10:35am. I was running late. If I chased the girl, then I'd miss my train and thus totally fuck my important client meeting. The pen would have to come with me.

"Know any shortcuts?" I asked the cab driver as I slammed the door shut. "I can't miss that train."

He instantly rose to the challenge, "Sure, what time does it leave?"

"10:55"

"Ha! Plenty of time!" We set off at grand prix speed and I leaned back in the big seat, juggling the fancy pen between my fingers.

"You don't know how I could find that girl again do you?" I asked, causing the cabbie to raise his eyebrows in curiosity.

"Why's that?" he asked with hint of amusement.

"She left her pen behind," I explained, waving the expensive pen in front of the rear-view mirror, so he didn't think I was going to hunt her down under the guise of a lost Bic ballpoint.

"All I know is that she's got an interview at Artemis Advertising," answered the driver in a fatherly tone.

"Thanks." Tracking down the curvaceous cutie would be easier than I'd expected. As I played absent-mindedly with her pen, I noticed an inscription on the back of it. "Hmmm...PB," I mumbled. Her boyfriend perhaps? That would explain why she didn't give me her number.

I was busy pondering the identity of 'PB' when my phone beeped in my pocket. It was a message from Gaz.

'Good luck today lad. I know you won't let me down.' Fuck. No pressure at all then.

'Cheers Gaz,' I replied simply. It was best to keep things simple and quick with Gaz.

'Do whatever it takes,' he responded.

'Will do,' I agreed, feeling the weight of the whole agency bear down on my shoulders. We were doing well, there was no doubt about that, but we were depending on this account to escalate us to a global scale. Gaz was aiming for a merger with an affiliate agency in the US so that he could finally retire. This account would make the deal a no-brainer for the Yanks.

I sighed and shoved both the pen and my phone into the front pocket of my satchel. Right now, the only woman who mattered was Sandrine Delfontaine. The cabbie wove in and out of traffic and, as promised, he got me to the station with five minutes to spare.

"Champion," I told him, handing over a massive tip before I jumped out and sprinted down the escalator with my suitcase above my head, as if I was an Olympic athlete. This meeting was going to make me an advertising legend, so I wasn't going to let it slip through my fingers for anyone.

At the check-in desk was a cute brunette sporting a name tag that said, 'Hi I'm Rachel'.

"Hi Rachel," I greeted her in my most charming tone, holding out my ticket with what I hoped was a flirty grin. "Am I too late?"

"Not at all Mr Stone," she answered with a sexy smile. I snuck a quick glance at her cleavage as she leaned over to take the ticket from my hand. Not quite as impressive as Dearest Ashley's, but still not too shabby. "We always allow extra time for our first-class passengers." She concluded with a wink.

"Thank god for that," I beamed, unable to keep my eyes off her ample rack. I couldn't help it. I was a boob man and there was nothing I could do about it. Rachel noticed my wandering eyes and smiled.

"I noticed that it's your birthday today," she said casually, as her long, fake nails began tapping at the keyboard.

"Yes, but let's keep that our little secret."

"Well in that case, happy non-birthday," she replied, handing back my ticket with a cheeky sparkle in her eyes. "Have a great day Mr Stone."

I took the ticket and noticed that she'd jotted her phone number on the back of it. "Well Rachel, it's certainly off to a good start." Maybe I hadn't lost my touch after all.

I strode through the gates to the waiting Eurostar and hurriedly boarded the first-class carriage. I found my seat and stowed my luggage with the help of the young stewardess.

"Can I get you any refreshments sir?" she asked, once I'd settled into the cushy recliner.

"A double-espresso and a bottle of Voss please," I requested politely as I set up my tablet on the little table and got to work on the final tweaks for my presentation. I was so engrossed in my pitch preparation that the train journey flew by.

"The next stop is Paris Gare du Nord," announced the driver over the PA system, what seemed like only minutes after our departure.

"Oh," I mumbled with surprise, as I looked up from my work. "Time flies." I packed up my belongings and readied myself for the biggest meeting of my career. As I exited the station gates, I spotted a wiry middle-aged man, holding a sign with my name on it.

"Bonjour," I greeted the man with an outstretched hand. "Je m'appelle Nathan Stone."

"Ahh bonjour Mr Stone. Je m'appelle Didier. Je suis le directeur des operations," answered the man with a friendly smile. His name was Didier and he was Sandrine's Managing Director, which made him the second most important person I was going to meet that day. I was surprised that he had been tasked with greeting me; I would have expected Sandrine to send someone less expensive than her right-hand man.

"Ravi de vous rencontrer Didier."

"Nice to meet you too Nathan but please, speak in English. It gives me good practice. I'm still learning," Didier admitted, as he led me towards a metallic black Rolls Royce Phantom. The expensive car was such a blatant show of wealth that I began to wonder whether I'd be able to pull this pitch off. Didier opened the automatic boot for me.

"You're doing very well so far," I told him.

"Thank you," he said proudly. "Just make sure you use Français when you meet Sandrine. She likes to see that people make an effort for her."

"Oh, okay," I chuckled, as I threw my suitcase into the trunk. "Thanks for the tip."

"The tip?" Didier asked, seeking clarification on my English slang.

"It means, advice. When someone tells you something useful you can say 'thanks for the tip' instead of 'thanks for the advice'. It's a little more casual."

"Ah, well thanks for the tip Nathan," he said with a wink. I got the feeling that Didier and I were going to get along well. We set off towards Sandrine's office and chatted amicably as we drove along the streets of Paris.

"I'm surprised Sandrine sent her second in-charge to pick me up," I said with a smile.

"She wanted to make sure you were well looked after," Didier said, looking me up and down with an amused smile. "I have a feeling she's going to eat you alive."

"Elle va me manger tout cru?" I repeated in French, assuming that he'd intended to say something different. Perhaps he hadn't gotten the English translation right.

"Oui," Didier nodded with a knowing smile.

"Oh." I fell silent, chewing on my nails as I stared out of the car window at the luxurious sights of Saint-Germain-des-Prés. Was that what Gaz had meant by 'do whatever it takes'? Was this all just a lavish charade to cover the fact that he was actually pimping me out?

"You don't look like the type to shy away from a challenge Nathan," Didier teased.

"No, I'm not," I agreed with a tight smile and as much confidence as I could muster.

"So why do you look so worried?" he asked with a grin, as we approached the massive stone building of Delfontaine headquarters, which also happened to be the home of Sandrine Delfontaine.

"I'm nervous. Not worried."

"You should be," Didier said with amusement, "but try not to let it show." A massive iron gate slid open to allow the black Rolls down the cobbled driveway and I was starting to wonder what I'd gotten myself into. I gulped loudly as we entered the inner sanctum of the tree-lined Delfontaine Compound. As with most of Paris, the estate entrance was punctuated with platane trees, but these ones had been hedged squarely as if they'd been decapitated. The gardens were beautiful but the harsh, square-topped platanes gave the place an undercurrent of harshness, and maybe even a tinge of violence.

We approached the building itself, and a large, black roller-door heaved upwards with a creak of displeasure. I glanced over at Didier who was mindlessly tapping the steering wheel as he waited. He seemed incredibly relaxed, but I got the distinct feeling that I was entering the lion's den as the sacrificial lamb. I peered inside the cavernous garage as the place lit up in a perfectly orchestrated sequence.

"Holy shit," I gasped at the sight before me. There were at least twenty-five high-end cars, including a Bugatti Veyron and a Hennessy Venom. "Are these all Ms Delfontaine's?"

"No, not all of them. Some of them are our staff cars, but the good ones are hers," he said, nodding towards the Veyron. "Sandrine is fond of the finer things in life."

"So it would seem," I said, in awe of the insanely expensive collection.

Didier parked the car, and we made our way inside the extravagant building. Everything about it screamed excess and over-indulgence. Even the light fixtures were over the top. Clearly Sandrine Delfontaine did not do anything by halves.

When we reached the reception area, I heard a sultry voice from behind me. "Nathan Stone. Lovely to finally meet you."

I turned to greet the mysterious woman I'd heard so much about. Sandrine was in her fifties, but there was something undeniably alluring about her. She was one of the most attractive older women I'd ever seen. Sexuality was oozing from her every pore, and it was clear that she was a woman who knew exactly what she wanted.

"Ms Delfontaine," I said, momentarily forgetting that I was supposed to be speaking French.

"Please call me Sandrine," she purred provocatively, offering me her hand. I wasn't sure whether she wanted me to kiss it or shake it.

"Okay," I agreed, deciding it was safer to shake her hand at this point. "Tellement agréable de vous rencontrer enfin. Merci de me recevoir."

"Your French is très impressive Nathan," Sandrine commended me in English, her tone not unlike a school teacher praising a small child for neat printing. Gold star for Stoner.

"Merci," I answered, with a sneaking suspicion that I was being seamlessly manipulated. There was something about Sandrine that made me want to please her, and I had the sense that whether I liked it or not, I was already under her control.

- KAT McPHERSON -

My desk phone shrilled sharply, and I glanced at the dial. It was Gareth Hemsworth, my demanding boss.

"Hi Gaz," I trilled, trying to pretend that it was a normal day and that I wasn't helping recruit my replacement.

"Our first interviewee is here," he said without preamble.

"Okay great," I answered, trying to muster enthusiasm for hammering a nail into the coffin of my own impending departure.

"I need to make a quick call before we start, so could you please go down and get her from reception?"

"Yeah sure."

"Great. Thanks. Her name is Ashley," Gaz said as I heard the shuffling of papers, "Ashley Granger."

"What?" I must have misheard him. He couldn't possibly have said Ashley Granger.

"I said, her name is Ashley Granger."

"Ashley Granger?" I asked, gripping the receiver against my ear in shock. "Did she used to work at Mareechi's?"

"Yes, that's right. Do you know her?"

"I know of her, but I thought she was…" I trailed off. It couldn't have been the same Ashley Granger that Ryan had told me about.

"Thought she was what?"

"Nothing, I must be thinking of the wrong person." Surely it couldn't be Ryan's Ashley.

"Does Ryan know her? It looks like they probably worked there at the same time. I'm about to call him and get his input."

"If it's the same girl then he does, but do you really need to call him now? Shouldn't we wait and see if she's any good before we waste time on references?"

"No, I'd rather know now. It will save time," he said firmly. "I'll meet you in the boardroom." Gaz said and then hung up abruptly. I slowly lowered the receiver and placed it gently back into the cradle with a sinking feeling in my belly... and this time it wasn't the baby. Ashley Granger had risen from the dead.

My mind flitted back to three years prior, when I'd first met Ryan. It had been the first time we'd spoken in detail about the mysterious woman, and the conversation had stayed with me. We'd been sitting on a large cushy daybed by the sparkling turquoise pool of Shoreditch House for Nathan's over-the-top birthday party.

"So, what's the vibe like at Mareechi's?" I asked Ryan as I sipped on my bright green cocktail.

"It's pretty good," he shrugged. "It's 'work hard, play hard', but that's pretty standard for an agency."

"Is the Creative Department any good?" I asked, tucking a wayward strand of curls behind my ear. It had been so long since I'd flirted with anyone I wasn't sure if I was even doing it right.

"Why? Are you looking for a job?" Ryan teased with a cheeky sparkle in his brown eyes, as he bumped his muscular shoulder against mine.

"Perhaps," I answered with a grin. "Are you looking for a Creative Director?"

"Yeah," he said nodding stiffly, "for the McEwan Account."

"You're kidding me?!" I said, nearly choking on my drink. "I ran the pitch for that account and you guys totally killed us."

"Yeah... we did," Ryan said apologetically. "Well, technically Ashley Granger did."

"I'd like to meet this Ashley Granger person," I said, amazed that Ryan had been one of the people responsible for stealing my dream account from underneath my nose.

"Err... well...it's sort of her position we're recruiting for," he said scratching his neck awkwardly. "She vanished three months ago."

"Vanished?" I asked, open-mouthed. That sounded a little melodramatic. "Did she get another job or something?"

"No one knows," Ryan replied with a shrug. "We haven't been able to track her down. She literally disappeared."

"Oh wow. Have you checked social media?" I asked, disbelieving that a human could simply just 'disappear'. How the hell could one vanish in our technological age? Surely if they looked hard enough they'd find some trace of the woman?

Ryan snorted indignantly, "Of course I have. She deleted all her accounts, her phone has been disconnected, her emails bounce back and her house is deserted. It's like she never existed. She's gone. Vanished."

"I'm sorry, were you close to her?"

He nodded solemnly. "She was my best mate."

"I thought Nathan was your best mate," I teased, trying to lighten the mood.

"Nathan thinks he's everyone's best mate," Ryan joked, nodding towards Ritchie and Nathan, who were at the bar doing shots together like best buddies. I studied Ryan for a moment. His pain was visible.

"You're in love with her, aren't you?" It was written all over his face.

"Who? Ashley?" he asked.

"No, the Queen the England," I teased with a smile, playfully nudging his shoulder with mine like he'd just done to me. He smiled shyly and looked down at his hands.

"Yeah, I guess I was."

"You still are." I told him assertively, "which is why Nathan is trying to get us together. He wants you to get over her."

"Nah, he doesn't know," he shrugged. "Besides... I don't think you can be in love with a ghost."

'A ghost'. That's what Ryan had called her that night and I'd known at that moment, that I would be the second love of Ryan's life. Now, three years later, on the anniversary of the day I'd met Ryan no-less, she had re-appeared as a candidate for my replacement. It was too bizarre to be a coincidence.

"Just breathe," I told myself calmly. Ryan and I were solid, and nothing would change that. Ashley Granger or not, we were happily married and Ryan wouldn't throw all of that away... would he?

I took a deep breath and made my way to reception. Of course he wouldn't. Ryan might have loved Ashley once, but he loved me now. Right? At the very least, I was his wife and I was having his baby, so even if Ashley was here to steal my man, Ryan's deeply-set morals would prevent him from cheating on me. I swallowed back my nerves and strode self-assuredly out into the reception foyer, stopping dead in my tracks when I saw Malibu Barbie loitering in the waiting area.

"Holy shit, please don't let that be her," I begged silently to any god that was willing to listen. Unfortunately, the tall, curvy blonde was the only person in the reception area so there was no doubt that it was her.

"Ashley Granger?" I asked hesitantly, as the woman began to take a seat. The Amazonian simultaneously rose and twirled with the grace of a (very tall) Bolshoi Ballet dancer.

"Yes?" she said with sparkly green eyes, as I gaped up at her with devastation. Oh dear god. She was gorgeous, and slim, and tanned, and tall - soooo tall - with the most amazingly long legs that I'd ever seen on a woman. It wouldn't be a hard decision for Ryan to make: his short, fat, pale wife; or this tall golden goddess from his past. "I'm Ashley Granger," the woman said with an outstretched hand. I momentarily fantasized about snapping her dainty wrist and kicking her perfect arse out the big glass doors.

"Wow, you're quite tall, aren't you?" I said, summoning all of my power to gently shake her elegant hand.

"Six foot without the heels, but I figure I shouldn't have to miss out on great shoes just because I'm tall."

"Very true," I agreed with a stiff nod. "I'm Kat McPherson. I'm the one you'll be covering. Gareth was caught up on the phone, so he suggested I show you to the boardroom."

"Okay sure."

I led her through the security gates and into the elevator foyer.

"So you worked at Mareechi's then?"

"Yeah, a while back. I've actually just returned from a three-year stint in Bali."

"Bali?" I asked as the lift doors opened. That would certainly explain why she had appeared to vanish off the face of the earth. "That's an odd place to go for our line of work isn't it?"

Ashley cleared her throat and followed me onto the elevator.

"I just wanted a change of pace for a while," she said smoothing down the front of her perfect dress.

I raised one eyebrow, "Couldn't handle the city pace?" I knew I was being bitchy but if she was a threat to my marriage in any way, I wasn't going to make it easy for her.

"I love the fast-pace of the city," Ashley replied, walking over to the full-length glass window that showcased the center tower of the building. "I just wanted to slow it down for a little while. Take a breather."

"Right." I said simply as the elevator began its ascent. Ashley stared out the window in awe of the sight before her. Our building was widely celebrated as one of the city's most impressive pieces of architecture, and from the inside it was clear to see why. The sun shone brightly through the massive round glass roof, and lit up the central shaft of the building as if it was an over-sized crystal chandelier. I remembered being awestruck the first time that I'd seen it too. I'd felt like Charlie, riding in Willy Wonka's magical glass elevator, and the look on Ashley's face mirrored mine from that day. Except that she was taller and way more gorgeous. "It's quite amazing isn't it?" I said, wondering why I was bothering to be friendly.

"It's breathtaking," Ashley agreed. "I bet you never get tired of it?"

I shrugged nonchalantly. "To be honest, you stop paying attention to it after a while."

"I don't think I'd ever stop paying attention to that view." Mercifully, the lift ground to a halt at the seventh floor, before I had a chance to gag out loud at her cheesiness.

"Here we are," I said alighting the lift, before leading Ashley down the window lined corridor to our chicly furnished boardroom. "Grab a seat. Gareth shouldn't be too long."

- RYAN McPHERSON -

I was busily perfecting a branding proposal in preparation for a phone conference with my sporting goods client, when my desk phone rang sharply. The screen said it was Gaz, so I greeted him with the brisk style he preferred.

"Yep?" I asked as cheerfully as possible.

"Ashley Granger," he grunted in his friendly tone. My chest cramped immediately.

"Pardon?" I spluttered, convinced that I'd imagined the words.

"Ashley Granger," Gareth repeated, "she used to work at Mareechi's. Did you know her?"

"Uhhh… yeah."

"Was she any good?"

"I'm not sure what you mean."

"Was Ashley a good Creative Director?" he asked impatiently.

"Umm…" I mumbled, trying to gather some words. I couldn't quite comprehend what was happening. Why was Gareth Hemsworth asking me about Ashley Granger? Why today? Maybe it was a prank and Kat was trying to wind me up.

"Come on McPherson, I haven't got all day. It's quite a simple question… is Ashley Granger a good Creative Director or not? I'm about to interview her for Kat's position so I want your opinion."

"She's coming in for an interview?" I spluttered in shock. Ashley was alive?

"She's already here. She's with your wife now, so I need a quick answer mate."

"Ashley's with Kat?" I squeaked, choking on the words.

"Jesus McPherson, keep up, will you?" he barked in exasperation. "I'm running late."

"Sorry. It's been a while since I've heard her name that's all."

"So, was she good?"

"Yes, she was a brilliant Creative Director. The best Creative Director I've ever worked with actually. Especially when it comes to digital. She knew - knows - more about websites and online marketing than some of the tech experts," I answered honestly. "In fact… it was Ashley who won the McEwan account. She was the Creative Director behind our pitch."

"Great, thanks." Gareth clicked down the receiver at his end and all I heard was the disconnection tone.

"No worries," I told the dead phone line. I was frozen in shock. Not only was Ashley alive, but she was in my office building… with my wife. I jumped up from my desk in a sprint towards the lifts when I ran straight into the solid, broad torso of my Project Manager, Ritchie Carlton.

"Oomph," I said as the air was knocked out of my lungs. The giant Australian looked down at me with a grin.

"You 'right mate?" he asked, slapping my back like I was a baby in need of burping.

"Yep," I whispered, trying to get some oxygen back into my lungs.

"You were bounding like a roo at a gate," he joked. Amazingly, after three years of friendship I'd finally begun to understand Ritchie's bizarre analogies.

"Yeah, there's someone I have to see," I said dodging around him to get to the lift before I lost my chance to see Ashley. If she was really here, I needed to see her for myself.

"No-can-do Sunshine," Ritchie said as he grabbed the back of my shirt and stopped me in my tracks. "We've got a phone conference with Jamie from Milner's Sports in about two minutes and Francesco has gone AWOL again."

"Ah shit," I sighed as Ritchie man-handled me back in the direction of my desk. Our oddball Creative Director had an annoying habit of vanishing right when we needed him. "How hard can it be to track down a six-foot Frenchman wearing a cowboy hat?"

"You'd be surprised," Ritch said with a deep, gravelly chuckle. "You get Jamie on the phone and I'll track down the crazy Frog."

I nodded and picked up my phone. "He's probably on the roof photographing pigeons... or maybe outside creating a collage with street rubbish... no wait... he'll be in the canteen sculpting the Tower of London out of mash." Sadly, there was about a 99% chance that I was correct on at least one of my predictions.

Ritchie laughed again. "Well, wherever he is... you're going to have to stall."

"Roger that," I agreed, pushing all thoughts of Ashley aside so that I could focus on the client who was solely responsible for my ability to pay my mortgage. "I'll stall for as long as I can, but we need Francesco back here ASAP because he's the only one on top of the TV commercial concepts."

After twenty minutes of seamless stalling by virtue of my God-given skill for making inane conversation, Ritchie had magically conjured up 'The Crazy Frog' and we proceeded with our concept presentation as planned. By the time it was over, I knew Ashley had probably left the building, but I had to try and catch her anyway. I plonked the phone down and sprinted upstairs to the boardroom just in time to see Gareth vacating the room.

"Is Ashley still here?" I asked him breathlessly.

"They've just gone down," he said, pointing towards the lift. The numbered lights above the occupied lift were quickly descending, while the other elevator had the 'up' button glowing. Fuck. The stairs it was.

"Thanks," I said, running back into the stairwell and down the endless flights of steps. My feet weren't carrying me fast enough, so I jumped onto the handrail and used it as a slide. I felt like an action star and I couldn't help making sound effects to ham it up a little. Eventually I came flying out of the stairwell on the ground-floor in a dramatic entrance to rival the best action hero, but Ashley was nowhere to be seen.

I spotted Kat heading back into the lift. "Is she still here?" I asked, puffing so hard I could barely breathe.

"You heard," my wife said flatly, as I peered out into the reception area.

"Gaz rang me earlier," I explained breathlessly, trying to catch a glimpse of Ashley.

"She's gone Ryan," Kat said stoically.

"Did you not think I might like to know that the woman was alive?!" I snapped without thinking. I wasn't angry at Kat, I was just annoyed that Ashley hadn't waited or even come past to say hi. Kat turned her back to me and boarded the waiting lift.

"I only just found out myself Ryan."

"Oh," I sighed, resting my hand against the open elevator door to catch my breath. "Well, what did she say? Where's she been? Why didn't she let me know she was okay?"

"She didn't say anything about you Ryan. I didn't tell her we were married. It was purely a business chat."

"Of course," I nodded, leaning against the door so it would stay open. "How did she go?"

Kat sighed heavily, "Gareth loved her. I'm pretty sure she got the job."

"Great!" I said cheerfully. I couldn't believe I'd be working with Ashley Granger again after all these years.

"Is it Ryan?" Kat spat incredulously, storming out of the elevator in a huff. "Is it really? Because as far as I see it, I'm being replaced by the only other woman you've ever loved, and you'll be seeing her every single day, while I'm at home nursing our baby."
I recoiled as if I'd been slapped in the face.

"Is that what you're worried about?" I asked in shock. "You think I'm going to cheat on you?"

"No. I know you'd never cheat," she paused, as I felt a wave of relief wash over me. "I think you're going to leave me for her."

My jaw dropped. It had never occurred to me that Kat might draw that conclusion. "Why would you ever think that?" I asked dumbfounded.

"Why wouldn't I think that?" she snapped angrily. I fell silent. Suddenly I felt like the shittiest husband in the world. I had no answer for her. I hadn't given her any reason to think otherwise with this crazy behaviour. I sighed and smiled at her apologetically.

"I'm sorry. I guess I was just in shock. I thought she was dead Kat, and now out of nowhere, she's not only alive, but in our fucking building. It was just a lot to process."

Kat nodded, "And now you're wondering if she's come back to find you." It wasn't a question. It was a statement of fact. She knew it, and so did I. I hung my head in shame and rubbed my face regretfully. I had indeed been wondering why Ash had reappeared, but leaving Kat had never once crossed my mind.

"I'm sorry. I didn't think about how this might have affected you." I took my wife's hand in mine. "I love you Kat, and I love our baby. I'd never leave you guys. Not for anything."

"Not even for a tall, gorgeous blonde?"

"She's blonde now?" I asked without thinking.

"Oh my god," Kat blurted in shock, pulling her hand out of mine as if I'd stung her.

"I'm sorry, I didn't mean it like that," I apologised frantically, wishing that I'd kept my stupid mouth shut.

"Yeah, well you're not really instilling me with confidence Ryan."

"I know. I'm sorry." I got down on one knee, and with Kat's pregnant belly poking out in front of my face, I couldn't resist giving it a kiss. I peered up at her with an apologetic smile and her frown began to fade. I took her hand again and looked her in the eye. "Katherine Isabelle McPherson... I love you now and forever, and I promise you that I will never leave you. Not even for a tall gorgeous blonde."

"Okay," Kat agreed with a tear in her eye, "but if she's going to be working here then you need to promise to be honest and open about what's going on in your head. If your feelings change you need to tell me Ryan."

"They won't change."

"Just promise me," Kat pleaded. She was starting to look peaky and it was hard to tell whether it was due to the pregnancy or an emotional overload. "If you ever find yourself wanting to be with her, then promise me you'll have enough respect for me to tell me. I can't bear the thought of living a lie."

"You won't have to babe. I promise you. We're a family Kat, and no one can change that." Kat nodded and began to sway on her feet a little. "Are you okay babe?" I asked, jumping to my feet just in time to catch Kat before her legs gave way beneath her. "Shit." Kat's eyes had rolled right to the back of her head and her body was completely limp. I grasped my wife as best I could without pressing on her huge belly. "Candice!" I shouted loudly to the receptionist as I carefully lowered Kat to the floor. "Candice!" I called again, but she couldn't hear me through the thick glass.

"Kat? Kat can you hear me babe?" I pleaded to my unconscious wife. "Kat," I repeated. "Candice!" I shouted again, unwilling to leave Kat lying there alone. "Candice!" I shouted even louder. She still didn't hear me, but thankfully Christian, one of my Account Execs, emerged from the lift with impeccable timing.

"Holy shit is she okay?" he asked in shock as he saw Kat lying on the floor.

"No, she's not mate, can you please ask Candice to call an ambulance?"

"Sure," he agreed and fled quickly out of the security doors.

"Kat, come on babe," I pleaded, patting her cheeks gently with the back of my hand. She was still breathing, which was a good sign, but Kat had never been prone to fainting, so I was worried that something might have been seriously wrong. "Please babe, open your eyes. I'm sorry. I'm so sorry."

Thanks to Christian's quick thinking, our First Aid rep, Lesley, appeared out of nowhere and sprang into action. She checked Kat's vitals as I continued to kneel on the floor cradling her head.

"Kat, can you hear me lovey?" Lesley asked, gently patting Kat's cheeks. Kat groaned quietly.

"Kat!" I exclaimed with relief. "Can you hear us babe?"

"Ryan?"

"Can you please get her some water?" Lesley asked Christian.

"What happened?" Kat asked, as we heard the ambulance sirens approaching.

"You passed out babe," I said, helping her to sit up.

"Oh my god. Is the baby okay?!"

"I don't know," I said honestly.

"What?!" Kat cried in a panic.

"I'm sure the baby is fine sweetheart," Lesley reassured her, casting me a 'what the fuck' glance. Clearly my bedside manner needed a little improvement. "The paramedics are here now, so they'll take care of you both." Candice swiped the paramedics through the security doors.

"Just in here," she directed them.

"Thanks," the female paramedic said, giving Kat a quick once-over. "What's your name love?" the woman asked Kat as she knelt down next to us.

"Kat."

"Okay Kat, I'm Fran. I'd like to do a few little checks before we get you up if that's okay?"

"Yeah sure," Kat agreed, glancing nervously at me. I smiled reassuringly, but I was panicking on the inside.

"And you're Dad?" Fran asked me as I kissed Kat's head.

"Yep."

"Great. You're doing a great job there. Keep supporting her like that," Fran instructed.

"Okay."

"I'm feeling fine now," Kat assured Fran as she poked and prodded at Kat's belly.

"Yes, it looks like it was probably low blood pressure, and I'd guess an iron deficiency too, but because you're so far along I need to make sure the baby is doing okay in there before we move you."

"Could there be a problem with the baby?" I asked, beginning to feel my panic rise.

"It's just a precaution," Fran explained.

"Okay," I nodded. Holy shit. What if something happened to the baby?

"Dave," the lady called to her partner calmly, "can you please grab the ultrasound?"

"Sure," Dave agreed, pulling a little white wand thing out of the bag.

"I'm just trying to pick up a heartbeat," Fran said as she lifted Kat's shirt and rubbed some gel on her tummy.

"There's no heartbeat?!" Kat asked with horror.

"It's sometimes very hard to hear with the stethoscope so I just want to be sure," Fran answered with an encouraging smile.

"Holy shit," I swore.

"There's no need to panic," Dave informed us as he handed over the small monitor. "We just need to cover our bases."

"Okay."

We all watched the little screen in silence, waiting to see some sort of movement that indicated our baby was fine. Fran moved the wand slowly around Kat's belly, and then we saw it.

"There," she said, pointing at a little pulsating black spot on the screen, "that's your baby's heart."

"Oh my god," Kat breathed, with tears in her eyes.

"That's our little girl," I whispered, kissing Kat on the cheek. It was the most amazing thing to see. "Is she okay?" I asked Dave.

"She's perfectly healthy," he confirmed with a smile.

"Thank god," Kat breathed, echoing my thoughts. The two of us tore our eyes off the screen and looked at each other with amazement and awe. Our baby was safe and healthy and nothing else mattered. I kissed her again with tears welling in my own eyes.

"I love you."

"I love you too," she answered, reaching up to gently wipe away my tears of joy. All the tension had dispersed, and we were back to being 'us' again.

"I'd still like to take you to the hospital for a full check-up to make sure," Fran told Kat as she began to pack up the equipment. "I don't think there's anything sinister going on, but I'd rather be safe than sorry."

"Okay," Kat nodded.

"Do you think you can walk to the ambulance or should we get the trolley?"

"I can walk."

"Or waddle," I teased with a chuckle, feeling relieved that we'd returned to normal.

Kat hit me playfully, "Not funny wise guy."

"Right Dad, let's get her up," Dave directed as he helped me lift Kat to her feet. "Then she can beat you up properly."

- ASHLEY GRANGER -

Full of enthusiasm after my interview that morning, I jumped on a train to Guildford en route to Granger Manor. I found myself a window seat and texted Kesha to tell her it went well. Within seconds my music was cut-off as the phone vibrated madly in my hand. I grinned and hit the green button.

"Oh my god!!!!" Kesha squealed down the line. I was pretty sure the other few passengers scattered about the empty carriage could hear her excited screams. "That's awesome! Tell me all about it!"

"Well the job itself sounds amazing; the CEO is really great, and the energy of the place is phenomenal," I replied quietly, trying not to be 'that person' on the train. "Kesh… I really want this."

"You'll get it. What's the salary like?" Kesh asked.

"I only got a ballpark figure thus far, but it's pretty damn decent. They've got to go via the recruiter, but he said he'd get back to them by close of play today."

"Oh my god that's so exciting! We have to go out and celebrate while we wait! I could meet you at Nama in twenty minutes?" She suggested, referring to our favourite raw food bar.

"I'm on the way to see my folks," I explained apologetically.

"Ooh unscheduled family visit, you must be excited."

"Yeah, I figured I should probably tell them, so they have some time to get used to it. What about Thursday night? I'll know by then and we can go drinking afterwards if I need to drown my sorrows."

"Sounds great, but we're going to be celebrating, not drowning sorrows."

"I hope you're right."

"Of course I'm right. Maybe I'll even invite my friend Jock," she teased. "He asked about you again.'

"No Kesh, I barely remember the guy."

"So I'll invite him out and you'll get to know him.'

"I don't think so."

"Why not? He's sweet, he's hot and he's got a sexy accent, what's stopping you?"

"I have trust issues with men."

"No shit," she chuckled. "Just think about it. You can't avoid dating forever and at least you'd be getting back on the horse with a nice guy."

"I don't need to get back on the horse."

"New flat, new job... new man?"

"I'll see you Thursday night," I said, keen to get off the phone. "Alone."

"Whatever you say boss. I'll see you Thursday," she conceded. "Good luck babe, not that you need it!"

"Thanks chick, love you."

"Love you too. Byeeeee," she said before hanging up. I snorted at her enthusiasm, and settled back into the scratchy seat, staring out the window at the changing scenery. I was deep in thought when my phone rang again, jolting me out of my ponderings. My heart leapt in my chest when I saw who was calling. It was my recruiter. Already.

"Hi Jennifer," I answered dubiously.

"Ashley, I have some great news," she said without even saying hello. "I just got off the phone from Gareth Hemsworth and he wants to make you an offer!"

My jaw dropped.

"Really?!" I asked loudly, not caring if everyone on the train heard.

"Yes! He absolutely loved you! Apparently, he feels like you're the perfect fit for Artemis and he was incredibly impressed with your technical skills too. He said that you had been given a glowing recommendation and that he'd never had a Creative Director with quite the same capabilities as you."

"Oh wow."

"So how do you feel about it? Would you be interested in considering an offer?"

"Of course I would!" I said with excitement, before remembering where I was. I immediately contained my jubilation, "I'd love to consider an offer."

"Great! I'll let him know and then send it through to you as soon as I get it."

"Perfect."

"Oh, and assuming you're happy with the offer, he asked if you'd be available to come in on Friday for an orientation."

"Friday?"

"Yes, they have their monthly company drinks and he thought it would be a good way for you to meet the team in a casual setting."

"Sure," I said, feeling like I was caught up in some sort of whirlwind.

"Great! Let me give him another call and hopefully we'll have this thing wrapped up by the end of the day."

"The end of the day?" I repeated like a mindless drone. I couldn't quite believe it.

"Chat shortly," Jennifer said chirpily, "and congratulations!" She hung up the phone and my music resumed playing through my headphones.

"Holy shit," I muttered under my breath. I couldn't believe it. That sort of thing happened to other people, not me. Maybe the tables had turned. The horrible chapter of my life was finally over, and I was starting afresh.

"Hi!" I shouted into the echoey foyer as I let myself into my parents house. The smell of Mexican food wafted through the house and I followed the scent emanating from the kitchen as my stomach rumbled.

"Hi love," Mum said, doing a double-take as she caught sight of my new look. "Oh, wow. Look at you!"

"Yeah, it's pretty white isn't it?" I chuckled, self-consciously running my hand through my newly bleached hair.

"No, it really suits you," she said, as I gave her a kiss on the cheek.

"Thanks Mum," I said, not entirely believing her.

"Where have you been all dressed up like that?"

"Out," I said as I peered into the bowl she'd been stirring. "Mexican is it?"

"It was the best I could come up with on short notice."

"Sorry. I got some news and I wanted to tell you guys in person."

"Never be sorry for visiting love. You don't have to wait for Sunday lunch to see us you know."

"I know. Thanks Mum," I agreed pleasantly, refusing to take on her guilt trip.

"I've made spiced black beans for you."

"Sounds amazing." My recent move to veganism had given my mother a whole new set of culinary skills. Being a good English housewife, her basic recipe repertoire had been heavily reliant on meat-based products, so it was sweet that she was embracing my new 'alternative' life choices.

"Not a problem love. I'm getting very good at this vegan-tarian cooking."

"It's just vegan mum," I corrected her as I taste-tested her special spiced black beans.

"That's what I meant," she replied smacking my hand away from the serving bowl. "Head straight through and have a seat at the table love."

"Okay," I said, as I wandered into the dining room where Dad was already sitting at the table waiting not-so-patiently for his lunch. He'd helped himself to a few taco shells, one of which was filled to the brim with nothing but minced meat. I fought back my urge to lecture him on his coronary health, and instead greeted him with a kiss on the cheek, "Hey Papa Bear."

"Hi Jelly Bean. You look lovely today."

"Thanks Dad," I said, as I pulled up a seat and grabbed a taco shell from the middle of the table. "So... guess what," I announced loudly enough for my Mum to hear from the kitchen.

"What Cookie?" Dad asked piling a forkful of jalapeños into his already over-flowing taco.

"Well-" I began to say, just as my Mum popped a bowl of grated cheese into the center of the table.

"Aww cheese," my father groaned loudly with the realisation that he hadn't allowed room for said cheese. He picked up his fork and started poking at the contents of his taco to make space for the additional ingredient, while Mum sat down and smiled sympathetically at me.

"Go on love," she prompted warmly, ignoring my father's antics.

"Well I've been offered-" I started to say, but was again cut short by my Dad, who let out a grunt of disappointment as his taco shell cracked in half under the weight of the cheese. The contents of his broken shell spilled all over his plate.

"Ah bollocks!" he grumbled, scraping up all the bits. Mum sighed and rolled her eyes.

"Geoffrey could you please stop fussing for one minute and listen to your daughter?"

Dad looked up as if only just noticing that we were waiting for him to pay attention. "Oh. Sorry," he put his fork down. "You have my full attention Petal," he said, throwing in a non-food related term of endearment.

"Well, pending an official offer... you're looking at the new Creative Director for Artemis Advertising," I announced proudly. They both stared at me blankly. "I've sort of been offered a job! I start on Friday."

"Brilliant!" Dad exclaimed.

"That's great news love," Mum agreed, with an uncertain smile. "But why Friday? That seems an odd day to start."

"Because they've got some sort of company drinks thing and my boss thought it would be a nice way to introduce me to the team," I answered, relishing the phrase 'my boss'. I had a boss again! I was adulting like a real grown-up person.

"Oh, okay," Mum replied, sounding less than thrilled by my news.

"I don't know much about my projects yet, but my boss mentioned a massive new account coming in that they would need a dedicated team for," I told them, grinning as I said, 'my boss' again. "I'm not sure whether they'd assign a newbie to that one, but the contract is ten million pounds."
My dad coughed on a piece of mince.

"Ten million pounds?!" he spluttered, hitting his chest to dislodge the meat. "Who spends that much money on an advert?"

"It's not just one advert dad, it will be a full-service solution."

"So, you start this Friday?" Mum asked warily, determined to communicate her disapproval.

"Yes Mum. I start on Friday. The day between Thursday and Saturday." I knew she was dubious about it, but I wasn't going to let her concern burst my bubble.

"How do you feel about that love? Do you think you're ready to go back?" I sighed patiently and pushed away the rising self-doubt that Mum tended to induce in me.

"Mum, I love you, and I really appreciate all the help you guys have given me…but I can't rely on you forever. I'm 33 now. I need to start earning some proper money so I can pay my own rent."

"But what about your yoga class?" Mum asked worriedly. Why did she always have to cling to the negatives? It was as if she didn't trust me with my own life.

"I'll still do it," I replied tolerantly, "…but one class a week doesn't pay the bills."

"Wouldn't you rather build the yoga business instead of going back to an agency?" asked Dad skeptically. I knew my parents had been hoping for me to make a complete career change after the whole Dom saga, but I'd always planned on going back to Marketing. I adored my work and there was no way I was going to walk away from doing something I loved so much.

"Dad you know how much I love my yoga, so I'll never give it up completely…"

"But?" he asked, with his broken taco poised in front of his mouth.

"…but Marketing is my life. I've worked so hard to build up a good reputation, and I can't just walk away from it now. I have to put Dom behind me, and the only way I can do that is if I get back to the real world. I need to reclaim my old life, as well as building my new one." I was doing it whether they liked it or not, but I so desperately wanted them to understand. "If I avoid going back to a career that I love, then I'm letting him win."

They both fell silent for a moment, staring intently at each other in some sort of telekinetic discussion about my unsanctioned decision to get a job. My eyes flicked between the two of them as I awaited their response, and at that moment, it seemed hard to believe that I was a grown woman. I felt more like a teenager needing approval to attend an unsupervised party.

"Oh sweetie, I'm so proud of you," Mum declared emotionally, as she stood up and gave me a kiss.

"We both are," my father agreed. "Like the pen says…the world is yours my love."

Ugh…the pen.

Where had my pen gone?

– *Chapter 2* –

THE DAY BETWEEN THURSDAY AND SATURDAY

- NATHAN STONE -

My pitch to Sandrine Delfontaine had gone far better than I'd ever expected, and the signed contract marked the beginning of our business relationship. Our personal relationship, on the other hand, had developed well beyond what it should have. Sandrine's flirting throughout my pitch had been less than professional, but she had managed to keep things at an acceptable level of respectability until the evening when Didier, either carelessly or purposefully, left the two of us alone in Le Crazy Horse Cabaret Club. As a general rule, I aimed not to shag my clients, but Sandrine had been way too persuasive to turn down. What should have been an overnight stay in Paris ended up turning into a three-night sexcapade for which I would soon be oozing with regret.

"Well Nathan," Didier had slurred in his smooth French accent, "merci for the fun night but it's time for me to, uhh, how you say…" he paused, as he searched for the correct English translation.

"Call it a night?" I asked, finishing his sentence.

"Oui. Call it a night" he agreed with a nod, as he rose on unstable legs. We were all heavily fueled by excessive amounts of cocaine, champagne and expensive whiskey, so given that Didier was in his sixties, I wasn't surprised that he was the first man down. I stood to offer him a steady hand.

"I look forward to working with you Nathan," he said grasping my hand tightly.

I clasped my other hand over his, "Likewise Didier."

"Bonne nuit Sandrine, bonne nuit Nathan. Have a safe journey home," Didier told me, as he kissed me on both cheeks.

"Merci Didier. Bonne nuit."

He stumbled his way to the door while Sandrine and I watched him make his inelegant exit. When we turned back to each other it was clear that all pretense of professionalism had been discarded. Sandrine grabbed my hand and pulled me down onto the leather seat next to her.

"See any girls you like Nathan?"

I surveyed the room, taking in all the gorgeous cabaret girls.

"They're all beautiful…but not as beautiful as you."

Sandrine's lips flickered into a sexy smile. Sweet-talking was second nature to me, but she saw straight through my charm. Ignoring my attempt at flattery, Sandrine leaned over and whispered in my ear.

"What if I said you could have me as well?" she asked with a devious glint in her eyes. I swallowed hard, and quickly re-adjusted my awakening cock. Was Sandrine suggesting what I thought she was suggesting? "Don't look so surprised Nathan… we French invented the phrase ménage à trois," Sandrine purred with a wink, "I thought you'd be up for the challenge."

"Oh…trust me. I'm up for it."

Sandrine glanced down at my straining crotch and grinned wickedly.

"So you are" she observed with delight. We shared a momentary silence. Our eyes were locked on each other in a Mexican stand-off. I had no idea why I was resisting such an alluring challenge when normally I wouldn't need to be asked twice. Sandrine knew she'd already won. "So, who do you choose?" she asked, nodding towards the girls.

"I don't think they do that do they? I thought it was a 'look but don't touch' sort of situation."

"Relax Nathan. I know the girls well." As if on cue, one of the dancing girls walked past and gave Sandrine a sassy wink. Sandrine nodded approvingly at the girl, who then vanished behind one of the plush black curtains. Sandrine turned her attention back to me. "Now choose."

I noticed a slinky, raven-haired girl with bright red lips. She wasn't my usual type, but she reminded me of a woman from my past who, outside of 'Dearest Ashley', had been the only woman in history to ever truly spark my interest.

"That one," I said, pointing towards her as if she were a puppy dog in a pet store.

"Aurélie," Sandrine replied with a pleased nod. "Très bien! You have very good taste Nathan. This will be a night you won't forget."

As it turned out, Sandrine was right. It had definitely been a night I wouldn't forget. Never, ever, ever… even though I desperately wanted to. Sandrine and Aurélie had certainly made an impression. Quite literally in Aurélie's case, as I now sported her teeth marks all over my thighs, and her leather paddle welts on my butt. When I'd chosen Aurélie, Sandrine had failed to mention that the girl was a professional dominatrix, and the kinky pair had proceeded to give me an education that I would happily never re-visit. They'd kept me locked up in Sandrine's mansion for three nights, in a room that could only be described as a sex dungeon. I'd suspected that Sandrine had held many an orgy in that room over the years.

In all my crazy sexcapades, BDSM was one area that I'd never branched into, and now I knew why. The torturous details were still replaying in my mind as I wearily boarded the Eurostar on Friday morning. I was absolutely exhausted, but I wasn't entirely sure how I was going to manage sitting for three hours. I stowed away my suitcase and flopped into my seat as gently as possible, cringing a little as my welted arse hit the cushion. Thankfully the seat was padded enough to make it bearable.

I felt like a seedy old man. On top of my sex inflicted war-wounds, my back was aching, my head was pounding, and my tired eyes were burning. What if I had to go back there again? Would Sandrine want a repeat? There was no way my body would be able to handle it.

I closed my eyes and let myself drift off with the steady rock of the train as the sun flickered across my face. We rumbled towards England, and flashbacks from my crazy pseudo-abduction circulated through my tired brain. Sandrine, Aurélie, cocaine, champagne, whips, chains, paddles, candle wax - holy shit, the hot wax. That had stung like a mother fucker. I rubbed the spot on my chest where there had once been hair. Did people really enjoy that violent shit? It seemed to be totally counter-productive to the whole sexing process in my humble opinion. Maybe I wasn't quite as wild as I had always thought myself to be. Or maybe I was just getting way too old for that shit. Maybe it was time for Nathan Stone to retire from the party scene.

- KAT McPHERSON -

I couldn't believe that I was stuck in bed while Ryan was at work with the Golden Goddess. Ashley was so beautiful, and I was so plain. How would Ryan feel when he saw her? Would he still love her? They had so much history that our relationship was still new by comparison.

I wondered how it would all go down. They'd probably have lunch and reminisce over old times. They'd laugh a lot and he'd remember how awesome it used to be. My face wouldn't even enter into his mind whilst he was staring into her big green eyes.

Oh god. I didn't stand a chance. My marriage was about to be demolished, and I was incapacitated in bed, helpless to stop it. Damn my body. Damn this pregnancy. Damn Ashley Granger.

With nothing better to do, I grabbed my phone and created myself a 'Miserable Music' playlist. It was self-piteous, but I was too busy wallowing to care.

"Dancing on my own...yep," I mumbled, reading out the names of all the songs I scrolled past. After adding every sad song that I found, I pressed shuffle and flopped back against the pillow hopelessly. "I hate you, I love you, I hate that I love you, you want her, you need her, and I'll never be her," I sang along with the music at the top of my lungs. I knew it was pathetic, but it was also quite cathartic and since I couldn't go for a run, singing my anger out was the next best option.

After ten minutes I started getting bored, so I flicked through my Facebook, and had a questionably brilliant idea. I could check out my competition. Surely, I'd be able to find some dirt on Ashley on the internet. After all, what else was the internet invented for?

I started doing some e-stalking, but I couldn't find the girl on Facebook or any other social media. No Snapchat, no TikTok, no Instagram... not even LinkedIn. Didn't everyone have social media? How could a 'digital superstar' like Ashley Granger not be online?

"What's your story Ms Granger?" I pondered to myself as I decided to try another tactic. I jumped back on to the Book of Face, and headed over to

Ryan's page. "You've got to be in here somewhere."

I skipped back through Ryan's timeline by several years, flicking over about fifty million photos. I saw all of Ryan's other Mareechi's friends, but I couldn't find one single picture of the Golden Goddess.

"Where are you hiding Granger?" I asked the empty room. How could she not be there? They used to hang out all the time. I was about to give up my search when I saw a pair of bright green eyes jump out of the screen at me. "No way!" I exclaimed, staring closely at the bony brunette in the photo.

The girl in the picture didn't resemble Ashley in the least. She was shockingly skinny, had pale skin, dark hair and bright red lips, but those green eyes were undoubtedly hers. No wonder Ryan had been shocked when I'd said Ashley was blonde. The girl in the picture didn't at all match the person I'd met on Tuesday. She was sullen and skeletal, with a vacant look in her eyes. "From Dark Temptress to Golden Goddess," I muttered curiously, suddenly intrigued by the mysterious woman that my husband was so besotted with.

I scrolled back over the other photos and now that I knew what I was looking for, I noticed the Dark Temptress in nearly every single picture. They were all fairly innocuous moments; chatting, laughing, drinking and dancing. She had big black sunglasses on her face in most of them, which is probably why I hadn't noticed her sooner. Night or day, inside or outside, those sunnies seemed to be a permanent accessory for the Dark Temptress.

I was almost done with my stalking, when I scrolled past a photo that hit me right in the stomach. It had captured what appeared to be a private moment between Ryan and Ashley. Ryan was sitting on a lounge with his arm draped protectively over the shoulder of the bony brunette, and her arms were wrapped around his waist. She was staring up at him adoringly with her big green eyes and their faces were so close together that it looked like they were about to kiss.

"What the hell?" I raged at the screen. Ryan told me nothing had ever happened between he and Ashley. Had he been lying to me all this time? I dialed his number, hoping to hear a perfectly logical explanation from his own mouth, but the call diverted to message bank. Why wasn't he answering his phone? He always had his phone on him. Where was he? I hit re-dial and got re-directed to voicemail again.

"Where are you Ryan?" I hung up the phone and jumped out of bed as elegantly as possible underneath the weight of my massive belly. I had to get into work ASAP. If Ryan wasn't going to answer his phone, I'd just have to go down there and see him. I took a step towards the wardrobe and the blood rushed to my head. I leaned on the bed to support myself until my eyesight returned. "Fuck," I swore in frustration and hopelessness. Why was my body letting me down? Before I knew what was happening, I felt tears streaming down my face. I flopped back onto the bed and bawled my eyes out. Why had everything come undone just when it was starting to go right?

- ASHLEY GRANGER -

I still hadn't wiped the grin off my face when I walked through the big glass doors of Artemis Advertising on Friday morning. My recruiter had been right about the job offer from Gareth. The whole deal had been signed and sealed within a matter of hours and the salary was well beyond anything I could have imagined. My exciting new life had finally begun! I made my way to the reception desk to collect my security pass.

"Hi I'm Ashley Granger, I'm starting today."

"Ashley. Right. Here's your Security Pass and your Orientation Pack," the receptionist informed me brusquely. "Just take a seat and someone will come down to collect you."

"Okay. Thanks," I said and turned to walk away. "Oh, I meant to ask…has anyone handed in a pen by any chance?"

"A pen?" the woman asked with confusion.

"Yeah, like… a gold pen. It's Mont Blanc. My Dad gave it to me for my birthday and this was the last place I remember having it."

"No, sorry," she said as a familiar voice echoed excitedly from behind me. "Ash!"

I spun in surprise.

"Ryza?" I gasped as he scooped me up in a massive bear hug. "What are you doing here?" It felt like only yesterday that I'd seen him last.

"I work here," he answered, placing me gently back down on the floor.

"Really? Since when?"

"Since they poached me from Mareechi's, which was about a year after you… err... left." Ryan shoved his hands into his jean pockets and shuffled uncomfortably on his feet. It was hard to tell whether he knew about Dom going to prison or not, so I remained silent. A saddened look shimmered in Ryan's big, brown eyes and regret oozed through every fiber of my being. I should have contacted him when I got back from Bali.

"What a great surprise!" I said, trying to keep the mood light.

"I hear you had an interview with my wife," he said.

"You're married?!"

"Yeah. To Kat," he answered awkwardly.

"Kat?" I was momentarily stunned that he could be married to someone so unfriendly. "Oh, wow, so that means… you're having a baby?"

"Well Kat is doing the hard work on that front, but yes we're breeding."

"Wow," I repeated, shell-shocked at the huge changes in Ryan's life. I'd missed out on so much.

"And what about you Miss? You look fantastic! Obviously motherhood is treating you well."

"Umm…" tears pricked at my eyes, but I refused to let them escape, "I lost the baby Ryan."

His face fell. "Oh," he stood silently for a moment. "I'm so sorry Ash." He squeezed my shoulder with a pitiful look on his face. It was the exact look that I'd pictured a million times over the past few years and it was the main reason I'd never called him. That look of sheer pity was the one thing that had prevented me from picking up the phone every time I'd wanted to hear his voice.

"It's okay. It's been a while," I smiled tightly.

"Seems like we have a lot to catch up on huh?"

"I guess we do," I agreed feeling off-kilter under the warmth of his big puppy dog eyes. It was bizarre to feel like a stranger with a man I'd once called my best friend… my rock.

"Ashley!" I jumped in shock when Gareth appeared out of nowhere. "Welcome to Artemis," he said, striding over to shake my hand.

"Thanks Gareth."

"Ryan will show you around this morning," he declared, getting right to the point. Gareth seemed like the sort of man who utilised every single second of his day.

"Oh great!" I agreed, "but what about Kat?"

"Kat's sick," Ryan explained in a very Gareth-like manner.

"And since you two already know each other I thought it would be nice for Ryan to step in."

"Works for me," I nodded.

"Of course it does," Gareth answered definitively. "This is the man who gave you the glowing recommendation, Ashley." He slapped Ryan on the back.

"You did?" I asked, feeling touched that after all these years he still had my back.

"Of course I did. You're the best Creative Director I've ever worked with."

"Careful not to say that when your wife is around," joked Gareth. "Anyway kids, I'm off to a Board Meeting. Enjoy."

"Will do Gaz," Ryan said, shooting me a wink.

"Great to have you on board Ashley," Gareth called as he strode towards the door.

"Great to be on board," I replied like an idiot.

Gareth vanished outside, and I looked at Ryan in disbelief.

He grinned, "Alright Miss Granger, let's get you settled in."

- RYAN McPHERSON -

It was hard to believe that Ashley Granger was right there in front of me, live in the flesh. She looked completely different, but she was still the same Ash I'd known all those years ago. Thankfully, we had the tour to distract us from the inevitable conversation. With thirteen floors housing over a hundred staff each, plus a canteen, a bar, a rec room, and fifteen meeting rooms, it took me all morning to show her through the office.

"Thanks for the recommendation," she said nervously as we queued for lunch in the canteen.

"I just told the truth," I replied with a shrug. I wanted to shout at her and ask where the fuck she'd been for the last three years, but my professionalism prevented me from doing so.

"Well… thanks. I really appreciate it."

"I was pretty surprised to hear your name Ash," I said pointedly. Did she have any idea how hard her disappearance had been for me?

"It's been a long time," she agreed cluelessly. Nope. She clearly had no fucking idea how worried I'd been about her, or how selfish it had been for her to just vanish like that. I couldn't speak, so I stared at her silently like a stunned mullet. "Do you still see any of the old crew?" she asked.

"Yeah, we try to catch up once a month, but it's getting harder now that we've all gone our separate ways. It was never the same at Mareechi's after you…" I stopped talking. What was the point? She'd never really understand the full impact of her disappearance anyway.

"After I left," she said, using my previous description of her absence. Well it was one way of wording it anyway.

"Is that what you'd call it?" I asked dryly, unable to filter my thoughts. We both fell silent, the tension hanging thick in the air.

"Kat seems nice," Ash blurted. She was grasping at straws and we both knew it, but at least she was trying.

"Yeah she is," I agreed.

"She's got amazing hair," she babbled superfluously. Same old Ash, with her nervous verbal diarrhea. "How long have you been together?"
We moved up the line.

"We met just after you… left," I said, rolling my eyes as I used the word again. "That's why I was offered the job at Artemis." The truth was that I'd been offered the job at Artemis because they found out that I was the Account Director on the McEwan pitch, but since that client brought up so many shared memories I thought it was best not to mention that particular fact. I didn't have the strength to re-live those times with her yet. Our work trip to Monaco for the Grand Prix had been one of the best weekends of my life. On our final night when we were at the McEwan wind-up party, drunk on free Grey Goose martinis, I'd gotten so close to telling Ash how I felt…until she'd vomited on my shoes. That had been a few months before she got pregnant, so it had been my last real opportunity to win her over.

"Oh right," Ash answered uneasily. Perhaps she could sense my veiled anger.

We were finally at the head of the queue, so I ushered her toward the till.

"I'll get the steak and kidney pie and a flat-white please," I told the cashier without even looking at the menu. "The meat pies are awesome," I assured Ash proudly. Meat pies were the one and only item that the canteen produced remotely well.

Ash cringed, "I don't eat meat. I'll get the vegetable curry please, and an almond milk latte." The woman nodded her head and vanished behind the bain-marie to fill our order. Ashley shrugged apologetically.

"At least you're eating something," I joked with a smile. "That's a vast improvement on nothing."

"Yeah I'm a bit healthier these days."

"You definitely look healthier," I agreed as the cashier brought our lunch to the counter.

"Is that a nice way of saying I got fat?" Ashley asked self-consciously. I shook my head in exasperation and followed her to an empty table.

"No Ashley, it was a compliment. You look really good… gorgeous in fact. The blonde hair, the tan… it …it really suits you," I admitted openly, clattering my tray down on the table. "The fact that your bones aren't sticking out anymore is an added bonus."
We slid onto the industrial metal bench seats.

"I think giving up the party lifestyle helped with that," she said, clearing her throat nervously. "I can't believe you're married."

I stared at her blankly for a moment, unwilling to discuss the details of my marriage with the only other woman I'd ever wanted to spend my life with. She dug around the curry with her fork avoiding my gaze, so I took a large bite of my meat pie. I had so many things to say to her that I didn't know where to start.

"I tried to find you Ash," I said once I'd swallowed my mouthful. "I tried everything to find you, but you'd vanished. I even went to your house and your neighbour said that you'd both moved out. A few weeks later I heard that Dom was in jail. Did that happen after you lost the baby?"

"You could say that," she answered with a macabre snort of amusement.

"What does that even mean Ashley?" I asked gruffly as my anger bubbled to the surface. "Please tell me something that actually makes sense, because I'm really struggling to understand where the fuck you've been for the last three years." Ashley looked devastated at my anger, so I took a deep breath to calm myself while she continued to push the food around her plate with the fork.

"It's a long story," she said quietly.

"I know you've had a rough time Ash, but seriously…what the hell? Why didn't you at least tell me that you'd lost the baby? I would've been there for you, but instead I've spent years wondering whether you were even alive." I paused and chuckled grimly, "I couldn't believe it when Gareth asked me about you. I felt like I'd seen a fucking ghost."

Ashley put down her fork with a sad sigh, "I'm so sorry." The regret in her eyes made me feel like a total arsehole. I sighed and pushed my plate to the side.

"You don't need to apologise Ash, just help me understand. I thought we were best mates, and for you to disappear like that..." I trailed off as I swallowed the lump in my throat. "Are you and Dom still together?"

"No."

"What happened Ash? Is there more to this story that I'm not getting, because none of this makes any sense to me."

"Yeah" she nodded. "There's a lot more to the story."

- NATHAN STONE -

Unenergetically, I plodded into my dry-cleaners en route to the office. All I wanted to do was go home and put my arse on ice, but I had to go in and lodge the contract with the accounts team, which meant that I needed a change of clothes. I trudged tiredly through the door and the little bell rang in greeting.

Lilly emerged from the back room.

"Oh my god Nathan, you look like shit" she said with brutal honesty. Lilly had been my dry-cleaner for the best part of five years and I would never go elsewhere. Partly because she was good at her job, but primarily due to the fact that she was an ex-fuck buddy and thus knew better than to question any of my dodgy stains.

"Thanks Lil, I can always count on you to say it like it is." I plonked my little suitcase on the counter.

"Rough trip was it?" she asked knowingly, as I extricated the dirty suit from my bag.

"You could say that" I nodded. "Can I give you this one too?" I asked referring to the stale, smelly suit I was wearing.

"Yeah, sure. Your white linen one is done and hanging in the back room if you want to go through and get changed."

"You're the best."

"I know," she answered as I ducked out the back. "So I take it I'll be scrubbing out some funky stains then Mr Stone?"

"Err, yeah, there might be a few. Sorry," I apologised, as Lil began sorting through my well-worn clothing. With a raised eyebrow, she held up the blue Versace shirt that had been an innocent victim of Aurelie's hot wax attack. "Don't ask," I responded with excruciating pain as I pulled the clean trousers over my mistreated bottom. It was hard to tell whether I was more pained by my paddled arse or the sight of the bright red candle wax on my favourite shirt.

"You know Nathan, there's something to be said for monogamy," Lilly chided as she continued rummaging through my dirty clothes. Ugh, there she went again. It was a conversation that Lilly instigated at any given opportunity.

"Just because you and Chen are deliriously happy, doesn't mean monogamy works for everyone."

"So, you'd rather spend the rest of your life jumping from one fuck buddy to another?"

"I would have been happy to continue jumping on you if you hadn't gone and got hitched."

"Nathan," she warned sternly. Lilly had a very strict rule about not mentioning our previous antics, due to Chen's blissful ignorance on the matter. Since I didn't want to find a new drycleaner, I willingly abided by her rule.

"Sorry," I apologised with a yawn." I'm too tired to think straight."

"See, you're getting too old for the party lifestyle babe."

"You're probably right," I agreed, rubbing my lower back like an old man. "I'm not as durable as I used to be, that's for sure."

"Oops, you might want to hold on to this," she pulled out 'Dearest Ashley's' pen from the pocket of my grey Armani jacket. In recovering from my foray into sex slavery, I'd almost forgotten about my green-eyed goddess. That cab ride felt like it had been weeks, not days ago.

"Thanks," I answered distractedly as she handed me the gold Mont Blanc.

"Seriously Nathan, when are you going to find a nice girl and settle down?"

"Maybe very soon Lil," I answered meaningfully, staring at the pen with an involuntary grin.

"I'll believe it when I see it."

"I'm serious Lil. I think this one could be a winner."

"Oh dear," Lilly snorted, shaking her head. "Just play nicely Nathan."
I gathered my remaining luggage with renewed swagger.

"Oh ye of little faith," I gave Lilly a quick peck on the cheek. "Thanks Lil."

"See you next week," she called behind me, as I dashed out into the bustling lunch time crowd.

I hurried out onto the street wheeling my near-empty suitcase behind me, slightly perturbed by my newfound preoccupation with a certain member of the fairer sex. I had never gotten caught up on an individual woman before. 'Women' as a collective sure. I mean, I rarely had a moment when sex wasn't on my mind, but I'd never had this obsession with one singular female of the species. I hadn't realised it back then, but 'Dearest Ashley' already had drawn me in before I'd even known her name.

As I traipsed out of the train station I spotted Amy Vaughan emerging from a coffee shop. Amy, or 'Red' as I called her, was one of the Art Directors from work and she was hot-as-fuck. A feisty red-head with a dirty Welsh accent and an attitude to match. We'd snogged once, way back when she'd first started at Artemis, but our meaningless interlude had caused a lot of drama, so we'd both done our best to pretend that it never happened.

"Yo Red!" I called with a goofy wave. She chuckled and made a beeline for me.

"Stoner, you're back! I was starting to think the French women might have locked you up and had their way with you."

"Bang on," I cringed with slight disgrace.

"No shit?!"

"No shit. But let's never speak of it again."

"It's not like you to be shy Stoner."

"Trust me. This one was bad even for me," I joked, keen to change the subject. I glanced at my watch, "You're arriving late today missy. Had a long lie-in?"

"Yeah, Ritchie had a long lie in me last night and I needed a recovery morning."

"Ugh, Jesus Red!" I laughed awkwardly. I loved that she was so blunt, but sometimes she even put Ritchie to shame with her crassness.

"What?" she asked defensively. "You asked me."

"I was expecting a polite response."

"Then you clearly don't know me as well I thought you did," she said, punching my arm playfully. She was right. In the four years that I'd known her, she'd never once given me a polite answer to any question.

"Fair call," I conceded, "but seriously woman, you need to tone it down or you'll get me in trouble."

"Aww Nathan, you still want to fuck me," Red replied as if I'd just given her the sweetest compliment ever.

"Who wouldn't?" I answered with a shrug, "but you can't say shit like that." A wicked grin flickered across her plump lips.

"Ooh am I a regular in your wank-bank?"

"I don't need a wank-bank thanks," I retorted defensively. "I have women to do that for me."

"Do you think about me when they're doing it?" she teased with a naughty wink. "Because I wouldn't mind if you did."

"No, but Ritchie would, so stop stirring."

"But torturing you is much more fun," she giggled evilly, running her finger across my shoulder.

"Just keep your filthy hands to yourself devil woman," I told her firmly, swatting her hand away from my bicep. I knew she wasn't serious, but we were now in very close proximity to the office, so I was worried that someone from work might spot us and take the moment out of context.

"Lighten up Nath, I'm just joking," Red answered with a smile.

"I know that, but other people might not. Besides, I don't want to hear about your all-night sessions with my best mate thanks."

"Sure you do," she winked.

I covered up a yawn. "I think I'll take a detour past the canteen for a Red bull if you want to join me?"

"Ooh, our first date," Red joked mischievously.

"Knock-it off you little trouble-maker," I laughed, playfully shoving her through the door, "or I'll tell Ritchie you've got crabs."

"That's fine," she shrugged with a grin. "I'll tell him you gave them to me."

- ASHLEY GRANGER -

Ryan listened so intently to my whole story that it seemed as if there was no one else in the room. People buzzed all about us as I recounted a toned-down version of my recent history. It was as if we were in a vortex, caught somewhere between the past and the present. Ryan sighed heavily when I finally finished my explanation.

"Wow," he said with wide eyes. "I don't know what to say Ash. I wish I'd known. I wish I'd been there for you."

"I'm sorry Ryan. I wanted to call you so many times..."

"No, I'm sorry," he said, before I had a chance to finish my sentence. "I'm sorry I didn't figure out what was going on. I should have seen it. Now that you've told me it seems so fucking obvious."

"How could you have seen it Ryan? I went to great lengths to make sure no one noticed," I patted his arm gently. "It wasn't your responsibility to save me Ryza, and you certainly don't owe me any apologies. You helped me in ways that you could never understand." I felt tears welling in my eyes as Ryza stared at his empty plate in silence. I wanted to know what was going through his mind, but I didn't dare ask. It was such a massive thing to lay on someone and I was amazed he was handling it so gracefully.

I waited silently, watching him process the epic information, until eventually he looked up with a smile on his face.

"I want to hear all about this Bali trip," he said lightening the mood. "I can't believe you're a yoga instructor."

"Yeah, I know, right?" I was relieved that our heavy conversation had come to an end. "Who would have thought?"

"Why yoga?"

"When I was recovering from the... attack..." I said, stumbling over the words, "...yoga really helped, so once I was better Mum and Dad booked the course and put me on a plane to Bali." I paused thoughtfully for a moment, "To be honest, I think it was mostly to get me out of the country and away from Dom's guys until it all blew over. It was the best thing they could have done for me. I never thought I'd become a teacher, but here we are."

"That's awesome Ash. You're amazing."

"Not really," I said, breaking eye contact with him. I began pushing food around my plate again. "I just decided that life was worth living."

"Well I'm glad you did," he said, "because the world wasn't the same without you."

I bit my lip nervously and noticed a random grayish lump in my veggie curry.

"What is that?" I mumbled to myself, as I continued to prod the weird chunk, hoping that it wasn't meat. At first, I thought it might've been some sort of root vegetable, but then upon closer inspection it didn't really look like any distinguishable form of plant matter, so I was stumped. "What do you think this is?!" I asked Ryan. Ryza squinted his eyes and leaned closer to investigate the lump.

"Hmm… it's hard to say. Potato maybe?" We both examined it closely.

"Maybe turnip or something," I hypothesised, stabbing my fork at the lump. Unfortunately, I used enough force to make the mystery chunk shoot off my plate, and straight into the air, splattering Ryan in the face with curry sauce as it flew past him. "Oh shit!" I squealed as the offending blob hurtled across the room. We watched in shock as the messy lump slammed smack-bang, into the leg of an expensive pair of cream coloured trousers. "Oh my god," I breathed in horror, as the blob slithered slowly down the pale fabric. What a fucking disaster.

I tore my eyes away from ground zero of the curry-sauce devastation and peered up to face my wrath. I reluctantly established eye contact with the owner of the stained trousers, and the words stuck in my throat. I was staring straight into the familiar blue eyes of my Thor. What was he doing there?

"Ashley," he blurted, breaking the silence.

"Hi," I answered.

"You two know each other?" Ryan asked in confusion, curry sauce still splashed across his face in bright yellow splashes, which looked almost fluorescent against his dark skin.

"No, not really," I said, distracted by the extraordinarily sexy red-head standing next to Thor. My heart sank. She must have been his girlfriend. The woman was stunning, she looked like Ygritte from Game of Thrones and I suddenly felt like an idiot for having thought that someone like Thor-man might have actually been interested in me.

"We met the other day," Thor explained with a cheeky smile. The red-head watched me with amusement as the awkward moment played out. There was curry sauce everywhere and I was the focus of everyone's attention. I surveyed the damage to Thor's trousers, but it wasn't just his trousers. The blob had sprayed his entire suit with the insidious yellow liquid so that it looked like an attempt at splatter painting gone wrong. Thor's eyes followed my gaze down the length of his sauce stained body.

"I'm so sorry about that," I said, gesturing at his ruined outfit. "So sorry."

He looked up, and his sparkly blue eyes locked onto mine. My heart thudded in my chest under his smouldering stare. I swallowed hard, expecting him to scream at me like Dominic would have, but instead of shouting or swearing, he let out a loud laugh. His warm, gooey laugh was so contagious, that I found myself giggling along with him. After a moment, it occurred to me that we'd barely spoken ten words the other day. I stopped laughing and eyed him suspiciously.

"Wait… how do you know my name?"

"I found your pen," he replied, flashing me a smouldering scrunchy-eyed smile that made my vajayjay announce her extreme interest in the beefy blonde.

"Oh, that's great! I was hoping it would show up somewhere," I said with relief.

"I was going to track you down to return it, but I guess I don't need to now."

"I guess you don't," I agreed saucily, before casting a quick glance at the red-head, who seemed completely unfazed by our flirting. Clearly, she wasn't his girlfriend.

"Great. We're all relieved the pen is safe," interrupted Ryan sarcastically, as he wiped the bright yellow curry sauce off his face with a napkin. Apparently, he wasn't finding the situation quite as amusing as the rest of us. I ignored Ryan and let my eyes wander back to the sexy blonde man.

"So do I get to know your name, or should I just call you Thor?" I teased with a smile.

The firey-haired woman snorted with laughter, "Oh my god, he totally looks like Thor," she agreed emphatically, wandering over to join Ryan and I at the table.

"Do I take that as a compliment?" Thor asked Ryan with bemusement. Ryan shrugged.

"I'm Amy," the girl introduced herself with a huge smile, as she slid elegantly into the seat next to me. "And Thor is Nathan."

"Guilty as charged," he agreed with a wink, before bending down and peeling the piece of road-kill off the floor. I watched him as he plopped the sloppy chunk down on the table in front of me. "I believe this is yours?"

"Yeah thanks, I was wondering where I put that," I joked. He laughed again and, with his waist at my eye-level, I accidentally glanced at his crotch. A blush swept over my face and I hoped that he hadn't noticed my crotchal perve.

Nathan grinned knowingly, and shoved his hands into his pockets, pulling the white fabric even tighter across his seemingly generous package.

"So Ashley, what do you do when you're not starting food fights?"

- RYAN McPHERSON -

The shameless flirting between Nathan and Ash, was making me angry, so I excused myself from the table, and headed to the bathroom to clean myself up. After splashing some water on my face, I returned to my desk to discover sixteen missed calls from Kat on my phone.

"Shit," I said, hitting the 'return call' button.

"Ryan?" Kat answered huskily.

"Babe, are you okay?" I asked in a panic.

"I'm okay now. I just needed to hear your voice."

"I'm sorry babe, is everything alright?"

"I tried to call," she answered tersely, "about twenty times."

"Sixteen actually," I attempted to joke. It wasn't well received.

"It's not funny Ryan. I really needed you."

"I'm so sorry honey. Gaz asked me to show Ash around, so I haven't been at my desk all day," I explained gently. "Did something happen?"

"Yes. No. Sort of. Can you come home?"

"Now?"

"Yes. There's something I really need to talk to you about." Kat never asked things like that of me, so I knew it was important.

"Okay my love. Just let me get organised and I'll be there." I quickly packed up my laptop and got myself back to my wife, as fast as I could. When I walked in the door, Kat was sitting on the sofa, surrounded by a garland of dirty tissues and empty chocolate wrappers. I ran over and knelt on the floor in front her.

"Babe, what's going on?" I asked, gently wrapping my arms around her as best I could. She sobbed and sniffed as she attempted to explain what was wrong.

"You were there with Ashley, and then you didn't answer your phone and then I tried to get out of the house, but my stupid body wouldn't let me, and then I tried to call again, and I just kept thinking…"

"Whoa, whoa, honey. Take a breath and calm down" I said stroking her hair. "I know you're worried about Ashley, but please trust me."

"How can I trust you Ryan?" she snapped through her tears. The venom in her tone took me aback.

"Honey, what do you mean how can you trust me? I'm your husband, and I've never given you any reason not to trust me." She was hormonal and irrational with the pregnancy, so I tried not to take it personally.

"That's not exactly true though is it?" she sniffed. Holy hell. Who was this woman and what had she done with my wife?!

"What?" I asked bewildered. "What have I done that would suggest otherwise Kat?"

"How about telling me that nothing ever happened between you and Ashley?" What the hell was she talking about? Had her pregnancy hormones turned her completely mental?

"Nothing ever did happen between us," I reiterated resolutely.

"Okay, then how do you explain this?" She asked, shoving her phone in my face. It took me a second to focus on the screen, but then as the full image came into view my heart thudded in my chest. I'd totally forgotten that photo even existed. That night felt like a whole lifetime ago.

"Where did you get that photo from?"

"Your Facebook."

"You e-stalked me?" I asked with shock. Maybe she really had gone insane because this was certainly not the behaviour of a well-balanced individual.

"Yep," she replied unapologetically, not even having the decency to pretend to be embarrassed by her childish and slightly sociopathic behaviour.

"Did it make you feel better?" I asked, lost for any other words. What was happening to us? When had we reached a point in our marriage that it had become necessary to cyber-stalk each other?

"Not really, because I found this."

"Right," I answered, stunned. I couldn't believe she'd actually stalked her own husband. "And what exactly do you think this photo means Kat?"

"That you two were together." I sighed and ran my finger across her cheek.

"We were never together babe."

"It certainly looks like you were," she retorted angrily. "If not then you at least kissed her."

"No," I shook my head, "I never kissed her."

Kat glanced down at the photo on her phone.

"But you wanted to. You clearly wanted to."

"Kat, you know I was in love with Ash," I told her honestly, "of course I wanted to kiss her, but that doesn't mean that I did."

"So, you didn't?"

"No," I replied firmly, "no Kat, I didn't."

I could see her brain ticking over, but there was still doubt in her eyes. Why couldn't she trust me? What else could I possibly do to convince her that we were solid?

"So how did you get from 'just friends'…" she shoved the phone in my face again, "…to that?"

I gently prised the phone out of her hands and put it on the coffee table. Regardless of whether this was hormones or some sort of deeper insecurity, the fact was, it was now officially an issue, so I had to deal with it. I took Kat's face in my hands, but she kept eyes on her phone.

"Look babe, that was a really messy night. We'd had a lot of coke, and a lot of alcohol, and neither of us was thinking straight. Besides, she was dating Dom by that time, so he would have had me killed if anything had happened between us." I paused, tilting her head up to face me so that she had to look me in the eyes. "That moment was just… well… it was just a moment. A very drunk, drug-fuelled moment that lasted for about as long as it took for someone to snap that photo." Kat fell silent and dropped her head against my shoulder. "Please Kat, can we go back to being normal because if we don't, this is going to tear us apart." I paused and waited for some sort of sign that my wife was still there, "I just want you to be happy."

She was silent for a moment, and then looked up at me and grinned mischievously. "Do you want to know what would really make me happy right now?"

"I can take a wild guess." I laughed as she wrapped her legs around my waist. Kat wriggled closer and kissed me seductively. Her lips were soft, and I could taste the chocolate still on her tongue. Why did we never kiss like this anymore? I missed it. I missed 'us'. I missed the days when we would lose hours, making-out and not even notice the time slip by. We used to do that all the time, but we'd been so volatile lately I was starting to wonder where I stood with her.

I felt Kat's hands on the back of my neck and wound my fingers through her hair. This was good. This was 'us'. This was how we'd always been, and it was nice to have it back again.

"Have I told you that these pregnancy hormones make me really horny?" she whispered with her lips still against mine. My cock instantly hardened.

"Not for a few days," I said croakily. We hadn't had sex since the morning of Nathan's birthday, so it certainly felt overdue.

"Well, are you going to do something about it?" she teased, tracing her finger along the crotch of my trousers.

"Absolutely," I breathed huskily, before running my hands up the outside of her thighs. My fingers crept up underneath her dress, and landed firmly on her bottom cheeks. Kat's breath caught in her throat and she snuck a hand down in between us to extricate my dick, gripping it hard for a moment.

Grasping her bottom tightly I pulled to her the edge of the sofa. She wriggled into a better position, and guided me carefully into her, groaning as I began to move slowly against her. My heart was thumping loudly in my ears, but then Kat's eyes rolled to the back of her head and she began to black-out again. I grabbed her around the waist to stop her from falling backwards.

"Whoa, stay with me baby." I held her tightly, until her eyes came back in to focus, "Are you okay?"

"I'm fine," she said, waving her hand nonchalantly as if nothing had happened. "It was just a little dizzy spell." She attempted to pick up where we'd left off, but I held her firmly.

"I think we should stop."

"Seriously, I'm fine Ryan," she assured me. "Let's just do this."

"Wow you're so romantic," I joked, a little concerned that she'd nearly fainted for the second time in less than a week. I pulled-out, and tucked my cock back into my trousers. The disappointment was written all over Kat's face. She looked totally betrayed, but I wasn't willing to risk it. Her health was worth more than our physical pleasure.

"Am I really that repulsive?" she asked smoothing down her dress.

"Sorry babe, it's not that I don't find you sexy, I'm just too worried about you. You just about passed out again."

"But I'm fine now," she assured me confidently, "so let's concentrate on getting back in the game." Kat fondled around in my trousers.

"No Kat," I told her firmly, pulling her hands out of my pants. "It's not worth the risk."

"Please?" she begged.

"I'm sorry babe. I can't," I said apologetically. "What if you faint again?"

"I'll be fine. We can do it on the bed if you're worried. You could go on top, then even if I do pass-out I won't fall."

I laughed at my wife's tenacity. I knew the pregnancy was making her horny as hell, but I couldn't risk her wellbeing for a quick roll in the hay.

"I just can't, okay. That was too close for comfort you know?" I explained, rubbing her arms affectionately.

"Yeah. I do know," Kat snapped. "I'm not Ashley, right?"
And there it was. Just when we were getting past the weirdness, she had to bring up the Ashley thing again.

"That's not fair Kat."

"She's so hot that you don't want to have sex with your frumpy wife anymore."

"What are you talking about?" I scolded her with a half-smile, knowing I'd played into her trap. "You're gorgeous and you know it." Without a doubt, Kat was hot in her own right and much more my type than Ashley had ever been.

"Not as gorgeous as her though," she argued.

"That's enough babe," I said, climbing onto the couch next to her. "Please just let it go now. This has nothing to do with Ashley and nothing to do with my attraction to you," I told her sternly.

"If you'd seen yourself the other day, you'd know why I'm worried. I know you don't believe me, but I love you more than anything in the world and nearly losing you this week just reinforced that for me."

"You didn't nearly lose me Ryan. I just fainted, that's all."

I sighed patiently. "Yeah for twenty minutes Kat. The whole time you were out, I was picturing my life without you and it scared the fuck out of me."

- NATHAN STONE -

I don't know of any other great love stories where our hero utters the phrase, 'She had me from, *Oh shit*', but she did. Ashley Granger was like no other woman I'd ever met and her 'oh shit', just made me fancy her even more.

Totally oblivious to the drama unfolding for Ryan, I remained in the canteen with Red and 'Dearest Ashley'. It seemed an appropriate time for me to sit down with the girls, but those hard metal chairs did not look appealing to my bruised rear-end, so I'd opted to remain standing.

"So, your first day huh?" I asked Ashley, "how's Artemis treating you so far?"

"Outside of throwing my curry at you, it's been pretty uneventful," she said with a glimmer in her green eyes.

I laughed, having momentarily forgotten about my stained suit. "Ah yes," I said with a smile, glancing down at the bright yellow stains. "It was certainly an original way to make an impression." She followed my gaze to the damaged trousers and I noticed her eyes pause momentarily over my crotch again. It was the second time she'd done that.

"Sorry again about your suit," she apologised, blushing slightly.

"Don't stress, it's all good. My drycleaner will be able to get it out."
I shrugged nonchalantly, shoving my hands back into my pockets so that the front of my trousers were pulled tight against my cock. I figured I might as well display my manhood in the most flattering way possible, since she seemed to find it so interesting. Ashley's eyes flicked back down to my crotchal region for another millisecond, but then she kept her gaze firmly focused on mine. I adjusted my stance ever-so-slightly to make my bulge more visible.

"Please make sure you send me the bill."

"No need," I said, grinning at her determined efforts to remain focused on my face. "But you could make it up to me by coming to the company drinks tonight."

"I think I could make that happen."

"I guess I'll see you there then," I said with wink.

"I guess you will," Ashley replied, as she stole one final glance at my groin.

"But in the meantime, I need to go get changed," I said teasingly. "See you tonight Ashley Granger." Ashley tilted her head and gave me a sexy smile that nearly brought me undone.

"Not if I see you first Nathan Stone."

I was speechless, so I gave her a weird salute and made a beeline for the exit with my roller-case in tow. When I reached the door, I glanced back over my shoulder at the only woman who had ever left me lost for words. Ashley didn't notice but Red did.

"Bye Thor," she called mischievously behind me.

After fleeing the canteen, I made a mad dash for the bathroom to try and save my curried suit. I filled the hand basin with warm water, stripped off my suit and then carefully soaked it in the tiny sink. I didn't expect it to work, but at least it would minimize the damage. I stood back to consider my next move, when I caught sight of my reflection in the mirror. I was standing in the men's toilet wearing nothing but socks, jocks and a vest top. It was not my most dignified moment ever, yet also not the least dignified moment I'd experienced over the last few days. The memory of Aurélie torturing me with hot candle wax was enough to make my whole body tense up. Even though it was hidden under my vest top, I tenderly rubbed the raw spot on my chest that had bore the worst of it.

How had I let that situation get so out of control? I'd wanted to leave by the end of the first night, so why I had let them keep me there for two more days was beyond me.

The bathroom door swung open and Francesco strutted in wearing a cape. I had no idea whether it was a fashion statement or a costume for one of his off-the-wall projects, but he was the only person in the world who could get away with it.

"Bonjour Nathan," he said cheerfully as if there were nothing abnormal about me hanging out in the toilet in boxers and a vest. "I hear congratulations are in order."

I scratched the back of my head awkwardly. "Yeah, thanks."

"Did you have a good time in my homeland?" he asked, giving no indication that he had even registered the fact I was standing there in my undies.

"Yeah it was very…" I searched for the accurate word, "…educational."

"I told you we Frogs are very friendly, no?" he said as if he knew exactly what I'd been up to for the past few days.

"Yes, you did," I agreed awkwardly as Francesco wandered over to the urinal and commenced a very loud slash.

"What was Madame Delfontaine like? As sexy as everyone says?"

"She was… umm, yeah, I dunno. I guess she's sexy for an older woman," I said loudly, so he could hear me over the sound of his power-piss.

"Ah, but older women are the cream Nathan," he said gesturing with his free hand. "They have the experience."

"Yeah, I guess that's true," I agreed, staring into the bottom of my empty suitcase. I rifled through it hoping that I'd magically find something to wear besides the pair of casual jeans that I'd bought on my first day in Paris. "Oh dear god."

Francesco finished his epic wee and zipped up his fly. "You have a problem Nathan?"

"Oui. I have no clothes," I said, closing the lid of my suitcase in defeat.

"Ah, I did wonder about les dessous," he said, pointing at my G-Stars as if it wasn't entirely abnormal for a man to be standing half-naked in a public toilet.

"Yeah I had a curry accident," I explained, gesturing towards my stained trousers soaking in the sink.

"You want mine?" he asked, beginning to un-zip his jeans.

I laughed and waved my hands frantically, "No I'm fine mate. Thanks though."

"Okay," he shrugged, re-zipping his fly. "I'll see you at the drinks tonight, no?"

"Oui."

"Magnifique!" he exclaimed. "Then you can tell me all about the Madame."

"Sure thing," I nodded stiffly and gave him a handgun point. Francesco winked and strutted out the door, with his cape floating behind him.

When I finally emerged from the bathroom, wearing nothing but the Paris-bought jeans and my vest top, I overheard one of the Account Executives from the other side of the room.

"I'll put a tenner on Stoner."

"A tenner on me for what?" I asked, walking over to the group of mischievous lads, who were huddled around Christian's desk.

"What the fuck are you wearing Stoner?" asked one of the guys as they all laughed at my get-up. "You look like a fucking bricklayer."

"Oh, he's a layer alright, just not of bricks," chimed in someone else.

"Okay, okay, laugh it up kids," I retorted, figuring it was something to do with Sandrine. "So what are you putting a tenner on me for?"

"That you'll be the first one to shag the new Creative Director," answered one of the onlookers.

"What the fuck?" Ryan blurted walking in the door at the exact wrong moment. "Are you guys serious?" He stormed over to us and the younger boys scattered hurriedly. "This is totally inappropriate! I should fire the lot of you on the spot." I stood my ground and put myself between Ryan and Christian who was staring at him like a deer caught in headlights. Unfortunately for him, Ryza was too furious to take pity. "Christian, you're a senior Account Executive, I'd expect you to know better than this," he raged.

"Sorry Ryza," Christian apologised from behind me, looking suitably ashamed.

"Go easy Ryza, it was all in good fun," I said, trying to cool him down. Clearly, he was not in a good mood.

"This isn't good fun Nathan. This is completely disrespectful. Ashley is not a piece of meat for your boys to profit from. Putting it down to 'a bit of fun' will only teach them that disrespecting women is okay."

"Well, when you put it that way…" I said, finally understanding where he was coming from. I turned back to Christian with a stern nod. "Ryan's right. I know you didn't mean any harm but this isn't okay. Shut this thing down and give the guys their money back."

"Okay," nodded Christian with relief. "Sorry."

"You *will* be sorry if I ever find any of you doing anything like this in future. You'll be back to coffee duties. Got it?" Ryza barked. All the boys nodded obediently.

Satisfied that they understood the error of their ways, I returned to my desk and left them to silently retrieve their cash from Christian. Ryan's words had hit me with a brutal realisation that I'd been a bit of a masogyinistic dick over the course of my lifetime. I watched Ryan as he returned to his desk.

"I've gotta say mate, you're getting good at this parenting thing. You even got through to me." I said, looking at him with a new found level of respect.

He sighed heavily and flopped into his chair. "Someone has to be the grown up here," he said with dismissive modesty.

"No, I mean it. You're going to be a really great dad," I said sizing him up. He wasn't his usual self. "But seriously MacDaddy, are you okay?"

"Nah, not really." He sighed again and rubbed his face. "Kat isn't well."

"Sorry to hear that man. Anything I can do to help?" I didn't have the first clue what one would do to help a sick pregnant lady, but Kat and Ryan were my best friends, so I wanted to be there for them.

"Thanks, but no. She just needs some rest. The bigger problem is that she's starting to lose it being stuck at home on her own while I'm here with Ash."

"That's not good," I paused wanting to know how Ashley fitted into the equation. "So what has Ashley got to do with it?"

Ryan sighed for the bazillionth time. "It's a long story."

"Well we've got about three hours until the company drinks start. Shall we go to the pub and grab a beer?"

"Yeah, why not?" he shrugged. "But then I'll need to get back to my hormonal wife."

I was surprised that he'd actually agreed. I'd genuinely expected him to spout some crap about needing to be responsible like he usually did, so I knew straight away that all was not well in his world.

"You're not coming to the company meeting then?"

"No sorry man, Kat needs me."

"Fair enough," I said, feeling both proud and impressed at the honourable man he had become. "You're a good man Ryza, and a good husband."

"Thanks Nath."

"Shall we go get our drink on?"

"Sure," he said, eyeing me up, "but for god's sake, could you at least put on a jacket?"

"Deal," I laughed, grabbing my spare jacket off the back of my chair. "Come on MacDaddy," I said ruffling his hair.

- RYAN McPHERSON -

Nathan and I settled into a cushy booth at the pub, with a pint each and a pack of salted crisps to share. I knew he was trying to perk me up, but it was hard to be cheery when Kat was struggling so badly.

"What's going on with Kat?" Stoner asked, trying his best to be a supportive friend. "Is the baby okay?"

"The baby is fine, Kat just had a little episode the other day," I explained, realising that Nathan wouldn't have heard about Kat's fainting incident. "She passed out in the foyer and Candice had to call an ambulance."

Nath put down his beer. "Oh shit. She's okay now though?"

"Yeah, it was just low blood pressure and low iron levels. If she takes her supplements and gets some rest, she'll be fine."

"Good, well that must be a relief."

"Yes and no. Her being at home is making her go a little crazy."

"Is that where the Ashley thing comes into it?" he asked curiously, shoving some crisps into his mouth.

"Yeah," I nodded, "she thinks I'm going to leave her for Ash." Nathan laughed wildly and then stopped abruptly when he realised I wasn't joking.

"Why on earth would she think that?"

"Ash and I are old friends. We worked together at Mareechi's."

"Oh," he nodded and sipped his beer, "and you guys had a thing?"

"No," I answered firmly, tapping my fingers lightly against the cold pint glass, "but Kat thinks we did."

"Ah, I see," Nath nodded understandingly. "You were in love with her."

I froze, my beer poised to my mouth. "Why would you assume that?"

"Because I know you Ryza."

"Am I that predictable?" I put my glass back down on the table.

"Mostly." He grabbed some more crisps out of the pack, "although I'm surprised that you never told me about Ashley back then."

"You're surprised?" I repeated sarcastically.

"Yeah," he said, "I would have expected you to tell me if you were in love with someone."

"That is exactly the sort of thing I would never have told you."

"But you never even mentioned her or invited her to any of our parties."

"Yeah, because you would have shagged her."

"Not if I knew you were in love with her."

"Stoner… I love you man, but you've shagged every woman that I've ever been interested in."

"Except Kat."

"With the exception of my wife," I amended, "whom you *tried* to have sex with before you introduced us."

"Okay," he said raising his hands in defeat. "Fair point. I used to be a shithead and a crappy friend."

"And it only took you a couple of decades to realise it," I teased. I was well-aware of Nathan's faults, but we'd been friends for a long time and I knew that his positive attributes far outweighed the shitty things he did sometimes.

"So, is Ashley single?"

"Ashley is off-limits Nathan."

"Why?"

"Two words… Becky Wheeler."

"That was five years ago Ryan, and you weren't even here then."

I surrendered with my hands in the air in the same way he had just done.

"Okay, point taken."

"Thank you."

I took a sip of my beer and then placed it back down on the table.

"So do you think you've changed since then Stoner? If you got involved with Ashley and pulled your usual shit, I would have to pay Ritchie to smash the shit out of you, and I can't really afford luxuries anymore."

"I get it Ryza. I've got a long history of fucking up. I can't argue with that, but there's something about Ashley and I can't explain it. I feel like I've met her before."

"That's because you have," I said without thinking, and then immediately regretted it.

"I have? When?"

The bar girl came over to collect our empty glasses. "Do you boys need anything else?"

"Another round would be great thanks," Nathan said with one of his most charming smiles. "My friend is about to become a dad so we're celebrating while we can."

"Aww that's lovely," she swooned, falling for Nathan's ploy. "How about I throw in a couple of shots on the house?"

"Well that's very generous indeed," he said, shaking her hand. "Does our beautiful barmaid have a name?" The woman eyed him up and down and giggled as if he'd just made the funniest joke in the world. She probably would have dropped her panties right then and there if he'd asked her to.

"I'm Kerry," she said practically fluttering her eyelids at him. How the fuck did Nathan do it? It was both sickening and impressive at the same time.

"It's very nice to meet you Kerry," Stoner said, glancing at me in triumph, even though he'd just illustrated my point for me. "I'm Nathan and this is Ryan."

- KAT McPHERSON -

I'd talked Ryan into going back to work for the afternoon because, as much as I wanted him to be at home with me, I suspected that his reluctance to have sex with me would have proved too frustrating for both of us. At least with him gone I'd been able to sort myself out and get on with my wallowing.

As soon as he'd left, I'd done what I needed to do, and had since been snuggled up on the couch with a fresh batch of choc-chip cookies, watching chick-flicks. I was trying hard to forget about Ashley Granger and her intentions for my husband, but I found myself continuously glancing at the photo of them on my phone. It was like a car-crash. It was painful to look at, yet I couldn't take my eyes off it. Was Ryan really telling the truth?

I shoved another cookie in my mouth and realised that I had nearly worked my way through the entire batch.

"Ugh," I moaned with my mouth full of the crumbly, sticky goodness. I could feel the sugary, chocolatey baked goods hitting my stomach and wasn't sure I'd be able to swallow the final remnants. I forced myself to swallow the mouthful, just as the front door buzzed. I glanced at my phone. It was 5pm. It seemed like a strange time for a visitor, especially given that most of my friends would be heading to the company drinks around about now. Climbing to my feet like a toppled hippo, I waddled over to the intercom to see who was there.

"Hello?" I asked dubiously.

"Yo Kitty-Kat, are you alive in there?" came the familiar American drawl of my Creative Partner and best friend, Beau Peterson. I smiled involuntarily. Beau was the one person who never failed to cheer me up. Next to Ryan, he was my favourite person in the world and, had it not been for the fact that he was gay, I would have happily bedded him in my pre-Ryan days.

"I must be, I'm pretty sure being dead would be more pleasant than this," I said pressing the buzzer to let him in. I unlocked the flat door and was hit with a wave of nausea. My stomach was not appreciating the tonne of cookies I'd scoffed. "The door's unlocked," I shouted, scrambling ungracefully to the bathroom to empty my stomach of all the cookies.

"Do you need any help?" Beau asked peeking his head in from the doorway.

"No, I'm fine. I'll be out in a sec," I replied as the heaving subsided momentarily. I climbed to my feet, lumbered to the basin tap and scooped up a handful of water to take away the bile taste. Within seconds of the liquid hitting my stomach I felt the chunky vomit rise in my throat and I quickly scrambled back to the toilet bowl to re-commence chucking.

"I'm coming in," Beau said, edging his way into the bathroom.

"No Beau. Trust me, you don't want to see this," I spluttered between heaves.

"Honey, there's nothing I haven't seen," he joked. The sound of his footsteps on the tiles echoed through my little bathroom.

"Beau. Seriously."

"Stop arguing and let me help," he ordered, gently rubbing my back. I heaved again and then stared up at him pathetically. "Oh my," he crooned, swishing a wayward strand of curls out of my eyes. "Let me go get you some water."

"Water makes it worse," I protested as he helped me to my feet. I caught sight of myself in the mirror. "Ugh, how am I ever going to compete with her?" I wailed, bursting into tears.

"Who's her?" Beau asked with confusion.

"Malibu Barbie," I spluttered through my tears as he soaked a wad of toilet paper under the tap. I knew I was being childish, but I couldn't help it. Beau smiled comfortingly and with one arm around my waist, led me into the bedroom and sat me down on the bed. He made sure that I was comfortable and then sat down next to me.

"You've totally lost me," he said, tidying my smudged make-up with the wet toilet paper. "Who's Malibu Barbie and why do we hate her?"

"Ashley Granger," I wailed hopelessly, flopping against his hard chest. Gay or not, the man was undeniably sexy. "The woman who's trying to steal my husband."

"Oh." He nodded and enfolded me in an inelegant sideways hug. After allowing me a moment to wallow in self-pity he prised me off his chest so that he could look me in the eye. "So is she actually trying to steal your husband or are you just being paranoid?"

"She's probably not," I admitted, "but Ryan is definitely in love with her."

"Come on Kitty-Kat, I'm sure it's not that dire."

"It is," I nodded obstinately, and my eyes drifted down to his shirt, which was nearly see-through and plastered to his chest with my snot and tears. My libido kicked into over-drive once again. Holy Mother of God, that chest. I'd seen his bare chest on many occasions, but for some reason it seemed so much more alluring when viewed through a thin, translucent layer of wet cotton. Hello Mr Darcy.

"Are you okay?" he asked, putting his hand to my forehead. "You feel quite hot."

"I feel like a fat, blubbering whale."

He laughed loudly, and threw his arm over my shoulder. "Well, you look beautiful."

"Flattery will get you everywhere," I bantered, wrapping my arm around his waist. As I snuggled into his shoulder, I got a whiff of his yummy aftershave. "You smell amazing," I said, sniffing his chest again. "You're going to make some guy very happy some day."

"Guy?" he asked with a shocked laugh. "What are you on about woman?"

"Just saying it like it is. You're hot babe, and any guy would be lucky to have you. If you didn't bat for the other team, I totally would have done you."

Beau stiffened, unwrapping his body from mine, as he studied my face with a look of confusion on his.

"I'm not gay Kat," he said with a bemused chuckle. For a minute I thought he was joking, but then when I looked up at his face I could see from his expression that he was deadly serious.

"What do you mean?" Of course he was gay. He'd always been gay. It was common knowledge at Artemis.

"I mean… I'm not gay. Why would you think I was?"

"You're well dressed, and sweet, and hot and all your friends are gay," I spluttered, grasping at straws as my brain tried to process this new information. How could I have misinterpreted that for so long? My gay best friend wasn't actually gay, but how could he possibly be straight? It didn't make any sense.

"Kat, please tell me you're fucking with me right now," he said, standing up from the bed. "I don't mind people questioning my sexual orientation, but you're my best friend."

"I know, but, but- I honestly thought. I mean, you know…" I paused and took a breath. "But you haven't had a girlfriend the whole time I've known you." But then again, he'd never had a boyfriend either. In fact, I'd never seen Beau interested in anyone.

"I haven't had a girlfriend because I can't find anyone who matches up to you."

"What?" I asked in bewilderment.

"I'm in love with you Kat. I always have been," he blurted with frustration. "I've never talked about women with you because it's too weird."

"So, our whole friendship has been a lie?"

"I never said I was gay. I had no idea you even thought that," he said, failing to hide a look of betrayal by turning away. He sighed and faced me with a grimace of pain on his handsome face. "I actually thought I was really obvious about my feelings for you. I thought you knew how I felt."

"No, I had no idea," I mumbled in a state of shock, as I played back the last few years of our friendship in my mind. All of the moments we'd shared together suddenly had a completely different meaning.

"Wait," I said, blushing with a mixture of anger and embarrassment as a few key memories replayed in my head. "I've been naked in front of you."

Beau blushed and dropped his eyes. "Yeah."

"You didn't think to mention it at that point?" I asked angrily. He shrugged sheepishly.

"I figured you were just, you know… really comfortable with your body."

"Oh my god!" I ran my hands through my hair. "This changes everything."

"But it doesn't change anything Kat. It is what it always was."

"Except that now I know you're in love with me," I said standing up from the bed too quickly and giving myself a head-spin. I gripped the edge of the bed tightly.

"Are you okay?" Beau asked, reaching out to steady me.

"I'm fine," I said, straightening myself up and removing my arm from his gentle grasp. "I think you should leave."

"What? You're kicking me out of your house because I'm *not* gay?"

"Yes. No. I don't know, but you need to go. You can't be here right now."

I ushered him towards the door, needing to get him out of there before my hormones took over and made me do something I would regret. He stopped in the doorway, and turned back to me sadly.

"So where do we go from here?"

"I don't know Beau," I replied. "I just need some time to work through this." He nodded silently, and I shut the door, feeling a mixture of relief, excitement and confusion. How had I never suspected that he was straight? Everything I thought I'd known was wrong, and if Beau wasn't my gay best friend anymore, who was he to me? And if he was in love with me, where did that leave us? I was in love with Ryan. He was my husband. We were having a baby. Beau was not an option.

- NATHAN STONE -

Ryza and I were well on our way to being toasted. I hadn't intended on getting drunk prior to the work drinks but Kerry, the barmaid, had been incredibly obliging with providing free shots, so it seemed rude not to.

"So, tell me more about Ashley," I probed Ryan as we downed our third round of free tequila shots. "When did I meet her?"

Ryan exhaled the tequila fumes; plonked down his shot glass; and pondered for a moment as if trying to find the right words. Finally, he looked at me poignantly and declared, "Nath, Ash is Dominic Doyle's ex-girlfriend." The words hit me like a punch to the guts.

"Oh fuck," I blurted in surprise. "She can't be."

"She is."

"But…" There were so many different thoughts whirling through my head that I wasn't quite sure where to start. Back when I'd met the girl I'd known as 'Dom Doyle's girlfriend' she was hot, but in more of a heroin chic kind of way, not the blonde bombshell she was now. "She looks completely different," I mumbled.

"Yep," Ryan agreed.

"Are you sure it's her?" I asked, unconvinced.

"Nathan, I know Ashley Granger well. Trust me; she's Dom Doyle's ex."
My mind slipped back to about five years earlier, when I'd first met 'Dom Doyle's girlfriend'. I remembered the moment well, because I'd never been so petrified in my life.

Dom Doyle was a man who always got what he wanted. No one ever refused him or disagreed with him because most people were scared of him. He was informally known as the Pablo Escobar of the London party circuit, because he was the biggest cocaine dealer in the city.

The night I'd met Dom's girlfriend, I'd been picking up a last-minute package from him at an underground club and, instead of risking his own neck to make the drop, he'd sent Ashley down to do the deal on his behalf. I'd genuinely thought I was going to crap my pants when I'd caught sight of his hot girlfriend. The woman was sultry to the 'n'th degree, and with her psychotic boyfriend scrutinizing our every move, I was overly conscious not to let my desire for her show.

Her dark eyes were fixed to me, while Dominic watched her like a hawk from the mezzanine platform above us. I was frozen to the spot as she worked her way through the packed dance floor towards me. Her intense stare made my chest tighten, and it wasn't until she got closer, that I realised her eyes weren't actually dark at all; it was just that her pupils were so dilated there was no colour left in them. Whatever pills she'd dropped, they were decent ones.

Under Dom's eagle-eye, I was too scared to move, so I stood stock still as his sexy girlfriend placed her hands gently on my hips. I glanced nervously up at Dominic and could see quite clearly that he was seething. As the girl closed the space between our bodies, I was convinced that I was about to feel the lead of a bullet.

She leant in close and whispered quietly into my ear, "Just put the money in my back pocket." She slid her hand into my front pocket and dropped the baggie, but her hand brushed a little too closely to my cock and the intimate action incited an involuntary jump from it.

A flicker of excitement flashed in her eyes, as she felt the movement. She tilted her head back and looked up at me with a sly smile. Electricity sparked between us, and the combination of fear and lust was excruciating.

I glanced up at Dominic with panic, positive that he could tell what was going on. He nodded stiffly, the rage building in his eyes, so I fumbled for my money and quickly shoved the cash into his girlfriend's back pocket, trying my hardest not to feel her arse as I did it. With the exchange complete, the girl wrapped her arms around my shoulders and leaned into my ear.

"Pleasure doing business with you." The feel of her breath on my neck sent shivers up my spine and, when she drew away from me, the air suddenly felt cold.

My gaze floated up towards Dom who was indicating in no uncertain terms that it was time for me to leave. I nodded my understanding and made an attempt to leave, but as I glanced at his girlfriend our eyes connected and something inside me refused to walk away. My steps faltered, and instead of fleeing for my life, I stood planted to the spot. I didn't move, didn't walk away like I should have. I just stood there staring into the big eyes of Dom Doyle's girlfriend. I was rooted in place.

"Go," she pleaded desperately.

"Come with me," my mouth blurted of it's own accord.

"What?" She asked, stunned.

"Come with me," I repeated, risking a glance up at Dominic.

"Do you have a death wish or something?"

"Maybe," I said, my confidence wavering.

"You need to get out of here. Now." The fear in her eyes was enough to break my spell of stupidity, so I turned and quickly vanished into the dancing crowd, wondering if I'd just made the dumbest mistake of my life.

Back in present time, I stared at Ryza, gobsmacked.

"Why did you never tell me that you were friends with her?" I asked with confusion.

"It never came up," he shrugged unapologetically.

"You don't think you could have mentioned it when I told you the story?"

"Why would I?" he replied blankly. "For starters, I was in love with her. Let's face it man, you would have just turned her into your next conquest." Ryza took a gulp of his beer. "And secondly, if Dom had found out that I knew you he never would have let me see Ash again."

"Thanks man," I said, crossing my arms like an obstinate child. "Good to know you've always got my back."

- ASHLEY GRANGER -

I'd been at the company drinks for at least forty-five minutes and there was no sign of Nathan Stone. I scanned the room for the umpteenth time, and Amy shot me a sympathetic smile.

"I'd be careful if I was you," she warned me knowingly.

"What?" I asked innocently, pretending that I had no idea what she was talking about.

"Stone," she answered bluntly. "He isn't a female-friendly zone."

"What's Nathan got to do with anything?" I said, shrugging casually as if I wasn't desperately waiting to see my Thor again.

"You and I both know he has everything to do with it."

"I'm not into Nathan."

Amy laughed, "If you believe that Ashley, then you're the only person who does."

I felt my cheeks flushing. "Am I that obvious?"

"Not to a blind person," she teased. "Look Ashley, I love Nathan but he's a player. He always has been, and he always will be. Hundreds of girls have tried to change him, but Nathan is what he is."

"Hundreds of girls?!" I spluttered, almost choking on my drink.

"Yeah," she confirmed with a nod. "If you want a bit of fun, or a one-night stand, then you'll be fine, but if you're looking for anything more than just sex, Nathan Stone is not your man."

"But I've already designed the wedding invitations," I joked in an effort to deflect from the fact that I was probably incapable of having a one-night stand. The truth was, deep down I already knew that Nathan was trouble. Mostly I knew that because I was attracted to him. For some reason I had an illogical attraction to bad boys and the more awful they were to me the more I loved them.

Dominic had been the worst, best example of that. At first, he had been charming and charismatic. With his tall, broad frame and his jet black hair, he'd stood out from the bougy club crowd like a lighthouse on a dark night.

At the time, I'd had no idea who he was but something stirred in the pit of my belly at the sight of him. From across the dancefloor, Dominic's eyes had locked onto mine and I swallowed hard as he assessed me with unashamed hunger. Unbeknownst to me, that was the moment that he'd decided he would own me. From that point onwards, I'd belonged to Dominic. In that one fleeting second, I had unintentionally changed the course of my entire life. Dominic was a hunter and I had become his prey.

"As long as you know what you're getting yourself into," Amy said as her eyes landed on something behind me, "but just remember that no one can tame Nathan Stone."

"Thanks, I appreciate the heads up." I knew what Amy was saying, but I really wanted Nathan. Did I care if it was just for one night? Could I handle casual sex with a work colleague? Hmmm. I wasn't so sure.

"And speaking of casual sex..." she nodded towards Ritchie Carlton who had just walked in the door, "I'm going to line-up mine."

"So, you and Ritchie are together?" I asked curiously.

"Nah, we just hook up."

"Oh, okay," I nodded, trying not to be judgemental. "So he's a bit of a Nathan then?"

"No not at all. If it was up to him I'd already have a ring on my finger," Amy answered rolling her eyes. "I'll catch up with you later." She patted me on the shoulder and sauntered over to Ritchie.

Rather than standing by myself, I ducked off to the bathroom and found myself in a toilet cubicle eavesdropping on a conversation between two younger girls. They each occupied a cubicle on either side of me, so I was literally in the middle of their conversation.

"I heard he only got the account because he shagged the client," one of the girls gossiped excitedly.

"Really?!" asked the other girl in amazement.

"Yeah apparently," the first one confirmed, feeding off the thrill of the gossip.

"Wow he must have been a good lay then!" exclaimed the second girl with a giggle. "But then again I'd happily give my left arm to be shagged by that man. Handing over a multi-million pound account would be a small price to pay."

"I know right?!" giggled the first girl. "He's totally lush. Except I heard he doesn't date anyone he works with."

"Honey that's because Nathan Stone doesn't date anyone...he just shags. The guy's a total player."

My heart sank.

"Yeah, but I'd still let him play with me any time," replied the other girl as they both giggled conspiratorially. I felt deflated. I didn't normally put much weight into gossip, but the evidence was starting to look pretty definitive. Nathan Stone was definately a man-whore.

I waited for the two girls to leave, then I escaped back out into the bar and I distracted myself by chatting to some of the developers. Half-way through the conversation, when I'd just about put Nathan Stone out of my mind, a drink appeared right in front of my face.

"Vodka soda, right?" My eyes wandered from the glass, to the strong hand holding the glass... and all the way up a bare bicep. A few of the guys chuckled with amusement at seeing Nathan's bizarre choice of wardrobe, but I had lost my ability to speak. I soaked in the magnificence of his shoulders and it took every ounce of my will-power not to reach out and squeeze his well-toned muscles. "Your glass was empty," he explained casually.

I smiled politely and took the drink from his hand. Before anyone had a chance to say anything further, a gorgeous, solider-like man appeared out of nowhere. He looked like the real-life version of G.I. Joe, minus the camouflage gear.

"What's with the Bob the Builder costume Stone?" G.I. Joe drawled in a thick American accent.

"Why don't you ask this lady right here?" Nathan answered, nodding towards me with a flirty sparkle in his eyes that made my lady-parts jiggle around excitedly.

G.I. Joe turned to me with a bright smile, "Hi I'm Beau."

"G.I. Beau," I joked, as I shook his strong hand. Nathan chuckled out loud, but G.I. Beau looked bewildered by my pop-culture reference. "I'm Ashley," I continued quickly, as if I hadn't said anything else at all.

"You're the new Creative Director, right?"

"I am indeed."

"I've heard a lot about you." I could see Beau's brain ticking over with some sort of hidden agenda. "I'm Kat's Creative Partner."

"Oh, I see," I answered, wondering exactly how much he knew about me.

"So, what did you do that led to Stone wearing that monstrosity?" he asked nodding toward Nathan. The group of men all looked at me for an answer and I suddenly felt quite flustered under the scrutiny of five rather attractive men.

"Ummm... curry blob," I blurted ineloquently. Nathan grinned in amusement while the other four stared at me blankly. I got the distinct feeling that he was enjoying my awkward moment.

"What she's trying to say," Nathan interjected with a wink in my direction, "is that she threw her lunch at me." He smiled at me mischievously, "and speaking of which, we need to discuss compensation for damages caused." With that, Nathan threw his arm over my shoulder, sending a waft of his tasty aftershave into my nostrils. He might have been dressed like a builder, but he certainly didn't smell like one. "Excuse us lads," he said to the group with a smug smile, before leading me out towards the roof terrace.

I cast an apologetic glance over my shoulder, and then let myself be guided out in to the open air. Nathan chuckled wickedly and subtly maneuvered me up against the balcony railing. It was a decidedly intimate arrangement and I was having all sorts of weird reactions to being in such close proximity to the sexiest man on earth.

"You owe me one Ashley Granger."

"Oh, really Nathan Stone? How do you figure that?" I asked leaning back slightly to create some air space.

"You mean besides the curry incident?" He had me there.

"Touché," I conceded in defeat.

"And now I've also saved you from being bored to death by the digi-geeks." Nathan subtly shifted his weight so that our thighs were touching ever-so-slightly. I had to swallow down the lump of desire that was rising in my throat. If he was aware of the effect that he was having on me, then he was hiding it well.

"They're lovely," I defended the digital boys with a slight wobble in my voice. In truth they were a little on the geeky side, but at least geeks were usually safe.

"That's because I got to you in time. Trust me Ashley, thirty seconds longer and your brain would have imploded from all the innocuous techno babble."

I took a long sip of my vodka soda while I pondered my response.

"So I take it you're not a fan of the digital revolution then?"

"Nope. I'm old school," he answered proudly.

"Well that's a shame, you seemed so perfect."

"You think it's a bad thing?"

"Of course it is. You old-school guys are so busy with your exclusive boys' club that you ignore the reality of your precious print-based business slowly eroding. If you don't accept and integrate new digital platforms, then your beloved offline accounts are going to be dead in the water."

Nathan gripped his throat, "Wow. Ouch. Straight for the jugular." I shrugged unapologetically. I'd spent so many years defending digital to arrogant advertising pricks, that I held no punches about it anymore. He scrutinised me closely. "You're a feisty one aren't you Granger?"

"I am when I'm right," I said with a wink.

"Well, you were right about one thing," Nathan replied with a mischievous grin.

"What's that?" I asked, taking a sip of my drink.

"I am perfect."

I nearly snorted my drink out of my nose, as I attempted to swallow and laugh simultaneously. "And clearly very humble," I said once I'd composed myself. Nathan's good-humoured banter was amplifying my desire for him, and my heart felt like it was lodged in my throat as we stood eye-balling each other. His thigh was still touching mine and the heat had spread from the point of contact, right up to my lady bits, which had become unexpectedly excitable since I'd met the infamous Mr Stone.

Nonchalantly, Nathan leaned against the railing so that our bodies were in complete contact down one side. He knew exactly the effect he was having on me.

"I have a question for you Dearest Ashley," he asked with a glint in his eye.

"Okay," I answered, swallowing the nervous lump in my throat. He pulled my pen out of his jeans pocket.

"Who is this PB character and why has he given you such a nice pen?"

I smiled and took the pen from him. "Can I let you in on a little secret?"

"Sure," he agreed with a grin as he leaned in closer to hear my earth-shattering secret.

"I'm a stationery addict and PB is my dealer," I told him as seriously as possible. "I can't get enough of it. Post-it notes, paperclips, pens... all of it. Artlines are my biggest weakness."

Nathan threw his head back and let out that velvety smooth laugh of his.

"I hope you're seeing someone about your addiction Granger, or this just won't work at all."

"Hey guys, Gaz is ready to do his announcement," called a well-dressed young woman from the terrace door. "Everyone inside please."

Nathan and I glanced at each other.

"That's Trish, the Office Manager," Nathan said as if reading my mind. "We'd better not tell her about your problem or she won't let you near the stationery cupboard."

- KAT McPHERSON -

It was rapidly becoming the Friday night from hell. Instead of going to the company drinks, Ryan had come home somewhat drunk and attempted to put the cot together, which was proving to be a serious test of our marriage. We might have survived the threat of Ashley Granger, but the fucking cot was going to push us over the edge.

"No babe, that one goes down there," I explained calmly, pointing between the instruction manual and the loose pieces of cot that were lying in disarray on the nursery floor.

"How can it go down there? It doesn't fit," Ryan replied with frustration.

"Why don't you just take a look at the instructions, so you can see what I mean?"

"I *am* looking Kat, but the picture doesn't look anything like these," he waved one of the wooden planks in the air. "Who the fuck writes these instructions anyway? They're not even in proper English."

I did my best not to smile. Ryan was adorable when he was angry. I had no idea why he was so hell-bent on getting the fucking cot built immediately, but he was a drunk man on a mission, so I wasn't going to get in his way.

"Maybe we should take a tea break?" I suggested, sounding eerily like my mother. Tea Breaks were the fundamental principle in The World According to Shirley Tailor. The woman believed that any problem on earth could be fixed with a nice cup of tea.

"Okay Shirley," Ryan replied tersely.

"There's no need to be mean," I said defensively. Of all the people in the world, my mother was the one person who I least wanted to emulate, and not because of her tea dependency. "I'm just trying to help babe."

Ryan looked up and grimaced in defeat, "I know. I'm sorry." I smiled at him as he sat on the floor like a frustrated toddler with mismatched building blocks. He was incredibly handsome, but a carpenter he most certainly was not.

"Why don't we have a Shirley cuppa and then come back to it?" I suggested again.

"But I really want to sort out this room."

"I know babe, but five minutes isn't going to hurt," I reached out my hand. "Are you having sympathy nesting or something?" I could see that this task had become a matter of pride, more than ability. Ryan sighed and glanced over at me sheepishly.

"I'm so sorry baby," he apologised, coming over to wrap me up in a bear hug. "I'm an appalling handy man."

"Yeah, you are," I agreed kissing him. "Luckily, I didn't marry you for your carpentry skills."

"Let's go have that cuppa then," he agreed. "Maybe Shirley is onto something with her tea philosophy." I grinned, and we headed into the kitchen arm-in-arm. Ryan offered me a chair, and fixed us a pot of tea in the exact way he'd been instructed by my mother herself.

"I'd never tell mum this… but you make her tea better than she does," I joked with a smile.

"Awesome. I can't build things, but at least I have career prospects as a tea lady."

"You'd make a very sexy tea lady," I teased.

"Would you like a bikkie with that?" Ryan said, cracking out his best Shirley impression. We both laughed and he set the teapot onto a tray and grabbed two of our nice teacups from the cabinet. "Hey listen, I was thinking…"

"Did it hurt?" I asked with an evil grin.

"Haha," he said, rolling his eyes, "I was thinking… that, since you're not at work now, maybe you should head up to Framlingham for a few weeks and spend time with your folks. Your mum would love that."

"Yeah she would," I agreed.

"Plus, you'd have her and Rosie to take care of you, instead of being here by yourself," he added, carefully carrying the tray of tea to the table.

"That's a good idea babe."

"Don't sound so surprised," he said, pouring our teas.

"I'm not surprised, I just thought you might feel a little left out."

"Baby, we've got the rest of our lives to spend time together. The most important thing is that you're not sitting at home by yourself."

I was strangely relieved by the idea, but couldn't help but wonder whether he was just trying to get rid of me for a while.

"Are you sure?" I asked.

"I did consider suggesting that your mum come and stay here but I don't think any of us would survive that." Oh god, I dreaded the thought.

"This is definitely the better option," I agreed. I took a sip of my tea, and it did somehow make me feel a little better to know that I'd have company. "Maybe I'll head up after the baby shower."

"Great idea babe," Ryan said smiling, with the teacup poised in front of his mouth. "The other thing we need to think about is a name. How's your short-list coming along?"

I placed my cup into its saucer with a delicate clink. "It's pretty short."

"Have you got any names on it yet?" he asked as I tapped my fingernails against my cup, avoiding eye contact. I had no explanation as to why it was so difficult for me to lock down a short-list of the name that we'd most likely be shouting repeatedly over the next eighteen years. "What about your mum's name?" Ryan suggested desperately.

"Shirley?!" I asked with amusement. "You want to call our daughter Shirley?"

"No, not really, but I thought you might like it," he admitted. I certainly didn't want to call our daughter 'Shirley', but I thought it was really lovely that Ryan was willing to name our child after my mother.

"The world doesn't need another Shirley, but I love your sentiment," I said, feeling a rush of lust for my beautiful husband. "You're being so sweet today."

- RYAN McPHERSON -

Kat put down her cuppa and maneuvered her large belly around the table so she could sit on my knee.

"I'm so lucky to have you," she said, draping her arms over my neck. "Despite your appalling handyman skills."

"I love you," I said, kissing her hard on the lips. Kat melted into me and returned my kiss with fervor.

"Prove it," she said with a sly grin. "I've been thinking about having sex with you all afternoon."

"Well let's make that happen then," I said as she wriggled the waistband of my sweatpants down. "Except this time, let's do it somewhere safe."

"Fine," she conceded, rolling her eyes playfully as she climbed off me. "Come on then big boy." Kat led the way into our bedroom and she stripped me naked before shedding her own clothes. Seeing her in her full pregnant glory took my breath away.

"God you're beautiful," I said, spellbound by her ripe figure. She smiled and silently pushed me onto the bed, lowering herself onto me carefully. With the reduced space in there, she was so snug that I could feel every inch of her. "Wow," I breathed as she began to move slowly on top of me, "you feel really different."

"In a good way or a bad way?"

"Neither. Just different. But I like it," I said as she began to rock back and forth.

"Me too," Kat agreed with a sigh of relief as she ground her pelvis against mine. I gripped her hips to give her some lower back support and revelled in the feeling of being completely encased by her. It was like nothing I'd ever felt before. I was getting closer to cumming, so I pressed my thumb against her clit and rubbed gently in time with her movements. "Oh my god. That's amazing," she breathed with sexy moan. The look on her face was pure ecstasy.

"My thoughts exactly," I agreed, watching the tell-tale red flush beginning to spread up her neck. "Pregnancy definitely works for you."

"It's definitely working right now," she retorted just before my cock hit a sensitive point inside her. Kat groaned loudly, and I felt her muscles starting to tighten around my cock. I was about to let myself go, when her belly began to lurch wildly like something out of an Alien movie.

"Holy shit!" I blurted as Kat's stomach moved uncontrollably from one side to the other as if it was being hit by a tidal wave.

"Ignore it," she pleaded, teetering on the edge of her climax.

"What's happening?" I asked in a panic, feeling my boner beginning to subside.

"Nothing. She's just moving," Kat said desperately trying to push herself to an orgasm. "She does this all the time. Just keep going."

"I can't," I answered trying to lift Kat off me. "She obviously doesn't like it."

"Ryan no!" Kat pleaded fighting to stay attached to my lap.

"Kat come on," I said, abruptly ending our session as I rolled out from underneath her. Her fierce eyes burnt into mine.

"Why would you do that?" she asked, appalled.

"Because we're traumatising our kid."

"We're not traumatising her Ryan. She doesn't know what's happening."

"I'm sorry babe, it's just too weird," I admitted more honestly than I should have.

"Well thanks, so now it's too weird to have sex with me?"

"No, that's not what I meant," I back-pedalled.

"It was exactly what you meant," she retorted accusingly.

"Yes… but not in a bad way."

"I don't know how that could possibly be intended in a good way."

"I just meant… you know... my kid is rolling around in there trying to escape the impact of my dick. It seems wrong to have my junk poking around my daughter's head."

Kat gaped at me with horror.

"Does that mean you won't have sex with me while she's in there?"

"Yes," I replied without thinking. The look on Kat's face said it all. "I mean no," I corrected myself. I was so flustered I couldn't think straight. "I mean… I want sex with you… I just don't want her to be upset when we do it."

"I'm having a shower," Kat replied flatly, as she waddled hastily to the bathroom. I sighed and flopped against the bedhead. What an idiot. I'd just made everything worse than it was before.

"Well done McPherson."

– *Chapter 3* –

THE BIRTH OF ASHLAN

- ASHLEY GRANGER -

On Saturday morning, I stood outside the studio door chatting with my yoga regulars, while we waited for Kesha's Body Pump class to finish. The door opened and people began filtering out, so I let myself in to get set-up. Kesha spotted me and grinned manically.

"Hey Miss Creative Director," she said nearly jumping out of her skin with excitement. "How was your first day at Artemis?"

I popped my backpack onto the stage behind her and gave her a hug.

"It was interesting."

"Interesting good or interesting bad?" Kesha asked as she disassembled her weight bar.

"Both I guess," I said, rolling out my yoga mat. "One of my mates from Mareechi's works there so that was a nice surprise."

"Awesome. Any hotties in the office?" she asked with a cheeky wink.

"Heaps of hotties," I replied as Kesh offloaded her weights into the rack. "In fact I think it might actually be a front for a high-class escort agency."

"In that case I expect an invitation to every single work function," she said as she tidied the weight rack.

"Done. Then you can come and suss out this guy for me," I said, trying to sound casual. Kesha stood bolt upright.

"There's a guy?!"

"Yeah. Maybe. I don't know. Kind of." I shrugged, but I couldn't hold back a tell-tale smile.

"Oh my god Ash! That's so exciting!"

"You haven't heard the bizarre part yet… do you remember that hot cab guy I told about?"

"Thor?"

"Yeah," I said, unlacing my trainers. "It turns out he works at Artemis."

"Shut up," Kesha answered, punching my arm with disbelief. "You work with Thor?" I nodded my confirmation of the news. "Well you know what that means," she declared grandiosely.

"If you say it's fate I'm going to hur-." My words were cut short when I noticed a little pink rabbit sitting on top of the speaker. The breath caught in my throat. It was exactly the same as the one that I'd thrown out the other day.

"Ash?" Kesha cocked her head, "Are you okay?" she asked as I stared at her with wild eyes.

"Is that yours?" I said, pointing at the rabbit as if it was the devil.

"No, that was here when I arrived," she replied with a shrug. "I guess some kid left it behind."

"Yeah, I guess so," I agreed distractedly, snapping out of my momentary daze. There was no way it was the same rabbit. There were probably millions of those things floating around Great Britain... yet for some reason I felt like it had been put there specifically for me.

"It looks well loved, I'm sure some poor mum will come back for it."

"Yeah. It's just…weird," I muttered under my breath, while Kesha gathered her belongings.

"Okay, I'm off honey," she declared. "We should catch up during the week and you can fill me in on Thor."

"Sounds good, I'll give you a call," I replied, at the exact same moment Thor's head pop around the door. My heart jumped in my chest as I did a double-take. What was Nathan Stone doing in my yoga class?

"Whoa, speaking of hotties," Kesha joked as she followed my gaze to the door.

"Nathan!" I said with surprise as he tried to sneak into the room unobtrusively. He looked damn cute in his gym gear.

"Sorry. Am I late?" he asked edging his way into the studio.

"Yeah, by about an hour gorgeous," Kesha piped up flirtatiously. "You missed my Body Pump class." Nathan scratched his neck and chuckled awkwardly as Kesha strutted past him towards the door. "Put it in your schedule for next week cutie," she instructed him with a wink before waving back at me. "Call you later Ash."

I waved at Kesh and shrugged apologetically at Nathan. "So… you're here for the yoga class?" I asked him disbelievingly.

"Sure am."

"Okay. Just grab a mat and find a spot on the floor," I told him, as I pointed towards the pile of mats.

"Yes coach," he joked, nodding obediently. He kept his eyes fastened on mine while he pulled a mat off the top of the pile. I watched him curiously as he found a space and wrestled with mat, attempting to unroll it in the most difficult way.

"Have you done yoga before?" I asked him with amusement. His confidence instantly faltered and he paused his fussing.

He looked up worriedly, "Err…no. Is that an issue?"

"Not at all," I assured him. "Just make sure you take the beginner options for every pose. They might look easy, but they can be quite taxing on your body if you're not used to it."

"Alright," he agreed, glancing self-consciously around the room.

"Okay guys, we're going to start with a very gentle sun salutation. Stand at the top of your mats in Tadasna and take a few deep breaths, inhaling through the nose." They all did as instructed, and I let the relaxing music wash over the room. I accidentally caught Nathan's eye and faltered for a moment, letting the silence string out for a little longer than I had intended.

"Uhh… breathe in deeply and fill your lungs right to the bottom," I recovered, finally regaining my focus. "Okay, as you take your next breath in, sweep your hands towards the roof and stretch them upwards with your palms together."

The class followed my demonstration and Nathan looked cocky about the ease of the moves thus far. Little did he know that the real challenge was yet to come. I could tell from the way that he moved that his hamstrings were tight – probably from all the rugby – and as such, he was staring down the barrel of a few painful stretches.

"Good, now stretch your arms as high as they'll go and then, bending from the hips, reach down and grasp your ankles." From my position I could see that Nathan was struggling. "If you can't reach your ankles, place your palms on your shins. The important thing is to keep your back straight."

Nathan peered up at me to see how I was demonstrating the move then corrected himself to the best of his abilities. His hammies were visibly protesting.

"If you can't reach your shins, place your hands on your thighs." Nathan looked relieved at being given an easier option, and I was pleased when he moved through the next few poses with relative ease. It wasn't until we reached the downward dog that things came undone for him.

"With your palms flat on the mat, push your bottom up to the sky, leaving your shoulders straight and your lower-back strong," I explained from underneath my own armpits as I maneuvered myself into the downward dog. Nathan looked appalled at the prospect of having to strike that pose, but proceeded to stick his bum into the air inelegantly. I bit my lip to thwart a laugh.

"Try to stretch out your hamstrings by pedalling your heels," I suggested. With his cute arse pointed in the air I couldn't help taking a quick peek. He was trying so hard, but he was way out of his depth. When he still wasn't catching on, I began a walk-around. "Try tilting your hips back Nathan."

"Like this?" he asked red-faced as he re-positioned himself awkwardly.

"Uh, not quite," I said, trying to hide my smile. "Here," I said gripping his hips to tilt them downwards.

"Oh," he answered bashfully, immediately collapsing onto the mat in a fluster. "I think I'll sit this one out."

"That's fine, just rest back into child's pose while we finish the sun salutations." Since he had no idea what a child pose was, I demonstrated it for him. "Like this."

"Thanks," Nathan huddled up with his forehead against the mat, while I continued talking everyone else through the sun salutation routine. I still couldn't understand why he'd come all this way on a Saturday morning just to do a yoga class. It seemed like a lot of effort for the chance at a quick shag and very unlike the notorious Nathan Stone I'd heard rumors about.

- NATHAN STONE -

What the hell had I been thinking going to a yoga class? I'd never gone to that much trouble for any woman before, so why had I suddenly decided to do it for Ashley? She was going to think I was a total git, especially after the untimely woodie I'd cracked when she'd corrected my position for the fucking downward dog. I'd always had a tendency to be quick to attention, but no one had ever had quite the instantaneous effect on me that Ashley did. Hopefully she hadn't noticed the movement…but then again, it wouldn't be the first time that we'd found ourselves in that situation.

Despite my embarrassment, I hung back at the end of the class to wait for her. Once everyone had cleared out, I wandered up to the stage and stood in front of Ashley as she rolled up her mat.

"Great class," I told her, trying to claw back some composure. "Yoga is way harder than I expected it to be."

She looked up and smiled, her green eyes sparkling with mischief.

"Was it purely coincidence that you ended up here, or did someone tip you off about my class?" Ashley asked with a sly grin. I nervously ran my hand through my hair. The woman always found a way to throw me off my game.

"I might have heard it from a little birdy," I admitted.

"Well I'm flattered that you'd give up your Saturday morning for it," she said, getting to her feet. "I hope it was worth it."

"That's yet to be seen," I replied with a flirty grin, as my mojo finally began to return. Ashley didn't respond. She just eyed me shrewdly, grabbed her bag and reached around me to flick off the lights. We stood face-to-face in the dim light for a moment.

"So what's the deciding factor then?" she asked provocatively. I took a deep breath. It was now or never.

"That depends. Have you got any plans right now?" I asked as casually as possible.

"I don't know," Ashley said, heading for the door. She peered back at me with a grin, "have I?"

I did my best to hold back my grin as I followed her out of the studio.

"I think maybe, if you have a look at your schedule, it will say that you're taking a jog down to Southbank with me," I said as she waved at a middle-aged lady floating gracefully on an elliptical trainer. "I'll even shout you lunch."

Ashley stopped and turned to face me. "A workout *and* a meal."

"I know an awesome vegan café," I said hopefully. She still hadn't actually said yes.

"You're vegan?" she asked with a raised brow.

"No," I shook my head and grinned. "I'm as carnivorous as they come but I thought you might like it."

Ashley nodded with an understanding chuckle as a teasing smile played on her pink lips. "Your little birdy certainly does know a lot about me."

"I have a very trustworthy flock," I said confidently. "So is that a yes?"

Absolutely," Ashley agreed with a devious smile, "but you'd better not slow me down," she said, sprinting out of the gym door before I even saw her feet moving. I laughed and bounded quickly after her, out the door and down onto the pavement. She was fast, but I was faster.

"Unfair advantage Granger," I called, jogging up behind her and grabbing her around the waist. She squealed with surprise, so I spun her around and plopped her on the ground facing in the opposite direction, then took off down the street the right way. "Now we're even," I teased over my shoulder.

"So chivalrous," she retorted, laughing as she tried to catch up. "I thought you were supposed to let the lady win."

"No way," I said glancing over my shoulder, "that's sexist. If you win it'll be because you earned it."

Ashley smiled, and I saw determination flare in her eyes. She pushed herself harder and very quickly she drew alongside me.

"No mercy huh?" she puffed with a grin.

"You'd better get used to that Granger," I retorted with a sly grin as we fell into step. "You're playing with the big boys now."

She peered at me sideways with an expression that I couldn't quite figure out.

"I guess I am," she agreed.

We jogged in comfortable silence, weaving through the relatively quiet streets towards the Thames. As we crossed Blackfriars Bridge, the sun was shimmering over the water and the reflected light gave Ashley's blonde hair an angelic glow. I still couldn't believe that she was the same raven-haired girl that I'd fancied all those years ago. Did she remember me? Had she felt the same spark that I had back then, or had I imagined it?

I glanced at Ashley for the fifth time in a row and I could see that she was beginning to tire. The look of dogged determination on her face told me that no matter how much pain she was in, she would never give up, so as soon as the Oxo tower came into view I slowed to a walk.

"It's just up here," I told her, pointing to a little row of shops at the bottom of the tower.

"Thank god," she said, stopping to catch her breath. "You win."

I laughed at her competitiveness and stretched my quads while I waited for her to collect herself. She was the most indomitable woman I'd ever met. Once she'd caught her breath, I threw my arm over her shoulder.

"Lunch time," I said, wondering what a vegan menu would entail. "I can't believe I'm about to eat vegan food for you."

She looked up at me with a cheeky half-smile. "Yeah, me either."

We found ourselves a table in the little eco-chic café that I'd found on Discover London, and Ashley skulled a pint of water without stopping for a breath. I waited for her to put down the glass and then asked her the one question I'd been dying to ask since Ryan had told me who she was.

"Did you know we've actually met before?"

She smiled and re-filled her water glass. "Yes, you stopped my tampon from doing a runner."

"Ha!" I snorted with amusement. "I was wondering if you'd ever bring that up."

"So, you knew it wasn't a lipstick then?"

"Of course I knew it wasn't a lipstick!" I answered with a grin. "I was trying not to embarrass you."

"How gentlemanly of you," she joked with sparkling green eyes. Even flushed and sweaty Ashley was sexy as hell. Probably more so in fact.

"I can be quite the gentleman when I want to be," I said casually. Her eyes bore into mine and momentarily threw me off-guard, so I broke eye contact and cleared my throat. "I wasn't meaning the cab day."

Ashley cocked her head, "Really? There was another time?"

"Well..." I paused, trying to find the right words, "your ex, Dominic...well, he used to be my guy...if you get my drift."

"Oh, you do have reliable birdies, don't you?" she answered with a tight smile. "Remind me to slap Ryan when I see him next."

"Meh, he didn't really have a choice. I'm very persuasive."

"I don't doubt that."

"So, Dom Doyle huh?"

"Mmhmm," she confirmed solemnly.

"Hey, no judgement here. I bought drugs off the guy for a whole decade."

"Yeah, Dom was 'the guy' for a lot of people around here before he went away."

"Well, to be fair... his coke was the best in town."

"He got it direct from Columbia," Ashley explained with a shrug, visibly uncomfortable with the conversation.

"Yeah, I'm not surprised he finally got busted," I said as our coffees arrived at the table. "Is that why you guys split?"

"Ummm… sort of," Ashley squirmed in her seat, "but...what's Dominic got to do with us meeting each other?"

"One night, it must've been a good five years ago now, I came out and met you guys for a last minute emergency run and you did the drop." I left it at that and waited to see if she would remember.

"Oh my go-" her words trailed off as the memory hit her. "That was you."

- ASHLEY GRANGER -

The image of Nathan's young face flashed vividly into my mind. He was Dom's hot client from that fateful night. It was so obvious, yet so bizarre. How had I not seen it before? His bright blue eyes had stuck in my mind for so long that it was hard to believe I hadn't clicked straight away. He'd looked different back then, with younger features and a floppy blonde hairdo, but I could still picture the petrified look on his beautiful face when my hand had brushed a little too close to his crotch.

"I remember you. Dom was…" I let my sentence trail off. I didn't think it was appropriate to tell Nathan that I'd copped a severe beating for our flirtatious interlude.

"Dom was what?" Nathan asked, smiling up at the waitress as she brought our lunch to the table. I waited for the girl to delicately arrange my plate of vegan lasagna.

"He wasn't happy," I replied tactfully.

"No, he wasn't," Nathan agreed, having no idea of the full extent of Dom's rage that night. A little spark of something intangible crackled between us as we assessed each other, both trying to communicate without speaking.

"I remember that night very clearly," I said, breaking the silence.

"I wasn't sure you would," Nathan admitted. "It seemed like you were on some pretty wicked gear that night."

"Nathan, I was dating a dealer. I was permanently on wicked gear. It kind of came with the territory."

"Yeah, I guess it would," he replied understandingly, "and speaking of dealers, you never told me who this PB character really is," Nathan probed with a cheeky grin. "Is he your new boyfriend?"

"No, he's not," I answered with amusement. "PB is my Dad. It's short for Papa Bear."

"Oh," he said, poking at his meal with the fork. "So you're single then?" He asked casually as he began scooping up a forkful of food.

I smiled and tucked my hair behind my ear, "Yes, I'm single." It was excruciating, like being back in high-school again.

"Good," Nathan nodded, "and this stationery addiction of yours. Is it terminal or do they have some sort of 12 step program you can do?"

"It's terminal I'm afraid."

"Hmm," Nathan mused before flashing his Colgate smile. "I guess I'll have to come to terms with that," he concluded. I shifted in my seat. I wasn't used to having someone be so openly interested in me so it made me wonder whether this was all an elaborate prank. "Enjoying the vegan lasagna?" he asked, as I quickly shovelled it into my mouth.

"It's a taste sensation," I joked and put my fork down with embarrassment. "But then again, I think most food is awesome."

"Besides meat," he joked with a wink.

I laughed at his wit and suddenly found myself feeling more relaxed.

"Considering I never used to eat at all, I'm doing pretty well."

"You never used to eat?" he asked, tilting his head and leaning his elbows on the table.

"I'm surprised your little birdy didn't mention that bit. It used to annoy him to no end."

"That sounds about right," he chuckled. Nathan held my gaze with his piercing blue eyes, and a smile flickered across his soft lips. "Well that explains why you were so scrawny back then."

I snorted with shock, "I wasn't scrawny."

"You were a walking skeleton" he said, glancing quickly at my now ample cleavage.

"Oh. I never noticed," I answered with a blush, sitting back in my chair so that my boobs weren't on full display. Nathan smiled and took a sip of his double espresso. I let my mind wander back to the night I'd first met him. Even back then we'd had sparks. A sly smile spread across my face as I remembered the obvious twitch in Nathan's trousers that night. "I couldn't have been too bad though," I teased, "you still seemed fairly impressed."

Nathan laughed just as he was swallowing his mouthful, and began choking on his coffee. For a minute I thought it was going to come out of his nose, but thankfully he collected himself before I bore witness to any coffee snorting.

"Gosh," he spluttered.

"Sorry," I apologised, handing him a napkin as he coughed. "Are you okay?"

"I'm fine," he said, thumping his chest. "Just clearing out my sinuses."
I laughed at his ability to crack jokes under pressure.

"People pay a lot of money to have their system flushed with coffee, although usually they start at the other end."

"Hmmm think I'll pass on the coffee enema thanks," he said wiping his hands with the napkin before looking up to catch my eye. "And for the record, you were still hot back then, but there wasn't much meat on you."

I shrugged awkwardly. "Yeah, I think my body image might have been slightly warped."

"Well, as an unbiased third party, I can honestly tell you that you're much hotter now." Nathan leaned back in his seat and rubbed the back of his neck. His T-shirt sleeve slipped down just enough for me to get a view of his toned bicep and my whole body surged with desire. I swallowed my urge to sink my teeth into his scrumptious arm and sipped on my coffee instead.

"Does that mean you think I'm hot?" I teased playfully. His eyes flickered with interest.

"Ashley, there wouldn't be a man in existence who thought otherwise."

"Ever the charmer Nathan Stone," I replied with a blush, embarrassed that I'd fished for a compliment.

"Oh, come on Granger, I bet you've had plenty of guys tell you that over the years."

"Dominic wasn't exactly the sort of guy to be forthcoming with compliments." That was a polite way to put it. 'Fucking cunt', 'spoiled princess' and 'rich bitch' had been Dom's most commonly used terms when referring to me. Nathan cocked his head quizzically.

"Surely there have been guys since Dom?"

"Nope, not one," I admitted with self-deprecating humour. "I've been completely man-free for three entire years now."

Nathan laughed, "I find that hard to believe."

"What do you mean by that?" I asked suspiciously. "Should I be offended or flattered?"

"What do you think Granger?" he asked, pushing his empty plate towards the centre of the table. At first, I assumed it was a rhetorical question, but then he picked up his coffee cup and took a long sip, as if waiting for me to respond. I felt obliged to fill the silence.

"I'm going to take it as a compliment?" I said with an inflection, making it sound more like a question than an answer. Nathan smiled and gently returned his coffee cup to the saucer.

"It's not a compliment Ashley, it's a statement of fact. You're a high-quality woman and there's not exactly a shortage of men swooning over you."

"Swooning? Do people still use that word?" I asked nervously.

"And now you're deflecting with humour," he noted with a raised eyebrow. It was possible that Nathan Stone was a lot more switched on than people gave him credit for.

"Well, how else am I supposed to respond to that?" I asked with an embarrassed shrug.

"Just say: 'Yes, you're right Nathan, I have guys queuing up to be with me,'" he teased, doing a bad impersonation of me. I laughed, feeling some of my nervous tension dissipate.

"That's sweet, but I don't have men queuing up to be with me."

"Yes, you do," he answered with a straight face. "GI Beau for example."

"Mmm," I mumbled, chewing on my bottom lip. "I don't think he was a fan of that name."

"No, he didn't seem to warm to it did he?" Nathan agreed with an evil chuckle. "But he seemed to be a fan of you."

"I heard he's gay."

"Ashley, that guy is about as gay as I am."

"Hmm." I replied, noncommittally. Gay or not, I still wasn't sure about Beau Peterson.

"And then there's Ryza…"

"Ryan's not swooning over me," I said defensively.

"Well he's hardly impartial when it comes to you," he said knowingly.

"That's just because we've been friends for a really long time."

Nathan raised an eyebrow. "And because he used to be in love with you." My stomach churned weirdly.

"What makes you think that?" I asked, pushing the remnants of my meal around my nearly empty plate to avoid eye contact.

"Because I've also been friends with him for a really long time," he said, hooking his arm over the back of his chair in triumph. "And because you're not denying it."

I patted my mouth with the napkin and looked Nathan in the eye.

"Nothing ever happened between Ryan and I."

"But you both wanted it to," he said. It wasn't a question.

I chuckled nervously and re-tied my hair. "Wow, this is like the Spanish inquisition."

"I just want to know if I'm in with a chance," he said bluntly, raising an amused eyebrow when I immediately ceased my fussing. He leaned forward over the table. "So are you still in love with him?" he asked, squirming a little as he awaited my answer. I paused, weighing up my answer. I decided it was best to be honest.

"I still love him," Nathan's smile faltered ever-so-slightly, "but I'm not in love with him anymore."

"Why not?" Nathan asked, leaning forward as if he actually cared about my answer.

"Once upon a time we had a spark," I answered, "but that's long-gone now."

"So, it's the spark that counts?" He held my gaze so intently it was disconcerting. I sipped on what was left of my lukewarm latte, recalling the day outside the cab when the static shock had zapped between us.

"It's always about the spark," I said eventually. "Without a spark how can there ever be a fire?" We assessed each other for a moment as I tried to subtly communicate my feelings.

"Excuse me miss, is this man bothering you?" Amy asked with a laugh as she appeared at our table, making the two of us jump in surprise.

"Amy?" I blurted, "What are you doing here?"

"I'm on my way to meet Ritch," she explained with faux innocence.

"Of course you are," Nathan said, raising a displeased brow at her. I grinned at Nathan.

"Let me guess, another one of your little birdies?"

"Sorry Ash, but he looked so pathetic I couldn't say no," Amy said, shooting a wink at Nathan. "Do you guys want to come along for a drink? It would be like a double date."

"Oh, this isn't a date," I explained quickly.

"No, we're just having lunch," Nathan agreed awkwardly, "as friends… like friends do."

Amy's eyes darted between the two of us.

"Okaaay," she said biting back a smile. "So how was the yoga class?"

"Total disaster," Nathan blurted with what appeared to be a slight blush.

"Actually, he did pretty well considering it was his first class."

"She's being nice Red. I totally sucked."

"I wish I'd seen it," Amy said with a wink.

"No. Trust me… you did not want to witness that. You'd have the images burnt into your retinas until the end of time."

"I didn't mind," I said with a shrug, catching his eye. Nathan looked at me with a sexy half-smile.

"You know Ashley, if you wanted to see my arse you, could have just asked. You didn't need to torture me with the downward dog."

"I'll remember that for next time," I retorted with a smile. Amy snorted with amusement.

"Yeah… sooooo not a date," she said checking her watch. Nathan and I peered at each other, but neither of us responded. "Well, would you two friends like to come and have a few drinks with some other friends?"

- NATHAN STONE -

Ritchie's eyes bulged out of their sockets when Ashley and I rocked up at the Slug & Lettuce with Red. I shrugged and tried to act nonchalant, as if it was normal for me to be escorting a work colleague around London on a Saturday morning, but I wasn't fooling anyone. In the decade Ritchie and I had known each other, I'd never once gone out of my way for any woman. Well, except for Becky Wheeler, but that had been quite a different kettle of fish.

"Well blow me down!" Ritch said in his typically loud volume, as he gave Red a mischievous grin. "You found some strays, did you?"

"Sure did," Red said, greeting him with a smack on the arse. "They looked thirsty, so I brought them along. Can we keep them?"

"I don't know… they're not up to our usual standard," he teased, eyeing our active wear. "Can I ask what you two were doing together that required gym gear?"

"We-" I began to respond before Red cut me off.

"They were on a date," she winked at Ashley whose face was as red as a beetroot.

"It wasn't a date," I said quickly, shrugging apologetically at Ashley. Ritchie patted me on the back and we commandeered a pair of big leather couches by the window. I casually ushered Ashley onto the smaller sofa but remained standing with the intention of ordering drinks.

"Nathan came to my yoga class," Ashley explained pointlessly. Little did she realise that we were going to get a grilling regardless.

"Oh, did he?" Ritchie asked with a chuckle, while Red lounged next to him. "And how was his flexibility? Did he perform well in all positions?"

"Knock it off Ritch," I said, punching his gargantuan bicep.

"No need to be embarrassed mate, we all have off days," he teased relentlessly. Fucker.

"You guys are arseholes," I said childishly. "Ashley won't come out with us again if you keep acting like this."

"My arse, she won't," Ritchie disagreed. "Granger can handle it. Right Granger?"

"It takes more than a loud-mouth Aussie to scare me off Ritchie," she retorted with a grin.

"See?" Ritch gloated pointedly, "Granger's fine. You're the one who's embarrassed."

"I'm not embarrassed," I rebuffed, "I just think you guys could take the grilling down a notch."

"Why? Is it ruining your date?" Red teased.

"It's not a fucking date," I reiterated. "If it was a date we certainly wouldn't be wasting it hanging out with you fuckers." Ritch and Red laughed with glee at the utter humiliation they were inflicting upon me. I turned my back on them and attempted to act unflustered in front of Ashley. She smiled empathetically and patted my hand in solidarity. "Vodka soda?" I asked, figuring that getting drunk would be the only solution.

"Yeah, thanks, but I'll get this round," she said standing up. Red grabbed Ashley's hand and pulled her back down.

"You'll do no such thing," she piped up, "you always let the man pay on the first date."

"I thought you were a feminist," I teased, rolling my eyes before making a quick escape to the bar. Ritchie jumped to his feet and trotted along behind me like an over-sized school-boy. He was having way too much fun at my expense. We leaned against the bar, waiting to be served, and he glanced over at me inquisitively.

"What are you doing man?"

"Getting drinks," I said, gesturing towards the bar.

"No, I mean what are you doing with Granger? Is this an actual thing?"

I shrugged, "I don't know."

Was it a thing? I had no idea. I really liked Ashley and I wanted to get to know her. She made me laugh, and she seemed to find me funny. Did that make it a 'thing'?

"You like her," he observed accurately.

"Yeah I do. She's pretty fucking awesome."

"Yeah she is," he agreed, studying me curiously. "And do you plan on fucking her tonight?"

"Jesus Ritch, it's not even a date," I snapped with disgust. "Besides I'd prefer if you didn't talk about her like she's a piece of meat." Did he really have to be so fucking crude about it?

"Holy fuck!" Ritchie spluttered, wide-eyed. "You're in love with her."

My head whipped in his direction. "I am not," I said defensively, as if he'd just blamed me for farting.

"Yes, you are. You're in love with Granger."

"I'm ignoring you now, so fuck off," I said, shooing him away. "I'll get this." I turned my attention to the bar guy to place my order and hoped that Ritch would get the hint and go away. He muttered something under his breath, but took his leave and let me ponder his accusation in relative privacy. Was Ritchie right? Was it possible I was in love with Ashley?

No way. I hardly knew her. We were just hanging out…and if it happened to result in sex then so be it. That was hardly the same as being in love was it? Not that I knew what being in love was.

I ordered drinks and some food for the table, then made my way back to the sofas. Ashley glanced up at me with a shy smile and my heart pounded a little bit faster. The woman certainly knocked me for six, but was Ritchie's theory accurate? Was I in love with her? Was that even possible for me? I handed Ashley, her drink and cozied up next to her on the sofa.

"I apologise in advance for anything that Ritchie says this afternoon," I said quietly to Ashley when I saw Ritch staring doe-eyed at the woman he was undeniably smitten with.

"He's harmless," Ashley assured me with a grin. "I've handled men much harder than Ritchie." Ritchie peered up from his conversation knowingly.

"So Granger, have you got any dirt on Ryza?" he asked mischievously. "He acts like he's got a stick up his arse, but I reckon he's actually a bit of a dark horse, isn't he?"

"Sorry Ritch, I can't divulge Mareechi's secrets." Ashley teased. "What happens on band camp, stays on band camp."

Ritchie leaned forward eagerly. "Come on, you've got to give us something. There must be at least one story you can tell."

"Oh, there are plenty of stories I could tell," Ashley answered with a laugh, "but I'm not going to. If Ryza hasn't told you himself then I won't be sharing."

"Give her a break guys," I said, casually draping my arm across the back of the sofa so that my hand was almost touching Ashley's shoulder. Red noticed my subtle move and grinned wickedly.

"You know, you two really do make a cute couple," she said and then turned to Ritchie. "Maybe we should start calling them Nashley."
Ashley put her drink down on the table and gave me a conspiratorial wink.

"No. I think I'd prefer Ashlan, what do you think Nathan?"

Ritchie guffawed loudly. "Granger, you're a keeper," he declared with a nod as he picked up his beer and raised his glass. "Here's to the newest member of the Artemis Crew."
It seemed Ashley had passed the test. Whatever the test was.

- ASHLEY GRANGER -

I'd never gone out for drinks wearing my yoga gear before, but Nathan was keeping me well supplied with vodka sodas so I'd stopped caring after the first hour or so. Besides, I was too busy enjoying the company to worry about it. Despite their incessant grilling, or perhaps because of it, Amy and Ritchie were rapidly becoming some of my favourite people to be around. I'd never laughed so much in my life, and it was nice to feel like a normal person for a while. I knew this was what most people did with their weekends. They went out, talked bollocks, laughed, drank and generally enjoyed life. It was something I hadn't done in so long, that I'd almost forgotten what it was like. I hadn't realised until that night that 'fun' had been seriously lacking from my life over the last few years.

"…so then Nathan wanders back inside, buck naked with Amy's beanie over his knob," Ritchie said, regaling me with the story of a ski holiday they all took a few years back. "The housekeeper nearly had a heart attack."

"It probably scarred her for life," Nathan laughed in agreement. "I bet she never picked up unattended clothes again."

"Forget her. It scarred me for life!" Amy said, taking a sip of her beer. "You do have a cute arse Nath, but I really liked that beanie and I could never bring myself to wear it again after that."

"You could have sold it on eBay for a profit," Nathan joked, leaning back against the sofa as he shot me a wink.

"Ego much Stoner?" Amy teased, before standing up abruptly. "I need to pee," she declared loudly, climbing over Ritchie to get off their sofa. "Want to join me Ash?"

"Why, do you need help?" joked Ritchie, slapping her bottom as she clambered to her feet. "Because I'd be happy to offer my assistance."

"No thanks stud. It's secret women's business."

"Like what?" Nathan asked with a laugh.

"We can't tell you or we'd have to kill you," I joked, standing up unsteadily to follow Amy to the toilets. The vodka was beginning to kick in and I was no longer in full control of my body. Nathan reached out and offered me a hand for balance as I negotiated my path between his feet and the coffee table.

"M'lady," he said gallantly.

"Why thank you, kind sir," I replied with a smile before Amy and I disappeared off to the Ladies'. I knew she wanted to grill me about my non-date, but I really needed to pee, so it was a price I was willing to pay.

"So, what's happening with you and Stoner?" she asked once we'd both finished our obligatory wees. "You guys are acting very date-y for something that's not a date."

"And you've been very encouraging for someone who was warning me off him." It had been less than 24 hours since she'd been telling me to steer clear of Nathan.

"It's possible that I might have changed my mind."

"Really?" I said dubiously, crossing my arms over my chest. "Overnight you've gone from 'Nathan Stone is dangerous' to: 'you make a cute couple'. How much did Nathan pay you to say this?"

"Not enough," she joked drying her hands under the noisy hand-dryer. "Ashley, the guy did a yoga class for you. I've never seen him make that much effort for any woman."

"That doesn't mean anything," I was trying to stay cool and detached about it, but I was starting to think that maybe there was more to this thing with Nathan than I'd originally assumed.

"You had lunch afterwards," Amy pointed out with raised brows.

"We're just hanging out," I answered with a shrug, but I couldn't stop a smile from spreading across my face. Amy grinned at my love-sick expression.

"Oh honey, you're in deep huh?"

"Yep."

"It's fine. He's clearly into you so just relax and see where it goes."

"Yeah. I can do that," I nodded. The movement made my head dizzy and I realised how drunk I was. "Ugh," I said, gripping my head.

"But first we need to sober you up," Amy concluded.

- NATHAN STONE -

When the girls returned from the bathroom, Granger was looking decidedly peaky. I probably shouldn't have been quite so liberal with her vodka soda supply, but I'd been trying to help her relax. I gave her a hand back to her seat and felt a rush of protectiveness over her.

"How are you going there Drunky?" I teased.

"I'm not drunk," Ashley denied, waving her hand about in a drunken fashion. "I'm just not very good at drinking."

"Okay, well that's completely different."

"It is different," she replied indignantly attempting to get comfortable. I sculled what was left of my beer.

"I think you could probably do with some fresh air. Want to go check out the festival?" I asked, figuring that it was our best chance at bringing her back from the brink of oblivion.

"Yeah that'd be good," Ashley agreed.

"I think it's time for us to make a move too, huh?" Red said to Ritch.

"Yeah," he nodded as they exchanged a meaningful look. We all fussed around, shaking hands and kissing goodbye. Ritchie pulled me in close and patted me on the back. "Take care of her man," he said quietly, nodding towards Ashley. "She's your beaver."

"Jesus Ritch, that's a bit much even for you."

"I'm not being dirty, you galah," he said punching my arm, "although that's applicable too." He gave me a mischievous wink, "But what I mean is, beavers mate for life and I'm telling you buddy… Ash is your beaver."

"Says the man with a regular fuck buddy," I retorted, playfully slapping his back.

"Yeah, we're more like skinks…" he joked. "Single for most of the year, then hook up with the same mate every breeding season."

"Right kiddies, it's been a great night but we're off to have sex." Red announced as she grabbed her bag.

"Point made," I joked quietly to Ritchie.

Ritch shrugged unapologetically, "It is what it is."

"Later daters," Red said with a cheeky wink aimed at Ashley.

"Later," I said, pushing Ritch towards the door.

"See you guys," Ashley waved goodbye with a drunk smile as she stood up to leave. "Whoa," she said with a laugh, nearly toppling forward so I quickly reached over to steady her.

"You okay?"

"Just a head-spin." She took my outstretched hand for balance then, still grasping my arms, she looked up at me and grinned, "Thank you Nathan Stone." She was an adorable drunk.

"That's okay Ashley Granger."

"You know you really are incredibly handsome," Ashley said, tapping her finger against my chest, "and very solid," she added, feeling my pecs with her entire hand. "I mean, really solid. Your chest is like a brick wall." She pressed on my torso as if testing its durability.

"Okay Drunky," I chuckled, peeling her hand away from my chest. "I know you'll regret this conversation in the morning, so let's get you outside for some fresh air." I grabbed our bags from under the table and led Ashley outside into the cool night air. Jubilee Garden was buzzing with activity. There were people everywhere. Tourists admired the London Eye; twenty-somethings milled about the food and drink stalls; and parents watched their kids run around in the playground.

"I forgot how much I love this place," Ashley said as I found us a quiet spot on the lawn, where we could sit and enjoy the festival atmosphere without being caught up in the excited crowds.

"Sit," I ordered her jokingly as I plonked our bags down on the grass.

"Yes boss," Ashley said with a crooked salute. I helped her get comfortable and knelt in front of her to make sure she was okay.

"Now, stay," I told her, pointing a finger as if I were training a dog. "I'm going to run to that stall and grab you some water."

"Okay handsome." She ran her hand ungracefully over the emerging stubble on my chin and I had to refrain myself from kissing her then and there. I laughed and removed her hand from my face.

"I'll be right back," I said making a dash for it. I needed to get her sober as quickly as possible because, if she kept on like this, my willpower wouldn't hold out for much longer.

- ASHLEY GRANGER -

The effects of the alcohol had hit me rather quickly and I was far drunker than I had originally estimated. Not so much that I was out of control, but enough that I'd lost my ability to employ a brain-to-mouth filter. I was ninety-nine point nine percent sure that I had embarrassed myself but at least the fresh air and water were helping to sober me up. Nathan leaned back on one elbow as we sat on the lush lawn drinking our bottles of slightly warm water.

"So what was it like dating a dealer?" he asked.

"It's not fair to ask me personal questions while I'm drunk," I said, lying back on the grass, unable to remain upright any longer. "I'm likely to divulge things I don't want you knowing about."

"Yeah I know," he grinned, "That's exactly why I'm asking."

"Dirty tactics Stone."

"Like I said Granger… you're playing with the big boys now." God he was sexy. I really wanted to kiss him. Did he want to kiss me? "So, my question still stands," he prompted, "what was life with Dominic Doyle like? Besides the endless supply of free drugs of course."

I laughed louder than necessary and tucked my hands behind my head as I remembered the days of life with Dom. He'd always had a way of convincing me to do things that I wouldn't normally do. No matter how uncomfortable I was, he'd somehow manage to talk me around. Dom had been like a tidal wave - once you were caught up in him, there was no use in fighting it.

I cringed as I remembered one particular night that still made me burn with shame whenever I thought of it.

Dom and I were at a Uni party - me as a student, Dom as the token dealer - and he talked me into having a quickie in the ladies toilets.

Dom had peered in to check that the coast was clear, and then pulled me in after him. I was dubious about the situation, but at that point, I had assumed he was planning on racking us up a couple of lines, so I went along with it. We slid quickly into the nearest of the dirty cubicles together and before I'd even had a chance to click the lock behind us, Dominic had me pushed me face first against the door. It hadn't been the direction I'd expected things to go. , so my heart pounded with a mixture of fear and excitement.

"Fuck you're gorgeous," he whispered into my ear as he pressed his body hard against mine. He kissed me madly from behind, and as his tongue forced its way into my mouth I could feel his cock straining hard against my back.

"We need to stop." I pleaded, turning my mouth away from his.

"Why?" He asked as his breath heaved in my ear. I had no answer. Why did we need to stop? The fact that it made me feel like a Grade A slut didn't seem like a legitimate reason, yet that was all I had. I liked him, but I had no desire to fuck him in a public toilet, especially not with my face pressed against a graffiti clad stall door. When I failed to give him an answer, his hands roamed my body. "Doesn't seem like you want me to stop," he said as his hand slipped inside my bra. My traitorous body quivered with pleasure but my gut was still telling me no. It felt like things had gone too far and I had no idea how to stop it.

In a panic, I did the only thing I could think of to avoid shagging him. Somehow I managed to maneuver my body around so that I was sitting on the toilet lid with Dominic's crotch right in front of my face.

He smiled in triumph, and rested his hands on my head as I got to work on unbuckling his belt. I sucked and licked madly in desperation for the moment to end and, thankfully, only minutes later Dom was shuddering in pleasure.

"Don't make a mess now," he said with a condescending smile as he pressed against the back of my head so that I couldn't move. With no other option, I obediently swallowed, trying my best not to gag as the thick liquid forced it's way down my throat. "Good girl," Dom said in a tone that made my skin crawl. He pulled his trousers back over his waist and lifted me to my feet.

"You've definitely earned this," he joked, as he racked up two lines of coke on the cistern and passed me a rolled banknote.

"Judging by that look on your face, I'm going to go ahead and assume that it wasn't particularly awesome?" joked Nath, bringing me back to the present. I shook my head and attempted a laugh.

"Not so awesome, no," I admitted vaguely as a bright glow emanated from the grass in between us. Nathan glanced down at my phone flashing brightly in the dimming light.

"I think you've got a text."

"No, it does that sometimes."

"That's weird. Maybe the battery is faulty."

"Yeah, I think the whole thing might be faulty to be honest."

"I'm not a phone expert, but I can take a look at it."

"Sure," I shrugged, and Nathan picked up the phone to investigate it.

"Wow, it's running super-hot," he said, feeling the heat coming off the back of it. "It's definitely working over-time." Nathan tapped a few things on the screen and, after a minute, he looked up at me with disbelief. "There's nothing on there," he announced with shock, "no Facebook, or Twitter or anything."

"I know. I don't do the internet."

"What do you mean 'you don't do the internet'?" he asked putting my phone back on down on the grass. "What about your digital revolution?!"

"Yeah I know," I nodded in acceptance. It was hypocritical, and I knew it. "I still stand by what I said. Digital is the future. Professionally I'm all for it, but personally I won't be participating. It's too dangerous."
He returned to his reclined position and tilted his head curiously.

"In what way?"

"Well if someone wants to find you, all they have to do is cyber-stalk you. Social media gives them everything on a gold platter. Current location, regular check-ins, work, photos, friends, relationship status, email address… they've got everything they need to find you."

"And I'm guessing you're referring to a particular 'someone'?"

"People don't usually run away from Dom Doyle and live to tell the story."

"Would he really do that?" Nathan asked in shock.

"Nathan, you've met Dom. I saw the fear in your eyes that night at the club. You can't tell me you didn't see the capacity for murder in his."

"Yeah I did," he agreed. "I guess I just never thought that shit was really real though, you know?"

"Either did I until Dom started using me as a punching bag." Ah shit. There was that can of worms that I hadn't wanted to open. Nathan looked gobsmacked.

"Dom hit you?" he asked as if he'd been unexpectedly slapped in the face. I nodded, mildly amused at his endearing innocence. Saying Dom used to hit me was like saying 'Antarctica is a little bit chilly'. Nathan ran his hand through his hair. "Did he…I mean, don't answer this if you don't want to but…did it happen a lot?"

"Daily," I admitted, feeling really odd about sharing my past with someone I was hoping to have a future with. Nathan's jaw clenched tightly.

"Badly?" he asked through gritted teeth.

I nodded again, "I wound up in hospital in the end. That's when I finally left."

"Holy fuck," he sighed breathlessly. It was all getting a bit deep and heavy for a first date - err, first non-date - so it was time to change the subject.

"And what about you Nathan Stone?" I asked with a sneaky smile. "What's your story?"

"In what way?" he said with a shrug.

"Well, you haven't really said much about yourself. You've been very good at asking me questions, but you've given nothing away, so it's your turn now."

"Well, no violence and no free drugs. Unfortunately, I had to pay your boyfriend for all of my drugs."

"Ex-boyfriend," I corrected him with a cringe.

"Sorry," he apologised. "So what do you want to know about me?"

"I don't know. Where did you grow up? What are your parents like? What do they think of your bachelor lifestyle?"

"Not a lot," he blurted with a snort. "My Dad died when I was thirteen and my mum doesn't even know me."

"Oh Nathan, I'm so sorry," I answered, feeling awful for him.

"No need to be sorry," he said nonchalantly. "That's just life, right?"

"I guess," I agreed hesitantly, "but it can't be easy losing a parent so young."

"Meh. He wasn't the first person to die of cancer and he won't be the last." I stared at Nathan in shock. "Sorry," he apologised again. "I don't really like talking about it, you know? It kinda makes it real. Before the cancer my Dad had always seemed invincible. He went from being this big ballsy guy to being so frail and sick that he couldn't even feed himself. Life didn't really make sense anymore you know? It just seemed so unfair," he paused for a moment. "Three years he was like that. In and out of chemo, sick as a dog. It was almost a relief when he finally went. Grieving for him was easier than seeing him so helpless."

I sat up and put my hand on his shoulder silently. I hadn't been expecting something quite so heavy. I couldn't imagine what it would be like to lose a parent, especially at such a young age. I tried my best to focus on his face, but unfortunately, I wasn't succeeding. Everything looked blurry, so I was probably making a weird cross-eyed expression.

"I'm so sorry Nathan," I said quietly, not knowing what else I could say.

"Like I said, it was a long time ago," he shrugged. "I was thirteen."

"You surprise me," I admitted. "You're not at all what I was expecting."

"I can only imagine," he replied rolling his eyes. "I know what people say about me."

"Oh, come on, everyone loves you," I told him honestly, lying back down.

"Yeah maybe so, but they still think I'm a man-whore." I bit my lip to stop myself from agreeing with him, and he sighed, having seen the answer written all over my face. "I suppose I've earned my reputation fair and square," he conceded with a half-smile. "But things change. People change. I've changed." Nathan flopped back to join me, tucking his hands under his head in the same way I'd done. In that position his bicep looked huge and my familiar urge to bite it returned.

I looked up at the London Eye to try and distract myself from my drunken desires. People laughed, chatted and wandered around us, but we remained together in comfortable silence, staring up at the massive, brightly lit wheel.

"Don't you find it bizarre?" Nathan asked randomly. I wasn't sure if I'd blacked out and missed some of the conversation, so I opted not to respond.

"I mean, we met by chance five years ago, and now here we are lying in Jubilee Gardens together. You can't tell me that's not weird," he said glancing at me over his toned bicep.

"Actually, we met by coincidence twice if you include the cab," I blurted nervously. "Three if you count working together. So that's even weirder."

"Yeah it is," he agreed, scanning my face with his sparkly blue eyes. God he was gorgeous, and that five o'clock shadow was killing me. Nathan rolled onto his side and the breath caught in my throat. I was too drunk to tell whether it was a kissing moment, but my heart was pounding all the same. He leaned his head on his hand and stared down at me with a look I couldn't discern. "You know… if this was an actual date I'd kiss you right now," he said with a sexy half-smile. Oh my god! I desperately wanted him to kiss me. "Except, this isn't a date," he said questioningly, "is it?"

I wanted to say yes, but something was stopping me. The word was right on the tip of my tongue, but I couldn't articulate it.

"I guess not," I replied eventually, unable to admit to him that I really wanted it to be a date, or more specifically, that I really wanted him to kiss me. Why couldn't I just say it? I bit my lip and Nathan nodded with a tight smile, sitting up abruptly.

"Do you want to go on the Eye?" he asked.

"What? You mean right now?"

"Yeah. I'll go get tickets." Nathan jumped to his feet and brushed the grass off his bottom, "unless you've got somewhere else to be?"

"There's nowhere else I'd rather be," I admitted without thinking.

"Good. Then stay right here until I get back."

- NATHAN STONE -

Being Great Britain, the Eye required two stages of queuing, and being me, I was unwilling to queue for anything so, unbeknownst to Ashley, I'd bought us a VIP pass to avoid the lines. I'd managed to sober her up somewhat, but she still looked a little worse for wear.

"Are you okay?" I asked. "You look terrible."

Ashley rolled her eyes and laughed, "Thanks Nathan, you're such a charmer."

"I didn't mean - I mean - you don't look well," I stuttered, realising that the words hadn't come out quite as intended.

"I'm okay," she said, touching my arm in reassurance.

"Do you think you're up to this?" I asked peering up at the over-sized ferris wheel.

"I'm fine, I promise."

"Alright." I didn't believe her, but she was an adult so if she said she was fine then I wasn't going to question it.

"So, what do I owe you for the ticket?" Ashley asked perkily.

"Nothing. It's my shout."

"Nathan, I haven't paid for a thing all day," she argued, continuing to open her purse.

"Well I guess maybe this is a date then," I said gently resting my hand on hers. Ashley ceased her fussing and bit her lip as I leaned in ever-so-slightly. She stared at me wide-eyed, like a deer caught in headlights. That same look had appeared on her face every time I'd attempted to kiss her that night so I chickened out for a third time. "I'll let you pay next time," I joked to try and ease the weird tension.

"Okay," she agreed with a stiff nod.

"Now follow me," I said, shoving her purse into her bag and grabbing her hand. "I have a surprise." I led Ashley past the long queue of people and up to the VIP window, handing the hostess our tickets.

"Thank you Sir," she replied. "Private capsule?"

"Well that part was supposed to be a surprise," I said, feeling a bit disappointed that she'd ruined it.

"You got us a private capsule?" Ashley asked in shock. I shrugged, hoping that I hadn't over-done it.

"I thought it would be easier to see everything that way," I explained quickly, "not because I'm trying to impress you."

Ashley cocked her head and shot me a sly grin. "So are you?"

"Trying to impress you, you mean?" I clarified and she nodded her confirmation. I smiled awkwardly. "Yes," I admitted bluntly, "is it working?" She looked down at her feet with a blush, and then caught my eyes again.

"Yes." So there it was. Just like the X-Files...the truth was out there.

"Okay sir, you're clear to board now," the hostess instructed, directing us onto the slowly moving glass pod. "Enjoy your flight."
We climbed on board, and Ashley ran straight over to the far window.

"Oh my god Nathan, this is breathtaking! Look at those lights!" The banks of the Thames sparkled and glittered, but not half as much as Ashley did. She was so beautiful, and I felt weirdly proud that I was the person who had put that look of awe on her face.

"And we've barely even left the ground yet," I laughed, joking with the on-board hostess.

"Oh sorry, I didn't see you there," Ashley apologised unnecessarily to the woman. "I'm a little over-excited. I've never been on the Eye before."

"I'm popping her cherry," I joked like an idiot, regretting the words as soon as they'd left my mouth.
Ashley blushed and turned her attention back to the view of our amazing city.

"Would you like me to point out landmarks, or would you prefer to enjoy the view?" the lady asked.

"Oh my gosh, look at Westminster Abbey!" Ashley said. "It's beautiful."

"I think maybe we'll just enjoy the view," I told the hostess with a smile as Ashley glanced over her shoulder at me.

"Come and look," she beckoned with a joyful smile that made my heart flip-flop. I wondered momentarily whether I was having a heart palpitation but then I remembered Ritchie's prediction that I was in love with Ashley. Perhaps he was right after all. Or perhaps was a mild case of angina.

I strolled over to join her at the window, taking in the scenery for a moment before I gazed down at Ashley. The view out there wasn't even close to competing with the view in front of me.

"You're right, it's beautiful."
Ashley leaned against the railing and turned to face me.

"So Mr Stone, tell me about this Becky Wheeler girl."

"Ah-ha, so people have been talking then," I said dubiously. Suddenly her repeated 'deer-in-headlights' reaction made perfect sense. She thought I was a player.

"Maybe I have a few little birdies of my own," she said with a grin.

"And what exactly have your little birdies told you?"

"All I've heard is that it was a pretty messy situation."
I laughed nervously. "Messy is a nice way to put it." It was probably the only nice way to put it. How could I tell Ashley the truth about Becky without sounding like a total cunt? "Becky Wheeler was a really nice girl. All I can say is that I fucked up. Well more accurately, I fucked up spectacularly... and at Artemis, nothing is a secret."

"So, what happened exactly?"

"The short story is that I cheated on her... with her flatmate." Ugh. It sounded so shitty when I put it like that. Oh, who was I kidding? It was shitty and there was no way around it. Younger Stone had not been the noblest individual.

"Ouch," Ashley replied with a cringe. Yeah that pretty much summed it up.

"Look Ashley," I began, feeling the need to further explain my personal growth. "I'll be the first to admit that I haven't been an angel in the past, but I sincerely regret what happened with Becky. If I could take it back I would… but I can't." It was the best explanation I could offer her, so if Ashley still thought I was a prick then there was nothing else I could do.

"I don't really know what to say Nathan," she replied, looking up at me with complete understanding. "We all make mistakes right? It's just whether you learn from them or not."

"That's very true," I agreed. "The truth is Granger…ten years ago when I was young and dumb, everything was about getting laid, but that sort of life just doesn't appeal to me anymore. I'd prefer to find myself a girl who can actually hold a conversation." I held her gaze hoping that she'd catch my not-so-subtle hint.

"Wow, so you mean you actually want a meaningful, adult relationship then Stone?" Ashley teased, nudging my shoulder with hers. "Someone needs to send out a press release." She peered up at me with those big green cat eyes of hers, and every bone in my body was telling me I should kiss her. All I had to do was lean down and touch my mouth to hers, it really wasn't hard. Come on Stoner you'll never get a better moment than this.

- ASHLEY GRANGER -

The big wheel turned slowly and if it hadn't been for the fact that I felt a wave of nausea wash over me, I would probably have kissed Nathan.

"Are you feeling okay?" Nathan asked as I put my hand to my mouth.

"Not really. I think the vodka is disagreeing with my stomach," I whispered, thinking that somehow whispering might help.

"Okay," he whispered in return, with one of his beautiful smiles. "Leave it with me." I concentrated on keeping my vodka down while Nathan wandered over to the hostess. I could feel the pressure rising into my chest and the gorgeous moving view was making it worse. Thankfully, Nathan returned with a couple of sick bags. "How about we sit you down?" He guided me to the wooden bench seat in the middle of the capsule, where I ungracefully plonked my bottom. Nathan opened one of the barf bags in preparation and I grabbed it just in time. My stomach ejected the vodka in an epic power-hurl.

"Sorry," I spluttered between heaves, feeling unbearably ashamed.

"It's fine Chucky," he said, rubbing my back. "It's better out than in. Just do what you have to do."

"Is she alright?" the hostess asked Nathan, passing him a few extra spew bags just in case.

"She's fine, it's just a bit of motion sickness," Nathan lied as I sheepishly hid my face in the full vomit bag. I was eternally grateful that he was covering for me, but even more so that he'd hired us a private capsule. Nathan handed me a fresh bag and pried the used one out of my hands.

"Sorry," I mumbled again, reluctantly relinquishing the paper bag full of sick.

"No need to be sorry," he said with his sexy, scrunchy-eyed smile, as I did my best not to breathe my vomit breath all over him. His five o'clock shadow highlighted his chiseled jaw and all I wanted to do was run my hand along his chin. So, I did. I'd never been so forward with anyone in my life, but with Nathan I seemed to lose my self-control. As my fingers brushed lightly across his stubbly face, I could feel the muscles in his jaw tighten.

"Just a few minutes to go if you'd like to make the most of the view," said the hostess politely. I removed my hand from Nathan's face.

"I don't think I can stand up yet, but you go take another look."

"I'm already enjoying the view," he said, sliding his arm around me and pulling me into his chest, still holding the barf-bag full of my vomit in his other hand. I leaned into him and stared straight ahead at the beautiful view of London through the big glass windows. We sat in silence and enjoyed the last few minutes of our 'flight'.

When the capsule pulled up to the flight deck Nathan lifted me to my feet.

"Right, Chucky, let's get you out of here." He handed the vomit bag to the hostess and looked at me with a grin. "Hold on tight."

"To what?" I asked in confusion. Nathan nobly scooped me off my feet and into his arms.

"To me," he said, before very carefully stepping off the moving wheel onto the platform, with me in his arms. I wrapped my hands around his neck feeling awkward. Not only because of my lingering vomit-breath, but also because no-one had ever carried me like that before. Dom had always thrown me over his shoulder and lugged me like a sack of potatoes, but I'd never been held with such care. Nathan gallantly carried me away from the London Eye and across Jubilee Gardens as if I weighed nothing. "You okay?" he asked, catching me staring up at his chiseled profile like a love-sick puppy dog.

"Besides a damaged ego you mean?"

Nathan laughed warmly. "At least you haven't lost your sense of humour."

"It's holding on by a thread..." I answered, feeling my cheeks blanching furiously, "...unlike my dignity."

"Dignity is over-rated anyway," he said with a smile. "Now lead the way boss. I'm taking you home."

- NATHAN STONE -

We made it back to Ashley's place with no further ado, or more accurately, a-spew. I found some Ibuprofen and helped her into bed, wondering whether I was supposed to stay or go. It was an unprecedented situation in 'The Life of Stone'. I'd never spent the night with a woman who I wasn't having sex with. In fact, I'd never even spent the whole night with a woman I *was* having sex with either. Usually I went home to the comfort of my own bed as soon as the deed was done.

I pulled the duvet up over Ashley's shoulders and her eyes fluttered closed. What was it about this woman that had me breaking my own rules? I stroked her hair and glanced dubiously out at the tiny two-seater sofa in the lounge room. Oh boy. It was going to be a long, uncomfortable night. I quietly backed away from my drunk, sleeping angel, and flicked off the light.

"Nathan?" Ashley asked croakily.

"Yeah?" I said, pausing in the doorway of the darkened room.

"Where are you going?"

"I was going to sleep on the sofa."

"Don't be stupid," she mumbled, "there's plenty of room in here."

"Ummm," I mumbled uncertainly. I had very little faith in my willpower and I didn't want to fuck things up. "Thanks but I'm fine."

"Seriously, you can't sleep on that couch, it's tiny," Ashley said, groggily patting the empty side of the bed. "I promise I won't bite."

"Oh well in that case there's really no point," I joked, shuffling on my tired feet. "Maybe I should just head home," I said, hovering in the doorway.

"I wouldn't have picked you as the shy type," she teased, sitting up as best she could in her fragile state.

"I'm not. I just don't trust myself lying in bed next to you," I answered way too honestly.

"You'll be fine," Ashley assured me. "The stink of my vomit breath will be enough to repel you."

"Well you've got a point there," I conceded with a laugh, making my way to her bed in the dim light. I crawled carefully into the vacant side. I could pretend that I was being chivalrous and trying not to wobble the bed, but the truth was that I was trying not to come into contact with Ashley. I wriggled around to get comfortable, but it wasn't easy since I was practically hanging off the edge of the bed.

"Thanks for looking after me," she said with a yawn.

"No worries," I said fluffing the pillow underneath my head. "It was my fault for getting you this drunk in the first place."

"I'm a big girl Stone, you didn't force me to drink."

"No, but I didn't exactly discourage you either."

Ashley rolled over to face me. "You're not like anyone I've ever met before Nathan." The room was dark, so I couldn't make out the expression on her face, but from the tone in her voice I could tell that she meant it as a compliment.

"Well, I am one of a kind," I joked.

"That you are," she agreed, rolling back over onto her other side. "'Night Stone."

"'Night Chucky," I said, feeling inexplicably smug.

"Stone?" Ashley said with her face snuggled into the pillow.

I peered at her through the dark, "Yeah?"

"Stop calling me Chucky."

I laughed, "Nah sorry love, that one's going to stick."

"I'm going to be Chucky forever, aren't I?" she asked with resignation.

"Yeah, you'll always be Chucky to me," I joked. "Although I also like Chuckster and Chuckinator."

"You're hilarious," she said, throwing her arm backwards to hit me playfully.

"Chuckilicious, Chucktard, Chuckenstein, Chuckle-Berry Finn-"

Ashley laughed, "I think I get the idea. Goodnight Nathan."

"Goodnight Chuck Norris." I relaxed and stopped worrying so much. Being with Ashley was really easy and, although having her warm body just inches away from mine was incredibly alluring, I managed to resist any urges that would have put an end to the wholesome relationship that we seemed to be building.

I was surprised when the morning rolled around, and I'd managed to actually sleep next to another human being. I opened my eyes and peered over at Ashley. She was still fast asleep and snoring lightly. I stifled a giggle. Fuck she was cute. Ugh. Ritchie was right. I was totally falling for her.

My stomach rumbled, so I checked my watch. It was 7:03am and I was supposed to be meeting Ryza for a jog in a few hours. I cast my eyes back over to Ashley and a sense of mischief crept over me.

"You awake?" I asked loudly, poking her in the ribs.

"No," she grumbled from underneath the pillow.

"Well wake up then. I'm hungry," I said, grabbing the pillow off her face.

"Noooo," she complained, rolling onto her side to get away from me.

"Pleeeeeease? I'll buy you breakfast."

Ashley opened her eyes and laughed tiredly when she saw me staring down at her with puppy dog eyes. "Fine," she conceded, "I'm up. I'm up."

"Yay!" I clapped like a retarded seal. Having never witnessed the wake-up routine of another human person, I'd always assumed that everyone was like me, but clearly Ashley was not a morning person. I stopped clapping when she still hadn't moved a muscle. "Come on Chucky," I prodded her impatiently.

"I'm working up to it," she mumbled with her face still firmly planted into her pillow.

"Then work faster. I'm starving." I waited patiently for a little while, but when she still hadn't moved, I jumped off the bed, grabbed her by the feet, and started dragging her off the mattress.

"Nathan!" she squealed in protest, desperately clinging onto the bed sheets with shocked laughter. "Please stop."

"Okay, I'm stopping," I agreed obediently, and promptly let go of her feet. Her bottom half plopped to the ground with a thud, so that the top half of her body was still in the bed, while her legs were hanging down on the floor. I had no idea why I was acting like a child, but I was enjoying it. Something about Ashley made me drop all the pretence of being suave and grown-up.

"Oh my god Nathan!" Ashley wailed tiredly, as I let out the most evil laugh I could muster.

"You're half way out of bed now so you might as well get up."

"Fine, but at least let me have a shower before you drag me out into public."

"Hmmm…I don't know. If I let you do that then you'll be clean and fresh while I'm stuck in my stinky gym gear."

"You're welcome to have a shower." she offered.

"Yeah, but I'm not sure I'd fit into any of your clothes."

"Good point," she replied with a giggle. "How about I cook you breakfast here instead?"

"Sounds awesome," I agreed as she climbed to her feet. Her make-up was smudged and her hair was messed up like a bird's nest, but she still looked sexy. I stared at her silently, feeling all sorts of weird things in my chestal region.

"What?" she asked, clocking the strange look on my face.

"Nothing." I didn't want to relay what was going on in my head, but Ashley raised a doubtful eyebrow which made it obvious that she wasn't going to let it go. "Okay" I relented, "I was just realising that this is the first time I've ever woken up with a woman."

- ASHLEY GRANGER -

Despite the unceremonious wake-up, I couldn't imagine a better way to start the day, than waking up next to Nathan. It felt strangely normal for his face to be the first thing I saw when I opened my eyes, and I hoped that maybe this would be the first of many. Nathan was, without a doubt, the sexiest man I'd ever met and I was starting to suspect that I was developing a serious Stone Addiction. It was funny that our little impromptu sleep-over was a first for Nathan, because it was also a first for me. It was the first time since Dom, that I'd shared a bed with a man. In fact, it was also the first time that a man to whom I wasn't related, had been in my flat.

"Well you popped my cherry, so now I'm popping yours," I joked stupidly. Was I really the first woman he'd ever woken up next to?

"I guess that's a fair trade," Nathan agreed with a deep, rumbly, belly laugh that made my ovaries twist with excitement. He glanced at his watch. "In fact we've now officially been hanging out for nearly 24 hours straight."

"Is that a subtle way of saying you've had enough of me?" I retorted, heading towards the kitchen to see what I could whip up for my accidental overnight guest.

"Quite the opposite actually," he said, tagging along behind me. "This technically now counts as my longest relationship."

"Oh no, I'd hate to ruin your reputation," I teased, rummaging through my cupboard to see what vegan delight I could create for my carnivorous visitor. Nathan casually hoisted himself up onto my bench.

"I think the boat sailed on my reputation a long time ago."

I laughed, and pulled out a packet of cacao. "Are chocolate pancakes okay with you?" I was secretly hoping that I might be able to impress him with my culinary skills.

"Sounds awesome to me."

"Withhold your judgment on their awesomeness until you've eaten them," I said as I offloaded all the ingredients for our pancakes. "They're vegan, sugar-free and gluten-free, so they might not be to your taste."

"Ah, so you're good for my health as well," he said with his sexy gravelly laugh.

"As well as what?" I asked, grabbing a mixing bowl out of the cupboard so I could measure out the flour.

"As well as being good for my soul." I froze mid-pour, attempting to fight off the burning blush that was assaulting my face. "Sorry. I didn't mean to embarrass you," he apologised.

"That's okay," I squeaked, trying to maintain my composure. "I'm not very good at taking compliments."

"Yeah, I've noticed that."

"I guess being treated like shit is more my comfort zone," I joked, trying to make light of the situation. "I can cope with being punched in the face, but give me a compliment and I freak out."

Nathan's face dropped in shock, "Jesus Chucky."

"Sorry. Too soon?"

"Yeah, maybe hold off on the abuse jokes for the time being," Nathan suggested, jumping off the bench and nudging up to me. I could feel the warmth emanating from his body, which rendered me motionless for a moment. "You know Granger, you'll have to get used to taking compliments if we're going to hang out." I peered up at him sideways, feeling nervous all over again. Even disheveled and wearing dirty, sweaty clothes he was still so handsome that he took my breath away. His blue eyes sparkled at me, and what had been merely a five o'clock shadow last night, was now fully formed stubble. "Right chef, what can I do to help?" he asked, breaking our little moment.

"Well..." I ran my hand through my hair, "the batter is under control, but you could cut up some fruit if you like?"

"Cool," Nathan said, grabbing a knife from the knife block. "Your wish is my command."

"Hmm... now that's a tantalising thought," I joked provocatively. It was so out of character for me to be brazen, but my guard seemed to drop when I was around Nathan. He paused, cleared his throat and began chopping the banana.

"So what are you up to today then?" he asked, changing the subject.

"Just the standard Sunday lunch with my folks, and then a workout with Kesha."

"Ah yes, the over-zealous Body Pump instructor," Nathan said with a cheeky smile. "If Ritchie wasn't obsessed with Red, Kesha would be right up his alley."

"Yeah, she's pretty much the female version of him," I joked with a nod. Nathan smiled and continued peeling an apple.

"Are you close with your parents?" he asked casually.

"Yeah, they're pretty cool as far as parents go," I said, omitting the fact that they regularly treated me like a five-year old. "What's today got in store for you then Mr Stone?"

"Not much. I'm meeting up with Ryza for a run in an hour and then going over to his place for lunch afterwards."

"A run? Who does that on a Sunday morning?" I teased with a laugh.

"Crazy people," Nathan answered, grinning like a crazy man. He peered into the pan at the batch of pancakes sizzling in coconut oil. "These smell amazing." From my stereo in the lounge we heard the first few bass riffs of an old Jet song. Nathan almost jumped out of his skin with enthusiasm. "What a tune!" he exclaimed, running over to turn up the volume.

"Agreed," I giggled as he began singing at the top of his lungs.

"Say 1, 2, 3 take my hand and come with me because you look so fine that I really want to make you mine," he sang as he bounced back to the kitchen doing some sort of bizarre, yet strangely sexy, fusion between Salsa dancing and head-banging. "I said you look so fine that I really want to make you mine," Nathan continued enthusiastically, grabbing my soup ladle from the utensil basket to use it as a microphone. "4, 5, 6 come on and get your kicks, now you don't need money when you look like that do ya honey?" He pointed at me like he was a rock-star on stage. I laughed at his frivolity and sang along with him as I finished off the pancakes. "Big black boots, long brown hair…." Nathan belted into the ladle, before shoving it in front of my mouth. I momentarily resisted and let a few lines slip by. "Come on Chucky."

I rolled my eyes and sang into the ladle, hoping that I didn't sound like a strangled cat, "I can see, you home with me, but you were with another man yeah."

"Nice work Granger," he nodded with approval, returning my ladle to the basket. "I can't believe you own an actual CD player. I didn't realise they still made them."

"I don't know if they do," I admitted. "I've had that one for years and I can't bring myself to throw it out, because I still have all my old CDs."
Nathan resumed his karaoke session minus the ladle.

"I said are you gonna be my girl?" he sang at me as I offloaded the last pancake onto the plate. My chest fluttered when he stuck out is hand towards me.

"What?" I asked, wondering what the hell he was doing.

"We're dancing," he declared, grabbing my hand and pulling me towards him. I laughed in shock as Nathan proceeded to drag me into his crazy dance. He threw me around with room with ease, and I was laughing so hard that my ribs were hurting. "You're a good dancer Chuckster," he said over the music. "Now let's see how good your cooking is."

"Better than my dancing, that's for sure."

- *Chapter 4* -

TROUBLE IN McPARADISE

- KAT McPHERSON -

In the early hours of the morning I was awoken from my restless slumber by a merciless kick to my bladder. My eyes flew open as I was hit with the sudden urge to pee. As if being the size of a small Mac truck wasn't uncomfortable enough, the baby had begun a strict routine of torturous workouts that primarily occurred when I was attempting to sleep.

I climbed quietly out of bed and waddled quickly to the loo in fear that I might actually wet my pants. Pregnancy was cruel and unglamorous. Every pee felt pointless, given I knew I'd be straight back to the toilet in another twenty minutes.

Instead of hopping back into bed and waking Ryan, I decided to get up and leave him to sleep. Maybe Beau would be up. He usually woke up early on the weekends for swimming training, but after the company drinks last night he might have decided to skip training. I sent him a text to check.

'Are you awake?' I typed and hit send.

'I am now.'

'Can I give you call?'

'Sure,' he answered simply. I pulled on my coat and Ugg boots and wandered out to the back courtyard so I wouldn't disturb Ryan. The sun was almost rising, and dew was glistening on all the leaves. It was actually a beautiful time of day to be awake. I breathed in the fresh morning air and dialled Beau's number.

"Hey," he said.

"Hey." I had no idea what to say. Everything had changed, yet nothing had changed. "How were the company drinks?"

"Yeah, good I guess. They announced Stoner's win on the Delfontaine account."

"Cool."

"Oh, and I met Malibu Barbie," he added. "You're right. She's pretty hot."

"Is that supposed to make me feel better?"

"No," he replied bluntly, "but you will be relieved to know that she and Stoner seem to have a thing going on, so I doubt she'll be chasing after Ryan."

"Ashley and Nathan have a thing?" I asked with surprise. I wasn't surprised that Nathan was going after her. He was Nathan after all, but I was incredibly surprised that she would entertain it. As much as I hated to admit it, Ashley seemed way too smart to fall for a guy like Nathan.

"Yeah, well, this is Stoner we're talking about," Beau said indifferently. I could almost hear him shrugging at the other end of the line. "If it's got breasts and it breathes then the chances are he'll chase after it like a horny dog."

"Yeah," I agreed, unsure what to make of this new revelation.

"So, what's up Kitty Kat? Does this phone call mean we're back to normal?"

"I don't think we can ever go back to normal Beau."

"Then what's the deal Boss? The ball is in your court on this one."

"I don't know Beau," I said with a sigh. "You're my best friend and I love you… which is exactly why I don't think we can be friends anymore. It's not fair on you."

"I don't care KittyKat. I'll take as much of your time as I can get. I want to be near you, even if it means just hanging out as friends."

"Let me think about it, okay?"

"Take whatever time you need, I'll be here whenever you're ready," he paused for a moment. "And Kat… just know that if you were my girl, all the Malibu Barbies in the world wouldn't distract me from you."

I hung up the phone feeling a little bit shell-shocked. That chat hadn't made the situation easier at all. I wasn't sure what I'd been hoping for, but if it was clarity, then I certainly hadn't found it.

I needed to take my mind off things, so I decided to make some muffins. I'd never been much of a baker, until a few weeks into my pregnancy when it had become a daily occurrence. My sudden baking obsession had been my first clue that I was pregnant. After months of failed attempts at baby-making, I'd let go of the hope that I might fall pregnant. So even though the physical signs had been there, I didn't let myself believe that I might actually be 'with child'. The bizarre change in my domestic routine however, well that was the thing that tipped me off.

It was funny how desperate I'd been to have a baby back then and now that the time was drawing closer, I was beginning to dread it. What sort of mum was I going to be? Would I know what to do once the baby arrived? Was there some sort of innate 'knowing' that appeared in women after they'd birthed a child? Oh god. The birth. How was I going to survive that? It was the stuff of nightmares. I didn't want my punani ripped to shreds for the sake of this child. Maybe it would be best if I elected to have a Caesarean. Could I do that at such a late stage? Maybe I'd call Doctor Murray on Monday and find out whether it was still an option.

I scoured the pantry for ingredients and pondered the possibility of a C-Section, while I whipped up a batch of blueberry muffins as quietly as humanly possible. I popped them in the oven and tidied up the kitchen while I waited for them to bake. It was 7am.

"Ugh," I sighed with frustration. There was no point in going back to sleep now. "Scones," I muttered, answering my own question. I pulled out another bowl and got to work on making some cheese scones. I was busily kneading the dough when Ryan emerged from the bedroom, rubbing his eyes against the bright light.

"What are you doing babe?" he asked with a yawn. He looked incredibly sexy when he was waking up, especially with his morning stubble. It made him look less uptight… almost relaxed even.

"Baking," I replied with a shrug, as I continued squishing the big ball of dough, trying not to think dirty thoughts about my unwilling husband.

"Yeah, I can see that," he said giving me a kiss on the cheek. "But why so early in the morning?"

"I couldn't sleep, and I didn't want to wake you," I explained, flattening the ball with the rolling pin. Perhaps if I concentrated hard enough on the dough, my hormonal body would get itself under control. It was a cruel irony that pregnancy made women horny, while the men got turned off by the big belly and the fact that their child was housed in the same general vicinity.

"So, you decided to make noise and create yummy smells instead?"

"Sorry. It made sense in my head," I answered, feeling bad that I'd woken him, and partly wishing that he'd go away so I didn't have to contend with my libido. "Why don't you go back to bed? There's no point in both of us being awake so early."

"But it smells so good out here," Ryan replied, peering curiously into the oven. "You make the best muffins in the world."

"I'll come and get you when they're done," I told him, pushing him out of the kitchen. It was easier to concentrate without him around. He was far too distracting, and given that having sex with him was now off the cards, the less I saw of him the better.

- RYAN McPHERSON -

I was worried about Kat. More so than usual. She wasn't quite herself and I got the feeling it wasn't just the pregnancy hormones. Kat had been baking a lot since she'd gotten pregnant, but 7am baking sessions were a new occurrence that I wasn't entirely sure how to handle. Besides the fact that it was making my stomach rumble, there was something disconcerting about it. Maybe she was still pissed about our failed sex attempt.

"Are you okay about last night?" I asked warily as she herded me back to the bedroom. "You seemed pretty upset."

"Why should I be upset that my husband doesn't want to have sex with me?" she replied with a fake smile.

"It's not that I don't want to have sex with you Kat," I explained hopelessly, taking hold of her hand in an effort to assure her of my affection for her.

"No, it's just that it grosses you out."
I sighed compassionately and ran my hand down her face gently.

"It doesn't gross me out babe, I think you're beautiful and I love having sex with you."

"But just not while I'm pregnant," Kat concluded with hurt in her eyes.

I kissed her softly. "I'm sorry if I made you feel like that," I apologised, cupping her chin in my hands. "I'm an idiot."

"Yes, you are," she agreed with a cheeky smile. It was nice to see her smile, even if it was because she was taking the mickey out of me. My Kat was back again.

"But I'm your idiot," I told her with a grin of relief, "and you're stuck with me whether you like it or not."

"I can live with that. But we seriously have to do something about this sex situation or I'm going to buy myself a vibrator."

"Well why don't you come into the bedroom and we'll see what we can do," I suggested, pulling her body into mine so that her big belly was pressed against my stomach.

"That sounds great, but I've got scone dough prepped and muffins in the oven," Kat answered, pulling away from me.

"How long will the muffins take?" I asked jokingly. "We could fit in a quickie before breakfast."

"Fifteen minutes," she replied with a chuckle.

"Meh, easy. We could be done in five," I teased.

"Go back to bed, you stirrer," she ordered, slapping me on the arse. "We'll revisit this conversation once the scones are done."

"Okay," I agreed with a tired laugh. "Sex and scones. Sounds like a kinky combo."

"Nothing sexier than baked goods," she said as I shuffled back to the bedroom.

"I love you," I called back to her with a contented grin.

"I love you too."

- KAT McPHERSON -

Unfortunately, we didn't get a chance to revisit our sex plan because Amy popped in to discuss details for the Baby Shower.

"Wow, it smells great in here. What are you cooking?" she asked as she let herself in the front door and dumped her stuff on the kitchen bench.

"Blueberry muffins, cheese scones, and I've just put a lamb in the oven."

"She's trying to fatten me up," Ryan said, emerging from the bedroom in his running gear, which admittedly did seem to be getting a little tighter around his middle. "I'm starting to wonder whether she's planning to roast me up too," he joked, giving Aims a kiss on the cheek.

"Well you would make a great casserole," Amy teased. "There's plenty of you to go around," she added, patting his belly.

"And on that note…" said Ryan, "I'm off to meet Nathan for a run."

"Okay honey," I said as he came over to give me a cuddle.

"We'll finish our conversation after lunch," he whispered in my ear, giving me a suggestive little squeeze.

"Deal," I agreed, feeling my lady-bits flare up again.

"Find out the goss, will you," Amy said as Ryan headed towards the door.

"What goss?" he asked, sliding his arms into his hoodie.

Amy grabbed one of the cheese scones out of the basket. "He had a date with Ashley yesterday."

I froze at the mention of her name. As did Ryan.

"Did he?" Ryan asked curiously, pausing mid-zip.

"They said it wasn't a date, but it clearly was," Amy continued oblivious to the mood change. "He even went to her yoga class. They were getting pretty cozy by the time we saw them," she said, biting into the scone. "They left together so I'd suspect he ended up taking her home."

"Hmm, so Beau was right after all," I mused out loud.

"Are you sure?" Ryan asked Amy.

"Very sure," she said with a mouth full of scone.

"Why don't you just ask him yourself if it's such a big deal," I snapped.

"To be fair, they're pretty fucking cute together," Amy said with a grin. I'd never heard anyone use the word 'cute' in relation to Nathan Stone. Many other words certainly, but never 'cute'.

"Okay I'm off then," Ryan said stiffly. "See you ladies later."

"Righto," I replied brusquely.

"Enjoy your run," Amy said chirpily as her eyes darted between the two of us. Ryan closed the door behind himself and she turned back to me. "What's going on with you guys?"

"Nothing," I said, not feeling ready to talk about it. "Did you want to stay for lunch?"

"Yeah, why not? It smells great." She took a seat at the counter. "So you're really getting in to this housewife thing huh?"

"Yeah. I think it's the hormones," I said as I pulled the lamb out to add the potatoes.

"Jesus that's huge!" she gawked at the sight of the massive roast. "I guess 'eating for two' really is a thing. What have you made for the rest of us?"

"You're a cheeky fucker," I laughed, throwing the potatoes into the pan. "So Ashley and Nathan huh? How long do you think that will last? I'd bet my life that it'll be over before they even get back to work tomorrow."

"Normally I'd agree with you," Amy said with a nod, "but honestly… I don't think this is one of Nathan's usual churn 'em and burn 'em things. I think he genuinely likes her."

"Yeah right. I'll believe that when I see it," I snorted in disbelief, "but as long as she keeps her hands-off Ryan then I don't care."

"Why would she go after Ryan?"

"They have history," I told her waving my spatula in the air. "Maybe she's come back to reclaim the one that got away."

Amy shook her head in disagreement. "Sorry hun, but you're being paranoid. Ashley is totally smitten with Nathan. There's no way she's into Ryan."

"We'll see." I wanted to believe it, but life didn't usually pan out that simply.

Aims rolled her eyes. "Kat, if Ryan and Ashley were going to hook up, they would have done it back then."

"They came close to kissing once Aims." I sighed and pushed the roasting tray back into the oven.

"That means nothing," she said, throwing her hands in the air. "I've snogged Nathan before but that doesn't mean I want to go out and shag the guy."

"Oh yeah, I'd forgotten about that." Amy and Nathan had had a very brief moment, back when Amy first started at Artemis. The whole thing had been a huge scandal at the time, but they'd both been coked-off their heads and united by their shared sluttiness. "That was hardly the same thing. Not to mention that fact that it was before you hooked up with Ritch."

"Yeah exactly," Aims said with a smug smile, "and whatever went on with Ryan and Ash was years ago before he met you."

"Maybe," I semi-agreed.

Amy leaned her chin on her hand, "You don't like Ashley much do you?"

"I don't even know the woman," I said, evading the question. "I've only met her once."

"Okay," Amy answered dubiously, "because I was going to suggest that we invite her to your baby shower."

"Why would I want to invite a stranger to my baby shower?" I was appalled by her suggestion.

"Well, you know… she's part of the crew now, so I thought it might be a nice way for you to get to know each other."

"Yeah fine. Whatever," I shrugged. I didn't want Ashley at my baby shower, but I didn't want to look like the unreasonable one. I'd just have to suck-it-up and hope that Ashley didn't accept the invitation.

"Great!" Amy said. "I think you'll really like her once you get to know her."

- RYAN McPHERSON -

The sun was shining brightly over the river by the time I met Nathan down at Southbank and I felt relieved to be out of the house and away from the tensions in my marriage. The chill hadn't quite lifted yet and with the fine white fog floating magically over the water, the Thames looked like a Monet painting.

"So, how's your weekend been?" Nath asked as we jogged along the promenade.

"A total nightmare," I admitted with a sigh.

"Why? What's going on?"

"I don't even know where to start," I said. "Sex has turned into an issue; I can't figure out how to put the fucking cot together; my parents are due back in town next week and Kat still thinks I want to leave her for Ashley."

"Eek," he replied with a cringe.

"Yep," I said, beginning to puff a little. I'd let my exercise regime slip over the past few months, so keeping up with Nathan was getting harder by the week.

"Are you going to catch up with your folks?"

"I don't know. I'd rather not, but they said they had something to discuss. I doubt Kat will want to see them again after last time."

"Yeah with fair reason, but what about you," he asked with a raised eyebrow. "Do you want to cut contact?"

"They're fucking cunts Nath, but they're my only family."

"No, Kat's your family… and I'd like to think that I am too."

"Thanks mate," I said, mulling over his words. Did I want to cut my parents off? Could I do that? Was I ready to admit that we were better off without them in our lives? What about our daughter? Wouldn't she want to know her grandparents? Realistically she'd probably be better off not knowing them, but then she'd also miss out on a rather hefty trust fund.

"You don't need them Ryza," Nath said as if he was reading my mind. "Every success you've ever had has been on your own terms. You've gotten this far without them, don't give away your power to fuckheads who don't deserve your time."

"You have a valid point," I said, wiping a stream of sweat from my forehead.

"Of course I do," he agreed, looking over at me with a grin. "I know it's hard, but it's time to walk away. They'll never give you what you need."

"What? Love and respect?" I joked with a puff.

"Yes, exactly."

"Hmm…" I mumbled, feeling a little weirded out that Nathan Stone was actually the bearer of wise words. "Anyway, let's talk about something else. How was your weekend? I hear you went out drinking with the crew yesterday."

"How did you hear that?" he asked, with a guilty look on his face.

"Amy's at my place."

"Of course," he replied flatly. "So what else did she tell you?"

I looked at him with a smug grin. "Everything."

Nathan rolled his eyes like a teenager.

"Okay go ahead and yell at me, I know you want to."

"What's the point man? You'll just do whatever you want anyway."

"That's true," he agreed.

"I can't believe you went to a yoga class," I laughed breathlessly.

"Yep. Go on. Laugh it up, just like everyone else has."

"Did she get any video footage of you doing yoga?" I teased, punching him in the arm.

"I fucking hope not," he laughed. "It was an epic fail."

"Can't have been too bad if you ended up taking her home."

"We didn't shag or anything," he said quickly. "Ashley got a bit tipsy, so I stayed and looked after her."

I rolled my eyes. "Ever the gentleman."

"Honestly Ryza. Nothing happened."

"Your sex life is none of my business Stoner…but if you hurt her, I'll fucking kill you." I had to admit that I wasn't overly thrilled at the news that Nathan had hooked up with Ash, but there wasn't a lot I could do about it. She was a big girl and she could make her own decisions, who was I to get in the way? But on the other hand… what would happen when Nathan did something idiotic and broke her heart? Because that was inevitable wasn't it? He'd accidentally slip back into his old ways, and I would be left to pick up the pieces. Then Ash would hate Nathan and I'd be forced to choose between my two best mates.

"Are you getting a bit out of shape mate?" Nathan teased as I puffed and panted beside him. I suspected it was mostly to distract me from the subject of Ash, but it didn't make him any less right.

"Yeah, I'm struggling man," I admitted breathlessly. "I think I might be developing a sympathy gut." I'd gained five kilos in the last three weeks thanks to Kat's baking and, since it had been caused by her pregnancy nesting, I could probably count it as a sympathy gut.

"Is that a thing?" Nathan asked with a laugh, peering at my growing belly.

"I don't know, but if it is I'm using it."

"Cop out," he teased.

"Nah, I'm serious man. Kat keeps baking," I said hopelessly. "Muffins, cakes, cookies…even fucking scones. I'm turning into a lard-arse."

"I don't know what to tell you man. You are getting a little soft around the edges, but I think that's pretty acceptable when you're about to become a parent. I guess you'll have to come and workout with Ritchie and me."

"Ergh," I panted in disgust at the idea of lifting weights. I'd never lifted weights in my life and I didn't intend to start now. I did need to do something about my rapidly expanding waistline though.

"Why don't you come along to rugby then?" Nathan suggested. "Those love handles will drop off in no time."

"Yeah, I could do rugby," I agreed, beginning to lag behind.

"Of course you could," Nathan said. He quickly took the lead as if we were in a relay race. "In fact, I remember you being quite good at Uni."

"That was a long time ago Stoner."

"Yeah it was, but I'm sure it's like riding bike," Nathan agreed with a nod, glancing back over his shoulder. "Come on tubby, step it up! That's one muffin down and only a hundred and seventy-four to go."

"Yeah right," I grunted with a chuckle. It was demoralising exercising with that guy. "Maybe I should start going to Ash's yoga classes," I teased with a grin. Nathan laughed and ran backwards so he was once again along-side me.

"I know you don't believe me, but nothing happened with Ashley last night," he said earnestly. It actually sounded like the truth, but I'd never known Nathan Stone to spend a whole night with a woman and not shag her.

"Like I said mate, it's none of my business. I just don't want to see her get hurt again that's all. She's gone through enough."

"I don't plan on hurting her Ryza."

"You never do Stoner," I told him with a puff. I wanted to believe him as much as he believed himself, but I'd known Nathan far too long to be convinced by his self-delusions. "You never do."

- KAT McPHERSON -

Amy and I were still hanging out in the kitchen by the time the boys arrived home. Our lunch was ready to go, and the smell of the lamb was making my tummy rumble.

"Hey baby, we're home," Ryan called happily.

"Wow, it smells great in here," Nath said, following Ryan into the kitchen. He was fresh-faced, clean-shaven and seemed relatively unspent compared to Ryan, who was flushed, sweaty and looked like he was about to pass out from exhaustion.

"Kat's made a roast," Amy said, as I tended to the cauliflower cheese.

"Oh, hey Red," Nathan said, giving her a quick peck on the cheek. "No Ritchie?"

"Nah, I wore him out last night."

"Oh god Amy, must you be so graphic?" I complained, seeing visuals in my mind that I would never be able to delete.

"I just like winding you guys up," she said with a grin before turning back to Nathan. "So lover boy, how did last night go? Is Ashlan official?"

"No comment," Nathan replied, before walking around to my side of the counter and greeting me with a hug.

"Did you even run? You smell like you just stepped out of the shower," I said, getting a whiff of his musky aftershave.

"Sundays are my easy runs," he said teasing Ryan with a wink.

"Well we can't all be as fit as you," Ryan said taking off his hoody to reveal some serious sweat patches on his T-shirt. Nathan gave my shoulder an affectionate squeeze.

"You didn't have to cook for us Tails, we could have gone past Marks & Sparks on the way home."

"Of course I did. I'm nesting," I joked, hugging him the best I could around my inflated belly. "It shouldn't be much longer."

"Great, I'm starving" he said, pulling up a stool next to Amy at the bench.

"Why don't you guys go watch some telly? I'll call you when it's ready."

"Nah, I'm going to have a quick shower," Ryan said, kicking his shoes off. "I stink."

"Yeah you do," I teased him with a grin, "but not too long, this is nearly done."

"Okay," he agreed, disappearing into the bedroom.

"So, who wants some wine?" I offered, pulling out a bottle I had stashed away for entertaining.

"It's not even twelve yet," Nathan replied.

"Since when has that ever stopped you?" Amy asked, as I handed Nathan the unopened bottle of red, on the assumption that he would partake.

"Good point," he grinned. "Wine it is." He set to work on opening the bottle while I grabbed the glasses.

"So… are you going to tell us how your date with Ashley turned out?" Amy probed as Nathan poured the wine. "Did you go back to her place?"

"Ah, I see what's happening," Nathan said, pausing mid-pour. "You two are trying to get me drunk so I'll spill all the details."

"Exactly," I agreed with a smile.

"It's not gonna work because there's nothing to tell," he said adamantly. "We just hung out."

"Nathan, you never 'just hang-out' with women." Amy said, taking the bottle out of his hand and finishing the pour. "Besides, you didn't answer the question… did you go back to hers?"

"Yeah, I did, but nothing happened. We just talked. She's really awesome."

"Yeah I've heard that," I said coldly, feeling another pang of jealousy. Why did everyone think Ashley was so fucking amazing? What made her so damn special?

"Are you jealous Tails?" Nathan teased. "You still don't like other women getting in on the Stoner action huh?"

"And you're still full of yourself" I snorted with amusement.

"And that's why you love me," he answered with a cheeky wink.

"Oi. Keep your dirty hands off my wife Romeo," Ryan joked, waltzing back into the room wearing nothing but a pair of jeans. Even with his dad bod he was still hot. He pulled his T-shirt over his partially wet torso as he joined the rest of us in the kitchen. "Smells amazing my love," he said, giving me a kiss on the back of my neck. My hormones started rampaging again.

"So, you're not going to tell us then?" asked Amy in confusion.

"Not all of us want to hear the details anyway," Ryan said, grabbing one of the roast sweet potatoes from the bowl. I smacked the back of his hand, but he was too quick, and gave me a cheeky wink as he popped it into his mouth.

"There's nothing to tell anyway," Nathan said with a shrug.

"What do you mean there's nothing to tell?" Amy asked, taking a sip of her wine. "You always have something to tell."

"Not this time," he said taking a swig of his own wine, "I already told you, nothing happened, so there's nothing to tell."

"Yeah right," Ryan retorted with a snort as he poured himself a glass of wine. "I've never known you to take someone home without shagging them."

"Except Becky Wheeler…" I said without thinking, "but we all know how that worked out."

"Wow, thanks Tails," Nath said sarcastically.

"Well…" I shrugged apologetically.

"Why is it so hard for you guys to believe that I've changed?" The three of us stared at him silently. There was no polite way to answer that question. "Ashley is different okay?" he said emphatically. "I really like her, and I don't want to fuck it up by shagging her."
We were all agape.

"You're actually serious, aren't you?" Ryan asked, with his glass of wine poised at his lips.

"Why would I lie about it?" Nathan asked, throwing his hands in the air.

"You wouldn't," Amy agreed, flashing me a smug smile.

"Wow, you really do like her then huh?" I asked, hoping that Ashley felt the same way about him so that she'd stay away from my man.

Nathan put his glass down on the counter. "Yeah. I really do."

"I give him two weeks," Ryan piped up, "then he'll either fuck it up or get bored."

"Geez, thanks for the vote of confidence mate. As if I'm not nervous enough as it is."

Ryan laughed loudly. "Nathan Stone is nervous about a woman? That's a world first."

Nathan rubbed his face with frustration.

"Seriously man, I'm not joking. I think I'm having some sort of mid-life crisis here."

"Why? Because you spent a night with a woman without having sex with her?" I asked him with amusement.

"Exactly," he replied. "Sex didn't even cross my mind," he added with a straight face. I raised my eyebrows doubtfully, calling his bluff. "Okay," he relented. "So that's not technically true. We slept in the same bed, so sex did cross my mind, but I didn't act on it. I didn't even kiss her."

"So, you're worried because you don't want to shag Ash?" Ryan asked with an expression of pure confusion, while Amy grinned at me like a maniac. She was revelling in being right.

"The girl is smoking hot Ryan, of course I want to shag her."

Ryan shook his head in bafflement. "Okay, well now you've completely lost me."

"My point is that I don't *just* want to shag her. I want to get to know her first," Nath said.

We all gawked at him speechless. They were words that none of us had ever expected to hear come out of Nathan Stone's mouth.

"So hypothetically speaking…" I asked curiously as I piled the carrots onto a serving plate. "You get to know her, then you have sex… then what happens after that?"

"Well hopefully I'd keep having sex with her."

"In a mutually exclusive manner?" clarified Ryan.

"Yes Ryan. In a mutually exclusive manner," Nath answered with irritation. "Is it really such a difficult concept to understand?"

"It is in relation to you," he said with a shrug.

"Harsh," Nathan retorted nearing the end of his patience.

"Wanna know what I think Stoner?" Amy interrupted.

"Not really," Nathan and I both replied simultaneously. Amy rolled her eyes and gave us her opinion anyway.

"I think you're falling in love."

"Did Ritchie tell you to say that?" Nathan asked.

"He didn't have to. It's obvious."

"I'm not in love with Ashley for fuck's sake," Nath snapped. "I just like her, that's all. Can we talk about something else now please?"

"Okay, whatever," Amy agreed with a wicked smile as the three of us exchanged glances. I stretched and rubbed my lower back. I'd pushed my body to its limits by standing in the kitchen all day. Ryan noticed and rubbed my shoulders.

"How are you feeling my love? Do you need to sit down?"

"Yeah I'm pretty tired," I agreed, ready to park my bottom and take the weight off my aching cankles. "This pregnancy thing is hard work."

"I bet it is," Nathan agreed. "I don't know how you women do it."

"Apparently the child makes it all worthwhile in the end," Amy joked.

"Yeah, I don't know how Ashley coped, going through all of this for nothing," I said stretching out my sore shoulder blades. I hadn't thought about what I'd said until after I'd said it and from the look on Nathan's face, it was the first he'd heard of it. "Shit," I swore.

"Kat!" Ryan blurted with horror.

"Whoa," Amy mumbled.

"Ashley was pregnant?" Nath asked, stunned.

"Sorry Nath, I didn't mean to say that. I just assumed everyone knew."

He shook his head. "No, it didn't exactly come up in conversation."

"That's not your business to share babe," Ryza said with embarrassment. "If Ash had wanted Nathan to know, she would have told him."

"Sorry, I thought since she was pregnant at Mareechi's that it was public knowledge," I said sheepishly. "I didn't think."

"Perhaps we should keep this to ourselves for now huh?" Amy suggested tactfully. "Ashley will share that when she's ready."

The rest of us nodded in agreement, but Nathan was quiet for the remainder of our meal. He looked like a kid who'd dropped his icecream, and I was the arsehole that had knocked it out of his hand.

- ASHLEY GRANGER -

After talking to Nathan about my phone over the weekend, I booked into the genius bar to get it looked at properly on my way to work on Monday. When I arrived at the Apple store, I was directed to my 'genius', who was a rather handsome ginger-haired man. He looked completely out of place in a sleek, elegant tech store, and according to his badge, his name was Jock.

"Ashley?" he asked, with a sexy Scottish accent that made my cheeks blush.

"Yes, that's me."

"I'm Jock," he said meaningfully, as if I was supposed to know him. I smiled at him politely.

"Hi Jock."

"You don't remember me do you?"

"Err..."

"I'm friends with Kesha," he told me. "We met at her birthday a few weeks back."

"Oh, that's right," I said as his face began to look vaguely familiar. "Kesh and I had a few of those fishbowl cocktails that night, so my memory is a little hazy," I admitted with a blush as I recalled our very messy night at Trailer Happiness. "But now that you've said it, I remember you. You're the cop right?"

"Ex-cop," he said with a shrug.

"Hey, well... nice to meet you soberly, ex-cop Jock. I'm yoga teacher - and now Creative Director - Ashley," I said, shaking his hand.

"So that interview went well then by the sounds of it?" Jock said, shaking my hand with a smile. I had zero recollection of telling him about my interview at Artemis, but I had been pretty drunk at Kesha's party, and very excited about my interview so I'd probably told everyone.

"It did indeed."

"Well, congrats," he said with his Scottish charm.

"Thank you." I blushed again. He was somehow the epitome of a rugged highland Scotsman, whilst also having a refined, royal air about him. He was like Prince Harry on steroids.

"I wondered if I was ever going to see you again," Jock said quietly, leaning over the table with a grin, "and here you are."

"Here I am," I agreed flirtatiously.

"So what brings you to the Apple store Ms Creative Director?"

"I'm having problems with my phone," I said stupidly.

"Well then you've come to the right place. What's the problem with it?"

I proceeded to explain the full details of my phone malfunction, as Jock listened intently. He wasn't traditionally handsome like Nathan, or model perfect like Beau, or even bad-boy hot like Dom had been. Jock was something else altogether. A tough, sexy geek. At Kesha's party I'd not really looked twice at him because I'd just assumed he was a meat-head rugby jock, but in the sober light of day, he was actually quite appealing.

I handed Jock my phone and stood quietly as he did some investigating. The concentrated look on his face made it seem like he was solving a problem of national importance rather than fixing a broken phone. After a few minutes of examination, he glanced up and smiled solemnly.

"I think I've found the problem, but I need to do some testing to be sure."

"Okay," I agreed with a curious nod. I was starting to get the feeling that it was more than a standard technical malfunction. He got to work on the phone and after five minutes of 'testing', he looked up with a serious expression on his rugged face.

"I hate to tell you this, but it looks like someone's installed spyware on your handset."

My stomach lurched and goosebumps tingled across my flesh. How could I have spyware on my phone when I'd only just bought the damn thing?

"What sort of spyware?"

"Literal spy-ware."

My jaw dropped as I suddenly understood what he was trying to tell me.

"Tracking software?" I asked quietly, as the air drained from my lungs and the familiar flash of red-hot panic surged through me.

"It's more than just tracking software, I'm afraid. Whoever's paired their phone to this handset can record your phone calls, access your microphone, read your text messages, and track your location using the GPS. Unfortunately, these apps are pretty common now, but this one is particularly insidious."

"But how?" I felt totally bewildered, but deep in my gut, I knew this had something to do with Dom. How could he have done it though? Dom was in jail. There was no way he, or anyone else, could have gotten hold of my new phone to install anything.

"Actually they're quite easy to install. It only takes a few seconds to download if you know what you're doing."

"But don't you need the handset for that?" I asked with confusion.

"Yes, that's right."

"But no one else has had access to this phone," I muttered in denial. "It's brand new."

Jock smiled understandingly, "Did you set up the phone from your cloud?"

"Oh my god," I blurted, realising how stupid I'd been. I'd used my old ID to set up the new phone. Why had I done that, when I'd been so careful with everything else?

"If someone had installed it on the old one, and you used the back-up to restore all your settings to the new phone, then it could have been downloaded along with everything else."

"Holy shit." I felt the blood drain from my face. Dom knew everything. Surely he couldn't have been tracking me from prison. Were they even allowed access to technology in there?

"You know Ashley, this is an act of cyber-crime, so you can report it if you're concerned about your safety," Jock suggested.

"Thank you, but the guy is still in jail, so I don't think there's any point."

"Och aye?" Jock muttered with surprise, his sexy Scottish accent almost distracting me from my panic.

"Sorry. That's probably too much info."

"I used to be cop remember? I've heard it all," he said with a sympathetic smile.

"So why are you working in an Apple store now? It's quite a career change from policing," I said, veering off-topic.

"Not so much. I was in the Cybercrime Unit so I still get to use my tech skills," he said looking around and then leaning close. "I'm actually only working here until I get a place in the Met," he said quietly, "but don't tell anyone."

"My lips are sealed," I promised, crossing my heart. Jock smiled and leaned back again.

"This is pretty serious stuff Ashley," he said, changing the subject back to my stalker issue. "Even if this guy was still in prison, he could have someone tracking you on his behalf."

I froze and studied Jock distrustfully.

"What do you mean, even if he was still in prison?"

"Oh, I don't know," Jock said with a casual shrug. "I just meant whether or not he's in prison, he sounds dangerous."

"Well he *is* in prison," I told Jock adamantly, "but I agree. He could have someone tailing me and that's what I'm worried about," I admitted honestly.

"I have friends in the department back home. I could call in a favour if you want me to investigate it further?"

"I couldn't ask you to do that," I declined, taken aback by his generosity.

"You're not asking. I'm offering," he replied with a smile. "Besides, it'll make me feel like I'm real cop again."

"Okay, that would be really awesome. Thank you."

"Not a problem, but I do have to tell you that this app has been active in the last few days. So if you think there might be a security risk then I suggest we get rid of it right now… and that means resetting your phone to factory settings."

"That's fine. Do whatever it takes," I said. "Hey, could you not mention this to Kesha? I haven't really told her much about my ex."

"Aye, for sure," he said. "You keep my secret, and I'll keep yours," he joked with a wink. It took Jock a total of about five minutes to wipe and reset my phone. "All done," he announced proudly as he unplugged my phone from the computer.

"Thank you," I said, accidentally brushing my fingers against his as he handed back my phone.

"Anything for a beautiful lady in distress," Jock joked with a flirty grin. "I'll send all the details over to my mates at Cybercrime but, in the meantime, I've put my personal number in your phone book so if you need anything please call me."

"That's really sweet, thanks," I replied feeling butterflies take flight in my belly. Was I being an idiot by trusting a guy I'd never met? What if he was somehow connected to Dom? I mean, what were the chances that in a store full of tech assistants I'd somehow ended up with the one who was a cop? Was it divine intervention or was it a set-up? It was hard to know. Jock rested his massive hand reassuringly on my shoulder.

"I mean it Ashley. If you need me just call."

"I will. Thanks Jock. I really appreciate it," I said, making a break for it.

"Take care Ashley," he called as I walked away. I smiled back over my shoulder and wandered out of the store in a daze. Was this really Dom's handiwork? Had he actually tracked me down or was this some sort of weird coincidence?

I glanced up to cross the road and noticed a beefy bloke standing on the opposite street corner who looked eerily like Dom. Great. Now I was so paranoid, that I was imagining Dom everywhere.

I shook my head to reset my brain and peered back towards the intersection. The man was gone. I was over-reacting. One little phone hack and neurotic Ashley had returned.

- NATHAN STONE -

I made my way up to Gareth's glass tower on the twelfth floor. This meeting meant only one thing… the Delfontaine account was kicking-off and my career was about to sky-rocket to a whole new level.

"Come in," Gareth called, as I knocked on the tinted glass doors. I let myself in and he gestured towards the big chesterfield sofas. "Have a seat mate."

"Cheers," I said, sitting on the hard leather seat. Gaz sat down next to me and patted my shoulder.

"Well lad, I've just spoken with Sandrine and she's keen to kick this off ASAP. She's offered to pay a fairly hefty retainer for us to allocate them with a full-time designated team, so we need to put together a suitable talent mix."

I nodded in agreement. "No worries."

"If we aim to get the team organised this week, then we should be ready to start in earnest by next Monday."

"Okay cool. I'll make it happen," I said confidently.

"I've got thoughts on the top-tier, but below that you're free to choose who you like. This is now our flagship account, so take whoever will fit best and we'll back fill the gaps later."

"Who are you thinking as leads?" I asked, already planning how I could extract my best team members from their existing projects.

"Cody for tech lead, Ritchie can project manage, and we'll team up Beau and Ashley as creative partners." My stomach lurched at the thought of Ashley working so closely with G.I. Beau.

"Would Beau be the best fit do you think?" I asked, failing to sound casual as my voice rose at least two octaves higher than usual. I cleared my throat to bring my voice back down to normal level. "Wouldn't Carine be a better option for a cosmetics account?"

"Nath, I want Beau on this one," Gaz said. "I think he and Ashley will work well together, plus Carine is across too many different accounts. It would be too disruptive to pull her off those and train someone new."

"I just don't think-"

"Nathan, this is not a debate," he interrupted matter-of-factly. "I've made up my mind. You're free to choose the rest of the team but I want Beau and Ashley together."

"Fine," I nodded stiffly, cringing at his choice of words. "I'll tee up a meeting to let them all know."

"Good," he paused, and studied me with his dad look. "Is there a reason you're specifically opposed to Beau?"

How could I explain myself without sounding like an idiot? I knew exactly what Gaz would say if he found out I had the hots for Ashley.

"Nope," I said shaking my head. He scrutinised me closely, and I could see his brain ticking over.

"Does this have anything to do with our lovely new Creative Director by any chance?"

"Why would it have anything to do with her?"

"Because I saw the way you were flirting with her on Friday night," he said in his all-knowing tone. "Just be careful mate."

"It's fine Gaz, I promise."

"Nath, I don't want another Becky Wheeler saga," Gaz said, rubbing his face. "It's a fucking HR nightmare."

"I swear… there's nothing to worry about."

"You know this would end up being worse than the Wheeler situation, right? You'll be her direct Line Manager as of next Monday so if anything goes wrong…"

"Gaz," I interrupted loudly, putting my right hand in the air and my left hand on my chest. "I, Nathan James Stone, do solemnly swear that nothing will go wrong."

"Geez you're a plonker," he replied, shaking his head with resignation. "Just don't fuck it up mate, or not only will I have to find another Creative Director, but I could also be looking down the barrel of a very damaging lawsuit."

"Gee, thanks for the vote of confidence Gaz," I shot back sarcastically.

"You know what I mean," he said waving his hands at me by way of explanation. He stared me down for a moment. "This is a big week for you Nath, and in case I haven't said it lately…I'm really proud of you lad."

"Thanks Gaz," I said as he patted me on the back in a half hug. I could tell he was going to say more, but I stood and strode to the door hoping to flee his office before the lecture began.

"Your mum's been asking after you," he said, as my hand landed on the door handle. "The nurse said they haven't seen you for quite a few weeks." His voice was dripping with disapproval.

"I've been a bit busy," I explained pathetically. I knew there was no excuse for not visiting her.

"You should go see her this weekend," Gaz suggested, rising to his feet.

"Maybe," I nodded. We both knew I had no intention of doing so. "Is that all?" Gaz closed the gap between us in three long strides. He put his hand on my shoulder and turned his parent-guilt machine up to full power.

"She loves you mate, and she misses you."

"She doesn't even know who I am," I snapped angrily. "Look, I know I'm a shitty son so I don't need you guilt-tripping me about it." I flung open the door like a stroppy child. "I'll go when I'm ready. I just need some time."

- ASHLEY GRANGER -

Even though I'd had my orientation on Friday, my first proper day felt completely different. Friday hadn't really felt real - like it was just a practice run - but on Monday, reality began to sink in.

"Welcome to your kingdom. Pease feel free to claim your throne," Amy joked cheerfully as she gestured to my very large workstation in prime position at the window. "You have the best seat in the house."

"But it's not made of swords," I kidded, putting my bag down on the desk. There was a fluorescent-coloured object sitting on my keyboard. "What's that?" I asked, walking around to the front side of my workstation to check it out.

"It's from Stoner," she said, pretending not to peer over my shoulder. I picked up the object and flipped it over. It was a CD case wrapped in Post-It notes, with big black words saying 'FOR CHUCKSTER'. I laughed out loud. "He said to tell you that he'd used an Artline… whatever that's supposed to mean."

I quickly pulled off the well-taped Post-It notes to reveal an actual real-life CD case with 'CHUCKY'S MIX' scribbled in Artline on the front of it.

"Oh my god."

"What is it?" Amy asked, as she stuck her head over my shoulder.

"He's made me a mix tape," I said, holding up the CD case.

"Oh my god," she echoed with a look of pure and utter amazement. "Do you even own a CD player?"

"Yeah. I actually do," I laughed, biting my lip.

Amy grinned, "I'll leave you to get settled in," she said, disappearing behind her large silver screen.

I read Nathan's note.

'Dear Chucky, just a few great tunes that I thought you would appreciate. Nath x'

My chest thudded. Not only had he gone to the trouble of making me a CD, but he'd signed off as 'Nath'. I chewed on my nails as I stared vaguely at the CD case. No one had ever done anything like that for me before. As if on cue, I heard Nathan's deep, sexy voice echo through the office.

"'Morning ladies," he called, striding out of the elevator foyer. My heart skipped a beat as his sparkly blue eyes caught mine. It had only been a day, but I'd almost forgotten how gorgeous he was.

"Morning Mister Stone, what brings you up to the tenth floor?" Amy asked him with a wink.

"This lovely lady actually," Nathan replied with a smile, as he headed towards my desk.

"I just got your gift," I said, waving it in the air.

"Do you like it?" he asked, rubbing the back of his head.

"I do." I chewed on my nail nervously, as Amy quietly hummed the Wedding March. I blushed and shot her a 'cease and desist' glare, then turned back to Nathan. "I'll give you a formal review once I've listened to it," I joked.

"I think you'll like it." Nathan either hadn't noticed Amy's antics, or he was ignoring them.

"Although…," I replied with a smile, "I am going to have to call my sponsor and tell him that I fell off the wagon."

Nathan gave a sexy half-smile. "I thought it was terminal."

"I decided I should at least try to kick my habit if we're going to make this work," I shrugged.

"That's a shame," Nathan said with a wink. "I kinda liked that you had a dark side."

"Is that right?" I asked with a blush. Amy shot me a cheeky look from behind her computer screen.

"That's not why I've come up here though," Nathan flipped back into professional mode. "I've actually come to give you some good news."

"Wow, a present and good news. I'm a lucky girl." I replied flirtatiously.

"More like a talented one. You'll be pleased to know that, as we speak, I'm looking at the new Creative Director for the Delfontaine account."
My eyes nearly popped out of my head.

"Seriously?!" I asked with a shocked laugh. I couldn't believe they'd actually given me the account! I was sure they were going to hand it to Francesco. He'd been at Artemis for nearly as long as Kat had, *and* he was French.

"Yep, you're the chosen one," Nathan confirmed. Amy cheered and bounded over to my desk with excitement.

"That's awesome news. Congratulations hun!" She squeezed me in a tight hug as I stared at Nathan in a state of elated shock.

"Wow, thank you," I said, once Amy released me from her vice-like grip.

"No need for thanks Chucky. You're the right person for the job."

"But what about Francesco?" I asked, "he's French, wouldn't that make more sense?"

Nathan shook his head, "Francesco is too ensconced in the Milner's account and Sandrine wants her own dedicated team. Besides which, he's not a good fit for a cosmetics account… especially one of this magnitude."

"Is that a nice way of saying he's too eccentric?" Amy joked.

"I didn't say that," Nathan answered with a conspiratorial smile. "Anyway," he turned his attention back to me, "I was thinking that maybe you'd like to come out for dinner to celebrate? It's a group thing. We're all going out for a curry on Thursday night if you're keen?"

"Sure, why not."

"Great," he replied with a wink. "Now, I need to go break the news to the rest of the team."

"The news of your second date?" Amy teased.

"Smartarse," Nathan rebutted before shooting me his beautiful scrunchy smile. "Later."

My first proper day passed in a blur as were working towards a delivery deadline for one of Kat's clients. It wasn't a difficult project but I felt the pressure of my first assignment and wanted it to go perfectly. Especially since it was Kat's client. Unfortunately, we hit a snag.

"Hey Jarrod, I don't want to be picky, but these banners don't seem to be displaying properly in Firefox." I informed my Flash developer, as I reviewed a set of banners that were due for delivery in less than four hours.

"Are you sure?" he asked, coming over to look at them on my screen. "I'm positive I tested them in all browsers."

"Here," I pointed to the issue and we both leaned in closer to the screen.

"Oh shit you're right. How'd I miss that?" Jarrod replied in a panic, as he trotted back to his work station. "Is it just the leaderboard?" he called from his desk.

"Umm..." I flicked through the other assets. "Nope, it's the MPU as well… and the skyscraper."

"Okay."

"…and the banner…and the super-sky," I added quickly.

"Bloody hell! What's the ultimate deadline on this delivery?"

"Five." Answered Amy from her desk.

"Fuck." Jarrod swore again, as he put his head down to begin his investigation.

"Should we call the media team and see if that time is solid?" I asked no one in particular.

"The more time the better," mumbled Jarrod from behind his big screens.

"I'll sort it," offered Amy, even though that wasn't her job.

"Thank you," I said appreciatively, as Jarrod started having a freak-out.

"I can't believe I didn't test that," Jarrod berated himself from behind his computer screens.

"Technology is a fickle beast Jarrod, you probably did test it," I told him calmly. "Don't beat yourself up. This is what makes digital so interesting."

"Yeah, I'll be more able to appreciate that once these banners are running properly," he answered distractedly, as he continued to study his code manically. "Oh fuck." He swore with a defeated sigh.

"That doesn't sound promising." I headed over to him to see if I could help.

"It's not," he admitted. "There's a massive logic issue in the Action Script."

"Bollocks. With that many banners, re-publishing will take hours."

"Yep." He agreed bleakly.

"Have we got an error reference?" I asked hopefully. If we did, it would make fixing the problem much quicker.

"Nope. I'll have to try and replicate it."

"Bugger," I muttered, knowing that it could take hours to isolate the issue.

"Media team said they can push it till six but no later," Amy told us.

"Okay, thanks hun," I called back. "Jarrod, I'll help with the replication. Hopefully with two of us we can get to the cause quicker."

"Awesome. But that's still not going to help with the re-publishing issue. There's no way to make that quicker."

"No, but if we split the assets then we'll at least be able to get several happening simultaneously."

"That could work." Jarrod agreed with an impressed nod. "It's nice to have a Creative Director who knows about Flash."

"Meh," I said with a blush, "I just know enough to troubleshoot."

"Well it's still cool," he said before turning his attention to his screen. I patted him on the back and returned to my computer to sink my teeth into a bit of problem solving. Maybe I was going to be okay at this job after all.

"Look at you go," Amy joked with a wink. "When you said you understood Flash, I didn't think that meant you could code."

"Ah yeah…I'm not exactly a pro, but I know enough to help."

"You're a woman of many talents Ms Granger!"

I blushed and shrugged off the compliment. "Let's just hope it pays off."

- NATHAN STONE -

After telling Ashley the good news, I did the rounds to let Cody, Ritchie and, unfortunately, Beau know that they had also been assigned to the Delfontaine account. It was finally beginning to feel real. As of next week, I would officially be leading a multi-million-pound account. I'd only just sat down at my desk, when Ritchie waltzed out of the elevator.

"Ready for lunch boys?" he called cheerfully.

"Yep," said Ryza, grabbing his jacket.

"Yeah I guess so," I nodded just as my desk phone rang. "No," I amended, picking up the receiver. "Hello?"

"Bonjour Nathan," Sandrine purred down the phone. Holy shit. Sandrine.

"Sandrine, hi," I spluttered, thrown off-guard. I really wasn't ready to speak to her yet. The memory of her torture flashed vividly into my mind and I could feel my face going red.

"So, you arrived home in one piece?" she asked cheekily. I tried to calm my fluster knowing that Ritchie was watching, but I could see that he'd figured it out. He raised his brows with intrigue and swaggered over to sit on my desk so that he could eavesdrop on my conversation. I didn't need another scandal against my name, especially not with Ashley around.

"Haha, yes I did," I replied nervously, doing my utmost to ignore Ritchie's intense scrutiny.

"We didn't damage you too much then?" Sandrine answered in English. Our conversations always tended to be an inconsistent fusion of French and English but, with Ritchie watching me like a hawk, I decided that speaking in a language he didn't understand would probably be safer.

"Vous m'avez vraiment donné une bonne séance d'entraînement!" I replied pleasantly, telling Sandrine that they'd definitely given me a run for my money.

"Well I'm glad you had fun Nathan. Perhaps we could do it again some time?" She chuckled suggestively. Oh shit. I most certainly did not want to repeat it again any time, ever. Period. I had assumed it was going to be a one-off, but perhaps I'd been a little short-sighted on that one.

"Err…maybe," I stuttered agreeably, as it finally occurred to me that I might have gotten myself in over my head with Sandrine. Had I inadvertently sold myself as a sex slave? Was I bound to service her every need for the length of our contract, or would she laugh it off and let it go? Fuck. What an idiot I had been.

"Now," she swapped to her business voice, "I'm sure you've spoken with Gareth by now, yes?"

"Oui," I agreed, relieved that she'd changed the subject.

"Great," Sandrine said. "I forgot to mention that I'd like the whole team to come out for a visit so that you can all see the factory and the Head Office." The breath drained from my lungs. That would mean having Sandrine and Ashley in the same room, at the same time. There was no way that situation would work out well for me.

"Oh, of course," I said casually as panic rose in my chest. "We're kicking off next week, so I'll touch base with you after that to arrange it."

"Très bien!" she said excitedly. "I'm really looking forward to working more closely with you Nathan."

"Yeah, me too," I agreed, wondering how close 'closely' would be and if it would involve any more painful S&M sessions with Sandrine and her sadistic dominatrix.

"Au revoir Nathan," she said cheerfully.

"Au revoir Sandrine," I replied, feeling a mountain of regret at my recent foolishness. It was a distinct possibility that I'd created myself a mess that I wouldn't be able to clean up. I sighed as I hung up the phone, forgetting that I was being closely monitored by Ritchie.

"You shagged her, didn't you?" he asked bluntly.

"No comment," I answered with a roll of my eyes.

"You did!"

"Ritchie," Ryan scolded.

"Oh, like you weren't thinking it," Ritchie shot back.

"Can we at least save it for the pub?" Ryan asked, ever the responsible one. "It's not really appropriate to discuss in the office."

"Fine," Ritchie agreed, "but I'm taking that as confirmation that you think he did too."

We wandered down to The Crown for a good old-fashioned pub lunch and Ritch was visibly eager to hear about my Parisian antics. The bloke had a finely tuned radar for detecting inappropriate sexual conduct, and it seemed that he was (accurately) sensing a juicy story afoot.

"Spill mate," he demanded, the second our bottoms hit the seats. "How did you manage to pull Sandrine?"

"Unintentionally," I admitted sheepishly, as I took a massive gulp of my beer.

"And?" Ritchie prompted.

"And what?"

"What do you mean 'and what'? What fucking happened Stoner?" Ritchie asked incredulously.

"I don't really want to talk about it Ritch. I shouldn't have done it in the first place," I said, feeling like a high-class hooker.

"Let me guess," Ryza interjected in his most judgemental tone. "She's now expecting you to ensure that Artemis is a 'full-service' agency?"

"I don't know. I think so," I said, rubbing the back of my head as if it would grant me a wish.

"Jesus, Stoner what were you thinking?" Ryza asked.

"I wasn't thinking," I admitted bluntly. "I was drunk and coked off my head and Sandrine was... determined."

"Nathan," Ryza groaned, cringing at the awkward situation I'd created for myself, "I swear you're compulsive."

"Stoner, your life has turned into a fucking soapie," Ritchie laughed.

"You don't know the half of it," I mumbled under my breath as our fish and chips arrived at the table.

"And I think I'd rather keep it that way," Ryza retorted, shoving a handful of chips into his mouth.

"Still working on that dad-bod mate?" I teased. He ignored me and shovelled even more chips in his gob to make some sort of childish point.

"So how did Sandrine rate anyway?" Ritchie asked curiously, as he followed suit and woofed down half a piece of fish in one go. "Are French women as wild as they say?"

"Honestly, she and her stripper friend just about fucking killed me. Literally. I've still got welts on my arse," I said without thinking.

"Her what?" Ryza spluttered, choking on his chips.

"You didn't?" Ritchie asked in awe. I nodded almost imperceptibly.

"You had a threesome with your client and a stripper?" Ryan asked once he'd dislodged the chip from his air-pipe.

"It wasn't so much a threesome as a kidnap and gang rape," I admitted with embarrassment. "They locked me in Sandrine's sex dungeon for three days, handcuffed to a weird sex table."

"Holy fuck!" Ritchie exclaimed amidst raucous laughter. "Only you Stoner. You, my friend, are pure entertainment."

"That doesn't go any further than this table though, got it?" I warned sternly. "I don't think I could survive another scandal."

"Sure mate," Ritchie agreed with a chuckle.

"Nathan, there's no way I'm telling anyone, or I'd be tainted by association," Ryza teased.

"I'm serious," I said adamantly. "I don't want Ashley finding out."

"And speaking of Ashley," Ritchie said with amusement. "What's happening there? Are you guys a thing yet?"

"I don't think so, but I'm working on it," I said honestly. "I invited her to curry night, so I was thinking I'd take her out for a drink afterwards."

"No can-do buddy," Ritchie piped up. "You invited that nightclub chick you shagged remember?"

"Oh shit, you're right," I said, face-palming. "I'd totally forgotten about her. What was her name again? Kylie?"

"Kellie, I think," Ritchie replied with an amused chuckle.

"Ah yeah, that's right," I answered with a nod. "How the fuck am I going to get out of that one?"

Ritch shook his head. "I don't know mate, but you'll have to come up with something before Thursday."

Damn my stupid antics. Past-Nathan was really starting to piss-off present Nathan. What had been going through my mind a week ago? Had I been deliberately trying to sabotage my future self?

Regardless, I had a few days to come up with a viable solution.

- RYAN MCPHERSON -

Amy had told me that Ash and Jarrod were chained to their computers fixing some issues on one of Kat's accounts, so I thought I'd help them out and deliver their lunch.

"I come bearing food," I announced, as I stepped out of the elevator.

Ash looked up from her computer screen, "oh my god, you're my hero."

"Mine too," Jarrod agreed. "I'm starving."

"Gluten-free veggie burger for you madame," I said handing Ash her burger, "and for the gentleman... The Works."

"I could kiss you dude," Jarrod said, cracking open the cardboard container.

"No need but thanks for the offer," I joked. "How's it all going?"

"We're getting there," Ash said with a smile, biting into her burger.

"Great," I said, shuffling on my feet. "Hey, can I chat with you for a moment?" I asked Ash.

"Sure," she said, studying me curiously, as I waited for Jarrod to get back to his desk. "I think the meeting room is free." I followed her into the empty meeting room and stood awkwardly as she closed the door. "Everything okay?" Ash asked, taking a seat so she could eat her meal.

"Yeah... kind of," I paused and took a deep breath. "Kat told Nathan that you lost a baby."

Ash put down her burger.

"Oh," she said, wiping her hands on her napkin.

"She didn't mean to, it just kind of popped out. You know - pregnancy brain and all that."

"How did he take it?"

"He was pretty shocked, but he seems okay today right?"

"Yeah."

"I'm really sorry Ash. I'm sure it will be fine."

"I'm sure it will," she said with a forced smile.

"Hey, I owe you another apology too," I said awkwardly. "I know it put a lot of pressure on you back then. My entire life revolved around you and you never asked for that. Then when you left, well, I guess maybe that's why you never called me."

"Is that what you think?" she asked wide-eyed, swallowing a mouth full of food. "Ryan... I never called because I couldn't stand the thought of letting you down. I was ashamed of my life. I didn't want you to know how spectacularly I'd fucked everything up, especially when you'd done so much to help me."

"You didn't fuck everything up Ash. Dom did." I told her firmly.

"Well that's certainly the truth of it isn't it?" she agreed with a sad smile. "Things got shitty Ryan, but you weren't responsible for me. It wasn't your job to save me, or look after me. It was my job. And I did a bad job of it," she paused and rested her hand on mine. "I was lucky to have a friend like you who looked out for me. I wouldn't have survived without you."

We both fell silent for a moment and then she looked up at me with a melancholy smile.

"Do you remember that insane night we had at Fabric?" she asked.

"You mean the night we knocked off an eight-ball?" I joked, remembering the drug-fuelled night that fateful photo had been taken.

"Yep."

"Amazingly... yes, I actually remember that night very clearly." We'd been so off our rockers that it was surprising either of us would remember anything. Ash took a bite of her burger and chewed on it thoughtfully before cocking her head and peering up with an expression that I'd never seen before.

"Why didn't you kiss me that night?"

"Besides the fact that Dom would have put a hit on me?" I said with a macabre laugh. "I guess I knew it wasn't right."

"Fair," she nodded, taking another bite of her lunch before peering up at me guiltily. "I wanted you to kiss me that night."

"I know," I admitted, "I wanted me to kiss you too, but it would have caused too much trouble for everyone."

"It would have," Ash agreed whimsically. What on earth was going through her mind?

"So why are we bringing this up when you're clearly keen on Nathan?" I asked with a knowing smile.

"I don't know," she answered honestly, shaking her head. "Closure I guess."

"Closure is good," I agreed with a nod, watching her for a moment. "I was in love with you back then. You know that right?"

"Yeah," she confirmed with a sly grin, "I was in love with you too."

"I know," I told her with a smile, "but then you left."

Ash looked down at her burger. "I did," she said quietly, "and life moved on."

"Exactly," I agreed, "I'm in love with Kat now. She's my whole world and I can't imagine my life without her in it, but you're always going to be my first love Ash… and my best friend."

"I feel the same about you," she replied with a smile, picking a sesame seed off her burger bun. "Can you imagine how the last eight years would have panned out if we had kissed that night?"

"Yeah, I can," I said smiling, "Dom would have had me killed and you would've met Nathan at my funeral and ended up with him anyway." One way or another, Nathan always got the woman. Ash laughed loudly.

"Nathan and I aren't together," she said, blushing as she picked at her burger with a bashful smile. The only person she was fooling was herself. I grinned and leaned back in my chair.

"Not yet."

- ASHLEY GRANGER -

It took Jarrod and I the entire afternoon, but we miraculously managed to fix and re-render all of the banners in time for our 6pm delivery. As the adrenalin began to wear off, the exhaustion set in, so I headed straight home. I dumped my bag on the kitchen table and fished out Nathan's gift from earlier that day. I was curious to see what music he thought I'd like, but more importantly, what music he liked.

I flipped open the cover, and popped the CD into my stereo, hearing my phone buzz inside my bag. I pressed play and some juicy bass chords wafted out from the stereo. I closed my eyes and enjoyed the sexy strums of the guitar kicking in. I'd never heard the song before but it was warm, and tinged with a rawness that made it feel simultaneously rough and smooth. Kind of like an aged whiskey. In fact, it was exactly how Nathan would sound if he was music.

With my eyes still closed, I did a quick yoga stretch and felt my heart radiating with happiness. Nathan was so sweet that it was hard to imagine him as the heartless womaniser everyone made him out to be. Maybe he'd grown up since Becky Wheeler. Or maybe he'd end up breaking my heart. Either way, it didn't matter to me; he made my chest flutter and that was all I needed to know for now.

I retrieved my phone from my handbag and my heart soared when I saw Nathan's name on the screen. I grinned and opened the message.

'I expect a review of the CD on my desk by Friday [winky face]'

'Will you be paying me over-time for that? [laughing face]'

'Yeah, I'll pay for your dinner on Thursday.'

'I thought it was my turn to pay.'

'Must be another date then??? [shrugging man]'

I paused and took a breath. I had no idea how to respond to that so I just sent a smiley face emoji. The three dots pulsated but he didn't reply. I hadn't really given him anything to reply to, so I changed the subject.

'Oh btw what's the first song on that CD?'

'Crash and Burn, by Angus and Julia Stone.'

'I really like it. It reminds me of you' I typed, poising my finger over the send button for a moment. Was that too needy? I was inexperienced at this text flirting thing, but given that Nathan had made me a mix-tape it was probably safe to be a little bit keen.

I took a deep breath and hit send, wondering if I should say anything else, but then I saw the telltale glowing dots that told me he was typing something at the other end. Hopefully I hadn't freaked him out. I watched the dots and waited for his response as the next song started. My heart fluttered at the first 'Ho'. This song I did know. 'Ho Hey' by the Lumineers. The chorus of the song was 'I belong with you, you belong with me, you're my sweetheart.' Was it intended as a message, or had he just thought that I'd like the song?

My phone vibrated in my hand. 'Number eight reminds me of you most'

'I haven't got that far yet,' I replied quickly. 'Only up to Ho Hey.'

'Appropriate'

Once again, I had no idea how to respond, so I resorted to another emoji and sent him a thumbs up. *Appropriate.* What did that mean exactly? Maybe Nathan was serious about this… about 'us'. Oh my god. Were we an 'us'?

I pinned my hair up and let the CD play as I got ready for bed. I wanted to hear the whole playlist in the order in which Nathan had created it. There were a few well-known songs like 'I Will Wait' by Mumford & Sons; Ed Sheeran's 'Kiss Me'; and 'Bloom' by the Paper Kites, followed by a couple of tunes that I had to Shazam. 'Stronger' by Ziggy Alberts and 'I'm with You' by Vance Joy, which were even more beautiful than the others. Nathan's message was coming through loud and clear. Or at least I assumed it was.

I paused my tooth-brushing and stood quietly at the basin with a mouth full of foam so that I could hear the next song. If I'd counted right, it was number eight.

"*Honey, you are a rock…*" Chris Martin sang from my loungeroom. I smiled and spat out the frothing toothpaste.

"Oh wow," I muttered. 'Green Eyes' by Coldplay was certainly not what I had expected Nathan to choose for me, but it was so unbearably sweet that my chest felt like it was going to burst.

- NATHAN STONE -

The shrill screech of my alarm clock woke me at the crack of dawn. After setting the stupid thing to snooze twice, I finally rolled out of bed with a groan and reluctantly pulled on my rugby kit. No matter how many years had passed since my father's death, I always found this day hard to cope with. Even my pleasant distraction with the gorgeous Ms Granger hadn't helped me wake up in a better mood.

I was late for training but I decided to jog there anyway. I needed to clear my head of noise. I grabbed a piece of toast and shoved a change of work clothes into my backpack, then took off. As I opened the front door I shivered at the gust of chilly morning air. I zipped up my hoodie and took a bite of my toast when I heard a quiet mew from the corner of the doorstep.

"Morning Fleabag," I greeted the little ginger mongrel who was curled up tightly against the wall. It looked hungry and cold. I glanced down at my peanut butter toast. "Here," I said handing it my toast. He meowed again and started licking at the peanut butter. "No worries buddy. Stay warm huh?" I told the cat before running off down the road toward the oval.

As my feet pounded against the dirty London pavement I focused on my body. I paced my breath and my stride and tuned in to my muscles as they worked to push me along smoothly. I savored the burn in my lungs and the tingle of lactic acid in my legs. When I was running I could forget everything else. Any emotional pain was forced to give way to the physical as I pushed myself harder and harder, faster and faster. I refused to stop until my heart couldn't actually beat any faster.

By the time I arrived at training my legs already felt like jelly, and my lungs were raw but it was good pain.

"Stoney. Thanks for gracing us with your presence," called Coach sarcastically, as I ran breathlessly across the field towards them.

"Sorry Coach," I puffed.

"Well at least you're already warmed up," he joked. "Get in there mate." I dumped my gear and joined the lineup.

"Hey, how you holding up?" asked Ritchie, as I slipped seamlessly into the training session.

"Yeah, alright," I nodded. "As good as I can be."

"Come on boys, pick it up," barked Coach in his usual drill-sergeant tone.

"So what's the plan for tonight?" Ritchie asked as he tossed the ball to me.

"Same as usual," I answered, catching the ball.

"By which you mean get smashed and wallow on your own?"

"Exactly."

"I know it's your tradition and everything, but do you think it might be time to start marking the occasion by doing something a less self-destructive?"

"Nope," I answered adamantly as I kicked the ball at him.

"Okay fine, but at least let Ryza and I join you so it's not quite so pathetic."

"No," I refused stubbornly, catching the ball as he kicked it back. Ritchie opened his mouth to respond when Coach bellowed at us for a second time.

"Enough gossiping ladies, this isn't high-tea at the Ritz."

We stopped our chatter and made an attempt to look less lady-like, but as soon as Coach was distracted Ritchie couldn't help himself.

"So what's the go with you and Granger?" he asked curiously, as I kicked the ball back in his direction. "You two seem to be getting very cozy."

"Yeah I guess," I shrugged, catching the ball. "I just don't know how to do this dating thing and honestly, I'm too scared to take it any further yet, because I know I'll probably do something to fuck it up."

"Well that's probably true," he teased heartlessly, booting the ball straight back again.

"Thanks for your support mate."

"So, did you univite Kelly to Dinner on Thursday?" He asked, to emphasise his point.

"Err...no." I said, failing to return the ball.

"Stoner, if you don't get rid of Kelly, then you'll definately fuck up everything with Granger."

"I know," I agreed pathetically, "I tried to univite Kell, but I felt like an arsehole, and then somehow I made it seem like I was confirming our date instead of cancelling it."

"You are an arsehole," he teased with a grin as he waved his hands impatiently for me send the ball back in his direction.

"It'll be fine," I assured him, finally kicking the ball.

"I don't know Stoner. I think you might need to grow some balls and tell Ashley you're in love with her."

"Ritch, we've gone over this... I'm not in love with her," I huffed loudly, causing Coach to lose his temper.

"Right you two, this is obviously too easy for you so drop and give me a hundred."

- ASHLEY GRANGER -

Day two at Artemis wasn't any less eventful than the first. It seemed the status quo for the agency was unrelenting chaos. Whilst I loved a bit of fluidity in my working day, Artemis was taking it to a whole new level. They lacked any real processes or procedures and, with my creative brain, I needed order and organisation to stay on track. Thus Tuesday was spent creating spreadsheets, flowcharts and process maps. It was going to be a challenge to get everyone on board with the new system, but that would be my concern for Wednesday. When six p.m. rolled around, Amy walked over and tapped my desk.

"You should go upstairs and have a drink," she suggested me with a sneaky grin.

"Why?" I asked, shutting down my computer.

"It wouldn't be any fun if I told you that," she said, as I collected my things and followed her out to the lifts. "Trust me, you need to go have a drink."

"Okay," I agreed with bewilderment, giving her a sideways glance. "You realise I think you're weird right?"

"And proud of it," she chuckled as the 'up' lift arrived. "I believe this is yours," she said, ushering me into the empty lift.

"You're not coming?"

"Nope."

"So, why am I having a drink on a Tuesday night by myself?" I asked as the doors began to close.

"Have fun," Amy sang through the small opening, as the doors closed between us.

"Weirdo," I muttered to myself as the lift ascended to the bar. Feeling like Ashley-no-mates, I wandered through the doors of the empty bar and, besides a guy slumped over the bar-top, the place was completely deserted. "Great, I really am Ashley-no-mates," I mumbled, hoping that I wouldn't have to converse with the drunk, depressed bloke at the end of the bar.

"Hi there," the barman greeted me merrily, as the drunk guy peered up. Oh shit. The drunk, depressed guy was Nathan Stone.

"What are you drinking luv?" asked the bar guy.

"Vodka Soda," answered Nathan on my behalf. The bar guy turned to me for confirmation, so I gave a quick nod and walked awkwardly over to Nathan. He nodded silently at me and then knocked back his shot.

"Hey," I said, hovering uneasily over the bar stool next to him, "mind if I sit?"

"Go ahead," Nathan answered with a shrug. I took a deep breath and sat down next to him.

"Rough day?" I asked, trying to dispel the awkwardness.

"You could say that."

"Okay," I said, as my vodka soda appeared in front of me. I handed a tenner to the bar guy and turned back to Nathan. "You want to talk about it?" I asked, desperate to put an end to the uncomfortable silence.

"I'm fine Ashley, if I wanted to talk about it I would," he said snidely, before knocking back the second shot that had been lined up in front of him. I recoiled slightly, taken aback by the venom in his tone.

"Sorry. I was only trying to help."

"I appreciate that, but not everyone wants to air their dirty laundry."

"Fuck you Stone,." I seethed, grabbing my bag from the bar. "Have fun writing yourself off." I pushed out my stool and it squeaked loudly against the polished concrete floor. If Amy had been trying to match-make then her plan had seriously backfired.

"Stop Chucky," Nathan called. I stopped but didn't turn around. "I'm sorry," he apologised humbly, "I didn't mean to be a dick. Please come back. Company would be good." I turned reluctantly, contemplating whether or not to let him off so easily. "Besides, you owe me one remember?" he said playfully.

"That's low Stone," I replied sternly.

"I know," he agreed. "A shot for Ashley please Brandon," he said to the barman.

"I'll stay," I relented, caving to his emotional blackmail, "but I'm not drinking shots."

"I can't drink shots on my own."

"Looks like you've been doing fine thus far."

"Yeah, and it's pathetic isn't it?" he agreed with a grin. "Come on, please?" He begged, as Brandon lined up two more shot glasses on the bar.

"Jack Daniels?" I asked with a cringe when Brandon poured the shots.

"Yep," Brandon confirmed.

"No way."

"Come on Chucky, it'll put hair on your chest." Nathan handed me one and I sighed heavily. Damn my need to people-please.

"I'm going to regret this," I told him sternly before we clinked glasses and gulped back our shots. "Holy shit." I spluttered, choking on the fumes of my bourbon. "Right then...spill it Stone. What's with the pity party?"
He looked up from his glass with those big blue eyes.

"Today is the anniversary of my dad's death."

"Oh Nathan, I'm so sorry," I breathed, resting my hand on his shoulder, "but is fucking yourself up on Jacks really the answer?"

"Probably not," he concurred with a shrug. "Drugs and alcohol don't solve anything, but they sure as hell make the pain go away for a little while right?"

"They certainly do," I nodded in agreement, "until they wear off and reality returns with a vengeance."

"True," he muttered before another short silence. "So what was your deal then Chucky?" he asked abruptly, steering the conversation away from himself as always.

"In what way?" I asked dubiously.

"Your daily coke habit," he teased.

"It was what it was," I said evasively. After his little dig ealier I wasn't sure that I wanted to share any more information with him.

"Okay," he agreed sensing my change of mood. "Hey look, I'm really sorry for what I said before. It was an arsehole thing to say and I didn't mean it. To be honest, I don't even know why I said it. I'm actually really glad you opened up to me, and I promise I won't ever throw it back in your face again."

"It's fine," I replied uneasily. That was exactly what Dom used to do to me.

"No it's not," he said kindly, "but thank you for accepting my apology."
I stared nervously at my lap. I wasn't very good at expressing my emotions.

"There's a lot of shit in my past Nathan and I've worked really hard to get over it all." I sighed and looked up at him. "It's not the sort of thing that I tell everyone you know? I told you because I trusted you."

"Uh-oh. Trusted, past tense," he said with a pained expression, "does that mean I've blown it now?"

I eyed him suspiciously. "I don't know Nathan."

"I'm sorry," he apologised again, "I was out of line."

"Yeah, you were," I agreed, not caring that I was probably being a bit harsh. Nathan stared into his glass as if he'd find the answer was at the bottom of it. I watched him distrustfully for a moment. Nathan wasn't Dom and, outside of this moment, he'd been nothing but chivalrous. "You've got to understand, that was exactly what Dom used to do to me."

"I didn't mean to do that," he said remorsefully. "No wonder you developed a coke habit," he joked, trying to lighten the mood.

"My coke habit was purely circumstantial," I said a little defensively. "I was trying to dull the pain of my reality. It was like being in a drug-induced emotional coma."

"I get that," Nathan said with an understanding nod. "Do you still partake occasionally?" he asked, tapping his nose.

"No. I gave it all up when I found out-" I instantly stopped talking when I realised that I was about to give him way too much information. Even though I knew Kat had told him about my pregnancy, I didn't want to offer him anything more than necessary. He may have had the ability to crumble my defenses, but there was no way I would intentionally let him glimpse that far into my story. "I gave it up before I left Dom," I amended.

"So you went cold turkey?" he asked with amazement.

"Yeah. It was a lot easier than it sounds." That part was the truth. It had been incredibly easy to give up snorting class A's when I'd found out I was responsible for growing a little human person.

"Have you been tempted to do it again?"

"I haven't felt the desire to do it again, but to be honest, I'd probably be too scared to try it again in case I liked it too much." We sipped our drinks in companionable silence for a short while, then Nathan peered up at me over the rim of his glass.

"I am really sorry about earlier though. I didn't mean to be a dick. I'm really glad you're here Granger."

- NATHAN STONE -

Of all the people who could have rocked up at the bar that night, Ashley Granger was the last person I would have wanted there… until I realised that she was the only person I wanted there.

"Hang on, how did this conversation turn back to me anyway?" she asked awkwardly. "We were supposed to be talking about you."

"We did talk about me," I teased with a wink, "and now we're talking about you again. You're way more interesting than me."

"You don't even know the half of it Stone," she agreed with a sexy smile.

"Maybe not...but I'd like to hear it."

"I'm sure you would," Ashley laughed, "but it's gonna take way more than a shot of bourbon to make me spill any more of my dirty little secrets."

"Well that can be arranged." I thumped on the bartop like they did in old movies. "Two more Jacks and coke please barkeep."

"Actually, can you make mine with soda water please Brandon?"

"Sure," he replied with a mocking laugh, pouring two double shots of Jacks.

"Jacks and Soda," I teased, shaking my head with a chuckle.

"Hey, I claw back the extra calories where I can." Our drinks were replenished, and she held up her glass in a toast. "Here's to your dad Nathan."

"Cheers to that," I agreed, as we clinked our glasses. "You know you're going to tell me your dirty stories right?" I teased with a huge grin as I handed her another shot. I'd never met a girl like her before. On the surface she was the girl-next-door, but secretly she had a wild streak, which I was somehow lucky enough to be privy to.

"No," she answered simply, as we sunk our next round of shots without breaking eye contact. It was a stand-off.

"Yeah, it's your turn to share again." I paused and waited for a response, but she said nothing. "Any lesbian moments?"

"Typical male." Ashley rolled her eyes dramatically.

"You're going to tell me eventually Chucky, so you might as well save yourself some hassle and tell me now." She had no idea how annoying I could be when I really wanted something. Ashley stared silently at me with a raised eyebrow, and I cheekily handed her yet another shot.

"Did I miss the section on information extraction in my orientation?"

"I can't tell you or I'd have to kill you," I answered, waggling my eyebrows. "So... you and your girlfriends were having a sleep-over..." I prompted. I was determined to keep the conversation away from me for as long as humanly possible. Plus I could tell there were a few juicy stories hidden behind this new, wholesome look of hers. Ashley laughed and shook her head unconvincingly.

"Not gonna happen," she answered, staring at the shot glass like it was the devil. She clearly underestimated my power of annoyance.

"Ahh...so there has been some girl-on-girl action then?" I asked, taking a stab in the dark as I downed my shot.

"You're not getting any more sordid stories out of me Stone."

"I'm pretty sure your stories will pale in comparison to the scenarios that I've already come up with anyway," I teased with a wink. She grinned and punched me playfully in the arm. I chuckled along with her and, for a moment, we were caught up in each others eyes. Her bright green gaze bore into me, and I felt my stomach do a little dance. Of course, that could have been all the bourbon shots slushing around in there. I was the first one to break the silence.

"Thanks for getting pissed with me Chucky, it's been nice having company. I normally do this on my own."

"My pleasure Stone," she said nudging my shoulder with hers.

"Yeah but seriously, you didn't have to, but you did and I really apreesherate – appreeshate – appr – fuck that's a dumb word," I grizzled, aggravated that I was unable to articulate the word 'appreciate' in my inebriated state.

"Yeah it is," she agreed with a heavy slur, "appresherate. Apreesherate." We erupted into drunken laughter and glanced at each other with open affection. It seemed as though we'd broken through our awkwardness. I slung my arm casually over her shoulder, and we leaned into each other. I was tempted to kiss her, but that scenario could only go one of two ways.

I peered sideways at her and weighed up my options for a moment. The small part of my brain that wasn't drunk, sent through a message loud and clear. 'No Stoner, do not kiss the woman. I repeat, DO NOT KISS ASHLEY.'

"Sometimes you just need someone to get drunk with," she declared, breaking the silence and snapping me out of my lustful thoughts. She grinned, and I stared at her with blurry drunken eyes, disappointed that the little sober voice in my head was right. "But call me Chucky one more time and we're going to have issues."

- *Chapter 5* -

THE BIG McMESS

- ASHLEY GRANGER -

On Thursday afternoon, Amy and I had gotten caught up with some beta testing for a website we were due to deliver on Friday, so we'd arranged to meet up with everyone at Brick Lane once we were done. I was looking forward to curry night, and also to meeting Kat again because I felt strange not knowing my best friend's wife, especially as I was the person delivering all of the hard work she'd done on her client portfolio.

"Where shall I drop you ladies?" the Uber driver asked.

"Just down here is fine," Amy said, pointing towards a restaurant where we saw Ryan, Kat, Ritchie, Nathan... and some young girl, standing outside of the restaurant. Nathan ushered the girl through the door in a very gallant and date-like gesture, and my stomach dropped.

"He brought a date," I said, stunned. Obviously, I had read too much into our situation.

"God he's a dick," Amy said with aggravation. "What the fuck is he thinking?"

"Ah well, it's not like we're dating or anything," I shrugged, eager to change the subject. It was hard to see Nathan looking so cosy with someone else. I knew the weekend hadn't counted as a date and that Tuesday night had been purely circumstantial, but I still thought it might have at least been leading to something.

"No, but-" Amy sighed and stopped talking mid-sentence, knowing it was a losing battle. We thanked the driver and climbed out of the car. "Are you okay?" she asked, as the Uber pulled away.

"I'm fine," I replied with a high-pitched voice that belied my words. "Let's just get in there." There was nothing I could do about it, so I just had to suck it up.

"Okay," Amy said threading her arm through mine. "Are you ready for this?" I took a deep breath and forced a smile to my face.

"Ready as I'll ever be."

Amy smiled and led me into the restaurant. Within seconds of walking through the door, Ritchie jumped up to greet Amy, and then kissed me on the cheek.

"You made it!" he exclaimed over-excitedly.

"I did," I laughed, thrown off by his enthusiasm. I was doing my best not to look at Stone and his date, for fear of exposing my disappointment, but I could tell I was coming across as rude. Not that I particularly cared. Avoiding eye contact with Nathan, I continued weighing up my seating options.

"Here love," Richie offered, patting the seat next to him with a kind smile. He seemed to have comprehended the situation and was doing what he could to stop it from being weird.

I smiled gratefully at him and slid quickly into the creaky wooden chair, cursing the fact that my seat also happened to be directly opposite Nathan. My lack of acknowledgement of Mr Stone was acutely noted and, as I shoved my handbag under my chair, he leaned right across the table and made a point of acknowledging me.

"Hi," he said, cocking his head questioningly. Feeling foolish, I peered up at him and forced a smile to my face.

"Hey" I said, gritting my teeth so as not to lose my smile.

"Glad you made it," he told me meaningfully. Or maybe there was nothing meaningful about it at all. I really didn't trust my own judgement after misreading the situation so catastrophically.

I smiled tightly. "Wouldn't miss it."

"I'm Kellie," announced Nathan's date chirpily. Her voice was so high pitched there were probably dogs in Edinburgh cringing in pain. I reluctantly shook her hand.

"I'm Ashley." I said with a forced smile. The girl couldn't have been more than 20 years old… and that was a generous estimate. Did her parents know she was out on a school night? Nathan raised an eyebrow at my frosty greeting.

"Hi all," a smooth voice interrupted. Oh god, it was G.I. Beau.

"Fabulous," Nathan muttered under his breath. His open annoyance at Beau's appearance made me feel childishly smug, and suddenly I found myself wanting to make Nathan jealous.

"Beau, hi," Kat greeted him casually, waving at him from her seat. "There's a seat down there next to Ashley," she pointed. He nodded and looked down at me with a warm smile.

"Hi again," he greeted me, sliding into the seat next to mine.

"Hey you," I replied super-sweetly, almost sounding genuinely happy to see Beau. "I hear you and I are going to be partners."
Nathan rolled his eyes at my blatant flirting.

"I hear that too," he said with a wide smile.

"Hi, I'm Kellie," repeated Nathan's date as she stuck her hand out at Beau.

"I'm Beau," he said, shaking her hand with a friendly smile.

"So do you guys, like, all work together then?"

"Ahh… yeah," he answered with easy charm. "What about you? Where did you meet Nathan?"

"At Fabric," she answered. We all stared at her blankly. "You know, the nightclub. I work there."

I glanced over at Amy who nearly spat out her water as she stifled a giggle. Maybe this dinner was going to be fun after all.

- NATHAN STONE -

I couldn't believe that I was stuck with a 20-something air-head while the woman of my dreams was sitting across the table with Beau-fucking-Peterson. All I could do was hope that I hadn't fucked my chances with Ashley entirely. I could tell she was pissed at me, but like a true English woman she was keeping the stiff upper lip. 'Keep Calm and Carry On' as they say.

"Shall I order a bunch of dishes for the table?" Kat asked no one in particular.

"Don't forget Ashley's vegan," I replied automatically. Red glanced at me with amusement and, for the first time all night, I was actually pleased that I'd invited Kellie.

"Oh my god you don't eat meat?" she asked Ashley with astonishment, as if veganism was a whole new concept to her.

"Nope," Ashley replied patiently. "I'm not super strict, but I aim not to eat any animal products at all."

"You eat chicken, though right?" Kellie asked. I had to physically restrain myself from face-palming.

"No. Chicken is an animal," Ashley answered calmly. Red choked back a laugh at Kellie's expense, but everyone else was pretending not to listen.

"What about eggs?" Kellie asked relentlessly. Did she really not get it?

"No, they come from chickens," Ashley explained.

"Oh right," Kellie nodded with confusion. "Aren't you hungry all the time?"

"Not really, no. There's plenty to eat without eating animal products."

"Like what?" Kellie asked dumbfounded.

Ashley sighed quietly but held her smile. "Vegies, fruit, tofu, rice, pasta, nuts, legumes…"

"What's legumes? Is that like tofu or something?" Kelly asked.

"No," Ashley replied, swallowing back a smile. "Legumes are lentils, beans, chickpeas… you know… legumes."

"Oh right," Kellie nodded, clearly still confused by the concept of legumes.

"So, what's it like working in a nightclub Kellie?" Beau interjected, coming to Ashley's rescue. It made me hate the guy even more that he was playing the hero. If Beau Peterson was gay, I'd eat my own socks.

"It's pretty cool, but I'm really just doing it to pay the rent while I study to be a hairdresser," Kellie told him proudly. I rolled my eyes. There was nothing wrong with being a hairdresser persay, but what had I been thinking when I'd asked her out? Besides sex, we had absolutely nothing in common. Past Nathan was an idiot.

"That's great," Beau answered tactfully, as my eyes wandered back to Ashley.

"Yeah, I actually found out today that I've been accepted for a hairdressing apprenticeship with Tony & Guy," Kellie continued. I didn't hear another word she said after that, because my eyes were fastened to Ashley. I wanted to be the one sitting next to her. I wanted to be holding hands with her under the table and sharing private jokes that no-one else would understand. Why the fuck had I invited Kellie? "What do you think Nathan?" Kellie asked, assuming that I'd been listening to the conversation, "Ashley should totally get some low-lights, right?"

"Umm…" I stumbled, not even sure what low-lights were.

"It would give your hair some texture, so it wouldn't look so fake," Kellie informed Ashley. I knew she wasn't intending to be rude, but that was how it came out.

"Personally, I think Ashley's perfect as she is," I blurted in Ashley's defence. Silence descended over the table as everyone stared at me open-mouthed. Ritchie rose from his seat, scraping the wooden chair legs against the tiles.

"Well I think it's time for a fag break," he declared loudly. "Fancy joining me for some fresh air Granger?"

- ASHLEY GRANGER -

Ritchie and I stood out in the fresh night air when and he lit up his cigarette, I peered back into the restaurant.

"Thanks for saving me back there," I said nodding casually towards the door.

"Tough night huh?" he asked with a knowing smile as he took a drag of his ciggy.

"Just slightly," I admitted. He offered me a cigarette and I shook my head politely. "No thanks, I quit a long time ago."

"No worries," Ritchie shrugged and shoved the pack back into his pocket. My head was starting to spin from the events of the day, so I closed my eyes and rubbed my temples. If Nathan was actually interested in me then why had he brought a date? And if not, why had he even invited me in the first place? And that whole, me being perfect thing… what the fuck was that? I opened my eyes again, to find Ritchie studying me with curiosity.

"What?" I asked self-consciously.

"Why don't you just tell him?" Ritchie had been so blunt that I hoped I'd misinterpreted his meaning.

"Pardon?"

"Stoner," he answered matter-of-factly, "just tell him how you feel."

"I don't have any feelings for him Ritchie. I barely know him," I said, defensively.

"Ha. Yeah and I used to be the president of Somalia," Ritchie replied with such a bizarre analogy that I had no response. "Look Granger, I'll give you a tip-off… the guy has the hots for you."

"He's on a date Ritchie," I said, not caring whether I gave my feelings away.

"He invited Kellie yonks ago and was too much of a pussy to un-invite her. I swear to you mate, he's not into her, he's into you."

"Oh."

Ritchie stubbed out his cigarette. "Nathan has the hots for you Granger, but he's not good at relationships so, if you want him, tell him." Ritchie glanced behind me to the restaurant door. "Just have a think on it mate," he said and smiled as he patted my shoulder. "I'll see you back in there."

"Thanks," I nodded as he retreated inside without another word. I stood alone in the bustling street, breathing in the warm night air. The smell of curry filled my nostrils and the sound of people, cars and music rang in my ears. I closed my eyes for another moment and I could almost imagine that I was in India.

"Hey," Nathan said right behind my head, making me jump in surprise.

"Oh shit," I blurted at his sudden and unexpected presence.

"Sorry, I didn't mean to sneak up on you," he replied with amusement as I turned to face him.

"Yes, you did."

"Yeah, I did," he admitted with a smile, "but only because you've been avoiding me all night."

"No, I haven't," I lied. Nathan raised his brows, amused by my attempt at lying.

"You're an appalling liar Chucky."

I rolled my eyes. I was caught out. "Okay, I have," I agreed, shifting my weight onto my other foot. High heels and cobblestones were not the best of friends. He smiled and looked me up and down very subtly.

"You look lovely tonight."

"Thanks," I answered awkwardly. "This is how I look when I'm not vomiting into a spew bag."

Nathan laughed, with that sexy rumbly laugh of his and, for a moment, I forgot I was angry at him.

"You make a cute drunk," he said, shuffling his feet.

"And you're full of shit," I teased with a flirty smile, as I caught a whiff of his scrumptious aftershave. "Anyway, I should get back in there." I made a move towards the door, but my heel wobbled on the cobblestones. Nathan reached out his hand to steady me and as our fingers touched, a sharp electric shock crackled between us.

"There's that spark again," Nathan muttered with a rasp in his voice. Instead of letting go of my hand, his fingers entwined mine. I stared at him with confusion, cocking my head with an unspoken question. Nathan cast his gaze back to the restaurant and when his eyes came back to mine, his hold tightened around my hand. He flashed another quick look back at the door and then pulled me further down the footpath with my hand firmly in his grasp.

"Nathan what are you doing?" I asked, jogging to keep up with him. He didn't answer, and once we were a reasonable distance down the road, he came to a sudden halt. It took my feet a moment to come to a complete stop and I nearly bumped into him. As he turned, his face was so close to mine that I could feel the warmth of his breath against my lips. He looked me straight in the eyes.

"Ash…"

I felt my breath catch sharply in my throat. He'd never called me Ash before. His blue eyes drilled into mine and goosebumps quickly erupted all over my flesh. My chest grew so tight that I'd almost stopped breathing. Was he going to kiss me?

- KAT McPHERSON -

Beau had been notably quiet during dinner, and every time I looked up he was staring at me. We'd catch each other's gaze, and then both look away. It was clear that we needed to continue our conversation, but tonight was not the night. I didn't know how to feel about Beau's revelation and I had a whole jumble of emotions going on simultaneously. I'd always fancied him under the assumption that he was unattainable, but now he was available and pledging his love, my heart was feeling completely confused. I was in love with my husband, so it should have been an open and shut case, but it wasn't.

The conversation flowed around me, but I wasn't able to focus on any of it. All I could think about was Beau. Why had he never told me before? If he'd said something before I'd met Ryan, then everything might have turned out very differently. But I loved Ryan, so I guess everything had worked out exactly as it was supposed to.

The waiter arrived at our table and the smell of the food sent a slight wave of nausea through my body.

"How you going there Tails?" Ritchie asked with a wink.

"Hanging in there Ritch, but I don't think I'll be eating tonight."

"Don't worry, I'll eat yours," he joked as the waiter placed the piping hot bowls down in the middle of the table.

"Vegetable korma, chicken tikkamasala, butter chicken and beef vindaloo."

"Mmm… vindaloo," Ritchie said rubbing his hands in excitement. "Vin-da-loo, vin-da-loo, and we all like vin-da-loo," he sang with a Cockney accent, sending Amy into a fit of giggles. "Come on everyone, sing it with me… 'Me and me Mum and me Dad and me Gran and a bucket of Vindaloo'…"

"Ugh," I swallowed back a small amount of vomit, as Ritchie's bowl of beef vindaloo steamed and bubbled in front of me.

"Are you okay babe?" Ryan asked, rubbing my back.

"No. That vindaloo is making me sick."

"Tails doesn't love vindaloo," Ritchie joked, causing Amy to giggle again. "Sorry Tails, I'll move it for you," he apologised, quickly removing the spicy dish from my line of sight.

"Thank you."

"Are you going to be able to sit through dinner?" Ryan asked with concern.

"Yeah I think so," I nodded.

"Okay," he agreed as the waiter brought bowls of rice and naan bread, "but as soon as we're done, I'm taking you home."

"Should we wait for Ashley and Nathan?" Beau asked politely, avoiding eye contact with me.

"Nah, they could be a while," Ritchie joked, not thinking about the fact that Nathan's date was sitting across the table from him.

"Maybe I should go get them," Amy said, rising from her seat.

"I'll go," Kellie said, quickly bouncing up from the table before Amy had even gotten to her feet. Aims looked questioningly at Ritchie.

"Is that going to end badly?" she asked, nodding towards Kellie.

"Probably," he said with a shrug. We all glanced over at Kellie, and watched her prance out the door. That girl had way too much bounce for one human person.

"She's like a puppy dog," I said with exhaustion.

"You mean cute, playful and endearingly stupid?" Amy joked at the same moment Ritchie shovelled a forkful of the piping hot vindaloo into his mouth. Ritchie laughed and nearly snorted the spicy curry out of his nostrils.

"Holy fuck," he spluttered in pain.

"I should go save her. Or them. Or whoever," Amy suggested.

"They'll work it out. They're all adults," said Beau.

"Well two of them are anyway," Amy joked with a cheeky grin, "but it's probably past Kellie's bedtime."

- NATHAN STONE -

Ashley stared at me wide-eyed as I stood silently holding her hand. I was so nervous that I thought no other words were even going to come out. I'd already started so I was going to have to say something more than just 'Ash'.

"I just wanted to apologise for Kellie," I stammered, still grasping Ashley's hand. It wasn't what I'd been hoping to say but it would have to suffice.

"Kellie's fine, I can handle her," Ash replied flippantly as if it was no big deal. "After living with Dom, I'm an expert at being insulted."

"No, I mean for her presence, not for her lack of social etiquette … although that bears apologising for as well." I took a breath. "I just want you to know that I invited her before-" My sentence was cut short by a sing-song tone from the doorway.

"Naaa-than," called Kellie with impeccably bad timing.

"Speaking of the devil," I mumbled, dropping Ashley's hand. "Yep, over here."

"Dinner's here," she chirped loudly.

"Okay," I called back with a forced smile, "we'll be there in a minute."

"Okay!" she said, before bouncing back inside. I let out an exhausted sigh and realised that Ashley was still watching me.

"I'm too old for this shit," I said, shaking my head.

She snorted, "Yeah well I wasn't going to say it." Her disdain was tangible.

"I'm really sorry," I said again, feeling like I'd lost my grasp on the situation. For the first time in my life, I actually cared what a woman thought of me.

"It's fine Nathan. You don't owe me an explanation. In fact, you don't owe me anything," she said dismissively. I felt a twinge of something unpleasant in my chest. What was that? Guilt? Fear? Nope... it was something else. Something I couldn't put my finger on.

"But I feel like I do," I disagreed, wondering whether I'd misinterpreted her signs. "I mean, isn't this kind of, you know... heading somewhere?"

"W-I don't- Yes? No. M-maybe," she stuttered. "I don't know. Is it?"

"I'd like it to be heading somewhere," I said, wanting to take her hand again. "Wouldn't you?"

Ash stared up at me. There was so much doubt and distrust in those bright eyes of hers that I was starting to think I'd blown my chance.

"Yeah, I would, but where's your 'somewhere' Nathan?" she asked unemotionally, "because I'm not sure we're aiming for the same destination." My heart pounded in my chest.

"Naa-than," interrupted Kellie's nasal voice again.

"Oh, for fuck-," I blurted with frustration before censoring myself. The woman had the shittiest timing in the world. "Yes Kellie?"

"Do you want me to order you a Grolsh?" she asked.

"Yes please," I called back impatiently. It was a crucial moment for Granger/Stone relations and Kellie was fucking it up.

- ASHLEY GRANGER -

Kellie bounced back inside for the second time, as Nathan and I stared after her with exhaustion. How was it possible for one person to be so fucking perky? I looked at Nathan, who was clearly at the end of his tether.

"You should go inside," I said coldly. "Your date's waiting for you." I knew I shouldn't have been pissed off at Nathan, but it was hard not to let my ego get the better of me.

"I don't care if Kellie's waiting," Nathan said adamantly. "This is more important."

"Is it?"

"Of course it is," he answered, as if I was crazy for thinking otherwise. "I'm not interested in Kellie. She's... well... she's barely an adult."

"So why is she here then?" I asked defiantly.

"I invited her before I went to Paris," Nathan said feebly. "We were sort of hooking-up."

"And then you realised you weren't interested in her anymore... but decided that it would be nicer to string her along, rather than be honest?"

"It sounds pretty shitty when you put it like that," Nathan said, shoving his hands in his pockets. "I didn't really know how to get out of it without looking like an arsehole."

"Yeah, you're right. It's much better to actually *be* an arsehole than to look like one," I said snidely. Nathan studied my face for a moment.

"You're right," he conceded as a huge grin crept over his lips. "Come with me," he said, holding out his hand.

"What… you mean right now?!" I asked in shock.

"Yeah, why not?"

"Because you have a date in there and I don't have my handbag."

"That was supposed to be a rhetorical question," he chuckled. "I promise I'll fix the Kellie situation tomorrow, and Red can look after your handbag for you."

"But I don't have any money, or my phone, or my keys," I argued.

"I've got plenty of money, and we'll have Red and Richie meet us later with your handbag."

"But…"

"Come on, let's go," he repeated with his hand still outstretched.

"Go where?"

"Anywhere but here," he replied with a grin. "Let me take you on a proper date, without ex-fuck buddies or annoying friends."

I glanced back at the restaurant hesitantly. I couldn't just drop everything and go with him, could I? That would be so reckless. And stupid. Mostly stupid.

"We can't run out on dinner," I blurted, feeling simultaneously panicked and excited at the prospect of a spontaneous date with Nathan Stone.

"Yes, we can," he said with a cheeky smile, offering me his hand again. "Let yourself have some fun Ash. Stop worrying about everyone else and just do what you want to do for once."

- RYAN McPHERSON -

Once again, Kellie returned the to the table Nathan-less and I could only imagine what she must have been thinking. I felt awful for her. The poor girl was just as mistreated in this whole situation as Ash was. They were both victims of circumstance. Or, more to the point, victims of Nathan Stone.

"They'll be back in a sec," Kellie said with a dignity that belied her age.

"Sorry Kellie," I apologised on Nathan's behalf, "he can be a bit flakey sometimes. He doesn't mean any harm."

"Honestly, it's all good," she said with a shrug, "but thanks Ryan. It's really sweet of you to care." She flashed me a flirty smile as everyone continued on eating and drinking merrily. If I hadn't known better, I would have thought she was trying to hit on me. I glanced over at my wife, who looked a bit green around the gills, so I rubbed her back and kissed her on the forehead.

"You sure you're okay?" I asked quietly.

"I'll be fine," she said with a smile. "I'll just stick to the plain rice and naan."

"Okay... but tell me if you want to leave."

"So, Ryan," said Kellie from across the table interrupting my private moment with Kat, "what do you do at Artemis then?"

"I'm a Client Services Director."

"Yeah he services all of our clients," Ritchie teased with a crude gesture.

"No, that would be Nathan's job," I retorted with a laugh.

"Our clients are always well serviced," Ritch agreed with an evil chuckle. Again, I realised that our banter probably wasn't appropriate around Nathan's date.

"Sorry again, Kellie," I apologised with a shrug. "We just like to wind each other up and Nathan's the easiest target."

"I get it," she said with a wicked smile. "At least Nathan is putting his talents to good use."

Richie guffawed. "Kellie, you're a ripper," he said, with amusement. "We'll have to bring you out with us more often." Kellie smiled and peered over at me with a flirtatious look in her eye.

"I might just take you up on that offer," she said, keeping her gaze trained on me. "And if you guys ever want to come to Fabric, I'll sort VIP passes for you."

"Sweet! Thanks Kell," said Ritchie, completely oblivious to the weirdness that was passing between me and Nathan's date. Or maybe I was imagining it.

- NATHAN STONE -

I wanted Ashley to myself without any interruptions so, even though I felt like a bit of a dick standing there with my hand outstretched, I was willing to make that sacrifice. My breath stopped for a minute when I thought she was going to say no, but then she cracked a smile.

"You're impossible to say no to."

"Does that mean you're saying yes?"

"Yes," she nodded, finally taking my hand. I smiled and wrapped my fingers through hers in case she changed her mind.

"Come on." I began running down the cobbled streets with Ashley's hand in mine, and we giggled like ninth-graders ditching a maths class.

"Why are we running?" she asked, breathless with laughter.

"I don't know," I replied, still sniggering like a child as we cut up the side lane, "but we can probably stop now." We slowed down as we neared the markets, and reduced our pace to a casual stroll, still holding hands as we headed into old Spitalfields.

"I can't believe we literally just ran out on dinner," Ash said, tripping over a bump in the pavement. I wrapped my arms around her, then lifted her off her feet and spun her around in a circle. She laughed and gripped my shoulders so that her chest was pressed tightly against mine. The feel of her warm body on mine was enough to get a reaction out of mini-Nathan and the involuntary twitch brought me to a rapid halt. The last thing I wanted to do was to begin our date with a boner.

I immediately stopped spinning, but it had made me dizzy, and with Ashley still in my arms it took me a moment to regain my balance. As my vision refocused, I found myself staring straight into her big green eyes and I suddenly felt like I was buck naked. It was as if she was looking past all of my bullshit and straight into my head.

I wanted to snog her so badly that my heart was thudding, and my palms were sweaty. I didn't want to scare her off by kissing her if she wasn't ready for that, but all my senses told me she wanted me to kiss her.

As I debated my next move, Ashley took the decision out of my hands by pulling my face to hers and kissing me hard. I let myself enjoy the taste of her lips, her mouth, her tongue. I could feel her heart beating fast against my chest and my brain vacated my body, leaving my sex-drive to take control. All I could think about was taking her back to my place and fucking her senseless.

No Stoner. Don't fuck this up, I scolded myself silently as I regained some of my faculties. I quickly disentangled myself from Ash and placed her gently on the ground, stepping back to put some distance between our bodies.

With a deep breath, I rubbed my face and ran my hands through my hair to try and bring myself back down. Ash stared up at me with confusion as I attempted to collect myself.

"Everything okay?" she asked nervously. The woman looked so fucking sexy with her flushed cheeks and pink lips that I nearly changed my mind, but

I knew how much was at stake.

"If we keep doing that we're not going to make it to dinner," I explained with an embarrassed chuckle. Ash smiled and bit her lip with an understanding nod. She reached out her hand.

"Then let's just stick to holding hands," she said with a sparkle in her eye. I took her hand and we walked to the restaurant in companionable silence. By the time we strolled into the quiet little laneway, most of the blood had returned to my head.

"Here we are," I said proudly, as we arrived at Benito's.

"Nathan, this place is lovely," she breathed as I opened the door for her.

"Wait until you taste the food."

We were greeted at the entrance by the owner Benito, who I had come to know very well. I'd spent so much money at his restaurant over the years that I was probably single-handedly putting his children through college. And he had four kids. Benito welcomed me, with a hearty hug.

"Ah Nathan, è bello vederti." Although my Italian wasn't quite as good as my French, I knew enough to hold a conversation.

"Ciao Benito," I replied with a smile, patting his back affectionately. "Come stai?"

"Molto bene!" he said in typical Italian style... loudly, with gratuitous hand gestures. "E tu?"

"Sto benissimo," I told him, nodding towards Ashley in explanation of why my life had been so great of late.

"Ahh si, si, si," he answered with a knowing grin, "and who's this beautiful lady?"

"Benito, this is Ashley."

"Lovely to meet you Ashley," Benito said, kissing Ash on both cheeks.

"And you Benito," she replied with a blush.

"Lucca, best table in the house for Mr Stone," Benito called to the young waiter, as he pointed us towards a table next to the window.

"Thanks Benito," I said, following Lucca to our special table. I showed Ash to her seat. "Signora," I joked, pulling out her chair. It was our first real date, so I was going to do it properly.

"Grazie," she said with a grin.

"I didn't know you spoke Italian," I said, sitting the chair opposite her.

"I don't," Ash joked with sparkly eyes. "That's about the extent of my knowledge, but I'm very impressed with your linguistic skills."

"My plan is working then," I replied with a wink. "Lucca, could you grab us a bottle of the Burlotto Barolo please?"

"Sure," he nodded, trotting off to organise our expensive bottle of vino.

"I'm a bit fussy when it comes to wine," I explained unnecessarily.

"In that case, you'll get along well with my Dad," she joked. "He's got a whole cellar full of expensive wine that he says Mum and I never appreciate properly."

"You mean, appreesherate?" I joked, sending us into fits of giggles. "You'll have to take me there some time," I said, once our laughter had subsided.

"Yeah," she agreed with a nervous smile, "I guess I will."

Lucca returned with our wine.

"Grazie Lucca," I said as he poured our wine. We patiently watched him fill our glasses and once we were alone again I raised my glass and clinked it against Ashley's. "To our first date."

"To our first date," she concurred with a smile, before taking a dainty sip of the wine. We both fell quiet, and I began to feel nervous again. I'd never been on a date that wasn't solely a precursor to getting laid.

"What do you think?" I asked, tapping my fingers against my wine glass.

"It's really good."

"And how am I doing on the first date scale?"

"Pretty well, although I do have to wonder whether you bring all your girls here," Ash teased.

"I've never brought anyone here. This is usually where I come when I want to get away from people."

"Oh," she said, looking pleasantly stunned, "well thank you for sharing it with me."

"There's no one else I'd want to share it with," I looked into her big green eyes and had to take a breath to collect myself. "Ash... there's something I want to know, but it's really none of my business."

"Okay," she answered with a nod, "how about you just try asking and see what happens."

"Sure," I agreed, gulping nervously. "The thing is... Tails said something on the weekend and I... well I guess I... umm..." Holy fuck, I sounded like Woody Allen. "Sorry, I'm making this really awkward, aren't I?"

"A little yeah," she agreed with a smile. "What did Kat tell you Nath?"

I took a gulp of wine for courage. "She said you'd lost a baby."
Ashley's stoic expression faltered slightly, and she nodded her head.

"Yeah that's true."

"I'm sorry. I shouldn't have asked. It's none of my business."

"It's fine Nathan. It was bound to come out sooner or later," she replied with a stiff smile. "I was six months pregnant when I left Mareechi's, so it wasn't exactly a huge secret."

"I'm so sorry Ash," I apologised, feeling like an arse for asking. "You don't have to talk about it if you don't want to."

She smiled sadly and looked me in the eye, "I just don't want you to think of me as a helpless victim."

"I don't think that at all."
She nodded and took a sip of wine, looking up at me uncertainly.

"He beat me so badly that he killed the baby."

"Who? Dom?!" I asked in shock. Ash nodded again. I felt like I was going to vomit. I couldn't believe that someone would do that to their girlfriend, let alone their own child.

"That was the real reason he ended up in prison," she confessed quietly.

"Fuck."

"Yeah."

"So what happened?"

"Honestly, I don't even remember what set him off that night but he was angrier than I'd ever seen him before. I didn't expect him to hit me while I was pregnant, so I wasn't ready for it. I never thought he'd do anything to hurt the baby. Mia was her name." I listened in stunned silence. "Whatever it was, Dom went absolutely mental. He pushed me down the stairs, and then beat me unconscious." Tears pricked at her eyes. "I tried to protect her, but once I was down he… he just kept kicking me." One of the tears escaped down her cheek, and her pain hit me right in the chest as if it was my own. "I knew after the first kick that something was wrong," Ash continued. "They told me later that Mia was dead before the ambulance had even arrived. I was unconscious, so they had to do an emergency C-section to get her out, and when I woke up… it was all over. She was gone, and I wasn't pregnant anymore."

"Holy fuck," I breathed, feeling like the wind had been knocked out of my sails.

"Nathan," Ash paused and looked down at her shiny nails. "I don't know exactly what we have going on here, but I have a really complicated past so I totally understand if you'd rather just stay friends."
I leaned closer to her, resting my elbows on the table.

"I don't know what this is either, but I do know that I don't want to be just friends."

- ASHLEY GRANGER -

I stared at Nathan silently, fighting my urge to dive across the table and kiss him. His perfect response, combined with our amazing kiss still fresh on my lips, had left me defenseless. Even though I was probably heading for a broken heart, there was some sort of magnetic force pulling me towards Nathan Stone and I felt incapable of resisting it.

"Okay," I said, unable to breathe properly, "so where do we go from here?" Nathan contemplated his answer for a moment.

"We get to know each other I guess." My heart melted. The man sitting in front of me was far from the heartless player who everyone had made him out to be.

"So much for your man-whore reputation," I teased, taking a sip of my wine. Nathan threw his head back and laughed.

"Granger you're the only woman I'd trade it in for."

"Why?" I blushed, peering at him over my glass.

"What do you mean 'why'?" he asked, cocking his head quizzically.

"Why me? Why not one of the million other girls you have falling at your feet?"

"Firstly, because you're not falling at my feet," he admitted with a sexy half-smile. "I like the fact that you don't just tell me what I want to hear. You challenge me to be a better person." My heart pounded and I could feel the blush beginning to spread up my neck. "And secondly, because they're all girls. You're a woman," Nathan said with fire in his eyes. I felt my blush flare hotter.

He grinned and lifted his glass to his lips. "The bigger mystery is why you're interested in me."

I smiled bashfully and shrugged, "I have a thing for bad boys."

"Clearly," Nathan snorted in amusement.

"Tell me more about your Mum," I asked, steering the conversation in a more 'first date' sort of direction in the hopes that it would allow time for my blush subside. "I take it you're not very close?"

"It's a long story," Nathan answered with a heavy sigh.

"We've got time," I said as Lucca brought our vegetable antipasto platter to the table. "Wow! This looks divine."

"Try the olives first," Nathan suggested, passing me the small bowl of olives from the board. "Benito makes them himself."

"Thanks," I said with yet another blush, as Nathan intently watched me pick out an olive and put it in my mouth. "Mmm," I said, trying not to have a food-gasm over the exquisite olive.

"Amazing huh?" he agreed, popping an olive into his own mouth.

"Uh-huh," I nodded and reached for a piece of fresh, crusty bread. "So, you were telling me about your Mum," I reminded him.

"Yeah," he agreed shifting on his chair, "there's not much to say really. She's got schizophrenia, so she literally doesn't know who I am. In fact, she thinks I'm my Dad most of the time."

"Oh, Nath," I breathed, leaning across the table to take his hand. "I'm so sorry."

"No need to be sorry," he reassured me with a sad smile. "It wasn't you who caused it." He took a quick glance at my cleavage, of which he had a fairly good view with me leaning that far forward.

"Do you see her much?" I asked, accidentally staring at his lips. I wanted so badly to taste those lips again.

"Every couple of weeks,"

"It must be hard that she doesn't recognise you," I said, unable to imagine how I'd feel if my Mum didn't know who I was.

"Yeah, it's really weird. Some days she recognises me, but they're few and far between. I never know what she's going to be like from one visit to the next."

"Nath that sounds awful."

"I missed my last visit," he said with a sigh. "I couldn't bring myself to go again after what happened the last time."

"Why? What happened last time?"

"She totally lost it," he explained. "She started punching me and screaming that I wasn't her son and accusing me of having kidnapped myself."

"That's horrible," I blurted, with tears welling in my eyes. My heart was breaking for him. No wonder he'd spent his adult life detaching from women.

"She doesn't know what she's saying but…"

"But it's hard," I finished for him.

"Yeah," Nathan agreed shamefully. "I feel so fucking helpless you know?"

"I can't even imagine, Nath."

"I think you'd get it more than anyone else I know," he said meaningfully.

"Yeah," I agreed. "We're quite a pair, aren't we?"

"We sure are." Nathan held my gaze intently, and I felt the butterflies taking off in my stomach again. "Tragedy gives you a different perspective on life though," he said. "I mean, it makes you realise that you have absolutely no control over anything."

"That's true," I agreed.

"Sometimes I do wonder why one person can get dumped with so much shit in their lives, while other people get to live in blissful ignorance until the end of eternity."

"Everyone has their own journey Nath. It's just that some of us have tougher lessons to learn than others." It was the only explanation that had ever resonated with me in order to make sense of my own messy life.

"Yeah, I suppose," he agreed with a shrug.

"But I do believe that the universe only gives us what we can handle."

"I don't know that I've been handling any of it to be honest," he joked, "especially when I look at you and see what you've been through, and you're so…" he paused, searching for the right word, "…so strong."

"You think I'm strong?" I chuckled with self-deprecation. "I'm a mess on the inside. I just look like I've got my shit together because I refuse to let my past define me."

"And that's exactly what makes you so strong," he said with a smile. "I, on the other hand, am a total coward. My Mum needs me, and I wimped out."

"You need to stop beating yourself up Nathan," I told him sternly. "How long has she been like this?"

"Since my Dad died," he answered quietly. "The doctors said it was brought on by a stroke, but I think it was because she couldn't cope without my Dad. The day he died, her soul went with him."

"That's a very romantic way of looking at it, Mr Stone."

"I suppose it is, he agreed. "I guess it's the only way I can make sense of it. She looked like Mum…but she was gone. She even tried to kill herself a few times, and that's when they admitted her."

I squeezed his hand, "I'm so sorry Nathan." My chest hurt with the weight of his sorrow, and I wanted to take the pain away for him. I couldn't imagine being so young and having both my parents torn away from me so horribly. It was as if the final piece of the Nathan Stone puzzle had fallen into place.

- KAT McPHERSON -

We were nearly finished our meals and Nathan and Ashley still hadn't come inside. Kellie seemed to be handling it well, but I was too preoccupied with Beau to notice or care. It was hard to concentrate when all I wanted to do was clear the air with him.

I glanced up at him again, and he caught my eye. His face softened with an expression that looked somewhat like a man in love. My stomach churned at the realisation that the look was aimed at me. Was he being brazen, or was it only obvious to the two of us?

Beau broke our gaze and peered under the table, then looked up and smiled. I felt my phone vibrate inside my bag. His eyebrows flickered, and I knew it was from him. Next to me, my husband ate, drank and laughed with our friends, oblivious to the intimate exchange that was passing between his wife and another man.

I subtly extracted my phone and read Beau's message.

'Can I escort you home?' My heart thumped. Was he suggesting what I thought he was suggesting? I peered up at him nervously, and seeing the hesitation in my eyes, he tapped out another text. 'Just to talk.'
The knot in my chest dissipated.

'Okay,' I replied. I put my phone away and leaned over to Ryan.

"Hey baby, do you mind if I head home?"

"Sure honey, let's go," he replied, putting his fork down.

"No, you stay and finish your dinner. I'll be fine."

"I can't let you go home on your own," Ryan protested.

"I can drop her home Ryza," said Beau from the other side of the table. "I need to turn-in early anyway. I've got to be at the pool first thing in the morning." I did my best not to look at Beau for too long, because I was having visions of him in his speedo. It was his swimming training that gave him such amazing abs and the thought of him wet and semi-naked stirred all sorts of reactions in my body.

Ryan turned back to me, "Are you cool with that babe?" I quickly focused on my husband and smiled reassuringly.

"Absolutely honey. You stay and enjoy your night," I said, patting his knee.

"Oh. Okay," he agreed with a nod. I grabbed my bag and Ryan helped me out of my seat.

"Sorry folks, but I need my bed," I announced to the rest of the table.

"Not feeling so well hun?" Amy asked.

"No, this baby-making process is pretty rough," I joked.

"That's why women do it love," Ritchie replied with a laugh. "We men are all wimps."

"Exactly," Ryan agreed, kissing me proudly on the head.

"Yet you wonder why I don't want to go through that," Amy quipped back at Ritchie.

"I'd just like to know if there's any lead in my pencil."

"Keep going like that and your pencil won't ever get near my sharpener again," Amy said as more drinks arrived.

"Whoa, that's big talk sunshine," Ritchie laughed loudly in response to Amy's banter. "Your sharpener wouldn't last a week without my pencil."

"That sounds like a challenge Mr Carlton," Amy replied with a smirk. "Shall we make it more interesting?"

"Please don't," I begged, positive that my stomach wouldn't hold out if I heard any more.

"Agreed," Beau concurred, sculling the remainder of his beer before plonking the empty bottle back on the table. Ritchie clinked his beer bottle against Beau's empty one in solidarity.

"Cheers to that," he said, proceeding to skull the rest of his own beer, which he then concluded with a massive burp.

"Charming," I teased rolling my eyes. "Anyway, I'm going to get out of here before I vomit. I'm trusting you guys to look after my husband."

"Of course we will," Aims said with an evil smirk.

"I want him back in one piece," I warned them with a smile.

"See ya folks," Beau said, taking Ryan's usual position at my side. "Don't do anything I wouldn't do."

"Well that doesn't leave much," retorted Amy.

"Hey, maybe you could send Nashley back in here on your way out," Ritch added with an evil chuckle. "They're going to miss out if they don't get back in here soon."

"Didn't we agree on Ashlan?" Amy joked.

The rest of us fell silent, glancing awkwardly at Kellie.

"Sorry Kell, they're just joking," Ryan assured her kindly.

"It's fine Ryan, it's not like Nathan and I are dating or anything," she replied with a surprising amount of dignity.

"I'll send them in," I said with a nod.

"Here's to getting drunk!" Ritchie announced, shoving a beer into Kellie's hand.

"And on that note, we're out of here," Beau declared with a wave.

"See you at home baby," I called to Ryan.

"See you soon gorgeous," he said, blowing me a kiss.

- RYAN McPHERSON -

Kat had barely left the restaurant before I saw her name pop up on my phone screen.

"Hey babe, everything okay?" I asked.

"Yeah I'm fine, I'm in the cab now but I just thought I'd let you know that Nath and Ashley are gone."

My jaw dropped. "What?"

"What's she saying?" asked Ritchie.

"What do you mean, gone?" I asked her in disbelief, holding up my hand to pause Ritchie.

"I mean, they're not out here. We've had a quick look around, but they're nowhere." It looked like our crew was dwindling rapidly.

"Thanks baby. You go get some sleep and I'll be home soon."

"No need to rush honey."

"Alright. I love you."

"Ditto," she replied strangely, before hanging up. In the three years that we'd been together, Kat had never replied to an 'I love you' with 'ditto'. She must have been more ill than I'd thought. I shoved the phone back into my pocket and realised that the remaining three were staring at me expectantly.

"What's going on?" Amy asked.

"Apparently Ashlan has left the building," I joked oddly, fighting a weird feeling in the pit of my belly.

"And then there were four," Ritchie laughed with amusement. "Shall we finish here and go get some shots?"

"Why not?" I agreed. With my two best friends off shagging each other, and my wife at home in bed, there was nothing left to do but get shit-faced.

"I'm up for that," Kellie agreed, skulling her beer. "You guys seem like the fun ones anyway," she joked.

"You can show us oldies how it's done Kell," Amy teased.

"Oh, I don't know," Kellie said, glancing at me quickly, "I think you've all probably got a few good tricks up your sleeves. Maybe you'll teach me a thing or two."

I felt a twinge in my belly. I was obviously misinterpreting Kelly. Why would she be interested in an old guy like me? Besides, she knew I was married.

"Right, let's do it then," Ritchie said with a clap of his massive hands.

- KAT McPHERSON -

I was feeling super-guilty, yet completely unrepentant for what I was doing. It wasn't like anything untoward was happening… but deep down I wanted it to. From the moment Beau had mentioned his swimming training, I couldn't stop thinking about his naked body. I'd coveted his six pack for years, and I already knew he was packing some serious heat in the downstairs department. For the first time in all the years we'd known each other, that fact was now suddenly of interest to me.

I breathed deeply and peered over at Beau, who was watching me with great interest.

"What did Ryan say?" he asked curiously, as our cab pulled out onto Liverpool Street.

"He's staying out for a while," I replied thankful that we'd grabbed the first mini-cab we'd come across.

"Okay," Beau nodded understandingly, "and what are we doing?"
My heart pounded. This was my chance to do the right thing.

"Well, I'm going to my house," I said, still undecided on whether I was going to succumb to my urges. Since Ryan had declared his disinterest in sex for the near future, Beau had become an extra-tempting offer. Beau's eyes held mine.

"And am I getting out with you or am I going home?"

I paused to think about my answer, but my mouth seemed to have a mind of its own.

"That's entirely up to you," I said, before I'd even realised it. I stared at Beau. The ball was in his court now.

"Right," he said, leaning back in his chair, "well, maybe I'll come in for a quick coffee."

And there it was. In the politest possible way, Beau was coming home with me. Obviously, that didn't mean we were going to have sex. I was six months pregnant after all. He'd hardly want to see me naked, but this was more than talking and we both knew it. Before long, the cab was nearing my street.

"Just up here thanks," I said, pointing to our house. "Anywhere you can find a spot is fine."

"Sure," the cabbie nodded, pulling into a parking bay a few houses down from mine. Beau grabbed some cash out of his wallet before I could get to my purse.

"Cheers buddy," he said, tipping the guy a fiver. Beau helped me climb ungracefully out of the cab and we walked silently up the steps to my place, arm-in-arm like an old married couple. It was the strangest feeling, going home with a man who wasn't my husband, yet Beau was so familiar to me that it seemed completely normal at the same time.

"Sorry you missed the rest of dinner," I said quietly as we reached my front porch.

"I'd much rather be here with you," he replied, playing with one of the wayward curls that had flopped over my face.

"Why?" I asked curiously.

"Because I love you," he replied huskily. My chest tightened, but I couldn't tell whether it was in excitement or agony. It was a perfect moment, but not the sort of moment that a married, pregnant woman should have with anyone other than her husband. Especially not on the front steps of her building.

I shattered our beautiful moment and quickly unlocked the door, pushing Beau through the entrance hall and into my place, before any of the neighbors saw us.

"Sorry," I apologised sheepishly once we were safely inside. "I know all the neighbours."

"It's cool, I get it," Beau replied, moving in close. My heart fluttered at the smouldering look in his eyes. He was so sexy, and so familiar that it almost felt right. But it wasn't right. I stepped back from him as guilt washed over me like a tidal wave.

"I can't do this."

- RYAN McPHERSON -

We paid the bill, gathered up our things (which included Ashley's abandoned handbag), and made our way over to the Big Chill for drinks. I was standing at the bar with Kellie, attempting to order our shots when her arm brushed casually against mine. I looked down at her and smiled.

"Hey, I'm sorry about how tonight panned out," I said apologetically.

"I'm not," she answered with a flirty grin.

"Well, I have to say, you're being a really good sport about it. I'm not sure I'd be so understanding."

"Meh, Nathan can do what he wants. Besides, I've got you all to myself now, so it's not all bad," Kellie replied provocatively.

"I guess not," I said, scratching my head awkwardly. She must have been taking the piss.

"So, are you having a good night?" she asked, leaning against the bar so that her cleavage popped even further out of her dress. I tried my hardest not to stare at her voluptuous boobs, but it was impossible not to look. Damn my male instincts.

"It's been eventful," I joked with a smile as Ritchie walked up behind me and patted me on the back.

"Ryza," he said, subtly slapping something into the palm of my hand. "These are for you."

"Yeah?" I took a quick glance and saw a little plastic baggie containing two white pills.

"Go nuts," he muttered with a cheeky grin.

"Cheers man," I said feeling a little bit nervous about taking Ecstasy at my age. Wasn't there some sort of cut-off age for recreational drug usage?

Amy walked past and pinched Ritchie's butt. "Let's go."

"Righto," he said obediently.

"Are you leaving too?" I asked him with exasperation.

"Nope, we're just gonna drop Ashley's bag and then we'll be back."

"Do you even know where they are?" I said, shoving the baggie of pills into my pocket.

"Yeah, Stoner texted," he answered with a shrug.

"Oh, right," I said, feeling slightly offended that he'd text Ritchie instead of me.

"You'll be in good hands with this man," he told Kellie.

"I'm sure I will," she replied, shooting me a flirty wink as Ritchie ran off after Amy.

"Sorry about my mates," I apologised.

"No need to apologise," she answered, twisting her hair around her finger. "I'm quite pleased they've left me alone with you."

My jaw nearly hit the ground. Holy shit. She was actually flirting with me.

"How long is this fucking bar guy taking?" I asked, hoping to deflect her attention as I waved at the bartender to no avail. Kellie turned around and leaned over the counter, grinning at the bar guy, who promptly came straight over.

"Two tequila shots, a Smirnoff ice and a…"

"Bourbon and coke thanks," I answered feeling quite in awe of her skills. I glanced sideways at Kellie. "That was quite impressive," I told her with a grin, "remind me to bring you along whenever I go to a bar."

"Invitation accepted," she said with a wink. I felt like I was looking at a different woman. At dinner she'd seemed so young and immature, but now she was sexy and confident. Up until this point I had been wondering how she and Nathan had ended up as fuck buddies, but now that I was seeing this side of her it made much more sense. She certainly wasn't my type, but this was more Nathan's speed and I suddenly saw her in a whole new light.

The bartender brought out our drinks and I paid for them. We downed our shots and I slammed my shot glass on the bar, breathing out the alcohol fumes loudly.

"Tequila!" Kellie sang with her hands in the air. I laughed and, feeling brave, I leaned in close to her and subtly flashed her the bag of pills.

"I don't suppose you'd like to join me for an Eccy, would you?" I asked quietly into her ear. She raised one well plucked eyebrow with interest.

"With such a chivalrous offer, how could I say no?"

- NATHAN STONE -

I stared at Ashley's elegant hand sitting gently on top of mine and I felt like my heart was in my throat. It was such an innocent touch, but it was igniting fires all through my body. I let my thumb gently rub against hers and for the first time in my adult life, I actually felt connected to another human person.

"Mi scusi Mr Stone," Benito said quietly, appearing beside me. "The couple outside wanted me to return this to Ms Ashley," he explained apologetically as he held up Ashley's handbag. I peered out the window to where Benito was pointing. Ritchie and Red were standing outside waving like idiots.

"Thank you Benito," Ashley said, sliding her hand off mine to take the bag.

"Are they not coming in?" I asked him.

"I don't think so sir."

I shrugged at Ritchie and he gave me a thumbs up.

"Excuse me for a second Ash."

"Sure. Say thanks for me."

"Will do," I squeezed her shoulder as I walked past. She peered up at me with a smile and I had to refrain myself from planting a kiss on her lips. "Back in a minute."

"I thought it was only going to be a second," she said with sly grin.

"Time me," I joked with a wink as I jogged out the door. Ritchie and Red met me at the entrance.

"Hey," I said, shaking Ritchie's hand. "Thanks guys, I owe you one."

"No, you owe us your first-born child," Ritchie joked, lighting up a cigarette. "There are some scary mother fuckers lurking around here."

I laughed loudly. "Ritch, you're six foot five, it's not like anyone is going to fuck with you."

"He thinks he saw Dom Doyle," Red explained mockingly.

"I fuckin' did," Ritch said adamantly. I chuckled again at my cowardly, beefy mate.

"The guy is in jail dude," I assured him.

"Thank you!" Red threw her hands in the air, "that's what I told him."

"I know what I saw," Ritchie replied shaking his head, "but let's just drop it."

"Hey, you're the one who brought it up," I said with a shrug.

"How's the date going?" Red asked eagerly.

"Good," I replied, glancing in through the window at Ashley, who was chatting animatedly with Benito. I smiled at the sight of her and turned back to my friends. "How was everyone after we left?"

"After you bailed on us you mean?" Ritchie retorted. I shrugged and scratched the back of my ear with embarrassment.

"Yeah okay, I'll cop that."

"It was fine," Red assured me with a knowing smile. "Kellie has been keeping herself entertained with Ryza."

"What about Tails?" I asked, having an inkling about how that situation might be playing out.

"She went home ill," said Red.

"Okay, well, just keep an eye on Kellie. She might seem sweet and innocent, but she's got a wild streak and I suspect she'll have Ryza for tea if Kat's not around."

"He'll be fine," said Ritch, waving his hand around as if I was being stupid.

"Okay," I said with a wary nod, glancing inside again.

"Get back inside dude," Ritchie said, slapping me on the arm. "Your date's waiting for you."

"Thanks man."

"You can fill me in at the gym tomorrow," he called.

"Maybe. Or maybe not," I teased with a wink, before heading back into the restaurant to rejoin my date. Ash looked up with a smile as I returned. "Sorry about that," I apologised, taking my seat.

"No need to apologise," Ash said with a smile.

"Now, onto more important topics," I said with a grin. "I still haven't received that CD report of yours."

"It must be in the mail room," she joked with a wink.

"Well… what did you think of it?"

"I loved it," she said with a blush. "I hadn't picked you for an indie folk-rock kind of guy though."

I smiled. "What had you picked me as then?"

"I don't know," she studied me for a minute. "I think I was expecting something EDM-y like Dirty-House, or dubstep or something."
I laughed loudly.

"Well, maybe back in the day," I admitted with a grin, "but only when I was off my rocker."

- KAT McPHERSON -

Beau and I sat on the couch awkwardly, drinking tea. I might have put the breaks on whatever that had been, but we still had a lot to discuss.

"I don't want to make life harder for you Kitty-Kat," said Beau, breaking the silence, "but you've got to know that I love you. If you decide you feel the same way about me, then I would do the right thing by you and the baby."

"Oh Beau, the right thing for the baby is to have her parents together."

Beau nodded humbly, "Yeah of course. I'm sorry." He fell silent for a moment. I sighed and rubbed my belly.

"I don't really know what to say Beau. If you'd told me this before I met Ryan, I feel like things would have turned out really differently."

"What are you saying? That you have feelings for me too?" he asked, moving closer. I looked up at him guiltily.

"I don't know," I said, and then, without thinking, I grabbed his face and kissed him. I was expecting that kissing him would make me realise that I had no feelings for him, but instead, it ignited my desire. Beau returned my kiss eagerly, and what began as a meaningless kiss, turned into a steamy snog. He wound his fingers through my hair, sending goosebumps across my flesh, before I felt his hand run up my thigh.

"I want you Kat," he said, as his hands roamed my body, "and I think you want me too." My chest was tight with panic, but my body was responding to him in ways that I hadn't expected. "Do you want me?" he asked. Desire was flaring in me and I found myself getting caught up in the moment.

"I do," I said in barely a whisper. Without any further discussion, he planted his mouth on mine again and kissed me as passionately as if we were the last two people on earth. I was a willing participant until he slid his fingers inside my underwear.

"Oh my god," I breathed, half wanting to walk away, but also not wanting him to stop, as my body lit up under his touch. I looked up at Beau uncertainly. He had an expression on his face that I'd never seen before, and I suddenly felt like I was with a stranger. He continued rubbing his fingers against the moist hair between my thighs, and the sensation was so intense that I lost all restraint. He unzipped his jeans and pulled his cock out.

I couldn't believe what was happening. We'd gone from zero to 100 in five seconds flat, but I felt like we'd gone too far to stop now. I fought against my conscience, but when I felt the tip of his penis against my skin, the physical pleasure was too much for me to refuse. He slid inside me and it felt so good that my whole body instantly surged with pleasure.

"Oh my god," I whispered breathlessly. We were in an awkward position so I maneuvered myself on top of him as best I could with my extra load.

"I love you Kat," he breathed, as I bobbed up and down inelegantly. I could feel guilt rising to the forefront of my mind, but I pushed it away and focused on the job at hand. My body was getting closer to its goal and I had to see it through now. Beau supported my back and tilted his hips upwards to get a better angle.

"Wow," I sighed breathlessly, "that's amazing."

"You're amazing." Well that clearly wasn't true. I was six months pregnant and fucking my best friend who, up until a few days ago, had been, for all intents and purposes, gay. If I'd ever been amazing, now was certainly not that moment.

I shook my head to clear the guilt. I couldn't have stopped even if I'd wanted to. I felt a wave of heat start to rise up from my core and my body felt like it was on fire in the most intoxicating way. Both of us were panting and I could tell that Beau wasn't far from blowing, but my back was getting sore.

"How about doggie?" he suggested seeing that I was losing steam. I nodded and re-positioned myself on the couch in a very unladylike fashion. Beau gently gripped my hips and continued where we'd left off. He proceeded slowly and carefully, but with the change of position he went deeper, and my body lit up like a christmas tree.

"Oh my god," I moaned in ecstasy as the fireworks in my body marked the end of my life as I knew it.

- RYAN McPHERSON -

I was so toasted that the night was becoming a total blur. It had been years since I'd popped a pill, and I'd almost forgotten how much fun it was. I fucking loved it. It was insanely brilliant. I felt invincible. Music sounded deeper, colours looked brighter and everything felt fucking sensational. Why had I let Kat talk me into giving it up when it was so much fucking fun?

"You're a great dancer!" I told Kellie over the thump of the music.

"So are you," she replied with a smile, wrapping her arms around my waist. "You're a lot of fun."

"Yeah. Normally I'm not," I admitted with a riotous laugh as I danced like an idiot. I knew I probably looked like a twat, but I felt like a legend. I glanced over at Amy and Ritchie with pride, as Kellie began gyrating along with me. It was all harmless fun, and everyone knew it, but it was nice to have some female attention none-the-less.

"You're killin' it MacDaddy," Ritchie called loudly with a 'thumbs up'.

"This is awesome," I said with a laugh as a few random girls joined our little dance circle. I'd never had so many women pay me so much attention before. I took it in turns dancing with them all, feeling like a total boss, when Kellie elbowed her way back into prime dancing position in front of me. The night was turning out to be unexpectedly epic.

"Here," said Kellie, holding out a little pink pill on the tip of her perfectly manicured finger.

"What is it?" I asked curiously. I'd never seen a pink pill before.

"LSD," she replied with a sultry grin. Feeling game, I nodded and moved to take the pill from her hand but instead, she slipped her finger straight into my mouth. I was a little taken aback by the intimate action, but I swallowed the pill with her finger still inside my mouth. Kellie's eyes flashed with lust and I suddenly realised that I might have been giving her the wrong idea. She wrapped her arms around my waist again.

"Have you ever had sex on pills?"

"Uh… no, but… Kell…" I began to say as she looked up at me expectantly, "I've got a wife."

"It's not a problem for me," she answered with a grin. My head began to swirl as a warm, fuzzy feeling crept over me and lit up every single nerve ending in my body. The LSD was kicking in.

"Oh wow," I breathed, in awe of the tingly feeling that was seeping through my body.

"Good pill huh?" Kellie said into my ear. Her warm breath sent shivers all over my body.

"Fuck yeah," I agreed enthusiastically.

The lights flashed, the music pumped, and our bodies writhed collectively in time with the beat. I closed my eyes and let myself get carried into the rhythm. It was such a visceral experience. I wasn't just hearing the music, I was feeling it. Coke was awesome, but pills were even better, and LSD was fucking insane. I felt like I was twenty again and partying in Ibiza with Nathan and the Uni boys. Life had been so much simpler back then. No stress, no mortgage, no responsibilities, just endless parties.

Kellie rubbed up against me and I felt little explosions of goosebumps erupt all over my flesh. It was mostly due to the pills more than her touch, but it was the best feeling I'd had that didn't involve sex.

"I love drugs!" I shouted happily, throwing my hands in the air. Cheers of agreement broke out from those within hearing distance. "Who else loves drugs?" I asked the crowd boisterously. Everyone on the dancefloor whooped and cheered and I felt like the king of the fucking world. The only thing that was missing was my queen. It sucked that she couldn't be here having an awesome time with me. Ritchie made his way over to us and shouted at me over the music.

"You need an equaliser dude."

"Huh?" I asked, unable to hear him.

"You need an equaliser," he repeated, pushing a bag against my hand.

"What? I can't hear you," I said loudly, throwing my arm over his shoulder. "Dance with us Ritch," I laughed, dragging him in to my drug-fuelled, dry-humping session. "I love you man."

"I love you too buddy," he replied, patting me on the back, as I began running my hand up and down his shirt. "What are you doing dude?" he asked, removing my hand from his chest.

"Your shirt is so soft," I said with wide eyes. "I bet that feels amazing to wear."

"Oh Jesus," he sighed with exasperation. Ritchie scooped out a bump of Coke and held it right up to my nostril. "Sniff." I did as ordered, and instantly felt my head clear.

"Thanks."

"That should at least straighten you out enough to face Kat."

"Oh fuck," I breathed with a laugh. "She's going to be soooo pissed at me."

"Yeah man," Ritchie agreed. "I'd say that's a fair guess."

"My wife is going to kill me," I explained humorously to Kellie.

"I guess you'd better not go home then," Kellie replied seductively.

"Where else would I go?" I asked with a chuckle. Kellie opened her mouth to respond when Richie interrupted her.

"Okay buddy, it's time to get you home to your wife."

- KAT McPHERSON -

Beau and I had been going for a while and I was feeling another orgasm about to hit me. I was so caught up in the moment that all thoughts of Ryan had vanished from my mind. As Beau's cock hit a certain spot, explosions of ecstasy burst through my brain and I let out a huge wail of pleasure. It was the biggest orgasm of my life.

"Oh my god," I cried for the millionth time, as my whole body shook uncontrollably. Beau was groaning loudly as the waves of pleasure continued crashing over me. I wondered whether it was him or the pregnancy hormones that had led to such a massive release, but either way I didn't care. It was exactly what I'd needed. Why couldn't Ryan have done this for me? Why had he left me hanging?

My body began to simmer down just as Beau shuddered with relief.

"Oh Kitty-Kat," he moaned as his penis jerked inside me and set off another little wave of explosions. "I've waited so long to do that," he sighed. "I hope that was sufficient to convince you I'm straight."

"I'm sufficiently convinced," I joked, gently removing myself from his spent cock. As I stood up I felt his warm jizz dribbling out of me and pooling in my knickers. What a class act I was. I'd been so caught up in the moment that we hadn't even used protection. Obviously, pregnancy wasn't an issue, but I knew absolutely nothing about Beau's sex life. What if he had some sort of disease that could affect the baby?

As reality sank in, it dawned on me that I'd turned into the sort of woman I'd spent my entire life trying not to become. I guess I was more like my mother than I cared to admit. Guilt oozed through me. What had I done? What sort of person would have an affair six months into a pregnancy? My change of mood must have been apparent, because Beau cocked his head and studied me.

"Are you okay?" he asked with concern. I needed him gone; I needed to clean myself up; and I needed to think clearly.

"Yeah. Just tired I guess," I lied as convincingly as possible.

"Okay. Can I get you something? Why don't you go lie down for a bit?"

"Actually, I think you'd better go," I replied more bluntly than I'd intended.

"What?" Beau asked, with hurt and confusion in his eyes.

"Ryan could get home any moment and I don't think it's a good idea for you to be here when he does." In truth, Ryan was still operating under the false assumption that Beau was gay, so he probably wouldn't have thought anything of it unless he'd actually caught us in the act.

"Doesn't he think I'm gay too?" Beau asked as if reading my mind.

"Yeah…."

"So, he wouldn't be suspicious right?" he said with a shrug. "I'm happy to put on a gay act."

"I appreciate that, but you still need to go. I really need to have a shower before he gets home."

- NATHAN STONE -

Once Ashley and I had finished our meal, she insisted on paying our bill, so I insisted on escorting her all the way home. It was probably a little old fashioned of me, but the one thing I had going for me was my chivalry, and I refused to let my standards slide. Admittedly, I usually walked girls home with the expectation that I'd probably get laid, but with Ashley it was different.

"Thanks for walking me home," she said, tucking her hair behind her ear as we stood on the front steps of her apartment building.

"Thanks for buying me dinner," I joked with a shrug.

"I mean it. It was really sweet."

I shoved my hands in my pockets. "It was self-serving really. It gave me extra time with you."

Ashley blushed and bit her lip, looking down at her shoes.

"I had a really nice time tonight."

"Ooh, nice? Is that a polite way of saying it was boring?" I joked. Ash laughed and hit me on the arm.

"Not at all. Nice is a novelty for me. It doesn't happen often, but I think I could really get used to it."

"Me too," I agreed, inching a little closer to her, catching a waft of her tasty scent. She always smelt so good. She shuffled on her feet, then rifled in her handbag and pulled out her keys.

"Do you want to come in?" she asked peering up through her white fringe.

"Yes. I do," I answered honestly, "but I won't."

"Okay," she agreed with a disappointed smile.

"Next time I will take you up on that," I said, feeling like a total plonker. I cleared my throat. "Tonight was the best date I've ever had."
Ashley blushed and swept her fringe out of her eyes.

"Me too, I'm really glad I came."

"Ditto," I replied, as we stood awkwardly waiting for something to happen.

"Well… goodnight," Ashley said with a little shrug.

"Goodnight," I replied huskily as my desire flared.
A kiss would have been the appropriate move for me to make, but that's not what I did. Despite my instinct to plant one on her, I knew after the intensity of our earlier kiss, that an innocent goodnight pash would most likely turn into a shag, and I didn't think either of us were ready for that yet. I took a huge step backwards and stumbled down her porch step.

"So… umm… I want to kiss you right now but I'm not going to," I explained like an idiot.

"Okay," Ash laughed as I backed away even further down the footpath. I knew I was being weird, but thankfully she seemed to find it amusing.

"I just wanted you to know," I said, grinning at her from my safe zone three feet down the pavement, "it's not that I don't want to, because I really, reeeeally want to."

"Okay," she repeated with an amused smile.

"...but if I kiss you now then I won't be able to walk away," I said walking backwards down the road, "... and I want to do this properly, because I like you a lot Ashley Granger."

"I like you a lot too Nathan Stone."

"And I definitely want to be more than just friends," I said with a grin.

"Me too."

"Awesome," I shouted happily while she watched me with great amusement. She was so damn sexy that I was tempted to run back up there and snog her, but it was imperative that I left while I still had some semblance of self-control.

"Sweet dreams Ash, I'll see you tomorrow."

"See you tomorrow," she said with a wave. With a huge grin on my face, I leapt jubilantly off the curb and jogged down the empty road towards the tube station, amazed and proud that I'd managed to control myself.

- RYAN McPHERSON -

Ritchie's pick-me-up had helped clear my head somewhat, but I was still a post-peak mess. A happy post-peak mess, but a big McMess none-the-less. I was struggling to construct a coherent sentence, and for some reason my legs weren't functioning properly. Unfortunately for Ritch, that meant he was left to haul my munted arse out of the building.

"I love you man," I told him for about the fiftieth time that night. "Have I ever told you that?"

"About five minutes ago," he said with an amused laugh as he began hauling me down the stairs. "Seriously dude," Ritchie groaned as he heaved my malfunctioning body with all his might, "you really need to come and work-out with me and Stoner. You're getting a dad-bod."

"That's because I'm going to be a dad," I said as if it was breaking news.

"I know," he replied with a grunt, "but that doesn't mean you have to look like one."

"I beg to differ," I argued with pride. "I've worked long and hard on this dad-gut and I won't have you putting it down."

"Okay tubby," he teased maneuvering both of us out of the club. There was a mini-cab waiting at the taxi stand, so Ritchie guided me over to it and piled me into the back seat.

"He looks blotto," grumbled the driver to Ritchie.

"I've had a few," I said, ignoring the fact that he hadn't seen fit to talk to me directly.

"But mostly he's pinging off his head," Ritchie added unhelpfully.

"Is he likely to vomit?" the bloke asked gruffly, continuing to act as if I was deaf.

"Not likely," I said loudly to make a point.

"Not likely," Ritchie concurred with a shrug. "He might declare his undying love for you a few thousand times, but he won't spew."

Ritchie laughed but the cab driver didn't find it so funny.

"Look mate, you might find this hilarious," he snapped at Ritchie, "but this cab is my livelihood and I can't drive people around with a backseat full of upchuck." Fair play to the guy, he did have a point, but I needed to get home to my pregnant wife.

"I promise man, I won't chuck," I promised with my hand on my heart. "Cross my heart and hope to die."

"See," Ritchie said to the driver in my defence.

"I love you Ritchie," I repeated with a heavy slur. "You're the best Australian I know."

"I'm the only Australian you know," he retorted with a laugh.

"That's true," I agreed with a nod as I noticed the feel of the seat under my hand. "Oh wow, have you felt this seat?" I asked the driver in amazement as I rubbed the leather. "It feels amazing."

Ritchie shook his head at me. "Shhh," he hissed.

"No way," barked the driver. "Get him out."

"Honestly mate, he'll be good as gold," Ritch assured the guy.

"It was just an eccy," I called from the backseat.

"Hmm," grumbled the driver.

"And some LSD," I added with a childish giggle. The driver shook his head.

"What if he pays you upfront?" Ritchie asked.

"Sure, but it still won't cover the cleaning costs if he does chuck," the guy said grumpily. Geez he knew how to drive a hard bargain.

"Okay, so how about I throw in an extra fifty quid?" I piped-up indignantly.

"Yeah okay," he nodded in agreement.

"Great! Thank you," I told him appreciatively. "So how much to Kensington?"

"Twenty quid."

"Fine," I nodded.

"See ya tomorrow Ryza," Ritchie said, patting me on the back before turning to the driver. "Get him home safely, his wife is pregnant." Ritchie slammed the door shut, and I handed £70 over to the entrepreneurial cab driver.

"So, what's your actual address mate?"

"It's Newton Court, just off Kensington Church Street. Cheers."

"That's funny. I've already dropped another couple off there tonight," the cab driver said.

"Yeah, that is funny," I replied, feeling time start to slip away from me. Damn those pills.

"So, you've got a kid on the way huh? Was this a last hurrah?"

I was usually up for a chat with a cabbie, but my brain was so fuzzy from the drugs and alcohol that I knew I wouldn't be able to keep track of an entire conversation. Time was ebbing and flowing in a very 'through the looking glass' sort of fashion, and it was hard to tell if my seconds were really seconds, or if they were actually minutes.

"Yeah. I guess it was," I agreed, half expecting the driver to turn into the Cheshire cat. "There won't be much time for partying once the baby comes along."

"Yeah, that's the truth," chuckled the cabbie, clearly having had first-hand experience, "and you can kiss goodbye to your sex life."

"Already have," I retorted with a chuckle. It could have been seconds, minutes or hours, but the next thing I knew, we were pulling into my street. "Just up here on the left thanks mate."

"Just up there?" he asked strangely, nodding towards our place.

"Yeah, cheers," I said as the cab came to a halt.

"Right," he nodded stiffly.

"Thanks mate," I said, opening the door. "I told you I wouldn't chuck." The driver laughed and handed back my extra £50 as I climbed unsteadily out of his unsullied taxi. I was glad to be home.

"Hey mate?" he called through the window.

I turned back curiously. "Yeah?"

"Ummm… take care yeah?" he said, with what was possibly the most bizarre farewell I'd ever received from a cabbie.

"Will do," I answered with nod, "and you," I said, not looking where I was going. I tripped up the first step and crashed inelegantly against the door.

"Fuck," I swore, dusting down my trousers. I glanced back over my shoulder but thankfully the cab had already pulled away so no one had witnessed my inelegant moment. At least I still had my dignity. I fumbled for my keys and dropped them on the floor, giggling as I bent down to pick them up. Well… maybe not my dignity, but at least I was home.

- KAT McPHERSON -

I awoke with a startle, as I heard a bang in the kitchen. It was 11:45pm, so if that was Ryan, then he was home much earlier than I'd expected. Thank god I hadn't let Beau hang around.

"Ryan is that you?" I called warily from the safety of my bed.

"Yep," he replied loudly, followed closely by a clatter.

"Are you okay?" I asked, climbing out of bed nervously. I was reluctant to see Ryan. What if he could tell? Would he know just from looking at me that something wasn't right? How was I ever going to look him in the eyes after what I'd done? Even though I'd showered after Beau left I could still feel the stickiness between my thighs.

"Yeah," Ryan answered drunkenly, as he attempted to pour a glass of water from the jug. He saw me standing in the doorway and looked up with the water jug in his hand. "Sorry, I was just trying to…" he began to explain as the water glass over-flowed. "Ah fuck…" he swore, and began trying to mop up the water with one hand.

"You're a mess," I teased. "How much did you drink?"

"A bit of a lot," he replied drunkenly, waving the water jug and splashing more water onto the bench, "and something of tequila." It made no sense, but I got the gist of his meaning.

He recommenced pushing the water around the bench with the cloth but instead of cleaning it up, he was just making it worse.

"Oh my god," I sighed with a helpless chuckle. "Go and sit down babe. I'll make you a toasted sandwich. That should soak up some of the alcohol." I looked him up and down, "Or at least give you something to throw up."

"Thanks," he muttered as he stumbled to his feet, breathing toxic-levels of alcohol fumes into my face. "I love you."

"I love you too," I replied, patting him on the shoulder. The guilt weighed heavily on my conscience. Ryan stumbled over to the cushy sofa and flopped down in the exact spot where, only hours earlier, I'd had sex with my not-gay best friend. I cleared my throat to swallow down my guilt. "I suppose the tequila was Ricthie's idea?" I said trying to change the subject in my own mind. When there was no response, I peered into the lounge to see Ryan fast asleep on the sofa. I switched off the jaffle maker and watched my husband dozing peacefully. I rubbed my face to stave-off the tears I could feel forming.

What had I done? I was a total monster to cheat on my husband three months before I was due to have his baby. I had enjoyed the sex though, so was I actually remorseful, or was that the story I was telling myself to feel less of a shit-head?

I pulled out a blanket and gently laid it over Ryan. There was no point in disturbing him now. It was best to let him sleep because tomorrow was going to be a rough day in more ways than one. He rolled over and snuggled up into the blanket, sending tears of guilt streaming down my cheeks. I was filled with shame and regret. Just thinking about it made me cringe. What had I been thinking? How had I let that happen? I had to come clean in the morning. Maybe if I owned up to it, Ryan would forgive me, and we'd be able to move on. Or perhaps that was wishful thinking.

- *Chapter 6* -

THE EYE OF THE STORM

- ASHLEY GRANGER -

It was just after 11pm when I walked in the door, and I couldn't wipe the smile off my face. I was crushing hard. My unexpected date with Nathan had turned out to be one of the best nights of my life. The fact that he'd decided not to come in actually made me fancy him even more. How could this sweet guy ever have been a player?

I sang the whole time I got ready for bed, and my smile widened when my phone buzzed with a text from the man in question.

'Best date ever' it said, followed by a giphy of Chuck Norris giving a thumbs up, with the caption "CHUCK NORRIS APPROVES". I laughed out loud (literally) and tapped my response.

'So now you're stealing my identity to approve your own date?', then added the shrugging lady and a winky face emoji at the end so he knew I was teasing.

'Haha. You've finally accepted Chucky! [hands in the air emoji]'

'Not exactly' I replied, and went into the bathroom to clean my teeth while I devised my next response. I was way out of practice with text flirting and I wasn't entirely sure whether I was coming off as funny and witty, or needy and lame.

Still lacking a sufficiently alluring response, I was relieved to see that there was already a message waiting for me when I got back to my bedroom. I unlocked my phone excitedly, but was paralysed with fear as I read the chilling words on the screen.

"Throw the Stone or he'll get crushed." Adrenalin flooded my body at the sight of the text and , without thinking, I deleted it and blocked the sender as if that would make the problem go away.

My heart was pounding. There was only one person in the world who would have sent that text. But how was that possible? Dominic couldn't have been sending a text from prison, so what did that mean? Did he have someone following me? Maybe he'd issued a hit on me when he realised that I was back in London. Was Nathan really in danger or was it an empty threat?

What the actual fuck was happening?

- NATHAN STONE -

I was happy to see a message from Ashley when I exited Notting Hill Station. Our date had been the most fun I'd ever had with a woman and we hadn't even had sex. I was starting to believe that Ritchie was right. I was falling in love.

'Are you okay?' Ash's text said. I cocked my head quizzically. That wasn't quite what I'd been hoping to read, but maybe she just wanted to know that I got home safely.

'I'm fine. Nearly home. Thanks for an amazing date.' I waited to see if the little grey dots would pulsate, but there was no response. Perhaps she'd fallen asleep. It was getting late after all. I shoved my phone back into my pocket and enjoyed the walk home in the night air. When I arrived at my building, the same ginger tabby was sitting on the doorstep.

"What are you doing here so late? I thought you had the morning shift," I asked the cat as if it was a person. The fleabag meowed and stared up at me feebly, looking scrawny and scared.

"Don't tell me you sleep out here?!" I asked, appalled that the flea-carrying feline had nowhere to go. I sighed loudly, knowing that I was going to regret what I was about to do. I stepped over the cat to unlock the front door, and stuck my head inside to make sure no one was around. Thankfully it was late enough that the doorman was off-duty. I stood back and let the cat inside the foyer.

"Just hide somewhere and don't tell anyone it was me who let you in," I ordered the cat, as if he was going to report me for aiding and abetting his trespassing crime. Fleabag prowled cautiously into the building, and sniffed around. "'Night Fleabag," I said, pressing the lift button. He followed me and began rubbing himself around my legs. "No, shoo cat. Go find a sleeping spot."

The cat ignored my instructions and, when the elevator doors slid open, he darted into the lift ahead of me.

"No, no. You can't come up. You sleep down here," I told Fleabag as he defiantly planted his bottom. "Seriously cat, get out of there before someone sees you." Fleabag didn't move. "Come on. Get out of there mate. The lobby is really warm I promise." As expected, my good deed was beginning to backfire. The cat clearly had no intention of moving. I stared down at it, debating my options, when I heard the front buzzer ring.

"Shit," I swore, peering over at the security monitor to see Stacy fumbling through her handbag on the other side of the big, wooden door. Stacy was the last person I wanted to see at that moment. Partly due to the cat, but mostly because I didn't want to put my new-found commitment to Ashley to the test. I'd managed to tame my over-zealous libido earlier on, but I wasn't confident that I would survive an onslaught from the Queen of Seduction in my fragile state. I looked up at the screen again as Stacy brandished her keys triumphantly.

"You win. Let's go," I told the cat as I jumped into the lift, madly pressing the 'close doors' button. Thankfully the doors slid shut before Stacy saw us. Fleabag meowed happily, weaving himself around my legs again.

"You're a cheeky little fucker, you know that?"

- ASHLEY GRANGER -

How could Dominic have tracked me down? Maybe Jock hadn't managed to remove the spyware after all.

"Jock," I mumbled, glancing at the clock. It was almost midnight, way too late to call him… but I needed to try. I had so many questions swirling through my brain, and he was the only person who would be able to answer them.

I pulled up his number in my phone and quickly dialled him before I chickened out. What the hell was I doing calling a complete stranger at midnight to ask questions about my stalker problem? The guy was going to think I was insane.

"Aye?" he said in his husky Scottish accent.

"H-hi Jock, its Kesha's friend Ashley, from the shop the other day. Sorry to call so late," I blurted, feeling like a total idiot.

"Ashley, hi," he replied with a smile in his voice. "Not a problem at all, I was awake anyway. Are you okay?"

"I think so. Oh god, is it weird that I called you? Yes… it is weird that I called, I'm so sorry. I don't know what I was thinking," I babbled like an airhead, instantly regretting making my midnight call.

"Ashley, no it's fine," Jock chuckled at the other end of the line.

"Are you sure?" I asked with embarrassment. I was acting like a total psycho.

"Aye, I'm sure," he said adamantly. "What's going on? Are you okay?"

"I just umm… something just happened, so I was hoping to ask you a few questions about this app thing that you found," I told him, feeling the weight of my worry unfold. "I haven't told anyone about the phone stalking situation and I really wanted to speak to someone who wasn't going to freak out on me."

"Sure," he replied gently. "What happened?" Jock was calm and steady, and it made me feel safer just having him at the other end of the line.

"He sent a text," I breathed quietly. "Well, someone sent a text. Obviously, it can't be from him because he's in jail, so…"

"So, perhaps someone sent it for him," Jock said, finishing my sentence.

"Yeah," I agreed, taking a deep breath to calm my rising panic. I couldn't believe that I was dealing with Dom again three years later and the more I talked about it, the more real it felt.

"Okay," he said. I heard the rustling of covers as if he was sitting up in his bed. "So he obviously thought to pull your number from the phone while he had access to it. Did you block the number?"

"I did…"

"But?" he prompted, correctly interpreting my unfinished sentence.

"He knew who I'd been with, and he sent the text once I was alone," I answered with a huge lump in my throat. It was sickening to admit that Dom might actually be back in my life again.

"Sounds like he does have eyes on you then."

"It seems that way," I sighed. "You said the app was able to access my microphone, what did you mean by that exactly?"

Jock switched into IT-mode. "Well, he could have logged in and activated your microphone at any time. It works in the same way as if you'd called him. He'd be able to hear anything in close proximity to the receiver."

"Which explains the random glowing," I said, realising that Dom had probably heard my entire conversation with Nathan that night at Jubilee Park.

"Aye. The phone would have glowed any time he connected to the app," Jock confirmed, switching back into cop-mode. "Ashley, I really think you should consider getting a Restraining Order against this guy. I know you said he's in jail, but the courts would still award you protection if you have evidence of reasonable cause for fear."

"But I don't have any evidence," I replied flatly, realising that my hasty reaction might have ruined my chances of getting a Restraining Order.

"You have a text message," he reminded me.

"But I don't," I admitted with tears stabbing at the back of my eyes. "I freaked out and deleted it."

"Okay," Jock said coolly, "but you blocked the number, so that means it'll still be in your phone records. We could pull it and trace it. It might not lead to much but it's worth a shot."

"That could work," I agreed hopefully, knowing that it would be a long shot. Dom was too clever to get caught-out on something like that. He would have had one of his guys buy the phone in a false name with cash.

"Plus, I've still got the guys looking into that app download, so we might even end up with an IP address or account ID," Jock said hopefully.

"Thanks for all your help Jock I really…" I trailed off as the tears finally spilled over. I swallowed hard to try and stem the flow, but it was too late, the sobs escaped me before I could stop them.

"Oh hey… you're okay. I'll keep you safe, I promise," Jock consoled me from the other end of the line. "Do you want me to come over?"

I froze. I wanted to say yes, but I hardly knew the guy, and I suspected that accepting his offer would send him the wrong message.

"Umm…" I mumbled unsurely.

"Sorry, I didn't mean for that to sound sleazy," he apologised quickly. "I just thought you might not want to be alone."

"No, that's fine," I said with a slight blush. "I appreciate the thought."

"No pressure, but the offer is there if you want it." The big question was… did I want it? The person I really wanted there was Nathan, but if Dom had someone watching me then Nathan could be in danger, and I didn't want to put him in harm's way. All I knew was that I didn't want to be on my own.

- NATHAN STONE -

When Fleabag and I arrived at my floor, the cat stuck so closely to me that I almost kicked him three times in the short distance between the lift and my door. I stopped to pull the keys out of my pocket, and Fleabag sat on my feet watching me intently.

"Wouldn't you rather hang out with someone else?" I asked him, as I jiggled my keys in the lock. I couldn't understand why the stray was so enamoured with me. I hated cats as a general rule.

I let Fleabag explore my house while I grabbed a drink from the fridge, and checked my phone again. Still no response from Ashley. I knew I was being needy about wanting her to text back, but I'd never had so much non-naked fun with a woman before. Ashley Granger had changed the game completely.

I cracked my beer and leaned against the bench, when my phone buzzed in my pocket. My chest pounded with excitement, until I saw what awaited me. Instead of a text from Ash, it was a text about her. My jaw dropped, as I stared at the picture on my screen. An anonymous person had sent me a photo of Ashley hugging a big ginger bloke outside of her apartment building.

"What the fuck?" I muttered, curious as to why someone had sent me the picture and what the point of it was. I could see that the mysterious sender was still typing something, so I waited to see what they had to say about the picture.

'Do you know what your girlfriend is doing right now?' said the words on my screen. My heart did one big loud thump in my chest, but I wasn't sure whether it was due to the fact that they'd called Ashley my 'girlfriend' or the possibility that she was shagging a guy who looked a lot like Prince Harry on 'roids.

Was the picture really from tonight? Why did this person think Ashley was my girlfriend? Most importantly... why were they taking photos of her in the middle of the night?

'Who is this?' I typed, ignoring all of the other questions that I'd rather have had answers to.

'A friend,' was the response.

'When did you take this?' I asked, unable to help myself.

'Ten minutes ago.'

My heart thudded again. Had Ashley lined up another guy after our date?

'How did you get my number and why are you at her house?' I tapped out quickly, wanting to ask all of the questions. For a moment the curser flashed as if I was going to get a response but then the number disappeared from my phone. The sender had blocked me.

"Fuck." What the fuck was this all about?

I studied the photo again. Who was the guy in the picture, and why was he at Ashley's house so late at night? Was I being played?

The cat wandered up and mewed at me.

"I think the player has been played Fleabag," I said, jumping off the bench to fix myself something stronger than a beer, "which sucks because I really like her." I grabbed a good bottle of Scotch from my liquor cabinet and snorted at the irony of the situation.

"Karma's a bitch huh?" Fleabag stared at me blankly. "I've spent my adult life trying to remain detached from women and the only one I've ever wanted to attach myself to, appears to be attaching herself to someone else." I cracked the Scotch and took a swig straight from the bottle, choking as the warm liquid burnt my throat.

"You want some?" I asked, slushing the bottle towards the cat. He didn't seem interested, so I took another swig, then flopped on the couch with the TV remote in one hand and the bottle of Scotch in the other. "You've got the right idea man," I told Fleabag. "Free and single and no one to answer to. No ties, no responsibilities, no owner. Just you." I looked down at him as he curled up at my feet. "I don't know why I bothered wanting anything more than that." Gulping back another few mouthfuls straight from the bottle, I flicked through the crappy television channels. Nothing was on.

"Forty-eight channels and it's all shit," I declared with frustration as I scanned through the guide. "Fuck this, I'm not going to sit at home and get drunk," I told Fleabag. "I'm going to find out what the fuck is going on."

The cat looked at me like I was insane…which I clearly was, given that I was conversing with a cat.

- ASHLEY GRANGER -

It had been an intense evening, but I hadn't realised exactly how wound-up I was until the moment I opened my front door to see Jock's handsome face smiling at me. My whole body immediately relaxed.

"Hi," I breathed with relief, giving him an awkward hug.

"You okay?" he asked looking sexily disheveled.

"I am now."

Jock smiled kindly, and then looked over his shoulder and nodded out to the street.

"I've done a quick sweep of the perimeter, but I didn't find anything."

"Thank you."

"Ashley," Jock said grimly, "if someone's watching you, then they're probably in one of these other buildings."

"But that would be impossible to narrow down."

"Not impossible, just unlikely."

My heart pounded.

"I can't believe this is happening."

Jock squeezed my arms reassuringly. "Let's get inside, huh?"

"Yeah." I nodded and stepped back from the door. "Thanks for coming over here Jock."

"My pleasure," he said nonchalantly, as I closed the door behind him. I directed Jock up the stairs, and suddenly felt quite embarrassed about having him there in the middle of the night. "Nice place," he said when I showed him into my apartment.

"Thanks. It pretty basic, but it's home." I ran my hands through my hair, knowing that I probably looked a complete mess.

Jock shrugged out of his hoodie and slung it over the back of the couch. I faltered at the sight of his broad shoulders. His tight T-shirt hugged his body like a second skin, and I could clearly see the outline of his rugby player muscles almost bursting out from underneath the fabric. I stared open-mouthed, trying desperately to think of something cool to say. Jock shoved his hands in his pockets.

"You look exhausted, why don't you go get some sleep?"

"Oh," I said, snapping out of my trance, "but you just got here. I can't disappear off to bed after you've trekked all the way across town."

"Yes, you can. I'm here to make you feel safe," he replied matter-of-factly. "You sleep, and I'll hang out on the couch. Consider me your own personal security guard."

I mulled it over for a minute. I did need sleep, but I was scared of what my dreams would bring.

"I might hang out here with you for a bit if that's okay?"

"Absolutely," Jock said with a smile. "Shall we see what's on telly?"

"Sure" I agreed, grabbing the remote control while he got comfortable on my little sofa. Jock wriggled around, trying to settle his large frame into the tiny couch. It was like watching Gulliver attempting to squeeze himself into Lilliput Manor. I flicked on the TV, and waited for Jock to position himself before I sat down next to him. With his broad shoulders it, was a tight fit, so I was practically sitting on top of him. He rested his giant arm on the back of the sofa and I found myself snuggling into him. Although my inner feminist was most displeased, Jock was so big and confident that it was hard not to feel safe with him around.

"I bet there's heaps of quality viewing at this time of night," he joked as I handed him the remote. I didn't want to be in charge of the channels. I didn't want to be in charge of anything. In fact, I didn't want to think at all. I just wanted to cuddle into him and not think. Jock flicked through a million home shopping infomercials, until the familiar theme tune of Sex and the City floated out of the TV. "That'll do," he said, balancing the remote on the arm of the couch.

"You like Sex and the City?" I asked with amusement.

He grinned and nodded, "I find it very educational."

I let my head fall against Jock's chest, and he rested his hand on my shoulder as the SATC girls chatted in detail about Sam's latest conquest. I must have drifted off because the next thing I knew, I was back in Twickenham, re-living the night that Dom had hunted me down.

I'd jumped on the first train that had arrived at the station and figured that Twickenham was probably a fairly safe distance. Had I known Dom would come after me I would have kept going all the way to Reading, but I'd been too naïve to pre-empt the lengths he'd go to. He found me in a busy little pub not far from the station, where I'd stopped to plan my next move. I'd only been in the pub for about twenty minutes when I saw Dominic walk through the door.

"Oh my god," I breathed, wondering if I was hallucinating. How had he found me? I'd fled the house when he'd gone out to the gym, so I'd had at least an hour headstart on him. How had he managed to get there so quickly, and more importantly... how had he known where I was?

My heart pounded as I sat motionless like a deer in headlights. I watched and waited for the moment to unfold, hoping that he hadn't seen me, yet knowing that I was caught.

Dom's eyes quickly fastened on mine and he grinned. A cold wave of fear washed over me as he prowled his way through the crowd. He moved with such grace and swagger that no-one would have suspected the impending attack... not even me. I knew without a doubt that he hadn't come to make amends, but I had nowhere to go. I was trapped in a cosy corner of this busy little pub on the edge of Greater London.

Dom descended on me so swiftly that I didn't notice the knife in his hand until he'd grabbed me by the waist in a possessive grasp. The smile on his face belied the menace in his eyes.

"Babe," he said cheerfully for the benefit of any possible witnesses. He kissed me on the cheek and leaned into my ear as if he was whispering sweet nothings. "No one leaves me Princess."

I attempted to pull away from him, but it was too late. I felt the cold, hard blade plunge into my ribs before I had a chance to react. The force of the puncture took the remaining breath out of my lungs, and my legs began to collapse beneath me. Dom scooped me up, threw my jacket over the bleeding wound, and carried me effortlessly out of the pub as if he was being chivalrous.

"You're mine Ashley," he hissed quietly. "You belong to me. Did you honestly think I'd let you run away?" he said with a fake smile.

I was in so much pain that I couldn't speak or put up a fight. Any onlookers would have assumed that I was drunk, and that he was taking me home. He swept me out into the deserted carpark and threw me unceremoniously into the back seat of his car. I could feel my voice beginning to return, so I cried out for help.

"Screaming won't get you anywhere Princess," Dom laughed, as he set to work tying his gym towel tightly around my mouth to stifle my screams. Regardless of his words, I screamed through the sweaty towel while Dom used his weight belt to restrain my hands. It was useless. There was no one around to hear me. The carpark was empty, and I was at the mercy of the psychotic man I'd once called my boyfriend.

"You know, you're actually quite sexy when you're scared," he said, as he closed the car door and climbed into the backseat on top of me. I was under no illusion as to what was coming next, so I fought hard to get away despite the searing pain in my ribs.

Unfortunately, Dominic was too strong for me. He laughed and pushed me back down to the seat with ease, pressing his finger against my wound. I howled in agony through the towel as tears streamed from my eyes.

"That cut is pretty deep Ash," he informed me, pinning me down with one hand as he adjusted his gym shorts with the other. "The more you struggle, the more it will bleed," he grinned, pulling out his cock and casually spreading my legs apart with his knees. I was completely helpless. There was nothing I could do to stop the impending rape. My heart pounded in my chest and Dom chuckled as I desperately tried to plead with him through the dirty towel.

"Please don't," I cried from under my gag, silently cursing myself for wearing a dress and making it so easy for him.

"I like you when you're begging," he laughed, sliding the crotch of my undies over to one side and pinning them hard against my thigh with his thumb. I attempted one final scream, but it achieved nothing.

"Don't fight it Princess, you're going to love it."

"No!" I shouted, sitting up abruptly as my head smashed against something hard.

"Fuck," I heard a male voice splutter. I was so disoriented that it took me a moment to figure out where I was and who the voice belonged to. I peered up at Jock who was grasping his face.

"Oh my god," I squeaked in horror at the sight of his bloodied nose. "Are you okay?"

"I'm fine," Jock said in a nasal voice. I grabbed a handful of tissues and shoved them under his nose.

"I'm so sorry."

"Don't be sorry. I'm fine. It's not broken," he replied with a smile. He dabbed at his nose with the tissues and then put the bloodied wad down as if nothing had happened. "Are you okay?" he asked, like I hadn't just head-butted him in the face.

I breathed deeply. "I was having a nightmare – more like a memory really."

"You're safe now," he said cupping my face in his hands. "I'm here and I won't let anything happen to you." My chest flooded with affection for the giant man. He was a complete stranger and yet I felt so safe and at ease with him. Our lips were only inches apart and without thinking, I tilted my head closer to his. Part of me wanted to kiss him, but there was something holding me back. Or, more to the point, someone.

I glanced at Jock's soft lips. "I was on a date tonight," I blurted in a whisper, feeling like I was betraying Nathan by being so close to another man.

"Oh," he said, his breath warm on my lips. "And was it a good date?" he asked, matching my hushed tone as the corner of his mouth turned up in a curious smile.

"Yeah, it was a really good date actually," I answered with a guilty nod.

"Okay," Jock said, sliding his hands away from my face. "So is this is your way of telling me that you're not available?"

"I guess it is," I replied, shifting away from him. "I'm really sorry Jock. I've led you on and there's no excuse for that."

"It's fine Ashley," he said, interlocking his strong hands over the back of his neck. "I didn't come here with an ulterior motive, you don't owe me anything."

"But I feel like I do," I said, amazed at how cool he was about it. "I totally understand if you hate me."

Jock laughed loudly. "Why would I hate you? I'm not going to pretend that I'm not disappointed, but I didn't come here for that. I just came here to help." I breathed a sigh of relief.

"Kesha's right. You are ridiculously perfect."

"Yes, I am," he joked with a grin. "So, why don't you tell me all about this date then. It must have been pretty amazing to trump my midnight security service."

- NATHAN STONE -

I grabbed my car keys and marched down to the garage. I knew the whiskey had probably put me over the limit, but I didn't care. I had to know what was going on.

I jumped into my Beemer and, as I pulled out through the security gates, I noticed a black Audi sedan following me up the street. It wasn't particularly unusual in itself, but I turned a couple of corners and the dark-tinted sedan was still tailing me. I figured I was being paranoid, but I was convinced it was an undercover cop, so I drove as responsibly as humanly possible, keeping within the speed limits and indicating at every turn. I didn't want to give them any reason to flag me down.

After ten minutes, I glanced into my review mirror and the car had gone. I assumed I'd either evaded them or they'd lost interest, but a few streets away from Ashley's place, they reappeared again out of a back street. A sinking feeling washed over me. Was I being tailed?

I turned into Ashley's street, peering in my rear-view mirror to see if the Audi would follow but it kept driving straight on. With a sigh of relief, I pulled into the parking bays across the street from Ashley's building and could see that there were still lights on in her flat. I checked my phone. She still hadn't responded to my last text, but she was clearly awake. I looked at the clock, 1:06am. I couldn't knock on her door at this hour, she'd think I was a psycho.

I sat and weighed up my options, when the street was lit up like a stadium. I squinted against the blinding headlights which were barrelling towards me at an alarming rate. The speeding car was hurtling straight for me, so I opened my door to jump clear of the impending accident, but it was too late. I heard the smash of glass, the crunching of metal, and a scream that seemed to be coming from my own mouth.

The world spun around me. I felt a searing pain in my leg and stinging all over my face, as glass shattered everywhere. Agonising pain wracked my entire body, and I felt like I was being squeezed in a vice, until everything turned fuzzy. I tried to fight against the blackness, but I was tired, cold and dizzy. I had lost control over my body, and I felt my grip on reality slipping, as I finally gave in to the pain. I slipped out of reality and into a world of ferocious agony. Nothing felt real, except for the pain. The pain was very, very real.

- ASHLEY GRANGER -

Jock and I were sitting at the kitchen table having a cuppa when we heard a massive crash outside. We both jumped up and ran to the window where we saw a white car flipped upside down in the middle of the road, as a black one sped away down the street.

"Holy shit," I breathed in shock.

"Call 999," Jock instructed me, as he immediately sprang into action. I grabbed my phone and trailed barefoot behind him as he ran out into the hall at the speed of light. He leapt over the railing onto the flight of stairs below, while I dialled 999 and ran down the stairs the normal way. I emerged onto the front steps to see Jock peering inside the crushed-up car, checking for any survivors.

"There's a guy in here!" he shouted over his shoulder. "He's alive but unconscious and pretty badly injured. Are the paramedics on the way?" I nodded silently and relayed all the information to the operator at the other end of the line, as sparks started crackling on the underside of the car. "I've got to get him out," Jock called as some of the other residents started spilling out on to the street.

I edged as close as I could, without cutting my bare feet on the debris that was scattered all over the road. One guy ran over to help Jock pull the driver free of the volatile wreckage, but I was at the wrong angle to see what was going on.

"The ambulance is on the way," I called to Jock as he crawled into the wreckage.

"His leg is stuck under the dash," my neighbour told Jock.

"I'll see if I can get it free," Jock said, wriggling his way further into the mangled car to help the trapped man. "Hold that up while I pull him out," I heard Jock instruct the other man. "Got him," called Jock. Moments later he emerged from the wreckage with the unconscious driver in his arms, and the world stopped for a split second as I saw the bloodied face of the man. Time decelerated into slow motion.

"Nathan!" I heard myself scream his name like a banshee, as I sprinted through the broken glass to get to him. The sound of my own voice was muffled by an intense ringing in my ears, and my vision was blurred by sheets of heavy tears that were streaming down my face. I wasn't thinking. I was being driven forward by a primal force inside me.

"Ash no!" Jock yelled loudly as my bare feet crunched over the shattered pieces of Nathan's crumpled car. I couldn't feel anything besides fear, as I ran full-pelt towards them. I came to an abrupt halt when someone grabbed me tightly around the waist from behind, and lifted me off the ground.

"Nathan!" I screamed again, kicking my feet desperately as the faceless person behind me tried to carry me to safety.

"Ash stay there," Jock shouted desperately, as he carried Nathan out of the danger zone. I heard sirens in the distance, and bright lights began flashing all around us, making the whole scene feel even more surreal than it already was. I sobbed uncontrollably as I watched people buzz frantically around Nathan, who was bloodied and lifeless. I felt like I was in a nightmare and there was nothing I could do but watch it unfold.

The ambulance doors opened and, against my will, whoever had hold of me heaved me into the back of it. I fought against the faceless arms.

"I don't need to be in here," I protested, struggling against the man. "I just need to know if Nathan is okay."

Jock helped the paramedics hoist Nathan up onto the stretcher next to me. He gave them all the details, with the confidence of a man who'd dealt with many a crisis. Seeing the concerned looks on their faces, I was starting to worry that I might actually lose Nathan.

"Ashley, I need you to calm down and let them look at your feet okay?" Jock said coolly. "You keep an eye on Nathan. I'll lock up your place and meet you at the hospital." I nodded obediently, and the ambulance doors slammed shut with an ominous thud.

The journey was a blur. The only image that was ingrained in my mind was the sight of Nathan's damaged, broken face, which was turning a strange shade of grey under the splatters of bright red blood. Sirens blared, and the paramedics scrambled around us, but all I could concentrate on was Nathan. Maybe, if I wished hard enough, he would be okay.

When we pulled into Accident & Emergency, the paramedics bundled me out of the ambulance and into a wheelchair so that they could transfer Nathan onto a hospital gurney. One of the paramedics gave the waiting doctors a run-down of his condition, and then they whizzed him off down a stark corridor out of view.

"Where are they taking him?" I asked desperately. "Can I go with him?"

"I'm sorry honey, he's going into surgery," said one of the triage doctors, "and we need to get these sorted out," she added, nodding towards my roughly bandaged feet. "I hear you've done some pretty nasty damage to yourself."
I didn't argue. I had nothing left in me. With the adrenalin wearing off, my whole body suddenly felt drained. My head was dizzy, and my limbs were weak. She wheeled me through a different set of doors and conferred with another doctor.

"She's sliced her feet nearly to the bone. There's still a lot of glass and debris in there so she'll need the wound flushed," she told the other doctor. I tuned out to what they were saying. I could finally feel the pain in my feet, and it was beginning to radiate up my legs. For the first time since I'd seen Jock pull Nathan from the wreckage, it finally occurred to me that I might have done myself some serious damage.

- *Chapter 7* -

THE SHOWDOWN

- RYAN McPHERSON -

I woke myself up snoring, and groaned in pain from the crink in my neck. Feeling disoriented, I studied the room to figure out where I was. Oh, bloody hell, I'd passed out on the couch, but at least I'd made it home. I was quite impressed that I'd even got that far. I looked around the house to get a grasp of the time. It was still dark so perhaps I hadn't actually been passed out for that long. I sat up slowly to get a look at the clock, and the whole room spun around me.

"Ooooh," I muttered to myself, trying to focus on something. Anything. Once the spinning had subsided, I squinted to see the time. Two a.m. I climbed to my feet and groggily shuffled into the bedroom to join Kat in bed.

"Ryan?" she asked sleepily as I climbed in next to her.

"Yeah, sorry babe. Go back to sleep," I told her, resting my pounding head on the pillow beside her.

"I can't. I have to tell you something," she whispered, wriggling closer.

"Can it wait until the morning?"

"Not really."

"Okay," I agreed, as my tired eyes drifted closed again.

"I slept with Beau," she whispered. I chuckled sleepily, assuming she meant years ago.

"Before he realised he was gay?" I teased, snuggling into the cosy duvet.

"Tonight," Kat answered bluntly, sobering me up instantly.

"What?" My eyes flew open and I sat bolt upright. "But Beau's gay." The information was not computing. She was pulling my leg, right? This had to be some sort of prank.

"No. He's not," she said shamefully as a tear rolled down her cheek. Holy shit, she was serious. I rubbed my face in shock, as I tried to absorb what she was telling me. I was feeling a million emotions at once and they were rotating so quickly, I couldn't settle on one. Furious and confused both appeared repeatedly.

"I don't understand," I muttered in shock, more to myself than to her.

"It just kind of happened," Kat said pathetically, attempting to touch me.

"You're fucking serious aren't you?"

"I'm sorry. It was an accident." My rage finally boiled over and I jumped backwards out of the bed to get as far away from her as possible.

"It was an accident?!" I shouted incredulously. "An accident?" I repeated, dumbfounded by both her stupidity and her lame explanation. Was she fucking kidding me? "So you just accidentally fell onto his dick?"

"No, I just… I've been feeling really awful about myself and you said you didn't want to have sex with me-"

"You're blaming this on me?!" I thundered with anger, not letting her finish her so-called explanation. "You fucked a gay man three months before you're due to have my baby, and you're blaming it on me?"

"Beau's not gay," Kat replied quietly. No, she did not just say that.

"Clearly not," I seethed angrily, too furious to shout. "How could you?"

"Please Ryan. We can work through this. Please," Kat pleaded with tears in her eyes. I fell silent for a moment as I tried to calm myself. Losing my shit wouldn't solve anything. I needed to be clear headed. "I love you Ryan." she spluttered desperately, rolling out of the bed to reach for my hand.

"Get out of my sight," I snapped, unable to look at her any longer. How dare she?

"But it's the middle of the night," Kat blurted in shock.

"You're right," I agreed. I couldn't send my heavily pregnant wife out on the street at two in the morning, no matter how much I hated her. "I'll leave." I stormed out of the room and grabbed my jacket off the couch.

"Please don't go Ryan," she begged as I marched towards the door. "If you leave now, we might never get through this," she pleaded, following me into the lounge room like a lost puppy dog.

"If I stay, we'll be over before the sun's up," I snapped before storming out the door. If I had to look at her for one more second our marriage would have no chance of surviving.

- KAT McPHERSON -

As Ryan slammed the door, my whole world crumbled around me. I burst into tears and sank hopelessly to the floor. Was he ever going to come back or would that be the last time I saw my husband? What had I done? What was going to happen to us? How was I going to get through this? Would he be with me for the birth? Would he be there to meet our baby? Would he want to be a part of our lives? What if he didn't? How would I raise our child without him?

The questions kept swirling in my head as I unceremoniously wept on the floor like a huge, blubbery whale. I knew I couldn't sit there all night, but I had no idea what to do next. If I got up off the floor, then I'd have to face the reality of my epic mistake, so I slumped on the wooden floorboards and gave in to my sorrow.

I had no idea how long I'd been there, but my legs had gone numb, and my bladder was madly protesting. I needed to get off the floor. That would be my first step. All I had to do was get up off the floor and go to the toilet. That was doable. I could do that. I grasped the arm of the sofa and ungracefully hoisted myself up. I was on my feet. Step one was successfully completed. Time for step two: the toilet.

I wiped my snotty nose with the back of my hand and took a deep breath as

I forced one foot in front of the other, all the way to the bathroom. I plonked myself down on the loo and cried as I peed. I'd fucked everything up. I'd made a stupid, selfish decision and I might never be able to fix what I'd broken.

I buried my face in my hands and sobbed loudly, until long after I'd finished my wee. What was I supposed to do next? I needed another step. Actually… I needed someone to tell me what to do.

"Rosie," I muttered out loud. It was a ridiculous time to call, but I needed my sister, so I hauled myself into the bedroom, and grabbed my phone from the nightstand, quickly dialling Rosie's number. "Please pick up," I begged as the phone rang.

"Kat?" Rosie said groggily.

"Rosie, I've done something really bad and I don't know how to fix it," I blurted, feeling the panic begin to rise in my chest. "I've fucked everything up. It's totally fucked and it's all my fault."

"Calm down kiddo," she cooed soothingly. "Take a deep breath and tell me what's happened."

"I cheated on Ryan." I was certainly not calm, and nor could I breathe, but explaining what happened had been surprisingly simple.

"Oh my god!" she replied with surprise. "So the baby isn't his?!"

"The baby is his. It was a little more recent than that."

"In the last 6 months recent?" Rosie clarified. I could hear the penny beginning to drop, so I took a deep breath and steeled myself.

"Tonight."

"Holy shit Kat, what were you thinking?" she asked with disappointment.

"I don't know Rosie, please don't lecture me," I begged pathetically. "I know I'm an awful person, I don't need your judgement, I just need your help. What do I do? How do I fix this?"

"Shit, I don't know Kat," she answered frankly. Oh god. Rose was my only hope so if she had no advice for me then I was totally fucked. There was no way I could tell Mum about this.

"I've made such a mess of things," I sighed sadly as we both fell silent.

"Yeah, well, promiscuity kinda runs in our family kid," she joked gently. "At least we know you're not adopted." I couldn't stop myself from laughing, even though it wasn't funny. As my laughter began, the floodgates opened and tears poured out of my eyes in some sort of dull hysteria. "Listen to me kiddo. Ryan's a good guy and he loves you… a lot. Maybe the best thing to do is just come up here and let it all blow over. Then, when he's calmed down, you might be able to fix it."

I processed her words and decided that her idea had merit. There was no way Ryan would be ready to face this yet, and I was officially on maternity leave so why not head back home to Framlingham for a while?

"Well…I've got three months to fix it, so I guess it's worth a try," I agreed, feeling slightly hopeful.

"I'll take tomorrow off and come down and get you in the morning."

"It is the morning."

"Yes, it is," she agreed, "so go the fuck back to sleep, and I'll see you after breakfast."

- RYAN McPHERSON -

My head was reeling, and I felt like I was floating outside of my body. I couldn't believe it. Like… I literally couldn't believe it. How could my heavily pregnant wife find herself accidentally having sex with another man? It just didn't compute. It was only a few weeks ago when she was worried I was going to leave her. Why would she go and fuck someone else? What had she been thinking?

I roamed the dark, quiet streets for a while, not knowing where to go. I couldn't go to Nathan's or Ashley's because, wherever they were, they would probably be together and I wasn't in the mood to see them loving on each other. Ritchie and Amy were the only other option, but they would probably be fucking.

What was I going to do? Not just in the immediate future, but long-term. I couldn't leave Kat three months before she was due to have our baby, but how could I possibly go back to her after what she'd done?

A vision of Kat fucking Beau flashed into my brain and my rage reignited with extra ferocity. I'd trusted that cocky American twat with my wife and he'd taken advantage of her. I was going to kill the fucker. I'd left my house in such a hurry that I'd forgotten to grab my phone and wallet, so it would to be a long trek to Beau's place, but it was doable.

I stormed purposefully across the south side of London and an hour later found myself standing out the front of Beau's terrace house. The cunt had ruined my marriage, so it was time for him to pay. I banged hard on the glossy white front door.

"Beau!" I raged loudly, not caring if I was disturbing the upper-class neighborhood. "Get out here you gutless prick," I shouted, continuing to bang on the door until it finally opened.

Beau stood in the doorway, half naked and completely unfazed by my drug-fuelled ranting. He ran his hand through his hair and leaned arrogantly against the door frame.

"I take it she told you then?" he asked calmly, almost as if he'd been expecting it.

"Of course she fucking told me. I'm her husband," I snapped aggressively, annoyed by his composure.

"Yeah, some husband you are," he snorted with disdain. "You let your wife hang out with another man and never once questioned it."

I shut my mouth immediately. Why hadn't I questioned it? Nathan had told me a million times that he thought Beau was straight, yet I hadn't heeded his words, nor thought to put any boundaries on Kat's friendship with him.

"We thought you were gay," I replied sheepishly.

"Then you weren't paying enough attention," he said, hooking his thumb into the pocket of his designer pyjama pants. "If you'd been paying attention to your wife, you would have seen it coming."

"You know nothing about me you Yankee prick," I growled, barely containing my urge to punch him, "and you know nothing about my wife."

"Well then I guess we have something else in common," he retorted with amusement, deliberately trying to rile me up.

"Who the fuck do you think you are?"

"I'm the man who sorted out your wife when you couldn't." I saw a flash of red and, before I'd even consciously thought about it, I'd swung my fist at Beau's pretty-boy face. "Fuck!" he cried in surprise, gripping his nose as I stood back and grinned in satisfaction.

"Stay away from my wife," I growled.

"You don't deserve Kat," Beau spluttered as he spat a mouth full of blood into the garden bed. "You don't even realise how good you've got it. If you'd looked after her properly in the first place she wouldn't have needed me," he added, re-aligning his nose. "I guess I should thank you really. She was a sensational fuck."

"Fuck you," I roared fiercely, and dove at him with the full force of my intoxicated body. I knew I was playing into his hands, but I was so furious I wasn't able to control myself.

This time he was ready for it, and he took a firm swing at my face as I hurtled towards him. His fist connected painfully with my cheekbone, and the punch shook my brain so hard that I was sent off balance. Already severely impeded by the remnants of the tequila, and various class A drugs in my system, I lost my footing and fell backwards onto the pavement, crashing to the ground with a thud. I gasped like a fish out of water as the wind was knocked out of me.

Beau stood over me, smirking like an arsehole while I waited breathlessly for him to punch me again. He bent down and grabbed the front of my shirt with his fist poised in the air. I stared at him wide-eyed, unable to do much else after the force of my fall. The dirty Yank looked me up and down with disgust and dropped his hand.

"You're not even worth it McPherson. You're pathetic," he drawled self-righteously, releasing his grip on the front of my crumpled shirt. I laid back against the concrete waiting for the air to return to my lungs. He was right. I was pathetic. I rolled over and groaned in pain as I felt my ribs twinge. "Go home and clean yourself up," Beau grunted with disdain, "you won't win your wife back like this."

"Don't act like you care about my marriage," I croaked, as I attempted to stand up. "You're the one who destroyed it."

"You're right. I don't care about your marriage," he admitted coldly, "but I do care about Kat and, if I win, I want it to be because I earned it, not because you were too pathetic to try. Now get the fuck off my doorstep, clean yourself up and fight for her properly."

- KAT McPHERSON -

I couldn't go back to sleep. Too much had happened. I had no way to get in touch with Ryan because he'd left his phone on the kitchen bench. I just had to give him some time to cool off. He would be back by daylight and then we'd sort out this whole mess, before Rosie even left Framlingham.

Inventing a whole host of unlikely scenarios in my head, made me feel better, but I knew I was fooling myself. There was no way of coming back from something like this. I really had turned into my mother after all.

I resigned myself to the inevitable and packed my bags with a constant stream of tears dripping from my chin. How had I let myself fuck things up so badly?

I had almost finished packing when I heard Ryan's phone ringing in the kitchen. Who would be calling at this time of the morning? Maybe it was Ryan. No, of course it wasn't. Why would he call his own phone? It was probably just Ritchie making sure that Ryan got home safely.

I hauled my arse up off the bed and began my long waddle towards the kitchen when the ringing stopped.

"Ugh," I grumbled, about to turn around and go back to the bedroom, as the phone started ringing again. I picked up his phone and looked at the screen. It was an unknown number. I hesitated for a moment, but something in my gut told me to answer it. "Hello?"

"Hi, I'm looking for Ryan McPherson," said an official sounding voice at the other end of the line.

"This is his wife," I said, reluctant to give any additional details to a stranger.

"I need to speak to your husband, is he there?"

"Can I ask who this is?" I asked warily.

"Sorry Mrs McPherson, my name is Adrian. I'm a registrar at King's College Hospital Emergency Department and we have your husband listed as the next of kin for one of our patients."

"Who? Has something happened to his parents?" I asked, feeling awfully guilty that I was somewhat excited by that prospect.

"I'm sorry, I really can't say," said Adrian, not sounding particularly sorry at all. "Is your husband there?"

"No, I'm afraid he left without his phone so I have no way of contacting him."

"Oh, I see," he said, mulling over his options. "Well, given that this is a critical matter and we haven't been able to contact the other next of kin…" I waited anxiously to hear who was in the Emergency Department. "We have a Mr Nathan Stone here in a critical condition, and we rather urgently need some details." The breath drained out of me.

"Nathan?" I squeaked. "What happened?"

"He was in a rather serious car accident."

"I'll find Ryan and we'll be there as soon as we can."

"Thanks Mrs McPherson," said Adrian, who gave me a list of things I needed to bring to the hospital. I jotted down his instructions, hung up Ryan's phone and dialled Ritchie's number. It rang out.

"Fuck," I swore, feeling completely helpless. What if Nathan didn't pull through this?

- RYAN McPHERSON -

After my fight with Beau, I'd wandered the streets aimlessly and had found myself standing outside of Ritchie's flat. I knocked softly on the door, feeling completely numb.What was happening to my life? How had it got to a point where Kat saw cheating as an option?

Ritchie peeked through the glass and then opened the door wearing nothing but boxer shorts. "Ryza?" he asked, scratching his bare chest. "What are you doing here man?"

"Kat fucked Beau," I said succinctly. How else would one explain showing up on a friend's doorstep at nearly four in the morning?

"Come in mate," he said, stepping back from the door to let me in.

"Thanks." In the light of his entry hall, Ritchie was able to see my bloodied, broken face.

"Holy fuck dude," Ritch blurted as he closed the door behind me. "What happened to your face?"

"Beau also fucked my face."

"Not literally I hope," Ritchie joked, trying to lighten the mood.

"That probably would have been preferable."

"You've had a big night, huh?" he said, patting me on the back as he guided me into the loungeroom.

"Ryza?" Amy asked as she came downstairs, wearing one of Ritchie's rugby shirts. "Is everything okay?" She cringed as she saw my damaged face, "Oh my god."

"Kat fucked Beau tonight," I repeated as if that was a sufficient response.

"What?" Amy asked. "That can't be right."

I shrugged, "She told me herself."

"I don't understand," Amy muttered.

"That makes two of us Aims," I agreed.

"We need drinks and an ice pack," she said, before promptly vanishing into the kitchen.

"Have a seat mate," Ritchie offered, leading me to the sofa. "So what are you gonna do?"

"I don't know," I admitted. "I can't stand the sight of her, but we're about to have a baby."

"Why don't you crash here for a while? You can have the guest room."

"Really?" I asked, as my eyes welled up with tears. Holy shit. I was going to cry.

"Of course," he nodded. "The room is all yours for as long as you need it."

I hugged him awkwardly across the sofa. "Thanks man,"

"Here," Amy said, returning with an icepack, a bottle of vodka and three shot glasses. Richie's eyes darted between Amy and the drinks.

"Err…coffee probably would have been more appropriate," he teased, as Aims handed me the icepack, and then proceeded to fill each glass.

"No," I shook my head and winced as the frosty icepack rubbed against my bruised cheek. "Vodka is perfect." I grabbed one of the shots with my spare hand and knocked it back, savouring the burn in my throat. It was a welcome distraction from the excruciating pain in my face and my heart. "I mean… how do you accidentally fuck someone?" I asked abruptly, waving my shot glass in the air. "Especially when you have a pregnant belly sticking out in front of you. And then she had the nerve to blame me for it. I mean what a fucking kick in the balls that was."

Ritchie and Amy exchanged worried looks and Amy patted my knee in reassurance.

"I don't know what to say mate," Ritch said sympathetically.

"Sorry guys, I shouldn't be laying all this on you. Kat's your friend too."

"It's fine Ryza. You need to get it off your chest," Amy said, pouring me another shot. A phone rang loudly on the kitchen counter and we all looked up in surprise. "That's mine," she said, handing me the bottle. I slugged back the half glass that she'd poured and then topped it up again. If it hadn't been someone else's vodka I would have just swigged it straight from the bottle.

Amy retrieved her phone and then looked over at me hesitantly. "It's Kat," she said with a grimace. "Should I answer it?"

"Doesn't bother me," I shrugged, feeling the effects of the vodka beginning to cloud my brain and dull the pain.

Ritchie nodded, "You should answer it."

Amy answered the call. "Kat," she said icily. "Yes he is," she said, glancing up at me. Kat was obviously talking at the other end, and Amy's face began to drop as she listened. "What?! When?!" She glanced between me and Ritchie with an indistinguishable expression, before nodding her head. "Okay, we'll meet you there," she said before hanging up.

"I'm not meeting her anywhere," I said stubbornly.

"Yes, you are. We're going to the hospital," Amy said, throwing Ritchie a T-shirt that had been draped over the radiator. "Get dressed."

"Is the baby coming?" I asked, as Amy kicked into action-mode.

"No," she said running towards the stairs, "Nathan's been in an accident."

Ritchie called an Uber, and we rushed down to the hospital to meet Kat. I felt hesitant about seeing my cheating pregnant wife so soon after her betrayal, but with Nathan's life hanging in the balance, our marital issues were irrelevant for the time being. I couldn't imagine the world without my best mate in it. Nath was arrogant, selfish and childish, but he was the closest thing I had to a brother, and losing him would be a burden that I wouldn't be able to bear. Nath and I had lived through our fair share of dramas and shenanigans over the years, but this was by far the worst. There was a distinct possibility that he wouldn't live through this one.

The Uber stopped outside the Emergency Department, and the three of us scrambled out and sprinted through the glass sliding doors.

"Hi, we're here for Nathan Stone," I told the nurse behind the desk, forgetting that I was sporting a black eye. The nurse eyed my damaged face.

"Sir do you need someone to take a look at that?"

"No, my face is fine, I just need to know if Nathan Stone is okay, and when I can see him," I said, wondering whether I'd ever see my best friend alive again.

"Okay, just one moment please," she replied, flipping through her folder.

Ritchie patted my shoulder, "We'll go sit with Kat. Are you okay here?"

"Yeah, I've got this," I nodded, patting him on the back. I tapped my fingers on the desk impatiently. "Is this going to take long?" I asked the nurse as politely as possible. "I really want to see him."

"I understand sir," she said with a sympathetic smile. "You're Ryan McPherson?"

"Yes."

"And you're his...?"

"Friend," I replied, trying to contain my frustration.

"We still haven't been able to get hold of his other next of kin, Gareth Hemsworth. Do you know how we might be able to get hold of him?"

"Yeah, I'll take care of that," I told her.

"Are there any parents we need to notify?"

"No, his mum's..." I paused, deciding that it was too hard to explain. "Never mind. Gareth is his... sort of dad so we'll be able to look after everything."

"Okay Mr McPherson," she tapped some things into her computer and then looked up at me. "It looks like your boyfriend is still in surgery, but I'll find out what I can for you."

"Oh, he's not my-"

"Ryan?" I heard someone say from behind me. I turned to see Ashley's mum, Mary, standing at the reception desk.

"Mrs Granger?" Seeing her, was like stepping back into the past. The last time I'd seen her was at Ashley's 30th birthday party, when Dom had cracked the shits and taken Ashley home before we'd even cut the cake. That was the night before she'd gone missing.

"Are you okay love?" she asked, inspecting my battered face.

"Oh, I'm fine. It looks worse than it feels," I said waving away her concerns for my health.

"It's great to see you again love," she said, giving me a tight hug. "I haven't seen you since..."

"For a long time," I said, saving her the trouble of re-living the memories of Ashley's Dominic days. Mary stepped back with her hands still on my shoulders.

"Ash said that you two are working together again. I'm so pleased you've reconnected."

"Yeah me too." I scratched my head. What was she doing here? Had Ashley introduced them to Nathan already? And speaking of Ashley, where was she?

"Geoff will be so pleased to see you," Mary said excitedly. "God knows where he's gotten to. He's probably emptying out a vending machine somewhere."

"Ryan," said Kat waddling up from behind us, "what happened to your face?"

"Nothing, I'm fine," I said dismissively.

"And you must be Kat," Mary exclaimed with delight, "Ashley told us about your pending arrival. Congratulations. You both must be so excited."

"Uh, yeah, we are, thanks," said the cheater, glancing at me awkwardly. Kat smiled at Mary and then turned to me, "I managed to get hold of Gaz and he's on the way."

"Okay, thanks. Maybe you should go home, you look exhausted," I said annoyed that I still cared about her after what she'd just done.

"Yeah, I am, but I don't think I could sleep anyway," she said, rubbing her lower back. "I'll just go sit with Ritchie and Amy."

"Okay," I nodded stiffly.

Kat smiled at Mary, "Nice to meet you…"

"Mary, I'm Ashley's mum," Mary said clasping Kat's hand gently.

"Well it was lovely to meet you Mary," Kat said with confusion and waddled off back to the waiting area.

"Oh, I'm so happy for you Ryan," she said, squeezing my shoulder. "Honestly I used to think maybe you and Ash would become an item, but she was always so hung up on that horrible man."

"Yeah," I said, still feeling confused by her presence. "What are you guys doing here Mary? Do you know Nathan?"

"Oh. No. We're here for Ashley, isn't that why you're here?"

I gawked at her, "Ash is here?"

"Yes, she was caught up in a car accident and they've got her in surgery," Mary said. "I assumed that's why you were here."

"No, I had no idea," I said stunned. "We're here for a friend of ours. I guess they must have been in the car together."

"Oh," she said with a furrowed brow. "The doctors haven't been able to tell us much."

"Mr McPherson?" the nurse called from the desk.

"Yes, hi," I said, "is Nathan okay?"

"He's still in the O.R, so we don't know for sure, but they said that they've controlled the internal bleeding, which is promising. I'll have an update for you once he's out."

"Okay, thanks."

"But in the meantime, I really need you to fill out this paperwork for your boyfriend," she said, holding out a clipboard.

"Your boyfriend?" asked Mary with surprise. I smiled and shook my head at her, then turned back to the misguided nurse.

"Sure," I said, taking the clipboard from her hands.

"I'll do what I can to get you in to see him," she said sympathetically.

"Thanks."

"Do you have any more details on Ashley Granger?" Mary asked the nurse hopefully. "When can we go in and see her?"

"I'll check for you ma'am."

"Thank you," said Mary, while I stared at the admission form. There were so many questions. Luckily, being Nathan's long-term boyfriend, I knew the answers to most of them. The rest I'd have to leave for Gaz. "Are you okay love?" Mary asked, studying me with a look of motherly concern.

"It's been a really long night," I admitted, sneaking a glance over at Kat, who was sitting with Ritchie and Amy.

"So, this Nathan man…" Mary asked, "Is he Ashley's boyfriend?"

"No apparently he's mine," I joked, tapping the pen against the clipboard. Mary smiled patiently and awaited an answer. I could see worry lurking in the depths of her eyes, so I cleared my throat awkwardly, "Umm… to be honest Mary, I don't really know."

"Oh okay," Mary said. "I just wondered, what with them being in a car together so late at night."

"They've been hanging out a lot," I told her honestly, hoping that it would end the conversation. Mary nodded anxiously.

"I see," she said, fidgeting nervously with her necklace. It was the first time she'd shown even a hint of panic bubbling under her well-composed exterior. I could see where Ashley got her stoic composure from. I put the clipboard on the reception desk and gently took Mary's shaking hands in mine.

"Nathan's a good guy Mary. I have no idea what happened tonight or what's going on between the two of them, but I've known him for a long time and I can promise you that he's not like Dom."

"Thank you love," she said, squeezing my hand. "I feel like I'm re-living it all over again. The last time we were in a hospital…"

"Yeah, she told me," I hung my head in shame. "Mary I'm so sorry. If I'd known what had happened back then I would have been there for you all."

"Oh love, you weren't to know," Mary said, putting her hand on my cheek. "She refused to tell anyone about losing the baby and we didn't want to go against her wishes. She just wanted to sneak away quietly and heal."

"Yeah, but I should have seen what was happening before it got to that."

"Ryan you can't blame yourself for any of that," she said adamantly. "Trust me, I've been there a million times and it doesn't fix anything." She smiled, "What's done is done love. Dominic is locked up in jail where he belongs and all we can do is move forwards in the best way we can."

"Yeah, I guess you're right," I nodded.

"Ryan, that beautiful lady over there," she nodded towards Kat, "she's working on your future right now. She's what you need to focus on." I peered over at Kat again. I was still furious with her, but with Ashley and Nathan in the hospital, Kat's one-off infidelity somehow seemed less significant. Kat looked up and saw me staring at her, so I attempted a smile. It wasn't my most genuine smile ever, but her face softened, and she rested her hand on her heart.

"Mrs Granger?" called a different nurse, emerging from the big double doors.

Mary turned expectantly. "Yes?"

"You can go in and see your daughter now."

"Thank you," said Mary with a look of relief. "Is she okay?"

"Her feet were badly damaged, so she'll need to be in a wheelchair for a few weeks, but she'll be fine."

"Oh, thank god," Mary said with a sigh of relief.

"We'd like to keep her in for a few hours so that we can re-dress the wounds, but we'll discharge her later in the morning."

"Thank you," Mary said again, before looking around the room for her missing husband. "Where on earth is Geoff?"

I squeezed her hand. "You go through Mary, I'll let him know where you are."

"Thanks love," she said appreciatively. "Will you come in later?"

"Sure," I agreed, "I'm just going to sort out this paperwork for my boyfriend."

Mary chuckled sadly. "Thanks Ryan. Even though it's not under the best circumstances... it's really nice to see you again."

"You too." I said. She headed towards the double doors just as Geoff reappeared at the other end of the waiting area with a tall ginger-haired guy in tow. "It's Geoff," I said, tapping Mary on the shoulder before she vanished through the ominous double doors.

"There you are!" she said to him impatiently. "Ashley is out of surgery."

"Sorry love," he apologised, giving her a kiss on the head.

"Hi Geoff," I said, pleased to see him again. He'd been more of a father to me than mine ever had. "Great to see you."

"Ryan my boy!" he said, slapping me on the back. "And you lad," he studied my black eye as he shook my hand, "did you get caught up in the accident?"

"Err, no," I shifted awkwardly on my feet. "This was separate."

"Ryan had another friend in the accident too," Mary explained.
The big red-headed bloke spoke up.

"Do you mean Nathan?" he asked in a thick Scottish accent.

"Yeah, how did you know?" I asked.

"Oh sorry, I should introduce you," Geoff said waving his hands in an introductory fashion. "Ryan, this is Jock. He's the guy with all the answers."

- KAT McPHERSON -

I sat and watched with curiosity as Ryan and Ashley's mum greeted a strikingly handsome older man, who I assumed to be Ashley's dad, and a huge ginger guy who looked like he'd come straight out of an action movie.

"What's going on there?" asked Amy.

"I don't know," said Ritch, rising from his seat, with his eyes firmly trained on the giant stranger. Ashley's parents vanished through the restricted doors, while Ryan followed the ginger giant towards the cafeteria. "But I'm going to find out," he added, striding purposefully after them like an over-protective bodyguard. When he reached the cafeteria doors, he looked back and gave us a nod. He stepped through the doors and we were left alone, sitting in silence, side-by-side, waiting to see if any of them would return.

I glanced at Amy, hoping she might say something, but she just stared silently at the doors. I sighed, and looked down at my hands, twisting my wedding rings nervously around my finger. I could tell Amy was pissed at me, but I didn't know what to say. I looked at her again and could almost see the anger emanating from her body.

"I'm sure Nath will be fine," I said, attempting to break the ice. "He's a fighter, he'll pull through this." Amy didn't say a word. She didn't even flutter an eyelid. It was as if I wasn't even there. "And I'm sure Ashley will be fine too," I added, trying my best to ease the suffocating tension. Amy still didn't respond. I sighed loudly. "Are you going to talk to me, or is this silent treatment some sort of punishment?"

"I've got nothing to say to you," she said unemotionally, keeping her eyes fastened to the cafeteria doors.

"I find that hard to believe," I said half-jokingly. "You always have an opinion on everything."

"Oh, I have an opinion alright," she said through gritted teeth, "but right now isn't an appropriate time for me to air it."

"Okay," I leaned back in my seat and rubbed my itching belly. "I appreciate that you're angry, but can't we just have a civil conversation about it?"

"Not really," she answered bluntly, still not looking at me. "We've got enough drama happening right now and the last thing anyone needs is a fight breaking out."

I wriggled my body around to face her.

"Are you really that mad?"

Her head turned sharply and she narrowed her gaze on me. I'd never seen so much rage in her eyes before.

"Are you fucking kidding me?" she hissed quietly. "You cheated on Ryan."

I bowed my head and nodded in agreement.

"It wasn't my finest hour," I admitted.

Amy snorted with disgust, "Well that's one way to put it."

"What do you want me to say Aims?" I asked, throwing my hands in the air.

"I don't know," she said with a sigh, rubbing her temples. I touched her leg lightly.

"I was an idiot," I admitted.

"Yeah you were," Amy agreed more harshly than necessary. I retracted my hand. "What were you thinking?" she asked, tapping her finger against her head.

"I wasn't thinking," I admitted. "I fucked up, but I can't take it back now. What's done is done."

"What's done is done?" she seethed, rising to her feet. "Kat, you must be the most uncaring, self-centred, irresponsible brat who's ever lived. Can you seriously not see the amount of damage you've caused?"

"Of course I can see it. I'm not proud of what I did. If I could go back to yesterday and change it I would. It's not like I planned for this to happen but there's nothing I can do to fix it."

"God Kat, just take some fucking responsibility for what you've done," she snapped.

"Aims," I pleaded, grabbing her hand to stop her from walking away.

"I can't do this right now," Amy said, shaking her hand out of my grasp. "Stoner is fighting for his life in there, and you're worried about what people think of you. It's time to grow the fuck up Kat." She stormed towards the exit, so I hauled myself off the chair and waddled after her as quickly as I could manage. Amy had just reached the glass sliding doors when Gaz came running through them.

"Where is he? How is he? What happened?" he asked so quickly that neither of us had time to respond. Gaz looked between the two of us as we stood staring at him like stunned mullets. When it was clear that he wasn't going to get an answer, he dashed over to the reception desk. "I'm here for Nathan Stone," he told the lady.

Amy glared at me and then turned on her heel and bolted straight out the door. I took a deep breath to swallow back my tears and then joined Gaz at the desk, resting my hand on his shoulder as the registrar filled him in on Nathan's condition. Once the woman had finished repeating her spiel, Gaz turned to me with a look of fatherly concern.

"You shouldn't be here in your state love. Why don't you go home and get some rest?" he suggested, squeezing my arm.

"Yeah," I agreed half-heartedly. "Ummm... I grabbed a bag of stuff for Nath, but I didn't know what to do with the cat."

"Cat?" asked Gaz with confusion.

"Yeah, there was a cat in his flat when I went to pick up his stuff," I said, stretching my aching back. "I couldn't find any cat food, so I just gave it a tin of tuna."

"Thanks love. I didn't know Nath had a cat, but I'll see if Ritchie can look after it," he said with a disdainful frown. "I'm allergic to those fucking things."

"Yeah, I'd offer to take it but things are a bit of a mess at the moment."

"That's fine love, you've been a big help already," Gaz said, patting my back affectionately. "You look like you need some sleep kiddo. Where's Ryan?"

"I'm not sure. In the cafeteria I think."

"I'll go find him."

"No, honestly it's fine Gaz."

"Nonsense love, you need to go home," he said authoritatively. "Just have a seat and I'll be back with your husband." He strode off through the double doors and I looked down at my wedding ring. Would I even have a husband by sunrise?

Stories from the City: Part 2

Heart of Stone

RECOVERY

- NATHAN STONE -

Through the darkness I could hear a steady beeping sound, but I couldn't figure out what it was. As I slowly floated back to reality, I started to become aware of my physicality again. I felt completely detached from my limbs, as if my body and my brain were separate entities.

I prised open my tired eyes, but the room was void of any natural light, so I had no idea whether it was day or night. I couldn't move my neck, and all I could see was the roof above. I could only assume from the relative quiet, that it was night-time.

How long had I been out for? The last thing I could remember was the blinding white headlights coming straight at me. Everything after that was a blur. I tried to make my body work, but it was too exhausting. The small amount of energy I had, was quickly zapped and my eyes floated closed again. I was so overwhelmed by tiredness that I couldn't fight it, so I let myself drift off again, and tried to tune into my body to take stock of the damage. I didn't have control over my limbs, but at least I was able to feel pain, so that was weirdly comforting. There was an itching sting in my left wrist, and something up my nose which was quite uncomfortable. My throat was raw; my face was stinging; my body was aching; there was a searing pain in my shoulder, but I didn't have any feeling at all in my legs. Were they still there?

Panicked by the thought that I might have been limbless, sheer will was enough to force my eyes open. With the limited movement I had, I nervously peered down at my legs and thankfully they were both present and accounted for. It wasn't entirely great news though. One leg was hooked up in a cast that was attached to some sort of pulley system, and the other one was serving as a pillow for Ash, who was fast asleep and delicately draped over my lap. Why couldn't I feel her there? Was I paralysed?

I tried to move my hand, but it wasn't working properly, so I had to channel all of my power to reach out and tap her arm.

"Ash," I said, struggling to find my voice. The breathing tubes in my nose weren't helping either. "Ash," I said a second time with a little more success. Ashley stirred from her sleep and peered up at me.

"Nathan," she said with a look of sheer relief.

I gestured to the breathing tubes as best I could and hoped that she would understand.

"I'll go get the nurse," she said with a nod. As Ash backed away from the bed, I noticed that the chair she was sitting in was actually a wheelchair. When she rolled out of the room I could see that both her feet were bandaged up. What the hell had happened? How had she ended up injured too?

The nurse came in and fussed about, removing pipes and flicking buttons as she chatted to herself. In the commotion, Gaz, whom I hadn't noticed sleeping on a chair in the corner of the room, awoke.

"Nath?" he asked in a daze, as he sat up in his chair. He rubbed his neck and rushed over to the bed. "Geez lad you gave me a good scare," he said, squeezing my hand as the nurse went about her business.

"Am I paralysed Gaz? I can't feel my legs."

"No, they've pumped you full anesthetic mate."

"Oh, okay." The nurse interrupted with a bunch of questions, and once all the tests and formalities were over, she left me alone with Gaz. Ash was nowhere to be seen. "What time is it? How long have I been out?"

"8am… on Tuesday. You've been out for five days," Gaz said with a look of fatherly concern.

"Shit," I said, feeling completely disoriented.

"Don't stress mate, we've got everything sorted," Gaz said, patting my shoulder. "We've put the Delfontaine account on hold until you get back, and Ritchie is looking after the cat."

"What cat?" I asked with confusion.

"Your cat."

"I don't have a cat."

"But Kat found one in your apartment."

"Oh shit, Fleabag," I said, remembering my furry visitor. "He's a stray."

"Oh," Gaz said with surprise, "let's not tell Ritchie that."

We both laughed, and then fell silent.

"So, what's the damage?" I asked, not sure if I wanted to know the answer.

"Broken ankle, shattered pelvis, dislocated hip, fractured femur, and a complete knee reconstruction," he said, not bothering to sugar-coat the truth. He paused and shrugged apologetically, "…and they had to shave your head."

"Fuck," I said touching my head to discover that my hair was gone. "Why?" I asked with horror.

Gaz cringed. "It was so matted with blood that they couldn't get the glass out."

"Did they even try?"

"Of course they did mate."

"This is fucked," I sighed hopelessly. I dropped my hands into my lap and saw that my wrist was bare. "Dad's watch?" I asked, hoping that it had survived the crash. Gaz pointed to the bedside table where my precious watch sat mangled and broken. My heart sank and the devastation must have been written all over my face.

"We'll get it fixed," Gaz promised, gently patting my arm. "I didn't want to take it in case you woke up." I nodded gratefully and swallowed back a lump in my throat.

"Any more bad news?" I asked Gaz sadly. "What's the ETA on recovery?"

"They think a month or two for the bones to heal, then another month or two of physio."

"Fuck," I repeated. There were no other words.

"What happened mate? Ashley said she saw another car flee the scene. Can you remember anything about it?"

"Yeah a little bit, but I do know that it wasn't an accident Gaz," I said as the memories started to filter back into my mind. "I was parked on the street and he came straight at me, head on."

"Okay, well you'll need to give the cops a statement when you're up to it but, regardless of what they find, your insurance is void because you had alcohol in your system," he said with a look of disappointment.

"Fuck my insurance, I just want my legs back."

"I know mate," Gaz said. "I haven't told your mum."

"Good. Please don't."

"She'd want to know."

"It'll just stress her out Gaz, she still thinks I'm a child."

"Okay," he agreed with a nod, "that's a fair point."

I leaned back and closed my eyes for a minute. I'd only been awake for ten minutes, but I felt exhausted.

"So what happened to Granger?" I asked with my eyes still shut. "Why is she in a wheelchair?"

"She ran barefoot into the wreckage when she saw it was you."

My eyes flew open, "Why the fuck would she do that?"

"Because she's in love with you."

"Yeah, that's why she had a guy over at midnight."

"You mean the big ginger guy?" He asked curiously. The mysterious photo flashed into my mind.

"Yeah," I said with a nod.

"Nath, that guy saved your life. Your leg was trapped under the dash. If he hadn't got you out… well let's just say we wouldn't be having this conversation." My stomach churned at the thought.

"Brilliant, I owe my life to Ashley's booty-call."

"Is that why you were outside her place?"

"Yeah," I said sheepishly. "Someone sent me a photo of them together and I wanted to go check it out for myself."

"Someone sent you a photo?" Gaz asked, standing bolt upright. "Nathan, something seems off about all this. What if someone wanted you at her building."

"It's probably a coincidence," I said, unable to believe that anyone would put so much energy into creating such an elaborate plan. "I mean, I know I've been a cunt to a few women, but I don't think any of them would go to this much effort to knock me off."

"Okay," he said with a sigh, we'll save this conversation for later, "but for what it's worth Nath… I don't believe there's anything going on between Ashley and her friend. She's refused to leave the hospital all week, even though she's been cleared for discharge." I opened my mouth to respond when there was a quiet knock at the door. "Come in," Gaz said in his work voice.

The door opened, and Ashley rolled hesitantly into the room.

"Sorry to interrupt."

"You're not interrupting love," Gaz said, patting her shoulder in a fatherly gesture. "He's all yours." Gaz left the room and Ashly wheeled her way over to me, veering off-course and nearly running into the bed-side table.

"I'm still getting the hang of this," she joked with a blush. "How are you feeling?"

"Like I've been hit by a car."

Tears sprang from Ashley's bloodshot eyes. "That's not funny," she said burying her face in her hands.

"Hey… Ash it's okay… I'm okay," I said, attempting to sit up, which sent waves of pain through my entire body. "Ah shit," I groaned, flopping back down against the pillow.

"Just lie still," she said, patting my hand, "I'll call the nurse."

"No," I said, grabbing her hand. Ash looked down at my hand on top of hers.

"Okay," she agreed.

"Gaz said you ran into the wreckage," I said, still not convinced that she and the big ginger guy weren't an item. "Are you okay? What made you do that?" I asked, with an annoying desire to wrap her up in my arms.

"I… I'm fine… I just… I…" She took a deep breath, "I thought I was going to lose you," she said, as another wave of tears rolled down her cheeks.

"What about the other guy?" I asked bluntly. "The guy who saved me."

"Jock?" she asked in confusion.

"Is that his name?" I asked flatly. "Why was he at your place after our date?"

"That wasn't what it looks like," she said awkwardly.

"So, what was it then? Do you normally invite guys around at midnight?"

"How did you know he was-" Ash paused. "Nathan… what were you doing outside my flat?"

"I…" I closed my eyes for a moment, beginning to feel the exhaustion catch up on me. The situation had gotten way out of control, and now I was the one behaving like a psycho.

"Nathan?"

I sighed. "Someone sent me a photo Ash," I said looking her in the eyes. "A photo of you and Jock."

"What?!" Ashley's eyes almost popped out of her head.

"I know it seems stalky, but I just needed to see it for myself because I couldn't believe it. Last night was the best date I've ever had, and I guess I was hoping that we were building up to something."

"Thursday night."

"Huh?"

"Our date… it wasn't last night, it was five days ago."

"Right," I sighed and rubbed my aching temples. "The point is Ash, I fancy you." Ashley stared at me in stunned silence while my words hung awkwardly in the air. She opened her mouth as if to say something, but then shut it again. I sighed and ploughed on, deciding that it was best to put all my cards on the table. "Like I told you the other night, I don't want to just be friends and I don't think you do either," I said earnestly. "Or has that changed?" I waited for her answer, feeling increasingly desperate as the seconds ticked past. "Come on Chucky, don't leave me hanging," I pleaded. "Please say something."

"Nathan-"

My face dropped at her solemn tone. It didn't sound like it was going to be the answer I was hoping for. "No, actually don't say it." I said, changing my mind. If she didn't want me, I didn't want to know. I held her gaze, searching her bright green eyes for a hint of the feelings I was sure she harboured for me. "I know you feel it too Ash. I can see it." She stared at me silently as tears shone in her eyes.

"It's too dangerous Nathan. You've already been hurt and I can't risk making another mistake."

"So, you're saying that our date was a mistake? Or just that I am?"

"Neither," she said in a fluster. "Nathan… I really like you, but I'm worried that if we get any closer then you're going to be in danger," she said sincerely.

"And what about Jock?" I asked, as jealousy reared it's ugly head again. "Do you consider him a mistake?"

"Nath, that's not fair."

"None of this is fair Ashley."

Ash wiped a wayward tear off her cheek and I felt a pang of guilt for being the arsehole who put it there, but I needed her to be honest. She took a breath and looked me square in the eye.

"Nathan, I promise there's nothing going on between Jock and I."

"Okay, so can you explain what was he doing at your place that late?"

"That's a really long story," she said, chewing on her bottom lip.

"Well, I'm stuck in here for three months," I scoffed, "so we've got plenty of time."

Ashley leaned forward in her chair and gently touched my hand.

"Who sent you the photo Nathan?"

"I don't know," I shrugged, "they never said."

"Oh my god," Ashley flopped back and ran her hands through her hair. "This really *is* all my fault."

"Ash, what's going on? What are you saying?"

She took a deep breath and collected herself.

"Nath… I think Dominic's back."

- RYAN McPHERSON -

Two weeks had passed since the night that ended the world as I knew it. It had only taken a few short hours for my universe to be destroyed, yet a fortnight later I was still reeling from the fall-out. My marriage was over; one of my best friends was in hospital, while another was in a wheelchair; and every single work day, I was forced to see the guy who'd fucked my wife and ruined my life. Quite honestly, if it hadn't been for the impending arrival of my first child, I would have given up on life altogether. All the joy had been sucked out of me, and I had nothing left to live for anymore. I'd lost the will to fight.

I stared unenthusiastically at my steak and kidney pie. I'd only ordered it to stop Amy from nagging me. Eating required more energy than I could muster. I'd completely lost my appetite since that fateful night because even chewing felt like too much of an effort.

"Are you gonna eat it or stare at it?" Ritchie asked from across the table, nodding his big bald head at my untouched pie. I shrugged and put down my fork, rubbing my newly bearded chin in despair. Shaving was another thing that I couldn't be bothered with anymore.

Amy glanced at Ritchie, and then leaned over to pat my hand. Her porcelain skin was a stark contrast to my dark skin, and it brought back an image of Kat lying in my arms, her delicate pale hand wrapped inside mine.

"Ryza we're worried about you," Amy said, snapping me out of my reminiscent moment. I rolled my eyes, too melancholy to even bother hiding my annoyance.

"Why? because I'm not eating my pie?"

"No, because you're a fucking head case," Ritchie said in his no-nonsense Australian manner. Amy shot him a dirty look and the smile vanished from his face. I glowered like a teenager who'd had their phone confiscated and Ritchie quickly shut his mouth. Amy cleared her throat, tucked her shiny red hair behind her ear and turned her attention back to me.

"Honey, you're not taking care of yourself," she said kindly. "Have you eaten anything in the last few days?" I thought about it for a moment, trying to recall the last time I'd bothered to eat a proper meal.

"I had a couple of Chocolate Digestives in our Project meeting yesterday," I said with a shrug.

"That doesn't count as a meal," she said unamused, ironically sounding exactly like I had five years ago when I'd lectured Ashley about not eating.

"Actually, they're reasonably nutritious," Ritchie joked to Amy's annoyance.

"You're looking gaunt Ryza," she said bluntly, ignoring Ritchie's light-hearted banter. "You've lost a lot of weight."

"The Dad Gut is no big loss," I said, feeling silently pleased at the fact that I'd at least had one win out of all of this.

"Technically it's quite a large loss," teased Ritchie. "It was getting pretty hefty."

"See," I said to Amy obstinately, too apathetic to care that Ritchie was taking the piss out of me. "I'm just goin-" My thought was cut short when I caught sight of Beau Peterson, as he strutted into the canteen. My eyes fastened to him, and I felt the same rush of rage that I had the night I'd gone to his house. My fist clenched so tightly that I could feel my nails digging into my palm. If I moved quickly, I could probably take him down.

Amy and Ritchie both turned around to see what I was looking at.

"No Ryza," said Ritchie sternly, "not at work."

Beau glanced over and saw me staring at him. He smirked and sauntered over to the counter as if my presence was nothing more than a mild amusement.

"Fucking prick," I growled under my breath. As I began to stand up, Ritchie's big hand clamped down on my shoulder, and pushed me back down to my seat.

"I said leave it, Ryan," he ordered resolutely. "You need this job man. You're about to have a kid. Don't let that Yankie prick get under your skin."

He was right. My job was the only thing I had left, and it was insanely brutal that I had to see Beau's face every day. He was the one who'd ruined my marriage, yet I had to suck it up and pretend like everything was okay, while that fucker continued life like nothing had happened. How was that fair? I didn't even know if he was still in contact with my wife or not. Feeling completely impotent, my anger exploded and I swiped my plate off the table with furious anger.

"This is fucked," I snapped, as the plate full of pie landed on the floor with a splat and a crash. Everyone in the cafeteria turned to look at me but I didn't give a shit any more. Why was I the one who always had to take the higher moral ground?

"Ryza," Amy cooed, trying to calm me down.

"I've got to get out of here," I said storming out of the canteen. I could hear Ritchie calling after me, but I didn't stop. I strode straight out of the canteen doors, through the reception area and right out of the building. I needed to get away from that place. Artemis had once been my safe zone; my home away from home, but now it was nothing more than my own personal hell.

- KAT McPHERSON -

"Jesus Kat," Rosie shouted from her tiny kitchen. "More muffins?! We haven't even finished eating the last four batches. I'm officially banning you from baking," she said, appearing in the lounge room with my latest batch of muffins in-hand. "I say this with love little sister, but this is fucking insane. You seriously need to get out of this house."

I'd been at her place for two weeks, and hadn't been outside once. I was in lock-down. The only person I wanted to see besides Rosie, was Ryan and he wasn't ready to see me yet. He'd asked for time to think, so I was respecting his space, but it was killing me to be away from him. I wanted to see him. I wanted to cuddle up with him on the couch and watch Netflix together while he wound his fingers through my unruly curls. I wanted to lose time, staring into his big, brown puppy dog eyes, and rest my head on his smooth, dark chest. I wanted my husband back… but all I could do was give him some time and hope that he would come around.

"I can't go out," I protested. "If I leave the house, someone will see me and tell Mum and Dad that I'm in town."

"I still don't see why that's such a big deal," she said taking a bite of one of the warm carrot and walnut muffins. I sighed and flopped back against the sofa.

"I can't face them yet. I mean… what am I supposed to tell them?"

"The truth," she shrugged with a mouthful of muffin.

"Now you're the one who's insane," I said, returning to my knitting. It was the first time I'd knitted since I was a kid, but I'd found all the supplies in the cupboard of Rosie's guestroom and figured it was probably like riding a bike. It definitely wasn't.

Rosie laughed. "How am I the insane one, baker-lady?"

"Because I can't tell our parents that I shagged my non-gay best-friend while I was six months pregnant with my husbands' baby."

"So water it down," she said with a shrug. "Just say that you and Ryan are having a break and don't go into details."

"Err… you've met our Mum right? When does she ever accept a vague answer to anything?"

"Fair point," she agreed, leaning against the doorframe and pondering on my dilemma. "You've got to do something though. You can't stay locked-up in here indefinitely. It's only been two weeks so far and you're already going mental."

"I'm not mental. I'm perfectly fine. See…" I said, holding up my dubious attempt at knitting. "I've nearly finished this baby blanket." We both eyed the wonky blanket, which was as a fairly accurate visual representation of how definitely she was winning our argument. I peered up at her to concede my defeat. "Okay, so… it's not awesome," I agreed, dropping the blanket, "but this is just a test run, the next one will be better."

Rosie's jaw dropped.

"No, no, no," she said, shaking her head as she hastily plonked the basket of muffins on the coffee table. "No." She repeated firmly as she sat down next to me on the sofa. Rosie sighed and took my hand in both of hers. "Honey… you know I love you right?"

I groaned and extracted my hand from hers.

"Yet usually that sentence is accompanied by something astoundingly offensive," I retorted with raised brows. She sighed patiently, but her voice remained calm.

"Kat, I can't sit here and watch you turn into a granny."

"Do you see me hunting down, and sexually accosting inappropriately young men?" I joked, referring to our lecherous grandmother.

"Not our grandma smartarse, I meant a generic granny," she replied throwing the remaining half of her muffin at me from close range. The half-eaten baked-good landed neatly my lap and I picked it up with a triumphant smile, taking a huge, over-exaggerated bite. "Oh my god," Rosie said, shaking her head in disgust.

"No point in wasting it," I replied with a shrug, as my phone buzzed on the table. Beaus name popped up on the screen and I rolled my eyes.

"Still ignoring him?" Rosie asked, glancing at the screen.

"He punched Ryan in the face," I said with my mouth full of muffin. I was furious at Beau. "I mean, how dare he? Ryan was the innocent victim in this. We're the ones who fucked up. Not Ryan. Beau had no right to be angry."

"That may be true, but he's obviously in love with you babe. He's rung you every single day since you got here."

"Not my problem," I said as the phone stopped jiggling around on the glass table-top. "He shouldn't have acted like such a meat-head."

"Mature," she said sarcastically. "You're going to have to talk to him at some point."

I stared at her blankly.

"I don't see why," I said, taking another bite of the muffin. "If I never go back to Artemis then I'll never see him again so it won't matter anyway."

"Kat, you can't hide from this. You made a mistake and now you need to clean up your mess," Rosie said standing up from the sofa. "You obviously had some feelings for Beau or you wouldn't have shagged him in the first place. At least put him out of his misery and tell him that it's over."

I dropped the remainder of the muffin into the basket and sighed. Rosie was right. I couldn't avoid Beau forever, but I wasn't ready to right that particular wrong just yet. Beau would have to wait.

- NATHAN STONE -

I'd been conscious for a week but being a vegetable for five whole days before that, made me feel like a stranger in my own life. Admittedly, I was still operating on a heavy cocktail of Tramadol, Naproxen and whatever else they were pumping into my IV, but so much had changed around me that I was finding it hard to sort through my feelings. Especially my feelings about my hair. Or, more specifically, my lack thereof.

I looked in the mirror and patted my spikey head. After the accident, my blonde mop had been so matted and tangled with blood and glass that the doctors had shaved the whole lot off. It was ironic that Ash had joked about me looking like Thor, because I felt exactly like the Son of Odin, when they cut-off his hair in Ragnarök. My trademark long blonde hair, was now a sandy-coloured number two.

As for the other changes that had occurred in the time that I'd been vegetating; the Delfontaine account had been put on hold; Ryan and Kat had split up; Dominic was wreaking havoc from inside his prison cell; and Ritchie was taking care of a stray ginger cat that had somehow become my fucking pet. Then there was the matter of the other Ginger Ninja who had elbowed his way into my life… Jock.

The guy was so fucking nice it was hard to hate him, but I was trying anyway. He might have saved my life, but as far as I was concerned, he was my competition. Everyone kept telling me that there was nothing going on between Jock and Ash but, from what I could gather, he had been acting very boyfriendy over the past few weeks. Besides which, he was clearly better boyfriend material than me and Ash was a smart woman so it wouldn't take her long to figure that out.

Being bed-bound and incapable of looking after myself wasn't helping to improve my mood, nor was the fact that I was staring down the barrel of at least three months of intensive physio just to walk again. Worst of all, until my shattered pelvis healed, sex was completely off the cards. My life as I knew it was over. One stupid, stalky, decision to go to Ashley's house, had cost me my hair, my manhood, my legs and my dignity. I was miserable.

I glanced at the bedside clock, it was 9:58am so I knew that in another two minutes, Ash would roll into my room like she had done every morning since I'd regained consciousness. And, according to the nurses, every day before then too.

Ash had been signed-off work for two weeks while her feet were healing, and she'd spent those days at the hospital, keeping me company so that I didn't go insane. Our relationship had become blurred after the accident, and neither of us really knew what we were doing. We weren't a couple, but we weren't not a couple either. We were caught in a strange twilight zone somewhere between friends and dating. Meanwhile, Jock was winning her over by acting the hero.

He had taken it upon himself to become her own personal bodyguard, and had even started investigating the Dom situation. The sneaky Scot was playing the knight in shining armor, while I was trapped in a hospital bed unable to fight for my woman. Hmm. Was she even my woman?

The clock hit ten, and right on cue, Ashley wheeled in on her blue chariot.

"Good morning Mister Stone," she said cheerfully, as she skillfully navigated her wheelchair through the doorway. She appeared to be happy, but the dark bags under eyes told a different story.

"Morning speedy," I said flatly, struggling to muster up any real enthusiasm for my crappy new existence. "Looks like you're a pro now," I said, nodding towards her chair, as she rolled up alongside my bed.

"Yeah I've finally got the hang of it now that I'm graduating to crutches," she joked, her green eyes sparkling, despite being slightly bloodshot.

"How much sleep did you get last night?" I asked, studying her gaunt face as she concentrated on parking her chair.

"Enough," she answered with a shrug. I stared at her without amusement.

"You haven't had one full night of decent sleep in the whole time you've been coming to visit me."

Ash leaned forward and rested her hand on mine.

"I'm fine Nathan, it's just the painkillers messing with my body."

"So it has nothing to do with Dom then?" Her eyes darted sideways. "You know you're a terrible liar so you might as well tell me the truth."

"Jock has the situation under control," she said evasively. I cringed at the mention of the Ginger Ninja. He seemed to pop up in every single conversation we had. "How are you feeling?" She asked chirpily.

I sighed, "you know my answer to that."

"Yeah, 'like you've been hit by a car'," Ash said, rolling her eyes, "it wasn't funny the first fifty times you said it, and it still isn't."

"You're the one who said it this time."

"Smartarse." She leaned back in her chair and scrutinized me, "why so perky today?"

"What do I have to be perky about?" I asked, sounding like Eeyore.

"That I'm here?" she suggested with a cheeky smile.

"Yeah," I agreed, "and then you'll be back at work next week and I'll be stuck in here by myself."

"Aww Nathan are you going to miss me?" Ash teased.

"At this point, your visits are the only thing preventing me from topping myself."

Her face fell and she rested her hand on mine.

"Are you being melodramatic, or do you actually feel that way?"

I looked up at the TV screen to avoid eye contact.

"I don't even know how I'd do it with the round-the-clock care here. They'd revive me too quickly," I joked half-heartedly.

Ash sat back and rifled around in her hand-bag.

"Well maybe this will make you feel better. I've been working on it all week," she said, pulling out an old iPod Nano. "I wanted to return the favour and make you a mix-tape. That way you'll sort-of have my company when I'm back at work," she said, proudly handing me the shiny pink iPod. "I hope you like it. I think I finally have a Nathan-worthy play-list."

"Thanks," I said glumly, putting the iPod in my lap without looking at it. I sighed and rubbed my shaved head. "Ash, we need to talk about something." The sparkle in her eyes quickly faded.

"What is it?"

"This whole Jock situation."

She sighed and crossed her arms over her chest.

"Nathan, there *is* no Jock situation."

"Isn't there?" I asked with a raised brow. "Who dropped you off here today?" Her jaw tightened and she dropped her gaze to the floor.

"Jock," she said with a heavy sigh.

"And there it is," I said as if it was some sort of pious victory.

Ash looked up at me exhaustedly, "he's just a friend Nath."

"A friend who looks after you like a boyfriend should."

She shook her head disbelievingly.

"You're pissed because he's being a nice guy?"

"No, I'm pissed because that should be me," I blurted angrily. She closed her eyes and dropped her head into her hands, raking her neatly polished nails through her fading blonde locks. The white in her hair had toned down over the last few weeks and I could see strawberry blonde roots beginning to peek through. Ash took a deep breath and looked up at me with regret in her eyes.

"I know this is totally fucked up Nath, but Jock's just making sure I'm okay given the whole stalking situation."

"Aren't the cops dealing with it?"

"They're not interested in my problems Nathan," she said with frustration, "they're investigating your accident and that can't be traced back to Dom."

"So, let me help you," I said stubbornly, "I'm the one who's been most affected by this but you keep running back to Jock."

"I didn't want to dump this all on you when you should be focused on recovering."

"And you think excluding me is the better option?"

"I'm not intentionally excluding you," she said, shaking her head, "it's just that you're in here and Jock's out there."

"Of course," I said with a pang of rejection, that felt like a knife stabbing into my chest. "Don't you find it weird that the guy just appeared from nowhere? I mean, you barely know him."

"I know him as well as I know you," she said defensively and I flinched at her sharp tone.

"What exactly does that mean?" I asked warily. "Have you kissed him?" Ash sighed and rolled her eyes.

"Please don't do this Nath. You're starting to sound like Dom and I don't have the energy to fight this battle with you."

"So you have kissed him then?" I asked, ignoring the fact that she'd just likened my jealous behavior to that of her psycho ex-boyfriend. She crossed her arms.

"No, I haven't. Jock is keeping an eye out for me and that's all there is to it."

"And what about that night Ash?" I asked obstinately, "I was there. I'd just left your place, so why did you call him."

"Dom had threatened you Nath. I didn't want you to get hurt."

I snorted at the irony. "Yet that's exactly what happened." The words had come out harsher than I'd intended and Ash recoiled in her chair. I was angry and there was no denying it. I'd been holding back my thoughts all week but now it was as if the flood gates had opened and I couldn't stop my thoughts from tumbling out of my mouth. "Maybe if you'd told me what was happening at the start, we could have dealt with it together, and I wouldn't be stuck in this fucking bed."

"I…" she opened her mouth to say something, but then closed it again as tears shimmered in her eyes. I powered on, ignoring the fact that I was upsetting her.

"Instead of trusting me, you went to Jock for help. I never had a chance to defend myself, because I didn't even know I was a target. All you had to do was tell me."

Ashley looked down at her hands.

"I never meant for any of this to happen," she whispered as a tear dripped off her cheek.

"No, but it did and now I'm the one who has to live with it."

Ash looked up at me with hurt and betrayal written all over her face.

"I'm so sorry Nathan."

"Yeah, me too." I said snidely. "I really thought we had something going Ash, but I don't know how I'm supposed to trust you after you went behind my back."

She stared at me defiantly, her eyes flashing fire.

"Then I guess we're done here," she said spinning her chair around, and wheeling out of the room at grand prix speed. I dropped my head into my hands and stared down at the pink iPod in my lap. Feeling like the world's biggest arsehole, I pressed the button and the screen lit up with 'Nathan's recovery playlist'.

"I'm such a cunt," I groaned with overwhelming remorse.

- ASHLEY GRANGER -

I wheeled angrily away from Nathans room, but I couldn't decide if I was angrier at him or myself. He was right after all. It *was* my fault... but he needn't have been such an arsehole about it. A million thoughts whirred through my head, and I was tempted to turn around and go back to him, but the fact was that we were both safer apart. Ashley Granger wasn't a story that would end well for Nathan. The closer we got, the more danger he would be in, so this really was the best outcome for everyone.

As I sped down the stark, sterile hallway, I nearly ran over Jock who was striding purposefully down the corridor with my phone in his hand.

"Oh shit," I swore, veering around his bulky frame. "Jock, I thought you'd gone to work?"

"You left your phone in my car," he said, handing it to me.

"Thanks, that's really sweet of you to drop it back," I said with a smile. He cocked his head and studied me inquisitively.

"Where are you going in such a hurry anyway?" he asked, shifting on his feet. "Is Nathan asleep or something?"

"No," I said with a clenched jaw. "We're done."

"Oh," he replied, furrowing his ginger brow with confusion. "Do you want me to drop you back at your parents place?"

"Thanks for the offer, but that's too far out of your way."

"Well what if I drop you at your flat?" he suggested with a shrug.

"No, I'm not ready to go back there yet," I said adamantly, "I was just going to call my Dad to come get me."

"You can't sit in the waiting area for an hour," he said with a smile, taking the handles of my chair. "Surely there's somewhere I can drop you while you wait?"

"Actually... maybe you could drop me at Kesha's?" I asked, peering up at him gratefully. "It's her day off today."

"Sure thing boss," he agreed, wheeling me towards the exit. "So are you nervous about going back to work next week?"

"Yeah a bit," I said with a nod, "but life has to go on right?"

"That it does," Jock agreed, clearing his throat. "And speaking of which..." he said, as we rolled toward the carpark, "there's something I need to talk to you about."

"Oh god," I sighed with a cringe, "is it bad news? Because if it is, could you save it for another day?"

"I don't know if I'd call it bad news..." he said, putting the brakes on my chair as we reached his car. He crouched down in front of me with a strange look on his face. "The thing is Ashley... I care about you," he paused, as if searching for the right words. "I know we agreed to just be friends, but my feelings for you have changed over the last few weeks."

"Oh," I said, hoping that I was wrong about what was about to come out of his mouth.

"I know this has been a really intense time, and I get that you feel a certain responsibility to Nathan..."

"Oh my god," I muttered, anticipating his next words. Nathan was right.

"...but I really like you Ash," he said, taking my hand, "and I want you to come away with me."

"What?" I stared at him, stunned.

"You're not safe here right now. We should take off for a few months while the cops figure it out, and then come back once it's all blown-over."

"I can't just take-off," I said wide-eyed with shock. "And what if it doesn't blow over? I can't walk away from my entire life."

"Why not? You did that last time right?"

"Yeah, but..."

"Come on Ash, it makes sense," Jock said with pleading eyes.

I shook my head solemnly. "I appreciate the thought Jock, but I can't go away with you."

He leaned back, staring doe-eyed at me like a sad puppy dog.

"But I feel like we have something good going here." He tilted his head with curiosity, "or is that just me?"

"Jock I-"

"Right," he said, as his head dropped. "It's just me." My heart sank for him.

"If things were different..." I said wanting to end his disappointment.

"But they're not different Ash," he said standing up. "Things are what they are, and you're clearly in love with Nathan."

"I'm sorry," I said pathetically, hating that I was hurting him.

"You can't help who you fall for," he said, giving me a firm kiss on the forehead. "Let's just get you over to Kesha's."

"Okay," I squeaked with a tight throat, overwhelmed by all the emotional revelations that had occurred in the space of 30 minutes.

It was a silent drive to Kesha's place and when we pulled-up outside her apartment block, I peered over at Jock with a heavy heart.

"Here we are," he said flatly, looking straight ahead, so as not to make eye contact with me.

"Here we are," I agreed with a quiet sigh. I stared at him with an overwhelming sense of loss. "Does this mean we can't be friends anymore?"

He smiled and et my eyes, then gently punched my shoulder.

"Of course we can still be friends," he said, unbuckling his seatbelt. I could sense the 'but' coming. "But I'm going to need some time."

I nodded sadly. "If that's what you need."

"It is," Jock said. "For self-preservation purposes."

"Okay," I agreed, "I'll leave you to get in touch with me when you're ready."

"Deal." He smiled sadly and climbed out of the car to get my wheelchair. His energy had completely shifted, and I felt him closing down. He helped me into the chair, kneeling down beside me to make sure I was in properly.

"Just promise me one thing," he said.

"Sure."

"Tell your parents about this whole Dom thing."

I shook my head. "I can't do that."

"Why not?"

"Because we don't know for sure that it was Dom."

"Are you fucking kidding me right now?" he snapped, swaying backwards with the force of his rage. "You *do* know that Dom's responsible for Nathan's accident. You've known that he's been stalking you since the day you came into the store. How can you suddenly not be sure?"

"I just-" I peered up at him like a shamed school kid, "I can't tell them until I have something solid."

"Ash," he said shaking his head, "this isn't a joke. You're in way over your head here."

I smiled and rested my hand on his shoulder gently, heartened that he cared so much.

"I can't live in fear Jock. I know this is serious but there's nothing I can do without evidence. If I freak out about it then I'm letting him win."

Jock exhaled loudly and leaned his elbows on the arms of my chair.

"You're underestimating Dom."

"I know exactly what Dom's capable of," I said defensively.

"Aye. So what about Nathan? Don't you care about him?"

"What do you mean by that?" I asked suspiciously, leaning back so that I could study his face. It seemed like Jock knew something that I didn't.

"What if Dom goes after him again?" Jock said, rising to his feet, "or your parents, or Kesha, or any of your other friends."

I dropped my head and stared at his huge shoes as he towered above me. He was right. I sighed with hopelessness.

"I don't know what I'm supposed to do Jock."

"You're supposed to lean on people Ash. You can't do this on your own."

"I also can't drag other people into my mess." I said as he walked around the back of my chair. He gripped the handles and pushed me up to Kesha's building.

"I'll see what else I can find out," he said unemotionally. "Could you at least get a restraining order?"

"Okay," I agreed as he pressed the buzzer for me. I had no intention of getting a restraining order, but I wanted the conversation to end.

"Thank you," he said with a relieved nod.

"Hello?" called Kesha through the intercom.

"Hey, it's Ash," I said, peering up at Jock sadly.

"I'll come down and get you babe," said Kesha.

Jock looked down at me, "I'd better get to work."

"Yeah, of course," I said with a nod, "thanks for driving me."

Jock patted my shoulder with a tight smile.

"Bye Ash," he said, turning to walk away.

"Bye Jock," I said quietly as he looked back over his shoulder. Kesha opened the door and he gave her a wave.

"Hey Kesh," he called, and then sadly climbed into his Volvo.

"What's up with Jock?" Kesha asked, watching him like a hawk as he pulled away.

"He wanted to be more than friends," I said, turning my chair around to face her.

"And you didn't?" she asked curiously. I shook my head silently and her jaw fell open. "Honey that man is tasty. Why on earth wouldn't you want to jump on him?"

I shrugged. "Nathan."

"Well if you're not going to sex up Jock, then I gladly will."

I smiled tightly, "he's all yours babe."
Kesha appraised me with a look of concern.

"What's on your mind chick?" asked Kesh, as she wheeled me inside. "I can tell this isn't just about Jock, so what's going on?"

"Life," I shrugged.

"Specifically?"

"Nathan, I guess."

"Why? What's happened with Thor? I thought you guys were clicking."

"We were," I said, "and now we're not. He unclicked us."

"Oh, I'm so sorry honey, I know how much you like him," she said, rubbing my arm. "Shall I go beat him up for you? Because I will. I don't care if he's an invalid, I'll pull-up if he's hurt you."

"Thanks hun, but it's my own fault. I think it's all over," I said sadly. Kesh stopped and wrapped her arms around my shoulders.

"I know what you will cheer you up," she said, resting her chin on top of my head.

"What?" I asked unenthusiastically.

"I have vegan Haagen-Daas in the freezer."

I looked up at her skeptically. "Which flavour?"

"Peanut butter chocolate fudge," she said with a grin and I smiled appreciatively.

"You're my hero."

- *Chapter 9* -

ONE MONTH LATER - LIFE GOES ON

- RYAN McPHERSON -

I trudged through the front door of my empty flat, throwing my jacket over the back of the nearest kitchen chair. I plonked my rucksack on the table and kicked off my shoes, leaving them sprawled where they laid. After all, what was the point of cleaning up, when there was no one else to see the mess?

I grabbed a beer out of the otherwise empty fridge, and stood aimlessly in the middle of my dark, empty kitchen. I was staring down the barrel of another lonely weekend. Six weekends had passed since Kat had left for Framlingham, and all I could do was wallow in self-pity.

The old days, when I'd looked forward to walking out of the office on a Friday evening, were a distant memory. Weekends were now nothing but a grim reminder of everything I had lost. The home that had once been so warm, welcoming and full of great smells, was now cold and taunting, yet I couldn't muster the energy to go out. It was a catch 22.

I sighed heavily, staring blankly at the floor as I replayed in my mind the pivotal events of the past few months. Every word, every moment, every conversation that I'd had with my wife... all of which had been missed opportunities for me to save my marriage.

My thoughts flitted back to the day she'd left for Framlingham. It had been a silent Uber journey home from the hospital after Nathan's accident. A night which had since become known as 'The Night that Kat Fucked Beau'.

The evening had been such an emotional tornado that it was hard to know where to even begin. Kat had wisely chosen to keep her mouth shut, and I did the same. It seemed like the safest option. The rage was still buzzing through me, however my anger felt slightly trivial while Nathan's life was hanging in the balance so I did my best to keep it at bay. We both remained silent as we let ourselves into the apartment, and by the time we were getting ready for bed, still not one word had been uttered. The silence felt ominous, but I was too scared to speak in case I lost control of my feelings and said words that I'd regret. Kat stood and watched me as I stripped off.

"Ryan, are we okay?" she asked quietly as I tossed my stinky, blood stained shirt into the washing basket. I ran my hands through my hair and sighed.

"I don't know," I answered honestly, avoiding eye contact with her. "I love you Kat, but I don't know if I can get past this."

She sobbed quietly, and sank to the bed.

"I fucked everything up," she whispered, almost to herself as she brushed a tear away from her cheek.

"Yeah you did," I agreed sitting down next to her, "but being in that hospital did make me reassess life a bit," I paused and looked her in the eyes. "I mean, we're both alive and the baby is healthy… maybe that's all that matters."

"Yeah," she said with a glimmer of hope shimmering in her brown eyes. I tucked my leg up on the bed and turned my body around so that I was facing her.

"Was this thing with Beau more than just a shag?" I asked, not sure if I really wanted to know the answer.

"It was for him," she admitted shamefully.

"And for you?"

"I thought he was gay," she replied flippantly, making the rage course through my veins again.

"That's your response?" I growled.

"No… it's not," she said, backpedaling in panic. "I'm not in love with Beau, Ryan. I'm in love with you."

I snorted in disdain. "Really? Then you've got a funny way of showing it."

"It was purely physical Ryan. I really needed-"

"No. Nope. Nope. I don't want to hear it Kat. It literally makes me sick to my stomach," I shouted, holding my hand up in her face like I was a traffic cop.

"What makes you feel sick Ryan? The thought of having sex with me, or the fact that someone else actually wanted to?"

"That's not fair Kat. My baby is in there and, eventhough I know it's stupid, I didn't want my dick flapping around her head," I explained defensively. "Apparently Beau didn't see a problem with that though."

"No, he didn't," she answered self-righteously.

"You have no right to be high and mighty. Maybe I've been a bit distant with everything that's been going on lately, but I've done nothing wrong here."

"No, you never do anything wrong Ryan," Kat retorted disdainfully. "How is life up on your pedestal? Is it breezy up there or does the hot air rise?"

"How dare you," I said wearily. All the fight had drained out of me. "You're the one who cheated Kat. What is it about this situation are you not grasping?" She looked at me blankly, like she herself didn't even know the answer. "Let's just go to bed," I said, getting up off the bed. Kat grabbed my hand.

"Have sex with me," she blurted, gripping tightly to my hand and stopping me in my tracks.

"What?" I asked, assuming that I'd misheard her.

"Have sex with me," she repeated as I gaped at her in shock.

"Are you for real?" I asked, stunned. "Have we been having the same conversation for the last twenty minutes or did you just not notice that our marriage is hanging on by a thread?"

"Please? We need this," she added illogically. I laughed dryly, and shook my head.

"How do you figure that?"

She stood up and moved closer to me.

"We need to reconnect, and if we don't do it now, it might never happen." I was silent. I had no words. "Please," she begged.

"You're serious, aren't you?" I asked, dumbfounded by her logic.

"Yeah I am. I don't want to lose you Ryan," she paused and waited to see if I'd say yes, but I didn't say anything. "Come on, it's worth a shot isn't it?"

I thought about it for a moment. Given the state of things, it certainly couldn't make the situation any worse.

"Okay," I nodded stiffly, feeling like an idiot for agreeing to her ridiculous plan. "Let's give it a try." She wriggled into my arms, but I didn't move. I was trying to rid my mind of visions of her fucking Beau.

"If you don't want to do this…" she whispered quietly.

"No. I do. Let's do this," I said, wrapping my arms around her awkwardly. Kat attempted to kiss me, but I couldn't do it, and I dodged her lips, lightly kissing her neck instead. Her mouth had been pressed against Beau's and I couldn't bear to taste her betrayal. She sighed quietly.

"Maybe this isn't a good idea," she said backing away from me, "you're not really here anyway."

"Sorry, I'm trying. I'll try harder," I said, taking off my jeans. "What's the best way to do this?"

"If you lie down… then I can…" she trailed off as she gestured towards the bed.

"Okay," I nodded, obediently lying down. It was arguably the most awkward sex attempt that had ever occurred between two humans. My cock was as flaccid, and I had no idea how I was going to snap myself out of it. She looked at my limp penis with determination.

"We can fix this," she said, and then proceeded to give me an enthusiastic blow job. She tried her best, but nothing worked.

"I'm sorry," I said, removing my cock from her mouth. "I can't do this."

"Please Ryan, don't give up on us," she begged pathetically.

"You're the one who gave up on us Kat," I said, grabbing a pair of tracksuit pants off the chair. "I think it's best if we have some time apart."

Time apart. That's what I'd asked for and that's exactly what Kat had given me. She'd gone up to Framlingham that same day. As soon as she'd gone, I knew that having time apart was going to be hard, but now that we were six weeks down the track, I was finding it harder than I'd ever imagined.

"I have to call her," I blurted to the empty room. I grabbed my phone off the bench and stared at Kat's name on the screen with my finger poised. All I had to do was press the green button and tell her that I wanted her to come home. That was it - nothing more and nothing less - just one little phone call and my life would be back to normal. Except that it wouldn't be normal. She'd fucked Beau, and there was nothing that would change that.

I put my phone back down on the bench and backed away from it. I didn't want our marriage to be over, but her infidelity had been such a big betrayal that I wasn't sure I could let it go. In fact, there was a small part of me that wanted to be angry at her forever.

- KAT McPHERSON -

I sat in the passenger seat of Rosie's car, staring woefully at my parents' house.

"I can't believe you ratted me out," I said sulkily.

"I didn't mean to," Rosie said defensively, "I just ran out of excuses for her not to come over. You know how hard it is to lie to Mum. She's like a fucking human lie-detector."

"Or you just wanted to palm me off on them."

"Don't be so melodramatic," she said rolling her eyes. "You can keep staying at my place, they just want to have you for a night or two. Besides which, I've covered for you for over a month, so I think I deserve some credit for that."

I sighed. "You're right. I'm sorry."

"I'll grab your bag," she said, unbuckling her seatbelt. "Oh dear. You better prepare yourself, because we've been spotted." Rosie nodded towards the front window where Mum was peering through the translucent white curtains, waving excitedly.

"Oh fuck," I said with a sigh as I unbuckled my own belt.

"It will be fine."

"Maybe for you," I said, opening the car door as Mum came flying out of the house like a puppy dog being re-united with its owner.

"Oh, Katherine, look at you," she exclaimed, seeing my massive belly, as I reluctantly hauled myself out of the car. She offered me a hand, "Andrew, she's here!" she called over her shoulder, but my Father didn't appear.

"Hi Mum," I said with as much enthusiasm as I could muster.

"Oh love, it's so good to see you," she said excitedly. Once I was fully on my feet, she gave me a million kisses and an inelegant sideways hug. In the last month and a half that I'd been hiding out at Rosie's house, my stomach had popped big-time. I was almost as wide as I was tall.

"It's good to see you too Mum," I said, already feeling emotionally drained.

"Come inside and sit-down love," she said, guiding me towards the front door. Rosie gave me her 'I told you so' look and followed us inside the cluttered house. Stepping into their place was like stepping back in time. Nothing had changed. Not the familiar array of ornaments crowded onto every visible flat surface (and also on the non-visible ones); nor the OTT floral theme that made it look as though a rose-bush had vomited on everything in sight.

"I don't know where your father has gotten to," Mum said, fussing about with a rose-patterned teapot, "I suspect he's out in the shed, tinkering as usual."

"I'll go find him," offered Rosie. While Mum's back was turned, I silently gesticulated at Rosie not to go, but she hand-signalled for me to sit down and talk. Rosie ducked out the kitchen door and into the backyard leaving me alone with my mother.

"Have a seat love," said Mum, popping the pot of tea and four matching tea-cups onto the rose-clothed table.

"Thanks Mum," I said, taking a seat at the old kitchen table, while she poured the tea. I'd sat and drunk a million Shirly Cuppa's at that table over the years, and it suddenly felt like I'd never left in the first place.

"So what's going on love?" Mum asked knowingly, as she took a seat next to me. It was the conversation I'd been dreading.

"I think my marriage is over," I admitted taking a sip of my tea.

"Oh honey, I'm sorry," she said, squeezing my hand. "What happened? Did Ryan cheat on you?"

"Why would you assume that?" I asked, unsure whether to be relieved or offended that she'd assumed Ryan would be the cheater.

"No reason," she replied quickly, "it was the first thing that sprung to mind, that's all."

"Wow, thanks mum," I said indignantly, insulted that my mother thought Ryan was that sort of man.

"Don't get upset love, it was just a comment."

"Yeah, a comment that insinuated my husband is a cheater," I answered a little too defensively. My mother had a habit of pushing all my buttons and I was starting to remember why I didn't come home for visits very often.

"Not at all love! It's just with his background..." Mum trailed off. I put down my cup.

"What do you mean, 'his background'?" I asked, hoping that she wasn't referring to his skin colour.

"He grew up rich love, he was always a bit out of your league," she said, waving her hands as if it was an obvious fact. I was stunned into silence, unsure whether that was better or worse than the racist reasoning. I couldn't believe that my own mother thought I'd married above my class.

"Wow," I breathed in both shock and offence.

"I'm sorry love, I didn't mean to offend you. I know you're probably feeling sensitive at the moment," she said unapologetically. "It's just, you know, well that's just the way of the world isn't it."

"Oh my god," I shook my head. I was speechless and I was seriously regretting my decision to come back to Framlingham.

"So what went wrong then sweetheart?" she asked gently.

"I cheated on him," I told her flatly, no longer concerned about what she thought, since apparently she didn't have a particularly high opinion of me anyway.

"What?!" Mum asked, nearly choking on her tea. "With whom?"

"Does it matter?"

"I suppose not," she agreed with a sigh. "I guess it was inevitable, but I honestly thought you'd escaped the Flemming curse. You've always been such a good girl."

"Infidelity isn't a curse mum, its poor self-control," I said snarkily, "and clearly the Flemming X-chromosome doesn't include an impulse control gene."

"Such is the curse," Mum replied, tracing the holy cross over her body. She was only ever catholic when it suited her. "You're now the fourth generation to succumb to it Katherine. This just proves it's real."

I was officially the fourth generation of cheating women on the maternal side of our family, but I was not going to let her use 'the curse' as an excuse for poor decision-making.

"No, it doesn't Mum," I disagreed vehemently, "it just means that the apple doesn't fall far from the tree."

"Well that's rude," she replied with horror.

"No, it's truthful," I retorted. "You've blamed the curse for your infidelity for the last thirty years Mum. When are you going to grow up and take responsibility for your shitty behaviour?"

"That's quite enough young lady," Mum said indignantly.

"Yeah, it would be awful to face the truth huh?" I snapped. My rage had been set free and now there was no controlling it. "You may feel okay about treating Dad like that, but I'm not going to invalidate Ryan by blaming my cheating on some horse-shit curse."

Mum stared at me with venom.

"I think you should leave," she seethed quietly.

"Fine by me." I pushed my chair out pointedly and the wooden legs screeched loudly across the vinyl floor. "I knew it was a mistake to come home," I said, before storming out the back-door to get Rosie. I knew I'd been hard on Mum. It wasn't really her that I was angry at, it was myself. All these years that I'd spent actively trying not to be like her and that was exactly what I'd become. It wasn't her fault, it was mine. I was the one who'd created this mess and I had to accept the consequences of that.

I opened the creaky shed door and stuck my head in.

"Dad? Rosie?"

"Katherine," Dad said running over to give me a hug, "it's so good to see you Poppet." He stepped back and scrutinised me with his hands on my shoulders. "What's wrong?"

"How long have you got?" I asked with a cringe, looking around the shed for my traitorous big sister. "Where's Rosie?"

"She's gone home. She thought you and your mum needed to talk."

"Great," I said, rolling my eyes.

"What's going on love?" he asked, guiding me over to the wooden bench at the back of his man-cave.

"I had a fight with Mum," I replied shamefully, "and I cheated on Ryan… but not in that order."

"Oh, I see," Dad nodded understandingly. "I suppose your mum thinks that confirms the curse then?" he said lightly, nudging my shoulder with his. I chuckled and sobbed simultaneously.

"Yep… and I told her what I thought of that," I said regretfully, "in a pretty brutal way." I felt so hateful towards my mother, but it was only because I was exactly like her. "I hate that I've become like her."

Dad wiped my tears away with his thumb, "oh dear."

"I was such a bitch Dad," I admitted shamefully, "I don't think she'll ever forgive me."

"Have faith Katherine. You and Mum will make-up," he assured me confidently as he wrapped his arm around my shoulder.

"Maybe, but that still won't change what I did to Ryan."

"Ryan will come around," Dad said with a knowing smile.

"I'm not so sure about that Dad," I replied with a sigh. "What made you forgive Mum?"

"I realised that I loved her, and my life wouldn't be the same without her in it."

"I don't know if Ryan will ever get over what I did, and honestly I wouldn't blame him. What kind of selfish psycho cheats when they're pregnant?" Self-flagellation felt like the most rational response to the situation.

"We all make mistakes love," he paused and glanced at my belly, "some larger than others, but that's called being human. No one's perfect. If we were, we'd never learn anything." He squeezed my shoulders and kissed my head affectionately. "Ryan's a good man. Once he's had some time on his own, he'll come to the same conclusion."

"I hope you're right Dad," I replied sadly, "I really hope you're right."

- NATHAN STONE -

"Ugh, fuck it," I swore angrily as my legs gave way beneath me for the fifth time. I'd been in active physiotherapy for two whole weeks and I still hadn't mastered the art of putting one foot in front of the other. I dropped to the crash mat and Wayne, my lanky Australian physiotherapist, helped me back up again.

"I've got ya." Wayne was one of the best rehab physio's in London and thankfully for me, he played AFL with Ritchie, so he'd agreed to take me on, despite his 6 month waiting list.

"Thanks," I said, tightly gripping onto the support rails. "Can't we just go back to doing massage and hydrotherapy?"

"Not a chance," he said with a smile. "You're doing great. Now try again," he added with an equal mix of compassion and 'don't fuck with me'.

"I've been trying all afternoon," I argued, feeling hopeless and pathetic.

"We've been going for thirty minutes, Nathan," he told me patiently.

"Fine," I said unhappily, as he helped me regain my grip on the rails. "What is it with you Aussies? You're all such hard-arses."

"We grow up with killer spiders in our back-yards," he joked, removing his hands from my waist, so that I had to hold my own weight. "Now let's try again."

"Sure," I agreed reluctantly.

"All you've got to do is take one step."

"Easy for you to say String Bean," I joked as I focused all my energy on moving my right foot and staying upright. With an excruciating amount of pain and many grunts and groans, I managed to take the step.

"Sweet," said Wayne, "now only nine more to go."

"You said I only had to take one step," I said, with shaky arms. It was fair to say that I'd lost a considerable amount of upper body strength in the month and a half that I'd been in hospital.

"I lied," he said with a huge smile.

"You're a cunt," I replied with a frustrated laugh.

"Yeah I've been told," Wayne chuckled, unphased by my banter. "Come on Nath, if you don't walk, then your pelvis won't get stronger and you'll never have sex again." I stared at him without amusement.

"You really are a cunt," I reaffirmed.

"Yes," he agreed with a grin, "and you're all-talk Stone. Come on. Less talky-talky, more walky-walky." I knew he was goading me, but it was working. I took a deep breath and forced my body forwards with dogged determination. One, two, three, four...

"Oh fuck," I stumbled and lost my footing but gripped tightly to the railings and saved myself from collapsing again.

"You've got this Nathan," Wayne encouraged me from the other end of the rails. "Only five more. You can do this."

"Yeah, I can do this," I agreed with a nod.

"Sorry, what was that? I couldn't hear you."

"I can do this," I said a little louder.

"Are you sure?" he asked, pulling a face, "you don't sound very sure."

"I can do this," I repeated adamantly.

"Good, then fucking do it," he said authoritatively. I gritted my teeth and smashed out my last five steps, almost falling into his arms with excitement, as I managed a couple of extras for good luck. We both cheered with glee as Wayne held me in his arms. "You did it!" he said, squeezing me tight.

"I fucking did it!" We both laughed and he patted me on the back.

"Wanna do it again?"

"Fuck no."

"Am I interrupting?" came Amy Vaughn's voice from the other side of the therapy room. Still wrapped together in our man-hug, Wayne and I looked over at the woman I called 'Red', as she stood in the doorway with a look of great amusement.

"Red!" I said excitedly, "I walked!"

"Well done babe, that's amazing," she said, clapping her hands with excitement.

"He's doing really well," Wayne told her, still holding me. He was surprisingly strong for a skinny guy.

"I'm proud of you Nath," Red said, hooking her bag over the handles of my wheelchair. "Seriously though, do you guys need a moment?"

Wayne laughed, "well we were just getting to the good stuff, but I suppose you could join in."

"Don't joke with her String Bean," I warned Wayne as he began maneuvering me back to my chariot, "or she'll tell Ritchie she shagged you."

"Meh," Wayne shrugged, "he may be a boofhead but I could take him."

"I'll tell him you said that, and we'll put it to the test huh?" Amy joked with a wink at Wayne. She looked back at me with a wicked grin. "See Nathan, it's not just you that I enjoy torturing."

"Aww, you're breaking my heart," I joked, as Wayne guided me into my chair.

"I'm sure you'll live," she retorted patiently, "besides, it looks like you have a beautiful Bromance happening here."

"Not really," Wayne piped-up, "he thinks I'm a cunt."

"That's because you are," I joked.

"A cunt that just got you walking," he replied with a smug smile.

"Fair," I conceded.

"Anyway, I'll leave you guys to it," said Wayne. "Well done today mate," he added, patting me proudly on the back before ducking out of the room.

"So how's Ash?" I asked unsubtly, as Red wheeled me towards my room.

She sighed impatiently, "Nathan, I've already told you that I'm not your messenger. If you want to know how Ash is, then you need to call her," she said firmly. "I know she'd like to hear from you."

"She has my number," I said childishly.

"How old are you Stoner?"

"Well, she could call me."

"Yeah but you're the one who keeps asking me about her, and I refuse to get involved anymore. If you really want to know how she is, pick up the fucking phone."

"Does that mean she never asks about me?"

Red groaned melodramatically. "Knock it off Nathan, I'm not your middleman."

"Fine," I said sulkily, as she navigated my wheelchair through the door of my room.

"So what's the real reason you don't want to call her?" Red asked, pushing my chair over to the little table, and taking a seat opposite me. I eyed her wearily. The determined look on her face told me that she wouldn't let it go until she got the truth out of me. I sighed and rubbed my aching neck.

"I don't want Ash to see me until I'm a proper man again," I said way too honestly.

"A proper man?!" she laughed, "Nathan, it's not like you got castrated. And even if you had, it wouldn't make you any less of a man."
I scowled at her, insulted that she was finding my predicament amusing.

"I can't have sex, so I might as well be a eunuch," I grumbled. Red sighed, but her face softened into something that looked a lot like pity.

"I can't believe I'm about to say this," she said resting her hands on the arms of my chair, "but it's not all about sex Nathan."

"I can't believe you just said that either," I teased my sex-crazed friend.

"I mean it," Red said with a smile, "being a proper man is also about getting over your ego, and stepping-up when someone needs you."

"Okay Yoda," I agreed obnoxiously. It annoyed me that she was right. Red sat up straight and rolled her eyes at my childish behavior.

"You know Ash as well as I do Nathan. She's too proud to admit that she needs help."

I snorted with arrogant amusement.

"Help? Ash never needs help from anyone."

"She needs you Nath," she said with a knowing smile. My chest twisted in an unfamiliar way.

"Why does she need me? Is she in trouble?" I asked with concern. Had there been a development in the Dominic situation that I didn't know about? Red shook her head.

"I don't know, but she hasn't been herself since the day she left your hospital room."

"I was pretty awful to her," I admitted.

"I know," she said sagely, as if she was a fucking psychic.

"I guess I should start referring to you as the Oracle then," I retorted snidely.

"Don't be a dick," she scolded gently. "You put me in the middle of this Stoner, so here's my advice… get over your ego, and be the 'proper man' that you want to be for her. It's time to step-up."

Feeling sufficiently shamed, I did the only thing I could think of in order to deflect the attention away from my own short-comings… I pointed out hers.

"Since we're talking about stepping-up," I said, knowing that I was indeed being a bit of a dick, "...have you spoken to Tails since you bailed on organising her Baby Shower?"

"Don't make me sound like a heartless bitch Nath," she said defensively. "I had the whole thing organised and then she disappeared back to Framlingham."

"She didn't have a lot of choice. She couldn't exactly stay in the flat with Ryan."

"So I'm supposed to just organize a whole other baby shower, two hours from London?"

"Like you said, you had most of it planned. It wouldn't have been that hard."

"We're not having this conversation again," she said angrily. "When you suck it up and call Ash, then you can lecture me."

"Okay, so we agree not to lecture each other anymore," I said with a nod.

"Fine," she said, rolling her eyes.

"How's Ritchie going with Fleabag?" I asked, changing the subject. Ritchie had been looking after Fleabag, whilst I'd been in hospital and he still had no idea that the cat was a stray.

"Ritchie's doing okay, but I think Fleabag is missing you."

I laughed, "I'm pretty sure he isn't. He barely knows me."

Red sat up straight.

"What do mean?"

"He was a stray," I said with a shrug, "I let him in that night before I went to Ashley's place and totally forgot about him."

She stared at me agape. "Fleabag is a stray?"

"Yeah."

"Does Ritchie know that?" she asked in shock.

"Nope."

Red laughed hysterically, "so you've let him look after a random cat for nearly two months?"

"Yep," I confirmed before bursting into laughter with her. We laughed to the point where we were nearly crying.

"Ritchie's going to kill you," Red spluttered between gasps.

"Probably," I agreed, wiping the tears away from my eyes.

"Please let me be there when you tell him."

"I'll be selling tickets for a tenner a piece," I said, as my laughter subsided, "and speaking of the loud-mouth Aussie... where is he this evening?"

"He's finishing off some prep for the Delfontaine account, and then he's on Ryza duty."

"Ryza's not doing so well huh?"

"Nope, he's a wreck," she said with a sigh, "I'm a bit worried he's going to top himself."

"That bad?"

"Yep."

"I'm sure Ritchie will set him straight."

"Nathan, he's sat at home watching Lord of the Rings every night since Kat left."

"Geez," I said with a wince, "maybe he needs to get laid."

Red's eyes lit up, "Nathan you're a genius!"

"I didn't mean you should do it," I joked, hoping that she wasn't planning to take advantage of Ryan in his fragile state.

"Eww, no," she said shaking her head emphatically, "but I know someone who would be up for it." She winked mischievously, and grinned at me like she wanted something.

"What?" I asked, feeling concerned by the look on her face.

"I need a favour..."

- ASHLEY GRANGER -

I pushed my veggie stir-fry around the plate, feeling my parents' eyes boring into me. The dread had been rising in my stomach for the last few days, and I could tell that they were getting suspicious of my unusual behavior.

"Are you looking forward to your yoga class tomorrow?" Dad asked practically inhaling his food.

"Yeah, I am actually," I said with a nod, "it will be nice to get back to it."

"And what time is Ryan coming to pick you up on Sunday?" Mum asked lightly.

"I'm not sure," I said flatly, looking up from the lovely meal that I wasn't eating.

"You know, we could help you move back home love," said Dad, shoving a piece of meat into his mouth, "Ryan doesn't have to come all the way out here."

"Thanks Dad, but Ryan offered. I think he needs the distraction."

"Poor boy," Mum said, shaking her head sympathetically, "he must be devastated."

"He is."

"Would you like to invite him for lunch? I'll make a roast."

"Sure," I agreed unenthusiastically. I didn't want to think about Sunday.

"Great," Mum said, scrutinizing me as I poked at my food.

"I'm sure you're probably looking forward to being back in your own space again poppet?" said my Dad chirpily, in an obvious attempt to lighten the mood.

"I guess," I agreed with a shrug. The truth was, I was dreading going back home, but I'd strung it out for as long as I possibly could. My feet had healed and I'd been off the crutches for two weeks, so I'd run out of excuses not to move back into my flat. Besides which, the daily commute from Surrey made no sense when my place was sitting empty.

"Everything okay love?" Mum asked, as I poked mindlessly at a piece of broccoli.

"Yeah fine," I said unconvincingly. Despite what I'd promised Jock, I couldn't tell Mum and Dad what was going on. I just had to suck it up and move back home.

"Have you heard from Jock lately?" my Dad asked randomly as if he'd read my mind. I shook my head.

"You should invite him down for lunch on Sunday too," Mum said. "We haven't seen him for such a long time."
I cleared my throat and put down my fork.

"We're not really hanging out anymore."

"Oh," Mum said as she exchanged a meaningful glance with my Dad.
"Why not?"

"It's a long story," I said, avoiding eye contact with either of them.

"I'm sure you'll sort it out," said Dad, ever the optimist.

I recommenced my food poking. "There's nothing to sort out."

"Right," Dad agreed, looking over at Mum for guidance. Mum took a deep breath and plastered a smile on her face.

"What about your friend Nathan?" she asked. "How's he recovering?"

"I don't know," I said, rubbing my temple with my spare hand.

"What do you mean you don't know?" Asked Mum with her fork poised over her plate. Dad was notably silent.

"Nathan and I aren't really friends anymore either."
Mum sighed, and placed her fork neatly on the plate with a clink.

"Ashley please don't do this to yourself again."

"Don't do what?" I asked defensively.

"Don't push people away," she said patronisingly. "You did this to Ryan and all of your Mareechi friends after Dom's attack, and look how much you regretted that. Nathan and Jock both care about you love, don't shut them out."

"For the record, I haven't shut anyone out," I said childishly. "Nathan blames me for the accident, and Jock doesn't want to see me right now."
My parents fell silent.

"Why doesn't Jock want to see you?" Dad asked, breaking the silence with genuine confusion at the idea that anyone wouldn't want to spend time with his one and only daughter.

"Like I said… it's a long story."

"Honey, it's been a stressful time for all of you," Mum said, resting her hand on top of mine. "Just give it some time and I'm sure it will all blow over."

"I don't think so, but thanks anyway Mum." I pushed out my chair with a scrape, and stood on my freshly healed feet. I forced a smile to my face, and gave her a kiss on the head. "I'm going to my room."

"Aren't you going to eat your stir-fry?" she asked, as I made my way around the table to Dad.

"I'm not very hungry," I said apologetically, as I kissed Dad on the cheek. "I love you."

"Love you too Cupcake," Dad replied. "Oh, by the way, there was some mail at your place today. I've left it on the hallstand for you."

"Thanks for doing that Dad."

"Anything for you my love."
I smiled half-heartedly and trudged out of the dining room.

"Do you want me to make you a peppermint tea?" called Mum with a tinge of hopelessness.

"No thanks," I said as I hobbled down the hallway. I slowed as I saw the mail on the hallstand. Sitting on the top of the pile was a brown envelope with nothing but my name handwritten on the front of it in big black letters. My stomach dropped at the sight of the familiar handwriting.

"Dom," I whispered under my breath. I glanced out towards the dining room to make sure neither of my parents had followed me. When I was sure the coast was clear, I picked up the envelope with shaking hands. I stared at it for a moment, then took a deep breath and peeled open the flap. Inside, there was a photo of Nathan in his hospital room.

My stomach lurched again. The picture had been taken from inside the hospital, which meant that Dom's guy had access to Nathan. I swallowed down the lump in my throat and flipped the photo over. On the back, in the same black writing, were the words: 'I'M STILL WATCHING'.

I felt anxiety gripping my chest. I took the threatening letter back to my room and shoved it inside my suitcase. Jock was right. I was in way over my head.

I sunk to my bed and closed my tired eyes. How could this be happening again? I ran over all the events of the past few months in my head. The spyware, the text message, the photo of me and Jock. My eyes flew open. It was Jock. His previous words reverberated through my head, 'I think you're underestimating Dom.' How could Jock possibly have known what Dom was capable of? More curiously still… why had he been so determined for me to go away with him? Was Jock somehow connected to Dom? Was he Dom's guy? It seemed too coincidental that he kept showing up every time something happened, and also that I'd just magically stumbled upon an ex-cop in the Apple store.

I needed to stop thinking, so I rolled out my yoga mat and worked through a few sets of sun salutations. As I focused on my body movements, the thoughts of Dom, Jock and Nathan started to fade away. I was mid-way into my cobra, when the sharp sound of the door buzzer caused me to nearly face-plant on the floor.

"Shit," I swore under my breath. My nerves had been so jarred by the noise that my heart was thudding loudly in my chest. I felt like I was back to the anxious, highly strung girl that I'd been all those years ago.

I heard the muffled sound of Mum's excited voice as she let in whomever it was, so I continued with my sun salutations, until footsteps echoed down the corridor.

"Ashley, you have a visitor," Mum called down the hallway. There was a quiet knock at my bedroom door.

"Ash?" It was Jock. My heart thudded in my throat. What was he doing here? "Ash?" he repeated, knocking again. I opened the door a crack. How was it that he'd turned up less than an hour after I'd got the photo of Nathan? "Hey," he said quietly, holding up a pink stuffed rabbit, "this was at the front door for you."

My heart stopped. It was Mia's pink bunny.

"Where did you get that?" I asked warily as he tried to pass the soft toy through the small gap.

"It was just sitting on the front step," he said with a shrug. "It has your name on it," he said showing me a brown label with the same black writing on it. "I figured someone had left you a gift."

"I don't want it." I said, grasping to the door handle tightly. "What are you doing here?"

"I need to tell you something," he said, looking back over his shoulder to see if my Mum was still standing there, "can I come in?"

"We haven't spoken for a whole month, but you drove out to Surrey at 8 o'clock on a Friday night to tell me something?"

"Yeah," he said with a nod.

"And you couldn't do that over the phone?" I asked suspiciously.

"Not really, no," he said, leaning his arm against the door-frame. "Can I come in so we can talk?"

"Here is fine," I said coldly.

"Have I done something to upset you?" he asked with confusion. I ignored him and powered forth.

"Jock, have you been to visit Nathan lately?"

"Yeah I went last week, but he was asleep," he cocked his head curiously, "Ash, what's going on? Has something happened?"

"What about Kesha?" I said, ignoring his question, "did you become friends with her just to get to me?"

"Why would you think that?" he asked more defensively than an innocent man would.

"Just answer my question Jock. Did you know who I was before you met me at Kesha's birthday?"

Jock stared at me agape. "What the fuck is happening right now?"

"Are you working for Dom?" I asked bluntly, leaving him no room for avoidance.

"Am I what?" he said, seemingly appalled. "Why would you think that?" I held the door handle so tightly that my knuckles were turning white.

"Because you've showed up every single time I've had contact from him."

"I can't believe you actually think that I would work for that psychopath," he said indignantly.

"Look at the facts Jock. You were at the Apple store when I went in to get my phone sorted; you were at my place when Nathan's car got totaled; you visited Nathan last week; and you're here right now… with that fucking bunny," I said, pointing at the rabbit in his hand. "You're the common denominator Jock." Jock dropped the stuffed bunny like it was on fire.

"Ash, you're being crazy," he said, stepping back from the door.

"Am I really?" I challenged, feeling confident that I'd figured out his secret. "It's interesting you should say that, because that's exactly what Dom used to tell me all the time."

He raised his hands in surrender, "I just came to tell you something."

"Well I don't want to hear it," I said firmly, "and I don't want to see you anywhere near here, or my flat, or Nathan, or Kesha ever again."

"It's not what you think …"

"Bye Jock," I said slamming the door in his face. I locked the bedroom door and flopped against it as the adrenalin coursed through my veins. I had no idea whether that little outburst would make things better or worse, but I was glad I'd stood up for myself for once. At least this time, Dom might realise that I wouldn't be such a push-over.

- KAT McPHERSON -

By the time dinner rolled around, Mum and I had made peace, but it was tenuous.

"I'm sorry for what I said earlier Mum," I apologised sheepishly as I helped her set the table, "I was angry at myself, not you."

"Apology accepted love," she said with a stiff nod, re-arranging the cutlery that I'd just set. "You have a lot going on right now."

I paused with the plates in-hand, waiting for her to offer an apology of her own, but it never came. It wasn't exactly the mutual apology I'd hoped for, but it was as good as I would get from my mother.

"Well, I appreciate that," I said as civilly as possible as I recommenced my plate-setting.

"I want you to know that this is a safe place love," she added as if she was the mother-of-the-year, "you don't have to be perfect here, we will never judge you."

"Thanks Mum," I said through gritted teeth, not wanting to re-ignite the argument.

"We're your parents Katherine, we will always love you no matter what."

I was on the verge of losing my shit, when my phone vibrated excitedly on the kitchen bench. I welcomed the distraction and waddled to the bench as fast as my burdened legs would carry me. It was Nathan. He was the only remaining friend I had, and he'd been checking-in on me every couple of days since he'd come out of his pseudo-coma. As much as it surprised me, I very much looked forward to our chats even though he was probably only calling because was going crazy in hospital. Regardless of his reasons, I enjoyed the momentary distraction from the depressing reality of my fucked-up life.

"Excuse me for a minute Mum," I said, stepping out into the backyard to answer the call. "Hey Mr Stone, you are now officially my favourite person in the world."

"Wow, I think that's the first time I've ever heard you say that," he replied with a laugh. "What's brought that on?"

"You saved me from having another argument with my mother."

"Another one? Does that mean there's already been one?"

"Yep, and it was a blinder."

"Oh dear," he said understandingly, "so they found out you're home huh?"

"Rosie blabbed," I said unimpressed, "and I'm now being held hostage at their place for the weekend."

"I'm sure it's not that bad," Nathan replied lightly. "Your mum always seemed really nice to me."

"That's only because she wanted to get in your pants."

"Wow, okay," he laughed. "This conversation just took a turn that I wasn't expecting."

"Sorry," I apologised, with a sigh. "I have no idea how I managed to fuck up my life so spectacularly."

"Don't keep beating yourself up Tails."

"And ironically, that nickname will actually become valid again soon," I said with a sad chuckle. Nathan was silent for a moment.

"I'm really sorry Tails, I honestly thought that you guys would be back together by now."

"The stupid thing is that I did too," I agreed quietly. "Anyway… tell me how the rehab's coming along."

"I walked today," he replied proudly.

"Nathan, that's amazing."

"Yeah, it was only about thirteen steps but it was a start."

"Not that you're counting," I teased, as my Mother stuck her head out the back door.

"Dinner's ready," she said pointedly.

"Okay," I said. "Sorry Nath, I've now regressed back to ten years old and have to do whatever my mother tells me, so I've gotta go."

"No worries," he paused. "Are you okay though?"

"I will be," I said with a nod, "I wish I could come and see you but I'm not allowed to travel. I'll come down once the baby is born."

"Hopefully I'll be walking before then and I can come up to visit."

"Katherine!" Mum shouted from the kitchen.

"Sorry, I have to go," I said, "thanks for being such a good friend Nath. No one else is talking to me."

"Give them some time, they'll all come around," he assured me confidently.

"It's getting cold," called Mum.

"Okay, chat soon," I said to Nathan as my impatient mother stuck her head out the door again.

"Chat soon," he agreed, and we both hung up.

"What are you doing?" Mum asked as I slid past her to return to the kitchen. "Didn't you hear me calling?" she asked, following me back inside.

"Mum the whole neighbourhood heard you calling," I said in what I hoped was a joking tone, although I was feeling far from amused. "I was just chatting to my friend Nathan."

"Oh yes, the handsome one who was in the accident," my Mum said, ever the cougar. "How is he doing?" she asked as we joined Dad at the dinner table.

"He walked today, so that's a pretty big achievement," I said, feeling a rush of pride for my determined friend. "They weren't expecting him to be walking so soon."

"Sounds like he's got something to fight for," said Mum with a smile.

"Yeah, his sex life," I joked, causing my Dad to choke on his roast potato.

"There are worse things to fight for," my Mum said primly. "Is he still single?"

"Yeah, sort of."

"It wasn't him that you…" Mum trailed off, raising her eyebrows in an attempt to get me to finish her sentence.

"No Mum," I said with disgust, "Nathan and I are just friends. Besides, he's hung up on Ashley Granger these days."

"Ashley Granger… isn't she the one that Ryan was fond of?"

Holy Hell. My Mum was like the fucking Terminator of the gossip world.

"Yes. She was. Is. I don't actually know where he's at with his feelings these days," I said, realising that I hadn't actually spoken to my estranged husband in over a month. Would he come around like everyone kept assuring me he would? I could only hope so.

- NATHAN STONE -

I hung up the phone from Tails and looked around my hospital room.

"Another wild Friday night for Stoner," I sighed, not knowing what to do with myself. I hummed quietly to the empty room. "No, you're not gonna get what you need." I'd been playing the same song from Ash's playlist on repeat for a month straight, and I couldn't get it out of my head. Every time I listened to it, I felt like Ash was talking to me.

I grabbed her iPod, along with my noise-cancelling headphones and pressed play on 'Honey'. I shoved the iPod into my hoodie pocket and wheeled my chair over to the desk to do some work on my laptop. The Delfontaine account was on-hold for now but I still had Marketing Strategies and Resourcing plans to lock down before we kicked-off.

"Come get your honey baby," I sang along to the song in a high-pitched voice, sounding somewhat like a cat being strangled. I had the music up so loud that I didn't hear the knock on the door, and nearly fell out of my wheelchair when Jock tapped me on the shoulder.

"Jesus," I said, taking off my headphones, "you gave me a fright."

"I did knock," he said apologetically. "Shall I go away and come back for your next show?"

"Heh, yeah," I laughed with embarrassment, shoving the iPod onto the table. I felt like a feeble, broken, little man in his presence. At 6ft 3", I wasn't short by any stretch of the imagination, but Jock was built like a Celtic warrior. I could only imagine how pathetic I must have looked in his arms, whilst he was carrying me heroically out of the car wreckage. "Ash made me a playlist."

"I see," he said with amusement, towering over me like some sort of Viking God.

"She thought I might need entertainment," I explained like a retard.

"That's grand," he said with a nod. "And have you spoken to her lately?"

"Err… no," I said, leaning back in my wheelchair to avoid getting a crink in my neck. "Not since she left the hospital."

Jock looked surprised, "why not?" he asked, crossing his huge arms over his chest.

"We just…" I trailed off, not having a sufficient explanation. Jock pulled up a chair and squeezed himself into it, re-adjusting several times before getting comfortable.

"Nathan, it pains me to admit this, but Ashley needs you."

"I doubt that," I said, as some jealous-ish emotions bubbled in my chest, "I'm sure you have it all under control."

"Stop being a fucking bairn," Jock berated me brutally. "You're sitting on your arse, feeling sorry for yourself, while she's going through hell."

"In case you hadn't noticed, this isn't exactly a walk in the park either," I snapped defensively. "Sitting on my arse is pretty much the only thing I'm capable of at the moment," I added, sounding like a five-year old. "And besides which, if you're so worried about her why don't you deal with it?"

"I can't," he said, scratching his ginger beard, "we're no longer friends." The tables had turned, and now it was my turn to do the interrogating.

"Why not?" I asked, sitting forward. He sighed heavily, and scratched the back of his thick neck.

"She thinks I'm working for Dom."

"And are you?" I asked suspiciously.

He shook his head, "would I be here if I was?" I studied him for a minute, wondering if Ashley's accusation could be true.

"Probably not," I agreed.

"Look Nathan, I didn't plan for this to happen, but I care about Ashley too much to see her hurting like this," he said, looking like a broken man.

"Okay," I nodded. I could see in his eyes that he was telling the truth. "So why are you here then?"

"I have some info on Dom that Ash needs to know."

"And what's that?"

"He's not where she thinks he is."

My jaw dropped. "Are you saying Dom's out of prison?"

"Well he's definitely not in prison, so one can only assume."

"How do you know that?"

"Because I went to pay him a visit," Jock said, clenching his jaw briefly. He seemed to be holding back. I scrutinized him intently, trying to figure out his angle.

"How could he have got out without the cops knowing?"
Jock squirmed in his seat.

"Because they think he's still there," he said, clearing his throat as he spoke.

"I really don't understand," I said, rubbing my face with confusion.

"There's a guy in prison who says he's Dominic Doyle," said Jock, leaning forward, "but he's not Dominic Doyle."

"Do you even know what Dom looks like? How do you know he's not Dom? " I asked doubtfully as my head reeled with the information.

"Because I'm a good cop," he said, fishing in his pocket for his phone. He tapped on the screen for a moment, then turned it around so I could see it. "This is Dom's mugshot from the night he got arrested," Jock swiped right to another photo, "and this is the guy in prison." It was a photo of a big dark-haired guy, who looked a lot like Dom, but was most definitely not Dominic Doyle.

"Holy fuck," I breathed, taking the phone from his hand so I could take a closer look. "It's not some hired goon stalking Ash," I mumbled as my brain went into over-time, "it's Dom himself."

Jock nodded stiffly. "Aye."

"And he's the one who tried to kill me…" I muttered, "and the one who sent me the photo of you and Ash and…"

"Stop," Jock said, raising his hand like a traffic cop. "There was a photo of me and Ash?"

"Yeah, that's why I was at her place that night," I explained sheepishly, "someone texted it to me."

"She never told me that," he said quietly. "No wonder…" he trailed off and sighed as I handed back his phone.

"Does Ash know about Dom?" I asked.

"No, I didn't get a chance to tell her."

"Right," I said, trying not to snigger at the image of Ashley slamming the door on Jock.

"Ash needs help Nathan, and I can't be the one to do it."

"Why not? You haven't had a problem getting involved thus far." Jock dropped his head and studied his gargantuan hands.

"Because I'm in love with her, Einstein." He looked up with a raised, ginger eyebrow, "and the problem is… she's in love with you."

I snorted in shock. "What makes you think that?"

Jock laughed. "I dinnae ken how you can't see it," he said, shaking his head in disbelief. "I think you must be the only person on the planet who hasn't figured it out yet."

"Relationships aren't really my forte," I admitted.

"No kidding," he teased, "well let me give you some advice," he said leaning forward as if he was going to share some sage wisdom, "man-up. Your woman needs you."

"Yeah, I've heard that one before," I replied sarcastically. "How exactly am I supposed to take care of a seven-foot psycho when I can barely walk?"

"I'm not telling you to fight him," he replied, rolling his eyes. "I'm working on getting the real Dom put away, but I can't look after Ash. I'm not her guy."

"Because I am?" I asked, wondering why he would bow out so gracefully.

"Exactly," Jock said.

"And you're just walking away from her without a fight?"

"Aye."

"Why?"

"I want her to be happy," he said, noisily extricating himself from the little chair he'd been sitting in, "and for reasons I don't understand, you make her happy Nathan." Once he was free, he walked over and patted my arm. "I know you'll do the right thing." It sounded more like a threat than encouragement.

"Hey," I said, grabbing his hand in a weird shake/hold/fist-bump combo. "Thanks man… and I mean for everything. I owe you my life."

"I'm a cop Nathan, that's what I do," he said modestly.

"Used to be a cop," I corrected him.

"Yeah," he agreed with a shrug. "Once a cop, always a cop." Jock cast me a tight smile and headed for the door. He stopped in the doorway and turned back. "If I had a woman like that waiting for me, I'd be walking already," he said, before vanishing down the hallway.

I looked down at my legs. He was right. If I wanted to help Ashley, I certainly couldn't do it from a wheelchair.

"Okay legs... let's see what you've got," I said out loud, and took a deep breath. "Come on Stoner, you can do this." I locked my brakes and gripped the armrests tight, letting my legs slide towards the floor, while I heaved the top half of my body upwards. I had a variety of different pains twinging through my lower body, but I gritted my teeth and breathed through the agony as if I was doing a workout.

A groan escaped my lips as my feet took the bulk of my weight. It was excruciatingly painful, but my legs were holding fast. I slowly prised my fingers off the wheelchair, and let the rest of my bodyweight shift into my legs.

"Yes!" I celebrated through gritted teeth, as pain wracked my body. I was standing on my own. It wasn't walking, but it was a start.

- RYAN McPHERSON -

Eight beers, and 'The Lord of the Rings' later, I was fairly toasted. Lying spread eagled on the sofa with a beer in hand, I stared hatefully at the the framed photos of Kat and I that hung mockingly on the loungeroom wall. The two of us had once been so proud of that fucking photo wall. As newlyweds, we'd spent an entire Saturday painstakingly hanging the purposely mismatched frames, so that they would look perfectly hap-hazard. Now, they did nothing but taunt me. In fact, I felt like the whole house was torturing me. Teasing me with reminders of my absent wife and our unborn child who would probably never live there.

My doorbell buzzed loudly. I looked at the clock. It was nine p.m.

"Fuck off," I mumbled drunkenly to the unwelcome visitor. Everyone I knew was either incapacitated or out partying. Or in fucking Framlingham.

I switched over to 'Fellowship of the Rings', snuggling into the couch for part two of my Lord of the Rings marathon when the intercom buzzed again. I turned up the volume to drown out the sound. The buzzing stopped, but then, after a few minutes of peace, there was a loud thump on my lounge room window.

"What the fuck?!" I swore with a jump.

"Ryza, open the door ya cunt!" Ritchie shouted loudly through the closed window.

"Ritch? What the fuck are you doing?" I asked with surprise, as I pulled open the blind to see him standing in my garden bed, with his face against the window.

"Your doorbell isn't working," he explained. I opened the window so we didn't have to keep shouting through the glass.

"Yes it is."

He threw his hands in the air, "well why the fuck didn't you answer it?"

"Because it's nine o'clock on a Friday night."

"Exactly Ryza... it's nine o'clock on a Friday night. What the fuck are you doing sitting at home?"

"Well I was trying to watch Fellowship of the Rings, until some psycho started banging on my window."

"Seriously Ryan, if you watch those fucking movies one more time, you're going to turn into a goblin."

"Hobbit."

"Whatever, I don't care, just let me in," he said with exasperation.

"Why?"

"Because we're going out."

"No, we're not."

"Yes, we are. It's time you had some fun," Ritchie replied sternly. "I've let you feel sorry for yourself long enough. It's time to get the fuck out of this house."

"What's the point?" I asked hopelessly.

"Holy fuck," Ritchie sighed, as he began to hoist himself through the window.

"What are you doing?"

"If you're not going to open the door, then I'll let myself in," he said, hooking his arm over the windowsill.

"Fine," I sighed in resignation, and stood back from the window so he could climb in. He stopped and looked up at me questioningly.

"You're not going to let me in the door?"

"You're halfway inside now, so you might as well keep going."

Ritchie swore under his breath and began wedging his large frame through the small window. There was so much swearing and banging that I wasn't sure whether my window would survive, but the fun of torturing him would be worth any damage bill. He finally made it inside, and flopped on my living room floor.

"You're a fuckhead."

"Yeah, but I am feeling a lot better after watching you do that," I joked with a half-hearted laugh.

He ginned mischievously, "and here's something else that will make you feel better." Still lying flat on his back on the floor, Ritchie rummaged around his jacket pocket, and pulled out a little baggie of cocaine. He waved it proudly above his face like it was a trophy.

"No Ritchie, don't you remember what happened the last time I did that?" He sat up.

"Yeah, you had fun."

I shook my head, "nope. I'm too old for that shit now."

"Fuck off cunt, you're never too old to have a bit of fun," he joked, as he crawled over to my coffee table and started tipping the coke onto the glass-top. "Besides, you can't blame drugs for Tails cheating on you."

I winced at the blunt reminder, but plowed forth regardless.

"I'm not doing lines with you Ritch, Kat would kill me."

"No offense Ryza…but Tails is gone," he replied, not unkindly, as he racked up two neat white lines. His words hit me right in the chest. Kat was gone. My stomach heaved at my new reality.

"She's really gone Ritch," I muttered stupidly, as if the thought had never occurred to me before. "I've lost my fucking family."
Ritchie patted me on the back.

"Cheer up mate. I know its shit, but it'll get better. If you can't forgive her then you need to move on. If you want her back, then you need to go and get her, but the one thing you can't do is sit here and feel sorry for yourself."

"You're right," I nodded as Ritch snorted up his line.

"Of course I'm fucking right," he sniffed, cleaning the remnants of coke off his nose, "why does everyone always sound so surprised when they say that?"

"Because you're a plonker," I teased.

"Ouch," he said with mock offence. "That makes me not want to give you your other surprise."

"There's more?" I asked sarcastically. I dreaded to think.

"Don't be so dismissive, you'll be pleased."

"Will I?" I found that hard to believe.

"Yes, because we're going to get you laid."

"No Ritch."

"Already sorted."

"Please don't tell me you've hired a hooker," I pleaded with a sick feeling in my stomach.

"No, of course we haven't," he said, waving his hand as if I was being ridiculous. "We've lined up Kellie for you."

My jaw dropped. "You what?"

"She's super-keen on you," he said enthusiastically, "so she and Amy are going to meet us out tonight."

I stared at him in horror, "why would you do that?"

"So you guys can finish off what you started that night."

"I didn't start anything," I said, with my hands in the air.

"No, but she did," Ritch said dabbing up a few coke crumbs with his finger, "she was ready to rape you before I interrupted and put you in a taxi."
I was stunned and horrified, but also the tiniest bit intrigued.

"Ritch, I'm still married." He looked at me with raised brows, but didn't say anything. "Yeah okay, I guess that's irrelevant now," I said, in agreement with his unspoken statement.

"Trust me," Ritchie said putting his hand on my shoulder, "once you get your end away, you'll feel a whole lot better."

"That's foul," I said, appalled that he was effectively pimping me out to a twenty-year old.

"But true," he replied with an unapologetic shrug. "Now…do you want a line or what?" Instead of instantly declining as I probably should have, I thought about it for a moment. What did it matter? Without Kat there was nothing stopping me.

"Fuck it," I said, reaching out for the rolled-up tenner, "give me that."

An hour later, our weird little foursome, was partying at some generic EDM club, filled wall-to-wall with trendy twenty-somethings. The coke was the only reason I was able to keep up with Kellie. She was young, enthusiastic and energetic. I was way too old to be with a girl like her.

Half way through the night, Ritchie and Amy vanished into the crowd somewhere, so I bought Kellie another drink and dragged her to a table to sit down for a bit. My body wasn't as durable as it had once been.

"I think it might be time to crack out some more Charlie," Kellie suggested, when I sat down with an old-man groan.

"I don't have any left," I said with a shrug.

"But I do," she said with a wink, subtly pulling out a little baggie of goodies underneath the table.

"Oh sweet," I said, unsure whether I should offer to pay for it.

"And I also got E's," Kellie added with a grin.

"Did you now?" I replied, clearing my throat nervously as she lithely slid her young, firm body onto my lap.

"Uh-huh," she nodded proudly, "but if you want one, you'll have to come and get it," she said, popping a pill on her tongue, and waggling it at me. My stomach flip-flopped. I hadn't kissed anyone other than Kat for three years, and it had been almost two decades since I'd been with a hot twenty year old. My hesitation seemed to spur her on and she ran her finger down my chest, searing me with a look that demolished my self-control.

I pulled her face to mine, and closed my mouth over hers. Kellie's tongue expertly ravished mine as we passed the bitter little pill back and forth between our mouths. It tasted awful but it was strangely sexy, and with her straddling my lap, I was finding it hard to control my excitement. My hands wandered underneath her tiny, skintight dress and up her bare thighs.

She smiled and whispered into my ear, "maybe we should move this party to the bathroom?"

"Sure," I agreed eagerly. My logical brain had officially disengaged and I was thinking exclusively with my dick.

"Meet me in the disabled toilet in two minutes," she said, climbing off me and slinking out into the foyer.

I waited for a few minutes - just enough time to gather my composure - and then, once the coast was clear, I escaped into the corridor and knocked quietly on the toilet door.

"Kell?" I called softly through the door, hoping like hell that I had the right toilet. The latch quickly unlocked, and like a ninja she reached out, grabbed my shirt and swiftly pulled me into the bathroom with her. "Hi," I said with a nervous laugh, as she immediately began unzipping my trousers. They dropped to the floor, and I opened my mouth to speak.

"Shhh," she whispered, extracting my already hard cock from my jocks.

"Okay," I agreed obediently. Kellie hoisted herself up on to the counter top, with her thighs spread and I felt a jolt of lust assault my body. "Oh my god. You're not wearing underwear," I breathed in awe as I was blessed with an unfettered view of her lady bits.

Kellie shot me a naughty grin, and hiked her dress up further for full impact. I stood staring at her in a state of elated shock as she hooked her legs around my butt, and pulled me towards her. I shuffled closer, with my trousers still around my ankles and with no pre-amble, she guided my dick inside her. I was starting to feel the effects of the ecstasy kick in as I grabbed her arse tight and proceeded to fuck her to the best of my ability. Kellie groaned with pleasure, but she wanted more.

"Harder," she instructed, desperately clawing at my shoulders to try and get more resistance. I gripped her hips firmly, and pressed her hard against my cock as I slammed in and out at a rate to which I was not accustomed. "Come on Ryan, fuck me hard," she goaded, as I pumped frantically, hoping I didn't have a heart attack before I finished the job.

"I think I need a line first," I admitted, running out of steam.

"No, we're almost there," Kellie argued with frustration. She wrapped her arms around my shoulders, and gripped her thighs tightly around me. "Let's swap. You sit and I'll fuck."

"Okay." I swung us both around, leaning my butt against the counter-top so that Kellie could sit on top of me. She rested her knees on the bench and moaned with relief as she began bouncing wildly on top of me. I could feel my own cum building, but I had a feeling that she still had a way to go so I slipped my hand between us and pressed my fingers hard against her clit as she ground up and down on top of me.

Kellie groaned with pleasure, and grabbed my hand, forcing my fingers right up inside her, alongside my cock. I wasn't sure whether to be offended or impressed, but as soon as they were in, her whole body began to shake, and she suddenly exploded in a very loud orgasm.

"Faaaaaahk," she wailed with pleasure as I waited for her to finish. I felt too weird about the whole situation to blow my load, and once she was done I removed my fingers slowly, feeling like they'd somehow been violated.

"You haven't gone," she said, looking down at me curiously.

"I guess I'm too exhausted," I lied. "I think I need a line."

"Tell you what," Kell said as she extracted herself from my still-hard cock, "I'll blow you while you're doing blow."

"Well, how could I say no to an offer like that?"

"You can't." She winked and pushed the bag of coke into my hand before sliding down my body to kneel in front of me. I fumbled with the zip-lock baggie but it was impossible to concentrate on opening the bag, with Kellies mouth around my cock. I quickly abandoned my efforts, as Kellie got into full swing.

"Oh god," I moaned as she worked her magic. "Fuck the coke," I mumbled as I threw my head back and enjoyed the best blow job I'd had in years.

Chapter 10

THE NEW NORMAL

- ASHLEY GRANGER -

It was my first day back at yoga, and despite my exhaustion, I was quite excited to get back to it. I squinted my tired eyes against the mid-morning sun as I jogged up the steps to the gym. I'd gotten used to not sleeping much, but last night I hadn't slept at all. Every time I'd closed my eyes, I'd had visions of Dom and Jock laughing as they hunted me down.

I stopped at the front door, took a deep breath, and shook my head free of bad thoughts. Yoga was about grounding and connecting so I couldn't run a class if my mind was elsewhere. I brought myself back into my body and focused on the present.

"You've got this Granger," I said to myself, summoning all my confidence.

When I walked though the door I was nearly moved to tears. I was face-to-face with a massive bunch of balloons, above which hung a big sign saying, 'Welcome Back Ash'.

"Aww you guys," I said tearfully, as the receptionist, Gretta handed me a huge bouquet of Daffodils, "this is so lovely."

"We've missed you," she said, giving me a quick hug. For the first five minutes after my arrival, I was bombarded by staff and clients wanting to welcome me back. With all the excitement, I almost forgot how tired I was. I was reeling in the love and good wishes when Kesha burst out of the studio.

"Ash!!!" she squealed excitedly, pushing through the crowd to get to me. People cleared out of the way and she threw her arms around my neck, "it's so good to see you back in here girlfriend."

"It's good to be back," I said with a laugh, as I peeled myself out of her grasp. I should have known she was the ringleader of this stunt.

"We've got another surprise for you," she said, grabbing my spare hand. "Follow me."

"That sounds mysterious," I said, grasping the big bunch of flowers with one arm, as she excitedly pulled me along with a crew of onlookers following closely behind us.

"I know you were looking forward to teaching your class today," she said with a grin, "but you'll have to wait until next week." She pushed the studio door open.

"Surprise!" everyone shouted. My class and Kesha's class were all in the

Studio, which was decked-out with streamers, balloons and a table full of food, including a chocolate cake. My hand flew to my face to combat the tears that had sprung to my eyes. I looked at Kesha and then took a step into the studio.

"I don't know what to say," I said, swallowing back my tears. I couldn't believe they'd gone to so much trouble for me.

"We couldn't let you come back without celebrating," Kesha said, leading me further into the room.

"This is amazing guys," I said, taking in the whole scene.

"The food is all vegan and refined sugar-free," Kesha told me proudly, "even the cake."

"You're all too much," I said gratefully. "Thanks guys, this looks great." Someone blasted the music, and the celebrations commenced. I tucked away my flowers, grabbed a piece of zucchini slice from the table, and enjoyed the company. Kesh draped her arm over my shoulder.

"You look tired babe," she said with concern.

"Yeah I didn't really sleep."

"Why not?"

"Jock came around last night."

Kesha's jaw dropped. "Oh really?" she asked with thinly veiled disappointment. "So does that mean you guys have made up?"

I smiled knowingly, "no actually, quite the opposite. We had a huge fight."

"Sorry to hear that hun," she said, looking decidedly not sorry.

"It's all good. It is what it is." I eyed her for a moment, intrigued by her new-found interest in Jock. Kesha had always been fond of men in general, but I'd never seen her get hung up on one particular male. "So you quite fancy Jock huh?"

"I mean… he's really sweet," she blushed, and popped one of the heart-shaped chocolates into her mouth, "and he's fucking hot."

"Yeah," I sighed and squeezed her arm.

"And, you know… since your accident we've been hanging out a bit more and I guess…well… I figured he was keen on you so I never did anything about it, but now…"

"Kesh, I'm not sure about Jock," I said as delicately as possible. If Jock was the man I'd previously thought him to be, then I certainly could have seen them together, but knowing that he was working for Dom changed the ball-game completely. It also explained why he'd been so interested in me from the get-go. Kesha eyed me suspiciously.

"Why?" she asked with slight distrust.

"How well do you actually know him?"

"Not as well as you I guess," she said with a hint of jealousy. "We met around the time that you started working here."

I winced with concern. It was all beginning to make sense.

"I don't think he's the good guy that he makes out he is."

She cocked her head curiously.

"Why would you think that? Is this just because you had a fight?"

"No. I can't tell you Kesh," I said with a cringe, "you've just got to trust me on this one yeah?"

She shrugged, "plenty of other fish in the sea." I got the feeling that she was just agreeing with me to end the discussion.

"Please babe?"

"Fine," she said with a fake smile. "Let's just enjoy your party."

- NATHAN STONE -

It was nearly midday when Ryan rocked-up for a visit. I was in the therapy room hobbling back and forth along the balance bars. I hadn't managed to walk without support yet, but I was determined to make it happen, if for nothing more than to shove it in Jock's face.

"Nice work Stoner," Ryan said, slinking into the room with coffees in-hand, and sunglasses on-face. He looked completely partied-out.

"Geez, it must have been a good night," I teased as he put down the coffees and helped me into my chair. "You look like shit."

"Yeah," he chuckled, picking up one of the cups and handing it to me. I took a gulp of the delicious hot brew.

"Oh proper coffee, how I've missed thee," I said, savouring the rich coffee taste before giving Ryza my full attention. "So MacDaddy, tell Uncle Stoner all about your night."

Ryan laughed and sunk down onto one of the chairs, sliding his sunnies up to the top of his head and squinting at the light.

"It was a fairly big night."

I sipped my coffee with a smile, "I heard you and Kellie hit it off pretty well."

"Heh. Gossip travels fast huh?"

I grinned, "of course it does. Haven't you learned anything over the years?"

"Good point," he said, leaning over the armrest like a ragdoll. It was an unusual role reversal. He was the one who'd been partying and sexing, while I'd been in bed stone cold sober.

"So tell me all about it," I prompted, "how did it go?"
Ryza chuckled and shifted in his seat again.

"She's pretty fucking crazy."

I laughed, "well I did warn Ritchie that she'd eat you alive."

"And that she certainly did," he said waggling his eyebrows.

"Oh Jesus," I said with another laugh, feeling weird about being on the receiving end of the sex-boasting. "Well, I'm glad you got sorted. You're definitely looking more relaxed than you have in a while."

"Yeah I think she'll be fun for a while," he said in a very Stoner-like fashion. I felt like I was talking to my old self, and it was starting to freak me out a little.

"Does that mean you're seeing her again then?" I asked, hoping that he wasn't going to go all 'Ryan' and get attached to her.

He nodded and yawned simultaneously, "yeah I'm seeing her tomorrow night."

"Oh right," I said with slight concern. Perhaps he hadn't quite reached full-throttle Stoner level yet. Twice in one weekend was pushing the boundaries of my fuck-buddy guidelines. "That's great," I said, trying to sound encouraging. He leaned his head on his hand.

"You don't approve, do you?"

I sighed, "look Ryza, it's not that I don't approve. I mean, Kellie's dirty-as-fuck and that's exactly what you need right now but…"

"But what?"

"Just don't turn it into a relationship," I said delicately. "I know you Ryza, you're a one-woman man and right now that's the last thing you need."

"It's nothing Nath, we're just fucking."

"Yeah," I agreed with a wince, "all I'm saying is, maybe just try to keep it that way huh? You've got a baby coming soon and having Kellie in the mix would just make the situation even more complicated than it already is."

"I get it Stoner," he said defensively. "I'm not attached, she's just… keeping my mind off everything."

"Okay," I agreed with a nod. He was a grown man and he was responsible for his own life. Who was I to judge? "Now, onto other matters…" I said changing the subject, "is Ash okay? I'm a bit worried about her and she won't answer my calls."

Ryan laughed and shook his head.

"Do you think that may have something to do with the fact that you blamed her for the accident and then ignored her for a month?"

I looked at my coffee cup feeling sheepish.

"I was a dick," I admitted bluntly. There was no point pretending otherwise.

"No surprises there then," he mocked.

"Ouch, bitch," I joked. Ryza smiled and put his coffee down on the table.

"So why has it taken you a whole month to come to that conclusion?"

"I came to that conclusion the second she left my room, I just didn't know what to do about it."

"Apologising is always a good start."

"Yeah," I agreed stiffly, "except she won't answer calls, which makes that difficult to do."

"If you really want to make amends, you'll find a way."

I rolled my eyes. "That's not helpful Ryza. You know I'm shit at this stuff."

"Yes I do," he agreed unsympathetically.

"So instead of lecturing me, could you fucking help me?" I pleaded, "I need to make this better and I really need to see her."

Ryan nodded like he was Don Corleone, granting me a request.

"I'm helping her move back into her flat tomorrow. I'll see what I can do."

"She's moving back home?"

"Yeah." Shit it was worse than I'd thought. She'd be a sitting duck staying there alone.

"Is that a good idea?" I asked desperately. I couldn't let her go back to her flat with Dom on the loose. "I mean, is she ready to be on her own yet?"

"She's fine Stoner, her feet are all healed. She doesn't need looking after."

"The thing is Ryza-" Ryan's phone rang loudly and cut me off.

"Sorry man, just give me a sec," he said, answering the call. "Hey Kell," he said, winking at me, "yeah I had fun too..." he continued, as he wandered out of the therapy room so that I couldn't hear the rest of his conversation. I sighed and sipped on my coffee. Ash was in trouble and Ryan was too preoccupied with his dick, to care. He really had been Stonerfied. So if Ryan was turning into me, did that mean I was turning into him?

Ryza appeared at the door, shoving his phone back into his pocket.

"I've got to fly, Kell's up for another session."

"Seriously?" I asked in disbelief. Who was the guy standing in front of me, and what had he done with my best mate?

"Yeah man, I'm not going to turn down dirty sex," he said with a shrug, sounding like me again.

"Right," I said, with a sigh.

"What's up? I thought you'd be proud of me Stoner," he joked, sizing me up curiously.

"Yeah, no, I'm glad you're getting back out there," I said with a forced smile. "Can you just make sure Ash is okay tomorrow?"

"I promise I'll make sure she's okay," he said with a Boy Scout solute.

"And get her to call me," I reminded him.

"Fine. I'll also get her to call you," he conceded, slapping me on the back, "but right now I've got a booty call to attend."

"Okay," I said, finishing off the dregs of my coffee, "I need to do another round anyway." I started hoisting myself off the chair, but must have forgotten to engage the break because the chair started rolling away from me. Ryan grabbed both me and the chair before we parted ways.

"Careful man," he said standing me upright. "Just go easy yeah? You still have limitations."

"Not for much longer," I said, taking my own weight, and letting go of Ryan. "Help me over to the rails."

"Okay," he agreed dubiously, supporting me while I walked. I cringed and winced and groaned the whole way there, but I made it. "How many laps do you have to do?" he asked.

"Three per round," I grunted, forcing my legs to move my body forwards.

"And how many rounds do you have to do?"

"Three today," I said, with determination.

"So how many have you done?"

"Six."

"Nathan," he said disapprovingly. "Don't push yourself too hard man."

"I have to," I said through gritted teeth as I finished my first lap, "I've got to get out of this place."

- KAT McPHERSON -

Saturday was overcast, and I still wasn't ready to be out in public yet, so my mother and I spent the entire day planning the Baby Shower. Amy had relieved herself of her Baby Shower duties, and I hadn't gotten anywhere with it. I got the feeling that her abdication was more about my cheating than my distance from London, but I'd destroyed so many relationships over the last few months I had no fight left in me to argue the point.

It was clear that Ryan would be getting custody of Amy and Ritchie in the divorce, and realistically, it was best for everyone if I let them go without drama. We'd all been through enough trauma over the last few months to last us a lifetime. I was the cheater, so it was my responsibility to leave as little damage in my wake as possible.

Amazingly, Mum and I had managed to not kill each other so I was considering the day a win. We finally seemed to be at a place where we could at least hold a civil conversation. Realistically, my cheating should have brought us closer together, but it seemed to have added another layer of resentment between us. Mostly because I was still repulsed by the fact that I had become her.

We sat next to each other, perusing a pamphlet of over-embellished Baby Shower cakes. They were all hideous and very Shirly-esque, so I sipped on my tea to hide any unfavourable expressions that might have crept onto my face.

I could feel Mums' eyes on me and I knew she was bursting to say something. There was one cake that was covered in an explosion of icing roses, so I suspected that she had already made up her mind, and wanted me to choose that one.

"Have you got a preference?" I asked, gently putting my cup into the purple rose-covered saucer.

"I think they're all lovely," she said in an oddly amenable manner.

"Okay," I nodded uneasily. Whatever she was wanting to say was right on the verge of escaping her mouth. It was probably worth bracing myself for another argument. I flicked through a few more photos of excessively decorated cakes whilst keeping one eye on Mum. I wanted to be ready to escape if necessary. After another five minutes of silence, she finally detonated, but not in the direction I had been expecting.

"Xavier Brownlough has moved back to town!" she blurted excitedly. My heart skipped a beat. Xavier had been my first love.

"What?" I asked, not wanting to encourage her, but also wanting to know everything.

"I bumped into his mum at the co-op this morning. He's a physiotherapist now."

"And his wife?"

"There's no wife. Xavier is divorced now too."

"I'm not divorced," I replied flatly. Mum picked up the biscuit tin and shoved it at me.

"Do you want a bikkie with your tea?"

"No thanks," I said, fighting against a smile as I recalled an eerily-apt Shirly impression that Ryan had once done. I felt a wave of loss wash over me. My husband was the only other person in the world who would have appreciated the hilarity of that brief moment. Mum put the tin back down.

"Apparently his ex-wife, oh, now, what was her name again? Aretha? No, Agnes I think."

"Agatha," I said, without thinking. Mum looked at me with a sly smile.

"Anyway, whatever her name was... Betty said that the horrid woman left him for a black man."

I choked on my tea.

"Mum, you can't say things like that!" I spluttered, trying to clear the tea from my airways.

"Like what?" She asked oblivious to her own political incorrectness.

"You do realise that your grandchild is going to be black don't you?"

"Well, she'll probably come out more caramel coloured, with your complexion."

I took a deep breath and plastered a smile onto my face.

"That's probably true, but the colour of someone's skin should not be a point of discussion."

"I was just relaying what I'd been told," Mum said indignantly. "The point is that Xavier is single again. I always thought you two made such a lovely couple."

I sighed in exhaustion, "I'm still married mum, and in case it's escaped your attention," I patted my massive belly, "I'm also incredibly pregnant."

"I'm not suggesting you have sex with the man," she said defensively, "just reconnect with him." I remained silent, pretending to study the hideous cakes.

Once upon a time, the thought of a single Xavi would have had me swooning. If Mum had imparted that little piece of gossip on me three years ago, I would have elbowed her out of the way to get to the door... but now, it felt redundant. The only man I wanted to reconnect with was my husband.

"He'll be at Church tomorrow," Mum said as if that was some sort of draw-card. I couldn't tell whether she was trying to sell me on church or on Xavi, or both. "You should come along with us. God knows you could benefit from a few Hail Mary's."

I huffed, indignantly. "Just when I thought you were becoming a decent Mother." The irony of her harsh judgment on my infidelity was not lost on me.

"You need to pull in your head young lady," Mum snapped back sternly. "Just because you've been living in London, doesn't mean it's okay for you to act like you're better than me."

"But it's okay for you to act like you're better than me?"

It was her turn to fall silent. She took a dainty sip from her cup and then placed it back down carefully onto the saucer, looking me in the eye.

"I will concede to that," she said stiffly. "Perhaps it's time we both stopped fighting the fact that we're so similar."

I nodded primly. "Agreed." I'd never seen my mother eat her words before and certainly never dreamed that she'd admit to having flaws.

"I'd still like for you to come to Church with us tomorrow."

"I'm not going to church Mum."

"It's about time you showed your face in town."

"I'm not going to Church," I repeated more forcefully. "I have no intention of showing my face in town whilst I'm heavily pregnant and estranged from my husband… especially not at Church." I was appalled at the thought, but clearly not as appalled as my Mother was at my defiance.

"Well, I have to say, I'm disappointed in you Katherine. I thought I'd raised you to be a braver woman than this."

"I came back here didn't I?" I mumbled under my breath.

"I understand that you're not ready yet, but think about coming next week okay?" she said, either ignoring or not hearing my juvenile jibe.

"Fine," I sighed, exhausted by the discussion.

"And maybe give Xavier a call. He's probably feeling the same way as you, so I'm sure he'd be delighted to hear from you."

"Maybe."

Mum nodded approvingly and fumbled through her purse. I watched with interest as she withdrew a pristine piece of paper.

"Here's his number if you change your mind," she said, pointedly sliding the lined paper across the table. "More tea?"

- RYAN McPHERSON -

On Sunday morning, I awoke face-down, lying sideways across my bed. My head was drooped over the edge of the mattress and I was still fully clothed, shoes et al. The blackout blinds had left the room in darkness, but I could tell from the slight glow around the edges, that it was daylight outside. I rolled over to look at the clock, and almost catapulted off the bed when I saw that it was after eleven.

"Shit," I swore, as I stumbled into the bathroom to spray myself with deodorant. I was expected at the Granger's in an hour and it would take me about that long to get out to Surrey. I'd have to go as I was.

I sniffed my pits and they smelt acceptable, but I sprayed another layer of deo just to make doubly sure. I quickly cleaned my teeth, and then rummaged in my pocket for some left over Charlie, snorting a quick lump to perk myself up. Feeling reasonably human again, I grabbed my keys and ran down to the car, tapping the address into my GPS.

Ash had always referred to her parents place as 'Granger Manor' and I'd assumed she was joking until, an hour later, when my sat nav instructed me to turn left into what seemed to be an endless wall of immaculate red bricks.

My eyes widened as I followed the map through a set of open wrought iron gates emblazoned with 'Granger' on one gate and 'Manor' on the other.

"Holy Shit," I breathed in awe as I took-in the full effect of the long gravel driveway, lined with huge Elm trees on either side. I'd always known the Grangers were well-off, but I'd never realized exactly how wealthy they were until that moment.

I rolled the car slowly down the driveway. My breath caught in my throat when the trees cleared, and I caught sight of the Edwardian Manor. It was breath-taking, not to mention, way too big for two retirees.

Still gaping in disbelief, I parked my car and ascended the grandiose front steps to the extravagant entrance. Granger Manor was a sight to behold. It was amazing that Geoff and Mary could be so down-to-earth with so much wealth behind them. My parents certainly hadn't grasped the concept of remaining humble in their life of privilege. It was probably the difference between earning the money and being born into it.

I pressed the shiny brass doorbell, and heard a loud 'ding-dong' echo through the large halls. Moments later, one of the big wooden doors opened to reveal Mary standing inside with a welcoming grin on her face.

"Ryan, it's good to see you again love," she said, embracing me in a tight squeeze. "Come in, come in." She waved me through the door like I was a prodigal son returning home from war.

"Thanks Mary," I said, handing her a box of chocolates that I'd picked up from the Service Station on the way.

"Aww, thanks love, that's sweet," she said, squeezing my arm, before leading me down the hall to the huge commercial-grade kitchen. "The other two have just popped down to Waitrose, but they shouldn't be long. Have a seat and we can chat while I finish off the yorkies."

"Can I do anything to help?" I asked, putting my wallet down on the shiny marble counter.

"No love, just sit and relax."

"Are you sure?" I asked, perching awkwardly on one of the white leather bar stools at the breakfast bar.

"Absolutely. Can I get you a drink? Beer, wine, soft drink?"

"Thanks, I'd love a soft drink. Anything is fine." Mary smiled in satisfaction and pulled out an icy cold can of IronBru.

"Would you like a glass?" she asked as she handed me the frosty can.

"No thanks Mary, this is great. I haven't had IronBru since I was a kid." The can hissed as I cracked open the ring-pull. I took a sip and the taste instantly transported me back to my childhood when I used to visit my relatives in Scotland. "Ooh that's good," I said, with a sigh of satisfaction. Mary smiled proudly and checked on the vegetables. As she opened the oven door, the scent of roast meat filled the kitchen. "It smells great Mary," I said, inhaling the enticing aroma, "I can't remember the last time I had a proper Sunday roast."

"Yes, you look like you need a good feed," she said, eyeing me up and down as she stirred the yorkie batter.

"That's what I keep getting told," I chuckled, but my smile faded as I remembered the day I'd eaten my last roast meal. It was the day that Nathan and Amy had come over for lunch. My chest tightened as I yearned to return to that blissful life before the night from hell. Mary furrowed her brow.

"Are you taking care of yourself love?"

I snapped myself back to reality.

"Not as well as I should be," I admitted. She stopped stirring and put down the bowl of batter with a look of concern.

"Our door is always open Ryan, whether you need a home-cooked meal, or an escape from London," she said as she placed her hand gently on top of mine. I was moved at her generosity and I had to fight back a tear that was piercing the back of my eyeball.

"Thanks Mary, that's really generous."

"I mean it love, our home is your home." She patted my hand and returned to her batter. "What about your parents? I heard they moved to the US, is that right?"

"Yeah, my Mother won a big contract with a New York Investment banker, so they've been living in Manhattan for the last few years."

"Have they come back to visit you?"

"Unfortunately."

Mary looked at me with horrified surprise.

"Ryan, that's an awful thing to say about your parents!"

"I know that sounds bad, but they're not like you and Geoff. They're empty, spiteful people, and every time we've caught up with them, they've done nothing but insult Kat. They think she's beneath me, and they have never let her forget that."

Her face softened, "I'm sorry to hear that honey."

"I guess they'd be pretty pleased with themselves if they found out what happened."

"Or they might surprise you."

"I doubt it, but thanks for the support," I said, fidgeting with the ring pull on my can of drink. "They're not talking to me at the moment anyway."

Mary looked up from her batter. "Why on earth not?"

"Because I refused to see them last time they were in town. Kat wasn't well with the pregnancy, and I didn't want to put her through that."

"Well I can't speak to what's happening with your parents, but I do know that you're a good man Ryan, I'm sure whatever you've done has been in the best interests of your own little family."

"Yeah, and a fat lot of good that's done me," I said with grunt, forgetting that I was talking to my best friends' Mum. I realized that I was being rude, and snapped my head up to look her in the eye. "Sorry Mary, I know you're just trying to help."

"No need to be sorry love. You've got a lot going on. Besides, it's good for you to get it out."

I opened my mouth to respond when we heard Ash and Geoff arrive home.

"Hi," Ash called down the hallway as the sound of the door banging closed echoed after her.

"Hi Love, we're in the kitchen," replied Mary in response. Ash stuck her head around the corner and grinned, but the worry in her eyes contradicted the apparent joy on her face.

"Hey Ryza," she said giving me a hug. "Did you find it okay?"

"Absolutely. GPS only sent me down one dodgy laneway," I joked.

"Ryan my boy!" Geoff announced heartily as he followed Ash into the room. "Great to see you again," he said, slapping me on the back enthusiastically. He grinned and kissed his wife firmly on the cheek. "This all smells wonderful love."

"It's ready, so how about you all take a seat in the dining room?" Mary suggested.

"You're the boss," Geoff guffawed happily.

"And don't you forget it," she replied with a cheeky wink. Ash smiled and led the way. She looked weary and worn, but her fake smile didn't falter once. It had been a long time since I'd seen her so anxious. She was obviously hiding something. Her uneasy demeanor was vaguely reminiscent of her Dom days. Back then, I'd always been able to tell when she'd had an argument with him before she'd even told me. Of course, now that I knew the full details of their relationship I could understand her previous skittishness, but that didn't explain her current malaise. Whatever was bothering her in that moment must have been something big.

- ASHLEY GRANGER -

For the entire length of our lunch, Ryan eyed me suspiciously across the table. Regardless of the conversation, his worry-filled brown eyes repeatedly drifted back to me, as if he was trying to send me some sort of ESP message. I did my best to avoid his gaze, which wasn't too hard thanks to my parents, who did a great job at inadvertently diverting Ryza's attention. They genuinely cared about Ryan, and it was nice to see him looking so at home. Parental love was exactly what he needed.

When it came time to leave, I felt a sinking feeling in the pit of my stomach Ryan and my Dad piled my luggage into the boot of Ryza's Vauxhall, and we said our goodbyes. Silently, we set off for the big city with full bellies and, in my case, a mind full of worries. Would I be safe now that I'd confronted Jock, or had I made the situation worse for myself? Knowing Dom, I'd probably just made it worse by antagonising him. What if Dom sent Jock after Nathan? He was an easy target whilst he was lying in that hospital bed, and there would be no way he'd stand a chance against a guy the size of Jock.

Ryan glanced sideways at me, and I forced a smile to my face. I could see that he was getting suspicious of my behaviour, but I didn't want him to know about Dom. He had so much of his own drama happening, and he'd finally started to come good, so the last thing he needed was extra stress.

I stared out of the passenger window, watching silently as the country laneways slowly turned into city streets.

"You've been quiet," Ryan said, glancing over at me for the five-hundredth time. "Are you okay?"

"Yeah, just nervous about going back to the flat I guess," I said with a shrug as I recommenced staring out the window.

"Have you spoken to Nath lately?" he asked casually, keeping his eyes on the road. I looked down at my phone in my hand, which told me I'd missed 28 calls from Nathan since yesterday.

"He's rung a couple of times."

"And what did he have to say…?"

"Not a lot," I said peering furtively at him, "I didn't answer."

"Why not?" Ryan asked, switching into his interrogation mode. "He's probably trying to apologise for what he said at the hospital. Why don't you hear him out?"

"I don't think it's a good idea," I said evasively. "I don't want anyone to get hurt."

"Ashley, I wouldn't encourage you if I thought he was going to hurt you," he said, glancing over at me. "In all the years I've known Stoner, I've never seen him serious about anyone. I never thought I'd say this, but I honestly think he's in love with you. Meeting you has changed him and that's got to count for something right?"

I exhaled heavily. "It's not that."

"Well what is it then?"

I chewed on my bottom lip and I was on the verge of telling him when his phone rang. I peered at the screen. "It's Kellie," I told him, wondering who Kellie was. "Do you want me to answer it?"

"No!" he said, pushing my hand away from the phone. "I mean… I don't want to take that right now. You're more important." He didn't have me fooled.

"Spill it Ryza," I teased. "Who's Kellie?"

Ryan scratched the back of his neck and kept his eyes glued to the road until the phone stopped ringing.

"Remember that night you and Nathan ran out on dinner?" he asked awkwardly.

"Yeah," I said, not getting his point.

"Well, she was Nathan's… date." My jaw nearly hit the floor as the penny finally dropped.

"Oh my god, the twenty-year old?!"

"She's actually twenty-five," he replied indignantly.

"Oh well, that's completely different then," I said, biting on the side of my cheek to stop myself from saying anything else. He did look much more relaxed than usual, so maybe she was good for him. "So when did that happen?"

"Friday night," he answered. "It's not a thing, we're just hooking up," he added dismissively, "she's keeping my mind off Kat."

"Fair enough," I agreed with a nod. "How's that all going anyway? Any news on the baby?"

"She's still got about six weeks to go so it's just a waiting game really."

"Are you going to be there for the birth?"

"Kat wants me to be in there, and I really want to see the birth of my child but…" he sighed, "I don't know, it's just all tainted you know?"

"Ryan, don't pass up that opportunity for the sake of your ego," I said, touching his arm, "you won't ever get that chance back again. This is the birth of your first child. You need to be there. Besides, you never know what might happen with you and Kat. Once you both see that baby you might realise that none of that other shit matters."

"I don't know if I'll ever get to that point, but I do want to be there to meet my kid."

"Well then, you have your answer." Ryan's phone beeped again, but this time with a text. "Kellie again," I said with a mocking grin.

"Don't open it," he instructed.

"Roger that," I agreed, picking up the hint. "Well she's certainly keen, I'll give her that."

"She's certainly something," he laughed as we pulled into my street. The road looked so calm and serene compared to the last time I'd been there. The only indication that the accident had happened was two missing bollards and a bent lamppost. My stomach churned, as the memories of that night flooded back to me. Ryza found a parking space and killed the ignition. "Home sweet home."

"Yeah," I said, trying to sound enthusiastic, but the dread was suffocating me.

Ryan unbuckled his seatbelt and looked over at me with concern.

"Are you okay?" he asked with a furrowed brow.

"I haven't been back here since the accident," I said quietly.

"Ah, I see," he said. "We can sit here for a bit if you like?"

"No I think I'd rather not," I joked half-heartedly. This was almost the exact spot where Nathan had been mowed down.

"Yeah me either," he agreed with a grim chuckle. "Let's get inside hey?"

- RYAN McPHERSON -

I helped Ashley settle back in, but I was worried about her. There was something going on and it was hard to tell whether it was to do with Nathan, or the accident, or both. The pair of them had been acting strangely, so maybe there was more to the story than they were sharing.

"Right, the heating's back, on and your parents have stocked up the fridge. Is there anything else you need me to do for you before I go?" I asked looking around the chilly little flat.

"No, I'm good thanks babe," she said with a smile that belied the worry in her eyes. "I'm just going to get into my PJs and watch Netflix."

"Okay, call if you need anything."

"I suspect you're going to be busy anyway," she teased as my phone rang.

"Speaking of the devil," I joked, seeing Kellie's name on my screen. "Sorry, let me just take this," I said, acting as if it wasn't a sex-related phone call.

"You do what you have to do," she said, flicking on the telly. I wandered into the kitchen.

"Kell," I said, peering out into the lounge to check that Ashley wasn't listening.

"I'm waiting for you, big boy," Kellie breathed into the phone like Marylyn Monroe.

"I'm just finishing up here," I told her quietly, "I should only be another twenty minutes."

"I'm super horny Ryan, if you take too much longer, I'll have to get started without you." I bit my knuckles. Damn, that woman knew how to tease me.

"Okay, but if you do, make sure you film it," I joked.

"Okay," Kell giggled mischievously before hanging up the phone. I shoved my phone into my jeans pocket and returned to the loungeroom where Ash was sitting on the couch with her legs tucked up beneath her. With her feet up like that, I could see the scars on her soles. Fuck, she'd really done herself some damage.

"Are you going to be okay?" I asked, perching on the arm of the sofa, "I'm really worried about you."

"I'll be fine," she assured me, patting my leg. "I have a lot of Netflix to catch up on.

"As long as you're sure, because I can cancel my plans."

"That's sweet, but there's no need to cancel your booty call for me," Ash joked. "Honestly Ryan, I'm fine. Just tired."

"Alright, but at least do me a favour and call Nathan," I said as my back pocket vibrated with a text message.

"I'll think about it," she nodded.

"Don't think about it. Just do it." I kissed her on the head, "rest up kiddo."

"Will do boss."

"I'll let myself out," I said, pulling my phone out as I headed towards Ashley's front door. "See you tomorrow."

"See you tomorrow," she called. I made sure the door was locked behind me and checked my phone on the way downstairs.

"Holy shit," I mumbled, nearly tripping down the stairs as I watched a video of Kellie masturbating. I hadn't expected her to take me seriously.

'On my way,' I texted back quickly, running towards my car.

- KAT McPHERSON -

While my parents were at Church, I settled onto the floral sofa and stared blankly at the moving pictures on the television. I couldn't get my mind off Xavi. When Mum had first mentioned his sudden singledom, and the fact that he had moved back to town, I hadn't been phased, but overnight I'd found myself drifting back to memories of days past.

Everyone had always expected Xavier and I to get married and settle down together, but fate had had other ideas. Was it just coincidence that had led us both home this time, or had destiny intervened yet again? The synchronicity seemed too hard to ignore, but I couldn't imagine risking my marriage for the sake of catching up with my high school boyfriend.

I closed my eyes and found myself transported back to the last time I'd seen Xavier. I was sixteen, and about to sit my final year of high school. Xavi was nearly eighteen and leaving Fram for his first year at Oxford University.

We had been best friends since we were born and, for the first time ever in our lives, we were about to be parted.

Tears streamed down my face as I stood on the platform at Ipswich station. My childhood sweetheart was off to do great things with his life, while I was stuck in Suffolk.

"Don't cry babe. I'll be back in Fram for Christmas," he whispered as he wiped the tears from my cheeks. I nodded sadly, and he tipped my chin upwards, to look me in the eyes. "You've got an important year ahead babe. The best thing you can do is study hard and blitz those exams. After that we can figure something out."

"But a year is such a long time," I replied tearfully.

"Not when we have a lifetime ahead of us," Xavier answered sagely, before kissing me firmly on the lips. He grabbed his suitcase and headed for the train, stopping at the carriage door. "I love you!" he called, blowing me a kiss.

"I love you too," I replied sadly, then he climbed onto the waiting train, and vanished from sight. I swallowed a sob, as a tear rolled down my cheek.

"He'll be back soon love," Mum assured me, rubbing my shoulder supportively.

"Not soon enough," I answered with teenage despair. Xavier tapped on the carriage window and waved forlornly. The look on his face, matched the pain I was feeling. Our hearts were mutually breaking. We were doing our best to pretend that we'd pick up where we'd left off, but we both knew deep down, that things would never be the same again.

I ran up to the window and placed my hand softly on the glass, against his.

"You've got my heart Xavi. It's yours forever," I promised, through the thick glass of the train window.

"I'll always love you Katie," he replied, as the train doors beeped. It was all very melodramatic, in the way that only teenagers could dramatize things.

"This train will now depart," announced the voice on the loudspeaker.

"I love you," I whispered, stepping back from the train as the engine began to rumble. With his hand still against the glass, Xavier stared at me sadly, and the train began to pull away from the platform. I sobbed involuntarily, as I watched my love vanish. That was it. That was the end of a lifelong relationship.

"Oh honey," Mum doted, as she wrapped me in a cuddle, "I know it seems like the end of the world, but it's only the beginning. You two will find each other again one day, I promise," she said, softly stroking my hair. I nodded into her chest. Her shirt was soaked with my sorrowful tears, but she continued to hold me tight until my sobs subsided.

"Thanks Mum," I said with a sniff, as I dried my cheeks with the back of my hand.

"That's what mothers are for my love," she replied warmly, guiding me gently towards the exit. "Now, how about we go have a nice, warm cuppa?"

The year that had followed, with all of its teenage angst, and heart-felt letters scribbled onto pretty pink paper, suddenly felt vividly real again. I had managed to keep those memories locked away for so long, compartmentalised, as if they had been part of someone else's life, but now, the raw emotions of those old wounds flooded through my body as intensely as if I was back on that train platform again.

Sitting curled up on the hideous sofa in my childhood home, I felt like I was that heart-broken, sixteen-year old girl, letting go of the only boy she'd ever loved. I let a tear roll down my cheek as I realised that I'd never really given Ryan a chance. I'd promised my heart to Xavi back then, and although I'd never consciously acknowledged it, I'd kept that promise and locked my heart away so that Ryan had only ever got the surface of it.

Regardless of whether or not my marriage was over, I had to see Xavi and put some closure on our relationship, otherwise I'd never be able to love anyone properly. I needed to let him go.

- NATHAN STONE -

It was late on Sunday afternoon, and I was anxious at the thought that Ashley was in her flat alone. I hadn't slept a wink over night because I'd had visions of her lying dead or injured in her flat. I was beyond exhausted, but I knew the best thing to do was distract myself in the therapy room. If I could get walking, then I could get out of there, and help Ash properly.

I managed my first round of bar-assisted laps fairly quickly, so I decided to bash out a second round. I knew my legs were getting stronger, because it felt much easier than it had yesterday. Even the two rounds in a row was manageable, so I quickly smashed out a third. After that I needed a break. I climbed back into my chair and sent a text to Ash. She wasn't answering calls, but perhaps she'd respond to a message.

'I'm worried about you. Ryza said you moved back home. Please let me know you're safe.' I re-read my text a few times, then hit send and leant back in my chair with a sigh. Did the woman have any idea what she was doing to me?

After a few minutes my phone beeped with a text. 'It's okay. I'm safe. x'

I breathed a massive sigh of relief and rubbed my face as I felt tears welling in my eyes. The lack of sleep must have been getting to me. I typed a response, then deleted it, then re-wrote it, then deleted it again, then dropped my phone into my lap. I had no idea what to say to her. Instead of responding, I climbed to my feet and did two more rounds while I figured out what to say.

Puffing and panting, I sank back into my chair and picked up my phone.

'I'm sorry', I wrote. I stared at the screen. Two words. That was all I had. There were so many things I wanted and needed to say to her, but 'I'm Sorry' was all I could think of.

"Fuck it," I said, shaking my head as I sent the message anyway. It was probably the only thing I could say. I put my phone down, and looked over at the support bars. I needed to walk without the rails.

Rising to my feet slowly, I balanced my weight evenly and remained upright. Standing on my own was getting easier, but I had to actually walk on my own if I ever wanted to get out of the hospital. I focused on the wall ahead of me, and took one small practice step. Good. Still standing. I took another, larger, step and nearly fell over when I heard Wayne cheer in excitement.

"Mate!" he exclaimed loudly, appearing out of nowhere.

"Fuck," I swore as I gripped the rail to steady myself.

"Nathan, you're walking!"

"Yeah, I was attempting to, before you scared the shit out of me," I said, leaning myself back against the bar. "What are you doing here on a Sunday?"

"I've got a few things to prep for tomorrow," he said chirpily, "although it looks like you're getting a head start on next week's sessions."

"Yeah, I've got to get out of this hospital Wayne."

Wayne clapped his hands cheerfully. "Great! Since you've skipped ahead of our therapy plan, I'm sure you'll be out in no time."

"No, I mean I need to get out of here right now," I told him, "and since you're here could you sign me off or whatever?"

Wayne laughed loudly, "I assume you're joking."

I stared at him blankly, "no, I'm completely serious."

"Nathan I'm not signing you off, you can barely walk."

"Please Wayne, I need to get out of here," I pleaded with him, "the guy who did this to me is out there, and he's after my…" I searched for the right word to describe Ashley, "woman, friend, Ash-Ashley," I stuttered, scratching my head. What was Ashley to me anyway?

Wayne sighed and ran his hand through his floppy brown hair.

"I'd love to help you out, but I just can't do it," he said apologetically, "I'd get sued for malpractice if I signed you off in this state."

"But I'm standing on my own," I disputed, "and I've been walking with the guide rails for the last few days."

"Yeah, 3 laps at a time Nathan."

"I did six rounds yesterday."

He sighed, "I can see how dedicated you are Nath, but it's not enough."

"So, what will it take for you to agree?"

He laughed again. "I'd need to see you at least walk across the room and back without falling over or breaking a sweat."

"Deal! I do a lap and you'll sign me off."

"No, not a deal," he argued, "you do that, and we'll talk about making a deal."

"Fine," I agreed, "let's do this." I gritted my teeth against the pain and walked very slowly over to the end of the room, one small step at a time. I made it to the wall and looked at Wayne with pride.

"Good, now up and back," he said with an encouraging nod.

"Didn't that count as the 'up' part?" I asked, feeling cheated.

"Nope," he said adamantly, "now up and back if you want to talk about that deal."

"Have I told you lately that you're a cunt?" I joked, beginning my first lap.

"Only every day," he replied with a grin, as I kept shuffling. One foot, stop. Other foot, stop, repeat. It was agonizing but I was doing it.

I'd have to take my mind off the pain if I was going to avoid breaking into a sweat though.

"So what will this deal entail?" I asked, trying to look like I wasn't hurting.

"Well, firstly you have to see this week out, and do an extra lap every day."

I stopped half way across the room.

"But I need to get out of here today."

"I'm sorry, but that's the best I can do Nathan," he said firmly, "keep going." I sighed loudly, but didn't argue. He had me by the balls, so I shut up and continued my excruciating journey.

"What else?" I asked dejectedly.

"You'll have to live with someone," he said sternly. "I don't want you living on your own for the time being."

"Okay," I nodded, "Gaz has already said that I should live with him for a while so that one's sorted. What else?"

"You need to hire all the equipment so you can do your exercises at home, and you need to come and see me at least three times a week."

"Fine," I agreed, finishing the first lap, "any other conditions on my release?" I joked as I turned and started plodding back the way I'd just come.

"No sex until the pelvic x-rays come back clear," Wayne said seriously.

I stopped in my tracks, "what?"

"They're my terms Nathan," he said sternly, "take them or leave them,"

I sighed, "okay, done deal."

"No," he said with an evil smile, "it'll be a done deal once you make it to the end."

- ASHLEY GRANGER -

I'd barely moved from my couch since Ryza had left for his booty-call. I still couldn't believe that he was shagging Nathan's ex-fuck-buddy. It was so out of character for Ryan, but if it was helping him get over Kat then it probably wasn't a bad thing.

I grabbed myself some food, admiring the bright yellow daffodils sitting on my kitchen bench. My surprise party had been so unexpected and so lovely. It made me wonder whether I should just give up my job at Artemis and take a full-time yoga teacher position. I didn't want to let go of my professional life, but once Nathan came back to work, we'd be working closely together and there would be no buffer between us. It wouldn't matter whether or not we were together, he'd be in my daily life and that would be dangerous enough.

I sighed and settled back onto the couch with my sandwich. There was no easy solution to the situation, so dwelling on it wouldn't help. I flicked through my Netflix menu and found an old Avengers movie which was arguably the worst film I could have chosen. Instead of cheering me up, all it did was remind me of Nathan every time Thor appeared on the screen.

My phone vibrated on the coffee table, so I peered over and saw that it was a text from Nathan. My heart jumped in my chest. I'd so badly wanted to answer every single one of his now, 36 phone calls, over the last 24 hours, but that photo from Dom had shaken me enough to stop me from caving. I couldn't risk Nathan's life for my own desire to speak to him.

I read his message and was really touched that he was worried about me. I had to admit, it was comforting to know that, even in hospital, he was looking out for me. At least I knew if anything did happen, or if I got too freaked out, that Nathan would be at the other end of the line if I needed him.

I replied to let him know that I was safe and then put my phone back down on the coffee table. I wanted to say more than, 'It's okay, I'm safe', but if I did then I'd be opening the door for a bigger conversation, and then we'd quickly hurtle into unsafe territory.

I turned my attention back to the movie, but I wasn't really watching it. My mind kept flitting back to Nathan. Unable to control myself, I checked my phone at least once every thirty seconds to see if Nathan had replied. He hadn't. To be fair, I'd been pretty succinct in my message, so there wasn't really much reason for him to respond, but that didn't stop me from wishing he would. I put my phone face down on the coffee table and forced myself to leave it alone while I half-watched the movie.

Twenty minutes later, my phone finally buzzed, and my heart fluttered with excitement as I scrambled to read the message.

'I'm Sorry,' said the message on the screen. That was it. Just, 'I'm Sorry'. What exactly was he apologising for?

I put my phone back on the coffee table so that I wouldn't be tempted to respond. Why was it so hard for me to stay away from Nathan? It had been a whole month since I'd last seen him, and I still felt as strongly about him now as I had back then. Weren't feelings supposed to fade with time? Or maybe in my case absence really did make the heart grow fonder.

Since I wasn't watching the movie anyway, I flicked off the telly and put on Nathan's mix CD. The music somehow conjured up the man himself, and my phone buzzed with another message from him.

'Can I call you?' asked my screen. I paused for a moment.

'I don't know Nath…' I typed hesitantly.

'Please? I know you haven't told Ryza, and I don't want you to feel alone.' A tear sprung from my eye as I realized how well Nathan knew me. For a moment, I stared at the phone in my hand, and then, rather than replying I hit the call button and held the phone to my ear.

"Hey," Nathan said, answering before the first ring had even finished. My whole body relaxed at the sound of his deep, velvety voice, and I had to fight hard to hold back more tears.

"Hey."

"Are you okay?" he asked with concern.

"Not really," I replied honestly.

"I had a feeling that might be the case," he said, with a calming warmth in his voice. "I'm glad you rang. How are you feeling about being home?"

"It's weird," I admitted in barely a whisper.

"Yeah, I bet it is," Nath empathized. I tried to stifle a yawn but he heard it as clear as day. "You're exhausted, you need sleep," he said kindly.

"It's only 7pm."

"Did you sleep last night?" he asked, ignoring my protest.

"Not really," I admitted, hiding another yawn.

"Nothing unusual there then," he teased. "I think you should get some rest anyway. I'll stay on the phone with you."

"You're going to stay on the phone with me while I sleep?" I asked, feeling a bunch of overwhelming emotions bubbling inside my chest. How had we gone from complete radio silence, to this exceedingly intimate conversation? It felt like we were picking up exactly where we'd left off the night of his accident.

"Why not?" he asked. I could almost hear him shrugging at the other end of the line. "It's not like I have anything important to do tomorrow," he chuckled, and then fell silent for a moment. "I'm sorry I was a dick that day."

I laughed, "I would've said 'arse' personally."

"I'll cop that," he replied humbly. "I was a dick and an arse, and probably a bit of a twat too. I'm really sorry."

"Well I appreciate the apology, but it's not necessary."

"So does that mean you're not angry at me anymore?" he asked hopefully.

"I was never angry at you Nathan."

"So why have you been ignoring my calls?"

"Because I've been trying to protect you," I said quietly.

"Protect me? I don't need protecting Ash," he replied firmly. "I can take care of myself." I shook my head, even though I knew he couldn't see me.

"I'm too dangerous Nath. You were nearly killed because of me."

"No. I was nearly killed because of Dom. Besides… you don't get to make that call for me," he said adamantly. "It was only dangerous because I didn't know what I was up against… now I do, and I'm prepared."

I knew Nathan well enough to know that there was nothing I could say to change his mind. He was the most obstinate, arrogant, pig-headed man I'd ever met. But he was also charming, caring, and amazingly sweet. I sighed and sank back against the sofa.

"You're infuriating sometimes," I said with resigned frustration. I was falling for a man who was hell-bent on self-destruction. "Is there anything I can say to convince you that I'm not good for you?"

"Nope," he said with a smile in his voice. "You're stuck with me Granger, whether you like it or not." My heart pounded in my chest. Lost for words, I searched my vocabulary for a suitable response but nothing came out. The only thing that escaped my mouth was a huge, unladylike yawn. "Get some sleep," Nathan instructed with concern.

"I can't sleep," I protested, finding my vocal chords back in working order.

"You need to sleep," he reiterated. "I'll be here. Just put the phone on your pillow and get some rest. I won't go anywhere."

"That's ridiculous," I argued, feeling stupid for wanting to take him up on the offer.

"God, you're so fucking stubborn," he huffed good naturedly.

"Funny, I was thinking the same thing about you a minute ago."
Nath laughed with a sexy, husky chuckle.

"Looks like we're perfect for each other then," he joked casually, as he started quietly humming the lyrics to 'Honey'. "…I have what you want, come get your honey baby," he sang under his breath. My stomach fluttered with butterflies. Did that mean Nathan had listened to my playlist after all? Silence abounded as I floundered for a response again. The man knew exactly how to floor me, without even trying.

"So you listened to the playlist?" I mumbled.

"I've had it on repeat," he admitted unashamedly.

"Oh," I said, lacking a better reply. When it was clear that I had no witty banter to retort with, Nathan spoke again.

"Now, stop being so damn proud, and take me to your bedroom."

- KAT McPHERSON -

I'd survived the weekend at my parents place, and although I had to admit that it hadn't been quite as awful as I'd expected, I was infinitely grateful to be back at Rosie's on Sunday night, where I could be myself without getting judged.

"I'm home," Rosie called through the door when she arrived home an hour after me, from yet another date. "Smells great in here!"

"Yep, dinner's on the table," I shouted from the bathroom, which was where I seemed to spend most of my time lately. "Get started and I'll be out in a sec."

I emerged from the bathroom feeling heavy and burdened - physically more than emotionally, but both applied. I waddled into the kitchen where Rosie was dishing up her spag bol. She looked up from scooping the pasta and cringed.

"Eek, are you okay?"

I was puffed and breathless, like I'd just run a marathon.

"I just want this baby out now. Everything is getting harder," I said, groaning as I lowered myself onto the chair.

"Oh honey, it's not long to go now," she said, slopping a ladle of bolognaise sauce into a bowl, and putting it in front of me, "it will be worth it in the end, I promise."

"Yeah, I know," I sighed, feeling my stomach churn, as a waft of the bolognaise hit my nostrils. "Ugh, I don't think I can eat."

"Do you want some plain spaghetti?"

"Yeah I'll give it a try," I said feebly. "I feel like my lifeforce is being sucked out by a blood-thirsty parasite. Oh wait… it is."

Rosie laughed. "Here wise guy," she said, swapping my bowl of Bol for a plate of pasta.

"Thanks," I replied with a weak smile.

"No more cooking okay," she told me with a concerned smile. "I think it's time that you just rest."

"Yeah," I agreed, "I think you might be right."

"Well, Hallelujah," she teased, raising her hands to the sky, "it must be a cold day in hell, because Katherine Tailor just agreed with me."

"McPherson," I corrected her. Rosie ceased her light-heartedness and looked at me with solemn curiosity.

"Are you going to stay a McPherson if you and Ryan don't get back together?"

"Yeah," I said, too exhausted to even think about the possibility of my marriage ending, "it would be weird if I didn't have the same name as my daughter."

"And speaking of names…?"

I shook my head. "Nothing."

"Seriously?" she asked, astounded. "There isn't one single girls name that you like?"

"Nothing that jumps out," I said with a shrug. "I'll know it when I see her."

"You could call her Agatha," Rosie joked with a wink.

"You know she'd be fat, with a name like that," I joked, mimicking her words from so many moons ago. We shared a laugh at our long-standing joke.

"And on that topic…" Rosie said, taking a large swig of wine, "guess who's back in town."

"Yeah, Mum might have mentioned that once or twice," I said flatly. Rosie leaned forward excitedly in her chair.

"Did she tell you he's a doctor now?"

"I thought he was a Physiotherapist," I said, putting a forkful of plain pasta into my mouth.

"Same thing isn't it?" she said with a shrug, "either way he's 'Doctor Brownlough' now."

"Right."

"And he's super-hot too," she added with a lecherous grin.

"How would you know?" I said dryly.

"Hey, I might be gay, but I still know a hot man when I see one," she said, playfully hitting me on the shoulder, "and Xavi, Dear Sister, is a very hot man."

"He always was," I said with a shrug. Xavi had always reminded me of a Ken Doll, with his thick brown hair and bright blue eyes. Ashley Granger would probably have been a perfect match for him. She'd won over all my other men so why would my childhood sweetheart be any different? Rosie studied me with a smug smile on her face.

"He's been asking after you," she said, breaking the momentary silence. I put my fork down.

"Oh my god, you're as bad as mum," I said with frustration, "she even gave me his number."

Rosie chuckled, "and…"

"And what?"

"Are you going to call him?" she persisted.

"Probably," I said. "Eventually."

"Maybe you could book an appointment with him," she suggested with an impish grin. "How's your neck feeling?"

I looked up at her unamused, "I'm still married Rosanne."

"On paper."

"And in reality," I said impatiently. "My marriage isn't done yet… plus I'm heavily pregnant. I'm not going to gallivant around town with my high school sweetheart."

"Fine," she said, shoving food into her mouth. "But you might change your mind when you see him."

"What part of 'I'm still married' are you not understanding?"

"Meh… you deserve to have a bit of fun," she replied with a cheeky wink.

"Having a bit of fun was what got me into this mess in the first place. Do you realise how much you sound like Mum right now?"

"Point taken," she answered with a formal nod, "but you'll have to get back on the horse some time and Xavi's a pretty fine specimen if you ask me."

"I didn't ask you."

"No, but I'm telling you anyway," she retorted quickly.

"Does that mean you don't think that Ryan and I will get back together?"

"Aww honey," she said apologetically, "that's not what I'm saying at all. I just think you need to accept that it's a possibility."

"I'm not ready to accept that," I told her adamantly, "I'm not ready to give up on my marriage, so until Ryan tells me it's over then I'll keep hoping."

"Okay," Rosie agreed, squeezing my hand, "but at least call Xavi so you can see what's on offer."

I stared daggers at my unrelenting sister. Perhaps my family had already moved on, but I refused to give up on my marriage.

- NATHAN STONE -

It was the early hours of Monday morning when I woke up in my darkened hospital room with the phone still in my hand. I rubbed my tired eyes and squinted at the bright screen. The call was still connected, which meant that Ash was at the other end of the line. I put the phone against my ear and could hear the sound of her steady breathing. I smiled and flicked the phone to speaker so I could listen to her sleep. Popping the phone on my pillow, I wriggled down the bed, forgetting that my broken body was still healing. The hospital bed squeaked loudly as I attempted to roll onto my side, and I gripped my waist when my ribs twinged painfully.

"Ah fuck," I groaned aloud. I flopped back over to the original position and grumbled at my own stupidity. Through my phone speaker, I heard Ashley stir. There was a rustling of fabric, and then the sound became more clear.

"Nathan?" she asked sleepily. "What are you still doing on the line?"

"I fell asleep," I said quietly, flicking the speaker off again, so I didn't wake the rest of the ward.

"Are you okay?" she asked with a yawn.

"Yeah I slept so well that I forgot I was broken for a minute there," I joked in a whisper, as I rearranged myself to a less painful position. Ash chuckled softly. Her voice was still husky from sleep, and it was so damn sexy that I felt another painful twinge in my body as my dormant libido re-awakened. I winced and tried to force my noncompliant cock back into submission.

"Sorry I woke you. You should probably go back to sleep. You've still got six hours before you need to be awake"

"Yeah. I can't believe I actually slept. And I really can't believe you stayed on the phone with me."

"If it helps you feel safe, then I'll stay on the phone with you every night."

"That's really sweet."

"It's also for selfish reasons," I said mischievously. "I enjoy sleeping with you Granger."

"Nathan…" Ash said breathlessly.

"Yeah?" I asked with a crackle in my throat. She fell silent and I could almost hear her weighing up her words.

"Thank you," she said eventually.

"My pleasure," I whispered. There was a long, drawn-out silence while I wracked my brain for something more to say… but I was speechless. I cleared my throat to dislodge the nervous lump that was beginning to form there, and wondered at exactly which point things had suddenly flipped back to being awkward. It was Ash who finally broke the silence.

"How's the therapy coming along?" she asked.

"Good," I said, relieved by the change of subject. "Looks like I'll be out of here soon."

"Really? But it's barely even been two months and they said it would take at least three."

"I don't like to be told what I can and can't do," I said, sounding oddly like her.

"It's possible that I might be able to relate to that," she said with a sleepy laugh. "For what it's worth… I'm really proud of you."
My stomach heaved with a feeling that I couldn't put my finger on.

"Thanks," I said croakily, wondering why I was having such a strange reaction to her kind words. "How are your feet?"

"They're fine now," she answered with a rasp in her voice. "Besides the scarring and the fact that I can't wear heels, life is pretty much back to normal. Well… as normal as they can be under the circumstances."

"Good," I mumbled, nodding to myself. "Ash, when I get out of here-" My words were cut off as an angry, hissing voice cut through the silence of the hospital room.

"Mister Stone," chided one of the night nurses. "What are you doing talking on the phone at this time of night? You're going to wake the other patients."

"Sorry," I muttered, apologizing to both Ashley and the nurse simultaneously. "I'll be quiet."

"I should let you go," Ash said at the other end of the line.

"No," I begged more loudly than I'd planned.

"Mister Stone, I need you to put the phone away," the nurse said firmly.

"You need to go," Ash agreed softly. "I don't want to get you in trouble."

"But I don't want to leave you alone," I blurted, before thinking about it.

"Mister Stone," sighed the nurse, holding out her hand for my phone.

"I'll be fine Nath. Thank you for keeping me company."

"I'll call you tomorrow."

"Ahem," the nurse cleared her throat.

"Why don't I just come and visit you after work and we can talk properly?"

"Please don't," I blurted ungraciously. Ash fell silent, but the nurse let out a huge sigh as she finally lost her patience with me.

"Mister Stone," she warned authoritatively.

"I don't want to see you when I'm like this," I quickly explained to Ash.

"I'll call you tomorrow." I hung up without waiting for Ashley to respond, and sighed guiltily, almost forgetting the nurse was still standing there.

"Ahem," she cleared her throat to remind me of her presence. "The phone Mister Stone."

"You're a poet and you didn't know it," I said, as I looked up at her without amusement. She raised her brows at me, so I reluctantly handed her my only lifeline to the outside world.

"I'll bring this back tomorrow," she said, as if I was some delinquent teenager, texting in the middle of an exam.

"Fine," I moped, playing my part like a pro. "I'll be right here waiting."

- RYAN McPHERSON -

I woke up with a pounding headache, wincing in pain as my alarm screeched loudly at me. I'd only crawled into bed a few hours prior, after an all-night, coke-fueled, fucking session with Kellie. The woman was insatiable.

I flicked off the wailing alarm, and rolled back over again. Fuck the snooze button, fuck work. I was going back to sleep. I closed my eyes and started to drift back off to sleep when my phone started ringing.

"Ugh," I grumbled in frustration. Without opening my eyes, I fumbled around on my nightstand for my phone and randomly pressed at the screen until I answered it. "Yeah?" I mumbled with my face still buried in the pillow.

"Ryza, can you go with Ash to work today?"

"Huh?" I asked, rolling over and rubbing my eyes. "Good morning Stoner, such a pleasant time to hear from you," I muttered sarcastically.

"Were you sleeping?"

"I was trying to."

"Aren't you going to work today?" he asked, sounding way too perky for that time of morning.

"Yes, eventually," I answered with tired annoyance. "Why are you calling me?"

"I need you to go to work with Ash today."

I sat up painfully. "Why the fuck would you need me to do that?" I asked with a groan as my entire body protested my upright position.

"I just want to make sure she gets there okay."

"You're being really weird about Ash lately," I said, unable to fathom why he'd gotten so clingy all of a sudden.

He sighed, "look Ryza, a psycho wiped me out in front of her place, so I'm worried about her being on her own okay?"

"You do realise she's an adult right?" I asked, wondering why he was being so strange about it.

"Yeah but-"

"I'm hanging up now Nathan."

"Ryza-" I hung up the phone. Nathan was going seriously loopy being stuck in that hospital.

I closed my eyes and tried to get back to sleep, but it was no use, my brain was wide awake. Unfortunately my body wasn't happy about it. I sighed, and then, with all the motivation I could muster, I rolled reluctantly out of bed.

"Hmmm… I think I still have left-overs," I mumbled, as I noticed my wallet sitting on the bedside table. I rifled inside the hidden pocket and pulled out a small baggie with the dregs of last night's coke. "Bingo!" I cheered, shaking the little plastic bag triumphantly.

I upended the bag onto my dresser and scraped out every last crumb. There was enough to rack up one little white line, which I promptly demolished. The powder quickly vanished into the rolled note, and when it was all gone, I sniffed hard to dislodge one large crumb that was wedged inside my nostril.

"Much better," I said to myself as I wiped my nose clean. Ritchie had been bugging me to tone down the coke, but I couldn't find a good enough reason to do so. Cocaine was the only thing keeping me functional. Without the party powder, I would have been a total train-wreck.

I cracked on with my day and headed straight to the office, figuring that since I was awake anyway, I might as well take the opportunity to get some work done. I was due to go out with Kellie again that night for her industry drinks and if I started early, I could knock-off at 4pm and have a quick nap before going out.

Unfortunately, my best laid plans had a down-side. In an almost deserted office building, I came face-to-face with the one person I least wanted to see. Beau 'perfect' Peterson, was already sitting at his desk, smirking like the prick that he was.

"Awesome," I muttered sarcastically under my breath. The ongoing tension between the two of us had reached an all-time high, and it took every ounce of my willpower to not punch him in the face again.

"Morning MacPherson," Beau said tersely, acting high and mighty, as if he was the one who'd been wronged. I ignored him and sat down at my desk, unable to engage with the cunt for fear of ripping him to shreds in my place of employment. "Still ignoring me then?" he asked in the same casual way you would ask someone about their weekend. I gritted my teeth to prevent myself from replying and acted as if I hadn't heard him. He snorted with disdain. "Need I remind you that you're the one who came to my house and punched me in the face?"

That was enough to elicit a response from me. My head whipped around violently, like a crocodile attacking its prey.

"You came to my house and fucked my wife," I seethed, pouncing to my feet. Beau smiled spitefully, like a cat who'd caught the mouse.

"So you *can* hear me," he said smarmily. I was on the verge of punching him when Ritchie strutted into the room.

"G'day benders!" he called from the other side of the room. Beau rolled his eyes.

"Ritchie, must you always be so vulgar?" he said haughtily.

"Yes, I must, Peterson," Ritchie retorted obnoxiously. It was awesome that he'd jumped on the anti-Peterson bandwagon in my defense. Beau glared at us both and Ritchie patted me on the shoulder. "Now MacDaddy, you have some details to spill." He said, as he gripped my shoulder firmly and guided me back to my desk. "Tell me all about your weekend Casanova. How was Kellie?" He asked with a grin, as he sprawled himself casually over Nathan's chair, plonking his feet onto the desk.

"What? Now?" I asked, glancing back at Beau, who was pretending not to be eavesdropping. Ritchie nodded with a wicked grin and I immediately dreaded what was about to come. I'd seen him interrogate Nathan plenty of times, but I'd never been at the center of one of his post-shag debriefs.

"So…?" he prompted eagerly. I sat down and decided that I didn't care if Beau over-heard us.

"Honestly… I'm lucky I didn't die of a fucking heart-attack," I admitted. Ritchie laughed loudly, and I couldn't help but join in. I stretched my back and groaned like an old man. "Seriously man, she's way too young and agile for the likes of me but… it was pretty fucking awesome."

"Details…"

"Really?"

"Abso-fucking-lutely."

"Okay, well you already know about Friday night, then she came over on Saturday and we shagged all afternoon… but last night…" I lowered my voice and peered around the room to make sure the prick wasn't listening. He was, but the look of disgust on his face spurred me on. "She sent me a video of herself… you know…" I made a fiddling gesture so I wouldn't have to say it out loud, "and then when I got to her place, she poured a line of coke from her neck right down to her…" I pointed at my crotch.

"No shit?"

"No shit," I confirmed.

"Then what?"

"I snorted the line and then… licked up the rest," I said with a wink.

"Aims will be pleased to know that you're eating again." He sniggered and we both laughed loudly at his crude joke, which usually would have disgusted me. "I think it's time to take it easy on the coke mate."

"So you keep saying, but it's not doing any harm."

"Not yet, but you don't want to turn it into a habit. Having a wild night on the Charlie is one thing, but three days in a row is starting to push it."

"I've got it under control Ritch," I said, silently amending his tally to four days in a row.

"Okay, if you say so," he shrugged doubtfully. "So what's the deal with Kell? Are you fuck-buddy's now then?"

"Yeah, it seems that way," I said with a shrug. "Unless someone else comes along."

"Ryza's back in the game," Ritchie said, punching me in the arm.

"I guess I am," I agreed with a nod. "Although I don't think I was ever technically in the game to begin with."

"You can take Stoner's spot," Ritchie joked, "I think he's out now anyway, even once his pelvis is back on-form."

"He's pretty smitten with Ash huh?" I said, remembering Nathan's weird phone call earlier that morning.

"He's in love with her," Ritchie said with a serious nod, as if someone had died. "You know what that means right?"

"Do I want to?" I asked with a cringe.

"Ryza... you're the new Stoner."

- KAT McPHERSON -

I sat at the kitchen, table staring at the little piece of paper with Xavier's number on it. I'd already been staring at that little piece of paper for at least fourty-five minutes and still not made the call. Why was it so hard for me to make one simple phone call?

"Because it's not a simple phone call," I told myself. "It's a very complicated one, and I don't think I'm ready for it."
Thank god Rosie had gone to work or she would have already done it for me. I could hear her voice in my head telling me to suck it up and make the call. I took a deep breath.

"Fine," I said to my sister's disembodied voice, as I tapped Xavier's number into my phone. The phone rang and my heart thudded. What was I doing?! Why was I putting myself through this? I quickly hung up before he could answer. "Shit," I said, throwing the phone down on the table with a clatter. Instantly it began ringing.

"Shit," I repeated, when I saw that it was Xavier's number. My hand hovered forwards and backwards over the phone as I debated whether or not to answer the call. "Fuck." I took a deep breath and grabbed the phone. "Hello?" I said as calmly as possible.

"Hi, this is Xavier Brownlough," said a deep, buttery voice, "I missed a call from this number."

"Hi, yeah," I said, not really knowing how to recover from my childish prank call, "Xavier, that was me," I said face palming at my stupidity, "it's Kat... Tailor," I said, feeling weird about using my Maiden name again. "I started to call and dropped the phone," I lied, in an attempt to salvage some level of dignity.

"Oh my god Katie," he breathed. He was the only person who had ever called me Katie. "It's so good to hear from you. I heard you were back in town, but nobody's seen you so I thought it was just a rumour."

"Yeah I'm back," I said, chewing on my lip, "I just haven't been out because I'm supposed to be on bedrest."

"Oh, why? Are you okay?" he asked with concern.

"Yeah, I'm fine, I'm just about to pop a baby out," I joked like an idiot. I cringed and rolled my eyes at my stupid comment.

"Oh wow," he said with surprise. "Congratulations."

"Thanks."

"So, how have you been?" Xavier asked, changing the subject. "Besides pregnant," he added with an awkward chuckle.

"Oh," I said, having no idea where to even start on the current state of my life. "Well, I've been good… I guess." I closed my eyes and shook my head to snap myself out of the childishness. "Life has been interesting," I concluded. "How about you?"

"I think interesting would sum it up fairly well for me too," he said with a half-laugh, and then paused for a moment. "I'd really love to see you. Would you fancy breakfast in the morning?" he asked, sounding more like the old Xavi. "I could bring around coffees and almond croissants."

"I'd really like that," I said, breathing a sigh of relief, "but I'll meet you somewhere. I need to get out of this house."

"Are you staying with your parents?"

"No, at Rosie's thankfully," I joked. "I did one weekend at theirs and that was enough to last me for the next twenty years." Xavi laughed understandingly.

"I can imagine," he said with amusement. It almost felt like no time had passed.

"So," I said chirpily, "where should we meet, and what time?"

"There's a little café on Market Hill called the Dancing Goat," he suggested, "they do good food, and there's tables outside so we could enjoy the sun. I have a gap at 10am if that suits you?"

"Sounds great," I agreed. "See you there."

"Katie…" he said before I hung up.

"Yeah?"

"I'm really glad you called."

"Me too," I said, feeling a weird mix of emotions rising in my chest.

"See you tomorrow," he said with a smile in his voice.

"See you then." I hung up the phone and exhaled a long, loud breath. Seeing Xavi was either going to be the smartest or the dumbest decision I'd made since I'd come back to Fram.

- Chapter 11 -

A BITTERSWEET SYMPHONY

- RYAN MCPHERSON -

On Tuesday morning, I once again awoke in severe pain. I'd been out with Kellie and her nightclub friends for Industry night, and boy, could those guys party. Monday nights were their night off so it was a massive blow-out. We'd drunk, snorted and popped so many different things that I couldn't remember much beyond the first hour of the night. I had a vague recollection of fucking Kellie in a back alley somewhere – at her request obviously – but even that memory was pretty foggy.

With my eyes still crusted closed I began to tune into the sounds of my surroundings. One thing was for sure… I hadn't made it home. I heard the shuffle of feet, the beep of ticket gates and a repetitive deep rumbling sound. What the hell had I done last night and where the hell was I now? From the noise I guessed I was in a train station.

"The next train to Stansted is departing in three minutes," said a voice over a loudspeaker. Yep. I was in a train station. Liverpool Street by the sounds of it.

I gradually began to feel my body again. It hurt. Badly. All of my muscles ached, my head was pounding, and I was shivering convulsively. I tore my eyes slowly open, and took a mental inventory of my surroundings… concrete floor, rubbish bin, feet… lots of feet. I forced my crusty eyes open wider. Flower stand, Starbucks, homeless guy. Hmmm…The homeless guy was staring at me.

I gingerly peered down at myself and realised that I was curled up against the brick wall on a pile of old cardboard and newspaper. Ahh. I'd stolen the homeless guy's bed.

I tried to get up, but I was pretty wobbly. I had absolutely no strength or balance left at all, so it took me about five attempts to get to my feet. Homeless Joe (as I had mentally named him) just stood watching me with an expression that looked akin to pity. Clearly my life had hit an all-time low when a homeless guy felt sorry for me.

"Sorry man, it's all yours," I apologised shamefully with a scratchy, gravelly voice. I rubbed my sore throat and then it came back to me… I'd smoked last night. In fact, I think I'd even bought myself a pack of cigarettes. I fished around in my pockets and found a half-empty pack of Marlborough Gold.

"Fuck," I groaned, shoving the fags back into my pocket. No wonder I was having problems breathing. I scrounged through my other pockets, and pulled out a fiver. "Here dude," I said handing the note to Homeless Joe. He assessed me momentarily, but finally decided that I was genuine and took the cash from my outstretched hand. He nodded his gratitude and I patted him on the shoulder.

I was in desperate need of caffeine and preferably, another line. I stumbled up to the service counter at Starbucks.

"Triple shot grande Americano please," I practically begged.

"That's quite an order," the girl teased flirtatiously, eyeing my dishevelled state with amusement.

"Tall, strong and black just like me," I joked with a wink, sounding strangely like Nathan.

"And hot of course," she said, with a cheeky smile as she made my over-caffinated beverage.

"Of course," I agreed chuckling.

"Have a big night did you?" she asked over the noise of the coffee machine.

"Yeah, except I can't remember much of it," I admitted, rubbing the back of my aching neck. "I woke up in the homeless guys bed," I added with a laugh as I pointed towards Homeless Joe. The coffee girl laughed as my new friend noticed us looking at him. I waved at him. "Want a coffee Joe?" I called over. He shook his head but gave me a salute of thanks.

"Wow, first name basis huh?" she teased with amusement.

"I actually just made it up," I said with a shrug, "I have no idea what his real name is." We both laughed.

"Well, he didn't seem to notice, so I think you got away with it," she said smiling. "There's your hot, strong, black coffee. That'll be £2.45"

"Cheers," I said, handing her a fiver, "keep the change."

"Thanks," she said.

"That's for putting up with my stink," I joked. "Catcha next time."

"See ya later, tall, dark and hot," she called after me. I smiled over my shoulder and she gave me a flirty wave, pointing at my cup. She had scribbled her name and number on it. I waved and smiled, then wandered off to find my way home. I noticed the time on the arrivals board and almost choked on my coffee.

"Fuck!" It was nine a.m. already, which meant that I had no time to go home before work. Thankfully Liverpool Street was only about 20mins from the office so I'd still get to work before 9:30.

I jumped on the tube, and squished into the busy compartment. I shoved my hand into my pockets to check that my coke was still there, and found a pair of red-framed sunglasses. I chuckled to myself as I pulled them out. I had no idea where they'd come from, but I was thankful. I was going to need those once I got above ground. I slid them onto my face, and yawned with exhaustion. I needed a quick bump of coke, but a busy tube was not the most appropriate place to do that. I looked around and figured that no one was watching me anyway so I licked my finger, stuck it into the bag and then rubbed it over my gums. I chased it with a mouthful of coffee and it instantly perked me up. I'd have a proper line once I got to work, and I'd be back on full-form.

- KAT McPHERSON -

It was 9:35am and with every minute that ticked past, my nerves kicked-up another notch. By the time the Uber arrived, I was a nervous wreck, and my anxiety was compounded by the familiar face of my driver. James Taylor was one of my old school friends. We'd bonded in seventh grade over our shared surname, even though his was spelt differently.

"Tails!" he said jubilantly as I climbed into the car. "I heard rumors that you were back in town young lady."

"JT," I said with a smile. "Long time no see. How are things?"

"Good, good, same old really," he said with a nod. "You know Fram, nothing much ever changes."

"Yeah," I agreed with a wry smile.

"Looks like you've had a few changes though," he joked, nodding at my belly.

"Yes, I definitely have."

"When are you due?"

"About six weeks."

"Wow. Is your hubby here with you or are you here by yourself?"

"Here alone. He's got to work," I confirmed, not willing to give him any additional info. The gossip-train would already have left the station.

"Right, right," he said casually. "So you heading into town then?"

"Going to meet a friend for breakfast."

"Nice, who are you meeting?"

"Xavier Brownlough," I said awkwardly, already knowing that he'd jump to conclusions.

"Wow… Xavi and Kat reunited huh?" he said with a reminiscent smile. "Just like the old days."

"Just catching up." There was no doubt that I was back in my small home town, and certainly no more hiding now that James had seen me in person. By this afternoon, my breakfast with Xavi would be the talk of the town. Like James had said… nothing much ever changed in Framlingham.

We pulled up outside the Dancing Goat, and I spotted Xavier immediately. He was sitting at one of the tables, reading a book with the morning sun shining on him like an Instagram filter. My breath faltered. Xavi was still that beautiful boy I'd fallen in love with all those years ago, except now he was all wrapped up in a grown man's body.

"He's beat you here," said James as he pulled on the handbrake.

"Thanks James," I said opening the door. "It was great to see you again."

"And you," he said with a smile. "I'm sure we'll see each other around."

"I'm sure we will," I agreed, climbing out of the car. As I closed the car door behind me, Xavier peered up from his book, and smiled. His smile was so warm and familiar, yet completely foreign, like I was staring at someone else's past.

He took his glasses off, put his book down and rested his hand on his chest, taking in the sight of me in my full pregnant glory. With the colourful maxi-dress that I was wearing, I imagined I probably looked somewhat akin to a hot-air balloon.

Xavi walked over to greet me, and I felt like I was watching the scene play out from somewhere up above us, as if I was indeed embodying a hot air balloon.

"Katie, you're still as beautiful as ever," Xavi said, offering me his hand so that he could assist me to the table.

"Oh, I feel a bit like a beach ball at the moment," I joked with a self-concious smile. "But thank you, that's sweet of you to say. You haven't aged a bit." I lied.

He'd definitely aged, but in a way that it was an improvement on the original version, like a fine wine or a good cheese. I never would have thought it was possible for him to get more attractive, but he'd done it.

Xavi sat down and leaned back in his chair with a smile, as the bright sunshine lit up his face.

"It's so good to see you," he said, staring at me with child-like awe. The moment was so surreal that I had to wonder whether I was dreaming. Xavi's blue eyes drilled into mine. "I can't believe you're actually sitting here in front of me," he said shaking his head in disbelief. "Do you know how many times I've imagined this moment?" I swallowed hard, feeling completely naked under his intense gaze.

"Probably as many as I have," I said, remembering all those years when I constantly played out our reunion in my mind. "Except I never saw myself being pregnant when it happened."

He looked down at his book sitting on the table, and gave me a sad little nod. "I left it too long," he said looking back up at me. "I should have come back for you fifteen years ago."

"You should have," I agreed with a melancholy smile. We sat silently for a long while. There was so much to say – twenty years of unspoken words in fact – but it was hard to know where to begin. Xavier leaned his elbows on the table, rested his chin on his interlocked knuckles, and sighed.

"Have I missed my chance with you Katie?" he asked curiously. I looked down at my hands, where my wedding and engagement rings were sparkling in the light. I twisted the rings back and forth around my swollen finger.

"Things are pretty complicated right now," I said with a nod.

"Yeah," he nodded, running his hands through his thick brown hair. "I suppose they are. Rosie said that you'd split from your husband?"

"Oh… no… not quite… you know…"

"Sorry," he apologised, "that's none of my business."

"No, it's fine," I said, looking down at my rings again. "I just don't really know where we stand at the moment."

"So what's wrong with him?" Xavier asked curiously. I looked up from my rings.

"What do you mean?"

"I mean, you're about to have his baby and you're here in Framlingham… so why isn't he here trying to win you back?"

"He… umm… I don't…" I sighed. "I did something pretty bad."

"It doesn't matter, he should be here doing everything he can to fix it."

"He has to work and honestly, I don't really blame him for not coming up," I said shamefully.

"If he doesn't, then he's an idiot," Xavi said, reaching over the table and resting his hand on mine. "And as another idiot who let you get away, I feel like I'm qualified to make that call."

"No," I shook my head. "What I did to Ryan was a deal breaker. He has every right to take some time."

The waitress brought our food over and we paused the conversation while we organised our meals. Once the waitress had left, Xavi looked up at me with those big baby blue eyes of his.

"No matter what you did… if you were my wife, I wouldn't be giving up so easily."

"Xavi," I warned with disapproval. His interest was flattering, but I didn't like his insinuation about Ryan's commitment to our marriage.

"Sorry," he apologized, leaning back in his seat, "but I feel qualified to say that. Trust me, life without Katie Tailor just isn't the same."

- RYAN McPHERSON -

When I got to the office, I veered directly to the reception toilets and racked up a good solid line on the cistern. I snorted it up in one go and then decided that I needed another one to even up my nostrils. I repeated the process and then wiped my nose clean. Much better. Now I could get on with the day.

I looked in the mirror. I didn't look fantastic, but I was passable. With a spray of deo I would be fine. I put the sunglasses back on and headed out to the elevator. As the doors began to close, Ritchie came flying around the corner.

"Wait!" he called, so I held the doors open for him. He took one look at me and cringed. "What the fuck happened to you?"

"Nothing," I replied sipping on my giant coffee as the doors slid closed.

Ritchie tilted his head, and read the number on my cup, "who's Jenni?"

"The coffee girl," I said with an arrogant smile. I was starting to realise why Nath had been such a cocky prick all those years. It was hard not to feel smug when you had sex offers being thrown at you from every direction.

"Right," Ritchie said, glancing sideways at me, "and what's with the sunnies?"

"Found them in my pocket," I said with a shrug.

"Okay," he said, frowning as he got a whiff of my body stink, "new cologne? Eau de homeless?" he teased, and I snorted with laughter.

"You have no idea how appropriate that actually is."

Ritchie turned to face me, "what the hell did you get up to last night McPherson? I take it you haven't made it home?"

"Nope," I said as the elevator doors binged our arrival at the 6th floor.

"I need to piss," he said, "and then you're going to tell me all about last night."

"Sure," I smiled and waved, as he peeled off in the direction of the toilets. I was almost at my desk when Beau Peterson saw me sneaking in.

"Big night?" he asked arrogantly. I rolled my eyes and turned around to face him, sliding the shades up onto the top of my head.

"Not that it's any of your business."

"You're right, it's none of my business," he said, raising his hands, "I just thought you'd be past all of this given you've got a child on the way." I was losing my patience with the guy.

"What the fuck is your problem?" I asked with annoyance. "You're the one who slept with my wife, who the fuck are you to be giving me lectures. If you've got an issue, just come out and say it, otherwise fuck off and leave me alone."

"My issue is your fucking attitude McPherson."

"My attitude?" I replied incredulously. "That's a bit rich coming from a homewrecker." Beau took a step back and ran his hands over his face.

"You have no idea how fucking lucky you are to have Kat. Instead of doing your best to fix things with her, you're out every night popping pills and boning teenagers."

"What gives you that idea?" I asked indignantly.

"Because I saw you on Kellie's insta page."

"Kellie's insta page? What the fuck is that? And why am I on it?"

"Getting insta-famous apparently," he said with disgust. "Looks like you're her new man-cessory."

"Fuck, I hope Kat doesn't see it," I said, having no idea how it all worked. I had a good grasp on Facebook, but Instagram was beyond my realm of social media knowledge. "How are you able to see it?"

"She connected with me after that last dinner."

"Why?" I asked, confused.

"Because Ryan, Kellie might seem sweet and innocent but she's a fucking deviant."

My jaw dropped, "don't tell me you fucked her too."

"I don't fuck young girls," he said harshly, "she was actually hitting me up to get info on you."

I laughed self-righteously, "and you thought she'd keep me distracted while you were fucking my wife."

"To be fair, it was the day after I'd fucked your wife."

That was the last straw. I finally snapped. In a split second I'd thrown my coffee on the floor and unleashed my rage on the slimy cunt. I exploded so fast that he never even saw it coming and he hit the ground hard. I punched and kicked with a fury that was so far beyond my control it was almost frightening. I'd never been a fighter until that prick had weaselled his way into my wife's pants and now I seemed to be developing a taste for it.

Shouts of concern began ringing out from every direction, but I had no idea who they belonged to, or where they were coming from. All I could see was my own rage, and Beau was at the centre of it.

"Stop Ryan!" I heard Christian shout, then felt hands grabbing at my back and arms to try and pull me off Beau. I was so crazed that it did nothing to thwart my vicious attack. Because that's what it was. It was an attack. It couldn't be classed as a fight, when Beau hadn't even swung once. He'd just dropped to the ground like a sack of potatoes while I'd gone at him with everything I had. I'd assaulted him and I had no intention of stopping.

"Ritch!" Christian yelled, calling in re-enforcements.

"Ryza!" Ritchie shouted from somewhere behind me. I heard the sound of his feet pounding against the carpet as he ran towards the fray from somewhere afar. "Get off him," he roared loudly at me, before hooking his hands under my armpits and lifting me up off the ground. I growled and fought against him like a wild animal as he pulled me off Beau, who was lying on the ground seemingly unconscious. "Settle down," he ordered gruffly, as a group of random people ran to Beaus aid. Ritchie carried me away down the hall kicking and screaming like a maniac. "Chill the fuck out Ryza," he said shoving me into the bathroom and throwing me into a stall so that I was trapped in between him and the toilet.

"What the fuck?" he snapped angrily. "You just knocked him out cold. The fucker could be dead, and if he's not, he'll no doubt press charges against you," he said, shaking his head in disbelief. "Not to mention the fact that this will probably cost you your job," Ritchie added, rubbing his bald head with concern. I remained silent, concentrating on calming myself down. "Look mate, in all the years we've been friends, I've never seen you in a fight, let alone start one, so what the fuck happened?"

"Do you really need to ask?" I snarled at him.

"I get it Ryza, trust me," Ritchie said loudly, "the guy fucked your wife, I'm not saying he didn't deserve it, but this isn't you, so what's going on?"

"That's what's going on," I said through gritted teeth, "he was winding me up and he got what was coming to him."
Ritchie crossed his arms over his chest.

"How much coke have you had today?"

"This has nothing to do with coke," I said obstinately.

"So then you won't mind telling me how many lines you've snorted up your nose this morning."

"A couple," I said with a casual shrug.

"Have you got any on you now?" he asked. I nodded. Ritchie rolled his eyes and stuck out his hand. "Give it to me."

"What? Fuck off."

"I'm serious Ryza, you can't have any of that shit on you if the cops show up. Hand it over," he commanded. I sighed. Ritchie was right. I reluctantly pulled my stash from my back pocket, and handed it over. "This shit is fucking with your head," he said, grabbing the little plastic bag off me.

"Says the king of coke himself," I sneered with disdain as Ritchie walked over to the basin and tipped the coke into the sink.

"I know how to handle my coke, but you're going off the fucking rails," he said, while I cringed at the sight of my precious powder getting washed down the plughole. "You've possibly destroyed two lives today. Four if you get put away. Do you really want your little girl to grow up without a Dad? And what about Tails? Do you think she'll want to raise a kid on her own?" he asked, throwing the empty bag into the bin. I shook my head sheepishly and Ritchie nodded approvingly.

"I'll do what I can to get you out of this shit-storm you've created, but this needs to end now, capishe?" he said, patting me on the arm. I nodded silently. "Good, now you stay in here and sort your shit out. I'm gonna go check on Peterson, and see what I can do to stop this situation from getting out of control." He strode out the door and left me in the toilet alone. I locked the cubicle door, dropped the toilet lid down and plonked my butt on it. As I sat on the toilet seat, playing over the incident in my head, my rage turned into a combination of fear and regret. What had I done?

Unable to contain the emotions that had been piling up over the last few months, I buried my face in my hands and cried like a baby. Was it possible that I'd killed Beau? Surely not. I hadn't hit him that hard had I?

- KAT McPHERSON -

"You know Katie," Xavi said as we finished our breakfast, "I always thought you and I would get back together in the end."
I put down my fork and pushed my plate away.

"I did too." I admitted, emphasizing the word 'did'.

"But you don't now?" he asked with perplexity.

"I'm still married Xavi."

"I know," he said with a huge, sad sigh.

"And you have to understand that I'm going to do whatever it takes to get Ryan back," I told him gently. "I want to be a family."

"Fair enough," Xavier nodded, then looked over at me with a melancholy smile. "When I left for Uni, I let go of 'us' but I never let go of you," he said quietly. "When you told me you were moving to London, I knew I had to let you go and that's why I ended up taking the job in Oxford. I didn't want to come home if you weren't here."

"But you're the one who left. You moved on to bigger and better things. Did you honestly expect me to stay in this little town, hoping that one day you'd come back?"

"No," he answered honestly. "I should never have gone to Oxford in the first place. I shouldn't have left you." My heart sank for him, but I knew, in time, he'd come to realise that, regardless of what we all thought back then, 'Xavi and Kat' were never meant to be.

"You had to go Xavier; or you would have spent your life regretting it. I mean, what would you have done if you'd stayed here? Worked at the Co-op?"

"At least I would have been with you," he replied bluntly. "I've never stopped wondering how life would have turned out if I'd stayed here with you."

"You want to know how life would have turned out?" I asked with a chuckle. "We would have got married and popped out a bunch of kids. Eventually you would've resented me for holding you back, and we would have lived unhappily-ever-after." Xavi balked at my grim prediction.

"Well that's not quite how I'd imagined it," he said indignantly. I shrugged dispassionately.

"That's the reality of it Xavi. If you hadn't gone to Uni, you would never have been able to make anything of yourself, and you would have always wondered what you'd given up. You were always bigger than this town. You needed to explore the world... and so did I."

"Okay," Xavi nodded stiffly and leaned forward with his elbows on the table, "I'll admit there's some truth to that, but I have to make my intentions perfectly clear." He reached across the table and took my hand. "I want you back Katie, and until the day you tell me that you're moving back to London to be with your husband, I won't stop trying."

"Xavi..." I said disapprovingly, as I removed my hand from his gentle grasp. "I'm not the person that I was twenty years ago," I paused and studied his lovely, familiar face. "London is my home now, it's part of who I am. I love being back here, and it's so good to see you again, but I don't belong in Fram. In this place I'm not me, I'm one half of 'Xavi and Kat'... and that's not who I am anymore."

He sighed and tenderly tucked one of my unruly curls behind my ear.

"Are you sure?" he asked hopefully.

"I am," I said apologetically. "I love you Xavi - I always have and I always will - but I'm in love with Ryan now, and I'm going to fix my marriage no matter what."

- RYAN McPHERSON -

I don't know how long I'd sat there crying on that toilet seat, but at some point, Ritchie came back in.

"Ryza?" he asked quietly, knocking on the cubicle door. I sniffed and wiped my eyes with the back of my hand.

"Yeah?"

"They need you to come out now," he said solemnly.

"Oh fuck, did I kill him?" I wailed in panic, as my head began reeling.

"No, he's alive…" he paused ominously, "but he's pretty messed up."

"Fuck."

"They've taken him to the hospital, but Gaz wants to see you."

"I'm not coming out man," I said pathetically.

"You're going to have to, or he'll come in and get you," he said.

"He's going to fire me."

"I don't think he's got any other choice," he said gently.

"I really fucked up," I sighed, as I unlocked the door and stuck my head out. "I never meant for this to happen Ritch."

"I know mate," he said, grabbing me in a man-hug. "I've got your back no matter what".

"Thanks Ritch," I nodded appreciatively and took a deep breath. "Okay, let's get this over with. No point in dragging it out."

Ritchie escorted me upstairs to Gaz's glass tower. I was expecting half the agency to be outside the toilet door but the place looked like a ghost town. Knowing Gaz he'd probably made everyone get straight back to work, and threatened to fire them if they left their desks. We stopped outside Gareths door, and I looked at Ritchie.

"This is it," I said as panic rose in my chest.

"Goodluck man," he said with a nod. "I'll wait out here for you."

"Cheers," I said turning toward the doors of impending doom. I took another deep breath and then looked back over my shoulder. It felt like the death march. "Thanks Ritch, for everything."

"No worries mate," he said with a tight smile, "you're my bro." I knocked on the door and Gaz called out for me to come in. I peered back at Ritchie one last time, and then opened the doors to face my fate.

"Gaz?" I said, closing to door behind me.

"Have a seat," he said with an unusual expression on his face. It was a combination of disappointment and concern. I perched stiffly at the end of the sofa, the leather creaking noisily as I sat down. "You know what I'm going to say," he said. It wasn't a question.

"Yeah," I nodded. Gaz sat down next to me.

"What's going on with you? This is so out of character."

"Beau fucked Kat," I blurted, "he's been torturing me over it for a while…

I guess I just finally snapped."

"Is that why she went back home?"

"Yeah," I nodded. He sighed and put his hand on my shoulder.

"I'm sorry to hear it." He paused while I stared at my knuckles, which were cracked and bloodied. Gaz rubbed his face. "You know I have to fire you right?" I nodded silently.

"I wish I didn't, but legally..." he trailed off and sighed again. "You're a good man Ryan. A good man who's been thrown into a shitty situation... but it's the way we deal with hardship that shows our true character," he patted my back. "I'm sure it probably feels like your world has turned upside down, but I believe in you and I know you can turn this around."

"Thanks Gaz."

"I'm going to put out a few calls on your behalf, see if we can get something lined up for you, but if I do that you need to promise me one thing."

"What's that?"

"You need to get clean," he said, looking me in the eye solemnly, "no more drugs."

"Okay," I agreed with a nod. "Thank you."

"I mean it Ryan. Take a month off, clean yourself up, clear your head, and then we'll get you a new job."

"Done," I agreed appreciatively. I was humbled that Gaz was willing to help me after what I'd done. "I'll do whatever it takes."

"That's the Ryan I know," he said with a nod.
We stood up and I reached out to shake his hand but he pulled me in for a hug.

"Call me if you need anything okay?" he said, slapping me on the back. "I can't be your boss anymore, but I can be your friend."

"Thanks Gaz, I really appreciate it," I said, opening the door. Gaz nodded supportively, and I let myself out of his office, shrugging at Ritch as he jumped up from the chair.

"How'd it go?" he asked worriedly.

"I've gotta go clear out my desk."

He nodded sadly, "I'll help."
We trudged back down to our floor, and when I walked in, the entire room turned to look at me. I hung my head in shame. What an undignified way to go out. Ritchie rested his hand on my back as a show of support and, as he walked me to my desk, like my own personal bodyguard, the whole floor fell deathly silent. I glanced over my desk and realised that I didn't need most of it so I shoved my few personal items into my rucksack and left everything else behind.

"Ryza?" I heard Christian say from behind me. I turned to face him, filled with shame and guilt.

"I'm so sorry," I said sheepishly, "I've let you guys down."

"Nah, you haven't let us down... but you are going to be missed," he told me with a nod and a sad smile. "I hope it all works out okay for you."

"Thanks Christian," I said, patting him on the arm.

"And for what it's worth... he deserved it."
I dropped my head and slung my bag over my shoulder. There was a

chorus of solemn goodbyes as I left the floor that had been my work-home for the last three years. As Ritchie and I waited for the lift, Ash came flying out of the stairwell.

"Ryza!" she called, throwing her arms around me with tears in her eyes, "are you okay?" she asked with her face pressed against my chest as I held her tight.

"Not really," I said into her hair, "but I will be."

She leaned back and held my face in her hands. "I'm worried about you."

"The tables have turned huh?" I joked with a grimace. Ash closed her eyes and dropped her head onto my shoulder.

"It's not going to be the same here without you."

"Yeah," I said, rubbing her back, "but I guess this will give me some time to sort my head out."

"True," she said, taking my hand and looking up at me. "I hope you don't mind, but I called my Dad… just in case."

"Thanks Ash, although I hope it doesn't come to that."

"I think it already has," Ritchie said, pointing out the window to where two police officers were heading towards the building.

"Oh fuck," I swore as my heart began pounding, "what am I going to do?"

"I think you need tell them that you've got a drug problem," Ritchie said.

"I don't have a fucking drug problem," I snapped. Ritchie gave me his 'cut the crap' look.

"Mate… whether you think you do or not, it's going to be your best bet for not going to prison. They may stick you in rehab for a while, but I know which one I'd prefer." I looked at Ash for support.

"Ritchie's right Ryza," she said, squeezing my hand apologetically. "I think regardless of how you feel… it will be your best option."

"Besides," said Ritchie, patting my shoulder, "this is your first offence, so they'd probably prefer to look at other options instead of prison."

"I think you should go down there before they come up here," Ash said, cupping her hand around my cheek.

"Yeah," I agreed.

"We'll come with you," she said, pressing the elevator button. I looked at Ritch.

"Like I said man, I've got your back no matter what," he said.

"Thanks guys."

It was the first time I'd been in the back of a cop car and let me tell you, it was not an experience that I'd ever wish to repeat. Besides the rancid, stale smell, and the array of dubious stains on the seat, being locked in a cage was the most dehumanizing feeling ever. They hadn't cuffed me though, so that was a good sign.

We arrived at the station, and the two cops escorted me through the clunky glass door. I did a double-take when I saw Geoff Granger sitting in the 70's style vinyl and lino clad waiting area.

"Geoff, how did you get here so quick?" I asked in shock as he stood to meet us at the door.

"Ashley rang as soon as she heard what had happened," he said as he turned to the officers. "Mind if we have a few moments lads?"
The two cops looked at each other and then the older one shrugged.
"Sure," he agreed dubiously, "but just a few minutes."
"Much appreciated," Geoff said with a nod, waiting for them to clear out of earshot. Once they were a reasonable distance away, Geoff put his hand firmly on my shoulder. "Ryan just be very careful about what you say son," he advised me in a fatherly tone, "there were a lot of witnesses, but don't admit to anything unnecessary. And for the love of god, please don't say anything incriminating. "
"Okay," I agreed solemnly as the gravity of the situation finally sunk in.
"Also… I agree that drug dependency is the best defence."
"I'd rather not."
"Ryan…" Geoff said in a parental tone, "you're a good kid and I don't want you to ruin your life over this."
I sighed and nodded my head, "okay."
"Come through please Mr McPherson," called the younger officer, waving me in the direction of a dingy looking question room. Geoff followed along behind me, but the policeman stopped him.
"I'm sorry Justice Granger, but I'm afraid you'll need to wait out here."
"I'm his acting counsel, so I'll be coming in," Geoff said sternly.
"Umm…" the young cop looked flustered, and he glanced over at the older one with a look of panic. The older guy nodded and we all continued into the interview room. I felt nervous, but I was doing my best to play it cool.
"So Mr McPherson, can you please tell us what happened."

– *Chapter 12* –

THE 'NASHLEY' REUNION

– ASHLEY GRANGER –

The clock ticked over to ten a.m, and Nathan still hadn't turned up in the Boardroom. I tapped my pen anxiously against my notebook. It was his first day back at work since the accident, and I wasn't mentally prepared for his return. I was still pissed at him for leaving me hanging. We'd had an amazing chat on the phone that night, and then he'd completely ghosted me. Two whole weeks of total silence with no explanation. Just... nothing.

It was going to be impossible to avoid him, particularly as we were kicking-off the Delfontaine account, but how would my pride hold out when I was staring into those clear blue eyes of his?

"Has anyone seen Stone?" Gareth asked impatiently. "I left him at his desk thirty minutes ago." Apparently in Gaz-land, physical disability was no excuse for tardiness.

"Yeah," Ritchie said, "he was on his way up."

"Righto," Gareth nodded. "He's probably still hopping along. Let's start without him or we could be here for hours." We all nodded in agreement. It was hard to believe that Nathan was actually fit enough to be out of bed, let alone back at work. No one had expected him to be up and walking quite so soon, but I suppose I shouldn't have been surprised. Nathan Stone was a determined man, so if anyone was going to put the doctors to shame, it was him. Gaz forged ahead. "So, now that you've all had time to-" he said before the boardroom door burst open.

"Sorry I'm late," Nathan apologised pushing the door open with one of his crutches. My heart stopped when I saw him, and my pen slipped out of my fingers, plopped onto my notebook and rolled onto the table. I didn't think it was possible, but somehow Nathan had gotten even sexier.

"I said be here at 10am Stone," Gareth reprimanded him sternly.

"I know Gaz, I'm really sorry," Nathan apologised. "I'm still figuring out how to drive these things," he said, casting me a cheeky glance. The sparkle had returned to his bright blue eyes since the last time I'd seen him. A far cry from the depressed man I'd spent time with in hospital. It seemed as if his joy for life had been reignited.

"Take a seat," Gareth said, nodding towards the chair next to me. Nathan hobbled his way to the spare seat and, as he passed behind me, the fresh scent of his aftershave hit my nostrils and caused a stir in the pit of my belly. Even in my anger, I still found him attractive, especially now that his hair had grown longer and he'd gained some extra bulk in his upper body. Quite honestly, he'd grown damn near irresistible.

I peered up at him as he tussled with the seat. His shirt strained tight across his muscled chest, causing my body to have an incredibly unprofessional reaction to him. I picked up my pen and scribbled random notes in my notebook to distract myself from the crazy effect the man was having on my libido.

Nathan maneuvered his gorgeous body into the chair, and fussed around with his crutches. Gaz waited for him to get settled, but every time he opened his mouth to get started, Nathan made another noisy adjustment.

"Are you good Nath?" Gaz asked after the third interruption.

"Yep. Sorry," Nathan replied, ceasing his fidgeting.

"Good," Gaz nodded approvingly. "Now, I want to talk about the-" Gaz's sentence was cut short by a loud clatter as Nathan accidentally knocked one of his crutches onto the floor.

"Sorry," he apologised reaching inelegantly downward to retrieve the runaway crutch. Gaz snorted with amusement.

"What am I going to do with you Stone?"

"I could think of a few things," I mumbled to myself, not realizing that I'd articulated my pervy thought out loud. The room fell silent and I looked up from my notepad to see all the boys staring at me open-mouthed.
Oh...My...God. How embarrassing.

"Watch out Stoner," Ritchie teased, breaking the stunned silence. "Granger's ready to take your new pelvis out for a test run."

Nathan coughed awkwardly, while Cody sniggered under his breath. My face flared red, and I felt Nathan's eyes boring into me but I was too embarrassed to look at him. All I could do was sink into my chair and recommence my scribbling in the hope that I might become invisible.

"Right," Gareth said, clearing his throat loudly. "First thing we need to tackle is a new Copywriter," he said, looking between Nathan and Ritchie, "and since you two guys put us into this mess, you can get us out of it," Gaz said sternly. The cover story was that Beau had been removed from the account because he was still recovering from Ryan's attack, but in reality, he was removed because Ritchie and Nathan both threatened to quit if he was allowed to retain his place on the Delfontaine team. "I'm leaving the recruiting in your hands," Gareth told the boys. "You can liaise with HR to sort it out, but we need to have someone in place by next week."

"Fine," agreed Nathan with a stiff nod.

"I'll help," I offered without looking at Nathan. It was probably better for me to have some input given that I'd be working the closest with the new recruit.

"Great," continued Gaz, moving on. "As you all know, Delfontaine is a high-profile client, and as such will now be our flagship account. Nathan, do you want to tell them about the move?" Gareth turned to Nathan, who was staring in my direction. "Nathan?"

"Huh?" Nathan asked, snapping out of his daze.

"The move date Nathan?" Gaz prompted. Due to our confidentiality agreement, we were going to be locked-down, which meant that we'd be moving to the 9th Floor, which had secure access.

"Oh right," Nathan chuckled nervously. "Monday," he informed us, as his eyes darted repeatedly back to me. Every time our eyes met my blush flared further.

"We'll need desks packed before you leave on Friday afternoon, so I need each of you to manage your teams on that," said Gaz, when Nathan failed to expand on the details. "The movers will come in on the weekend, and you'll have your updated security tags waiting for you at reception on Monday morning. We'll have a full team brief mid-week, once you're all settled in."

"Awesome," said Cody.

"Yeah. Awesome," I agreed half-heartedly, still reeling with the humiliation of my verbal diarrhea. How was I going to avoid Nathan once we were locked in a room together?

"Anyway," Gaz pushed on, "I assume you've all had time to prepare your resourcing plans, so I'd like to hear your thoughts."

"Probably best to start with Granger," Ritchie piped up, "apparently she's been doing a lot of thinking."

- NATHAN STONE -

"Any more questions?" Gaz asked, at the end of our kick-off meeting. He looked between the four of us, and we all shook our heads. "Great. Let's get cracking then." He made pointed eye contact with both Ashley and I, and then abruptly left the room.

I glanced over at Ash, who was hurriedly collecting her things. She looked up and smiled uncomfortably, then tucked a wayward strand of hair behind her ear. Her hair had grown since I'd last seen her, and it wasn't white blonde like it had been before. It was more of a sandy colour now, which was more natural. Plus, it had a cute wave to it that made her look more laidback, almost as if she'd been at the beach all day.

"Your hair looks good," I said, balancing my weight evenly on the thin silver poles.

"Thanks," she replied, touching her hair, before running her eyes over mine. "So does yours." It was a far cry from the blonde mop I'd always prided myself on - more Captain America than Thor - but it had grown whilst I'd been in hospital, so it was looking slightly more respectable.

"Thanks." We looked at each other silently for a moment. Unable to stop myself, I reached out and stroked a silky smooth strand of her wavy locks. "I mean it, this really suits you."

Ash stepped back and eyed me suspiciously.

"What are you doing Nathan?" she asked with a hint of irritation.

"Err… I don't…" I let my words trail off. I couldn't very well tell her I had no idea what I was doing. I dropped my head and studied her conservative blue pumps. Quite different to the stiletto heels she used to wear, but again, the flats suited her better.

"You never called," she said sternly.

"I know," I said, shamefaced.

"Why not?"

"It don't know," I admitted with an embarrassed shrug. Ash rolled her eyes and quickly grabbed her notepad off the table.

"See you Nath," she said, making an abrupt dash for the door. I attempted to follow her on my invalid sticks but I was slow and clunky.

"Ash," I called after her, fighting with my unwieldy crutches, as I tried to scramble out the door. "Ashley," I called again, but she powered on. The flats also made her much more agile. "Ashley please stop," I begged with a frustrated laugh, as I hobbled down the window-lined corridor after her. I couldn't believe she was literally running away from me. What were we? Five?

"Could you please stop?" I pleaded to no avail, so I did the only thing I could think of. I broke into song, as if I was a character in High School Musical. "It was not your fault but mine…" I sang at the top of my lungs. "… and it was your heart on the line…" Ashley stopped in her tracks and turned around awkwardly. "I really fucked it up this time, didn't I my dear?"

"What are you doing?" she hissed with embarrassment, glancing self-consciously at the various onlookers who had stopped to watch my impromptu performance.

"Little Lion Man," I told her with a shrug.

"I know the song," she said in shock, "I just don't understand why you're singing it in the middle of our office."

"Because you were running away from me," I said, catching up to her.

"I wasn't running away from you," she lied, as we stood staring at each other. A little spark flickered between us.

"You're still a shitty liar," I teased with amusement. She rested her hands on her scrumptiously curvy hips.

"Okay fine. I was running away from you."

"Well are you done running?" I asked with amusement, leaning against the glass wall to recover from my exertion.

"Not really," she answered snidely, before swallowing a wry smile. "I'm trying to reach my cardio target for the day."

My chest did a little flip, and I laughed loudly.

"There she is. That's the woman I've been missing."

"I've been right here," Ash said leaning her shoulder against the window so that we were face-to-face.

"Yeah," I agreed with an apologetic nod, "you have. And I flaked out on you."

"Yeah you did. Again." Her emerald eyes held mine as I gave her what I hoped was a piercing stare.

"What can I do to make it up to you?" I asked hopefully.

"How about you tell me what the fuck happened."

I rubbed the back of my aching shoulder, like it would grant me a wish.

"I was scared," I confessed with embarrassment.

"Scared?" Ash asked with confusion.

"Yeah, I have some feelings." I nodded, humiliated. "For you," I clarified unnecessarily. "You make me feel things Ashley. I've never really liked any woman before, so I didn't know what to do, especially while I was incapable of being a real man."

Ash laughed with shock.

"Nath, you don't need two working legs to be a real man."

"My legs weren't the appendage I was concerned about," I said with unfiltered honesty. Her jaw dropped.

"You didn't call me because..." her words trailed off as she processed my meaning. "That's ridiculous."

I smiled, despite the sting of her words.

"Yeah, it is," I agreed, inching slightly closer to her. "I wanted to call you so many times, but then the longer I left it, the harder it got."

"Pardon the pun?" she mocked sarcastically. I couldn't hold back a grin. Even amidst her anger, she still had a good sense of humour.

"You have no idea how much I've missed you Granger."

Ash blushed and looked down at the floor.

"I've missed you too," she said quietly.

"So do you think we could stop messing around and just admit that we like each other?" I asked, leaning in closer. She looked up slowly, and her bright green eyes pierced through my defenses. Our mouths were nearly touching and I could feel her warm breath ripple across my lips.

"Nathan, this Dom thing..." she muttered quietly.

"Ash, it's okay," I said, putting my hand on her shoulder, "I know more than you think I do, and I don't care."

"But-"

"No buts, we're in this together now," I whispered, my lips almost brushing hers. I was conscious of the fact that my timing was awful. Standing against a massive glass panel in the third-floor hallway, was not exactly the most appropriate place to be initiating a private moment, but unfortunately now that the ball was rolling, it seemed impossible to stop it.

"What are you saying Nath?" she asked, wide-eyed.

"I'm saying that I'm only here because of you," I said quietly, glancing at her lips again. "I pushed myself to walk, so that I could get back here to see you again." I swallowed hard. "And so I could do this..." I grabbed the back of her head with my spare hand and closed my mouth over hers. For a minute Ash was taken aback, but then she quickly melted into me and returned my kiss with equal enthusiasm. I leaned most of my weight against the wall so that I could pull her close without falling off my crutches.

"What the fuck?!" Gaz said, appearing out of nowhere.

"Umm..." I stuttered, as Ashley and I disentangled ourselves in a clatter of crutches, while Gareth stared wide-eyed in dismay.

"What the fuck is going on with everyone at the moment? You've all gone bonkers," he hissed irately. "First Ryan and now you two. You're all senior members of staff. You're supposed to be setting a good example for these kids, not starting fights and romping around like hormonal teenagers."

Ash and I exchanged embarrassed glances. There was nothing either of us could say that would salvage the situation. Gaz sighed disappointedly.

"I know there's a… 'thing' going on with you two, but you both know better than to let your personal lives interfere with your work."

"It was my fault Gaz," I fessed up.

"I don't give a fuck whose fault it was," he hissed angrily, "if I ever have to tell you two about appropriate office behavior again, I won't think twice about firing either of you."

"You can't fire me." I snorted with amusement.

"Try me," he said with resolve. I took a moment to bide my words, tempted to argue my position as part-owner of the company, but decided it was better to remain silent. Gaz waved us away. "Get the fuck out of here."

- ASHLEY GRANGER -

After publicly embarrassing ourselves, Nathan and I escaped in opposite directions as quickly as possible. He vanished off to his desk, while I retreated upstairs to the tenth floor, where I hid in the bathroom to collect myself. My whole body was reeling from that amazing kiss.

I closed the stall door and leaned against the back of it, touching my mouth gently as if I might still be able to feel a trace of him there. We'd kissed once before, but this one had been different. There had been a raw intensity in it that had been entirely different to the last time.

My heart was still pounding, but my breath had slowed, so I exited the stall to dab some water on my face and chest. I took a few deep breaths and fanned myself down, as I waited for the cool water to dry on my hot skin. I stood with my eyes closed, silently reciting a calming meditation and breathing deeply to slow my heart-rate. It was working, until Amy's voice broke the silence.

"What's the deal with you and Stoner?" she asked, bursting into the bathroom.

My eyes flew open, "how did you even know I was in here?"

"I made an educated guess," she teased with a grin.

"Oh great," I said sarcastically, wondering how many people had witnessed our little show. "News travels fast around here doesn't it?"

"You do realise that we work in a glass building right?" Aims teased with great amusement, "and you were standing against the window. I think at least 80% of the office saw you guys snogging."

"Fuck," I said, running my hands through my hair.

"So what's the deal with Nashley?"

"Nothing. There is no deal."

Amy ran her finger across my sweaty chest.

"That's not nothing," she said, wiping her now damp finger on my T.shirt. I bit my lip and conceded defeat.

"It's all a bit complicated."

"Yeah I can see that," she said grinning. "So whatcha gonna do about it?"

"Continue to avoid him," I said honestly.

"Nope. Avoidance is a bad plan. You guys need to fuck."

"Wow, you're such a lady," I joked, knowing that despite her crudeness, she was probably right. "But even if we did… how would that even work right now? He's pretty much shattered from the waist down."

"You have no imagination," she said pulling out her phone and tapping in a message. I heard the swoosh of the text and Amy looked up at me proudly.

"What did you just do?" I asked with slight trepidation.

"I did you a favour."

"No, no, no, no, no, no," I said quickly, waggling my finger at her. "I don't think I want whatever favour that was."

"Trust me," she eyed me up and down, "you want it." Her phone beeped with a text. She read it and smiled with triumph.

"What? What is it? Who is it? What does it say?" I babbled anxiously, wondering what on earth she was getting me into.

"It's Ritchie," Amy said, putting her hand on my shoulder. "All will be revealed in good time. Your fairy god-fuckers have it under control."

My stomach lurched, "oh my god."

"Stop stressing and trust me, I've got this," she laughed, "and I promise you will be pleasantly surprised."

"Why do I find that hard to believe?"

"Ashley, stop fighting it. You need this." She wasn't wrong. I did need it, but having her and Ritchie in control of my sex life, felt a little pimpy. Plus it had been a long time since I'd had sex. Three years to be exact.

"I can't do it," I said, shaking my head emphatically.

"Of course you can."

I took a deep breath, "Amy, no one's seen me naked in like, three years, and I'm a lot chubbier these days," I said with a rush of panic at the thought of Nathan seeing me in my birthday suit. "He's been with a lot of girls, and I mean a loooot of girls. What if I don't make the grade?"

"It's not a test Ash, you won't be getting scored on your ability."

"How do you know that?" I asked frantically. "Maybe he has some sort of grading system."

Amy sighed, "hi, hello, crazy lady?" she said waving her hands in front of my face, "you need to chill the fuck out. Everything is going to be fine. I'll even help you avoid him for the rest of the day," she said gripping my shoulders to snap me out of my freak-out. "Now, more importantly… have you waxed lately?"

I shook my head with embarrassment. "Nope, it's like a jungle down there."

"Okay, I'll book you an appointment with my lady," she dialed a number into her phone, and looked me up and down while she awaited an answer, "and then at lunch, we're going dress shopping."

- NATHAN STONE -

I was embarrassed that Gaz had seen our snog, but I was totally unrepentant about doing it. I'd been wanting to kiss Ash again since the night of our date, but so much had happened in between that it had never been the right time. As inappropriate as our hallway window kiss was, it had finally felt like the right time.

When I returned to my desk all the young guys hooted and hollered. Not knowing how else to handle the situation, I took a bow.

"Okay, settle down, that's enough," I said loudly, channeling my inner Ryan, and eventually they all calmed down and got back to work. Ritchie strutted over and sat down at Ryan's desk. Or, more accurately, Ryan's old desk. I still couldn't believe he wasn't there anymore. I found it very hard to imagine him starting a fight. I'd known him for so many years, and I'd never once seen him hit anyone. I guess we'd all had some life changing moments of late.

"Welcome back mate," Ritchie said with a grin.

"I can't believe Ryan's in rehab," I said with bewilderment. I'd heard about it, but now that I was actually in the office, and he wasn't there, the reality was beginning to sink in.

"Better than being in jail," Ritchie shrugged.

"Surely he can't have been that addicted in such a short time."

"He was on quite a bender," Ritchie said with a nod. "I think Kell was getting ropey blow from her nightclub mates and it fucked with his head."

"It's so hard to imagine. He's been so straight laced. He hasn't done any coke since he hooked up with Tails."

"And he certainly made up for it."

I sighed, struggling to process it all, "did he really beat-up Beau that bad?"

"Yeah he went bezerk," Ritch said with a wince. "I had to pull him off Peterson in the end. He was like an animal, I seriouly thought the cunt was dead for a while there."

"Fuck."

"Yeah."

"It's not going to be the same around here without him."

"That's for sure," Ritchie said with a grin, "although it's proving to be very entertaining having you back."

I cringed, "you heard about that huh?"

"I saw it," he said, leaning over the desk.

"Brilliant."

"You know you've gotta get that under control right?"

"Yeah I know Ritch," I said defensively. "It was the first time we'd seen each other since she left the hospital and we had a few things to deal with."

"Like eating each other's faces off?" he teased.

"Among other things," I said, not bothering to argue.

"Amy reckons you need to fuck and get it over with."

"And Red's an expert at being professional in the workplace, is she?"

"Whoa there," he said protectively. "Have you ever seen us mauling each other up against a huge glass window?"

"Fair point."

"Besides, I agree with her. You guys need to shag."

"Wayne said I can't have sex until my x-ray comes back clear."

"You have two hands and a mouth."

"Jesus Ritch," I said, shifting awkwardly in my seat, as my cock reacted to the graphic visions playing through my mind.

"Deny it all you want, but you two need to bump uglies soon or it's going to get worse."

"You make it sound like we both have a disease."

"You do. Needafuckitis." Ritchie said, cackling at his own joke. "Don't drag it out any longer mate. It's been a long-time coming," he said, laughing again as he realized his double entendre. "Speaking of long-time coming… when was the last time you actually got laid?"

"68 days ago," I said immediately, "in Paris, with you know who."

"Not that you're counting."

"Not at all," I laughed.

"This must be some kind of record for you."

"Yep…longest drought since I was about 15."

"You've been in hospital Nathan. I don't think that counts as a drought."

"If I'm not having sex, then it's a drought," I joked as Ritchie looked down at his phone and grinned. He clapped his hands together loudly.

"Let's break that drought," he said, slapping me on the back. "You and Ash are coming out with Amy and I tonight," he said with an evil grin. "We've got a plan."

"Does your plan involve swinging, hookers, sex clubs or strippers?" I asked, counting them off on my fingers.

"No."

"Okay then." I agreed dubiously.

"Does that mean you're coming?"

"Sure, why not," I agreed with a sigh. "Just promise me that you're not going to embarrass me in front of Ash."

Ritchie shook his head, "I can't make that promise."

"You're a prick."

"Yeah," he agreed with a proud grin.

- ASHLEY GRANGER -

As I walked through the massive archways of Club Bordello I was awe-struck. The club was unbelievable. It was decked out like an old-school cabaret club, with thick velvet curtains, patterned wallpaper, dim lighting and posh furniture. It was the perfect venue for the intended purposes of our impromptu evening out. I stopped in the lobby and turned to Amy anxiously.

"I don't know if I can do this," I said, tugging nervously at the hem of the very short, skin-tight white dress that she had bullied me into buying.

"Of course you can," Aims said, slapping my hands away from the dress. "Stop fussing. You look hot."

"I don't look like a hooker?" I asked, unaccustomed to wearing such figure-hugging clothes.

"Are you kidding me?!" she laughed, "you look like a Greek Goddess in that dress." She paused and smiled, "like Artemis in fact."

"I'll take your word for it," I said, feeling incredibly self-conscious.

"Also, she was the Goddess of chastity and virginity, so it's fairly appropriate, given you're a born-again virgin," Amy teased with a laugh.

"Not after tonight," I rebutted with blush.

"There's my girl," Amy said proudly, linking her arm through mine. "Come on then Artemis, let's go find Thor so he can pop your cherry."

I laughed loudly as my nerves kicked up a notch. Amy squeezed my arm reassuringly and we made our entrance into the main room which was even more decadent than the lobby. It felt like stepping into a high-class brothel.

"Whoa," I breathed, taking in the opulence of the room.

"What did I tell you," Amy said nudging me with a pleased grin, "now are you happy you trusted me?"

"Yet to be seen," I teased, at the same moment as I caught sight of Nathan. My heart fluttered.

"Target acquired," Amy joked from beside me, but my gaze was firmly fixed to Nathan. He was so incredibly sexy. The top few buttons of his shirt were undone, and I could see small wisps of his chest hair sticking out from underneath it. I wanted to know exactly what he was hiding under there. His broad shoulders were perfectly outlined in his tailored jacket, and with his short hair, he looked refined yet ruggedly handsome. It should have been illegal for one man to look that hot.

Ritchie spotted us, and nudged Nathan with his elbow. Nath looked up and took my breath away with a smoldering stare.

"Oh boy," I whispered, swallowing down my nerves.

"I think it's safe to say you've caught his attention," Amy teased.

"Yeah," I agreed, unable to say anything more. I was so nervous I could barely breathe.

"Go get him tiger."

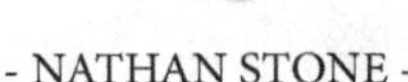

- NATHAN STONE -

"Hold on to your hat 'cause there's no turning back now," Ritchie chuckled, nudging me with his elbow as he nodded towards the door. I looked up to see Ashley standing in the entrance, and I was hit by sudden jolt of excitement.

"Holy fuck," I breathed in awe. The woman was a million shades of hotness. White dress, dark tan, bright eyes, nice curves and amazingly long legs. I'd never seen anyone make a dress look so fucking sensational.

The music pumped loudly, saturating my senses so I took a deep breath and tried to calm myself as Ashley flashed me a sultry smile.

"You okay mate?" Ritchie asked with a cringe. "You look like you've got jock itch."

"Yeah. No. I don't know," I muttered anxiously. "I feel a bit weird."

"Pop some more pain killers and you'll be right," he said, patting me on the back. "Oh by the way," he added, rifling in his pocket, "a little present from Amy and I." He pulled out a small gold gift box, slapped it down on the table and slid it towards me.

"What for?" I asked in confusion, as I picked up the box.

"Just open the box," he said. I pulled the lid off the gold box and inside there was a key card and a condom. I looked over at him for an explanation and Ritchie beamed. "Room 55 is yours for the night. Have fun," he said, glancing over at our women, who were crossing the room towards us. "There are more frangers in the top drawer of the bedside table. Just in case."

From the vast array of Australian slang words that Ritchie had taught me over the years, 'frangers' was probably my favourite. In addition to the fact that other people didn't seem to realise what we were talking about, it also gave the little rubber shields an element of mischief.

"Thanks Ritch," I said, slipping the door card into my trouser pocket, then shoving the box containing the condom into my jacket.

"Game on," Ritchie said, slapping me on the back, as he stood up to greet the girls.

"Yeah," I agreed quietly as Ash caught my eye again.

"Ladies," Ritchie said, escorting our women to the table, as I wrestled with my crutches to get to my feet. Red slid into the opposite end of the booth, where she and Ritchie huddled together conspiratorially. If they were trying to be subtle, they were failing miserably.

"Hey," Ash said, still standing.

"Hey," I replied. "You look… breathtaking," I said, reaching out for her hand and dropping one of my crutches in the process. It hit the table with a clatter and then fell to the floor barely missing her feet. "Fuck, sorry," I apologised with embarrassment.

"It's okay," she said with a smile.

If it wasn't for the crutches, I would have grabbed her and kissed her right then. She leant down to pick it up, but I intercepted her with my free hand.

"Leave it there," I said, hobbling out from the booth on one crutch. "I can do this without it."

Ash nodded and held my gaze intently. No further words were exchanged. They didn't need to be. We both knew what was coming. I discarded the other crutch, and Ash rested her hands softly on my hips. Her touch was feather light, but it was enough to keep me balanced. All I could hear was my heart thudding in my ears as I let my hands slide around her waist, hoping that my legs didn't give out. Ash stared up at me with her big green eyes, so I smiled reassuringly and ran one hand up into her hair.

Her sweet smell was engulfing me, and I couldn't take it anymore so I crushed Ashley's mouth to mine. It was a fierce kiss and the force of it took us both by surprise. It was as if all the emotion and tension of the previous few months had finally escaped, and neither of us were capable of stopping it. Ash pressed her body hard against mine and grabbed the back of my neck. I could feel her heart beating fast against my chest. I wrapped my arms tightly around her waist with a desperate need to feel her even closer.

"That's what your room is for," Red shouted over the loud music. We quickly ceased our snogging, and Ash rested her head on my chest in embarrassment.

"Oh my god," she whispered in mortification, "they got us a room?"

"Yeah," I said nodding. "Sorry."

"What are you sorry for?" she asked, looking up at me with a confused smile.

"I don't know… Ritchie mostly," I said, laughing nervously. "Should we get out of here?" I asked, not caring how sleazy I sounded.

"Yep," she nodded, staring up at me with flushed cheeks. I stalled briefly as I contemplated kissing her again, but with our pervy friends watching us, I thought better of it.

"Let's do it then," I muttered, as I peeled my body off hers. I shoved my wallet and phone into my jacket and double-checked my trouser pocket to make sure the room key was still there. Ash handed me the crutches and we looked over at Ritchie and Red.

"We're off," I said honestly. Given that they were the ones who'd booked us the room, there was no point in trying to be subtle.

"Go have some fun," Ritchie said with a salute. "And remember Stoner… No glove, no love."

"Thanks Ritch," I replied sarcastically, not entirely sure whether my body would even be up to the task anyway.

"Play safe kiddies," Red joked with a sly wink, as she reached over and slapped Ashley on the arse.

"Always do," I said, wishing they would shut the fuck up.

"Shall we go?" Ash asked, ducking under my arm and threading her hand around my waist for added support.

"Yeah," I agreed, adjusting my grip on the crutches to account for the added balance.

"No erection without protection," Ritchie proclaimed with a laugh as we made our slow exit. "Cage the snake before you shake."

"You're a tool," I said over my shoulder.

"Ah yes… don't be a fool, cover your tool," Ritchie added loudly as we negotiated our way through the crowd. "Don't be silly, protect your willie," Ritch shouted after us, causing much amusement amongst the onlookers. "Wrap your pickle before you tickle." I should have known his gift would come at a price. Humiliating me was Ritchie's favourite form of compensation.

"I think Sex Ed is different in Australia." I joked, to hide my embarrassment. Ashley laughed and shrugged it off. We finally made it out to the elevator lobby and I apologised awkwardly. "Sorry about Ritchie, he gets joy out of torturing me."

"It's fine Nath," Ash answered with a chuckle, "I'm getting used to Ritchie," she said studying the signs on the wall. "So what's our lucky number?"

"55. The key card is in my trouser pocket," I said, nodding toward my front pocket. Ashley stuck her hand in and fished around for the key card. She glanced sideways at me with a mischievous grin on her face.

"This brings back some memories," she teased with a wink. I laughed at the reminder of our first encounter.

"Only this time I don't have to leave you behind," I said, as the mood between us became more solemn. I leaned down to plant a kiss on her shiny pink lips and she returned it eagerly.

"I wish I'd gone with you that night," she said quietly, with her face against my chest.

"Me too," I said, giving her a little squeeze. I felt Ash retrieve the key from my pocket, and she peeled herself away from me to call the elevator. We only had to go one floor up, but I wasn't ready to tackle the stairs on crutches.

When the elevator reached the lobby, we shuffled our way in. Ash swiped the card and turned to face me as the doors began to close. She smiled and edged closer, running her hand up my thigh and letting it rest low on my hip.

I pulled her close and kissed her hard as my cock strained so much that I felt a twinge in my problematic pelvis. Fuck. What if my body wasn't up to sex? I pushed the thought aside and hungrily mauled Ash. Half a decade after meeting her, I was finally taking my dream woman with me.

- ASHLEY GRANGER -

As we groped and kissed frantically, Nathan leaned me up against the elevator wall. We were pressed so tightly together that I was locked between the warmth of his solid body, and the cold, hard mirror behind me.

"Caught between a stone and a hard place," I joked between kisses. Nathan laughed his yummy warm laugh.

"Do you think this counts as appropriate behavior?" he asked, as I felt his hand run up my thigh.

"This is incredibly appropriate," I answered breathlessly. The elevator binged, the doors opened, and we momentarily paused our fondling session to find our room. We located room fifty-five, and swiped ourselves in, letting the door slam closed behind us. I threw my handbag on the bedside table and Nathan discarded his crutches. Once his hands were free, they quickly made their way to my bottom, as we resumed our frenzied groping. I whipped his shirt up over his head, and the sight of his chiseled body stopped me in my tracks.

"Holy shit" I breathed quietly, suddenly feeling incredibly self-conscious about my own, slightly squishier figure. What was this Greek God doing with someone like me? "You're perfect," I muttered nervously. I ran my hands over his rock-solid chest and Nathan let out a husky chuckle. He gave me a moment to admire his body, then unzipped my dress in one swift move. "Oh," I gasped with shock as my dress fell to the floor.

"Wow," Nathan said with a smile, appraising my fleshy figure, as I stood awkwardly in front of him wearing nothing but my lacey white thong. "You're beyond perfect," he concluded with a sexy grin.

"And you're a fabulous liar," I teased. With my scars, stretch-marks and post-pregnancy wobbly bits, I was far from perfect.

"Just shut up and kiss me Granger," he said with a smile, pulling my body tightly against his. Nathan's warm tongue explored my mouth, making my heart thud even faster. I threaded my arms around his waist, and he ran a hand up my back, stopping at the base of my neck, where he wound his fingers through my hair. My whole body reacted to his touch and within seconds, we were getting hot and heavy again. My heart was pounding and damp heat was throbbing between my thighs. I got to work on unbuckling Nathans belt, but he caught his trousers before they fell to the floor.

"The scars are pretty bad," he said with a cringe. I ran my finger along his stubbly jaw.

"I'm not going to judge."

"No but they look pretty awful."

"Nath... I've got my fair share of gory scars," I said, running my hand over the scars on my stomach and lifting up my feet so he could see my scarred soles.

"Oh," he said, looking at my old wounds, as if he'd only just noticed them. He ran his hand gently over the big squiggly scar on my ribcage then pulled my body against his, nuzzling his face into my hair. I wrapped my arms around him, sensing the change in his mood.

"Are you okay?" I asked.

"I don't know how this is going to go," he whispered into my ear, "I might not be able to do this."

"We'll figure it out," I said, leaning back and taking his face in my hands. "Let's just take it slow."

"Yeah," he nodded. He let go of his trousers and they dropped down around his ankles, revealing the burgundy scars all over his legs. I tried not to react but I felt a huge wave of guilt. It was my fault that he had those scars. Out of nowhere, a tear sprang from my eye. "Hey," he said, wrapping me up in his arms again.

"Sorry," I sniffed, and angrily wiped the tear off my face. "You were right at the hospital… this is my fault."

"No Ash, I was just angry and frustrated. It was wrong of me to put that on you," he said gently. I closed my eyes and leaned my forehead against his chest. I couldn't bear to look him in the eye. "Ash," he said, tilting my chin up to face him, "I'm alive. And that's all that matters." He brushed his lips against my neck and trailed his hands softly down the length of my body. Goosebumps erupted on my skin again and I let my head roll back as his gentle fingers teased my skin. A quiet moan escaped my lips, and the sound spurred Nathan on. He let his hands brush softly over my nipples, as he continued kissing my neck. I moaned again, and arched my chest further into his strong hands. "I've been waiting for too long to do this and I'm not going to let a few injuries stop me," Nathan said quietly, breathing warm air down my neck.

"Okay." I gulped back a lump in my throat, and bit my lip as he hooked his fingers through the waistband of my underwear.

"But if my body does let me down, I have a few other tricks up my sleeve." My heart thudded loudly.

"I bet you have," I said in scarcely a whisper as my lacy thong dropped to my feet. It was the first time since Dom that anyone had seen me naked, and my chest was so tight that I could barely breathe.

I stepped out of my panties and peered up at Nathan, pleased that Amy had sorted the waxing appointment for me. Nath smiled reassuringly, and raised his arms out to the side so that I could do the same to him. He was so confident that I faltered for a moment. Chewing on my bottom lip, I pushed aside my insecurities, and slowly traced my fingers down Nathan's six-pack, and across his hips to where the scars began. I stopped at the thick elastic band on the top of his G-Stars and looked up at him.

"We don't have to do this if you're not ready," he said, misinterpreting my pause as hesitance.

"I'm ready," I told him with a smile before carefully freeing him of his underwear. Nath laughed nervously, as his penis jumped excitedly to freedom. I froze, stunned when I saw the size of it. "Whoa," I breathed with surprise. I could certainly see why he'd never had a problem with the ladies. "That's…" I looked up at Nathan and burst into nervous laughter.

"Well that's the first time I've ever had that reaction," he answered with an awkward chuckle, scratching the back of his neck.

"Sorry. I'm nervous. You're perfect, just, really..." I gestured my hands to indicate his large size, but then decided that it would be easier not to speak. I slid my hands around his neck and kissed him hard.

Nathan wrapped his arms around me, and the feel of his naked flesh against mine sent instant shockwaves down to my already excited vajayjay. We eased ourselves cautiously onto the bed and, with our bodies entangled, we let our hands explore each other until we were breathless. My whole body was straining for his.

"You'll have to take the reins on this," Nath said hoarsely, as he rolled flat onto his back. I nodded and kneeled over him, lapping-up the sight of his well-toned torso. "My side pocket," he said, pointing to his jacket, which was slumped in a pile on the floor along with the rest of our clothes. I fumbled around inside the pocket and found a little gold gift box. I looked up at him questioningly. "Another present from Ritchie and Red," he said with a nervous laugh. I popped the lid off the box and laughed out loud as I saw the little blue packet.

"Well that was very thoughtful of them," I said, as I pulled out the condom and tossed it to Nathan. It had been so long since I'd used one that I wasn't sure I'd even be able to put it on him properly. I ditched the gift box, and climbed back onto the bed, straddling Nathan as he sorted the condom. "What if I hurt you?" I asked, noticing the bruises on his hips. He let his eyes wander appreciatively across my naked body and then returned to meet my gaze.

"Then we'll stop," he said logically.

"Okay," I nodded, carefully positioning myself above him. Nathan grasped my hips and guided me gently downwards. I moaned with relief as we connected. We fitted perfectly together. Pleasure washed over me, and I felt a hot flush sweep across my skin. Although my body was urgent with need, my brain was still worrying about Nathan. He groaned quietly and I froze. "Are you alright?"

"I'm very alright," he said, breathing heavily. "That was a good noise."

"Okay," I whispered with a nod, and begun to move slowly against him. I was so scared that I was going to damage his newly healed pelvis, that my movements were almost imperceptible. Nathan sat up and cupped my face in his hands.

"I'm okay, I promise," he said, before shoving a pillow behind his back. I nodded and Nathan wrapped his arms around my waist, pulling me closer and guiding me deeper. I could feel every inch of him inside me and, as we held eye contact, it almost felt like he was inside my head too. My heart was racing in my chest as I began to move steadily on top of him. My need for him was growing, but I could see that the exertion was beginning to take its toll on him. He was eagerly soldiering on, but there was a definite mixture of pleasure and pain on his face.

"This is too much for you," I said, ceasing my movements. He sighed with disappointment.

"Yeah," he admitted, flopping back against the pillow. "Sorry."

"Hey, it's okay… we'll wait until you get better," I said, delicately climbing off him. "Let's just chill and watch a movie or something."

"Yeah," he agreed with a nod. I laid down next to him and let my fingers trail up and down his body. Nathan pulled off the condom and dejectedly threw it at the bin. I expected it to splat against the edge and slide onto the floor, but it flew straight into the center of the bag.

"Impressive shot," I said with a smile, trying to lighten the mood.

Nathan sighed. "This isn't exactly how I was hoping this would play out."

"It is what it is Nath, don't stress," I said, leaning up on my elbow. "It's more important that you heal properly."

He rolled over and pinned me down playfully.

"And in the meantime…" he said with his lips brushing mine, "we'll just have to find other ways to stay entertained." I was expecting him to kiss me, but instead, he smiled and let his right-hand slide over my body. His fingers trailed up my thigh, over my hip, across my stomach, and up to my breast, where they stopped and circled over my nipple. I let out an involuntary moan as my body tingled under his touch. He smiled again, his mouth still hovering above mine, and then let his wandering hand trail its way across to my other boob to repeat the action. My breath was heavy, and I swallowed back my craving as I enjoyed his soft touch. With his body pressed tightly against my side, there was no mistaking his desire either.

A naughty smile flickered across his lips, and his mouth tilted ever-so-slightly towards mine, but he still didn't kiss me. Instead, he gently squeezed my breast, sending a spasm of pleasure through my entire body. My gasp was stifled by his lips as they finally closed over mine. Nathan's tongue explored my mouth, and my body involuntarily strained towards his hand, which had started roaming between my thighs. His fingers felt so good that another louder moan escaped my lips. He was setting off fireworks in my brain which were radiating through my entire body. Just when I thought I'd hit the peak, he rubbed his thumb against my clitoris and slid his finger further inside me. My whole body exploded, and I let out a loud groan. My breath caught in my throat, and my body felt like it was glowing from the inside out.

"Oh my god," I whispered, as my thighs began shaking. I arched my body upwards to meet his touch, feeling overwhelmed by all the sensations, yet not wanting them to end.

- NATHAN STONE -

I kept my fingers working between Ashley's thighs until I was satisfied that she was satisfied. Her cheeks were flushed, her lips were bright red, and she was completely breathless, so I felt like I'd succeeded in my mission. I trailed my fingers back up her stomach.

"Oh wow," Ash said, as she took a moment to recover. "That was… amazing," she added with an exhausted laugh.

"I aim to please," I said, glad that I'd at least been able to achieve something for her following our failed sex attempt. A mischievous smile crossed her face as she rolled over and crawled to her knees.

"Hmmm… I wonder what I could do to thank you," she said, pushing me flat onto my back before disappearing down the bed.

"What are you up to?" I asked croakily as she gently ran her hands up my scarred thighs, making my hair stand on end.

"Take a guess," she said as she lowered her head towards my straining cock.

"Oh my god," I mumbled involuntarily. Ash looked up with a glint in her eye and let her mouth hover just above the tip. Her eyes held mine for a moment and then she flicked her tongue teasingly over my penis. "Oh my god," I repeated. I sank back onto the bed as her mouth clamped softly around me. "Oh wow," I moaned when Ashley proceeded to treat me to the best blow job of my life. Her tongue swirled around and around. I gripped the sheets tightly. "Holy fuck!" It was so sensational that I thought I was about to blow my load, until she grabbed the base of my shaft and pulled gently downwards. "Ohmyholyfuckinggod," I blurted incoherently, as she brought me back from the brink. Apparently, I'd become deeply religious in the last few minutes. My orgasm subsided slightly and then Ash recommenced her sucking. She seemed to know exactly what she was doing to me, and she took me right to edge and back again so many times that I thought my brain was going to explode along with my body.

Just when I thought I couldn't handle anymore, Ash squeezed with her hand while her tongue moved quickly up and down the underside of my cock.

"Fuuuuck," I moaned with indescribable ecstasy, gasping and shuddering underneath her mouth. The movement sent a twinge of pain through my pelvis, but the gratification was so intense that I barely noticed it.

"Holy shit," I said with an astonished laugh, as she crawled back up to join me. "That was mind-blowing."

"I also aim to please," she mimicked with a wink, as I wrapped my shaky arms around her. With the countless blow jobs I'd had over the years, not one of them had ever come close to being that intense. It had been more than a blow job… it was a blow-masterpiece. We snuggled into each other, and I breathed deeply, feeling more relaxed than I had in months.

"See… we figured it out," she said, letting her hands trail up and down my arm.

"Yes we certainly did," I agreed. "Although… I thought you didn't eat meat." We both giggled like naughty school kids.

"There was no animal cruelty involved," she said with a grin.

"And for that, I'm thankful," I laughed, remembering my tortuous liaison with Sandrine and her psycho stripper friend. "Where did you learn how to do that?" I asked without thinking.

"I'm not sure you really want to know the answer to that," she replied, peering up at me with a cringe.

"Probably not," I agreed, "but I think we should schedule that in, once a week for the rest of eternity."

Ash rested her elbows on my chest.

"You're planning to hang around for that long are you?"

I shrugged, "if you'll have me."

"Let's see if we make it through this week," she said, peering down at my bright red scars. Ash propped her head in one hand, and then let the other one run down my chest, over my bruised hips and down my right leg. "I'm sorry you got dragged into my mess," she said resting her hand on my leg.

"Your mess is mine," I said with a smile.

Ash grinned. "You're plagiarizing Vance Joy now?"

"Ah you've learned well young Jedi," I chuckled, pleased that my Indie-Folk education had made some sort of impact on her. "I don't think he'd mind. It's for a good cause."

"Yes, I'm sure Nathan Stone's sex life is right at the top of his charity list."

"Ash…" I said, changing the tone for a moment. "I mean everything I've said you know? This is more than just sex for me."

"Technically we haven't *really* had sex yet," she teased with a wink. I winced at the reminder of my sex fail and she smiled apologetically. "Sorry, I resort to humour when I'm nervous."

"I know you do," I agreed with a nod, "but why are you nervous?"

"Just this type of conversation," she said awkwardly. "Feelings and stuff. I'm not very good at sharing mine. Dom used to use everything I said against me so, you know... I kind of got good at shutting down."

"Well... you don't have to share anything if you don't want to, but if you do... I promise that I will never use it against you," I told her adamantly. "I will be yours whenever you want me, wherever you want me, for as long as you want me."

"Honestly?" she asked, sitting up.

"Yes, honestly. Why else would I have worked so hard to win you over?"

"To get laid," she answered matter-of-factly, "I thought it was just part of your whole playboy thing."

I laughed loudly, "Ashley… I am very much looking forward to having proper sex with you, but if it was just about getting laid, I could've got that elsewhere for a lot less effort."

"Oh," she replied quietly, "and you wouldn't have been hit by a car either," she joked. I shook my head and she blushed. "Sorry. Again."

"You don't have to apologize," I said, rubbing her arm, "I'll stop talking about it, but I need you to know that you aren't just another conquest for me."

"Okay," she nodded, "but just so you know… I'm only using you for your body."

I laughed and kissed her gently to emphasize my point. We sank back down to the bed together and I ran my fingers down her body, tracing them softly across her flesh, until I came to the long, thin scar at the bottom of her stomach.

"So this one is your c-section?" I asked, tracing the tidy straight line.

"Yep," she nodded. I lingered on it for a moment and then trailed my fingers up to the thick jagged scar at the top of her rib cage.

"What's this one from?"

"That was my punishment for leaving Dom the first time," she answered shamefully.

"He came after you?" I asked stunned. She nodded solemnly and my stomach twisted in disgust. "What happened?"

Ash grimaced. "How much of this story do you want to know?"

I thought about it for a moment and wondered whether I'd be able to handle the reality of her past.

"Tell me all of it," I said, deciding that I wanted to know everything there was to know about her, no matter how awful it was.

"Okay, I'll tell you, but only if you promise that it won't change anything."

"Of course it won't," I agreed, wondering what could be so bad that she'd think it would change my opinion of her. She nodded and sat up, modestly tucking her legs to one side.

"He tracked me to Twickenham… I didn't realise he'd installed that tracking spyware on my phone."

"The same thing Jock found on there?"

"Yeah," she said looking down at her hands. "Then he stabbed me with a knife in the middle of a busy pub."

"Fuck," I breathed, unsure how else to respond.

"It gets worse," she said, and took a deep breath before continuing. "The wound was pretty deep, and I was in a bad way, so I couldn't fight back. He carried me out to the carpark, gagged me, tied me up in the back of his car… and then raped me."

I felt like I'd been slapped in the face.

"Shit…" I said, unable to find my words. I sat up and wrapped her in my arms. "I'm so sorry you went through that," I said, hugging her into my chest as I kissed her head. "We're going to find Dom and put him back in jail for good," I said without thinking. "I won't let him hurt you again."

Ash froze in my arms, and looked up at me with piercing eyes.

"What do you mean, 'put him back in jail'?" she asked shakily. "He's already there."

- ASHLEY GRANGER -

Nathan's body went rigid as I awaited his explanation.

"Nathan?" I prompted him, as I pulled back to study his panic-stricken face. "What do you mean about putting Dom back in jail?"
Nath sighed and ran his hand over his face.

"Fuck. Okay, I guess we're doing this right now," he said with a nod. "I would have preferred to be fully clothed while we had this conversation."

"What conversation?" I asked, bewildered by his response. He wriggled around to a more comfortable position, and took a deep breath before his bright blue eyes locked on mine.

"Dom escaped," he said with an air of solemn calmness. My throat closed up and I felt like I was suffocating.

"How? When? How did you find out when I didn't even know?" I squeaked, forcing sound out of my vocal cords.

"Because Jock came to see me at the hospital." His words snapped me out of my shock and moved me straight into panic. I grabbed his hand.

"No. Jock's working with Dom."
Nathan shook his head and cupped my cheek in his hand.

"I honestly don't believe that he is."

"None of this makes any sense," I said, running my hand through my tussled hair. "How did Dom escape and how did Jock find out? And why would he go to you a rather than me?"
Nathan grinned with amusement.

"He tried, but you slammed the door in his face."

"Oh yeah," I said, trying desperately to piece it all together as Nathan swallowed a smug smile. "But how did Dom get out?"
He shifted stiffly, his mouth twitching as if he was fighting the words.

"It looks like he either paid, or blackmailed someone to take his place. The guy they have locked up isn't Dom."

"No." I whispered, as the rest of my breath drained from my lungs. "Why didn't you tell me sooner."

"I thought it would be better to wait until I was out of hospital so I could be there with you. I didn't want to freak you out while you were in your place all alone."

"So you just deserted me, knowing I was in my flat alone, while Dom was out there stalking me?"
He scratched his face awkwardly.

"Not exactly," he admitted. "I had security guys watching your flat. And work. And the gym."
I balked at his nerve.

"You hired a security team to stalk me, but you couldn't pick up the phone to give me a call?"

He shrugged nonchalantly, but I could see shame burning in his eyes.

"I'm not saying it made sense… or that it was particularly mature."

"Well that's an understatement."

"I didn't know what else to do. I was stuck in there, and I needed to know that you were safe. That was the only solution I could think of."

"The only solution that didn't involve talking to me, you mean?"

Nathan blushed. It was possibly the first time I'd ever seen him blush at anything.

"It was meant with the best of intentions. Please don't be angry at me."

"I'm not angry at you," I said with a smile. "It was really sweet, even though it was completely misguided."

"I'm sorry." Nathan took my face in his hands, and looked me in the eyes. "I promise it will be okay," he said as if it was no big deal.

"You can't make promises like that Nathan, you have no idea what Dom's capable of."

"Yes, I do," he said adamantly, gesturing towards his damaged legs. "In fact, I think I know better than most people exactly what he's capable of, but we're in this together so we'll get through it." Nathan ran his hands down my arms. "Ash, I want you to come and stay with me for a while."

I was momentarily stupefied.

"Stay with you?" I asked with disbelief.

"My building has tight security, and video surveillance, so there's no way Dom would be able to get to you."

I smiled and shook my head.

"It's not me that I'm worried about Nathan, it's you."

"I'll be fine," he said with a cheeky smile. "Besides, you'd be doing me a favour. It's only been a few days and I'm already sick of living with Gaz. If you're at my place, then I'm allowed to be at home." He scrutinized me hopefully, as I sat in stunned silence. When I didn't respond, Nath cocked his head and gave me puppy dog eyes. "Come on Granger, don't make me beg. You've got to admit it's a good solution." He awaited my answer, with eyebrows raised in anticipation. I opened my mouth but nothing came out. He faltered for a moment, before a mischievous smile flittered across his handsome features. "You'd have me at your disposal as a dedicated sex slave. I'd be available for your personal pleasure twenty-four seven." He waggled his eyebrows, and grinned like an idiot, which was enough to snap me out of my temporary shock-coma. I laughed and took his stubbly face in my hands.

"That does sound like a tempting offer," I said, ignoring the fact that my wanton body was most excited at the prospect. "But moving in together?" I asked breathlessly. "That's crazy Nath."

"Maybe," he said kissing me softly on the lips, "but it would probably be the least crazy thing that's happened since we first met."

With our faces almost touching, I held his gaze for a moment, searching the depths of his eyes for any sign of deception or doubt, but there wasn't any. My chest tightened with a mixture of excitement and anxiety as Nathan rested his forehead against mine. Every fiber of my being yearned to accept his offer, in spite of the fear and panic that raged through my mind. The beautiful man before me, sparked a reckless desire deep inside my heart, and I had to fight hard against my shameless inner-vixen who urged me to ignore the looming threat of Dominic Doyle to play happy families with Nathan.

"I don't know," I muttered quietly as my head reeled at the rapid pace our relationship was progressing.

Nathan slid his hands up my arms and ran them softly through the back of my hair, sending tingles through my entire body. His fingers twisted delicately through the matted strands of hair at the back of my neck.

"Do you trust me?" he asked croakily, as his gaze quickly darted to my lips. I nodded almost imperceptibly, not wanting to break our exquisite trance.

"I do."

- NATHAN STONE -

They were the magic words I needed to hear, so I pulled Ashley's face to mine and kissed her hard. A quiet moan escaped her lips when I let my tongue explore her sweet, warm mouth. I felt a tiny bit guilty about my deliberate distraction, but she was so damn tasty I couldn't help myself. I pulled her close and wound my fingers through her hair, eliciting another eager whimper from her. Spurred on by Ashley's enthusiasm, I let my hand wander down to her breast and brushed my fingers lightly over one of her perky, pink nipples. Her body jolted in response and she arched herself against my hands like she had the last time. I repeated the action on the other nipple and then I lowered my head and let my tongue trace the same path.

Ash gasped in pleasure and sunk her nails into my shoulders. I twirled my tongue around her nipple a few times and then took the whole thing into my mouth.

"Oh," she moaned breathlessly, pressing her body to meet my touch as I did the same to her other breast. Our awkward seated position was beginning to test the limits of my aching body, so I carefully maneuvered us back down to the bed, making sure that I avoided placing weight on any of my broken bits.

Ash kissed me eagerly as we laid facing each other. She slid her hands across my bare flesh, leaving no part of me untouched. When her finger trailed over my cock, it was my turn to groan with desire. Her touch awakened my senses, as if she was switching on every single nerve-ending in my body.

"I think I just figured out how we could make this happen," I said hoarsely into her ear, as I pulled her top thigh over mine.

"Mmm-hmm," she agreed breathlessly, re-positioning her leg for a better angle. I seized the opportunity to explore the most sensitive part of her body and let my finger brush along the moist hair between her thighs. Ash drew a sharp breath and wriggled closer, guiding me carefully inside her. Our bodies fitted together like two erotic puzzle pieces.

My heart began racing in my chest, as I felt her body encasing mine, and the sensation was so overwhelming that I let out a loud groan of pleasure. I gripped her bottom tightly and pulled her body hard against mine, but the move sent shards of shooting pain through both my pelvis and my hip.

"Shit," I swore, cringing in agony. I wanted to throw her down and climb on top of her, but unfortunately that would have to wait until my body was fully healed.

"I don't think this is a good idea," she said, her pink lips darkened from our relentless kisses.

"Sure it is," I said, guiding her hips back towards me. She was about to protest when I readjusted my bottom, and unintentionally sent a shudder of pleasure through her body.

"Oh," she moaned as her body arched of it's own accord. I let my hands roam over her breast as a red flush crept over her chest. As the waves of her orgasm crashed between us, the movement pushed me over the edge. I grasped her hips tightly, as my whole body surged with a mixture of relief and intense pain. I pulled Ashley tightly against me so she wouldn't see the look of agony on my face. She draped her arm over me and softly nuzzled my chin with her nose. She was sweaty and spent, and more beautiful than ever. I kissed Ash hard with the last of my remaining energy.

"Whoa," she laughed, touching her forehead briefly against mine.

"I hope I was worth the wait," I said insecurely, as she cuddled up under the duvet and nestled into my chest.

"Nathan I would have waited for you forever," she said without thinking. I paused and looked down at her, shocked that she'd actually talked about her feelings. Ashley's eyes flew open when she realized that she'd dropped her guard. I chuckled quietly, and titled her chin up so she had to look at me.

"Don't worry Chucky," I said with an amused smile as she peered up and cringed melodramatically, "I'll pretend I didn't I hear it."

"Thank you," she said with a blush.

"Ash… you're like no woman I've ever met."

"I guess I am one-of-a-kind," she said with an embarrassed shrug.

"That you are," I agreed, brushing some vagrant hair off her face.

"What am I going to do about Dom?" she muttered, almost to herself.

"Generally, guys don't like it when women talk about their ex-boyfriends straight after sex." I teased, hoping to distract her from the heavy burden of reality. "Besides… we already have a plan. You're going to move in to my place until he's back in prison, where he belongs."

"I don't think I ever agreed to that."

"No, but it makes sense and you know it."

"Yeah maybe."

"Put it this way Granger, if you don't, then I'm going to drive down to Surrey and tell your parents what's happened."

"You wouldn't," she said confidently.

"Turn me down and you'll find out for sure."

"That's blackmail."

"No. It's me protecting my own," I said logically. Ashley's head snapped up, her lips parted in surprise as her bright green eyes bore into mine.

"I'm 'your own'?" she asked with a sexy half smile.

"If you want to be."

"I do."

I smiled joyfully. This amazing woman was all mine.

"Does that mean you'll move in with me?" I asked again.

Ash rested her elegant hand on my cheek.

"I will," she said, making my chest wrench violently with all sorts of unfamiliar feelings. My whole insides lurched with that heart attack feeling again. Not that I had a clue what a heart-attack felt like, but as Red had so kindly pointed out, I was approaching middle age so it was a distinct possibility. Ash cocked her head quizzically.

"Are you okay?" she asked with concern.

"Yeah," I said with a nod, "just having some more of those feelings."

She chewed on her lip nervously and rested her head on my chest as I ran my hands through her soft hair, and inhaled deeply to try and dislodge the unusual lump in my chest. Ashley made me feel things that I'd never felt before. In fact, she made me feel things, period, which in itself was an extraordinary feat.

– *Chapter 13* –

LOVE, INTERRUPTED

- ASHLEY GRANGER -

When the sun peeped through the blinds the next morning, Nathan and I were spooned together in the small bed. I could feel his warm, steady breath on the back of my neck, as his chest moved gently in unison with mine. Waking up in his arms felt so normal that I struggled to remember what life had been like before this moment. Outside, reality loomed - waiting for us to leave the safety of our hotel room, and the little love bubble we were hiding in - but in here I could pretend that we had our happy-ever-after. I forced the bad thoughts away, and took stock of the beautiful moment, letting a happy sigh escape my lips. Nathan stirred, squeezing me in gentle hug.

"Morning," he mumbled, sounding sleepy but content, as he snuggled in closer.

"Morning," I answered with a smile as I felt his hard-on press firmly against the back of my thighs. Even though I was still half-asleep, desire flared in the pit of my belly. It was certainly an effective wake-up tactic.

Nath softly kissed the back of my neck and without saying anything else, I wriggled my bottom so that his excited cock slipped easily inside me. I moaned quietly as our two bodies became one again. Nathan groaned with his 'good noise' and gripped my top hip, as he began moving gently against me. It felt deliciously intimate having his warm breath on the back of my neck, as we moved slowly together. I couldn't have imagined a better way to wake up.

He picked up his speed and then let his fingers trail over my hip and down between my thighs, breathing heavily into my ear as he did it. I let out a weird sound of pleasure and then bit my lip to thwart it as Nathan's fingers began exploring body.

"Oh," I moaned loudly, unable to contain myself when his penis hit my g-spot. Fireworks began exploding through my entire body, and my breath caught in my throat. I reached back urgently, and grabbed his bottom to pull him tightly against me. I was so caught up in my own pleasure that I'd completely forgotten about his broken pelvis. He groaned loudly into my ear, and at first I thought he was in pain until he gripped me tighter and increased his efforts. Waves of ecstasy were crashing over me, and I urged Nathan on by squeezing my thighs tight.

He moaned and shuddered as my muscles tightened around him. I felt him explode inside me, causing my own body to surge again in response to the movement. Nathan grunted, and kissed me from behind.

"You certainly know how to do a good wake-up call," I joked breathlessly.

"I definitely prefer that to my alarm," Nath agreed, as he wrapped his arms around me. He snuggled his face into my hair, with a happy sigh. "I've spent my entire life feeling lost, and I never knew why until I found you," he said, rolling me over to face him. "You're the missing piece Chucky."
My breath faltered.

"Wow," I whispered, otherwise speechless. I cupped my hands around his stubbly jaw, and pulled his face to mine, kissing him softly and slowly. Nathan encased me in his arms, and let his hand slide up and cradle the back of my head as he returned my gentle kiss. With our bodies pressed together, I could feel my desire reigniting again. "We'll be late for work if we keep going like this," I said with a grin. Nathan peered over at the clock.

"It's only seven, we've got plenty of time," he said, kissing my neck.

"Not really. I've got to go home first. I didn't bring a change of clothes, and I can't rock up at the office wearing that," I said, pointing at the crumpled white dress. He followed my gaze to the heap of clothes on the floor.

"To be fair you did look fucking sensational in it," he said with a mischievous grin, "but… legitimate concern," he agreed with a nod. "I'll order you a town car. You'll get home quickly and avoid a walk of shame."

"You have a solution for everything don't you?"

"That's what I do… I'm a problem solver," he said, sliding his fingers down between my thighs. "And right now I'd like to solve some more interesting problems for you." His touch lit my body on fire again, and my breath caught in my throat. I closed my eyes and lost myself in the moment, but then I came to my senses and removed his hand.

"No Nathan, after yesterday I can't afford to fuck up again."

"It'll be fine," he said confidently into my ear, almost melting away my resolve.

"I don't want to give Gaz any more excuses to fire us," I argued, beginning to care a lot less about my job, as I felt Nathans fingers tracing gently over my skin.

"He can't fire us Ash," Nathan snorted with amusement.

"Err… yes he can," I disagreed. "He was right about yesterday. It was totally inappropriate."

"Hmm, yes. He'd probably say that this is inappropriate wouldn't he?" he said with a smile, as his hand began to roam towards my breast.

"You're playing dirty Stone," I said breathlessly, as he rubbed my nipple between his fingers.

"Yeah, but it's working isn't it?"

"Uh-huh," I nodded, feeling the moistness swelling between my thighs again. "But I need this job Nath. You can get away with it because you've proven yourself, but I've only been there for two months and I was away for two weeks of that."
Nathan ceased his tantalizing torture and looked me in the eyes.

"I promise you won't get fired," he said adamantly.

"Why are you so sure of that?"

He exhaled loudly, and rolled back against the pillow, giving up his attempts to seduce me. "As well as being best friends, my Dad and Gaz were also business partners. They started Artemis together and I own my Dad's share."

"What?" I was stunned.

"I'm a silent partner in Artemis," he explained, tucking his hands under his head with a cocky smile. "Gaz runs the show, but I get a share of the profits."

"So… you don't really need to work then?"

"Not for financial reasons no," he said with a shrug. "But I don't know who I'd be if I wasn't working."

"Does anyone at the office know?" I asked, wondering how he could fly under the radar in a place with such an efficient gossip train.

"Some of the Finance guys, the other shareholders and the Legal team."

"But no one else?"

"Besides you? Nope."

"Not even Ryan?"

"Not even Ryza. If people knew, they'd treat me differently."

"Wow," I said with amazement. It was like real-life Undercover Boss. "You're full of surprises Mr. Stone," I said, admiring his beautiful face.

"Does that mean I can keep doing this…?" he asked with a grin as he rolled onto his side and recommenced his breast fondling.

"No, I still need to get going," I said, removing his hand from my over-excited boob. "Even with a town car it will take me at least an hour at this time of day."

"Don't stress. I've got this under control." Nathan edged his way out of the bed inelegantly to a soundtrack of pained grunts and groans. Once he was on his feet, he smiled at me triumphantly. He limped slowly over to the pile of clothes on the floor, and plucked up his Jacket with one impressive, and surprisingly graceful, movement.

"I'm not going to put your jacket over-top of the dress and pretend it's an outfit," I said hoping like hell that wasn't his amazing solution.
He glanced sideways at me with a raised brow.

"Oh ye of little faith." He rummaged in the pocket, and brandished his phone. I raised my hands in surrender, and let him tap out his message uninterrupted. He finished typing, hit send and looked over at me proudly. "All sorted," he said, throwing me his phone before hobbling off to the toilet.

I admired his scrumptious arse until it disappeared into the bathroom and then glanced down at the text on his phone. My jaw dropped with horror.

"Oh my god Nathan!" I cried in disbelief. "You can't say that!"

"I already have," he called from inside the bathroom. "And it will be fine, Gaz gets it. Plus, he really likes you, so he'll probably go easier on me if he knows you're involved."
I re-read the message he'd sent to Gareth and I could feel a blush burning in my cheeks.

'I've taken Granger hostage as my sex-slave. Please tell everyone we're on a client visit today so as not to alert the authorities.'

- NATHAN STONE -

When I emerged from the bathroom, Ashley was staring at me agape.

"What?" I asked, standing stark naked in front of her.

"I can't believe you sent that message to Gareth," she said indignantly. I sighed and rested my hands on my bruised hips.

"Ash, please trust me. I know Gaz, and I know how to handle him. I promise this will be fine."

"What makes you so sure of that?" she asked as my phone beeped in her hand. We both glanced down at the phone.

"What does it say?" I asked, already knowing what the response would be. Ash opened the message and, as she read it, her mouth curved into a reluctant smile. She shook her head with disbelief. "So…?" I asked, knowing that I'd won. Ash rolled her eyes and read the message out loud.

"Fine, but I want you both in tomorrow."

I grinned and raised my arms victoriously.

"What did I tell you? I'm the king of problem solving."

"Don't gloat," she said, throwing my phone back to me, "it doesn't suit you." I caught my phone as it hurtled towards me.

"What's the point of being right if I can't gloat about it?" I said with a wink. Ash laughed good-naturedly, and then glanced down at my cock. "Enjoying the view?" I teased, throwing the phone back onto our pile of clothes.
She blushed at getting caught perving.

"It's definitely a highlight of the room."

"Would you like to get a closer look?" I asked, waggling it in her direction. Ash laughed. "Will it cost extra?"

"No, I'm very cheap," I joked, crawling on top of her like a lame crab as I tried not to put any weight on my freshly reconstructed knee. Ash chuckled and wrapped her thighs around my waist, but with all my weight on my good knee, I lost my balance and we fell sideways, giggling like children. Her leg was hoisted up over my hips so with only a few minor adjustments, I slid straight into her. Ash gasped loudly. "Is this close enough for you?" I asked as I felt her heart pounding against my chest.

"It's perfect," she answered with a husky laugh. I did the best 'sexing' that my fragile pelvis could manage, and thankfully we both came fairly quickly so I didn't have to test my limits. "We're getting good at that," Ash said, catching her breath.

"Yes, we are," I agreed, slapping her butt playfully. She looked at me with a mischievous grin.

"Imagine how good we'll be once you're fully recovered."

"So good they'll have to make it illegal," I joked, as my stomach rumbled. "I'm starving. Let's order room service."

"Good call," Ash said, rolling over to get the hotel guide out of the bedside table. "Oh," she said quietly.

"What's up?" I asked when she fell silent. She pulled out the box of condoms that Ritchie had left in the drawer for us.

"We didn't…" Ash let her sentence trail off, not needing to finish her thought out loud.

"No, we didn't," I agreed, wondering how the fuck I'd managed to forget that rather crucial step in the sexing process… three times. "Are you… okay?" I asked, as we both tiptoed awkwardly around the subject. She nodded, catching my drift.

"I've got an implant," she said, tapping the inside of her left arm, "but…"

"I'm usually much more vigilant than that," I assured her, knowing that she was probably wondering whether I'd given her a host of venereal diseases from my playboy days. I felt like an idiot. I couldn't believe that after all of Ritchie's protection-shaming last night, I'd forgotten to use the fucking frangers.

"So… we're good?" she asked, putting the box down on the bedside table.

"All clear."

- RYAN McPHERSON -

I was sitting in Group Therapy, staring out the window at the morning sunlight. I'd been in rehab for a month and it was still beyond my comprehension why they would schedule the torturous session twice a day.

"Ryan?" said Byron our therapist, in a tone that indicated he'd been trying to get my attention for some time.

"Huh?" I asked, snapping out of my thoughts.

"I asked if you're ready to share with us yet? How are you feeling about not your time here so far?"

"I'm feeling great about it," I said sarcastically.

"Sarcasm doesn't achieve anything Ryan," Byron scolded me, as if I was an insolent child.

"No, but it is a coping mechanism right?" I shot back, using his wanky psychological jargon against him.

"Noted," he said, unimpressed, yet unable to argue. "This is a safe space for you to share, and I think it's important for you to do so, especially given the impact that your recovery will have on you and your impending family."

"Well…" I said, fed up with having to share my every thought and feeling with these people, "…it fucking sucks."

"Okaaaay," Byron said with a sigh, "and what are the feelings that it brings up for you Ryan?"
I gritted my teeth together and rolled my eyes.

"Anger, injustice, guilt, shame…"

"Shame," said Byron, "that's an interesting one. Tell us more about that. What are you feeling shameful about?"

"My behaviour that landed me here in the first place," I said, not willing to expand any further.

"Good, but what about your behaviour do you find shameful?"

I sighed and leaned back in my chair, resting my ankle on my knee.

"I'm not sure there's much that I don't feel shame for to be honest," I said, tucking my hands behind my head. "I snorted so much coke up my nose that I didn't even know what day it was; I repeatedly had unprotected sex with some random party girl who was a full decade younger than me; and I punched a guy in the face so many times that I nearly killed him. Should I not feel shame about all of that?"

"No, I think that's healthy," said Byron as everyone else sat silently. "Shame indicates that your actions weren't in line with your morals, which shows that you understand the destructive nature of your behaviour. They key is, now that you've identified it, you need to work through the shame and forgive yourself."

I snorted. "Forgive myself. Right. I'll be sure to do that."

"Ryan, if you keep shutting down every time you get close to a breakthrough then you'll be in here for longer than any of us would like."

"Byron, I was really hoping to share today if that's okay?" interrupted the bolshy blonde bombshell sitting opposite me. She quickly shot me a conspiratorial wink, before Byron sighed and turned his gaze on her. I smiled gratefully, thankful that she'd diverted his attention away from me.

"Okay Sloane, what's on your mind?" Byron asked with a patient smile.

Sloane Sutton was our resident pop-star and she'd been there for longer than the rest of us. She'd been dubbed as England's answer to Miley Cyrus, and she certainly had the bad girl routine down-pat. I did have to wonder how much of it was an act designed to generate PR, and how much of it was actually real.

"Well," Sloane said with a mischievous glint in her eyes, "I've been thinking about how I use sex as crutch. You know, like, when I stopped using, I replaced it with fucking, and that's just switching one addiction for another isn't it? And in some ways, sex is more self-destructive than drugs, especially when you start venturing into, like, threesomes and gang bangs and stuff… and don't even get me started on SM." She flashed me a subtle smile as Byron rubbed his face. She was deliberately winding him up.

I bit the inside of my cheek to thwart my grin, but a quiet snort escaped through my nose, as Byron looked up at her with complete and utter exhaustion.

"Err… yes, that's true," he said, momentarily caught off-guard by her brazenness.

"So, I guess what I'm saying," Sloane continued, "is that I finally get why we have the abstinence rule, it makes perfect sense now, and I think, once I get out of here, I'm going to follow that through and maybe even go to, like, Switzerland and spend some time in a nunnery. Or maybe I'll go to Tibet and hang out with the monks. Just something that connects me back to myself you know?" Sloane said with a straight face, before cocking her head thoughtfully. "You're still allowed to, you know, sort yourself out though right?"

I knew she was teasing, but her acting skills were impeccable, and it looked as though Byron didn't know whether or not to take her seriously.

"Okay… well… let's talk about… why you think you need to do that," he said, regaining some composure.

"Why I need to masturbate?" she asked with faux innocence.

I let out a quiet snort as I attempted to hold back my laughter.

"Umm… no, but maybe that's a good thing to talk about with your psych at your one-on-one," suggested Byron awkwardly. "I'm referring to your belief that you need to abstain completely. Do you not trust that you can have a meaningful connection with someone without turning sex into a crutch?"

Sloane pretended to think about it for a minute.

"I guess I just really like sex," she said, playing the part to perfection, "and once I get started, I just find it really hard to stop."

"Right," said Byron, taking a deep breath. "I think we should probably park this one for now and, uh, maybe that might be a good discussion for your one-on-one."

"Maybe you and I could have a one-on-one Byron," Sloane suggested with a seductive wink, giving her game away.

"Okay, Sloane that's enough," Byron said, finally catching on, "has anyone else got any real issues they'd like to discuss?"

- KAT McPHERSON -

I rung the hem of my flowy maternity dress around my hand repeatedly as I sat and listened to Mums friends gossiping about every person in town. It was under the guise of a bridge game of course, however the only reason the Country Women's Guild ever got together was to rumormonger. These women could easily put the gossip-train at Artemis to shame and I had to wonder how many times I'd been the subject of their conversation over the years.

"And then Cynthia said she saw Nigel leaving something in Audrey's letterbox," one of the ladies said with all the self-importance of a Lady in court for the season. It was certainly easy at that moment, to imagine that I was back in the 1800's. In fact most of the women in the Guild looked weathered enough to have been alive back then.

I tuned out their blabbering, and stared out the window. It was raining. Again. We'd had a constant mist of fine rain for the past two weeks, whilst London had been bathed in sunshine. Although the rain made the countryside fresh and green, it also caused me to wonder whether I'd been too hasty in leaving my beloved city. I missed London almost as much as I missed Ryan. Not just because of the slightly warmer weather, but also the anonymity. It was nice to be able to walk down to the local Tesco in my tracksuit knowing that I wouldn't see anyone that I knew.

That would never happen in Framlingham. You could never set foot outside your door without bumping into several familiar faces. I felt so conspicuous in this tiny town, like every move I made was being monitored and judged. Oh who was I kidding? Every move I made *was*, being monitored and judged.

"Margaret said that young Doctor Brownlough just put in an offer on the old farmhouse on Brook Lane," Martha said, casting a pointed glance in my direction.

My spine straightened at the mention of Xavi, but I made a distinct effort not to show interest. I suspected that old Martha had thrown that in to test my reaction, and I didn't want to give them any extra gossip.

"Apparently, he's planning to restore it to it's former glory," she added, trying to elicit any sort of reaction from me.

"Wouldn't that be a trip down memory lane Katherine?" Said my mum whimsically.

I didn't know what memories my mum held of Brook Lane farm, but I expected that they were not the same as the ones I had. The Brook Lane farm was where Xavi and I had spent much of our time as children, fishing in the pond and chasing rabbits through the barley fields. Then as teens, engaging in much less innocent activities out in the back paddocks.

"He's such a lovely boy," swooned Beatrice. "I imagine he won't stay single for very long. All the young ladies in town have been getting themselves in a twist trying to gain his affection."

"Yes, it's a shame he only has eyes for one," agreed Martha, turning her beady-eyed gaze back to me.

All eyes were trained on me, waiting expectantly for a response that would give them another morsel of tasty gossip to share amongst themselves. I scanned their faces, and felt almost crushed under the weight of their anticipation. My breakfast 'date' with Xavier had generated enough excitement around town as it was, even before he'd begun his relentless, and incredibly public, 'wooing'.

Xavi had been determined to win me over despite my constant rejections, and he was quite open about his intentions. His blind persistence was growing tiresome, but with the whole town on his side, he was being spurred on to continue his misguided pursuit. I cleared my throat delicately, and clasped my hands in my lap.

"Katherine is still married," my mother said, obviously sensing the anger that was seething beneath my forced smile.

"Xavi and I are just friends," I informed them primly. "Now if you'll excuse me, my child is currently kicking on my bladder like it's a football."

I rose as elegantly as was physically possible, and waddled towards the toilets with my head held high. Refuting Xavier's affections was one thing, but disappointing an entire town was a heavy burden to bear.

I snuck out into the church foyer, and tended to my urgent business. I took my time, reluctant to rejoin the vultures, but I'd procrastinated for as long as possible. I stuck my head around the door and peeked reticently into the hall. The ladies had resumed their card game, and accompanying gossip, and didn't seem to have noticed my extended absence. With a spark of genius, I decided that the only course of action was to make a run for it. Admittedly, it was an adolescent stunt, but I couldn't go back in there.

I peered out through the church doors to the castle grounds. The air was still misty with the gentle rain, but the castle called to me, offering me a private safe-haven away from the watchful eyes of the town elders. My coat was hanging on the coat-stand at the other side of the foyer, so I took an inelegant jump across the open doorway, hoping that my bulky figure hadn't been spotted. I peeped back into the hall, but the vultures were too busy feeding on another scrap of scandal to notice my movements.

I smiled smugly to myself and quickly turned to grab my coat, when I came face to chest with Xavier Brownlough.

"Ooph," I said as I gently bounced off him. He grabbed my arms to stop me from toppling over.

"Are you okay?"

"Shh," I hissed quietly, peering back into the hall, to make sure no one had heard us. The coast was clear, so I grabbed his hand and dragged him out of view. "What are you doing here?" I asked in an angry whisper.

"Why are we whispering?" he whispered back, failing to answer my question. I rolled my eyes, beginning to lose my patience. I'd almost escaped and now the primary source of my distress, was standing right in front of me, blocking my only escape.

"I don't want them to hear me," I told him in an irate hiss.

"Why not?" he said at a similar volume.

"Because I'm trying to escape."

His brow furrowed in amused confusion.

"Why do you need to escape a bridge game?" Xavi asked at a slightly higher volume.

"Shh," I repeated in panic, as I heard a stir of movement from within the hall. We stood stock still for a moment, listening for any sign of discovery, but the babble continued undisrupted. I breathed a silent sigh of relief, and turned back to Xavi. "It's because of you, if you must know. You've made my life a living hell."

"How so?" He asked with a raised eyebrow, as he crossed his arms over his chest.

"They all want us to get back together." Xavi's face softened and he grinned with triumph. "Don't get any ideas," I said quickly. "I don't negotiate with terrorists."

"Now I'm a terrorist?" he asked with a mocking grin.

"Well you're terrorizing my life, aren't you?" I paused and cocked my head quizzically. "Actually… what are you doing here anyway? It's ladies day. I assume you got a tip-off as to my whereabouts?" I said coldly as Xavier blocked my exit with his slim but solid frame.

"I may have been given some insider information," he admitted shamelessly.

"You can't keep following me around like a puppy dog Xavi. I'm not going to change my mind."

"Maybe not," he agreed with a shrug, "but if that's the case then I intend to spend as much time with you as I can until you vanish from my life forever."

He crossed his arms over his chest, and set his jaw. I sighed. He had an answer for everything, and it was obvious that he wasn't going to give up. "So can I buy you a coffee?" He asked, taking my elbow as if we were characters in a Charlotte Brontë novel.

"Would you take 'no' for an answer?" I said wryly.

"No."

"Then I guess you're buying me a coffee."

- ASHLEY GRANGER -

After our room service breakfast, we packed up the few belongings that we'd brought with us, plus the box of condoms, and headed downstairs to check-out. Despite having mocked the idea earlier, I'd opted to wear Nathan's jacket over my white dress after all. It wasn't the height of fashion, but it made my walk of shame feel slightly less shameful.

I followed along behind Nathan as he hobbled down the hallway on his crutches. He looked like he was in quite a lot of pain, but he was doing his best to cover it up. I knew his ego would prevent him from admitting that he'd pushed his body too far. I could only hope that he wouldn't end up regretting our night together, because I certainly didn't. Admittedly, I did feel super-trashy walking around a hotel in my mismatched morning-after ensemble, but it was worth it.

I smoothed down the dress and tried rolling up the sleeves on Nathan's jacket but there wasn't really any way to make the outfit look better. How was it that he still managed to look hot in his crumpled shirt, while I looked like a homeless person who had raided a goodwill bin? Nathan stopped at the lift and looked back at me.

"Quit fussing Ash, you look great."

"That's sweet, but I look terrible," I said, flattered that he'd even noticed my fussing.

"No, you look cute," he said, pressing the lift button, "besides, it's not like we're going to see anyone we know." We hopped onto the elevator and he hooked his arm around my shoulder, wincing as he did.

"You're in pain," I said, taking some of his weight on my shoulders. "We pushed it too far."

"It was worth it," he said, bending down to plant a lingering kiss on my lips. My heart fluttered in my chest, and it was hard to tear my mouth away from his when the doors slid open. I helped Nathan into the reception area and we exchanged awkward glances when we spotted Ritchie sitting at a small table in the lobby. So much for not seeing anyone we knew. Ritchie looked up and grinned when he saw us.

"Hey, it's the lovebirds," he called loudly. "I'd ask how it went, but from the look of you both I'd guess it was a success."

"Ritch, what are you doing here?" Nathan asked.

"Waiting for Amy," he said with a shrug, "the woman takes forever to get ready."

"No, I mean why are you here in the hotel."

Ritchie smiled like the Cheshire cat.

"Did you think we'd let you have all the fun? We decided to make a night of it too," he said, waggling his ginger eyebrows.

"Fair enough," Nath nodded. "Let me sort out your bill then."

"Nah man, it's already sorted," Ritchie protested. "It's our gift to Nashley."

"Ashlan," I corrected him with a teasing smile.

"Either way. We're just glad that you guys finally fucked."

I cringed at his brutal honesty, but such was Ritchie's charm.

"Ritch…" Nathan started to say, but he was interrupted by his phone as it beeped with a message. He glanced at the screen and looked at me. "The car is nearly here."

"I'll wait outside," I suggested with a nod. I began sliding out from underneath Nathan's arm, when he gripped my waist to stop me.

"Before you go…" he said pulling me into him for a long, sexy kiss. When his lips eventually left mine, I was ready to take him back up to the room. "See you out there beautiful," he said as he ran his thumb along my chin.

"You're such a charmer Nathan Stone." I squeezed his hand and gave Ritchie a pat on the arm on my way out the door. "Thanks Ritch," I said with an embarrassed smile.

"No worries love," he replied with a proud nod. I made my way outside and squinted against the bright sunshine, wishing that I hadn't left my sunglasses at the office. It was 9:30am, and the peak-hour human-traffic was in full swing, so I found a spot next to the door where I could keep out of the way. I leaned against the wall and fumbled in my handbag for some breath mints or peppermint oil, or anything that would help me feel less morning-after-ish. I located my little tube of peppermint beadlets, as I heard the chilling tones of a voice that I'd long since forgotten.

"Well there she is."

My chest tightened reflexively.

"Dominic," I whispered with dread, looking up to see the one person who could instill fear in me with only a few words. Besides a little more facial hair and some extra bulk in his shoulders, he still looked exactly the same.

"The one and only," he answered arrogantly, swaggering proudly towards me. I should have run back inside, but I was frozen to the spot. "Aren't you pleased to see me?" he drawled sarcastically, casually lighting up a cigarette with his tattooed hands. His dark eyes were still filled with that same familiar mixture of rage and contempt.

"How did you get out?" I asked breathlessly. I couldn't believe he was standing right there in front of me. It was like a nightmare had come to life.

"Come on sweetheart. Did you really think I'd let them keep me locked up? I thought you knew me better than that." His tone was dripping with disdain, and he was clearly enjoying his psychotic little game.

"What do you want Dom?" I asked with a slight wobble in my voice.

"I came to see you Princess," he answered with an amused shrug. He took a purposeful step closer. "Did you like the rabbit?"

"That was you?" I asked with revulsion, remembering how awful I'd been to Jock about the fucking stuffed bunny. I felt like I was going to either vomit or pass-out. Or maybe both simultaneously.

"Of course it was," Dom admitted proudly. "I'm surprised you didn't figure that out."

"But – how did you-" I asked incoherently, desperately searching for words as Dominic savoured my obvious terror. He smirked and stood over me, blowing cigarette smoke into my face. I remained planted to the spot in horror and disbelief.

"You can't hide from me Princess. No matter where you go…I'll always hunt you down," he said ominously, making my stomach drop like I was on a rollercoaster. "I know everything about your new life. Where you work, where you live… who you're fucking," he fake whispered with a triumphant smirk. He was reveling in his own evil genius. "You'll never escape me Ashley, you know that right?" he goaded, stubbing out his cigarette right next to my feet.

I watched him squish the butt with his heavy black boot, and a wave of calm swept over me. Although I was clearly out-matched in physical strength, Dom wouldn't be expecting me to put up a fight, and he didn't know that Nathan and Ritchie were inside, which meant that I had a tactical advantage. I looked up at him defiantly

"You're psychotic," I said unemotionally.

"Yet you don't seem to take me very seriously," Dom replied with mock confusion, "I told you to steer clear of Stone, and yet here you are, fucking him like the dirty little whore that you are."

"Who I see is none of your business Dom," I snapped, momentarily losing my fear. "And if you go anywhere near Nathan again, I'll-"

"You'll what Ashley? Put me in jail for good?" he snorted indignantly. "You're pathetic. And if you think Stone gives a shit about you, you're sadly mistaken Princess. You're nothing more than a piece of arse to that guy."

"You don't know anything about Nathan," I replied tersely.

"I know a lot more than you think I do," he whispered, as if it was a secret. Revulsion and despair blazed through my body.

"Ash? Are you okay?" Nathan asked from behind me. My body instantly relaxed at the sound of his voice.

"Ahh Nathan Stone, right on cue," Dom announced with morbid amusement. "Looks like you've had a nasty accident."

Nathan huffed with disgust, and hobbled over to us, so that he was standing in between Dominic and I. "I think we all know who was responsible for that."

"Do we now?" Dom said, eyeing Nathan up and down, as if measuring him up for a fight. Dom's eyes flicked over Nathans shoulder to me, and then back to Nathan again. "I see you've been taking good care of my ex while I've been away." If Nathan had been shocked by Dominic's attempt at intimidation, then he did well not to show it. He looked totally unfazed.

"I think it's time for you to clear out Doyle," Nathan warned him boldly. My stomach lurched with fear for Nathans safety.

"Oh do you now?" Dom retorted with amused sarcasm, squaring his solid shoulders in preparation for a rumble.

"Nathan, let it go," I pleaded, touching his shoulder. Nathan looked back at me, visibly debating his choices. After a moment, he nodded his head.

"Okay," he agreed.

Dom's shrewd eyes darted from me, to Nathan, and back to me again.

"So you were fucking him then."

"That's enough Doyle," Nathan growled, standing his ground. I could see his jaw clenching on and off, betraying his calm exterior. "Get out of here mate."

"I'm not you fuck'n mate…mate," Dom seethed at Nathan before turning his attention back to me. "I shouldn't have gone so easy on you that night, you lying little slut."

"Get the fuck out of here Doyle," Nathan snapped angrily, as he re-positioned his body so that I was completely blocked from Dom's eye-line.

"You University cunts, think you own the whole fucking world," Dominic hissed at Nathan. "I should've figured out you were the one who knocked her up."

"The baby was yours and you know it," I snapped angrily, pouncing toward Dominic in an attempt to scratch his eyeballs out. Nathan instinctively reached out and grabbed me tightly, dropping his crutches to the floor with a loud clatter. I stopped immediately, worried that Nathan would topple over and hurt himself. Dominic laughed sadistically.

"That's what you say Princess, but we all know you're a liar."

Nathan looked simultaneously dumfounded and disgusted.

"Get pleasure in bullying women do you Dom?" he asked, guiding me behind his back to re-claim his position as my human shield.

"Only when they deserve it Stone," Dom answered with a slimy smirk.

Nathan's fist clenched ever so slightly, but he didn't move.

"Well that's a matter of opinion isn't it?" he replied through gritted teeth. I knew he was trying to stay calm, but I could see the rage building inside him, and he wasn't in any state to get in a fight. Especially not with Dominic Doyle.

"Nath," I said quietly, putting my hand on his waist. "Let's go. He's not worth it."

"Oh, I see she's the one who wears the pants in this relationship," taunted Dominic. He was trying to rile Nathan up. "You have no idea what you're in for with this one mate. Trust me, she's not worth it. You're better off walking away and leaving her to fight her own battles like a big girl."

"I'll take my chances," Nathan countered sternly, not buying into Dominic's games. Dom sniffed in scorn and stood right up in Nathans face. Nathan's arms flew backwards as he pushed me gently away, so that I was safely out of Dom's reach.

"Nathan, no," I begged as I saw his rage bubbling to the surface.

"You can have her," Dominic told Nathan snidely, "she's a slut anyway."

I heard the crack of Dom's nose, before I even saw Nathans fist move.

"Oh my god," I cried in shock. Nathan shook his hand in pain, while Dominic wiped the blood from his nose. He turned back to Nathan, grinning sadistically like something out of Terminator. The bright red blood dripped from his nose and trickled down over his mouth.

"Go inside Ash," Nathan instructed me tersely, but I refused to move. There was no way I was going to leave him alone with Dom. "Ash, get back inside," Nathan barked with frustration, as Dom wiped his face with the back of his hand. The beast cracked his neck, readying himself for a fight that he knew he'd win easily. "Ash," Nathan snapped. Ritchie appeared from behind us with the security guard in tow.

"Have we got a problem here?" the security guard asked authoritatively, while Ritchie planted himself in front of Nathan.

"Ash are you okay?" Amy asked, running up and throwing her arms around me.

"Yeah," I nodded, breathing a sigh of relief. Dom sized up Ritchie and the security guard, then took a step back.

"Nah," he conceded, realizing that the odds were no longer in his favour. "No problem here."

"Good, then I suggest you get the fuck out of here," Ritchie ordered, squaring his bulky shoulders.

"Fine," Dom agreed angrily. The five of us stood silently and watched Dominic back away. His eyes darted suspiciously between us, and once he was at a safe distance his cold gaze settled on me. "You can't hide behind you boyfriends forever princess." Dominic sneered, and then jogged away. Immediately, the air felt lighter, until Nathan turned to me with annoyance blazing in his eyes.

"Why didn't you go inside?"

"Pardon?" I asked incredulously.

"I told you to go inside Ashley," he barked rudely. Without any conscious thought from me, I planted a swift, hard slap across his face.

"How dare you," I seethed with indignation, "you're just as bad as him." Nathan stood, stunned, and I turned on my heel, and stormed down the street to where the town car was waiting. It was hard to tell if I was more upset about the fact that Dominic had found us, or that Nathan had spoken to me like that, but either way, I needed to get out of there.

- NATHAN STONE -

Ash jumped into the town car and slammed the door shut.

"Ash-" I called, as I felt Ritchie's hand clamp down on my shoulder.

"Let her go man," he advised wisely. "She needs some time to cool off."
Ash glanced out the back window as the car pulled away.

"But what if Doyle's waiting for her?" I asked frantically.

"She'll be fine," he said confidently, "just jump in a cab and meet her there."
Red picked up my crutches from the ground.

"Here babe," she said, helping me back onto them.

"I really fucked up," I told them with a sigh. Ashley's words had hurt as much as her slap had. "I shouldn't have spoken to her like that."

"Ash will be fine Stoner," Red assured me, "she's just running on adrenalin. Once she's had a moment to think, she'll realise that your heart was in the right place."

"Yeah I guess," I replied with a shrug.

"When did Doyle get out of the lock-up?" Ritchie asked.

"I don't exactly know. Maybe a few months, maybe years."
A grim expression crossed Ritchies face.

"So it probably was him I saw that night when we dropped Ash's bag off."

"Yeah probably," I nodded. His lips turned up at the corners slightly, as he fought a smug smile. He then glanced at Red.

"See, I told you I wasn't going crazy," he told her, before turning back to me. "Did he have anything to do with your accident?"

"Yep."

"Fuck man. Why didn't you tell me?"

"I thought it was under control," I said, realising how stupid that sounded.

"Well it clearly fucking isn't."

"Yeah," I agreed and we all fell silent. Ritchie turned to me with a sly grin and broke the silence.

"She's got a good arm huh?" he chuckled, doing his best to lighten the mood. "How's your face feeling?"

"Fucking sore actually," I answered with a half-smile, rubbing my cheek.
I was actually kind of proud that Ash had such a good swing on her.

"She got you a good one. You'll have that hand-print on your face for a few days I reckon."

"Probably," I agreed solemnly. I was finding it hard to be cheery after that encounter with Dom. "I'd better go and make sure she's safe."

"No worries man," Ritch said, patting me on the back. "Want me tell Gaz you'll be late?"

"Nah, it's already sorted, but thanks," I told him with a sheepish smile. "If anyone asks, we're on a client visit today."

"Gotcha," he said with a grin, turning to walk away. He stopped and turned back. "Don't worry Stoner, we're not gonna let this prick win."

"Cheers man."

I said my farewells, and grabbed the first cab I saw. I tried calling Ash a few times on the way to her flat, but she didn't answer. I dialed again a fourth time and when she didn't pick up, I decided to leave a message.

"Ash, I'm sorry, please pick up," I said to the voicemail, "I need to know you're okay," I sighed. "Please let me know you're home safe." I hung up and rubbed my face with my hands. I was tired, sore and worried. Seeing that prick standing over Ash like that had ripped me apart. The look on her face had been painful to see…and I mean it had actually physically hurt.

I sat with my head in my hands, re-living the moment, and wishing that I'd been able to get in more than one punch.

My phone vibrated in my pocket.

"Ash," I breathed with relief as I answered her call, "are you okay?"

"I'm okay Nath," she said. "I'm home safe."

"I'm sorry for what happened back there, I wish I could take it back," I said, before re-thinking. "Actually no… not all of it," I reneged, pleased that I'd gotten to punch the cunt, even if it was only once. "I'd still hit the prick, but I wouldn't have yelled at you."

"It was an intense situation Nath. I'm the one who should be sorry," she said with a sigh. "I've dragged you into my mess, even though I knew I should've walked away from you."

"You didn't drag me into anything," I said adamantly as the cab pulled into her street. "I made my choice, and I stick by it."

"No Nath, this is too dangerous," she replied quietly. "I won't be able to live with myself if anything else happens to you."

"Fuck Ash," I breathed, trying to process the severity of the situation. I was way out of my depth on this one. Psychopathic drug dealers were well out of my scope of reality. I thought about it for a moment. "What if we get a restraining order?"

"That will just antagonize him," she said stubbornly.

"We have to at least let the cops know what's going on Ash."

"How do you think he got out in the first place Nath? He's probably paid them off… or blackmailed them," she said with frustration. "That's what he does. No one's safe from Dom, and if we try to alert anyone we'll just make things worse for ourselves."

"So what do we do then?"

"Maybe Jock was right," she said. "Maybe I just need to go away again."

"That's not a solution," I said as the cabbie pulled over to the curb. "You can't keep uprooting your life for him."

"What else can I do Nath. I don't want him to hurt you again."

I handed the driver some cash.

"Cheers," I told him, climbing out of the taxi.

"Cheers?" Ash asked with a shocked laugh.

"No, sorry, I was talking to the cab driver," I explained hobbling up the street towards her flat.

"Why, where are you?" she asked.

"Look out your lounge room window." I heard a rustling at the other end of the line and then saw Ash appear at the window. "Hey," I said, with a single wave.

"Hey," she replied, leaning against the window frame. "What are you doing here?"

"Making sure you're okay."
She chewed her lip and looked down at me sadly.

"We can't do this Nathan. It's better for everybody if we just end this now."

"No," I said decisively, "I'm not going to let you run away from me."

"I'm not running away, I'm trying to protect you," she said.

"Wow, de ja voux," I teased. "What did I tell you the last time you said that?"

"It doesn't matter what either of us said before Nath," she said, shaking her head. "Today changed everything."

"Today changed nothing."

"Dominic wants us both dead. He'll keep coming for me no matter what, but he'll stop coming after you if we end this."

"I don't care about Dom. I'm not letting you walk away," I told her adamantly. Ash fell silent, and I could see her wipe a tear off her face. I leaned my armpit on my crutches and ran my hand through my hair. "What did he mean about knowing there was something going on with us? Was he talking about the night we first met?"

"Yeah."

"So, when he said he shouldn't have gone so easy on you…" I said grimly.

"Yeah… he beat me," Ash nodded almost imperceptibly. My stomach lurched at the thought of what he might have done to her and I rubbed my face angrily.

"How bad was it?"

"You don't want to know Nathan."

"Fuck," I swore, trying to hold down my vomit. "I'm sorry. If I'd known- "

"Stop," Ash cut me off. "There was nothing you could have done differently Nath. Dom always found a reason whether there was one or not, so don't beat yourself up about something that you couldn't have changed."

"I'm so sorry," I said again quietly.

"Why are you sorry?" she asked, peering down at me with confusion.

"Because I'm not a very good knight in shining armour, am I? Just a bloke with shining crutches."

"I never believed in fairy-tales Nath," Ash said with a smile. "I always thought it was pathetic that the Princess needed a man to ride in and save her.

"Only you Granger," I said, proud of my strong-willed, independent woman.

"Ironic really that Dom always called me Princess," she said as a smile crept over her face. "The only Princess I ever wanted to be was She-Ra."

I laughed loudly. "The Princess of Power," I said with great amusement. "Now why doesn't that surprise me?"

"You remember She-Ra?"

"Of course! I had a huge crush on She-Ra as a kid…" I told her with a wink, "which was a bit dirty really, because I always wanted to be He-Man, and he's her twin brother."

"That is a bit dirty," she agreed with a smile. "but, you know… I always had a crush on He-Man too. That man-kini was pretty hot."

"Then I guess we're as dirty as each other," I said with a grin, as I stared up at her from the pavement. Ashley's smile faltered and she sighed quietly.

"What is this thing Nath? I mean… what are we doing?"

"I don't know what you're doing, but I'm pretty busy falling for you."

"Oh," she said quietly.

"Does that freak you out?" I asked, unable to interpret her silence.

"No," Ash shook her head, "because I'm falling for you too," she said without cracking a nervous joke.

"You are?" I asked, staring up at her beautiful face through the window.

"I've already fallen, if I'm honest," she replied bashfully, playing with a vagrant piece of her wavy hair. My chest heaved.

"I so badly want to kiss you right now," I said, swallowing back the lump in my throat. Ash vanished from the window. "Where are you going?" I asked, standing in the middle of the footpath, staring up at the empty window.

"There's someone at the door," she said, hanging up the phone. I looked around the busy street, confused. There was no one at the front door, so maybe someone was inside. What if Dom had gotten in to her building?

I sped to the porch as fast as my crutches would let me, but I'd only made it to the front steps when the front door flew open, and Ashley ran out, still wearing my jacket over her white dress. My breath caught in my throat at the sight of her. Ashley's eyes bore into mine, and I suddenly felt overwhelmed with the intensity of my feelings for her.

"I'm in love with you Ashley Granger," I said, shuffling closer to her.

"I'm in love with you too Nathan Stone," she said with a smile as she threw her arms around my neck. We leaned in closer to each other and, although our lips weren't quite touching, neither of us moved any further. It was as if we were suspended in slow motion, while the rest of the world sped on around us. Eventually one, or both, of us closed the gap and our lips finally met. I had no idea how everything was going to pan out, but as long as we were together, we would make it work. After a long, slow kiss, I pulled away from her.

"Let's get inside," I said, squeezing her shoulders, "this place gives me the creeps." I let my hand slide down her arm as I took stock of our location. The last time I'd been on that street I was fighting for my life.

"Me too," she admitted, taking my hand. "So I guess that's that. Looks like I'm staying with you for a while."

- RYAN McPHERSON -

I had a brief reprieve while everyone else in the group took their turns at sharing. I had just begun to think that I'd escaped further interrogation, when Byron turned his attention back to me.

"Ryan, I'd like to circle back to you," he said calmly, as five expectant faces followed his gaze in my direction. I squirmed under their close scrutiny.

"Awesome," I replied, with a fake smile on my face.

"You said you feel shameful for your behaviour, yet you're resistant to therapy. Why do you think that is?"

"I'm not resistant, I just don't see the point."

Rodney snorted, "are you too good for therapy Rich-boy?" Rodney was a bitter and twisted Ex-Soapie Star/heroine junkie, hailing from the East End of London. Although he'd done alright for himself in TV-land, he seemed compelled to harp-on about his 'ghetto' roots, to tedium.

"Enough Rodney," warned Byron, "I'd like to talk about why you're so riled up by Ryan. I feel like perhaps his upbringing is a point of jealousy for you."

"Why would I be jealous of that arrogant prick?" Rodney huffed, "I'm a fucking TV star and what's he? Nothing but some sort of sad-arse marketing prick who's wife fucked a gay guy."
I stood up abruptly and my chair screeched loudly in the quiet room.

"What the fuck did you just say?" I asked, ready to punch his lights out. He was a weedy little junky so he'd go down quickly.

"Ryan, cool it," Byron snapped, standing up in case he had to intervene, "or do I need to remind you that fighting would be a breach of your court orders?"
I ground my teeth for a moment, keeping my eyes on Rodney.

"No, you don't need to remind me," I said through clenched teeth.

"Right, then sit down and cool off." I sat down like an obedient puppy dog. I had to comply or I'd end up in here for longer, or worse, I'd end up in prison.

"Pussy," mumbled Rodney.

"Rodney," barked Byron, who was having a hard day at the office. "That's enough."

"Sorry," Rodney apologised insincerely.

"Now, let's look at your behaviour shall we? You say that you're proud of your roots, but is there a small part of you that would have liked to have a privileged upbringing like Ryan did?"

I grinned smugly, and leaned back in my chair as Rodney fidgeted. His eyes quickly darted around the room, and I hooked my arms behind my head, interested to hear what Rodney had to say about Byron's apt observation. After a moment of silence, Rodney puffed out his chest and stared Byron in the eyes.

"Why would I want to grow up like a pussy?"

"Why wouldn't you?" said Byron curiously. "I would have loved to grow up without money troubles."

One point to Byron, I thought haughtily.

"Money isn't everything," shrugged Rodney, like a sulky child.

"Very true," agreed Byron, "so why, in your mind, is Ryan's defining trait his money?"

"Well look at him," said Rodney pointing at me angrily, "he obviously thinks he's better than the rest of us."

"I can't pretend to know what Ryan thinks, and neither can you," said Byron, "but even if that is the case, why would it be because of his money? Let's face it, everyone here is doing fairly well for themselves financially, otherwise you'd be in a cheaper facility."

I leant forward with an intrigued smile, pleased that Byron was on my side.

"Yeah, I do alright," Rodney mumbled.

"So why would Ryan think he's better than you because of money? I find it interesting that that's the conclusion you've drawn."

"That's just the feeling I get."

"My interpretation of the situation is quite different," Byron said assertively. Rodney shrank in his chair, but I was keen to hear what Byron had to say. "I think Ryan makes a distinction between himself and the rest of you because he doesn't believe that he's an addict."

"Wait what?" I asked, thrown off-guard by the fact that Byron seemed to be agreeing that I was arrogant. "I don't think I'm better than everyone else."

"Okay Ryan," said Byron, "so why don't you tell us how you feel about your drug dependency."

"I don't have a fucking drug dependency," I said defensively. "I had a shit time, so I went on a bender to try and numb the pain. That's it. I was off my tits for about a week and I made some shitty decisions." I stopped and checked myself on that one. "More like big mistakes," I corrected myself, "but that was it, I didn't take drugs before that and now… after what I did, I certainly won't be taking them again. So no, I'm not an addict, I was just temporarily fucked up."

"That's an interesting way to see it," said Byron in an aggravatingly condescending tone. "There are a lot of men who get cheated on Ryan, but they don't all go out on a bender, as you put it, then beat a man unconscious." He paused and let his words sink in. "Why do you think you chose to go down that particular route? Why were drugs your escape?"

"Because my mate came around with a bag of coke," I replied flippantly.

"And he forced it up your nose?"

"No."

"Then did he make you snort the next lot? Or pop the pills? Or tip the vodka down your throat?"

"No."

"So what made you do that to yourself Ryan? Why did you see that as your only option?"

I sighed and sank down in my chair, looking at my hands in my lap.

"I guess I didn't want to feel the pain anymore."

"Good," he said encouragingly. "I think that's the first honest answer you've given us in the whole time you've been here. Maybe there's hope for you yet."

I stared up at him like an obstinate child. I was starting to understand what having real parents must have been like, and I wasn't so sure that I'd missed out on much.

- KAT McPHERSON -

Xavi escorted me to the Castle Pub and we settled in to one of the squeaky leather booths inside. It was warm and cozy, and very quiet being a weekday. Besides a few tourists, we were the only ones in there.

"Tell me all about your husband then," he said as we drank our coffees.

"What do you want to know?"

"What's going on with you two?"

I sighed and stared him in the eye. "Do you want the truth?"

"Full truth."

I nodded and clenched my hands in my lap.

"He's in rehab."

"Oh," Xavi said, taking a sip of coffee to hide his shock. "Is he an addict or something?"

"No... well at least, he wasn't. Not until recently anyway. He went off the rails when I..." I trailed off.

"When you what?"

"You're going to think I'm a horrible person," I said, shaking my head in shame.

"I bet I won't."

"Hold that judgement until you hear what I did," I said shamefully. "I cheated on him."

"I see," he said without judgement.

"When I was six months pregnant," I added to make a point of just how bad it was.

"Okay," he said, un-perturbed by that fact.

"See... I'm a horrible person," I told him adamantly.

"Katie you're not a horrible person," he assured me, touching my hand.

"A nice person doesn't cheat on their husband with a gay man when they're six months pregnant."

"The guy was gay?" he asked with a laugh, his hand still on mine.

"Yeah. Well... No. I thought he was gay, but then it turned out he wasn't."

"Or you turned him," Xavi joked with a wink as I extracted my hand from beneath his.

"It's not funny," I laughed half-heartedly. "I was awful," I said shaking my head. "I hurt him too. In more ways than one. He's the reason Ryan ended up in rehab."

Xavier cocked his head with curiosity. "How so?"

I proceeded to tell him the whole sordid story about me, and Beau, and

Ryan, and the Lodge, and he didn't once make me feel bad about any of it. It was so easy to talk to Xavi. With Ryan so far away, I'd almost forgotten what it was like to hang out with someone who knew all of your deepest, darkest secrets, and loved you unconditionally regardless. Coffee turned into lunch as we continued our catch up.

"So I heard you bought the Brook Lane farm," I said, over my salad.

"Yeah I did," he said with a sad nod, "it was mostly a nostalgic purchase," he admitted. His eyes caught mine and we both blushed simultaneously at the memories of when we used to sneak out to the barn at night and fumble around in the dark, clumsily learning our way around each other's adolescent bodies. Xavi broke eye contact and cleared his throat nervously.

"I'm going to restore it," he said running his hand through the back of his hair. "It will be a work-in-progress, but I think I can get it back into working order."

"You're doing it up yourself?"

"Of course I am. Why do you sound so surprised? I've always built stuff."

"Yeah I know," I agreed, "I just assumed that after so many years in the city you'd have lost your… err… rustic nature."

"You can take the boy out of the country, but you can't take the country out of the boy." He joked.

"I guess not."

"What about the girl?" he asked, taking a small, polite bite of his burger. Ryan would have inhaled the whole thing in one go. "She seems to be pretty happy in the city," Xavi continued once he'd finished chewing. "Is there any country girl left in her?"

"I don't think so," I said, picking a chip off his plate without thinking. His blue eyes sparkled as he watched me with amusement. I suddenly realized what I'd done and blushed furiously. "Sorry," I spluttered, instantly regretting my over-familiar action. "Old habits die hard I guess."

"That they do," he replied, reaching over the table to take my hand again. I pulled away.

"Xavi, I can't do this," I said standing up. "Pretending to be friends isn't good for either of us."

"I didn't realise we were pretending," he said, motioning at me to sit down when I grabbed my coat off the back of my chair. "I'll stop. I promise. Just please don't leave." I exhaled lightly and studied his face. It was so familiar, that it was all-too easy to fall back into old patterns without even realising it. "Please?" Xavi repeated, patting the table. I nodded silently and plopped my coat back over my chair. He breathed a sigh of relief and smiled. "Thank you. I'm sorry if I made you uncomfortable, it's just that when I'm with you it's easy to convince myself that we're still together."

"But we're not," I reminded him sternly, "and I don't want to do anything else that might jeopardize my marriage."

"Point taken," he said, raising his hands in defeat. "From now on I'll be a perfect gentleman."

- ASHLEY GRANGER -

I felt quite anxious as I followed Nathan down the elegant hallway towards his apartment, wheeling a suitcase of clothes behind me. I couldn't believe that I'd agreed to live with him. I had zero doubts about being with Nathan, but I was worried that our temporary co-habiting could ruin what we had going. He swung the door open and flicked on the lights.

"Mi casa es tu casa," he said with a grin. I was stunned at the sight of the lavish apartment. It was like something out of a lifestyle magazine. Sleek white tiles, shiny black furniture and huge glass windows that over-looked the park.

"Wow," I breathed, leaving my suitcase by the door, as I walked over to the floor-to-ceiling window, and peered out at Holland Park. "This place is beautiful."

"You haven't seen the best bits yet," he said with a grin. "Follow me."

I did as I was told, and followed along behind him, past his big commercial-grade kitchen and into his luxurious bedroom. I was lost for words. The black and white décor, flowed seamlessly with the rest of the house, and his bed was large enough to accommodate several overnight guests. I dreaded to think how many women he'd 'entertained' in it.

"Keep coming," he said, beckoning me forward, before vanishing through a mirrored door. I peeked my head through the door, into a massive walk-in wardrobe. "Here!" Nathan said proudly as he pointed to an entire empty section, which included hanging space and a couple of shelves. "Tada!" he joked as he opened an empty drawer, "I cleared these out for you."

"Oh," I laughed nervously, "when did you do this?"

"When I got out of the hospital," he said with a shrug. I was speechless again. His smile faltered slightly, and we stood silently for a moment. "Are you okay?" he asked, leaning on one crutch, as he removed the other one, and propped it up against the shelf.

"Yeah, this is just..." I searched for the words. "I wasn't expecting you to go to so much trouble."

"If we're going to do this, we're going to do it properly," Nath said, running his spare hand through his hair. "Ugh, I really need a shower," he joked, pulling a face as he got a whiff of himself. I'd showered and changed at my place but he was still in the same stale suit that he'd been wearing since yesterday. He leaned his other crutch next to the first one and whipped his shirt off over his head. Even though I'd spent the night staring at his bare chest, I still got a thrill of excitement at the sight of him standing half-naked in front of me. I swallowed back the lump in my throat as Nath threw the dirty shirt into the laundry basket. He grinned and took my hand.

"Follow me again."

"Okay," I agreed with a smile, as he led me, very slowly, to the bathroom. "What are you up to Mr Stone?" I asked curiously.

"Nothing bad I promise," he joked as he reached for the door handle. "Now close your eyes," he said, putting his other hand over my eyes.

"Fine, I'm closing them," I laughed, shutting my eyes tight as he removed his hands from my face. I could hear the rustle of plastic.

"Okay you can open them now," Nathan said proudly.

I opened my eyes to find a basket of toiletries in front of my face. It wasn't just the basics, it was a full array of bathroom necessities, complete with toothbrush, hairbrush, shampoo, conditioner, deodorant, perfume, body wash, razor, and even facial products.

"I figured you should have all the comforts of home," he explained with a grin.

I stared at him with astonishment, "Nathan, this is... something."

"Do you like it?" he asked anxiously.

"It's really sweet. I love it, thank you," I reassured him happily as I took the basket from his hands. "I just can't believe you did all this for me."

"You're worth it," he joked, quoting the L'Oreal slogan, even though the brand wasn't present in my personalised basket.

"You must have really been hoping to get in my pants," I joked, grinning up at him with great affection.

"No, there was never any doubt that I'd get in your pants," he said with a cheeky wink. "That was always a given."

"Is that right?" I asked with a laugh, putting the heavy basket down carefully on the bench so I could slide my hands around his bare waist. "And what made you so sure of that?"
He smiled, running his hands underneath my T.shirt and up my back.

"The moment you threw your lunch at me, I knew you wanted me," he said, squeezing my body tightly against his.

I laughed, "you realise that was an accident right? I had no idea you were standing there."

"Sure you didn't."

"No, I genuinely didn't," I said with amusement. "The blob flew off my plate and then I saw you."

"Well that's disappointing," he said with a grin, "here I was thinking I was special."

"You are special," I said, giving him a soft kiss. "I'm glad it was you that I hit with my curry blob."

"And I'm glad that it was you who threw it," he replied with his lips against mine, "otherwise it would have been a devastating waste of a good pair of trousers."

"Your drycleaner couldn't save them huh?"

"Sadly not," Nath said shaking his head, "but it was a worthwhile sacrifice," he added before resuming our kiss. His hands ran along my body, and as he reached up to remove my shirt, he paused and let go of my top. "Nope, I stink," he said peeling his body away from mine. "If I wasn't crippled, I'd do you in the shower right now, but given the state of my body, it would be a health hazard for both of us."

"Yeah probably," I agreed with a laugh. "In that case, I'll go unpack while you de-smell yourself."

"Then we'll resume this," Nath said as he balanced against the counter to carefully strip off his trousers. I took a quick moment to admire his body, while he jiggled around awkwardly on his unsteady legs. He was so chiseled that he looked like a more generously endowed version of Michelangelo's 'David'. He looked up and grinned. "You're quite the perve aren't you Granger," he teased, when he caught me watching him. "Just wait until I'm all better. When I'm back to full strength, I'm going to blow your mind," he said with a cheeky wink,

I smiled and blushed a little, "Nathan you've already blown my mind."

His bright blue eyes bore into mine, and the look on his face made my stomach flip. I bit my lip and backed out of the bathroom, closing the door gently behind me. I exhaled and looked around the lavish room. It was immaculate. Everything was perfectly placed and well ordered, which was a stark contrast to my chaotic and quirky little flat.

How were Nathan and I going to merge our worlds? We were so different. His life was neat, tidy and black and white while mine was... well... it was a mess quite frankly. A big crazy, colourful mess.

I wandered around the room, trailing my hands over all of his shiny, perfect things, until I came across an old acoustic guitar that looked out of place in his pristine apartment. I cocked my head and admired the colorful patterns on it, tracing them gently with my finger.

"That was my Dads," Nathan said, making me jump, as he emerged from the bathroom, dripping wet, with a towel wrapped around his waist.

"It's beautiful," I said, running my hands over the well-worn strings.

"He got it from a street stall in Mexico when he was twenty," Nath explained as he limped over to join me. "Dad said that he spotted the patterns on it from across the road and knew he had to have it." He stopped right behind me. "The shop owner made all his guitars by hand, and he told Dad that they always picked their owners."

"I love that," I said with a whimsical smile as I looked over my shoulder at Nathan. A droplet of water dripped from his short hair and landed on his damp, bare chest. He leaned in and reached around me to pick up the guitar. I could feel the length of his wet body, pressing against my back, and butterflies erupted in my belly.

"Dad said that the man told him this one was special," Nath said quietly into my ear, sending goosebumps across my flesh. He rested his freshly shaven chin on my shoulder and placed the guitar in my hands. "Apparently he made this one in the memory of his lover, who was 'muerto', as they in Mexico."

"That's so beautiful," I said as Nathan arranged my fingers carefully on the strings. His breath was warm against the skin on my neck, and my body was having all sorts of reactions to him.

"He believed that this guitar would bring the sound of her soul to the living world, so that he would never have to be without her again."
I peered up at Nathan and my cheek brushed against his.

"So why did he sell it your Dad?"

"Because his guitars picked their owners, and that one had called to my father," he breathed quietly. "The man trusted, that for some reason, it had to go home with my Dad."

"Wow," I said in a whisper.

"That's not even the best part of the story," Nath said, strumming the guitar with my hand inside his. "Two weeks later, when Dad was back home, he took his new guitar out to Hyde Park, where he was meeting up with some friends. They were sitting around having some sort of hippie, kumbaya, sing-along, and he saw a beautiful lady walking towards him, wearing a skirt with exactly the same pattern as the guitar."

I glanced down at the intricate patterns on the varnished wood.

"Then what happened?" I asked, engrossed in his story.

"Well, the woman spotted my Dad - probably because he was staring at her - and she smiled when she saw his guitar. My Dad said that at that moment, they both knew."

"Knew what?" I asked breathlessly.

"That they were meant to be together," he said quietly. I looked up at Nathan, our lips nearly touching.

"The woman was your Mum."

"Sure was," he said as his lips curled into a sexy smile. "And because of that, my Dad always believed that this guitar was magic. He called it the Guitar of Destiny," Nath declared in a big movie narrator voice. "Dad was convinced that one day it would bring me my soul mate, just like it brought him his."

I stared at Nathan, holding my breath, and for a moment I was speechless. Our eyes were locked, and our faces tilted ever-so-slightly closer. I paused to study his face and realised that he'd probably told the same story to a million other girls. I leaned away from him and smiled with amusement.

"Oh you're good at this."

"Good at what?" he asked innocently.

"You nearly had me for a minute there," I said with a quiet laugh. "How many times have you told that story?"

Nathan delicately removed the guitar from my hands and turned me around to face him.

"I've never told anyone that story," he said grasping the guitar in one hand and my waist with the other. "I actually used to think it was a load of bollocks. I hadn't even thought about it for years... until I saw you standing there admiring it," he said using the guitar to pull me in closer. "Now I know my Dad was right."

"So it would seem," I said, deciding to let myself be swept away in the romance of it all.

Nath leant down and pressed his lips to mine, as we melted into each other. I slid my hands down the bare, damp skin on his back, while Nathan attempted to return the guitar to its cradle without interrupting our kissing session. He waved the guitar about with one hand, but couldn't locate the holder whilst his face was attached to mine. I laughed and took the guitar from him, tucking it back into the stand, before peeling my T.shirt up over my head. I smiled and let it drop to the floor.

Nathan stepped towards me, but I put my hand on his chest to stop him coming any closer. I summoned my inner-stripper, and tried my best to look sexy as I unzipped my skirt, stepping backwards out of it when it slid down around my feet. Nathan's eyes flashed with desire, so I took off my bra and threw it onto the armchair.

"Wow," he said, taking another step towards me. I shook my head, and wriggled out of my little black thong, crawling teasingly onto his giant bed, and arranging myself in the sexiest pose possible. He cocked his head and looked at me with an expression that I couldn't interpret.

"What?" I asked, instantly feeling self-conscious.

"I can't believe you're in my bed," he said, resting his hands on his bruised hips.

"Technically I'm on your bed," I joked, before sliding between the silky white sheets. "Now, I'm in your bed."

Nath smiled. "So you are," he agreed, standing beside the bed staring at me.

"If you always knew you'd get in my pants, why is it so unbelievable that I'm in your bed?" I asked curiously, propping my head on my hand.

"Because I've never had a woman in my bed before," he said, rubbing the back of his damp hair. "You're the only other person, besides me, who's been between those sheets."

"Why? Because you normally have sex in the loungeroom?" I teased.

"No," he said playfully, taking my jesting in his stride. "Because I've never brought a woman home."

I laughed loudly, assuming he was joking.

"I find that hard to believe, especially given the size of this bed."

"No, I'm serious," he said with a nod. "I don't like women knowing where I live, so my number one rule was 'always go back to her place.'"

"Wow. There were so many things in that one sentence, that I don't actually know where to start," I joked. "You have sex rules?"

"I used to," he said, furrowing his brow, "but they've all gone out the window with you."

I smiled and sat up.

"So why are you ignoring all your rules for me?"

"It would seem that they don't apply anymore, so I'm making things up as I go along now," he said as he pulled off his towel and threw it at me. I giggled and threw it back at him.

"That makes two of us."

"You're a Game Changer Granger," Nathan joked with a grin as he climbed carefully onto the bed, grimacing when he put too much weight on his bad knee. He readjusted his position and looked up at me with a mischievous grin.

"Plan B," he said, as he ripped off the covers.

"What are you doing?" I asked, laughing.

"You'll see," he replied, grabbing my ankles to pull me down the bed.

"Oh," I breathed in surprise, as I felt the warmth of his tongue between my thighs. I wasn't normally a fan of that particular activity, but I had a feeling that Nathan was about to convert me. "Wow," I said breathlessly, gripping the sheets as his tongue worked its magic.

Nathan ran is hands up my thighs and let his fingers join the party. There were so many sensations happening that my brain felt like it was going to explode. I arched my back, writhing beneath his mouth. I was teetering on the edge of an orgasm so I put my hands over my face to stifle a moan that was so loud I thought the neighbours might complain. My enjoyment seemed to spur Nathan on, and whatever he'd been doing down there, he began doing it faster until my thighs started to shake uncontrollably.

"Oh my god," I sighed, feeling a massive wave of pleasure crash over me, but Nathan kept going, while my whole body shuddered repeatedly. "Okay," I pleaded with a croaky laugh, once the massive orgasm subsided. "You can stop now. You've got my thighs shaking."

Nathan took his cue and came back up to join me with a proud grin on his face. "You approve?" he asked, already knowing the answer.

- RYAN McPHERSON -

We all filed out of the group therapy room for a much needed lunch break, and I tried not to make eye contact with Sloane until we were out of earshot. Once we'd made it safely to the loungeroom we looked at each other and exchanged smiles.

"Thanks for your help earlier," I said, elbowing her affably.

"No stress," she said as we shared a giggle at her antics. "I did it for myself as much as you," she answered with a cheeky grin.

"Well it was fucking priceless. You should consider an acting career."

"I'd probably be better than Rodney," she agreed with a laugh as we both peered cautiously in his direction. He was out of earshot, so we had another quick chuckle at his expense.

"Seriously though, I owe you one Sutton," I said, punching her arm.

"No way. It was worth it just to watch Byron squirm."

"Yeah, I suspect he'll probably avoid being alone in a room with you from now on."

"I don't know, I think he might have a hidden kinky side," Sloane joked. "I might have intrigued him."

"That wouldn't surprise me," I agreed with good humour, "you'd have to be pretty fucked in the head after hanging out with crazy people all day."

"You coming to the dining room for lunch today?"

"Nah, I'm going to grab a sandwich and eat in my room."

"You know you're going to have to join us for a meal at some point right?"

"Why? It's only three months. I was planning to keep to myself, do my time and get out of here."

"They won't discharge you if you don't integrate and socialize."

"That was never specified. I'm sure they wouldn't take something like that into account."

She raised her eyebrows. "Ryan, I've been here for a long time."

"Voluntarily."

"Yes, exactly," Sloane said pointedly. "I know how to get out."

"So why don't you?" I asked, curious to know why anyone would actually choose to be in this hell-hole.

"Because this is where I need to be right now." I opened my mouth to ask another question but she silenced me with her hand. "I'm going to the dining room for lunch. If you'd like to continue this conversation, you know where to find me." She smiled tightly and swanned in the direction of the dining room. I momentarily contemplated following her, but thought better of it, and turned towards the kitchen. As I stepped out into the hallway, I bumped straight into Rodney, who was walking down the hall in the direction I was about to go.

"Oi, watch where you're going rich boy," Rodney snarled. I stood silently for a moment, debating my words, then decided not to respond. I shook my head and stepped around him to go the opposite way down the hall, even though it wasn't the direction I'd planned to go. "I'm speaking to you, cunt," he called after me.

I stopped in my tracks, feeling the rage beginning to bubble to the surface. I took a deep breath, knowing that he was just trying to wind me up. Rodney wanted me to snap so that I'd end up in prison, but I wouldn't give him the satisfaction. I had too much on the line. I ground my teeth and forced myself to walk on, without turning around.

"You too good to say sorry are you?"

"No Rodney," I muttered peevishly over my shoulder.

"Well stop fucking ignoring me and apologise," he said, storming after me.

"Sorry," I called insincerely, increasing my pace. I needed to get to the dining room where there would be witnesses, and he wouldn't be able to pick a fight. Being alone with Rodney was dangerous. It would be his word against mine.

"That's not a fucking apology," he snapped.

"That's the best you're going to get," I replied brusquely, hurrying down the long corridor which suddenly seemed endless.

"Not good enough," Rodney growled, grabbing my arm.

"I don't know what else to tell you mate," I said, wrenching my arm out of his tight grasp.

"How about you say it like you mean it."

I turned away from him and resumed walking.

"I'm not going to fight with you Rodney."

"You seem to think you have a choice," he hissed, clamping his hand down on my shoulder. "But here's a news flash for you rich boy... whether you choose to fight or not, I'm still going to kick your arse."

"Knock it off Rodney," barked Sloane stepping out of the ladies bathrooms. Rodney released his grip on my shoulder.

"Fuck off Sloane, this has nothing to do with you."

"Yeah, you're right," Sloane said with a shrug, "I'll just go let Byron know that you punched Ryan, and he'll kick you out. I mean, you'd be doing us all a favour really. I'm sure Ryan would be happy to take a punch for the benefit of the team."

"You're a cunt," Rodney mumbled through gritted teeth.

"Yeah I am," Sloane agreed, unphased by Rodney's aggression. Angelica walked around the corner and saw the scene before her. Angelica was a sweet older lady who was addicted to something called Quaalude's. Although she was softly spoken, she was a total bad-arse. Apparently she'd smuggled pills into the country from South Africa more than a decade ago, after Quaalude's was banned in the UK.

"What's going on?" she asked with concern.

"Rodney just needed some help making a decision," Sloane said without taking her eyes off Rodney. "So… what's it going to be CockRod? You staying or going?"

Rodney looked between the three of us and growled.

"Fuck the lot of you," he said, storming off down the hallway. We stood and watched him vanish towards the kitchen. It seemed I managed to make enemies wherever I went.

"What was that all about?" Asked Angelica.

"Just Rodney being Rodney," Sloane said with a shrug.

"As long as everything's okay," she said, studying me.

"It's fine, thanks Angelica," I assured her with a smile.

"Alright love," she said patting my cheek, "but you just let me know if he causes you any trouble and I'll kick his scrawny little arse." She was like a bad-ass version of Betty White. I smiled at the woman's tenacity.

"I will."

"Good," she said with a sweet smile. "I'm going to get my lunch now." She wandered off down the hall towards the dining hall. Sloane and I looked at each other and grinned.

"She's my idol," Sloane said with a chuckle.

"I know, right? Gangsta Granny or what?"

"I want to be like her when I grow up," she joked.

"Hey, thanks for that," I said gratefully, "as much as I hate it here, I really don't want to end up in prison."

"We won't let that happen," Sloane said, punching me in the arm, "besides, you've got Gangsta Granny fighting in your corner."

- KAT McPHERSON -

Lunch with Xavi had progressed without further incident, so afterwards we took a walk around the castle grounds. Despite the hoards of tourists that usually inhabited that area, it always felt calm and peaceful. Even in childhood it had been the place I'd retreated to whenever I needed to collect my thoughts.

Xavi walked silently alongside me, sharing my reverence for the place. He knew better than disturb me whilst I was deep in thought. He glanced over at the church and spotted the illustrious Country Women's Guild emerging after their bridge game.

"Do you need to get back there? They'll probably be worried about you?" He said, as we watched the ladies cackle and natter with naught a care in the world.

"I think they're fine," I replied with a smile. "They probably suspect that I'm with you."

He smiled bashfully. "Sorry," he apologised with sincerity. "I've made things worse haven't I?"

"It's fine," I said, waving away his concerns, "I know how to handle a bunch of vultures. I've been living in London, remember?" We both chuckled and continued walking.

"I've had fun today," Xavi said, glancing at me sideways, with so much adoration in his eyes that I felt guilty.

"Yeah, it almost feels like…" I said, letting my sentence trail off, as I realized that he could misconstrue my meaning.

"Old times?" he asked, finishing my sentence for me. I nodded silently, and he stopped walking. "Look, Katie," he said, touching my arm softly. "I know you've got a lot going on in your head at the moment, but this could be the only chance I have to win you back, and I don't want any more regrets." Xavi paused and took my hand. "I'm in love with you Katherine Tailor. I've loved you since we were five, and I will continue to love you until the day that I die. I don't expect anything of you, but I need you to know that I'm an option for you. If you want me, I'm here, and I'm prepared to do whatever it takes to make you happy."

"Oh Xavi," I breathed sadly, my heart breaking for him. Before I knew what was happening, his mouth closed over mine. He braced his hand gently against the back of my head, kissing me with so much angst and passion that it took my breath away. It had been a long time since we'd last kissed, yet it felt exactly the same. The intensity had increased, and there was a desperation in his lips that hadn't been there before, but he still tasted the same.
I stepped back abruptly.

"I have to go," I said, backing away from him as if he was a rabid dog.

"I'm sorry," he apologised, "I didn't mean to do that."

"No, I'm sorry Xavi. I should never have agreed to lunch." I turned around and fled as quickly as my large belly would allow me. I waddled across the road to the church, where the vultures all stood by their cars, eyes wide and mouths agape.

"Katie," Xavi called from the other side of the quiet street. I ignored him and kept walking, unsure whether he was chasing after me or if he'd regained some of his senses.

"I'm sure that will provide you with a few weeks of gossip," I snapped snidely at the ladies, and continued marching straight past them and down the hill as I fought against the hot tears that were threating to fall. I refused to shed even one tear in front of those people. My mother, who had been uncharacteristically quiet all day, had finally found her voice.

"Katherine!" she called, running along after me. "Where are you going love?"

I clenched my jaw tight and forged ahead, biting out my response over my shoulder. "Anywhere but here."

– *Chapter 14* –

REALITY BITES

- NATHAN STONE -

I awoke in the morning to the smell of fresh coffee. Ash wasn't in the bed so I glanced over at the clock radio. It was seven a.m. I'd slept though my alarm. I rolled out of bed with a yawn, and limped groggily to the kitchen, rubbing my eyes when I saw a gorgeous goddess pottering around my kitchen. Ash was wearing my one of my work shirts, with the sleeves rolled up, and one button fastened at the front.
I leaned against the doorframe and watched her making coffee.

"Wow, you look great in my kitchen," I joked, alerting her to my pervy presence. She looked up with surprise.

"You don't think it makes my bum look big?" she retorted, pointing her very fine, barely covered arse in my direction.

"Not at all…but I do like your bum better when it's in my bed," I joked. "What are you doing awake? I thought you didn't get up until 8."

"Your alarm woke me and I couldn't get back to sleep. I figured I might as well get some coffee brewing," she said, as I hobbled over slowly and kissed the back of her neck. She tilted her head to the side and let out a quiet little whimper as I pushed her hair aside and trailed my lips over her soft skin.

"Hmmm. I could get used to waking up to this," I said softly into her ear, as I squeezed her around the waist, ensuring that my hard-on rested firmly against her bum cheeks.

I ran my hands up the inside of her shirt - or my shirt as the case may have been, and her breath faltered. I grabbed one of her boobs in each hand and tweaked both her nipples. Ash moaned and bit her lip, as she let her head drop back against my shoulder. I continued to let my hands slide slowly down her stomach and between her thighs.

I grabbed the bag of coffee out of her hands and slammed it distractedly onto the sink. It slumped and tipped over, noisily spilling coffee beans all over the bench. We ignored the ever-growing coffee mess, and I swiped a clear space amongst the beans. Ash slid up onto the kitchen counter and wrapped her legs carefully around my waist. Without pre-amble, I was in. It wasn't an ideal position for my broken body but I was determined to make it work, so I pressed my palms into the benchtop to take my bodyweight.

"Oh wait," I said, feeling like I should mention our repeated slip in precautionary measures. "We haven't used anything. Maybe we should…"

"It's fine Nath," Ash interjected, wrapping her thighs more tightly around my hips so that I couldn't move.

"So you're not worried about my history?"

"You said you're normally careful," she answered breathlessly. "I trust you."

I grinned and kissed her hard, as we recommenced proceedings. It was reckless, but at that point in time, unprotected sex was the least of our concerns. The bigger threat to our health, was Dominic Doyle. We could shack-up together and play house for a while, but it wasn't going to stop Dom in the long-term. What we needed was a plan.

My body continued tending to the task at-hand, but my brain trailed off onto thoughts of how I could solve our Dom problem. Getting him arrested wasn't a realistic option, since the cops already thought he was in jail, plus he'd already managed to get out of prison once, so he'd be able to do it again. Would he take a bribe? Probably not. It wasn't about money for him, it was about revenge, and he wouldn't stop until we were dead. Or until he was dead. Now there was a thought.

I shook my head to clear my Dom-related thoughts. That psycho was the last thing I wanted to be thinking about whilst I was having sex with his ex-girlfriend so I turned my full attention back to Ashley, kissing her hard as we both puffed and panted. Once we were done, we slumped against each other to recover and Ash looked up at me with concern.

"Where'd you go just then?" she asked, studying my face with a serious expression.

I sighed and kissed her forehead, "I'm sorry. I'm just worried about this Dom thing," I admitted, dropping my head onto her shoulder. "I can't shake the feeling that there's more to it. I mean… how did he know we were at the hotel yesterday?"

"I don't know," she said quietly. "He said he knows where I work, so I guess he's been following me and biding his time."

"Yeah, but we were there all night," I said, going over it in my head. "He would've had to sleep outside."

"I wouldn't put it past him," she said, putting her hand on my cheek. "Nathan, Dom will go to extraordinary lengths for the thrill of scaring someone. He gets-off on it. When we first got together, he told me that he stood outside his ex-girlfriend's house for three days, just to freak her out."

"Holy fuck. And you stayed with him?"

She winced at my words, and lowered her eyes in shame. "I was already in too deep to get out."

"Sorry," I apologised for my own insensitivity. "I'm not judging you, I just can't get my head around it." I kissed her forehead gently and then ran my hands through my fluffy hair with a sigh. "So how do we win against this psycho?"

"If I knew the answer to that, we wouldn't be having this problem right now." Ash looked up at me solemnly. "Nathan if you want out, I'll understand. This isn't your battle and you're under no obligation to fight Dom with me."

"But this is my battle," I told her grimly, channeling my inner Thor. "He made this my battle the first time he hit you. I wasn't there to help you then, but I'm sure as hell here now, and I'll never walk away without you again."

Tears shimmered in her eyes and she dropped her head to my chest.

"I have no idea how to fix this Nath."

"Me either," I said, stroking the back of her hair. "But we've got Ritchie, Jock and a lot of money, so that's a fucking good start."

- ASHLEY GRANGER -

We got ready for work like a normal human couple, except that we were weighed down with the burden of the battle that lay ahead of us. What the hell were we going to do? How were we going to put an end to this game of Dom's? We had no idea where he was; how he'd found us; or when he would show-up next. All we knew was that he would be back. What else could we really do besides wait for him to re-appear?

"So what's the best way to get to the office from here?" I asked, stepping into my skirt, as I attempted to pretend that this was just a normal day like any other. "Central line to Oxford Circus?"

"Car," he said with a wink, as he buttoned up his shirt. That wash-board chest of his was still a sight to behold. "I have my own parking space so it's quicker and easier to drive."

"And since your car is at the wreckers, we'll take the central line?" I teased, heading to the bathroom to do my make-up.

"My old car is at the wreckers," he agreed as I rifled through my make-up bag. "But my new one is downstairs in the garage."
I stuck my head back out of the bathroom door.

"What new one?"

"I bought a new one."

"When did you do that?" I asked, confused.

"When I was in the hospital."

"What? Why? How did you even buy a car when you were in hospital?"
"I have a guy."

I raised my brows. "You have a guy who buys cars for you?"

"Uh-huh," he said, combing his hair. "I have a guy for everything."
I stared at him like a stunned mullet, unsure if I wanted to know exactly what other things he had guys for.

"Should I be worried by that?" I asked, looking at his reflection in the bedroom mirror. Nath looked back at me.

"Probably," he teased with a confident smile. Twenty minutes later, we were heading down to the parking garage. Nathan looked me up and down and smiled.

"You're so hot."

"You're not so bad yourself," I replied with a smile as I threaded my hand around his waist, "even with the crutches."
He laughed and pulled me into him.

"Nathan," a husky voice purred from behind us. We both turned around to face the owner of the sexy voice, and my jaw dropped when I saw a super tall, super curvy, Prada-clad redhead, who looked like she'd just stepped off the pages of Vogue. Oh… My… Fucking… God. I was face-to-boob with Jessica Rabbit.

"Stacy, hi," said Nathan awkwardly, as he ever-so-slightly tightened his grip around my shoulder. Stacy shot Nathan a saucy smile, before looking me up and down with a disdainful, well-plucked eyebrow. Clearly the two of them had history. "This is my… uhh… Ashley," Nath stuttered, stumbling over the introductions. "Ash this is Stacy, she lives in the penthouse."

"Hi," I answered with a forced smile, as I felt a mad blush creeping up my neck and over my face. I couldn't believe how tall she was… and I was taller than most women. It was very unnerving to be quite literally looking up to another woman.

"Charmed," Stacy replied disingenuously.

"So where are you off to looking so lovely?" Nathan asked with nervous charm. The woman must have really been something if she was able to rattle Nathan Stone.

"Just coming in actually," Stacy replied with a sexy wink. How the hell did she manage to make the walk of shame look sexy?! She looked like she'd just spent three hours in the salon; while yesterday I'd looked like something the cat had dragged in.

"Oh right," Nathan nodded stiffly.

"Looks like you had an interesting night too," Stacy teased, looking me up and down again.

"Actually, Ashley's staying with me for a while," Nathan replied awkwardly.

"Oh," she said with a very slight tinge of disappointment, hidden beneath a much thicker layer of 'challenge accepted'.

"Well, we'd better get going," he said, using his crutches to guide me swiftly towards his car. "Have a nice day," he called to Stacy over his shoulder.

"Nice to meet you Stacy," I waved behind us.

"And you Shelley," she said snidely, as we escaped, at a slow limp, around the corner.

"Have a nice day?" I teased him with a laugh. "That's certainly not up to usual Stone standards. She makes you nervous," I pointed out with amusement. He was actually quite adorable when he was flustered. It made him seem more human.

"Err…well…yes, she does," he admitted, "Stacy can be a bit of a viper."

"No? Really? But she seemed so lovely." I joked.

"We used to… you know," he blurted guiltily.

"Yeah I figured," I said with a teasing smile. "It's okay Nath. There's no need to feel bad about it. Well besides the fact that Jessica Rabbit now knows you're slumming it with me."

"She is a bit Jessica Rabbit-ish isn't she?" Nathan chuckled, "but I'm certainly not slumming it. She-Ra wins hands-down. She fights evil. Jessica Rabbit just plays pattycake with all the bad guys," he said, pausing to fumble in his pocket. "Here," he said, handing me his car keys.

I stared at him blankly.

"You want me to drive your new car?"

"Yeah, I can't drive remember?"

"That's true," I agreed as he gestured towards a shiny new metallic blue, 2-door Tesla. My eyes widened at the sight of the ridiculously expensive car. "You can't be serious."

"Of course I'm serious," he answered, pressing the car beeper in my hand. "You've driven before haven't you?"

"Yes but-"

"But nothing," he said, popping the boot and sliding his crutches in between the front seats, "you'll be fine. This car practically drives itself... apparently."

"Fine, but I take no responsibility for any damage that may occur whilst I'm in control of your fancy vehicle."

"Don't stress Chucky, I have insurance. If you crash, just do your best not to hurt us."

"Great. Thanks," I answered sarcastically, "and don't call me Chucky."

"Okay Shelley," he joked with a wink. "What should I call you anyway? Are you my girlfriend?" he teased.

"I don't know... being your 'Ahh... Ashley' sounded so perfect."

- RYAN McPHERSON -

When the orderly announced that I had visitors first thing on a Wednesday morning, I'd assumed it would be Nathan or Ritchie popping by before work – or perhaps even the Grangers, who'd visited a couple times – but I'd never expected that it would be my parents. My jaw dropped in sheer amazement when I saw them standing in the visitors lounge.

"Ryan," my mother said stiffly, as she caught sight of me standing in the doorway, gawking. "I'd love to say that it's good to see you, but this is hardly a pleasurable circumstance."

"Great," I said sarcastically. My mother's disdain had effectively snapped me out of my stupor. "So nice to see you guys." I crossed my arms over my chest, and remained in the doorway. I wasn't ready to enter the lions den. Or, more appropriately, the dragons den.

"Son," my Father nodded rigidly. "Come and sit down," he ordered, taking control of the situation as usual. "We've got a few matters to discuss."

"I'm fine standing thanks," I said coldly, as I planted my shoulder against the doorjamb.

My mother sighed impatiently.

"Must you always be so obstinate?" she asked huffily.

"Yes Mother, I must." I replied snidely.

"Fine then," snapped my father. "If you're not going to be civil, we'll get to the point."

"Yes, lets," I answered obnoxiously. My parents exchanged a glance, and my Father nodded at my Mother to take the lead. They made quite a good team, despite the fact that they were cold, heartless bastards. Like the Joker and Harley Quinn.

"We've been thinking about your situation," my Mother began, "and although it's regretful, the woman wasn't a good fit for the family anyway."

"Absolutely," my father jumped in. "She did us all a favour son, at least now you can find yourself someone more suitable, and we can all move on." I stared at them, gob smacked. Just when I thought they couldn't get any worse, they'd hit an all-new low. "How much do you think will it take to make the problem go away?" My father asked callously.

"The problem?" I muttered in horror.

"Yes, your wife." He confirmed stonily. "How much should we offer her?" I balked at his arrogance, and then took a very deliberate step into the room.

"Kat's not a problem," I said, astounded, yet not surprised, by their heartlessness, "she's my wife."

"Would she take a hundred?" My father said, as if I hadn't even spoken.

"A hundred pounds? To sign divorce papers?" I asked incredulously. The nerve of the guy astonished me.

"No," he said, as if I was being preposterous. "A hundred thousand. And she'd need to sign an agreement to take the baby and walk away with no future contact or demands."

Nausea washed over me.

"Are you fucking serious?" I asked, feeling my anger explode to the surface. I wanted to throttle him, but I couldn't. If I attacked my parents, I'd be sent straight to prison, and would never be able to see Kat again.

"I told you we shouldn't have let him marry her without signing that pre-nup," my mother told my father self-righteously.

"I know my love, but he refused to do it."

I was livid. I felt a flash of red hot hatred, coursing through my veins.

"Get. Out." I snarled through clenched teeth. Both my parents turned to look at me as if they'd only just noticed me standing there.

"I beg your pardon?" my Mother asked me indignantly

"I said get out."

My father snorted pompously. "You must be joking."

"Do I look like I'm joking?"

"He's obviously having withdrawals from the drugs," my mother said by way of explanation.

"It's not the drugs, it's you," I seethed, barely containing my rage. "You're awful human beings. I've spent my life doing everything I could to try and make you proud of me, but nothing I do, will ever be good enough for you."

"Maybe if you didn't make such stupid decisions all the time, we wouldn't have to come down on you so hard." Barked my father as if he was the pinnacle of great parenting.

"Don't pretend that you give a fuck about me," I snapped. "All you care about is protecting the family fortune."

"Which won't be a fortune for very long if you don't play your cards right with this divorce," he replied, either oblivious or completely uncaring of the fact that he sounded like a heartless cunt.

"Get the fuck out of here," I growled.

My mother gasped in horror, "you can't speak to us like that."

"I just did. Now, walk out that door and never come back."

"We will do no such thing," argued my pretentious father.

"Then I will," I told him. I turned on my heel and stormed out of the visitors area. I furiously barged through the double doors that led to the residents halls and stomped down the empty hallway.

I needed to speak to Kat, goddamn it. What if the bastards went to see her? I had no way of stopping them. Blast the stupid technology ban. Would my parents know where to find Kat? Would they bother making the effort to go to Framlingham to track her down?

"Urggh," I growled, and swung my fist against the wall. Pain splintered through my hand as my knuckles collided with the hard brick. "Fuck," I swore, shaking out my bleeding hand.

"Ryan?" Sloane said quietly from behind me. I looked up, blinking back unwanted tears at the sight of a friendly face. "Are you okay?" she asked, resting her hand gently on my shoulder. I shook my head, unable to speak. "Come on, let's go outside before anyone sees you like this." Sloane suggested, taking my good hand and leading me quickly out into the lush gardens.

I trailed along behind her like a lost little puppy dog. I felt totally helpless. Just when I'd thought my life couldn't possibly get any worse, my parents had swooped in and proved me wrong, yet again. How would I be able to stop them while I was stuck in that godforsaken hell hole with no access to the outside world? There would be no chance of salvaging my marriage if they got to Kat first.

- KAT McPHERSON -

Rosie knocked quietly on my bedroom door, and when I didn't answer she poked her head into the darkened room.

"Hey kiddo, I've got to get to work. Are you going to be okay?" she asked with concern.

"I'll be fine," I mumbled, and pulled the covers over my head. She sighed, and I heard her soft footsteps against the carpet as she crossed the room. I felt the bed sink on one side as she sat down.

"I'm worried about you Kat," she said, rubbing my leg, "I've never seen you like this before. I think I like the psycho knitting lady better than this. Please promise me that you're not going to do anything stupid."

"I'm not going to top myself if that's what you mean," I muttered from under the duvet. "I'm not moving from this bed until the baby comes and then I'm going back to London where things make sense."

"As long as you don't ruin the bed," she joked, patting my mess of curls that were sticking out from the top of the cover. She stood up. "I'll see you when I get home."

"Okay," I said, curling my knees up to my big fat belly. "Have a good day."

"You too." Rosie closed the door, and I squeezed my eyes shut, wishing the day away. My interlude with Xavier yesterday had completely broken me. Despite all of my best intentions to win Ryan back, I'd gone and blown it all over again. If he heard about the kiss, there would be no saving us.

How could I have been so stupid to have let that happen? And in front of the vultures at that. The entire town would have heard about our kiss before breakfast was even served. There was no way I'd ever be able to bring Ryan back to Framlingham. But then again, after yesterday I never wanted to come back to Framlingham anyway.

I wiped away a shameful tear. All I wanted was Ryan. I wanted to see his face, snuggle into his chest and hear his voice as he told me that everything was going to be okay. But I was stuck in Framlingham and Ryan was stuck in rehab. How had I let our wonderful life go so horribly wrong?

An abrupt, loud buzz interrupted my wallowing, and I nearly jumped out of my skin. It took me a moment to realise it was the intercom, but I decided that whoever it was, would have to come back another time, because I was not going to get out of that bed. The door buzzed again, and when I ignored it a second time, my phone rang sharply from the nightstand.

"For fuck sake," I muttered angrily, as I picked up my phone. "What?" I grunted rudely.

"Katie?" asked Xavi caught off-guard by my gruffness. "Are you okay? Rosie said you're at home, but I've just buzzed and there's no one there."

"I'm here."

"Oh," he said, humbled. "Can I come up?"

"No."

He sighed and I could almost hear him rubbing his face in frustration.

"I'm sorry for yesterday," Xavi apologised meekly. "I shouldn't have kissed you. I didn't mean to do that, it just kind of… happened."

"You just accidentally stuck your tongue in my mouth?" I asked facetiously.

"Yes," he said without a hint of irony. "It was instinctual and I lost myself for a moment. I should have had some self-control. I'm really sorry that I upset you. Can I please come in so that we can talk about it."

"We are talking about it."

"I don't mean on the phone."

"The phone is safer."

"What if I promise to remain three feet away from you at all times?" He joked. "Please Katie, I can't leave things like this."

I sighed exhaustedly.

"Fine," I agreed against my own better judgement. "Just give me five minutes."

"Okay."

I rolled out of bed and tidied myself up just enough to look like a functional adult, but it still wasn't a pretty picture. My eyes were puffy from crying, my face was blotchy, and my curls were so frizzy that all I'd been able to do, was pull them back into a messy bun.

I let Xavier in, and watched him warily, as I backed away to the other side of the kitchen table. He was true to his word and kept a decent distance between us.

"Thanks for hearing me out," he said with a stiff nod. "I'm really sorry about yesterday."

"You've said that already," I blurted coldly, wishing he would get straight to the point.

"You're right, I have." Xavi smiled tightly, and leaned his hands on the back of the chair in front of him. "I've been so selfish these past few weeks," he said humbly. "I was so wrapped up in my own need to win you back, that I never stopped to think about how much I might be hurting you."
I peered up to meet his gaze and could see genuine regret in his eyes.

I nodded. "I appreciate you acknowledging that."

"I don't want to be a complication for you Katie. I never meant to add to your problems… I just wanted to be the answer to them." He looked abashed as he held my stare, "but you have a husband whom you love, and I need to respect that. It will kill me to walk away from you again, but my happiness depends on yours, so if that means I have to let you go forever, then I will." Xavier stopped talking as a tear sprung to his eye. He wiped it away quickly and stared into my eyes. "But if you and your husband can't work things out, then I'll be waiting here with open arms." He stopped talking and rifled around in his pocket to pull out a weary looking box.

I looked at him questioningly as he opened the lid to reveal a beautiful gold ring, with a delicate little diamond set elegantly on top of it. I stared up at him in shock, searching his eyes for an explanation.

"Is that…" I whispered, letting my sentence trail off.

"I know it's not very impressive, but I bought this for you when I graduated from Oxford," he said sadly. "I was going to propose to you when I got home, but then you left for London before I made it back."

I stared at him agape, "Xavi, are you proposing?"

"It's more of a pre-proposal I suppose," he said with a nod. "If you came back and took me up on the offer then I'd buy you a better ring of course, and ask you properly, but I need you to know how serious I am about you. You're the woman of my dreams Katie, and I want to be the man of yours."

- NATHAN STONE -

"Oi, oi!" Called Ritchie loudly from the reception area, as Ashley and I emerged from the parking garage. We both looked at him, but continued walking, not bothering to slow down for the raucous Aussie. I rolled my eyes good-naturedly as Ritchie boisterously bounded up behind us. "You two will start rumours arriving at work together."

"People need someone to talk about," I said, with a wink at Ashley. "We're providing a community service, right Granger?"

"Haha, absolutely," she agreed. "Today is a freebie, but we'll start charging after this."

Ritchie fell into line with us as we wandered towards the lifts. He looked back and forth between Ash and I with a big grin on his face.

"Good client meeting yesterday?" he asked with the intent of embarrassment. Ashley blushed furiously and jumped straight onto the elevator as soon as the doors opened. I shot Ritchie a warning look, as I stood in between the doors.

"Ritchie and I will get the next one," I told Ash, with my hand firmly planted on Ritchie's broad chest, to prevent him hopping aboard. "I'll see you at lunch."

"Okay," Ash nodded. I planted a quick kiss on her soft lips, and stepped away from the elevator.

The doors slid closed, and Ritchie immediately commenced his torture.

"Holy shit mate," he hollered with a laugh, slapping me on the back, "she stayed the night again huh?"

"She did," I confirmed without amusement, "and I've managed not to fuck anything up so far, so I appreciate it if you didn't try and sabotage me."

"Whoa," he said raising his hands, "I was just having a bit of fun Stoner."

"Well don't do it in front of Ash."

"Geez... okay. Sorry," he replied sulkily. The second lift arrived and we rode it in silence. Ritchie remained quiet until I sat down at my workstation. He plonked his big arse on my desk, and settled in for our standard post-shag debrief. "Granger isn't here right now, so... how was yesterday?" he asked way too loudly. A few people looked up from their desks with a chuckle or a knowing smile.

"Please don't," I replied exhaustedly. Whilst normally I would have filled Ritchie in on every gory detail, it didn't feel right this time.

"Why not?" He teased, glancing down at my crotch with raised eyebrows. "...don't tell me it doesn't work?"

"It works Ritch," I snapped, in defense of my perfectly healthy erectile function.

"Why so touchy today?" he teased good naturedly.

"It's not appropriate right now," I told him, sounding very much like a grown-up adult person.

"Stoner… appropriate went out the door the moment you two started snogging in the hallway window," Ritch teased with a smirk. I rolled my eyes at him, and he raised his hands in surrender. He peered around and then lowered his voice. "So how about that Dom thing yesterday… that was pretty crazy huh?"

"Yeah it was," I agreed. "Thanks for stepping in. I thought he was going to kill me."

"Me too," he agreed. "Is Ash okay?"

"She's pretty freaked out, but she's going to stay with me until Jock can track him down."

"You both staying at Gaz's?" he asked with confusion.

"No, mine. I had to be at Gaz's because Wayne wouldn't let me live by myself," I said with a shrug, "but with Ash at mine I can stay there too."

"Well in that case you can have your fucking cat back," Ritchie said.

"Oh come on, you love Fleabag," I teased.

"Meh, he's okay, but he's too high maintenance."

"Really? I'm surprised a stray would be that fussy."

"Well he – wait, what? What do you mean 'stray cat'?" Ritchie asked.

"Fleabag's a stray," I told him, unable to contain a grin.

"You cunt," Ritchie swore, as I laughed. "You let me look after a fucking stray for two months?!"

"Yep," I said, grabbing my crutches to make an exit, before he pummeled me.

"Get back here you little shit," Ritchie said, catching me in two strides. "You're in so much fucking trouble," he said, grabbing me in a headlock. "Carlton Crush," he said, shoving my face into his armpit, while I laughed like an idiot.

"I don't care, it was worth it," I teased, muffled beneath his pit.

"Oh, there will be more," he warned, gripping me tighter, "I just need time to think up a suitable punishment."

"It's okay, Red is going to torture me for telling you when she wasn't here."

"Amy knew?" he asked, abruptly letting me go.

"Yep," I admitted proudly. "So did Gaz… and Ryza."

"Oh, you're all pricks," he said shaking his head. "I can't believe you all kept that quiet. Is this how you thank someone for getting you laid?"

I straightened up. "Actually, I do owe you for that," I said sincerely. "Thanks man."

"Good friends look after their friends," Ritchie said factually.

"Yeah they also look after their friends stray cats," I teased, bursting into another round of laughter.

"You're such a fuckhead," he said with a laugh, as his eyes wandered towards the door behind me. His smile faded instantly, and his jaw clenched tight. "Beau's back," he said through gritted teeth. I glanced over my shoulder to get a look at the smarmy Yank.

"Oh fuuuuck," I breathed, getting a load of his ruined face. "Ryza did that?"

"Yep."

"Holy shit," I swore in disbelief.

"He fuck'n deserved it," Ritchie said protectively.

"This isn't our fight man," I told him, patting his chest to calm him down.

"Fuck with one of us, fuck with all of us Stoner."

"Not if it's a work colleague," I replied patiently, as Beau glanced in our direction. "Besides, it looks like Ryza's punished him enough."

"Boys," Beau greeted us solemnly, as he walked past. He was playing the victim well, but there was an underlying cockiness to his demeanor that made me want to punch him in the face myself. Neither of us replied, but I nodded my acknowledgment in order to keep the peace.

"He's enjoying this way too much," Ritchie muttered angrily as we watched Peterson wander over to his desk.

"Yeah he is," I agreed, no happier about the situation than Ritchie was. My desk phone buzzed. It was Gaz, so I picked up the receiver without bothering to talk. I had the feeling it was going to be one hell of a long day.

"Nathan come up to my office please," he requested before hanging up.

"Gaz?" Ritchie asked knowingly, as I put down the phone without saying one word.

"Yep," I confirmed, with a slight feeling of dread.

"May the force be with you," Ritchie laughed before strutting away. "Oh by the way, I'm bringing Fleabag back tonight."

"Fine," I agreed, "why don't you and Red come for dinner?" I suggested. "As an apology."

"Okay, but you better have beer… and whiskey too," he said as I walked away.

"Sure thing."

"And not the cheap shit… it better be that really fucking expensive whiskey that you're always banging on about. And dessert."

"Got it," I said with a salute, as I exited to the elevators. I stopped outside Gareth's office door, and took a deep breath before knocking.

"You took your time," he barked at me tersely when I eventually let myself in.

"Sorry," I apologised humbly. Gaz seemed grumpier than usual.

"Right lad," he began as I took my place on the black leather sofa. "We've got a few things we need to discuss."

"I know," I agreed hesitantly, waiting for my bollocking to begin.

"Monday morning was unacceptable… on so many levels," he said sternly, getting right to the point. "I have to say, I'm really fucking disappointed in you." I nodded shamefully but remained silent. "And taking the day off yesterday…" he sighed and rubbed his face. "I get it, and I know you needed to get whatever it was out of your systems… but if you pull that shit again, I'll fire both of you, and don't think I won't," he said seriously. "Your position as a silent partner is completely separate from your role as a Client Partner, so there's nothing to stop me from kicking your arse out of that door."

"Understood," I agreed with a nod.

"I know it's been a weird time lately Nathan, but I've never seen you act so unprofessionally. I've always given you a lot of leeway, but Monday was pushing the envelope. If it had been anyone else, I would have fired them on the spot."

"I know," I admitted with embarrassment, wondering what he'd say if he ever found out about my little encounter with Sandrine. "I'm really sorry Gaz."

"Nath," he sighed, rubbing his hand over his face again. I was starting to worry that I'd broken Gareth Hemsworth. "This thing with you and Granger… just be very careful lad," he warned. I nodded solemnly, unsure whether it was my turn to talk or not. "Living together is a very big step up from where you've been."

"I know Gaz, but it will be fine. I promise." Part of me wanted to tell him about the Dominic situation, but he was stressed enough as it was. Ritchie and I would figure something out, and then once I had a solution, I'd tell Gaz.

"Look, I know things are different with Ashley, but I don't want to see you do anything to risk your position on the Delfontaine account. I know exactly how hard you've worked for this success, so please don't blow it by doing something stupid."

"I won't."

Gaz nodded, seemingly appeased by my promise.

"Speaking of doing stupid things," he said, joining me on the chesterfield, "how's Ryan going?"

"He's been better, but it's giving him time to sort through some shit." I sighed guiltily. "I feel like I let him down."

"You didn't let him down Nath, you were in hospital," he said patting me on the back. "Just keep an eye on him huh?"

"Yeah, I will."

"We still need to replace him too," Gaz added, "we need to keep the Milner's account running smoothly or we're buggered."

"Christian seems to have everything under control for the time being," I assured Gaz. "He's really stepped up since I've been back."

"Enough for a promotion?"

"Yeah, I think so," I said with a shrug, "I'd like to give him a chance at least."

"Okay," agreed Gaz, "I'll take your lead on that one. Now we just need a new copywriter for Delfontaine, and we'll be sorted."

"Ritchie and I have it under control," I lied.

"Great! I just spoke to Sandrine, and she wants to meet the leads, and introduce them to her team. She asked if you could take them out there for a visit ASAP."

"Okay," I agreed reluctantly, "I'll set it up for a few weeks time. That will give us a chance to find our Beau replacement." I didn't really care about finding a new Copywriter before our Paris visit, I just wanted to buy myself some time. With all the Dom drama, I'd forgotten about the Sandrine situation and I needed to figure out a way to clean up that mess before Ashley was thrown into the snakepit.

"I think she was hoping it would be sooner than that," Gaz said, eyeing me suspiciously.

"How much sooner?"

"Next week."

"Oh, that's quite a bit sooner."

"I would've thought you'd be excited about that lad," Gaz said.

"Yeah. I am. I mean, it's quite last minute that's all."

"Why don't you give her a call and see what you can figure out."

"Yeah of course," I nodded with a cool smile, whilst freaking out on the inside, "I'll pick it up with Sandrine. I'm sure she'll be fine with two weeks."

"Good," he paused again. "Make sure you keep her happy Nathan. We're counting on this client."

I nodded obediently, hoping that Gareth didn't realise exactly what his sentiment might entail.

- RYAN McPHERSON -

My body was still shaking with rage, but by our third lap of the main garden, I'd calmed down enough to speak.

"We've got twenty minutes before group therapy so you'd better talk quick," said Sloane, leading me over to a wooden bench seat that was tucked away underneath the old oak tree. We sat in silence for a while, taking in the lush gardens, until Sloane fastened her piercing gaze on me like a laser beam.

"What happened?" she asked, eying my bloodied knuckles.

"My parents came to visit," I explained, leaning my elbows on my thighs, and flexing my aching hand. We'd had enough discussions in Group Therapy about the state of my family, so I knew she'd be able to draw an accurate conclusion to that scenario.

"Oh," she said with complete understanding, "and I take it the visit went about as well as you'd expect?"

"That would be the understatement of the century," I joked half-heartedly. "Today they reminded me exactly why I cut them off in the first place," I said, feeling my hackles rising at the memory of my fathers words. "They're such cunts."

Sloane laughed in shock.

"Well that's fairly definitive," she teased, "but from what you've said in Group it sounds well deserved."

"Yeah," I agreed with a nod, as I clenched my damaged fist. "But they hit an all-time low today." I looked up at her and huffed disdainfully. "They offered to pay Kat a hundred grand to take the baby and run."

Sloans jaw dropped.

"Whaaaaaaat?" she asked, stunned.

"Apparently she was never good enough for the family, and she's done us all a favour by cheating on me."

"Holy shit Ryan," she swore in bewilderment. "They really are cunts."

"Yep. And I have no idea whether they're going to go after her. While I'm stuck in here without a phone, they could be making their way up to Framlingham to pay her off, and I might never see my child."

"They wouldn't sink that low would they?"

"I have no idea anymore," I admitted, rubbing my face, "but I wouldn't put anything past them." I glanced sideways at her, feeling tears stinging the back of my eyes. "I don't want to lose my family."
Sloane wrapped her arm around my shoulder and rubbed my arm.

"I won't let that happen Ryan," she said adamantly, pulling a phone out of her pocket. My eyes bulged at the sight of the contraband, and I looked quickly around the garden to make sure no one could see us.

"Where did you get that from?" I hissed, not knowing why I was whispering. "Didn't they confiscate it when you checked in?"

"Yeah, they did," she said with a sneaky grin, "but like I said, I've been here for a while, so I know how to work the system." Sloane held out the phone in front of me, and I surveyed the garden again to make doubly sure that we weren't being monitored. "Call your wife," she said, pushing the phone at me so I'd take it from her. I clutched the little white rectangle in my hands as if it was a lifeline. "Then go clean up that hand." Sloane stood up with a smile and squeezed my shoulder. "I'll see you in Group."

- KAT McPHERSON -

After Xavier left, I'd retreated straight back into my bed. Whilst I was pleased that he'd agreed to cease his efforts, I was left rattled by his non-proposal. Was he really so stuck in the past that he thought I was his best option? Or perhaps his pride was wounded after being cheated on by his wife.

"Hmph," I muttered out loud at the irony of the situation. Of all the women in the world, why on earth would Xavi want marry another cheater?

I snuggled into the duvet and tried to get some sleep. I wasn't tired as such, just physically and emotionally exhausted. How was I going to explain any of this to Ryan?

Just then, my phone rang again. I sighed and rolled over to check who it was. I didn't recognise the number so I let it ring out. If it was important they'd either call back or leave a message. I rolled back over when my phone rang again.

"What's with people today?" I grumbled, repeating my side roll like a beached whale. Just as I reached for the phone, it stopped ringing. "Damn it," I swore with frustration, moments before it began ringing again. Whoever was calling, was desperate. I answered the call and lifted the phone to my ear.

"Hello?"

"Kat," Ryan breathed with relief at the other end of the line. I sat up against the headboard.

"Ryan?" I asked breathlessly, "how are you calling? I thought you weren't allowed to have phones in there."

"I'm not, I borrowed it from a friend," he explained quickly in a hushed tone. "I wish I could talk with you properly but I don't have long."

"But I've got so much to say," I said, feeling tears welling in my eyes.

"I know. Me too, but right now I just need to warn you that my parents came to see me."

"Oh god," I said, feeling sick to my stomach. "You're going to leave me aren't you?"

"No, if there's one thing I've figured out, it's that I want to make this work," he whispered, "but they have other ideas. I just need you to know that if they approach you, it's of their own accord. Whatever they say, it's not coming from me."

"Why, what are they going to do?" I asked with panicked confusion.

"Possibly nothing, but they want you gone Kat. I just wanted to get in first in case they tried anything. I told them to – shit – I've gotta go." I heard him fumble with the phone and then the line went dead.

There was nothing but silence at the other end, but I sat with my phone clasped to my ear. A lump rose in my throat and, until that moment, I hadn't noticed that there were tears pouring down my cheeks.

The MacPhersons wanted me gone, but Ryan wanted me back. The latter was all that mattered.

- ASHLEY GRANGER -

Nathan and I were in the kitchen, prepping the food for our dinner. I peered over at him as he checked on the meat. There was something I needed to tell him and I wasn't sure how he was going to take it.

"Hey Nath…" I said hesitantly. He looked up and froze when he saw the look on my face. I gulped, "there's something I need to tell you."

"Okay," he said dubiously, as he closed the oven door and leaned against the bench. "Am I going to need wine for this?"

"I spoke to Jock today," I blurted, figuring it was best to go for a 'ripping the band-aid' approach. "I called him to apologise for being a psycho-bitch."

"And…" Nathan asked worriedly.

"And we chatted, and cleared the air."

"And?"

"And… well that's it really. I just wanted you to know."

"Oh," he said, exhaling loudly. "I thought – never mind. I'm glad you guys made up," he said, obsessively wiping the bench with a wet cloth.

I smiled. "You thought what?"

He sighed and stopped his manic cleaning.

"I thought you were going to say that you wanted to be with him."

I laughed, surprised that Nathan would jump to that conclusion after everything that had happened between us.

"Nathan Stone, are you jealous?" I teased, as I wrapped my arms around his waist. Nathan nodded and smiled awkwardly.

"He's in love with you."

I sighed and stared blankly at Nathan's chest.

"Yeah I know," I admitted, feeling a little embarrassed. "He told me that day at the hospital... after you and I had that fight."

"It's just a one-way crush then?"

"If you don't know the answer to that by now then you haven't been paying attention," I joked quietly, as I stroked the hair at the back of his neck. "You said it yourself yesterday... I'm yours Nathan."

He smiled and bent down to kiss me, but the intercom buzzed before our lips touched.

"You're kidding me," Nathan said, throwing his head back with frustration. "Ritchie is so good at torturing me, he does it without even trying." Nath hobbled off to buzz our guests in. "Hey man, come on up," he said into the intercom before returning to the kitchen. "We'll finish that later," he told me with a wink.

"Damn straight we will," I agreed, flicking him playfully with the tea towel.

"On the plus side, you finally get to meet Fleabag."

"Nath, you can't keep calling the cat Fleabag."

"Why not?" he asked, kissing my neck, "he's probably used to it by now."

"I don't know, it just seems cruel," I replied, feeling sorry for the cat.

"Why don't you name him then?"

"He's your cat, you should name him," I answered with a laugh. I'd never had a guy ask me to name his pet before. Or at least not in a literal sense.

"Then I choose to call him Fleabag," he answered stubbornly.

"Okay fine," I relented with a chuckle, before blurting the first name that popped into my head. "What about Fred?" I suggested half-jokingly.

"Fred?" Nath laughed loudly in amusement.

"Yeah. Fred," I repeated with a grin. It was a ridiculous name for a cat, but anything would be better than fleabag.

"What sort of cat's name is Fred?!" Nathan asked, "I might as well just call him John."

"It's better than Fleabag," I answered with a shrug, "and better than John."

"I guess it is," he conceded with a smile. "Fred the cat."

"Fred the cat," I repeated.

"Okay then. Fred it is," Nath agreed, shaking his head with amusement as we heard a knock at the door. "Come on then, it's time for you to meet our new flat mate." Nath opened the door, and there was Ritchie standing in the hallway cradling a fluffy ginger cat.

"Your cat sir," said Ritchie with a half-bow, as he shoved Fred into Nathan's arms.

"Jesus Ritchie, he's huge. How much have you been feeding him?"

"Just breakfast and dinner," Ritchie shrugged, squeezing past Nathan into the flat as Amy stood at the door, smiling with amusement.

"Hey Fleabag," Nathan said, promptly placing the chubby cat on the floor. Fleabag wound himself around Nathans legs, seemingly pleased to see him. "Guess what buddy... you've got a new name," Nathan told him. "From now on, you're Fred the cat."

"Fred?" laughed Amy, following Ritchie through the door.

"Ashley's idea," Nathan was quick to point out, as he closed the door behind them all. "So who's hungry?"

"Starving," said Ritchie, grabbing a beer out of the fridge and nearly finishing the entire bottle in one go. "What have you got cooking?"

"Prosciutto wrapped rump beef with roasted honey and mustard parsnips, potato dauphinoise and steamed mange tout, all courtesy of my good friends Marks & Spencer," Nathan said with a grin, as he started piling the food onto the table. "And a vegan roast for the lady."

"The vegan crap is all yours Granger," Ritchie joked, "I'm going to demolish that meat," he added. Nathan poured the wine, and we all took our seats as Fred explored his new home. "So, we have two orders of business," Ritch declared, as if he was conducting a business meeting. "Firstly, it's the Baby Shower in a couple of weeks, so while the girls are doing their girly things up in Framptonshire..."

"Framlingham," Nathan corrected him.

"Framlingham," Ritchie repeated with a posh British accent, "we should do something for Ryza," he directed that comment to Nath. "You know, take him out and get his mind off things."

"Agreed," Nathan said with a smile. "Let's take the boy golfing. You guys can come here first. Ash and Red can take my car and we'll hire a bigger one."

"I'm not going to the Baby Shower," Amy said, as she gulped a mouthful of wine.

"Why not?" I asked worriedly, "I can't go on my own, I barely even know Kat."

"You'll be fine," she said, "but you're under no obligation to go either."

"I kind of am," I disagreed, "Nath told her I'd be coming."

"Plus, I don't want Ash going all that way on her own," said Nath. "What if Dom follows her?"

"Just tell her Ash can't go now," Amy said with a shrug.

"No Red," Nath said firmly, "you've gotta go to the baby shower, Kat's your best friend."

"Not anymore, she's not."

"Since when?"

"Since the night she cheated on Ryan," Amy said angrily.

"Aims," Ritchie said, touching her arm, "can we not do this tonight? It's not our business."

"It is our business," she disagreed, "she ruined Ryan. He's gone off the rails and he pretty much destroyed his life because of what she did and she just gets to wander off into the sunset like nothing ever happened."

Nathan's jaw dropped, and I had a strong feeling that he was about to say something he'd regret, so I stepped in.

"Look Amy, I don't know Kat," I said, patting Nath's leg under the table, "but I do know what it's like to be pregnant, and I don't think she would be having the best time doing it on her own."

"Well she brought it on herself," Amy said unforgivingly.

"Wow," Nathan said in disbelief, "of all the people Red, I would have thought that you would be a little more understanding."

Amy shot Nathan a warning glare, "don't even start Stoner."

"Okay, so I think maybe we need to leave this order of business alone for now," I joked, trying to diffuse the tension, "what's the second order of business Ritch?"

Ritchie looked at me as Nathan and Amy glared at each other.

"Ah... I don't know if it's a good topic to bring up anymore."

"Well I don't think it could get any worse," I said through a fake smile.

He nodded, "I was going to suggest we come up with a plan to deal with your ex-boyfriend."

"Oh, yeah, umm... I don't think there's anything we can do," I said firmly.

"So, you want to sit back and do nothing?" Nathan asked with a tinge of annoyance.

"No," I said patiently, "I just don't see what we can do right now."

"Restraining Order would be a good start," Amy piped up.

"That would antagonize him," I said, shaking my head.

"But at least you'd be safe," she argued. I snorted with amusement.

"Amy, the guy just managed to get out of prison without anyone knowing about it, do you really think he'd let a piece of paper stop him from coming at me?"

"Good point," she agreed. "Can't we at least let the cops know that the guy in prison isn't Dom?"

"And how would we prove it?" I asked, shaking my head. "It's Fake Dom's word against ours, and as far as they'd see it, he has zero reason to be lying about his identity."

"There's four of us who've seen the real Dom, plus the security guard at the hotel. They'd at least have to investigate it," argued Ritchie. Nathan was interestingly quiet on the matter.

"Okay," I agreed, "so we report it, and they investigate but we have no idea where he even is."

"No, but that's for the cops to find out right?" asked Aims.

"Look guys," I said, with a sigh, "I appreciate your support, but this is my problem to handle, and I don't want to do anything that will put any of you in danger."

"You don't have any choice Granger," Ritchie said with a shrug, "you're part of our crew now, and we stick together."

"We always have each other's backs no matter what," added Amy.

"Unless you're Kat," Nath muttered under his breath.

"For fuck sake Nathan," she snapped, pushing back her chair, and storming out the sliding glass door onto the balcony. Ritch looked up awkwardly and smiled.

"Excuse me for a minute," he said, standing up.

"It's okay Ritch," I said, "I've got this one." I joined Amy outside and leaned quietly against the bannister next her. "So what was that all about?" I asked curiously, "or do I not want to know?"

Amy sighed. "It's probably not what you're thinking."

"So you haven't shagged Nathan then?" I asked with a smile. I was getting used to the fact that my boyfriend had slept with most of the women in

London.

"No," she assured me, "but we did snog a really long time ago."

"Okay," I said, wondering where this was leading, "and did that have anything to do with what just happened in there?"

"Sort of," Amy said with a sigh, as she leaned up against the railing next to me. "When I first started at Artemis, I was seeing this guy Alex, from my old work. He thought it was serious but, like... I'm not a relationship person, right?" she said with a nervous laugh, "anyway... Nathan and I, and few of the old crew were out partying. We were all pretty messy," Amy cleared her throat, "someone posted a photo of Nathan and I snogging on Facebook and Alex saw it."

"Oh," I said, turning around to look out at Holland Park, "so what happened?" I asked peering out into the darkness.

"Alex killed himself," she said, causing my eyes to bulge out of my head.

"Oh my god," I said, wondering how Nathan had failed to mention that.

"That's partly why I won't commit to Ritchie," she said, "I can't be responsible for someone else's happiness. I'm not equipped for that. I mean, I was already pretty messed up before I met Alex, but he added a whole new layer of crazy."

"That was a pretty extreme response though Aims," I agreed, trying to offer her some comfort. "He clearly must have had some issues for suicide to even be an option."

"Yeah." Amy looked inside at the boys, "but don't we all?"

"True," I agreed with a nod.

"You've found your tribe here Ash," she joked with a smile, "we're all so fucked-up that even your psycho-ex doesn't scare us."

I laughed and looked inside at Nathan who was chatting animatedly with Ritchie.

"So you and Nathan..." I ventured, wondering how far their relationship had gone.

"There was never a me and Nathan," she said, touching my hand, "and that's actually the worst thing about the whole situation. It was all over nothing. There was never anything between the two of us. It was one snog, which was purely force of habit because we were both so whorey."

"Okay," I nodded.

"Plus, it was a lifetime ago," she said, tucking her shiny auburn hair over her shoulder, "things have changed a lot since then."

- NATHAN STONE -

Ritchie and I watched as Ash joined Red on the balcony. I hadn't intended to upset her, but she was being ridiculous. She of all people should have known how heavy it weighs on your conscience when one stupid mistake fucks up the course of someone else's life.

"I hope I wasn't too hard on her," I said to Ritch, feeling a little guilty.

"She'll be right," he said with a smile, "she's tough."

"Yeah," I agreed. Ritchie looked outside to make sure the girls were still out of earshot. They were talking intently, so it looked like they'd be out there for a little while.

"So what's the real plan for Dom then?" he asked, knowing that I wouldn't just sit back and do nothing about it.

"We're all going to Paris in a few weeks right?"

"Yeah…" he said, not entirely catching my drift.

"So we'll make sure that a lot of people see all three of us together… a long way from London."

"Right, and we'll be doing that because…?"

"I'm going to get rid of the cunt for good," I said honestly.

"I'm still not getting it."

"Dominic is a dead man walking, Ritchie."

Ritchie laughed nervously, "I assume you mean metaphorically?"

"No," I said seriously, "I mean literally."

"Are you saying what I think you're saying?"

I nodded, "I'm going to have him knocked-off."

"Nath," Ritchie said with a look of sheer horror, "please tell me you're not serious."

"I'm as serious as a heart-attack," I assured him. "I just have to find someone to do it."

"Nathan, you can't murder Dom."

"Firstly, I won't be the one doing it," I paused and took a sip of wine. "I considered it. I know a guy who can get me an unlicensed gun, but then I realized I don't even know how to shoot a gun."

Ritchie stared at me with raised brows.

"And that was the only reason you decided not to physically kill a man?"

"Well that, and the fact that I probably wouldn't have been able to go through with it," I admitted with a shrug.

"Good, because you had me worried for a minute there," he said taking a large gulp of his wine. "But you still can't have someone else kill him. That's crossing the line man."

"But that's the thing, I won't be killing Dom," I said with a smile, "Dom Doyle is in prison remember? And if he's in prison, then he won't really be dead will he?"

"Holy fuck," Ritchie breathed, as he rubbed his face, "do you have any idea how psycho you sound right now?"

"I do, but there's no other solution Ritch," I told him adamantly as I glanced out at Ashley. "I've gone over and over all the options in my head and none of them are viable."

"I'm not sure if I'm more worried about the fact that you've thought this through so well, or the fact that you seem to be quite excited at the prospect of his death."

"I'm not excited, I'm-" I thought about it for a minute. "Okay I'll admit I'm a little excited," I said honestly, "but only because, while Dom's alive, Ash will never be free. He'll keep chasing her until she's dead. Or until he's dead. Which is the option I prefer."

"But you will have killed a man," Ritchie said grimly. "Will you be able to live with that on your conscience?"

"When it comes to that man… yes," I told Ritch. "Look, the cops think he's in prison, so no one will even know he's gone. It's not like the guy has any family, and all his friends are criminals."

Ritchie cringed, "that's not the point Stoner."

"No, I know," I agreed, "the point is that Ash will be able to stop living in fear, and we can get on with our lives without being hunted like animals."

Ritchie skulled the remnants of his wine, "I think you're gonna need to crack out that whiskey."

"Okay," I said with a chuckle, heading to the liquor cabinet to pull out my £200 bottle of Nathan Stone's Private Stock 105 Proof Bourbon Whiskey. It wasn't the smoothest whiskey ever, but I liked the fact that it had my name on the bottle. I poured two large glasses and handed one to Ritch. He took a massive swig and put the glass down on the table.

"Right, so what's your plan then?" he asked, with a deep breath.

"Well, I have to find someone to do it," I said logically. "I have a contact who might know how to put me in touch with someone but I have to be careful about making too many enquiries. I can't let this trace back to me, just in case someone does notice that he's missing."

"This is insane Stoner," Ritchie hissed, looking over his shoulder at the girls.

"Yeah, well, Dom's insane, and this is the only way I'm going to be able to end it."

"I can't believe you're even considering this," he said, running his hands over his bald head. "What if Ash finds out?"

I leaned over the table and looked him in the eyes.

"She can't know. At least not until it's done," I told him sternly. "The less everyone knows, the better."

"Fucking right about that," he agreed, taking another large mouthful of bourbon. Ritchie leaned back in his chair and crossed his arms, studying me with concern. "Fine," he said, "what do you need me to do?"

- ASHLEY GRANGER -

After Ritchie and Amy left, we cleaned up the kitchen and settled down on the sofa together.

"So we have officially hosted our first dinner party together," Nathan said, as he draped his arm over my shoulder.

"Yeah, we have," I agreed. The whole Amy and Nathan thing was still lingering on my mind.

"It wasn't a total disaster," he joked.

"Just a minor one," I agreed with a laugh. "Hey… Amy told me something tonight and I need to ask you about it."

"Okay," Nath said, shuffling around so he was facing me. "This sounds serious."

"Not serious, just…" I paused and sighed, "she said you guys have kissed."

"Oh," he nodded in understanding, "yeah we did, once, a really long time ago. There was nothing to it though I promise."

"No, I know," I said with a nod. "I'm just wondering why you didn't tell me."

"I'm sorry," he said, taking my hand. "It was so long ago and with everything that's been happening… I honestly hadn't even thought about. It's not an excuse, I know, but it was so insignificant in the scheme of things that it hadn't occurred to me."

"Except that a guy killed himself over it."

"Well, yeah, there was that," Nath agreed sheepishly, "but I promise you, there was nothing between Red and I. We were both just coked out of our minds and in the habit of playing around."

"Yeah she mentioned that," I said, trying not to sound like a jealous girlfriend.

"I'm sorry I was such a man-whore."

"Nathan, you don't need to apologise for your past," I told him, rubbing his leg, "you've just really got to warn when it's going to pop into our present."

"Okay, I will. I'm sorry anyway," he said with a smile as he put his arm around me again. He kissed the top of my head and squeezed me gently. "Did we just have our first fight?"

I scoffed. "If that counts as a fight then we're doing okay."
Nathan stopped and thought for a moment.

"Actually I think our first fight was yesterday when you slapped me in the face." He said, rubbing the side of his cheek with an impish grin. I laughed, and kissed his cheek.

"I'm sorry."

"You're forgiven," he teased, turning his head to catch my lips with his, before leaning further down to kiss my neck. It sent shivers all over my body, and the breath caught in my throat as his hands wandered downwards to cup my breasts.

"Mmmm," I mumbled as he bent in for another kiss. Just as our lips met, Fred sat down in front of us and mewed loudly. We stopped in our tracks and looked down at the interrupting cat.

"Ah yes," Nathan said with a wry smile, "we have a cat now."

"No, you have a cat now," I teased, patting Fred. The cat jumped up into my lap as if to protest my rejection of him, and Nathan laughed his yummy chocolate laugh.

"I think he might disagree," Nath teased with amusement. I swept Fred up in my arms and snuggled into Nathan's chest with a happy sigh.

"Okay, I guess we have a cat after all," I conceded. Nathan wrapped his arms around me and patted Fred's head affectionately.

"Perhaps having a cat isn't so bad," he joked, resting his chin on my head as we all cuddled together like a happy little family. "It's been a crazy few days huh?"

"It's been a crazy few months," I said glancing up at him with slight despair. "I can't help but think everyone would have been better off if I'd just stayed in Bali."

"I wouldn't," he disagreed adamantly.

"Nathan, you'd still have two working legs and an uninterrupted sex life."

"Yeah, but I wouldn't have you."

- *Chapter* 15 -

THE BABY SHOWER

- RYAN McPHERSON -

I was ready and waiting in the reception area by the time Ritchie and Nathan rocked up at the Lodge. I couldn't wait to get out of there, even if it was only for the day. I'd been in that place for over a month, and I was already going crazy. The biggest irony, was that one day in that place, could push anyone into excessive drug usage. It was nothing but continuous therapy sessions; Group Therapy, one-on-one psych, Art Therapy, Hypnotherapy, Acupuncture, the list went on. One session after another. Every. Single. Day. Not to mention the rather annoying cockney cock-head who seemed intent on making my life miserable.

"Stoner!" I called excitedly when he walked in the door. I ran up and gave him a hug, "I could kiss you right now."

"I'd prefer if you didn't," he laughed, patting me on the back. "How you going in here?"

"I'll fill you in on the way," I said, keen to get out of there. "Where are we going anyway?" He and Ritchie still hadn't told me what they had planned for the day, and after having dreamed up a million dodgy outings that Ritchie might have come up with, I'd been slightly dreading it.

"Ah, patience my dear Ryza," Nath teased with a smile. "Let me sign you out and all will be revealed." Nathan filled out the thousand page manifesto that was required in order for me to be a free adult human for one day, and as we walked out the door, a horn beeped in a cheery tune.

"Let's get going cunts," called Ritchie happily from the driver's seat of a silver station wagon. "Say hello to the Mum-Mobile, Ryza."

"Where's the new Tesla?" I asked Nathan, feeling a little disappointed that I didn't get to check-out his new ride.

"We wouldn't have fitted the three of us and golf gear," Nathan answered with a smile.

"Golfing?" I said, pleasantly surprised.

"Yep," Nathan said proudly.

"You know me too well," I answered with a smile. "Thanks."

"No worries. It could be ages before we get another chance to do this."

"Yeah. Life is changing huh?"

"Sure is," he agreed, as we joined Ritchie in the Mum-Mobile. As we pulled out into the Saturday morning traffic, I inhaled deeply, reveling in my freedom, even though it was only fleeting.

"So which course are we going to?" I asked casually, trying to convince myself that everything was the same as normal.

"Royal St George," Nathan announced proudly.

"As in… the Royal St George, in Kent?" I asked, gobsmacked. Royal St George was one of the best clubs in England.

"Yep," Nathan answered with a grin.

"Hand me some bread because it's Sandwich time baby," joked Ritchie, referring to the fact that the course was in the town of Sandwich.

"You've been hanging out to say that all day haven't you?" Stoner teased.

"That's just the beginning," Ritch replied, waggling his eyebrows. "I have a whole list of Sandwich related puns to work through."

"Great," I said with a smile. It almost felt like a normal weekend. "Is Amy going up for the shower?" I asked Ritchie.

"Errr… no," he said awkwardly.

"Don't tell me they're still fighting?"

"Amy's pretty angry with Tails for… well… everything," Ritch explained. "She'll cool down eventually, but at the moment she's feeling pretty protective of you."

"I don't need her to protect or defend me," I said, feeling touched that Amy had taken my side, "but it is kinda sweet."

"Ash is going," Nathan blurted. I turned to him with my mouth open, like one of those carnival clown heads.

"Ash is going to the Baby Shower? Do you think that's a great idea?"

"Why wouldn't it be?" he asked.

"Kat's not her biggest fan. She could be walking into the lions den."

"Tails seemed fine with it when she invited her the other day."
My jaw dropped.

"It was Kat that invited her?" I asked, stunned.

"Yeah," Nath shrugged. "When I was chatting to her."

"You've been chatting to her?"

"I call her every few days to make sure she's okay."

"Oh, I see," I wasn't sure how I felt about that. I was surprised that Amy had sided with me, but I thought for sure that I would get to keep Nathan. We had, after all, been friends for longer.

"Look Ryza," said Nathan, reading my vibe correctly, "Tails and I have been friends for a long time, and just because you guys aren't together any more, doesn't mean I'm going to stop being friends with her."

"I know, it's just… I was your friend first," I said feeling hurt.

"Dude, we're not in high school," he said, shaking his head. "We're adults. Tails is my friend and I'm not going to abandon her for making a stupid mistake. God knows I've made enough in my time, and she's never ditched me once."

"I'm glad someone is keeping an eye out for her," agreed Ritchie, "I'm just trying to keep out of it to avoid an Amy-rant."

"Jesus Ritch, you really need to grow a pair," teased Nathan.

"I know," Ritchie agreed. "I hate myself, but the woman has me whipped. I'm her bitch."

"I thought you were just fuck buddies," Nath said.

"Yeah... except I'm in love with her," Ritch said hopelessly.

"What?!" I asked in shock. "I thought Fuck Buddies was your idea. I thought you preferred it that way."

"No, it was Amy's idea. She prefers it that way."

"Oh," I answered simply. I was astonished at the revelation. I'd always assumed it was Ritchie putting the brakes on their relationship. "Have you told her you want more?"

"Of course I have," he admitted, "she says we're too young to tie ourselves down."

"Ouch," I winced on his behalf, "harsh."

"I know right? How is nearly forty too young?" he sighed. "Every time I propose, she rips off my balls."

"Holy fuck," said Nath, echoing my thoughts. "When did you ask her to marry you?"

"Last December," said Ritch, "then January, then February..."

"Okay, okay," I said, waving my hand at him unable to hear anymore. "So what are you going to do about it Ritch?"

"Not much I can do," Ritch shrugged, "it's either this or nothing, and I'd rather be her fuck-buddy than her friend."

"Fair enough," I agreed, "there's nothing wrong with fuck buddies."

"And on that topic," said Ritchie, changing the subject, "Aims called Kellie and told her what happened, apparently she wants to come and see you."

"Why? I assumed she would have moved on to the next guy by now."

"I dunno," Ritchie said with a shrug, "maybe she actually likes you."

"I doubt that," I said with a smile, "she's a party girl through and through."

"I'd agree," agreed Nathan. "It's probably best if you just let that one go."

"Yeah, you've got that right," I said with a nod, "it was never meant to get that out of control in the first place."

"So just like that huh? Cut and run," Ritchie said with a sigh. "I wish I could walk away that easily."

"You could if you wanted to," said Nathan, "the problem is that you love her. You've got to decide if being half with her is worth the pain."

"Listen to the man. Three weeks in a relationship and suddenly he's a love guru," I teased, still finding it hard to believe that Nath and Ashley were a proper adult couple.

"So...it's going well then huh?" I asked stunned at the change in Nathan.

"It's going really well actually."

"You're living with a woman and you're not freaking out?" I teased, still finding it har to believe that Nathan was actually in a committed relationship.

"Correct."

"And you haven't done anything dumb yet?"

"Nope."

"Well not yet anyway," muttered Ritchie under his breath. Nathan rolled his eyes at Ritchie.

"I haven't done anything dumb that would fuck up my relationship at least," Nathan clarified sheepishly.

"So what happens now then?" I asked, sincerely interested in Nathan's plans.

"We're just taking it slow."

Ritchie and I exchanged amused glances and erupted into laughter. Nathan's eyes darted between the two of us as if he was genuinely confused about why that might be funny.

"What?" he asked befuddled, "why is that so funny?"

"You're taking it slow?" I teased, "Nathan, you moved in together the day after you hooked up."

Nathan blushed, which was an event I'd never witnessed before.

"Yeah, well that was due to extenuating circumstances," he mumbled.

"I guess I shouldn't mention that you're meeting her parents tomorrow then?" Ritchie piped up, shooting me a wink.

"You meeting her folks?" I asked, in disbelief. Nathan sighed and gave in to the jovial teasing.

"Yep, we're going down there for lunch."

"Fuck Stone. That's huge. And that's your idea of taking it slow?" I laughed again. "You two are incredible."

"It's not like we planned it. It just sort of worked out that way."

"Oh Stoner. You don't do things in halves do you?" I said with an amused chuckle.

"What's that supposed to mean?"

"Nothing buddy," I said patting him on the back, "I'm happy for you."

"You know what that means Stoner?" Ritchie asked with amusement. "You and Ash are now the only functional couple in our group."

"Well that's a strange turn of events," Nathan laughed.

"Yeah…who would have guessed that you two would end up the emotionally stable ones?" I teased.

"I don't think I'd call it emotionally stable," said Ritchie, casting a judgmental glance at Nath.

"Why is that?" I asked with curiosity. Ritchie stared at Nath, who peered over the headrest like a guilty puppy dog. "What's going on?" I asked.

"Err... we've got a bit of a... Dom issue," Nathan answered quickly.

"Well that's one way to put it," Ritchie balked.

"A Dom issue?" I asked with surprise. A sick feeling began to churn in my stomach. That was a name that I thought I'd heard the last of. "What do you mean?"

Nathan took a deep breath and shuffled his body around to face me.

"Don't freak out," he said condescendingly, "but Dom's back."

I gaped at Nathan, hearing his words but failing to compute them.

"How can Dom be back?" I asked as my brain went into over-drive. "Isn't he in prison?"

"Not anymore," Ritchie said.

"What? How?" I asked in shock. How the fuck could they just let him out of prison?

"It's a long story," said Nathan.

"Lucky we've got a long drive then," I said, not letting him get out of it that easily. "Start talking Stone."

- KAT McPHERSON -

It was the day of my Baby Shower, and my belly was feeling so heavy I could barely move. The baby had moved into a horrible position, and she was so big that it felt like she was using up every available space inside my body.

I was sitting at Mum's kitchen table, skewering little cubes of cheese and cocktail onions onto toothpicks. It was hardly high-class catering, but Mum refused to veer from her tried and tested party food, which meant a menu straight out of a 1980's Good Housewife magazine.

My mother flapped around me like a chook without a head. This baby shower was more about her than it was about me or the baby.

"Did you pick up the cake Rosie?" she called out towards the living room, where Rosie was setting up some of the games.

"No, I thought you were getting it," Rosie called back.

"What?!" Mum exclaimed in horror, "that was your one job Rosanne, how could you possibly forget to pick it up?"

Rosie stuck her head into the kitchen with a smile, "I didn't. It's in the back fridge," she teased with a wink. "I just wanted to see you flip out."

"That's an awful thing to do," Mum scolded her.

"True," Rosie agreed, "but also incredibly fun," she said grinning ear-to-ear. "I'll go get the cake."

"Thank you," said Mum, not sounding very thankful at all. Rosie rolled her eyes, and vanished out the kitchen door to get the cake from the back fridge, when the doorbell rang.

"Oh good heavens, it's still too early for guests," Mum said in a fluster. "I'm not ready yet."

"Chill Mum, it will all be fine." I said, heaving myself up off the chair, "I'll get the door and you go get ready." I waddled out to the hall and opened the front door to find Ashley Granger standing on the doorstep, holding a massive pink gift basket.

"Ashley!" I said with surprise. I'd reluctantly invited her for the sole reason that she now appeared to be Nathan's girlfriend. They'd only been an item for a few weeks, but technically it was Nathan's longest relationship, and given he was the only friend I had left, I felt like it was important to get to know her.

"Hey Kat, thanks for inviting me," she said with a nervous smile.

"I'm so pleased you came," I said, genuinely touched that she'd had made the effort to come all the way to Framlingham. I hadn't actually expected her to show up.

"This is from Nathan and I," she said, handing me the massive basket.

"Thanks, it's lovely," I said, looking inside the ridiculously lavish and no doubt expensive, gift basket.

"Nathan chose it," Ashley said with an embarrassed laugh.

"Yeah it certainly looks like a Nathan present," I agreed with a chuckle as

I tried to see inside the window of the bright blue sports car parked in my parents' driveway. "Did Amy come with you?"

Ashley stared down at her feet and my heart sank.

"Sorry," she said awkwardly.

"It's not your fault," I said with a disappointed shrug as I stepped back from the door. "Come in." I gestured for her to come inside. "Welcome back to the 1950's," I joked as she took in the décor.

"It's sweet," Ashley replied with a smile, "and Framlingham is lovely."

I ushered her into the house and popped the basket on what my mother had decided was the gift table.

"So you drove up?"

"Yeah, Nathan loaned me his new car," she said with a cringe.

"He already has a new car?" I asked with a laugh.

"Yeah, apparently he has a guy," she joked, mimicking Nathan aptly, when my mum flapped into the room excitedly.

"Ah, our first guest!"

"Sorry I'm so early, the traffic was a lot better than I was expecting," Ashley apologised unnecessarily.

"Don't be silly," said Mum, waving her hands about.

"Mum this is Ashley," I said, hoping that Mum wouldn't mention anything about Ryan's previous fondness for her.

"Oh yes, Nathans girlfriend," my Mother exclaimed loudly, as she grabbed Ashley in an over-enthusiastic hug. "So lovely to meet you," she said squeezing Ashley's arms.

"Thanks," Ashley said, taking it in her stride. "You have a lovely home."

"Oh aren't you sweet," Mum said, glancing at me pointedly. She was endlessly offended by my open distaste for her interior design. Looking back at Ashley, she plastered the smile back onto her face. "How's Nathan?"

"He's good," Ashley replied, with a look on her face that told me exactly how much she loved my friend. "He's still got a lot of physio ahead, but the x-rays came back clear yesterday, and all the bones have healed now."

"Well isn't that fantastic," Mum exclaimed. "I've got to get myself ready for the party, so I'll leave you girls to it." She squeezed Ashleys arm and then quickly darted up the stairs and out of sight.

"Do you want a drink?" I asked Ashley, not really knowing what to say to a woman whom I barely knew, yet whom had also inadvertently played a pivotal role in my life to date.

"Sure, but I'll get it," she said indicating for me to sit down. "You must be exhausted."

"Yeah, I'm pretty ready for this baby to come out to be honest," I said taking a seat as she poured us both a glass of pink lemonade. "My body hurts in places I didn't even know I had."

Ashley laughed, "I never got quite that far along but I do remember the aching bones and the constant need to pee," she joked, as she handed me the little plastic cup. We fell silent for a moment as we drank our fizzy pink liquid. "How are you going?" Ashley asked, breaking the silence.

"Besides the peeing and the body pain?"

"No, I mean… how are you actually going? With moving up here and everything. It must be hard not having Ryan around." I was a little taken aback by her question, but also moved by the fact that she cared. I felt a tear welling in my eye but refused to let it take hold.

"This isn't exactly how I'd seen the last few months of my pregnancy playing out," I answered, rubbing my belly, "but I don't really have any right to feel sorry for myself. I'm the one who caused it."

"Kat," Ashley said, placing her elegant hand gently on my arm, "you made a mistake, but that doesn't mean you're not allowed to have feelings."
I sat back in the chair and sighed.

"How come you're being so nice to me?"

"Why wouldn't I be?" she asked with confusion.

"Because I've never made any effort to be nice to you."
Ashley smiled warmly and squeezed my arm.

"You've had a lot going on since we met."
I looked down at my hands in shame. She had no idea about all the horrible things I'd said and thought about her over the last few months.

"Yeah but, I was a bitch, and I've been secretly hating you for a really long time."

"Oh," she said with a little nod. I felt like I owed her a better explanation than that.

"I hated that Ryan used to love you," I admitted a little too honestly.

"That's understandable," she agreed, "but you know that nothing ever happened between us right?"

"Yeah, but I should have given you a chance in the first place, and I'm really sorry that I didn't. I think we would've got along well," I said, peering up at her, as all of my previous hatred dissipated. She was really nice, and no matter what had happened, or not happened, with her and Ryan in the past, it was long gone.

"We still can," she said.

"Really?"

"Kat, you're having my best friends' baby and, well, you're also really important to my boyfriend, so that makes you really important to me."

I snorted, "it's so weird hearing you call Nathan your boyfriend."

"Yeah it still feels weird saying it," she admitted with an embarrassed giggle.

"For what it's worth, he's really in love with you."

She bit her bottom lip, "I'm really in love with him too."

"So how are you coping living with him?" I asked, knowing how OCD Nathan was about his immaculate apartment, "is he driving you insane?"

"Well, it's only been a few weeks, but so far we're doing okay," she said with a smile, "as long as I don't leave anything out of place."

"I'm glad everything is going well for you two," I said sincerely, "and I've got to tell you that you've been really good for him. He's been a better person since you showed up at Artemis."

"He was always a good person," she said with a knowing glance, "just a good person who made a few stupid decisions."

"Yeah," I nodded, understanding her meaning. "And speaking of which…

have you seen Ryan lately? How's he doing?"

"Yeah, he's doing okay," she said with a nod. "I think he's pretty embarrassed, but rehab is the best place he could be. The boys have taken him out golfing today as a pre-baby celebration."

"That's good," I said feeling pleased that his friends were taking care of him. "I imagine he could probably do with a day out. And has Beau recovered okay?"

"Oh, you haven't spoken to him?"

"No, we're not really talking anymore," I told her shamefully, feeling the irony of the fact that Beau and I were the whole reason that this mess even happened in the first place. "We were pretty strained anyway, but this was the last straw. I can't believe he had Ryan arrested."

Ashley took a breath, "yeah, although to be honest, Ryan was pretty brutal." I suddenly felt very protective over the father of my child.

"I think we both know that Beau was goading him." My words came out a little more terse than I'd intended.

"It seems that way," she agreed with an awkward shrug. "I've never seen Ryan like that before. I can't imagine him going that far without some prodding."

"I still can't imagine him hitting anyone at all," I said, unable to believe that my gentle Ryan could attack someone to the point of nearly killing them. "Thanks for calling in a favour with your Dad. From what Nathan said, it sounds like Ryan would have ended up in prison if it wasn't for him."

"None of us would have let that happen," Ashley said, not disputing the fact that Ryan could have ended up in jail.

"I need to pee," I said, rubbing my face. I stood up and felt liquid running down my thighs. "Oh my god," I mumbled in embarrassment. My bladder had been pretty bad over the last few months, but I'd never wet myself before. The fact that I had a witness, made it all the more mortifying.

"Oh my god!" repeated Ash, as she saw the massive puddle at my feet.

"Sorry," I apologised with shame, "my bladder has been really bad lately but I've never …"

"I don't think that's wee Kat," Ashley said, looking at the sticky liquid that was continuing to trickle down my legs.

"What do you mean?" I said in panic.

"I think the baby's coming!" she said excitedly.

"No it's too early," I muttered in a daze.

"It might be early, but that looks to me like your waters have broken."

"But Ryan isn't here… and I haven't had any contractions," I disagreed with panic. I'd literally just said that I was ready for the baby to come out, but now that it was a possibility, I realised that I wasn't ready at all.

"Maybe not…but there's about five pints of amniotic fluid running down your legs, that says you're having this baby," she said, standing up to help me.

"Oh," I gripped on to Ashley's shoulder, yelping in pain as my first contraction hit. "Rosie!!!" I squealed wondering where the hell my sister had disappeared to. The kitchen door burst open and then slammed shut as Rosie bolted in from outside.

"What's wrong?" she called in panic as she ran in through the kitchen door with the cake in her hands.

"Kat's in labour," Ashley told her, as I found myself breathless with pain.

"Oh my god!" gasped Rosie, spotting the growing puddle.

"Can you grab a towel?" Ash asked Rosie, as she grasped my hefty waist.

"Sure," Rose answered, quickly plonking the cake down onto the table. "Where's Mum?"

"In the shower."

"I'll go get her."

"No," I said firmly, "I don't want her fussing, just let Ashley take me to the hospital and meet us there when she's ready."

"Okay," Rosie agreed. "I'll go find a towel," she said, running upstairs.

"Is that okay with you Ashley?" I asked, realising that I'd just forced her into being my chauffer.

"Of course."

"Sorry, I didn't even ask, I just don't think I could deal with my Mum right now."

"It's fine Kat, I'm happy to do it." Ashley started maneuvering me towards the front door, when Rosie came back with a towel.

"Wow, that stuff just keeps on coming doesn't it?!" she asked with a laugh, as I left a trail of amniotic fluid in my wake. "Here," she said, handing Ashley the towel.

"Thanks," Ashley said, as they both took an arm each and guided me carefully out the door. "Just take it one step at a time," Ashley instructed me calmly.

"Okay," agreed a flustered Rosie. I looked at my sister sideways.

"I think she was talking to me Rosie."

Rosie laughed nervously. "Oh, yeah," she said, looking at me apologetically, "I think I'll have to tap out on this one kiddo. It's a bit out of my scope I'm afraid."

"What?! But you're supposed to be my birth partner," I said with panic. "You can't bail on me now."

"Your friend seems to have it under control," Rosie argued calmly, and leaned over to look at Ashley. "You're okay to be the birth partner right?"

"Umm…" Ashley replied uncertainly.

"You can't ask Ashley to do that," I said, appalled.

"I honestly think she'd be much better than me."

"No Rosie, I need you," I pleaded desperately.

Ashley seemed nice but we weren't quite at a point where I'd be comfortable with her seeing my vagina.

"I won't be helpful Kat, this is totally freaking me out already so I'd just end up making it worse. I could go and get Mum?" Rosie suggested.

"No!" I shouted in panic. I most certainly didn't want my mother in the room, and I couldn't do it on my own. "Ashley, would you be okay with that? Just until Ryan arrives. I know it's a huge ask."

"Okay," Ashley agreed with a calm smile.

"We'll meet you at the hospital," Rosie told me, "but what about Ryan? Is someone going to tell him?"

"I'll call Nath on the way," Ashley suggested, as she unlocked Nathans brand new car. "He's with Ryan." Ashley threw the towel onto the seat and helped me into the car.

"I can't do this," I said as a rising panic struck me. "I know I said I'm ready but I'm not."

"Honey, there's no turning back now," she said, closing the door and climbing into the driver's seat. "Come on Mrs McPherson… it's time to have a baby."

- RYAN McPHERSON -

I couldn't believe that we were playing on one of the most prestigious courses in England, but then again, it was typical Stoner-Style to go over-the-top, so I shouldn't have been surprised.

"Can you believe we're playing holes that Ernie Els and Greg Norman have played?" I said as we made our way to the third hole.

"Nah, Stoner's only interested in one hole these days," Ritchie joked.

"Geez Ritch," Nath said, punching him in the arm, "that's my girlfriend you're talking about." It made my stomach churn a little, hearing Nathan refer to Ash as his 'girlfriend'.

"Toughen up sunshine," Ritchie said, slapping Nathan on the back, "you can't go all grown-up on us and not expect to get ribbed."

"No, I think he's more of a magnum guy, than 'ribbed for her pleasure'." I joked.

Ritchie laughed loudly. "And he's also a fan of glow-in-the-dark ones, aren't you Stoner? They're always good for a laugh hey?"

"Huh, yeah," Nath agreed awkwardly. It was unusual for him not to banter back. Ritchie and I exchanged a glance, as Nathan pretended to practice his swing. "Anyway, who's tee is it?" Nath said, changing the subject.

"Stoner," prodded Ritch, studying him as he concentrated on refining his technique.

"I'll just take a go then," Nath said with a shrug.

"Why are you being cagey?" Ritchie asked.

"I'm not being cagey."

"Yeah you kind of are," I agreed.

"Okay fine," Nathan said, propping his golf club over his shoulder, "Ash and I might've let it slip once or twice."

"Seriously? Even though I gave you a fucking jumbo pack of frangers?"

"To be fair, we've had a lot of sex in the last few weeks, so a couple of times isn't too dramatic."

"A lot of sex?" I asked, impressed by Nathan's determination. "With a broken pelvis? That's impressive."

"I'm not saying it was easy," Nathan joked, "or that I was any good, but we made it happen."

"So what did Wayne say yesterday when you got the x-rays back?" Ritchie asked, giving me a quick wink that told me he was up to mischief.

"I got the all-clear, but apparently he could tell that I'd been putting stress on it, so I got a sex lecture from him too," Nath said, using the golf club to stretch his back. "I have to do extra physio with him every week to make up for breaking our deal."

"He could tell that you'd been having sex from an X-ray?" I asked, wondering how that was even possible.

"Technology is pretty amazing isn't it?" Ritchie said with fake amazement. Nathan stared agape at Ritchie as it dawned on him.

"You told Wayne?" Stoner said, punching Ritchie in the arm. "Why would you do that?"

Ritchie grinned proudly, "because I wanted to get you back for Fleabag... plus, I enjoy torturing you Stoner, and so does Wayno."

"Fucking Aussies," Nathan said, shaking his head. "Did he tell you to lecture me about safe sex too?"

"No... that's just common fucking sense," Ritchie said, swinging at the golf ball.

"It's fine Ritch, Ash has that implant thing and normally I'm careful," Nath explained, "plus I get tested all the time and I always come back clean."

With all the safe sex talk, I started thinking about my time with Kellie, and as I replayed all of our interludes in my mind, I had zero recollection of ever using any protection whatsoever.

"Actually now that you mention it," I muttered out loud, "I was pretty slack with Kellie," I said, thinking back over our crazy week of drug-fueled fucking. "In fact I'm not even sure if we ever used anything." The other two looked at me stunned. I shrugged my shoulders, "I was pretty high for most of it," I admitted figuring there was no point in hiding my excessive drug usage, since I was in rehab anyway.

"Well in that case you've definitely got scabies," Ritchie teased, which brought back a vivid memory of that final night in the laneway outside the club.

"Down there," Kell had suggested, nodding to a dark alleyway full of rubbish bins, that came off the back of the club.

"We're not fucking in an alley," I'd said with a nervous laugh, hoping that she was joking.

"Come on," she'd goaded me. "It'll be hot."

"It'll be dirty," I'd rebutted.

"Exactly."

"No I mean bad dirty," I'd clarified, "like we'd probably get bitten by rats and end up with scabies."

"I think you mean rabies," she'd said, "scabies is an STD."

"Yeah, they'd both be a possibility if we had sex in there," I'd replied with a disdainful nod, as she'd pulled me towards the laneway, having already made her decision.

"Fuck I did some stupid shit," I said, rubbing my face in shame. I couldn't believe how low I had sunk since Kat left.

"I'm sure it will be fine," Nathan said, patting me on the shoulder.

"It wasn't just that Nath," I said, having some sort of 'breakthrough', as they called it in therapy. "I've hit rock-bottom, and I don't know how I'm going climb my way back out again."

"Hey, being at the Lodge is a fucking good start," Ritch said, punching me on the arm.

"Yeah I guess."

"You'll sort it out Ryza, and we'll be here for you," Nath said, giving me a sideways man-hug, "but I do think it might be a good idea to get tested just in case."

"God I don't even want to think about it," I said with a cringe.

"You boys disappoint me," said Ritch, "don't they teach Sex Ed in England?"

"Let it go Ritch," Stoner said protectively.

"Do you know what they call people like you guys?" Ritchie asked. We both ignored him. "Parents," he said, when neither of us responded.

"Not far-off," Nath laughed, "Ryza's about to have a baby and I now own a cat."

"Yeah MacDaddy," Ritchie agreed, as the song 'Honey' emanated from Nathan's back pocket. We both looked at Nath, surprised by his choice of ring-tone. He put his club down and shrugged.

"It's Ash," he said, with what appeared to be another blush.

"You gave her a special ring-tone?" I teased, struggling to process how smitten Nathan was with my other best-friend.

"Yeah," he said, answering the call. "Hey babe, did you make it to Fram okay?" he said into the phone. It was weird hearing him call her babe. "Really?!" he said with wide-eyes. "Okay, we'll be there as soon as we can," he added, hanging up the phone.

"Be where?" I asked.

"Ipswich Hospital."

"Why, what's happening?" said Ritch with slight panic. The last time we'd had a call like that, it was because Nathan was fighting for his life.

"The baby's coming!" said Nathan with an excited laugh, "Ryan really is a parent."

- NATHAN STONE -

We grabbed our clubs and ran to the golf buggy, or limped in my case. I hoisted my enfeebled body into the front seat, while Ritchie loaded up the clubs in the back. He hadn't even made it onto the cart when Ryza took off at full-speed.

"Oi!" Ritchie bellowed, as he threw himself onto the back seat like Indiana Jones.

"Sorry," Ryza called over the sound of the whirring engine, which was revving like a hotted-up lawn-mower. "I can't believe the baby is coming," he said, looking over his shoulder to check that Ritchie was still with us. "What if I miss it?"

"Don't worry," I said, patting his shoulder, "we'll get you there."

He nodded stiffly, "I hope so."

Ritchie wriggled himself around so that he was sitting properly in the seat, and his movements wobbled the buggy back and forth.

"Sit still Ritch, or this thing is going to topple," Ryan barked.

"Sorry to be an inconvenience," Ritchie retorted sarcastically. Thankfully the third hole wasn't far from the clubhouse, so we made it back fairly quickly.

"Righto," said Ritchie once we were all in the Mum-Mobile, "let's see how fast this thing can go. Buckle-up lads."

"I'll check-in with the girls," I said, dialling Ash.

"Hey babe," she said chirpily.

"Hey, I just thought I'd let you know that we're on the road now, where are you at?" I asked as a painful wail reverberated down the line. It sounded like a wild animal was being mauled to death.

"Jesus," said Ritchie, as I moved the phone away from my ear.

"Is everything okay?" asked Ryan. The scream subsided, so I put the phone back to my ear.

"Is everything okay?" I asked, relaying Ryan's question.

"Fine," said Ash, "we're nearly at the hospital."

"Okay," I said as Kat began wailing again.

"Just breathe honey, you're doing great," said Ash.

"Is Kat okay?" I asked with concern. I'd never heard a human make a noise like that before.

"This is what childbirth sounds like Nath," Ash said dryly.

"Wait, she's not having it right now is she?" I asked in a panic. Partly because I didn't want Ryan to miss the birth, but mostly due to the fact that I didn't want my new car ruined before I'd even driven it.

"No Nath, she's just having contractions," Ash said calmly, "your car is fine," she added teasingly. She could read me too well.

"I'm not worried about the car," I lied, "I just don't want Ryza to miss it."

"Sure," she said with a laugh. "Is Ryan there? I've got you on loud speaker if he wants to say hi to Kat?"

"Yeah, I'm sure he would," I said, handing Ryza the phone, as we heard another shriek emanating from it.

"Fuck," said Ritchie, "it sounds like they've got a stuck pig on board."

"Shut up Ritch, we're on loud speaker," I said, slapping him over the head.

"Sorry for Ritchie," Ryan said once the screaming had died down. He listened and then signalled that the girls hadn't heard Ritchie's comment. "Oh nothing, just being a dick as usual," Ryan said, rolling his eyes at the outspoken Aussie. "How are you doing babe? Are you okay?" he asked kindly. "Alright, well hang in there, we're on our way, so we'll see you at the hospital." He nodded his head, "I promise. We'll be there as soon as we can."

"Can I talk to Ash again?" I asked, reaching for the phone.

"Yep, I'm just going to put Nathan back on okay?" Ryan said as another wail filled the car. I waited for things to go quiet, and then put the phone to my ear.

"Hey, it's me again," I told Ash.

"We're nearly at the hospital Nath, but I think she's quite far along, so be quick okay?"

"We're going as fast as we can."

"Okay, just drive safely," she said as another shriek echoed through my head. "I'll give the nurses your number and get them to keep you updated."

"That'd be good. Good luck Tails, you'll do great," I said loudly down the phone.

"Thanks Nath, I'm really looking forward to having my vagina ripped apart," called Kat in the background.

"Right," I said, not quite sure how to respond to that.

"She's in a lot of pain right now," Ash explained with a laugh. "See you there babe."

"See you there. I love you."

"Love you too," she said. When I hung up the phone and both the boys were silent. Ryan was staring at me with his jaw almost on the floor, and Ritchie kept glancing at me in the rear-vision mirror.

"What?" I asked, wondering what was happening.

"You said 'I love you,'" muttered Ryan.

"Yeah I did," I replied with a nod. I hadn't actually thought about it. The words had just come out of my mouth automatically.

"Wow," Ryza said, "maybe you really are the grown-up one now."

- KAT McPHERSON -

I felt better knowing that Ryan was on the way, but they were still nearly two hours away. What if this was all over before they even got here? Ash pulled the car into the drop-off bay, and ran inside to get some help. She emerged minutes later, with a nurse and a wheelchair.

"Let's get you inside hun," Ash said, opening the door and helping me out of the car.

"Hi Katherine, I'm Sally," said the nurse. "It sounds like you're a fair way along love, so we'll get you straight up to the birthing suite okay?"

"Okay," I agreed with a nod, "but my husband isn't here yet."

"That's fine sweetheart, let's not worry about that right now."

"Alright."

Ashley parked the car, while Sally took me upstairs to the maternity ward. I'd never been in hospital as a patient before, so I was feeling a little overwhelmed by it all. Not to mention the reality of what I was about to do. This massive thing in my belly was going to be coming out through my vagina. My body would never be the same again. Sally helped me up onto the bed.

"Since your waters have broken, we need to pop on the heart-rate monitor and make sure bubs is okay in there."

"Okay," I agreed with a nod. "Is it likely that something is wrong? She's quite early."

"Your membranes can burst for a lot of reasons love," she said as she put a blanket over my legs and pulled my dress up to get to my belly. "Sometimes they're just ready to join us early, and sometimes it's stress induced..."

"That's the one," I said interrupting her, "I've been pretty stressed lately."

"Listen," she said with a smile, turning a knob on the machine. "That's your baby's heartbeat. It sounds like she's strong and healthy in there."

"Oh, thank god."

"Now you get comfy, while I get the room set up for you."

Ash stuck her head in the door. "Everything okay in here?" she asked, coming over to my side.

"She's doing great, and the baby is strong and healthy," repeated Sally.

"Great," said Ash, squeezing my hand. Sally pulled a massive blue bucket, out from underneath the bed.

"What's that for?" I asked

"It's a vomit bucket love," she answered gently.

"Why would I need a vomit bucket?"

"Your body has strange and wonderful ways of dealing with pain."

I looked at Ashley in horror. "I don't think I can do this Ashley," I told her helplessly. If vomiting would be the easier part, how bad was the bad part going to be? "How can I have this baby when Ryan and I are such a mess?"

"Whatever happens, Ryan won't leave you to do this on your own," Ashley told me sincerely, "and once he sees that baby, everything else might fall into place. He misses you Kat. This might be what he needs to get his head on straight."

"You really think soooooooooaaaaaaaaagghhhhh?" I wailed, as a much stronger contraction assaulted my body.

"Breathe through it hun," Ashley said, as I grasped her hand for dear life. Weirdly, I was glad she was the one beside me in Ryan's absence. "You're doing great," she added reassuringly. The pain finally subsided, and I sank back on the bed in exhaustion.

"Those contractions seem to be building quite quickly," said the nurse. "Could you whip off your knickers please love, I'd like to take a look at how you're coming along."

"Sure," I answered dejectedly. The baby really was coming, and there was nothing I could do to stop it.

"I'll give you some privacy," Ashley said, quickly vacating the room.

I stripped off the last of my dignity, and leaned back on the bed, with my feet in the stirrups as instructed. I knew it was routine, but I cringed with embarrassment as I sat there with everything on show. I wasn't in enough pain, to make opening my legs feel less awkward. After a few minutes of prodding around in my vagina, the midwife popped her head out from between my thighs.

"Well, you're moving along nicely. You're six centimeters already, so it looks like this is going to be a speedy labour. Do you want me to call your husband and see how far away he is?"

"Yes please," I said gratefully, "could you also send Ashley back in here please?"

"Sure love."

"Thanks," I said, as Sally covered me back up with the sheet, for the illusion of modesty. She left the room, and I'd finally gotten comfortable when I was viciously attacked by another violent contraction. "Uggggggghhhhh!" I growled loudly, like a wild animal. The pain was getting worse and worse. It felt like my whole body was being squeezed in a vice.

- ASHLEY GRANGER -

Sally the midwife, popped out into the hallway and smiled.

"This is going to be quite a quick labour," she told me quietly, "she's already six centimetres so if her husband doesn't get here in the next few hours then he's going to miss it."

"Okay, thanks," I said, peering into the room to check on Kat. "Would you mind calling him please?"

"Sure love," she said as I heard a guttural scream come from Kat's room. I ran in and grabbed Kats hand.

"Breathe hun, breathe," I instructed her calmly. "You're doing great." As I rubbed Kat's back, I felt a weird mix of sadness and relief that I'd missed out on this experience with Mia. It was magical and yet excruciating at the same time, but I could only imagine how much worse it would have been if I'd gone through all of this, and then still lost her. How did women bounce back from that?

The contraction subsided, and Kat looked up at me exhaustedly.

"This must be really weird for you."

"Not at all, it's really special," I told her with a smile. "I didn't get to experience this bit so it's nice to be a part of it."

Kat sighed and cringed, "I'm so sorry. I hope this isn't bringing back too many bad memories?"

"Please don't worry about me. I'm perfectly fine," I assured her. "I'm really glad to be here."

"Did you get to see her? Your daughter I mean?" Kat asked with a sad expression. It was a moment of shared pain between two almost-mums.

"Yeah," I said, feeling my throat tighten. "They kept her body, but by the time I came around she was long-gone. I just remember thinking that she was so tiny... and so blue," I said, with tears threatening to shed. "When I held her she was stone cold."

Kat grabbed my hand, with tears in her eyes, "Ash I'm so sorry."

"Thanks, but it was a long time ago now," I said, squeezing her hand again. "Besides, it's always felt so surreal, like it never really happened you know? Or like it happened to someone else. But honestly, when I think about it, Mia was better off not coming into that life anyway."

"Mia? Was that her name?"

"Yeah," I said, nodding sadly as I wiped a tear from my eye. "If I could do it all over again, I would have run away from Dom as soon as I saw the little blue plus sign on the pregnancy test. If I'd done that, Mia would be alive."

"Oh my god Ash," Kat said with tears streaming down her face. "You can't blame yourself. Dom is the only one at fault heeeeeeeeeeeeeeeeeeeeeeeeeeeeeeeee eere," Kat wailed as another contraction hit her. She squeezed my hand hard.

"Deep breath in.... and out..." I said, breathing along with her. I couldn't

and played around with my private parts from behind. If I thought I'd had no dignity before, we'd now gone into deficit. My fanny was on display in the most inelegant way, while a million people buzzed in and out of the room, in preparation for the impending arrival. I was mortified, but all I could do was focus on my breathing.

"I can't do this. I'm not ready for this," I spluttered, as I vomited violently into the spew bucket again with my naked bum in the air for everyone to see.

"Well you'd better get ready sweetheart, because this baby is nearly here," declared Sally from behind me. "You're already eight centimetres."

"I can't do this Ashley," I told her in a panic, as another wave of contractions hit me. "Aagggh!"

"Yes you can. I know you can," Ashley reassured me calmly. "You've got this Kat. You're superwoman."

"I want the epidural!" I wailed in pain.

"It's too late now love," the other mid-wife laughed heartlessly, "you're too far along. Its gas only from here on in."

Ashley squeezed my hand, "you can do this."

"I need to push," I pleaded helplessly, as my body attempted to purge the child.

"Not yet lovie or you'll end up with tearing," instructed the midwife calmly, rubbing my lower back as I knelt semi-naked over the fitball. "Try to hold out for a little bit longer if you can. Do you want to lie down?"

"Yeah," I nodded exhaustedly. Ashley and the midwife helped me climb onto the bed, moments before the next contraction hit me. "Agggggggggghhhh!" I bellowed manically. My whole body was begging me to push, but I gripped tight and tried to breathe through the pain.

"You're doing well," Ashley reassured me.

"And you haven't even sworn once," joked Sally, "most women have usually worked through their entire swear-vocab by now."

"See, I told you, you're superwoman," Ashley said, rubbing my back. "Have you heard from my boyfriend yet?" she asked the midwife.

"They're not far away now," Sally said from between my legs. "You're doing well lovie, and you're nine centimetres now so if you need to, you can push with the next contraction."

"Oh my god, it's coming!" I screamed, simultaneously howling like a wild animal. The sound was guttural and primal. I'd never known I was capable of making noises like that, but my body was in control and I was going with it.

"Okay, and… push," directed the midwife, as she held my thighs up to my chest. "Push into your bottom like you're doing a poo," she said graphically.

"I can't," I cried loudly, "I can't do it!" I wailed like a banshee, as I tried to push downwards in the way that the midwife had instructed, but my brain couldn't figure out how I was supposed to push into my bottom, whilst I was sitting on it.

"Why don't you get back on your knees babe?" Ashley suggested once the contraction was over, and I was no closer to freeing my body of the little instrument of torture. "You were laboring really well on your knees. Maybe gravity will help."

"Yeah," I agreed breathlessly, using the last of my energy to clamber back onto my knees. I was beginning to tire, and hoped to God that I'd have enough strength to make it through the home stretch... pardon the pun. "I can feel another one coming," I told the midwife.

"Right, use the bed head for leverage, and remember what I said...push into your bottom as if you're doing a poop."

"Okaaaaaaaaaaaaaaaaaaaaaaaaaaaaaaayyyyyyyyy," I agreed loudly, as my entire body pushed hard to try and expel the tiny intruder. I was pretty sure I'd actually pooped myself, but there was so much going on down there it was hard to tell. I felt hands wiping at my bottom, so I assumed they were quickly discarding any evidence of such.

"Okay, good love. Now rest for a moment. The head is almost out so with one more push you should have it," the midwife instructed as I nodded exhaustedly. "Just try to relax."

"Relax?" I snorted tiredly, "I have half a head sticking out of my vagina... relaxing isn't physically possible right now."

"You're doing well honey," Ashley told me, massaging my back.

"I just want her ooooooooooouuuuuuuuuuuuut!" I groaned wildly with the next contraction, just as the doctor arrived. "Aaaaaaaaaaaaaaaaaaaaaghhhhh!" I continued to scream, as I tried to push the melon-sized head out of my vagina, while an audience looked on. I was beyond caring about my privacy. I just wanted that baby out.

- RYAN McPHERSON -

When the midwife led me into the birthing room, I almost recoiled at the horrific sight in front of me. It looked like a horror movie. Kat was kneeling on the bed, half naked, in an insanely huge puddle of bright red blood, which was up to her knees and overflowing onto the floor. Beside the bed, was a vomit bucket and what appeared to be a poop bin. But then I saw the baby's head.

"Oh my god that's our baby!" I said running over to Kat. "I'm sorry I took so long," I said, kissing her on the forehead, as Ashley quietly slipped away. "I'm so proud of you."

"Okay, the head's out now but we're going to need another big push to get these shoulders out," the doctor instructed. "This is the hard part, but you're nearly there."

"Harder than that?!" Kat cried, exhausted and emotional, "I just want her out."

"I know love but keep going, you're almost there," the midwife encouraged her gently.

"You can do this babe," I told her, as I brushed the sweaty hair off her forehead. "Look how well you've already done."

"Okay...push," directed the doctor.

"Aaaaaaaagggggggggggggggggghhhhhhhhhhhhhh!" Kat wailed.

"You're doing awesome babe," I encouraged her as she roared like a lion, "keep going."

"Use the contraction Katherine. Let's get this baby out," said the Doctor excitedly.

"I can't," she wailed as the contraction subsided.

"You can," I told her. "Just one more big push."

"Okay," she nodded.

"Are you ready Katherine?" asked the midwife. "Here it comes love, push hard."

"Aaaaaagggggggghhhhhhhhhhhh!!!!!!" Screamed Kat, and after a few massive pushes, our daughter was in the world.

"You did it!" I cried.

"Well done love," the midwife praised her proudly.

"A gorgeous little girl," the Doctor announced, as he handed me the scissors. "Here Dad, would you like to cut the cord?"

Oh my god. I was a dad. I looked into the big brown eyes of my baby girl, and my heart swelled.

"Wow," I breathed in awe. "Hey baby, I'm your daddy." As I cut the gristly cord, a tear sprung to my eye. I cradled the baby tight and took her over to Kat, who had been flipped around and tidied up a little. "Isn't she perfect?" I said as I placed the baby on her chest as instructed.

"Oh my god, she is perfect," Kat agreed, stroking the baby's cheek. "Aren't you gorgeous?"

"You did good babe," I told Kat, but she didn't respond. She was too wrapped up with the baby. It was as if no one but the baby existed to her, and she didn't even seem to notice the fact that the doctor was busily stitching up her lady bits. I suddenly felt quite left out. The midwife interrupted their magical moment.

"Right love, we need to take the baby to the special care unit to make sure she's okay, so why don't you get up and have a shower while we clean the room?"

"Okay," Kat agreed, reluctantly handing over Baby McPherson.

"She's so beautiful," I said in awe, as I stroked our baby's soft head.

"She is," Kat agreed, with her eyes glued to our gorgeous daughter.

"Does she have a name yet?" the midwife asked.

"Not yet," I said.

"Actually Ryan…" Kat said, looking up at me, "how do you feel about Mia?"

I smiled, "I love it…but wasn't that the name of Ashley's baby?"

"Yeah," she nodded, "I thought since Ashley played such a big part in the birth it might be nice."

"It's a nice idea, but do you think she'd be okay with that?"

"I don't know," she answered, "but it won't hurt to ask right?"

"Okay," I agreed, helping Kat up from the bed, as the midwife took the baby away. "Mia McPherson. I like it." We looked at each other with affection, and I wrapped my arm around her waist for support. Kat was flushed and sweaty, but my heart thudded as I realised how much I loved her, and how much I'd missed her over the past few months.

"I'm so…" I paused, not entirely sure what I wanted to say to her. There were so many words to be said. "I'm sorry, I wish I'd…" I stopped again. "Kat… I've missed you so much."

"I've missed you too," she said with an exhausted smile, "and I'm glad you got here."

"Me too."

- ASHLEY GRANGER -

I slipped away quietly when Ryan arrived in the birthing suite. I took one final glance at the two of them together, and them left them to their private family moment. I couldn't believe what I'd witnessed. Childbirth was amazing. It literally was a miracle. I wandered out in to the waiting area in a bit of a daze.

"Babe," Nath said, striding over to greet me with a hug.

"Hey," I said taking a proper breath for the first time since Kat's water had broken. "It's good to see your face."

"I know the feeling," he said with a smile, kissing me gently on the lips. "How's it going in there?"

"It's amazing Nath," I said as he ran his hand down my face. "I've never seen anything like it. She's doing so great."

"You look tired," he said with concern. "Are you okay?"

"I'm fine," I said with a smile, "maybe a little shell-shocked, but fine."

"So that didn't bring up anything for you?"

"Oh," I said with a nod, catching his drift. "Honestly, it was kind of therapeutic. I feel like that gave me some closure."

"Good," he said, wrapping his arms around my waist, "I'm glad."

"How was golfing?" I asked, draping my arms over his neck.

"Short," he joked. "We've spent most of the day in the Mum-Mobile, so my whole body is aching."

"Aww, poor baby," I teased, kissing him playfully, "maybe we should get a hotel room and drive back in the morning."

"We've got lunch with your parents tomorrow remember? That would be a four-hour drive from here."

"Oh yeah," I said looking up into his big blue eyes as a bunch of emotions welled in my chest. "I love you."

Nathan grinned happily. "I love you too," he said, pulling my body against his as he bent down to give me a soft, sexy kiss. "You're getting much better at feelings Chucky," he teased, resting his forehead to mine.

"I guess you bring out the best in me," I said, flinching as Shirly squealed from somewhere behind us.

"Ryan!" she exclaimed, jumping up from her seat when she spotted Ryan emerging from the birthing suite.

We all turned to Ryan.

"We have a baby!" he announced with pride.

"How are they doing?" Kat's Dad asked.

"They're both doing great," he announced proudly. "The baby's been taken for a once-over, and Kat's having a shower. She was amazing," he said proudly. We all congratulated him, and the place was abuzz with pats on the back and general cheer.

"So is it as bad they say?" Ritchie asked.

"It's worse," Ryza joked.

"Like watching your favourite pub burn down?" Ritchie said.

"Truthfully, it was like a horror movie," Ryan answered honestly, "but it was the most amazing thing ever. That little girl is so beautiful, that none of the rest of it matters."

"Awww! I can't wait to meet her!" Rosie squealed excitedly.

"We'll be heading up to the room shortly, so you'll be able to meet her very soon."

"No name yet?" Asked Nathan, as he slung his arm casually over my shoulder.

"We have an idea," Ryan said, cocking his head with an unusual expression on his face. He smiled at me, "Kat wants to see you."

"Me?" I asked, detangling myself from Nathan.

"Yeah," he said with a nod and a grateful smile. "Thanks for being there Ash."

"No need to thank me, it was… awesome," I said, squeezing his arm, "but I'm glad you got here for the important part."

"Me too," he nodded, stepping aside so I could get past.

"Wait!" said Rosie, "I've got clothes for her," she said, handing me a rucksack. "She'll probably want those."

"Yeah, I suspect she will," I agreed, heading back down the corridor. I knocked quietly on the door. "Kat?"

"Hey Ash, come in," she called happily. I let myself in, and Kat was sitting on the bed in a hospital gown, towel-drying her beautiful curly hair.

"Rosie brought some clothes for you," I said, handing her the bag.

"Oh, thank god," she said, ditching the towel, "I'm definitely not going to start any fashion trends in this thing."

"Revival of the moo-moo?" I joked. Kat laughed, but she looked shattered. "How are you feeling?" I asked, rubbing her arm.

"Exhausted."

"I bet," I said with a nod, "you did great."

"You should see her Ash. She's perfect."

"I don't need to see her to know that."

"She makes that horror worth it," Kat paused and gave me a hug. "I think you're really amazing Ashley."

I smiled awkwardly, not knowing how to respond.

"You're pretty amazing yourself hot Mumma," I joked.

"Ash, I've got something to ask you."

"Okay," I said curiously.

"Well… Ryan and I were thinking… only if you're okay with it… that we'd really like to call her Mia."

"What?" Tears instantly sprung to my eyes.

"I'm sorry, it was a bad idea," Kat apologised quickly. "I just thought it might be a nice thing – but – no, it's stupid. I'm sorry I asked."

"No," I blurted, as a tear rolled down my cheek. "It's not a stupid idea, it's lovely."

"Really?" she asked as tears welled in her eyes too.

"Yeah, Mia is perfect," I re-assured Kat with a hug. "It's perfect."

"They're ready for you to go up to your room now love," a new midwife said cheerfully, as she appeared in the doorway with a wheelchair. "Where's your husband?" Kat and I wiped our tears and pulled apart.

"I'll go get him," I offered, giving Kat one last quick squeeze, astounded at how close we had become, when five hours ago we'd barely known each other.

"Thank you, Ash."

I stepped out into the corridor and all the emotions began welling in my chest. So much was happening in my head that I couldn't sift through all the feelings quickly enough to grasp onto one. Perhaps I was picking up on Kat's hormones because it reminded me of the crazy emotional roller-coaster of pregnancy. I closed my eyes and took a deep breath to collect myself.

"Come on Ash, get it together," I told myself sternly. I took control of my erratic emotions, and headed out to the waiting area where Nathan was standing with the boys. The moment I saw him, my strong façade completely shattered and the tears began welling again. With Nathan there, I was safe to fall apart. With him I was home.

- NATHAN STONE -

While Kat's family chattered and giggled with excitement in the waiting area, Ryza, Ritchie and I stood by the water cooler in a state of shock. What a huge day it had been. It was probably the first time in history that all three of us were lost for words.

"So," Ryza said, breaking the silence, "you and Ash huh?"

"Yep."

"You guys look good together," he said, punching me on the arm. "I'm sorry I gave you such a hard time about it."

"To be fair, you didn't have much to go on," I said with a smile.

"Well that's true," he teased, "but honestly Stoner, now that I've seen you together... I get it. You two make sense."

"Thanks buddy," I said, getting a little choked up at his sentimentality.

He sighed, "I hope Kat and I can work it out."

"I'm sure you will," I told him, looking to Ritchie for some back-up.

"Of course you will," he agreed with a nod. "You guys have a family now.

Nothing else matters."

From the corner of my eye I saw Ash emerge from the corridor. Her eyes were bloodshot, and it looked like she'd been crying. I hobbled over to her as fast as I could.

"Are you okay?" I asked, reaching out to her. She nodded, but wrapped her arms around my waist and buried her head into my chest. I was taken aback, but I engulfed her in my arms and squeezed her tight. "I've got you," I said, stroking her hair. I peered over at Ryan, who shook his head with confusion.

"I'll go check on Kat," he said, vanishing quickly down the corridor. I had no idea what had happened, but I'd never seen Ash like that before. Even with everything that we'd been through, she'd never broken down in public. I'd seen her shed a few random tears, and I'd seen her angry; I'd even seen her scared; but this was different. This was raw and real. This time she wasn't hiding her feelings or pretending to be okay. This time she was allowing herself to need me. I leaned my chin on her head and pulled her close.

"I've got you," I repeated quietly. At that moment, no one else existed. I didn't care what was going on around us, all I cared about was Ash.

At some point, the midwife came out to tell us that Ryan and Kat were ready for visitors. Kat's family went up to see them, and so did Ritchie, but we remained standing there, wrapped up in each other. My knee and hips were starting to ache but I pushed the pain aside. For once, I was able to be Ashley's Prince Charming, so I wasn't going to let her down.

"Sorry," she said quietly into my chest, as she gripped the back of my polo shirt.

"Don't be sorry," I told her, rubbing her back. "Did something happen with you and Kat?"

"No," she said shaking her head against my tear-soaked shirt, "she was really lovely."

"Okay," I said with a confused nod. I kissed the top her head, not sure what else I could say. Ash glanced up at me with mascara running down her face.

"I don't even know why I'm crying," she admitted with a laugh/cry. I smiled and took her face in my hands, wiping away the smudged make-up as best I could with my thumbs.

"You're adorable, and you don't need a reason to cry."

"There were so many emotions going on and I'm happy, but I'm sad and then I saw you and I just..." she sobbed again and buried her head back into my chest. She was so damn cute that I had to swallow back a laugh.

"Hey, it's okay," I said, squeezing her against me again, "you can cry as much as you want."

"Kat and Ryan asked to call the baby Mia," she said into my chest.

"Really?" I asked, unsure whether that was a good thing or not. "Are we happy or unhappy about that?"

"Happy," she said as she burst into another round or tears. "It's such a lovely gesture."

"It is," I agreed trying my best not to chuckle. Although I loved and admired my independent woman, it felt really nice to be needed for once.

- KAT McPHERSON -

"Knock, knock," called a midwife at the door. "Here's your baby," she said excitedly, as she rolled a basinet into the room. I caught sight of my daughter for the first time since she was born, and my heart thudded with joy. Tears welled in my eyes. She was beautiful.

"Awww our baby," Ryan whispered happily.

"Mia," I said, looking up at Ryan with a smile. "She's our little Mia."

Ryan gave me a cuddle and we both leant over the bassinet to get a closer look at our beautiful, sleeping daughter.

"Shall I let your family know you're ready for visitors?" asked the midwife. Ryan and I looked at each other, and without speaking, agreed that we'd get it out of the way.

"That's fine, you can send them through," I said tiredly. I really wanted to snuggle up in bed with Ryan and Mia, but everyone had been out there waiting all afternoon, so we couldn't leave them hanging any longer.

"You ready for this?" Ryan asked, rubbing my shoulder.

"Yeah," I said with a smile. Moments later, Rosie appeared in the door with a bunch of bags.

"Hey guys, congratulations," she said, giving us hugs and kisses before plopping the bags on the side bench. "I've got some pressies for her."

"Oh my god Rosie, how much did you get her?!" I asked, looking at the huge pile of presents. She turned and shrugged.

"It's just a few essentials. Don't ruin my fun."

"You're as bad as Nathan," Ryan laughed, as Rosie peeked her head over the side of the crib.

"Rosie, this is Mia," I said quietly with a smile, "Mia, this is your Aunty Rosie."

"Oh my god!" Rosie whisper-squealed when she caught sight of our beautiful daughter. "She's the most gorgeous thing I've ever seen. I'm so proud of you little sister."

"Thanks Rose."

"She did great," Ryan said, putting his arm over my shoulder. I looked up at him, and felt such a rush of love for the man. I really wanted to kiss him, but I didn't know whether we were at that stage yet. He smiled and kissed me gently as if reading my mind. Rosie looked up and grinned, then turned her attention back to Mia.

The three of us were still huddled around the crib when Mum and Dad came in.

"Kath-" Mum started to say, but we all looked up and shushed her simultaneously.

"She's sleeping," I whispered, beckoning my parents over.

They came over and peeked into the crib. Mum peered up at me with tears in her eyes, and then hugged me tightly.

"She's beautiful love," she whispered adoringly.

"She is," I agreed, smiling involuntarily at the sight of my gorgeous daughter. "Her name is Mia."

Mum grinned, "that's perfect." We exchanged hugs and kisses with everyone, and then we all resumed staring at Mia as she slept peacefully. It was amazing that one tiny, sleeping human could keep five grown adults occupied for so long, but it was abundantly clear that we were all very much in love with her.

- RYAN McPHERSON -

Once Kat's family had left, we had a quick visit from Ritchie, and then we had a moment to breathe. I felt a bit sad that my parents weren't here sharing in the joy, and embracing my child with the love and care that Shirly and Andrew had done, but I'd never expected that of them. They were cold people, and a grandchild wouldn't change that. I knew I'd done the right thing by cutting them out of my life, but it didn't make the disappointment and hurt any less.

"Are you okay?" Kat asked, sensing the slump in my mood.

"Yeah, just wish that my parents were more like yours," I said sadly. "I know your mum can be a handful Kat, but she loves you, and she loves Rosie and she loves little Miss here."

Kat nodded, "you're right, but you know what? You now have the chance to be the father that your Dad never was."

"Yeah," I agreed, "and I promise you both, that I'm going to be the best fucking Dad on the planet."

"I know you will."

There was a quiet knock on the door, and we tore our eyes away from the baby.

"Are we interrupting?" Ash asked from the door.

"Not at all," I said, as Nathan popped his head around the door behind her.

"Nath! It's so good to see you," Kat said excitedly, standing up to greet him.

"It's good to see you too Tails," he said, giving her a kiss on the cheek. I felt a bit guilty that I'd given him a hard time about staying in touch with her. If nothing else, Nathan was a loyal friend, and I couldn't begrudge him that. "So this is my cute little niece," he said, running his finger gently down her cheek. "Welcome to the world kiddo."

"Oh my god, she's gorgeous!" Ash said, edging closer. "Can I hold her?"

"Of course," Kat agreed, delicately handing over our precious cargo. Nathan peered dotingly down at Mia over Ashley's shoulder. "She's beautiful Tails. You did good love."

"Thanks babe, so did your girlfriend," Kat replied with a wink, as Ashley continued swooning over my daughter. "I couldn't have got through it without her." Ash blushed and ignored the compliment in her usual, modest way. Nathan rubbed her shoulder lovingly, and as he gently kissed her on the forehead, my heart wrenched with a bitter-sweet mixture of happiness and sorrow. I was pleased that Ashley and Nathan were happy, but with my marriage in tatters, it was hard not to feel a little jealous.

I glanced over at Kat, and I could see that she was feeling it too. We'd never had what Ashley and Nathan did, in fact, we'd never had even half of what they had. We were good together, sometimes we were even great, but what Ashley and Nathan shared, was the sort of bullshit fairy-tale love that didn't come around very often. Kat and I were an interesting sub-plot at best… but despite that very clear fact, every fibre of my being told me that it was worth trying to save our less-than perfect, non-fairy-tale romance.

Eventually, 'Ashlan', left for their long trip back to London, looking as weary as we felt. We said our goodbyes, and finally we were alone. Kat, Mia and I. My imperfect little family.

"Gosh," I said flopping onto the bed. "It's nice to be alone."

"Yeah it is," she agreed, popping Mia back into the crib, and joining me on the bed. "Thanks for being here."

"Babe, I wouldn't let you do this alone."

Kat smiled nervously and peered over at me. "Are we…" she let her words trail off. I sat up and took her hand in mine.

"I want to give this a go," I said with a smile.

"Really?" she asked, as tears glistened in her eyes.

"Really," I nodded, getting on to the floor, and kneeling down in front of her. I looked up into her eyes, feeling the sparkle of love that had been missing for so long. "Katherine Isabelle McPherson… will you stay my wife?"

"Yes," she said, shedding a tear. "I will."

"I love you so much," I said, gently pulling her face to mine, and kissing her hard.

"I love you too," she said, her cheeks wet with tears. "I'm so sorry for what I did."

I looked deep into her eyes. "And I'm sorry I let you down."
Kat looked surprised.

"You didn't let me down Ryan."

"Yeah, I did," I said, wiping the tears from her face. "I should have done this two months ago, but I was too busy feeling sorry for myself."

"I guess we still have a lot of things to talk about."

"Yeah we do," I said guiltily. "I'll go get us something from the coffee shop, and then we can have a good chat and get everything out in the open."

"Sounds like a good plan." I grabbed my wallet and headed towards the door when a thought hit me. I stopped and turned back to Kat.

"I wonder if anyone told the Lodge that I wasn't coming back tonight?"

"I'm sure Nath took care of it," she said with a nod.

"Yeah," I agreed dubiously, "but maybe I'll give them a call just in case."

"Good idea," Kat agreed. "My phone's on the bench."

"Cool thanks," I said, going back in to get the phone. "I'll be back in five with some food for my beautiful wife," I told her with a wink.

- KAT McPHERSON -

I was still staring at Mia in her cot when Ryan came back with our food. I tore my eyes away from Mia, and turned to greet my gorgeous husband with a contented smile.

"I can't take my eyes off-" I stopped mid-sentence when I saw the look on his face. "What?" I asked, petrified of what was to come next. How much could have gone wrong between here and the coffee shop?

"Xavier?" he asked, holding my phone up questioningly. "As in, your ex?" I dropped my head and sighed, then looked him in the eyes.

"Like I said, we've got a lot to talk about."

He nodded and sat down on the bed next to me. We were long overdue for a chat. We talked for a long time, and no stone was left unturned. It was warts and all, with brutal honesty. Sharing the unbridled truth, was the only way our marriage would survive. I wasn't thrilled to hear that Ryan had hooked up with Kellie, but I was in no position to get angry about it. At least his affair had happened after we'd broken up. Whatever had happened between them, was over now, and if he was able to forgive my adultery, then I needed to let go of his little post-break-up-fling. Mia started to grumble so Ryan rolled off bed to tend to her.

"It'll be nice to get home," he said, gently lifting her out of the crib.

"Yeah it will," I agreed. "I've missed home."

"Me too," he said as a look of realisation crossed over his face. "Except I can't go home with you, because I have to go back to the Lodge in the morning."

"Oh yeah," I said disappointedly, as he lightly bounced Mia in his arms. Her beautiful caramel skin looked so pale against Ryan's dark hands. "Let's just enjoy being together tonight and deal with reality tomorrow."

"Yeah," he agreed sadly. "I really fucked up, Kat."

"We both did."

He gently kissed the top of Mia's head and looked at me with a smile.

"Our new life starts now," he said, "…or at least our temporary new life starts now. You stay with Rosie, and then once I'm out of rehab we'll move back home together and start the next chapter," he suggested. "It won't be much different from the original plan, except I'll be involuntarily incarcerated in hell instead of at work."

I laughed. "Okay," I agreed. It was the only option we had. I wandered over and gave Ryan a kiss. "We'll make it work."

"Of course we will," he said positively. "This is the start of the rest of our lives." He might have had a rough few months, but Ryan had gained a confidence that he'd never had before. It was as if he'd finally stepped into himself.

"Fatherhood suits you," I said as he passed Mia over so that I could feed her.

"Yeah, it's weird. I feel like this is what I'm here for you know. Like it was my life purpose to become a Dad."

"I love you Mr McPherson."

"I love you too Mrs McPherson."

I sat down on the chair to feed Mia, when my bladder suddenly protested with a very urgent need to be emptied.

"Can you take Mia again please? I need to pee."

"Sure," Ryan answered, as he carefully slid his hands underneath Mia.

"Quick," I pleaded desperately. My bladder wasn't willing to wait. It was too late. By the time we'd exchanged Mia, I'd already started peeing.

"Oh my gosh," I breathed in mortification, thankful that I was wearing a massive surf-board sized pad to soak up all the excess liquid.

"Are you okay?" Ryan asked in confusion, as he moved out of the way with Mia.

"No, not really," I replied, fleeing into the bathroom. Sitting on the loo was totally pointless by that stage, but it seemed like the only thing I could do. "I just need a few minutes," I called from the bathroom.

"Okay, sure," he answered understandingly through the door. "Take your time, I'll take Mia around the ward for a quick walk."

"Okay, thank you," I called gratefully. I heard him leave the room, and within seconds, tears erupted from my face. I didn't even know why I was crying. It could have been relief, embarrassment, overwhelm or all of the above. I was getting used to the mood swings, and I could come to terms with the relentless bleeding, but incontinence? That was more demeaning than words could describe.

Once my tears began to subside, I tidied myself up, and left the safety of the bathroom. One of the midwives knocked on the door and walked through it simultaneously, in the way that only nurses and midwives seemed to get away with doing.

"You ready for your obs love?" she asked casually, as if she hadn't just invaded my privacy. I had no idea why they even bothered putting doors in hospitals.

"Yeah sure," I agreed reluctantly, as I laid down on the bed and pulled down my pants, once again.

"The stitches are looking good," she told me casually, as if she was inspecting something less personal than my vagina.

"Good."

"And how's the pelvic floor? Is it holding okay?" she asked, going through her observation check-list.

"No, not really," I admitted.

"Oh, okay. A bit of leakage?"

"Nope," I admitted. "I did an entire wee in my pants," I said bluntly, annoyed that I had to share my own personal shame with a total stranger.

"Okay, I'll write you a referral to the physio," she replied, without battering an eyelid. "And your bowel movements have returned to normal?" she asked, working her way down her check-list.

"Seem to have."

"No urgency with that?" she asked

"Well I haven't shat myself, if that's what you're asking," I replied snidely. I knew I was being rude, but I was exhausted, sore, embarrassed and completely fed up with having people between my legs. The midwife nodded, and silently jotted something down on her notepad, while I got myself decent again.

"Sorry," I apologised sheepishly.

"It's fine love," she answered understandingly. "I'll leave you alone now, and I'll have this referral ready for you when you're discharged in the morning."

"Thanks," I said, as Ryan returned with Mia, who was crying for a feed.

"Sorry," he apologised, "She's still hungry."

"Hey beautiful," I cooed dotingly at my little girl, as I rearranged myself to give her a feed.

"How's the breast feeding coming along?" asked the midwife curiously, as she hovered in the doorway.

"Yeah good," I said, as I attached Mia to my nipple in the way the previous midwife had shown me. I was feeling pretty pleased with myself for having gotten the hang of it so quickly.

"Oh. Why are you doing it like that?" the midwife asked, closely investigating my breastfeeding technique.

"Because that's how the other lady showed me to do it."

"No, it's much easier if you hold her like this," she said, rearranging the baby and my boob simultaneously. Why did people suddenly think it was perfectly acceptable to man-handle me?

"Okay, thanks," I answered politely, wishing that she would just fuck off and leave me alone.

"See it's not so hard is it?"

"Not at all," I answered dismissively, but the midwife didn't seem to get the hint.

"I think maybe Kat just needs some time alone with Mia," Ryan told her firmly. I smiled gratefully at him, thankful that he was there.

"Okay, I'll leave you to have some family time," she said, finally leaving us alone. We watched her leave, and then Ryan came over to rub my shoulders.

"Are you okay," he asked, kissing the top of my head. "Can I get you anything?"

"No," I said with a smile, "I have everything I need right here."

- RYAN McPHERSON -

We didn't sleep much during the night. Partly due to the fact that Mia was awake every hour or two for a feed, but primarily because Kat and I wanted to make the most of every second we had together before we were separated again. We were dreading the arrival of the morning, knowing that our little bubble of family bliss would burst, and we'd be facing the reality of our recent fuck-ups. Sex was not on the cards after the horrors her lady bits had been through, but after being apart for so long, we had a lot to talk about, so we laid in bed together, cuddled up under the shiny hospital sheets.

"So the cat wasn't even Nathans?" Kat asked with a laugh when I'd finished regaling her with the story of Ritchie and Fleabag. Err... Fred.

"Nope, he'd just let it in for the night."

"Well that would explain why I couldn't find any cat food at his place," I laughed. "Ritchie must have been furious."

"Yeah, I don't think he was impressed."

Kat sighed and snuggled into my chest, "I feel like I've missed out on so much."

I squeezed her shoulder and pulled her in close.

"Yeah I know how you feel," I said, kissing the top of her head, "I've only been in rehab for a few weeks and suddenly Ash and Nathan are a couple." Kat looked up at me with concern in her eyes.

"And how do you feel about that?"

"Honestly... it was a bit weird at first, but then seeing them together today made it clear how much they love each other," I told her honestly. "They're so obviously meant to be together."

"I know right?" Kat said with a sad smile. "Do you think that's what we have?"

"I don't know," I said, shaking my head, "I think what we have is different, but not in a bad way."

"Yeah," she agreed. "I know we haven't been perfect, but I love us," she said, reaching up to run her hand along my stubbly chin, "and I've missed us."

"Me too," I said, giving her a kiss.

"I'm sorry I fucked us up," said Kat, rolling over and leaning her chin on my chest.

"Babe..."

"No, I mean it," she said adamantly. "You didn't deserve what I did. You were always a good husband and you loved me with your full heart... I was too caught up in my own shit to see it."

"Wow," I replied, pleasantly surprised. It sounded like Kat had been doing some serious soul-searching.

"I've had a lot of time to think over the last couple of months, and I realized that I never really gave you a chance Ryan. I never loved you properly, and that wasn't fair."

"I don't know what to say," I said, feeling like there might have been something that she was trying to tell me. "I never felt like you weren't loving me properly… well… until…" I cringed at the memory.

"Yeah," she agreed with a wince. "I'm sorry."

"That's behind us now," I told her, tucking a strand of her bouncy curls behind her ear. "The only way we can move forward is if we let it all go, and that means you too. You need to stop beating yourself up. It was shitty, but what's done is done, and now we just need to focus on our future."

"Agreed," she said with a nod. "I just want you to know that this time, I'm all in," she paused and wriggled around so that she was sitting up. "But first, there's something else that I need to tell you."

"Okay…" I said warily, leaning up on my elbows, "should I be worried?"

"No, I just want to tell you in the interests of full disclosure."

"Alright," I said with a nod, "I'm ready to hear whatever it is."

She took a deep breath, "Xavier proposed to me," she said with one long exhale. My stomach churned. Oh god had she slept with him too? I sat up and leaned against the squeaky bedhead.

"He what?"

Kat looked down at her hands.

"I said no, obviously, but he was very persistent and… he kissed me in public."

"Oh," I said in shock.

"There was nothing in it and I as soon as I realized what was happening I ran away. I just wanted to tell you so you didn't hear it from someone else."

"Okay," I nodded, processing the new information. Her eyes held mine, as she silently pleaded for me to believe her.

"You're my home Ryan, and I'm lost without you. I'd never do anything to risk us ever again."

My chest heaved with relief and I took her face in her hands.

"I love you."

"I love you too, and I need you to know that you can trust me. I'll do whatever it takes to prove that to you."

"I do trust you," I said, kissing her hard. Mia stirred in her cot, and we both froze, waiting to see if it would turn into a full cry. She was silent for a moment and then more crying rang out.

"I think it's my turn," I said, reluctantly letting go of Kat and rolling out of the bed to make Mia her bottle. Much to the disgust the midwives, we had decided that we would supplement Mia's feeds with a bottle, so that Kat would be able to have some help. Things were going to be hard enough as it was, so if including a bottle in Mia's routine would enable Rosie or Shirly to help out, then it seemed like a no-brainer to us.

I fixed the bottle and sat down on the chair with Mia, while Kat relaxed as best she could in the squeaky hospital trundle.

"Hey honey, are you hungry again?" I asked Mia quietly as I put the bottle to her lips. She drank hungrily, so I sang softly to her while she ate. I heard Kat stifle a sniff and I looked up to see her crying. "Oh babe, what's wrong?"

I asked, wanting to give her a hug, but loathed to disturb Mia now that she was settled.

"This is so perfect," Kat said, wiping her eyes. "I'm so happy."

"Yeah I can tell," I teased with a smile.

"I just want this to last. I don't want you to have to go back tomorrow."

I looked at the clock. It was 3:46am.

"Technically it's today," I said sadly.

"Oh god, don't say that."

"Sorry," I apologized, "but I promise it will all work out."

Kat sat up in the bed.

"Maybe, I should move home now," she suggested. "At least then we'd be close and we could come visit you every day."

"I mean… that would be great for me babe, but you'd be on your own most of the time. Would you really want that?"

"Yeah if means we can see you."

"Maybe your Mum would come down and stay with you for a while?"

"Oh god, I don't know if I could handle my Mum," she joked, "but I could try doing it on my own. It's not like I have to go back to work or anything."

"Alright," I agreed with a nod. "Maybe you should stay up here for the next few days while you get your bearings though?"

"Okay, good idea," she agreed with a smile. "Does that mean we actually have a plan?"

I grinned and nodded, "we actually have a plan."

- KAT McPHERSON -

When the morning rolled around, we were both blurry-eyed, weary, and absolutely dreading Ryan's departure. He rolled over and wrapped his arms around me, taking a long sniff of my unruly hair.

"Your hair smells amazing," he said with a sigh. "I missed waking up to this."

"Yeah," I agreed, wriggling around so that I could snuggle into his chest. "I can't believe you have to go in an hour."

"Me either," he said, threading his arm around my waist, laughing as his hand brushed past my flatter but much wobblier tummy. "I keep forgetting the bump's gone," he joked, squeezing me affectionately.

"Yeah, it's nice to be minus the wide load, but I don't know about this flabby skin. I hope that goes back to normal. It's awful."

"Babe, you should be proud of this body," he said, as he ran his hand up and down my side.

"It's a little hard to love it right now," I said rolling my eyes. "It's not just the flabby tummy, it's the bladder, the bleeding, the sore boobs, the whole lot. I don't know if my body will ever be the same again."

"Maybe not, but it just made her," he said, pointing at Mia who was sleeping peacefully, "so if you ask me, it's pretty fucking amazing."

I peered up at his beautiful face. "You always know the right thing to say."

"That's because I'm your husband."

"That's true," I said with a smile, feeling like I was home, as I stared into his big brown eyes. What was I ever thinking when I threw this away? Ryan was the other half of my soul, and it was crazy that I'd ever doubted him. He kissed me softly, and then sighed.

"I guess I should go have a shower before everyone gets here."

"Yeah," I agreed. "Do you have a change of clothes?"

"Nope, but I'll get changed when I get back."

"Okay," my heart wrenched with the thought of him leaving. "Maybe Mia and I should come down with you guys."

"I'd love you to, but I think a four-hour round trip would be too much for both of you right now."

"True," I said sadly, "I just don't want to be away from you again."

"Let's assume it will only be a couple of days while I sort out a sentence deferral," he said, sweeping my hair off my face, and tucking it behind my ear. "I think, given the circumstances, they'll let me postpone my sentence, but if they don't then we'll cross that bridge when we come to it."

"Okay," I nodded.

"It was really nice of your parents to offer to drive me back," he said. "I wasn't really looking forward to the train ride."

"Babe, there's no way they would have let you catch the train back," I told him with a smile. "You're the father of their grandchild after all."

"That I am," he said with a grin as Mia stirred.

"She must have known we were talking about her," I joked, as we both climbed unenergetically out of the lumpy, squeaky bed. "Come here little one," I said, getting Mia out of her cot to discover an explosion of sticky black poop all through her jumpsuit. "Oh my gosh."

"Oh wow," said Ryan as he turned to see what I was making a fuss about, "that's quite impressive young lady."

"Maybe you should take her in the shower with you," I suggested, not particularly keen to deal with the tar-like gunk.

"Leaving me to clean up the mess huh?" he teased.

"Exactly," I smiled. "I'll get her out of this and bring her in when you're ready."

"You could always join us too," he offered with a cheeky wink, as he stepped into the bathroom. I laughed and peeled Mia out of her ruined jumpsuit, as the sound of running water emanated from the bathroom.

"Right missy," I said to Mia, "let's get you in the shower." I held her with two hands, making sure I was supporting her head, whilst avoiding getting poop on myself.

"I'm ready when you are," called Ryan from the shower.

"On our way," I said, carefully navigating around the open bathroom door which used up about 50% of the available floor space in our small room.

"Oh," I said out loud, when I stepped around the door and saw Ryan naked. It wasn't as if I'd never seen his body before, but after not seeing it for such a long time, it was certainly a sight to behold. He'd trimmed down a lot since I'd left, and the Dad-Bod that he had started to develop, had completely disappeared. He actually looked more toned and muscular than he ever had. I suppose a lifestyle of non-stop drugs and dancing would do that to a person. Ryan looked up and grinned when he saw the expression on my face.

"Pass over the little poop-machine," he joked. I smiled and carefully handed him Mia without saying a word. I felt like I was seeing Ryan for the first time, rather than the fifty-six millionth. He smiled lovingly Mia, and gently washed all the gross poop off her little caramel body. "I can't believe something that disgusting could come out of something so beautiful," he said with a chuckle.

"Yeah, they did warn us in pre-natal class that the first few poos were going to be awful," I agreed, feeling inexplicably pervy for watching my own husband in the shower.

"Well they weren't wrong," he said, cleaning the last of the thick black goop off Mia. He cradled her gently, protecting her eyes from the shower spray, and my heart melted like ice-cream in the summer sun. Ryan had always been a softie, but the way he handled Mia was something different. Those big strong hands of his, that had apparently been powerful enough to knock a man unconscious, were so tender and delicate when it came to her. The contrast between his strength and her fragility was beautiful.

"I should leave you to it," I said, backing away from the shower, "this could be the last time you'll have together for a while."

"No, please stay," he said with a sad smile. "I want to spend time with you too."

"You don't feel weird about me seeing you naked?"
Ryan laughed loudly, which jiggled Mia about on his chest.

"Why would I be weird about you seeing me naked?"

"I don't know," I said with a blush. "It's been a while."

"Yeah it has," he agreed, staring at me with Mia's little head tucked under his chin. "Too long." Butterflies fluttered madly in my stomach.

"Don't get any ideas Mister," I joked nervously, "there won't be any action happening down here for a while," I said, waving my hands around my nether-regions.

"That's not what I meant," he said with a smile, "I was there remember? I saw what happened to it, so there's no way I'd be brave enough to try until you gave me the green light." I blushed again, but this time at the thought of what he must have seen yesterday.

"It can't have been pretty from that end," I joked awkwardly.

"It was amazing babe," Ryan said genuinely, "it was the most amazing thing I've ever seen."

"Really?"

"Yeah," he nodded. "I mean, obviously it looked painful… but it was almost magical. Ugh, that sounds so corny," he said with a laugh.

"No, it's beautiful," I said, smiling bashfully. "Is it weird that I feel like our time apart might have actually done us some good?"

"Not at all," he said, shaking his head. "I feel the same. It would have been better if we'd got to this point without all the drama, but I think maybe we needed to break in order to heal."

I snorted, "you've obviously been listening in your therapy sessions."

"Yeah, I guess rehab isn't all bad," he said with a shrug. "Hey, can you take Mia now? I want to kiss you but I really don't want to drop her."

"Sure," I said with a laugh, grabbing a towel and carefully taking Mia from Ryan's slippery hands. Once I had her safely wrapped in the towel, Ryan leaned out of the shower and pulled my face to his. His lips were warm and wet from the water, and it was such a scrumptious kiss that I never wanted it to end.

"I love you so much," he whispered quietly, leaning his damp forehead against mine.

"I love you too."

– Chapter 16 –

THE NEXT CHAPTER

- ASHLEY GRANGER -

Blurry eyed and shell-shocked, Nathan and I sat cuddled up on the couch after breakfast. It had been a crazy twenty-four hours, and so many things had happened that neither of us really knew what to say.

"So... do we mention the fact that we both said the L word in public, or are we just going to let that slip under the radar?" He asked, stifling a yawn.

"I was going to let it slip under the radar," I answered honestly.

"Of course you were," he said with a smile, "but then your quirky nature is part of why I love you. Because I do Ash... I love you." Silently, Nath bent down to kiss my neck gently, sending shivers all down my skin. He continued trailing kisses over my neckline, and my whole body melted beneath his touch.

"I love you too," I breathed, as Nath began to trail his hands down the length of my body. With dreadful timing, Fred sat down in front of us and mewed painfully.

"Hey buddy what's up?" Nath asked the cat, stroking him gently. Fred rubbed his head against Nathan's leg for reassurance. "He doesn't seem quite right," he said, just as Fred wretched all over the floor. "Oh shit."

"I'll sort it," I said, jumping up to grab the paper towels from the kitchen, while Nathan tried to comfort the distressed cat.

"It's okay mate." Nathan reassured Fred, scooping him up to move him away from the growing pool of pungent cat upchuck. "Should we take him to the vet?"

"Probably," I said as I finished cleaning up the gross vomit, "I'll google and see if there's one close." I found a local vet and jumped on the phone to book an appointment. Nath was cradling the cat so tenderly anyone would have thought he was holding a baby. So much for 'Fleabag the Stray'.

"Hello, Holland Park Veterinary Practice," answered a friendly lady.

"Hi, our cat is vomiting and unsettled. Is it possible to bring him in?" I asked the lady, as Nathan teasingly raised his eyebrows at me.

"What?" I mouthed at him.

"Nothing," he whispered, shaking his head with a smile, as he continued to cuddle Fred.

"Sure," the lady replied, "what's the cats' name?"

"Fred," I answered, supremely pleased that I didn't have to say 'Fleabag'.

"Fred?" The woman repeated curiously.

"Yes that's right," I confirmed, beginning to feel a little embarrassed about the pedestrian name I had bestowed upon the poor cat.

"Okay and what's Fred's surname?" she asked.

"His surname?" I said dumbfounded. Did pets use surnames?

"Yes love, what's his surname?" the lady repeated patiently.

"Ummm…Stone," I answered with a stunned chuckle. If I'd known Fred would inherit Nathan's surname, then I'd probably have thought a little harder before coming up with his name.

"Fred Stone," the receptionist replied, as I swallowed back another chuckle. Nathan glanced at me curiously - probably wondering what I was finding so amusing about the whole situation. "Okay, we'll see you and Fred shortly."

"Great. Thanks," I hung up the phone with a laugh, as Nathan waited for an update. "They can see Fred now," I said with a smile.

"Great," Nathan replied, heading towards the door.

"Fred Stone," I said randomly before erupting into hysterics. After a moment of shock, Nathan joined in my laughter, "I'm sorry," I apologised between gasps, "I had no idea pets had surnames."

"Don't apologise to me lady, its Fred you're making fun of," Nathan laughed, as we headed down to his car.

"Sorry Fred, I'm not laughing at you buddy, I'm laughing with you," I told the cat. "Maybe Fred wasn't such a cool name after all."

"No, this makes me like Fred even more. I'll even make his middle name Flint," joked Nath, sending us both into another bout of childish laughter.

Once the Stone boys were securely fastened into the passenger seat together, I shut the door and turned around to find myself staring into the voluptuous chest of Jessica Rabbit.

"Stacey, hi," I said trying my hardest to sound friendly as Miss Devil-wears-Prada, stood in front of me, in a perfume cloud of spiciness. The smell was so strong that it took my breath away.

"Shelley," she answered, deliberately getting my name wrong, as she bent down to wave at Nathan through the car window. The queen of snobbery was dressed to the nines, obviously on her way home from some sort of high-flyer's party. "So you and Nathan are still an item then?" Stacey said snidely, with a huge, fake smile plastered to her face. Passive Aggressiveness oozed from the woman, but I couldn't be bothered putting up a fight.

"Yes we are," I responded curtly, "and right now we really need to get our cat to the vet." I strutted around to the drivers side and put on my best fake smile. "Anyway, great to see you again," I waved as I climbed into the car. Nathan glanced over at me with a knowing smile as I navigated my way out of the parking bay.

"So Fred is our cat is he?" he asked teasingly, as I concentrated hard on not hitting any bollards with his expensive car.

"You heard all that did you?" I chuckled self-consciously.

"I did," he confirmed with a smile, as I risked a glance in his direction. "I think that officially makes us parents."

"I guess it does," I laughed.

When we arrived at the vet clinic, Nathan carefully carried Fred inside and took a seat while I saw the receptionist.

"Hi, I called about the cat," I told her.

"Fred Stone?" She clarified, as I did my best to keep a straight face.

"Yes," I replied formally, biting the inside of my cheeks to prevent myself from giggling again. "Fred Stone," I said with a nod, as I heard Nathan snorting in amusement behind me. The receptionist handed me some paperwork to fill out and looked over at Nathan in bemusement. "Sorry," I apologised on his behalf, "it's the first time we've used his full name."

"Right," she answered dryly, "if you could fill that out, we can get Fred in to see Dr Klein."

"His first name isn't Calvin is it?" Nathan joked, causing me to snort loudly. The receptionist stared at me with shock.

"Sorry. Thanks," I apologised with a blush, before quickly fleeing to Nathans side like a naughty school child. We filled out the paperwork together as quickly as possible, and I handed the forms back to the lady at the desk, just as Fred started mewing unhappily.

"The doctor won't be long," she assured me, with a sympathetic glance towards Fred.

"Thanks."

"Don't worry buddy, you'll be okay," Nathan reassured Fred.

"Yeah," I agreed, "I'm sure Calvin won't be long."

- NATHAN STONE -

"So what seems to be the problem with Fred?" Doctor Klein asked, as I gently placed Fred down on the clinic bench.

"Well he's been off his food for a few days, and he's just started vomiting," I told the doctor, as he read through our registration forms.

"You've only had Fred for a few months?"

"Sort of," I confirmed. "He was living on my doorstep and then my friend looked after him while I was in hospital." I peered over at Ashley and we both sniggered at the fact that Ritchie had been suckered into looking after the stray cat.

"Hmmm," Calvin nodded, "it certainly looks like you've all been taking good care of him," he said, putting down the file and taking a closer look at Fred. "Hmmm," he repeated again, as he examined Fred, "and this is the first time you've brought Fred to see a vet?"
Ashley and I glanced at each other with concern.

"Yes," I said solemnly, "should I have got him here sooner?"

"It's always good to get animals checked if you don't know their history, but it's not an issue," he answered, as he pressed and prodded Fred's belly.

"Is he okay?" I asked anxiously.

"Well I'm pleased to say that there's nothing wrong with Fred Mr Stone… however you may wish to reconsider the name."

"Haha, yes, but it was better than Fleabag," I joked self-consciously. Ashley laughed, but Calvin didn't find me funny.

"No I mean, you may wish to reconsider the name because Fred is actually a female."

"Oh," I answered in shock. It had never once occurred to me that *he* might have been a *she*.

"Wilma?" Ashley joked, causing me to laugh loudly in the tiny, echoey room. Calvin smiled patiently, but was obviously not charmed by our childish sense of humour.

"Mr Stone…Fred is pregnant," he stated bluntly. Ashley and I immediately shut up.

"Oh," I said again, staring at Ashley.

"From my examination, I'd say she has a litter of about four kittens, but I'd like to do an ultra sound to confirm that."

"Do you know how far along she is?" Ashley asked.

"I'd say she's about five or six weeks Mrs Stone. Full gestation is around 60-70 days, so she's probably only a few weeks away from giving birth."

"Oh no, we're not marr-" Ash began to explain our marital status, but Dr Klein interrupted her, mistaking her clarification of our relationship for a reluctance to deal with kittens.

"I know it seems overwhelming Mrs Stone, but we can give you all the information you need on how to look after the kittens, and how to care for Fred in the final weeks of her pregnancy. We'll also be happy to help you find homes for the kittens once they're old enough." Ashley and I remained silent, staring at each other in shock. "It's lucky you took her in, or these babies might not have survived," the vet said, patting me on the back. "Although it might be worth getting her spayed once she's had this litter."

"Absolutely," I nodded in agreement. I wasn't even sure I wanted to deal with one litter of kittens, let alone a second round.

"Are you happy for me to do the ultrasound?" Calvin asked, looking between Ashley and I for approval.

"Yeah sure," I nodded, as he proceeded to pull out a little ultrasound machine. The vet gently held Fred down, and ran the wand over her belly.

"There's one, two…three…four…" he counted, watching the little screen. I glanced up at Ashley, who looked as stunned as I felt, "…five," the vet finally concluded, "but that fifth one is quite small, so I'd be surprised if it survives."

"Oh that's so sad," Ash said with a look of sheer horror. "Is there anything we can do to help it?"

"Not really Mrs Stone, this is just the way it goes with cats, particularly strays," the vet answered unemotionally. He'd called Ash, 'Mrs Stone', so many times that I was beginning to think it was her name.

"So…what do we do now?" I asked dumbfounded.

"Just take her home, make sure she's got a quiet, cosy place to give birth, then wait. If you're worried about anything during the labour then give me a call, but generally she'll do all the work herself. Like I said, I'll give you some information so you know what to look out for."

"Right," I answered feeling overwhelmed.

"Has she got a basket?" Dr Klein asked.

"Err... no, she just sits on my couch," I replied, unsure whether that was the answer to the question he was asking. From the look on his face, it wasn't.

"Okay, well given that she's now a permanent part of your family, might I suggest that you to go into our shop and pick up a few basics for her before you leave? Some specialised food and a carry cage would be a good start, then at least you can get her home safely."

"Okay," I agreed. After all, how much stuff could one cat need? Roughly £400 worth of stuff apparently.

"That comes to £386 all together," the receptionist told us calmly, as we took Fred and all of her new high-tech 'essentials' up to the counter. The two of us nearly choked at the price.

"Sorry, how much?" I asked politely.

"£386 Mr Stone," she repeated, as I reluctantly handed over my Black AMEX. "£195 for the pet store purchases, £24 for the consultation, £35 for the registration fee, £40 for Fred's vaccinations, £12 for the microchip, and £80 for the ultrasound... and that includes VAT," she explained condescendingly, as she handed me a copy of the itemised account, "it's all broken down on the bill for you Mr Stone."

"Right. Okay, thanks," I nodded. Perhaps pet insurance should be our next job. We exited the vet surgery, under the heavy weight of Fred's fancy supplies, and bundled them all into the car. "Well that's one way to blow nearly four hundred quid in less than an hour."

"Yeah, pretty good for a cat that's not yours."

"I guess I can officially call him my pet now," I agreed with a chuckle, "Oops, I mean her," I corrected myself, "it's going to take me a while to get used to that."

"Yeah me too."

"Can you believe we're going to have a little fur family?" I joked in shock.

"Does that mean you're planning on keeping them all?" Ash asked sounding surprised.

"I don't know Mrs Stone, what do you think?" I teased. "Do you want to start a family with me?"

"Sure, but don't expect me to give up my job to raise your children," she teased, watching the road. "I've only just got my career back on track, and I bet you won't even change one dirty litter tray."

"Oh come on…Fred hasn't even popped yet, and you're already turning me into a deadbeat dad," I said in mock offence. "At least give me a chance."

"Okay, okay," she agreed, "but if I have to clean up after the birth, then we're getting a divorce."

- ASHLEY GRANGER -

Once we'd got Fred back home and settled, Nathan and I showered, dressed and headed down the country lanes of Surrey towards Granger Manor. We were only a few weeks into our relationship, and Nathan was about to meet my parents. Eek. Everything was moving so fast. I could sense his nerves mounting as we pulled into my parents' street.

"Are you honestly okay with doing this?" I asked self-consciously, hoping that he wasn't having second thoughts.

"Ash… this is important and I want to be here for you," he reassured me.

"I still don't know how I'm going to tell them about Dom," I said nervously. The one thing I did know is that they weren't going to take it well.

"You'll figure something out, and I'll be here to back you up," he said running his hand through my hair. "We're in this thing together remember?"

"Ummm… about that…" I replied, as I turned into the long gravel driveway that led up to my parents' property, "how would you feel about being just a friend today? It's just that my parents are a bit… umm… how do I put it?"

"Protective?" he offered.

"Over-protective might be a better word," I said apprehensively. I wanted them to meet him before I broke the news of… well… everything. "After what happened with Dom, and then the accident…"

"Ash its fine," he interrupted, "I get it. You're their baby girl, and they don't want to see you get hurt again. I'll be subtle I promise. Today we'll just be friends."

"Thank you," I said, patting his leg as the row of trees ended and the massive house came into view.

"Whoa," Nathan breathed in awe, "you didn't tell me you were loaded."

"I'm not," I answered truthfully, "but my parents are."

"Right, well that makes me feel a whole lot better," he laughed nervously, as I turned off the ignition.

"Says the silent millionaire," I teased him with a smile. "Anyway there's nothing to be nervous about… we're just friends today remember?"

"Friends who shag a lot," Nathan retorted before I helped him out of the car and up the front steps. He stood awkwardly on the porch, so I stopped to give him a quick kiss.

"You'll be fine," I reassured him confidently. "If all else fails, just talk to my Dad about wine," I suggested, before unlocking the front door. Nathan smiled nervously, and gripped tightly to the bottle of wine he'd insisted on bringing along. "Hi," I called loudly, as we walked down the long, extravagant hallway.

"Hi love, how are you?" Mum shouted from her usual hiding place in the kitchen. I led Nathan through the high-ceilinged reception room, and into Mum's den of good smells, as she fussed about the oven. I dumped my handbag on the kitchen bench and gave her a kiss. I was about to introduce

Nathan when she caught sight of him and beat me to the punch.

"And you must be Nathan," she said excitedly, giving him a massive hug.

"Nice to meet you Mrs Granger," Nathan said politely, while Mum squeezed him as lovingly as if he was her own child. I would have been embarrassed if it wasn't so funny. Nathan looked flabbergasted. He clearly wasn't used to open displays of parental affection, but he was doing his best to go with it. Mum smiled warmly and then stepped back to get a better look at him.

"Well aren't you a handsome one?" she declared as proudly. "How are the legs love?"

"They're healing well thanks Mrs Granger," Nath answered with a smile, "I'm still restricted in what I can do," he glanced at me with a sparkle of amusement in his eyes, "but the X-rays came back clear on Friday, so I'll be back to normal soon enough."

"Well that's fantastic! But please call me Mary love," Mum instructed him, pinching his cheek.

"Oh my god, Mum," I groaned in embarrassment.

Nathan handed Mum the bottle of wine. "This is for you Mary. Thanks for having me over." Despite his nerves, Nathan was as charming as ever.

"Oh that's sweet love, thank you, but honestly it's lovely to have you here," Mum replied, taking the wine, as she gave me a subtle yet knowing nod. "Geoffrey... they're here!" she shouted over her shoulder to my father. There was no response from Dad. All we could hear from the depths of the lounge room was the blaring television. "Geoffrey?" Mum called again, and while she was distracted, I took the opportunity to give Nathan a quick wink before Mum turned our way again. "He's deaf as a door-nail these days," Mum joked, missing our little exchange, "although, according to him, he has 20/20 hearing."

"20/20 hearing?" I asked with a laugh, "is that even a thing?"

"I don't think so," Mum answered with a chuckle. "Why don't you two go through to the lounge room and make yourselves comfortable."

"Okay," I agreed cheerfully, taking Nathan through to the lounge room where my father was relaxing in his big leather recliner. "Hey Papa Bear," I greeted Dad, who hadn't even heard us walk into the room. 20/20 hearing my arse.

"Oh hiya pancake," Dad replied, getting up from his chair to give me a kiss. He noticed Nathan standing uneasily behind me. "And who's this strapping young lad then?" he asked, as if I was seventeen and introducing him to my prom date. I got the feeling that Dad was deliberately trying to embarrass me.

"Dad this is Nathan."

"Thanks for having me Mr Granger," Nathan told Dad, as they shook hands.

"Not a problem son, but please call me Geoff. I know it doesn't look like it, but we're not big on formality in this house," Dad told him with a playful nudge. "So Nathan, you're back at work now then?" my Dad asked like a normal human-person. Work. Yes. Good. Work was a normal-people conversation.

"Yeah, I've been back for a weeks," Nathan said flashing me a subtle smile and I felt a slight blush creep over my cheeks as my mind flicked back to the day he'd returned to the office. So much had happened since then, that it felt like much longer than a few weeks ago. "It's good to finally be using my brain again and we kicked-off our new account this week so it's all systems-go," Nathan said, doing an exemplary job at keeping up the pretense of a business-only relationship.

"Dad, Nathan's in charge of that new account that I'm working on," I explained, trying to make our friendship sound purely professional.

"Ahh... so you're the hotshot who sold a make-up advert for ten million pounds." And there it was. My father skipped right over the pleasantries and dove straight into embarrassment territory. Nathan laughed but I was mortified.

"Dad!"

"What muffin?" he asked innocently.

"You know what," I answered, rolling my eyes.

"Well Geoff, I think that makes only two of us who think I'm a hotshot then," Nathan joked with a wink, making Dad laugh his big, amused belly laugh. He slapped Nathan on the back jovially.

"Do you drink wine hotshot?" he asked Nathan. Was the Pope Catholic?

"I sure do Geoff," Nath replied eagerly.

"Come with me then, I'll show you my cellar," my Dad said excitedly, as he dragged Nathan away towards his hallowed man-cave. Oh my god. Dad was showing Nathan the wine cellar.

Nath glanced back at me with a grin, and I laughed as they tottered off happily together like two toddlers who had just agreed to be best friends. I couldn't believe Dad was showing off for Nathan. He never usually got out of his chair, let alone took a guest down to see the wine collection. Apparently, I wasn't the only Granger who was falling for Nathan Stone.

Feeling slightly left out, I slipped back into the kitchen to help Mum while the boys went off to play.

"Where are the others?" Mum asked, as she checked on the lamb.

"Dad's showing Nathan the cellar."

"Really?!" Mum asked in amazement, gawking at me in disbelief.

"Yep," I nodded with a shrug.

"Wow, Nathan must have impressed him," she mused thoughtfully, and then paused for a moment, before pouring some frozen peas into a microwave dish. "He's certainly a good-looking young man isn't he?"

"Yeah he is," I agreed casually, trying not to blush.

"Are you two...you know?" Mum asked curiously, causing a mad blush to spread across my face. It was one of the more excruciating conversations my mother had ever attempted to initiate with me.

"Nathan and I are just...we're just..." I spluttered, struggling for words that weren't lies.

Thankfully Mum interjected before I finished my sentence.

"Well, he's clearly keen on you."

"You spent about two minutes with the guy, how could you possibly come to that conclusion?"

"Call it Mother's intuition," she said with a wink, "and you like him too." I rolled my eyes but didn't say anything. Mum peered at me sideways and smiled. "He makes you sparkle Ashley, and that's something that I haven't seen in you for a really long time."

- NATHAN STONE -

Geoff's wine cellar was extraordinary. I'd never seen a personal collection of that magnitude before. It was like a radioactive bunker, filled to the brim with racks of rare and expensive vino.

"This is impressive Geoff," I said in awe, as I wandered around the room full of quality wines.

"Thanks hotshot. It's just a hobby, but I do love it," he replied proudly, studying me carefully as I admired his impressive collection.

"Wow, you've got the 1955 Grange," I swooned, as I spotted a bottle of the revered vintage sitting in the fridge, along with several other rarefied wines. The guy certainly knew a thing or two about viticulture.

"You know your wines hotshot."

"My clients tend to enjoy the finer things in life, so it pays to have a bit of knowledge," I answered modestly, "I also have a uselessly vast knowledge of whiskey and cigars," I added, figuring I should probably omit hookers and cocaine from that list. Geoff studied me again for a moment, and then nodded with a satisfied smile.

"Yep, you'll do," he muttered almost to himself.

"Sorry?" I asked innocently, suspecting that I knew exactly to what he was referring.

"Never mind hotshot," Geoff answered, as he patted me on the back in a fatherly gesture, "I'm just remembering what it was like to be young."

"I heard you helped Ryan stay out of jail?" I asked, keen to change the subject before I gave away too much about my relationship status with his daughter. "Are you a lawyer of some sort?"

"Not really, I'm retired, but I used to be a Supreme Court Justice," he answered modestly. Holy fuck. Ashley's Dad was a High Court Judge?! How the hell had Ash gotten mixed up with a low-life criminal like Dominic Doyle?

"Well that would explain why Ash is so smart then," I laughed nervously.

"Yet she still thinks we'll believe that you two are just work friends," he joked with a wink.

"Umm…we're - it's not - she just…" I stuttered, sounding like Ash as I tried to come up with a reasonable response. Geoff chuckled and patted me on the back again.

"It's okay lad, I know how persuasive my daughter can be, and I realise it was probably her idea to keep it quiet."

"I think she just wanted to ease into it after…" I let my words trail off.

"Yeah," he said with a nod. "So she's filled you in on Doyle then?" he asked, as a look of suppressed anger washed over his face.

"Yeah."

"What a piece of work he was," Geoff sighed angrily, "but at least he'll spend the rest of his life in prison, where he belongs."

"Hmm," I agreed dubiously, feeling guilty that we were about to shatter his peace of mind.

"Come on hotshot, let's choose a bottle to go with lunch," Geoff instructed, patting me on the back for a third time.

"Everything okay down here?" Ash called, peering down the cellar stairs, "he hasn't bored you to death has he Nathan?"

"Far from it," I said, trying to ESP her that we'd been busted.

"See shortcake, some people actually appreciate my wine," Geoff teased. Ash and I shared a smile at the word 'appreciate'.

"I appreciate your wine dad," Ash bantered, "especially when I'm drinking it."

"Cheeky little bugger," Geoff retorted before turning to me, "she gets that from her mother you know."

"Anyway," Ashley interjected, "I was just coming down to tell you that lunch is ready, so if you two are done playing, we can go eat," she said, flashing me a quick smile. I grinned with amusement. She didn't have the slightest inkling that Geoff was onto us.

"On our way," Geoff nodded, as Ash bounced back up the stairs. I had to consciously remind myself *not* to check out her arse, as I followed slowly behind her, one step at a time.

"Prepare yourself for the best roast in Surrey," Geoff told me as the delicious smell of home-cooked roast hit my nostrils.

"Here you are," Mary said, when we returned to the dining room. "Nathan brought this," she said, handing Geoff my bottle of wine.

"Ah... the '99 Boroli. Good choice hotshot," he nodded, with approval, before he turned to Ashley. "This one's a keeper cupcake," he told her, holding up the bottle of wine with a cheeky wink. Ash glanced at me awkwardly, then looked back to Geoff, and then back to me again. She was clearly unsure whether her father was referring to me, or the wine. Geoff shot me a conspiratorial wink, and I grinned involuntarily. It looked as though he was planning on torturing his daughter.

"Shall we eat?" suggested Mary.

"It smells great Mary," I said, as she began dishing up the steaming roast.

"Go ahead and tuck in love," Mary instructed, piling vegetables onto my plate. "There's a nut roast if you're vegan too."

"No, I'm a meat-eater, Mary," I assured her.

"In that case, eat up," she said happily, plonking a forkful of lamb down next to the vege pile she'd constructed on my plate.

"That's plenty, thanks Mary."

"Nonsense," said Geoff with a huge smile, "I'm sure you two have been working up quite an appetite," he joked. Unfortunately it was at the same moment I took a sip of my wine. My nervous laughter happened quicker than

I could swallow, so I came very close to snorting expensive wine out of my nostrils.

"Dad!" Ash exclaimed, handing me a napkin, "are you okay Nath?"

"I'm fine," I spluttered, with burning nostrils.

"Behave yourself Geoff," Mary scolded him under her breath.

"So Nathan," Geoff piped up with a huge grin, "it sounds like you'll be keeping Ash pretty busy?" This time it was Ash who nearly choked on her drink. Mary cast Geoff a warning glance, but he continued with an impish grin. "With this big make-up account and all," he added with an unrepentant shrug.

"Aah, yeah, it's going to be pretty full-on for a while," I replied neutrally, not wanting to get myself into trouble. Ash was trying to stay cool, but the blush was slowly spreading over her cheeks. "We'll actually be going to Paris for a client visit on Tuesday."

"Yes, Ashley mentioned that. How exciting," said Mary.

"I guess with all the travel and work it doesn't leave much time for a girlfriend does it Nathan?" Geoff asked mischievously.

"Please stop," Ash pleaded with him, as I chuckled and scratched the back of my neck awkwardly.

"Although, I'm sure a hotshot such as yourself does just fine with the ladies" Geoff added with a wink.

"Oh my god," Ash groaned, shaking her head with humiliation. "How about you just let Nathan eat his lunch in peace?

"Where's the fun in that?" teased Geoff, with another wink in my direction. "Do you see yourself settling down and having a family Nathan? Or are you more of a career man?" he asked, ignoring Ashley's fruitless plea.

"I guess I've always been pretty career focused, but I'm at a point now where I'm ready to settle down and have a family," I replied honestly, making an effort to catch Ashley's eye as I said it.

"Really?" Ash asked with surprise, paying no heed to the fact that her parents were present.

"Yeah," I replied, holding eye contact with her, "especially after meeting Mia yesterday."

"Mia?" Mary asked, with her fork frozen mid-air.

"Oh, I haven't told you guys yet," Ash said, face-palming. "Kat had the baby yesterday."

"Oh how fantastic!" Mary said, looking less pale, "I bet Ryan is so chuffed."

"He is," Ash said.

"Ash helped deliver the baby," I said proudly.

"Really?" asked Mary wide-eyed.

"Not exactly," Ash said, waving her hand dismissively, "I got Kat to the hospital and stayed until Ryan got there."

"Which was only the very last bit," I clarified, "she was there for most of it."

"And so they asked if I'd be okay with them calling her Mia," Ash explained to her parents, "to sort of... honour my Mia."

"Oh how lovely," Mary breathed with a tear in her eye, "what a beautiful thing to do."

The one thing that had become abundantly apparent to me, was just how far the fall-out from Dominic Doyle had reached. That psycho hadn't just damaged Ash, he'd also impacted her whole family. They needed to know that he was back.

I looked at Ash, hinting with my eyes that now was the time, but she subtly shook her head. I nodded. She shook her head again. It was like a ninja tennis match. I rolled my eyes and then nodded again and Ashley sighed. She looked at her parents, who were watching us with great interest.

"There's something I need to tell you guys," she said reluctantly.

"We already know, Cupcake," said Geoff, "you and Nathan are dating."

"Errr… no. I mean…" she took a deep breath. "Okay, fine, we are but that's not what I need to tell you."

"Oh," Geoff said, taking a big gulp of his wine, "what is it then?"
Ashley looked at me for reassurance and I nodded my encouragement.

"Well… you know how Jock used to be a cop?" she said nervously.

"Yeah," said Geoff, as he and Mary exchanged confused looks. Ash turned to me again, so I stepped in to help.

"Jock came to see me before I left the hospital," I told them. "He found out that Dom isn't in prison anymore."

"What?" said Geoff.

"How can he not be in prison?" Asked Mary, "surely they have to tell us if he's getting released?" she asked Geoff.

"We should at least have been notified," he confirmed with a nod.

"They don't know that he's missing," I explained quickly. "Dom's either hired or blackmailed someone to impersonate him. As far as they know, he's still locked up."

"There's something not right about this," said Geoff. "I'll follow it up with my contacts before he shows up again."

"Geoff, I know you don't know me, but I can promise you that I have this under control," I told him earnestly. "Just give me a week and I'll have this whole situation sorted out. If not, then I'll leave it in your hands."

Geoff scrutinized me for a moment and disconcertingly, he seemed to catch the depth of my meaning. He nodded.

"Okay hotshot, you've got a week."

"I think you should come back and live here honey," Mary said to Ash, "it's not safe for you to be living by yourself if he's out there."

"Actually…" Ash said, glancing over at me, "I'm staying at Nathan's until this all blows over."
Geoff and Mary looked at each other.

"My place is near work and it's a secured complex," I explained when I saw the uneasy looks on their faces. "Jock's working on tracking down Dom, but in the meantime… Ash will be safe at my place."

"Sounds like it's all under control," Geoff said chirpily, as he rose abruptly from the table. "Now come with me hotshot, I've got another bottle of wine I think you'd like."

- RYAN McPHERSON -

I got back to The Lodge just in time for Group Therapy. Yay. The session had already started, so the orderly told me that I had to go straight to the Therapy room, which meant that I didn't have time to change out of yesterday's stinky clothes.

"The prodigal son returns," said Rodney snidely as I tried to sneak quietly through the door. "Decided to come back did you?"

"Hi Ryan," said Byron, ignoring the giant dick sitting next to him. "I hear congratulations are in order."

"Yes, thanks," I nodded, edging my way into the room.

"Take a seat and you can tell us all about it," he said.

"Why did Ryan get a night out?" asked Rodney, trying to stir shit.

"Because his wife had a baby dumb-ass," Sloane interjected, with her trademark sassiness.

"So what?" Rodney said with the maturity of a five-year-old. "The rest of us aren't allowed to leave at all, so why should he be allowed out for sleepovers?"

"Well for a start he's not a fucking smack-head like you," Sloane said in my defense, although I felt like it wasn't so much about standing up for me as it was a convenient opportunity to fight with Rodney.

"Yeah, and he's not crack-whore like you," Rodney retorted.

"Okay guys, that's enough," said Byron, taking control of the situation.

"But he's still in detox phase," argued Rodney, "how do we know that he didn't snort some Charlie or go on a bender while he was out?"

"We don't," Byron replied patiently, "but we trust that he respected himself and the program, because... why?" he asked the room, expecting us to parrot back his stupid mantra.

"The only person he'd be harming is himself," we all chanted unenthusiastically.

"What a crock of shit," mumbled Rodney under his breath. For once we were in agreement.

"Is it a boy or a girl?" Asked Angelica.

"A girl," I told her with a smile. "We called her Mia."

"Oh how lovely," she said, squeezing my leg affectionately as I sat down next to her.

"Must have been rough. You look like shit," teased Sloane.

"Yeah it was pretty intense."

"I imagine that would have brought up quite a lot of emotions for you Ryan," prompted Byron, always in the mood for psychological torture regardless of the situation. "Seeing your wife again, and meeting your child... how are you feeling?"

"I'm feeling exhausted," I said, resistant to his head-shrinky ways.

"Come on Ryan, you've been here for a while now, I expect more than that from you," Byron scolded me. "You need to acknowledge that there were some pretty hefty hurdles in front of you when it came to your wife. A few weeks ago, you weren't sure if you could forgive her. Has that changed now?"

I sighed and rolled my eyes. "Yes it has," I said, playing along with his game, "we've decided to get back together."

- KAT McPHERSON -

I strolled through Framlingham in the midday sunshine, appreciating the fact that I could walk without hauling an over-sized load on my front. It was much easier to push a baby in a pram than it was to lug them along in your belly.

The beautiful little town was alive with colour, but I was finding it hard to appreciate the beauty without Ryan by my side. We'd only been back together for one day, yet now we were being forced to live apart. Hopefully the Medical Director would agree to defer the rest of his 'sentence', so that he could spend some time with Mia and I.

I glanced down at our gorgeous daughter and my heart lifted. Her big brown eyes were just like Ryan's, so as long as I had her, then Ryan would never be far away. I looked around the town, feeling like I was caught in a time warp. It was as if time had stood still in this place. It was exactly the same as it had been when I'd first left, except that I was now 'me and a half'.

I'd made it as far as the Co-op when my boobs began to tingle. Uh-oh, my milk was coming in, and I'd forgotten to wear breast shields.

"Oh dear," I mumbled to Mia, desperately hoping that her food supply would hold off for long enough to get off the High Street. "Right missy, we'd better get home, because Mummy forgot to put in her breast pads" I joked. Motherhood was certainly not a glamorous lifestyle.

"Katie," called a deep voice, from behind me. I spun around self-consciously, to see Xavi jogging across the street.

"Xavi," I said with apprehension.

"I was just wondering how you were, and here you are," he chuckled nervously. "Congratulations."

"Thanks Xavi," I was flushed and flustered, feeling the tingle of milk in my breasts and hoping that it wouldn't break-through my bra cups.

"And who's this?" he asked, bending down to the pram to get a peek of Mia.

"This is my daughter, Mia," I said, bending forward over the pram to try and stop my T. Shirt from touching my dampening bra.

"She's gorgeous Katie," he said with a smile, "looks just like her Mum."

"Besides the brown skin," I joked nervously. What a fucking stupid thing to say.

"Right," he laughed awkwardly, "did your hubby come up?"

I nodded, "yeah, he did."

Xavi sighed and nodded.

"Well I'm glad he came to his senses," he said and then pulled a weird face. "No, actually, I'm not. I'm quite disappointed, but I'm glad for you and Mia." I was stunned into silence for a moment.

"It's the best thing for everyone," I said eventually, as I felt my boobs begin to leak through to my T. Shirt. "Anyway, I'd better get back," I said in a rush, "the little one needs a feed."

"Oh, okay," Xavier answered with surprise, as I turned around and maneuvered the pram past him. "Catch up soon?"

"Yeah, sounds good. I'll call you," I said as I fled away, with milk seeping through my T. Shirt. "Oh my god," I mumbled in mortification, "I'm so classy." I practically ran home and by the time we got there, I had two big wet stains on the front of my T. Shirt.

"Jesus," said Rosie with a laugh, as I burst through the door. "What's going on there?" she asked, waving her hands around my boobs.

"Ugh, don't," I said, quickly getting Mia set up to feed. "I forgot to wear nipple shields and this happened in front of Xavier."

"Well at least you're giving him a sneak peek," she teased as I attached Mia to my boob. I rolled my eyes at her.

"Ryan and I are going to make it work Rosie, it's what's best for everyone," I said again, frustrated about being back in a place where I was seen as nothing more than Xavi's other half.

"No offence babe, but Ryan is stuck in rehab, what sort of a relationship is that?"

"It's a marriage Rosie," I said, "and in a marriage you make it work no matter what," I told her. "A few months out of an entire lifetime is nothing, and Xavi... well that ship sailed a long time ago."

"I think you'll find that it's back in the harbour, and it's waiting to be boarded."

"Enough," I warned her, "besides, my vagina is still in recovery so no-one will be going near her any time soon."

Rosie cringed. "I've never been so thankful to be a lesbian," she joked with a wink.

"Lesbians can still have babies Rose."

"Yes, but not accidentally. It takes a lot of planning for us to make one of those things," she pointed at Mia. "And there is no scenario in which I will ever plan to have my vagina ripped open." Rosie patted Mia's head lovingly, "no offense babe," she told her quietly. I had to hand it to my sister, she always knew her mind. Even as a kid, she'd always been so focused and so sure of herself, whereas I'd always flitted about from one thing to another, never really knowing who I was, or what I wanted.

I suppose that was symptomatic of the fact that I'd spent my entire childhood and teenage years as one half of 'Kat and Xavi'. Firstly as his best friend, and then as his girlfriend. I'd never had the opportunity to find out who I was without him until I'd moved to London.

In that year after Xavi had left, I'd started to realise that I had no idea who I was without him. Being in a small town like Fram, had condemned me to being the person that everybody thought I was. I hadn't been able to break free of the half-Xavi Kat that I'd become, and it had been suffocating. When I moved to London, I finally felt like I could breathe, which was ironic given that London air is notoriously thick with pollution.

Despite the smog, I loved it. For the first time in my life, I was able to be the person that I actually was, rather than the person that everyone else wanted me to be. I could do anything, and be as crazy as I wanted because in London, no one cared. I was finally able to shine, and unleash my creativity on the world. I made all my own funky jewellery and found my quirky, creative style. I was able to be me, inside and out.

With freedom of anonymity, I'd discovered the true me, and it was quite a revelation. Many of the things I'd previously thought that I'd liked, were actually not to my liking at all. There had been so many things that I'd only liked because Xavi had, and not because I actually enjoyed them. I'd molded myself in his shadow because he'd always been my idol, and I'd never thought to make any of those decisions for myself.

I thought back to earlier, when I'd bumped into Xavi and the sad look on his face when I'd told him that Ryan and I were staying together. I felt sorry for him. He was stuck in the past, and trying to reclaim something that was long-gone. Xavi thought he loved me, but he had no idea who I really was. Ryan, on the other-hand, knew exactly who I was and he loved me because of that.

I looked down at Mia, then across to Rosie. I was happy to be with them, but sad that Ryan wasn't here with us.

Rosie looked at me with a smile, "I'm so proud of you kiddo," she said rubbing my shoulder. "You've done the most amazing thing."

"Yeah I have," I agreed, cuddling Mia closer. "I just wish that Ryan was here."

"I know this is not how you'd ever planned it, but I'm glad you guys are here. It's been really nice spending time with you both. We haven't spent this much time together since we were kids."

"That's true," I agreed.

"Every cloud, as they say," she said, kissing me on the top of my big pile of curls. "How about we put on Netflix and get drunk together?"

"Sounds perfect."

- NATHAN STONE -

I followed Geoff as he silently led me towards the cellar. He was so stoic that I was beginning to wonder if he was luring me down there to kill me. Perhaps he wasn't happy about Ash moving in with me. He gestured for me to go down the stairs ahead of him and, as I hobbled down the wooden steps, I heard the door close behind us. I turned back to look over my shoulder, and Geoff was following me with a grim expression on his face.

"Everything okay?" I asked nervously, wobbling slightly on my unsteady legs. It would have been incredibly easy for him to give me one little nudge and put an end to Nathan Stone.

Geoff silently moved around me, and helped me finish my descent down the stairs. My heart began pounding in my chest. I swallowed hard but smile as he stood right in front of me so that we were face to face.

"Whatever you have planned Nathan," he said, resting his hand firmly on my shoulder, "I want in."
My jaw nearly dropped to the floor.

"Pardon?" I asked in shock. There was no way he'd have said that if he knew exactly what I was planning.

"I know you're planning something big, I can see it in your eyes," he said squeezing my shoulder. "You don't work in the law courts for forty years and not pick up a thing or two."

"Oh," I said, not knowing what to say next.

"Does Ashley know?"

"No," I admitted, wondering if he understood exactly how extreme my plan was. "I don't want her to know."

"Good," he said, taking a deep breath. "So what's the plan and how can I help?"

"I… err…" I laughed nervously, and then shook my head, "I really don't think you want to know Geoff."

He nodded and smiled tightly. "Are you planning what I think you're planning?"

"That depends on what you think I'm planning," I said evasively, still not sold on sharing my murder plot with a retired Judge.

"If it involves killing the bastard then I'm in," he said bluntly.

"What?" I asked, unable to believe my ears.

"Nathan, that monster killed my granddaughter, and nearly killed my daughter. He tortured Ash for ten years, and I had no idea what was going on. When I sat in the courtroom and heard everything that he'd done to her over the years…" he sighed and clenched his jaw, "I was ready to kill him right then and there. He was lucky he got locked up."

"Okay," I breathed, with a nod, "I'm still working out the kinks to be honest. I haven't really done anything like this before."

"And for that I'm glad," he said with a smile. "It'll happen while you're in Paris?"

"Yeah," I said awkwardly, "only… I don't have anyone to do it yet. I have a lot of connections, but hit-men don't seem to be on that list."

"I'll take care of it," he said firmly.

"You know a hit-man?" I joked.

"No," he said, "I'll take care of it."

"Geoff…" I argued.

"The less you know, the better hotshot," he said cutting me off. "Does anyone else know?"

"Just my mate Ritchie, but he's safe."

"Okay," he said, pacing the room. "Don't tell anyone else, and don't discuss it over the phone, not even to me."

"I won't," I agreed. "So how should we communicate?"

"We don't, not about this at least," he said, continuing his pacing. "I want you as far away from this as possible."

I shook my head, "I appreciate that Geoff, but I want to do everything I can to keep Ash safe."

"I know lad," he said, ceasing his marching, "which is why I need you safe and out of jail."

"But-" Geoff held up his hand and interjected before I could argue.

"You won't be any good to her if you're locked up in jail Nathan," he said solemnly. "I won't be around forever, and I can see that she's very much in love with you, so I need you to keep yourself out of trouble. You get her to France and I'll sort the rest."

"But, you're a Judge, what happens if you get caught?"

"I *was* a Judge. And that's exactly why I'll be able to get away with it."

"Fuck," I sighed and rubbed my face. "Are we really doing this?"

"We sure are," he replied with a nod. Holy fuck. I'd just pre-meditated a murder with a High Court Justice.

- ASHLEY GRANGER -

Besides the Dom bombshell, lunch had gone amazingly well. I hadn't fooled anyone with my 'just friends' stance. As Nathan had pointed out on many occasions, I was an awful liar, so I felt much better once it was out in the open. I was pleasantly surprised that my parents were okay with the whole thing, especially with me staying at Nathan's place. I was a little surprised that they actually seemed pleased by the news of Nathan and I being a couple.

Dad seemed to be on some sort of mission to get Nathan drunk, and thus far he had been succeeding.

"You're going to love the next one hotshot," he boasted, as he emptied the remnants of their third bottle of red into Nathans glass. Both of them were pretty jolly by that point, so another bottle wasn't the most sensible idea.

"No Geoff, you'll both be under the table if you drink anymore," Mum jumped in, as she yanked the fourth bottle of wine from my dad's hands.

"Aww...just one more?" My father whined like a child. "I've got some port downstairs that Nathan would love." I'd never seen my father warm so quickly to someone. Particularly when he was excruciatingly aware of the fact that I was shagging that particular someone.

"No Geoff, leave the poor boy alone," Mum scolded, "Nathan has to work tomorrow."

"And on that note… I think it's probably time to go," I declared, patting Nathan on the back.

"Already?" Dad asked with disappointment.

"Dad, I'll bring Nathan around to play again another time okay?"

"Cheeky," Dad replied good naturedly, as he and Nathan sniggered like naughty school boys. "She gets that from you," Dad informed my mother factually.

"Yes Geoffrey," Mum agreed patiently, as she rolled her eyes behind his back. "He thinks he's a comedian after a few drinks."

"See! Cheeky!" Dad accused, pointing at her in a drunk-judge sort of way.

"Okay Papa Bear," I said, trying to lift Nathan to his feet. He was so solid that he didn't budge, until he realised what I was trying to do and stood up obediently. I gave Dad a kiss on the cheek as I guided Nathan past him. "I love you."

"I love you too cupcake," Dad answered with a drunk smile, before shaking Nathans hand.

"Thanks for having me Geoff, and thanks for the… wine," Nathan slurred, giving my father a weird nod.

"Not a problem hotshot, we'll see you when you get back from Paris," Dad told him, "and next time we'll crack open the port." We all seemed to be in agreement that there would definitely be a 'next time', so that was a good sign.

"Sounds good," Nathan agreed. "I'll bring you some great whiskey too," he added, before giving my Mum a kiss on the cheek and she looked pleased at his unprompted affection. "Thanks so much for lunch Mary, it was lovely."

"Not a problem love. You're welcome any time, so don't be a stranger okay?" she told him, squeezing his cheeks excitedly. I would have been embarrassed if Nathan hadn't been so tipsy.

"I won't. Thanks," he said drunkenly, "in fact, if you guys would like to come to ours for lunch next week, I could cook for you."

Mum and I exchanged glances at Nathan's use of the word 'ours'. It was hard to tell what she was thinking, but my heart had skipped a little beat when he'd said it.

"Thanks love," she said with an amused smile, "well chat with Ash later in the week."

"Night Kids," said Dad with a drunk wave.

"Bye. Love you," I said loudly, leading Nathan towards the front door.

"Oh wait!" Mum called, before disappearing momentarily. I sighed patiently, and continued herding Nathan down the entry hall to expedite our escape. Seconds later Mum returned with two massive plastic bags, laden with Tupperware containers full of left-overs.

"Seriously Mum," I chuckled, shaking my head in amusement.

"You're busy people, you need to eat," she answered defensively.

"This is enough to keep us fed for a week," I joked, taking the bags from her gratefully.

"You need to keep your strength up," Dad teased, giving Nathan a wink.

"Oh my god Dad," I replied in mortification. "We're going now." I shoved Nathan gently out the front door before my Dad said anything else embarrassing.

"Thanks Mary," Nathan stopped and waved appreciatively, before I led him towards the car.

"Oh Ashley?" Mum called with amusement.

"Yeah?" I asked, turning back to them.

"You forgot your handbag love," she answered teasingly, holding out my bag.

"Oops," I replied with a blush, as I ran back up the front steps. "Thanks Mum."

"No worries love," she responded with a chuckle, handing over my bag. "He's lovely sweetheart," she whispered into my ear, "and if his invite still stands when he's sober, then we'd love to come for lunch next week."

"Yep. Okay. Bye," I replied awkwardly, before running down the steps to join Nathan at the car. I piled our food into the boot, while Nathan stood, staring up at one of the big pine trees. "Nathan, what are you doing?"

"Just admiring the tree," he said as if it was a rare and unusual sight.

"I think the wine is messing with your meds," I laughed.

"No, really," he said, peering over the car roof at me, "London's like this weird little microcosm of existence, and sometimes I feel like the we're all so brainwashed and caught up in the bullshit that we're completely missing the point of life."

"Wow. Where did all this come from?"

"I guess my accident just made me look at things a little differently," he said with a shrug.

"Okay, let's continue this in the car Drunky."

"Right you are boss," Nathan said, doing his best Dick Van Dyke impersonation, which he ended with a grin and a salute, before plonking himself ungracefully into the passenger seat. I glanced up at Mum and Dad, who were standing in the doorway watching us with great amusement. They both smiled and waved.

"Drive safe," my mother called cheerfully.

"Will do. Bye," I said with a wave, before climbing into the driver's side of Nathans flashy Tesla. I glanced over at my man as he struggled with his seatbelt. "All buckled up?" I teased. I heard a click, and he looked up proudly.

"Am now." he said with satisfaction.

"Oh my word, remind me never to leave you alone with my Dad again," I joked, as I started up the car.

"Geoff's a legend," Nathan blurted with a childish grin.

"Yeah, you seemed to make quite an impression on him too," I chuckled. "What were you two doing in the cellar anyway? Should I be concerned?"

Nathan laughed, "no, but maybe your Mum should."

I glanced over at him and smiled happily. After ten years of bringing a psychopath home to my parents, it was nice to finally show up with someone who they actually liked. Dominic had been a nightmare from the beginning.

The very first time they met him, he had done his best to alienate me from them. I remembered being completely stunned, as I watched a guy who had been relatively charming to that point, suddenly turn into an obnoxious, arrogant prick. He had been so over the top, that I'd thought he was joking at first.

"So Geoffrey, looks like you've got a few bob stashed away then old man?" Dom had blurted as we'd sat down to dinner.

"I'm doing okay for myself thanks Dominic." Dad answered sternly.

"Looks like you are," Dom had answered leering at my mother. I'd been so shocked, that I'd just sat there and stared at him in astonishment, as he'd winked lecherously at mum.

"So Dom, what do you do?" My Dad asked brusquely, diverting Dom's attention away from my mother.

"Distribution mostly," Dom had answered honestly, "but I've got my fingers in a few pies."

"Such as?" My father inquired in his judge voice.

"Eh, you know, this and that."

"Right," Dad said unamused. I'd suspected at that point, that he'd already concluded Dom's business wasn't exactly legal. Mum and I had both remained silent while the men continued their stilted conversation.

"I'm actually thinking about branching into the property market," Dom declared as he took a massive, inelegant gulp of his wine.

"Really?"

"Yeah, there's a nice little place in Stockwell that's just come up for sale, and

I reckon it'd be perfect for Ash and I." Dom said as he stretched, arrogantly draping his arm around my shoulder. It was the first I'd heard of it, but I did my best not to look surprised.

"In Stockwell?" Mum asked with disbelief. My father was notably silent. I could tell that he was seething. Stockwell was one of the less desirable areas of London to live, and one of the more dangerous areas at that. It would be the perfect location for Dom's business.

"Yeah." Dom grinned, which in retrospect was probably because he knew that he was achieving his goal of causing trouble in the Granger camp.

"And what do you think about that Ashley?" Dad asked pointedly.

"I…uhh…" I looked at Dom who was nodding his head firmly at me, before I glanced over at Dad, as he offered me a chance to stand up for myself. Dads strength was almost enough to make me speak my mind, but as I looked back at Dom he gave me a warning stare, and I knew that disagreeing with him wasn't an option. "It's fine." I finally said.

"See, she's happy." Dom added, patting me on the back as if I was a dog that had obeyed its owners command.

I'd often wondered how I didn't see through him that night. Maybe I hadn't wanted to. I sighed heavily. I hated that the awful memories had returned. My life had moved forward so nicely until Dom had showed up at the hotel. I had honestly believed that I was finally free of my past. I liked this version of my life and I didn't want Dom to ruin it.

"What's on your mind?" Nathan asked, snapping me out of my thoughts.

"Oh," I said with a jump. "Nothing."

"That doesn't look like nothing," he said running his finger along my furrowed brow.

"I was just thinking about Dom actually." I admitted.

"Well that explains the angry face," he joked.

"What do we do Nath?" I asked with a hopeless sigh, "he's never going to leave me alone." Nathan reached over and stroked my hair.

"Don't worry babe, I have a plan."

My stomach lurched, and I momentarily took my eyes off the road to shoot him a warning glance.

"Nathan," I said reproachfully.

"What?" he asked innocently.

"You know what."

He crossed his arms and set his jaw sternly.

"I'm not going to let that psycho ruin your life again."

"I don't want you, or any of the boys, doing something you'll regret."

"We wont," he told me adamantly, "I promise there will be zero regret," he muttered under his breath.

"No Nathan."

- RYAN McPHERSON -

Dinner was one of my least favourite times at the Lodge, second only to our Group Therapy sessions. Even after having a day away from the place, I could quickly feel my life-force being drained out of my body. Particularly by Rodney.

"Decided to join us plebs did you?" he asked snidely under his breath when I put my plate down next to Sloane. I ignored him and took my seat. Sloane bumped my shoulder with hers and glanced sideways at me with a smile.

"Glad you decided to join us," she said quietly. I smiled and took a mouthful of my tasteless meal.

"How are you going love?" asked Angelica. "It must be hard being stuck in here when your wife's at home with a brand new baby."

"Yeah," I agreed, putting my fork down, "I wish I was home with them."

"They might let you out for a few weeks," suggested Sloane. "This would have to count as extenuating circumstances wouldn't it?"

"I'm going to talk to my Lawyer about lodging an Application for Deferral, but it will come down to the Medical Directors discretion."

"It's worth a try," Angelica said with an enthusiastic nod.

"I shouldn't even be in here anyway," I said with a sigh.

"But the rest of us should?" Rodney shot back.

"I didn't say that."

"No but you thought it," he seethed.

"I just meant that I made one stupid decision that landed me in here."

"And that's different to the rest of us how?" he asked angrily. "You think you're so much better than us don't you? You ponce around here with your fancy clothes and your big sob-story about how your wife cheated on you, like your shit doesn't stink," he said with disdain, "I've got news for you sunshine, your wife cheated on you for a reason, so maybe you should cut your crap and think about what drove her away in the first place."

"You don't know anything about me and my wife," I said through gritted teeth. He was trying to stir me up, but I wasn't willing to risk my freedom for that arse-hat.

"If you have an issue Rodney, then I suggest you bring it up at Group Therapy tomorrow," said the orderly, asserting his authority over the situation.

"Then I shall do so," Rodney said snidely, attempting a posh accent.

"And we'll all be looking forward to it," I mumbled sarcastically.
Rodney glared in my direction, and stood up from his seat.

"I'm sorry rich-boy, have you got a problem with me?"

"I have so many problems with you Rodney, that I wouldn't even know where to start," I said without thinking.

"Is that right?" he replied, puffing up his chest like the cock that he was. "Well then how about you come over here and say it to my face."

"Sorry, I thought I was," I retorted, "but now I can see I'm actually talking to your arse. My mistake," I said with a shrug, causing Sloane to snort loudly, while the others all sniggered quietly under their breath.

"Are you fucking kidding me?" Rodney snarled, as he pushed out his chair so hard that it fell to the ground with a loud clatter.

"Whoa, enough!" shouted the orderly. "Dinner time is over for you two boys. You're both on wash-up duty."

"I'm not hungry anyway," I said, standing up from the table with my plate.

"But he started it," whined Rodney, like a baby.

"How old are you?" hissed Sloane, "besides, technically you started it."

"Shut up slut-face," snapped Rodney.

"Hey, don't call her that," I said. Rodney ignored me and continued to address Sloane.

"You know he was insulting you too. He thinks he's better than all of us."

"You're the only one who thinks that Rodney," she said, unphased by his anger. "Maybe that's something that you need to think about."

"Come on you two, into the kitchen," said the orderly, herding us both out of the dining room. "If I hear any fighting in here, I'll be reporting you both."

"Fine," I agreed with a nod, as I began loading dirty dishes into the dishwasher.

"Great work Rich-boy," Rodney said under his breath, once the orderly had left the kitchen.

"I'm not going to fight with you Rodney," I told him calmly, as I loaded the pots into the dishwasher, "I just want to do my time and get the fuck out of here."

"And until that day," he said, leaning into my ear, "I'm going to make your life a living hell."

I stepped away from him. "You're a fucking psycho."

"I ain't the one who nearly beat a man to death rich-boy."

I glared at him, unamused.

"I'm going to my room," I said, pushing past him and out the door. I had to get in touch with Geoff and see if he could get me the fuck out of that place. I didn't need proof of an afterlife. I knew it was real, because I was already in hell.

- KAT McPHERSON -

As much as I'd loved spending time with Rosie, Ryan and I had already been apart for two months, so I couldn't bear living two hours away from him any longer. Much to the disapproval of my entire family, I decided to move back home. On Monday morning, wired and drained after my first night of solo motherhood, I packed up the few belongings we had at Rosie's house, and she drove us back down to London.

I had a suspicion that I was being overly optimistic about my ability to single-parent a new-born baby, but I was determined to make it work. This was our family now and being so far from each other felt wrong.

Geoff had told Ryan that they should have a decision on his sentence deferral within the next few days so, with any luck, he'd be home before the end of the week.

It was the first time I'd been home since the morning I'd left for Framlingham, and it felt strange to be standing at my own front door again. So much had happened since the day I'd walked out that door that it felt like a lifetime had passed in between. Ryan and I had both made a lot of mistakes, but our marriage was back on track now, and we had a beautiful baby girl.

I peered down at Mia in her carrier and a smile sprang to my face. Soon we would all be together again and finally have the chance to be a proper little family. This situation was certainly a test of our grit, but when I looked at that precious little face, it made all the pain worthwhile. I knew with every fiber of my being, that everything was going to be fine. We were a family now and it was the start of a whole new chapter.

I took a deep breath, and unlocked the door. I stood for a moment and took stock of the entry hall before I stepped over the threshold. It felt like an abandoned crime scene. As well as dirty clothes decorating the house, there were half finished mugs of skanky black coffee, empty beer bottles and the pièce de résistance... a rolled-up tenner with remnants of cocaine sprinkled across the dusty glass coffee table.

Rosie stuck her head inside and stepped around me, as I stared in revulsion at the state of the messy flat.

"Jesus," she said, waving her hand in front of her face to deflect the funky smell that seemed to be emanating from the kitchen, "doesn't smell like he did any cleaning while you were gone."

"Doesn't look like it either," I said, eying the random debris spread throughout the house.

"Let's figure out where that smell is coming from, and then we'll tackle the mess," Rosie said, plopping my bags down on the floor.

"Okay," I muttered in mild shock. Was this really how Ryan had been living without me there? It was so unlike him. Normally he was the tidy one in our relationship.

"Holy fuck," I heard Rosie swear from the kitchen.

"Oh no," I mumbled, dreading to know what she'd found.

"Sorry babe, but you married a pig," she called, making a bunch of noise that would indicate she was cleaning up something pretty rank. I sighed, and placed Mia's carrier on the floor, gently pinching one of her chubby little cheeks.

"Looks like we've got a lot of work to do young lady."

- NATHAN STONE -

Given our eventful weekend, the big move to the 9th floor on Monday morning seemed to pale in comparison. What once would have been a massive deal to both Ash and myself, was now just another slightly notable event in our chaotic lives.

The rest of the Delfontaine team buzzed around the floor, setting up their desks and exploring our new home. There was excitement all around me, but I was in a world of my own as I called Sandrine to confirm our visit. Our Eurostar tickets were booked, and we were set to go to France in the morning, which meant there was no turning back now.

My stomach was in knots about it, and not just because of what Geoff would be doing while we were away. I still hadn't told Ash about what had happened with Sandrine in Paris. I'd planned to tell her on the weekend, but then with Mia arriving, and the whole plotting-a-murder thing, I hadn't found the right time to do it. If I was being honest, I didn't really want to tell her at all. It hadn't exactly been my proudest moment.

"We'll see you tomorrow then Nathan?" Sandrine purred down the line in her sexy school teacher voice. "I've been waiting very patiently for you."

I cleared my throat awkwardly and glanced over at Ash, who was at the desk opposite mine.

"Oui," I agreed, "we'll see you tomorrow."

"Tres Bien!" she said happily, "shall I arrange for Aurelie?"

"No!" I said urgently, causing Ash to look up at me curiously. "I mean..." I cleared my throat again, "no thank you," I said more calmly.

Sandrine let out a husky chuckle, "she was a bit too much for you Nathan?"

"Yeah, you could say that," I said awkwardly, trying not to draw too much attention to myself.

"Okay, just you and me this time then," it sounded like an order rather than a question.

"Ummm...."

"See you tomorrow Nathan."

"Au revoir," I said, hanging up the phone. I looked up at Ash who was concentrating on her big screen. I had to tell her sooner rather than later. There was no knowing how Sandrine was going to behave when we got there, or how she would respond when I told her that we wouldn't be repeating our dirty little tryst. I leaned across the desk to get Ashley's attention.

"Hey," I said nervously, as she looked up with a smile. "There's something that I need to talk to you about."

"Oh god," Ash cringed and leaned back in her chair. "Nothing good ever follows that sentence."

"It's not great." I glanced around the room. "Come in here," I said, leading her into the small meeting room.

"I'm getting worried now," she said anxiously, as I clicked the door shut behind her. "What's this all about Nath?"

I sighed and turned to her earnestly. "Ash," I said, not quite sure where to go next. "I did a lot of stupid things before I met you, and I'm a bit worried that some of it is going to come back and bite me in the arse." I paused and gulped down the nerves that were rising in my throat. What if this was a deal-breaker for her? A three-day S&M sexcapade wasn't exactly a minor infraction. She smiled understandingly, although I was willing to bet that she had zero comprehension of exactly what I was about to tell her.

"Nath I'm fully aware of your past."

"Not entirely," I groaned with a grimace. "I've done some pretty dodgy stuff and I don't want it to fuck up our future."

"Is there something in particular that you're worried about?" she asked, reading me like a book.

"Yes," I admitted. "I had sex with Sandrine."

"Oh," she said, calmly tucking her hair behind her ear.

"And it wasn't just a one-off," I blurted guiltily. Ashley's jaw dropped, and although every fiber of my being wanted to gloss over the details and pretend it was nothing, I owed Ash the truth, no matter what it would cost me. "Actually it was a one-off but we did it more than once. It was like, quite a few times actually, but only one session, you know? But not a normal one night stand situation. It went on for three days and there was someone else involved too," I babbled quickly. Her brow furrowed in what looked to be a mixture of confusion, disgust and hurt, but she didn't utter a word. I cleared my throat nervously and tried to explain better. "The two of them tied me to a bench in Sandrine's sex dungeon, and had their way with me for three days."

Ash stared at me wide-eyed. I didn't know what to make of her silence and I began to spew forth more apologies when she hushed me.

"Did you ask to be tied up?" she asked, appalled.

"No, it was more of an abduction if I'm honest," I admitted with embarrassment.

"Oh my god Nath"

"Does that mean you're not upset about it?" I asked with concern, as I edged closer to her.

"Well I think it was pretty fucking stupid to get involved with a client," she answered frankly, "but no, I'm not upset. I'm concerned. That's basically rape, Nathan."

"I guess," I shrugged sheepishly.

"So is she expecting you to..." Ash paused with a grimace, "...do it again?"

"Yeah, I think so, but I can't exactly have that conversation with her in the over the phone, and I don't know how she'll react when I tell her in person."

"Okay," Ash nodded. "So how do you want to handle this then?"

"I guess I'll just have to get her alone when we get there," I said, running my hand through my hair. Ash cringed at my use of words. "Sorry, I didn't mean it like that."

"I know," she said with forced smile. She'd taken the news much better than I'd expected. Ash hooked her thumb into the back pocket of her jeans. "So are there any other dirty little secrets that I should know about while we're at it?"

"Probably."

"Oh well," she sighed, "let's just deal with one Stone sexploit at a time."

"Solid plan," I agreed. She looked me up and down for a minute.

"That bitch will have a fight on her hands, if she tries to take advantage of you again." Ash was attempting to come across stern, but the sparkle in her eyes gave her away.

"Aww, you're going to defend my honour?" I joked, shoving my hands in my pockets to prevent myself from grabbing her around the waist.

"I sure am," she said with a lopsided smile. "No one messes with my man." I took a step closer to her, and tilted my head like a puppy begging for a treat.

"I love you She-Ra."

She laughed and rolled her eyes.

"That smile will only get you so far Mr Stone."

"I'm sorry past Nathan was such an idiot" I said, realising that I'd never be able to charm my way out of trouble with Ash.

"What's done is done babe," she said, catching sight of our audience, who were not-so-subtly, peeking in the meeting room window. "Now... was that everything boss?"

"That and I wanted to let you know that I've got a board meeting tonight, so you might as well take the car. I'll call a town car later on."

"Don't be silly. I'll just catch the tube."

"No," I said in panic. I didn't want her exposed and vulnerable with Dom lurking around. "Public transport is too risky."

Ashley's face softened and she stepped forwards, about to place her hand on my cheek before she remembered that we had an audience. She stopped in her tracks and dropped her hand to her side.

"I love that you're worried about me, but I'll be fine. There's nothing he could do on a crowded tube."

"You're underestimating Dom again," I said, finding it hard not to reach out to her. "We both know that crowds don't perturb him."

Her eyes studied every inch of my face and I thought she was going to launch into an argument, but instead, she nodded her head in resigned agreement.

"You're right," she said with a humble smile, "I'll take the car, but at least let me come and pick you up."

"Nah, I don't know how long the meeting will take. They're a bunch of Old School Advertising boys remember?" I teased. "They like the sounds of their own voices."

"Very true," she agreed with a smile. "Well in that case, I'll head straight home and sort dinner."

I grinned like an idiot. "You called it home," I said with a little thrill.

"I did."

"Does that mean we might be able to make this a permanent thing then?"

"Let's just see how we go Romeo."

"You're breaking my heart Chucky."

"I'll break something else if you keep calling me Chucky."

"You always say that, but I think deep-down you love it," I said with a smile, dying to kiss those shiny lips of hers. I peered out of the meeting room window to see if anyone was still looking, but sadly most of the team were watching. They were probably waiting to see if we'd put on another show for them. "If we didn't have an audience, I'd kiss you right now."

"How about we save that for later?" she teased with a smile, as she peered over her shoulder at our unsubtle onlookers. "I think they've had enough free entertainment from us lately."

"Agreed," I grinned, shoving my hands in my pockets again. "So you're going to be okay with Sandrine tomorrow?"

"I'll be fine Nath," Ash said waving her hand, "I've survived Jessica Rabbit, I'm sure I can handle two days with Sandrine."

"You're a saint."

"Yes, I am," she joked with a smile, "and you can make it up to me when we get home."

"You called it home again," I teased.

"I'm leaving now," she said, heading for the door.

"You taking your ball and going home?" I teased with a laugh.

"Just get back to work boss."

- ASHLEY GRANGER -

The problem with driving home after work, was the peak-hour traffic. I'd been sitting in pretty much the same spot for twenty minutes, wishing that I'd caught the tube. I stared at the barely moving cars ahead, and started running through a check-list in my brain of all the things we still needed to organise for our trip tomorrow. Cat was sorted, bags were packed, tickets were in Nathan's possession and passports...

"Oh shit," I muttered to myself as it occurred to me that I'd left my passport at my flat. I engaged the high-tech blue-tooth system and dialed Nathan.

"Hey, you've reached Nathan Stone. I'm not able to answer your call right now, so please leave a message and I'll get back to you as soon as possible."

"Hey, it's me," I said loudly into the car blue-tooth. "I just realized that my passport is still at the flat, so I'm going to swing by and grab it on my way. I'll see you at home. Love you."

I detoured out of the traffic, and towards my flat, which was only fifteen minutes from where I was. I parked the car on the street, fighting with that same uneasy feeling the flat now elicited in me. Wanting to get out of there quickly, I trotted down the wonky footpath towards my building. The place felt different than it had before. It didn't feel like home anymore.

I pulled out my keys, but when I approached the front steps I noticed that the door was ajar, which was unusual. The front door was never even left unlocked let alone open.

"Hello?" I called into the empty entrance foyer, assuming someone must have been planning to go back out. I scanned down the hallway, but no one was around, and all the apartment doors on the ground floor were shut. "Hello?" I called again. The place was silent, so I closed the front door and climbed the stairs to my flat. I had a sinking feeling in the pit of my belly, but as I reached the landing, nothing seemed awry. I was probably being paranoid.

I unlocked my door and as I turned the handle, a massive hand clamped down over my mouth, gripping my face so tightly that I could barely breathe. Panic flooded my body as a big arm grabbed me around the waist. I tried to scream, but the sound was so muffled it was barely audible. I kicked and screamed as hard as I could, while the assailant dragged me forcefully through my door.

"Hello Princess," he said, shoving me so hard that I stumbled and fell painfully to the floor, momentarily winded. Dom slammed the door behind me, cutting off the light from the shared hallway.

I remained frozen to the spot while my eyes adjusted to the dim light. My heart was pounding wildly as I realised that I was now a prisoner, trapped inside the cold, dark place I'd once called home.

Dominic clicked the lock, and the sound rang out like a gunshot in the deathly quiet flat. I held my breath, and rolled over slowly, as if moving too fast would draw his attention. All I could make out through the dark was the silhouette of his hulk-like body hovering ominously in front of the door. I carefully crawled to my knees, waiting for my eyes to adjust to the darkness. The silence was deafening.

"I've been waiting to get you alone," he said with eerie amusement. The malice in his voice sent chills up my spine. I was in serious trouble.

"How did you know I'd be here?" I asked breathlessly, hoping that he couldn't see me edging cautiously to my feet. Dominic flicked on the light and I shielded my eyes against the unexpected brightness.

"Nice place you've got here," he said, ignoring my question. "Very quaint." I waited for my confused eyes to readjust again, and then held his gaze. Dom's dark eyes bore into mine. He was the predator and I was the prey. His tattooed hand rested menacingly on the door handle as he scrutinised my living room slowly and deliberately, like he was taking a mental inventory of everything I owned.

"Dominic, how did you know I was going to be here?" I asked again, finding some inner strength hidden under my many layers of fear. Dom grinned sadistically, as if it was all a big game to him.

"I think you'd be able to figure that out if you really put your mind to it," he said, as he prowled towards me with his piercing gaze locked on me like a missile locked onto its target. "You and I have a score to settle sweetheart."

"Really? Because I thought we were pretty even," I retorted snidely, feeling too brave for my own good.

Dominic growled and lunged at me so quickly that I didn't realise what was happening until it was too late. His big fingers dug tightly into my arms as he effortlessly lifted me off my feet, and threw me over the couch. I tumbled back onto the floor, banging my elbow on the coffee table as I went down. He peered over the sofa, and snarled like an animal, while I stared at him, wide-eyed with shock and immobilised by fear. He smirked and turned away, stalking around my lounge room like a hungry lion. I held my breath and cowered in the small gap between my sofa the coffee table.

"You obviously don't take me very seriously Princess," he said calmly, noticing Nathan's Mix-CD sitting on the top of my stereo. Dom picked it up and read the note that Nathan had written on the cover. He looked over at me with disdain, and then glanced back down at the CD with a repulsed look on his face. "I told you to steer clear of Romeo… and now you're living with him."

"How do you even know that?" I asked, in barely a whisper.

"I thought putting Stone in hospital was a pretty fucking clear indicator of how serious I am, but you and all of your little boyfriends still seem to think that you can win this game."

"What game Dom?" I asked, finding my voice, "you're the only one playing a game, you know that right?"

"Little miss innocent huh? Poor little Ashley," he paused and stormed across the room, still grasping the CD case. He leant right down so he was hovering above me. "Let me tell you something Princess… I've never done anything that you didn't bring on yourself."

I pushed him away from me and sat up in agony.

"You kicked me down the stairs and killed our baby," I hissed with venom, letting my anger take hold.

"It wasn't my kid you little slut," he growled with rage, gripping the CD case so hard, that it started to crack. I shuffled backwards on my bottom to put some distance between myself and the monster.

"The baby was yours," I said defiantly.

"Stop fucking lying!" he bellowed, throwing the CD case across the room. I flinched as it hit the wall and smashed into pieces. The situation was escalating quickly, but I was determined to stand up for myself this time. I steadied my breathing and looked him dead in the eyes.

"I never cheated on you Dom," I said calmly.

"I don't believe you Chucky," he said with an arrogant smirk. I recoiled at the word 'Chucky', as if he'd slapped me in the face. Nathan was the only person who called me Chucky.

"What did you call me?" I asked breathlessly, wondering whether I'd heard him right.

"You don't like being called 'Chucky'?" he teased with amusement. "I thought that was your nickname now." A blaze of red-hot rage, flared though my body, and momentarily obscured my vision with a blinding flash of light, that exploded from somewhere deep within me.

"How do you know that?" I snarled through gritted teeth. "Did you do something to Nathan?"

"I told you Princess... I know more than you think I do."

"Dom, what have you done to Nathan?" I asked, barely a whisper. All the air in my lungs had evacuated, and I felt like I was suffocating.

"Relax Chucky, your boyfriend is fine," he goaded arrogantly. "Use that pretty little brain of yours and you'll figure it out. Deep down you already know the answer." He was right. I did know the answer and I was furious at myself for not realizing it earlier.

"You put spyware on Nathan's phone," I said trying to steady my breath.

"Bingo."

"When he was at the hospital," I added unnecessarily, angry that I'd been so fucking stupid. He winked, reveling in his power over me.

"You're not really as dumb as you make-out are you Princess?"

My heart thudded violently in my chest, pounding out a frantic rhythm like the double bass drum at a Metallica gig. I couldn't believe that Dom had been privy to every private moment Nathan and I had shared since he'd left the hospital. In a matter of seconds, I'd replayed our entire relationship in reverse. My conversation with Nathan about Sandrine; our new living arrangement; random private moments we'd shared in his apartment; the night Nathan had stayed on the phone; the day at my flat right after Dom had first reappeared; waking up together in the hotel room; our fleeting visit to Club Bordello; and our kiss in the Artemis hallway. I lingered briefly on that beautiful but now sullied moment and felt a warm tear roll down my cheek. All of our memories - every single moment we'd shared together since that day - had now been tainted with the possibility that Dom had been listening.

I took a breath and continued my relationship replay. Then I saw it. Nathan looking down at me with a self-assured smile as he said, "I know more than you think I do." My stomach churned at the realisation that Dom had been five steps ahead of us the entire time.

"That's how you found us at the hotel," I whispered breathlessly.

Dom let out a loud, mocking laugh. "And wasn't that an entertaining evening?" he said, clapping his hands with amusement. I snapped out of my daze, and stared my demon in the eyes.

"What else do you know?"

Dominic grinned again. It was obvious he was enjoying his twisted little game.

"I bet I know a few things that you don't," he taunted.

"Like what?" I asked, fully aware that I was taking his bait.

"Like the fact that Stone had some plans of his own."

I was sure Dom was bluffing, trying to cause a wedge between Nath and I, but I had to continue down the rabbit hole to find out for sure.

"What plans?"

Dom smiled gleefully, visibly pleased that he was reeling me in. He took a calculated step closer to share his secret.

"Your new man is a murderer sweetheart."

I shook my head. "You're the only psychopath around here Dom."

"Are you sure about that?" he asked with an evil smile.

"Yes," I replied, less confidently than I would have liked. His determination was disconcerting. He huffed with amusement and cracked his knuckles. The sound sent shivers down my spine.

"Your boyfriend organized a hit on me Princess."

"He what?" I blurted in shock, still sitting ungracefully on the floor. I couldn't fathom the idea of Nath participating in a murder plot, but I knew he'd been putting a lot of thought into the Dom situation so it wasn't entirely far-fetched.

"He's been trying to have me killed," Dom explained condescendingly. "Which means that you have him to thank for this," he said gesturing proudly towards himself and my flat. "I was going to string it out for a few weeks and have some fun messing with the two of you, but Stone and your Dad forced my hand."

"My Dad?" I asked, stunned.

"Papa Granger and Stoney Smurf are best pals," he sneered. "They were down in the bunker plotting a murder, and you and your Mother were none the wiser." I didn't know whether any of that was true, but it finally dawned on me exactly how fucked I currently was. I searched the room for some sort of escape plan as the panic rose further in my chest. Dom was standing between me and the only exit, and my phone was lying on the floor behind him. I glanced over at it, wondering whether I could reach it quickly enough.

"Don't even think about it sweetheart," Dominic warned menacingly, as if he'd read my mind. I was running out of time.

I crawled backwards towards the bookshelf, where there was a big chunk of Rose Quartz on display. It wasn't exactly a scary choice of weapon, but it would still hurt if I hit him with it. I reared slowly towards my only defense strategy, but Dom closed the distance between us in a single step. He bent down and leaned right into my face.

"You can't escape me Princess. You're in way over your head this time."

"Maybe," I agreed, "or maybe not." Dom thought he was still dealing with the old Ash, but he had another think coming.

"Who do you think you're fucking with Ashley?"

"I'm not trying to fuck with you Dom, I'm just trying to get on with my life," I replied quietly. "Maybe you should get on with yours too."

Dom's eyes flashed with rage as he finally snapped. He grabbed me by the throat and yanked me to my feet.

"You put me in prison you fucking slut," he snarled angrily, shoving me up against the bookshelf with his hand pinned firmly around my neck. His grasp was so tight, that he was blocking my air supply. I gasped frantically, trying to get air into my lungs as the dizziness began to take hold. Desperately, I clawed at his hands, but his grip was too strong. Dom smirked arrogantly, and his eyes lit up with excitement as he watched the colour drain out of my face.

I reached backwards and grabbed the Rose Quartz off the shelf then, with the last of my strength, smashed it sharply over the side of his head. The beast howled, and released me from his grasp as his hands flew to his head. He sunk to the floor in a daze, and I noticed a trickle of blood run down his temple. The stone of love had never been used for such heinous purposes.

I sprinted towards the door, but Dom grabbed my ankle and I crashed to my knees. Even half concussed, he was too strong for me. I tried to wrestle my leg free, but he had a tight grasp on it. With adrenalin pumping through my veins, I rolled onto my back, and kicked at Dom as hard as I could. It was enough to throw him off balance, so I ripped my foot free, and commando crawled to my phone, hurriedly dialing 999. I scrambled to my feet when Dominic dove ferociously at me sending me back onto my knees.

"Fuck," I swore as the phone flew out of my hand and skidded across the floor. "Please don't hurt me Dominic," I shouted loudly, hoping that my voice was loud enough to carry to the person at the other end of the phone.

"It's too late for that Princess," Dom growled ferociously, as he grabbed my hair from behind and dragged me viciously to my feet. "I'm going to finish this thing once and for all."

"Get off me," I said, kicking and punching backwards as vigorously as my disadvantageous position would allow.

"Get up you little slut," Dom snarled, nearly ripping my hair from the scalp.

"If you're going to kill me, you'll have to work for it," I said, flailing like a speared octopus. He twisted my right arm, and pinned it behind my back so that I was locked backwards against his solid body.

"Oh I'm not going to kill you yet Princess," he chuckled evilly, "we're going to have a bit of fun together before I do that." My belly dropped like I was on a roller-coaster.

"Over my dead body," I growled, wriggling so hard to escape his grip that I almost dislocated my shoulder in the process. I cried out in pain and Dom laughed.

"That can be arranged," he drawled with calm confidence. "I do like it when you fight Ash, but there's really no point." With that, Dom slid his hand down my stomach and popped the button on my jeans with his thumb.

"Get off," I shouted, swallowing back the bile in my throat, as I jerked my body away from his touch. I attempted to writhe free of his grasp, but with my shoulder twisted painfully backwards, I couldn't get away. Dominic flicked my zip down and chuckled evilly, as he yanked me tighter against his body. My resistance was doing little more than amusing him.

"The slut has gone shy, has she?" he sniggered huskily into my ear. His warm breath smelt like stale beer, and I had to hold back another wave of nausea as I felt his cock harden against my back.

"Fuck you Dominic," I seethed with a combination of rage and panic.

"That's what I was hoping you'd say," he whispered arrogantly as I heard the jingle of his belt being unbuckled. "How do you think Romeo will feel when he finds out I fucked his woman?"

My heart thudded in my ears and revulsion washed over me as the futility of my situation finally hit home. I was helpless again. Dom was too strong for me.

"Please don't do this," I begged quietly. Dom laughed and, keeping a firm grip on my wrists, he shoved me to my knees so that my arms were pinned behind my head, execution style.

"Consider this my last gift to you," he said condescendingly as he ripped off his belt. It cracked loudly, like a whip, right behind my head and the sound sent shivers down my spine. He wrapped the warm leather belt tightly around my wrists, tugging on it to make sure my hands were securely fastened. I fought against the heavy-duty binding, but he'd tied it so tight that my hands were turning a very slight shade of purple. There was no way to escape the inevitable.

Dom knelt behind me and breathed heavily into my ear as he let his free hand slide into the front of my jeans.

"Dom, don't," I pleaded again, unable to stop his fingers from roaming inside my underwear regardless of how many different ways I contorted my body. I twisted and turned but it did no good. I couldn't avoid his touch.

"Come on Princess, you know you want it," he drawled lecherously into my ear as he pressed his fingers harder inside me. I blushed with anger and shame. Even though it was beyond my control, I felt like I was cheating on Nathan.

"Dom stop," I begged, as he continued to violate my body with increasing determination.

"Shh," he said into my ear, "I know what you like Ashley, so there's no point fighting it." His breath on my face was hot and oppressive as he leaned even closer. "You know I'm going to kill you, so this will be your last chance to get-off."

"I'd prefer if you just killed me now," I snarled through gritted teeth.

"We'll see about that," Dom said, shoving his fingers further into me as he rubbed hard on my clit with his thumb. Although my brain was fighting it, my body was succumbing to his touch. I fought against the wave of pleasure that began to wash over my body, but it was no use. My body was too far beyond my control. Hot tears stabbed at the back of my eyes. Why was my body betraying me? "Ahh, there she is," Dom laughed teasingly from behind me as my traitorous body shivered with an orgasm. My tears broke and rolled down my flushed cheeks. I hated that I had no control over my body. I hated that I had no control over the situation. And I really, really hated that Dom was the person in the driver's seat. "Still the same slut you always were," he mocked with glee. "Come on slut, you're going to fuck me one last time."

Dom removed his fingers from my underpants and momentarily released his grip on the belt. I knew it was now or never, so I yanked my wrists forwards and attempted to make another run for it. Without missing a beat, Dom caught me with one arm and kicked me back down to the floor.

"Stay there slut," he growled, grabbing the dangling belt strap and turning me over with excessive force, "I want you to see my face while I'm fucking you."

I ceased fighting, and ran my bound hands over my tear-soaked cheeks as Dominic jammed his elbow into my sternum, and yanked my jeans off me. I knew I wouldn't be able to make an outright escape, so I would have to be smart if I wanted to get out of this alive.

Dom removed his own jeans, leaning hard on my chest, whilst keeping a tight hold on the belt to ensure that I didn't attempt another escape. He kicked off his pants, and proudly presented his disgusting boner. He wedged his knees between mine, forcing my thighs apart. Vomit rose in my throat as the memories of his previous rape replayed in my mind. I closed my eyes, wondering whether I'd be able to get my foot to his groin before he realised what was happening. The odds were against me, but it was the only chance I had.

"Open your eyes and look at me slut," he barked. When I didn't obey, he slapped me hard across the face. I gritted my teeth against the pain and swallowed back my tears before I opened my eyes. I refused to let him to see my fear. I was petrified, but I stared up at him defiantly.

"Fuck you," I snarled. Dom smiled and ran his stiff cock up my bare thigh. Terror flared in my belly and despite my best efforts not to let it show on my face, Dom could sense it. His eyes flashed with lust every time the fear gripped me, so I tried not look scared as he ground his groin against mine and breathed heavily in my ear.

"I know you want this Princess," he said huskily, as I felt a drip of pre-come land just above my pubic hair.

"I couldn't think of anything worse," I said through gritted teeth. Dom paused and studied me with amusement, shifting his weight slightly as he reached down and slid his fingers inside me.

"You can't lie to me Ashley," he said with a smirk, pulling his fingers out and holding them up to my face to show me the slimy liquid, "you want me and we both know it." He rubbed his fingers together with a look of smug amusement, then wiped them against my cheek.

I jerked my head away from him in disgust, but all it did was encourage his sick game. He laughed sadistically, and thrust his cock straight into me before I could retaliate. Sorrow wracked my whole body as he grunted on top of me and, unable to prevent it, a loud sob escaped from my lips as a decade of rage and grief erupted from my soul. Dom stopped his rutting and pushed himself upright so that he was kneeling over me with his boner on full display.

"I like it when you cry but this is ridiculous," he scolded me, as if he was a teacher telling off a misbehaved student. "Quit with the hysterics Princess," he said, stroking himself slowly and deliberately, "and admit that you've missed this." Through my tears I smiled involuntarily as he provided me with the perfect escape.

"I promise I won't miss it this time," I said solemnly, and without a second thought, I contorted my leg around his body and kicked him hard in the dick. Dom squealed like a banshee and rolled onto the floor in the fetal position, while I clambered to my feet, grabbing my jeans with my hands still tied together. I threw my jeans over my shoulder and scooped up my phone with both hands.

"Hello, are you still there?" I panted desperately into the phone, shoving it between my neck and my shoulder as I awkwardly tried to pull my jeans on.

"Hello, are you okay?" replied a lady at the other end.

"Not really," I said frantically, stumbling towards the door with one leg in my jeans.

"The police are on the way to you. Do you need an ambulance as well?"

"No, I'm not hurt," I blurted breathlessly, as I successfully pushed my other foot into my jeans, "but I don't have long before he recovers."

"They should be there soon," she said. "What's your name love?"

"Ashley, Ashley Granger," I said, jiggling to get the jeans over my bottom. I reached for the door handle with my bare bum still on show, figuring that getting to safety was more important than my modesty.

"Okay, Ashley, are you somewhere safe?" she asked as something sharp sliced through the back of my shoulder blade. I opened my mouth to respond, but all that escaped was a guttural scream. The phone once again clattered to the floor.

"You fucking bitch," Dom spluttered, as I turned with terror to see him doubled-over, holding his penis in one hand and his bloodied pocket knife in the other. "Now I *am* going to kill you," he said, still catching his breath, "and then I'm going to kill Stone," he added with an evil, breathless laugh.

"Not if he kills you first," I hissed, wincing in pain, as my shoulder dripped with blood. Dom snarled and lunged towards me, forcing me to jump away from my only exit. I ducked the knife, and ran towards the kitchen in the hope that I could climb out of the window or, at the very least, arm myself with a make-shift weapon. I gripped my jeans at my waist and fled into the kitchen as fast as I could, grabbing the biggest knife out of my knife block. I gripped it tightly in my bound hands, and Dom appeared in the doorway, still half-naked. He snatched one of the other knives from my set and roared like an animal as he dove at me with it. The shiny blade flashed with the reflection of the street light outside the window, but I dodged him, and madly flailed my own knife in his direction. Blood splashed everywhere and I couldn't tell if it was his, or mine. It was literally a matter of life and death, but I had no idea who was winning.

- NATHAN STONE -

When I got home, the house was dark and silent.

"I'm home babe," I said loudly, flicking on the lights and half expecting to see Ash sitting naked in the dark to surprise me; but the flat was empty and silent except for Fred who was mewing madly for her dinner.

"Are you home?" I called out. "Ash?" I said again, wandering through all the rooms to see if she was hiding somewhere. I was getting a bad feeling in the pit of my stomach, so I grabbed my phone and dialed her number. It diverted to voicemail. I left a message and hung up before I noticed that I had a voicemail waiting.

"Any idea where she is?" I asked Fred as I dialed my mail box.

"Shit," I said, as I listened to Ashley's message. I could feel in my bones that something was wrong. I rang the town car driver and hobbled downstairs, as fast as my legs would carry me.

Having only just left my building, the driver was pulling up out the front as exited the doors. I begged him to speed all the way to Shorditch, but when we approached Ashley's street, we were stopped by a police barricade. There were police lights flashing and people everywhere.

"I'll get out here," I told the guy, before flying out the back door and jumping over the barricade. I found myself hoping that it was a bomb threat, but a voice in the back of my head told me that this had something to do with Dom. As I got closer, I noticed the hub of activity was outside of Ash's apartment block. There were two cop cars, an ambulance and a coroner's van all parked near the front steps.

"What the fuck?" I mumbled to myself as my stomach churned with dread. Coroners didn't show up for run-of-the-mill bomb threats. In a split second I was running full-pelt towards the building, desperately needing to know that the sickening circus had nothing to do with Ashley. I didn't even think to ask anyone what was going on, I didn't care, all I wanted to know was that Ash was safe in her apartment.

I pushed my way through the fray of onlookers, and ducked under the police tape, scrambling for the front door as fast as I could. A burly cop appeared out of nowhere to block the entrance.

"Sorry sir, you can't go in there," he said, as I attempted to get around him.

"But I live in there," I lied, hoping that it would grant me access into the building, "I just want to get home and make sure my girlfriend is okay."

"No one can go in or out until the coroner has removed the body," he told me firmly.

"The body? What's happened?"

"I'm sorry sir, I'm just here to secure the crime scene," he apologized, "I'm sure they'll debrief all the residents once they're finished."

"Can you tell me which apartment it was?" I pleaded, as he maneuvered me away from the door.

"Number eight I believe," he answered dismissively. His words hit me like a punch to the stomach.

"Number eight?" I asked breathlessly. Ashley's flat was number eight.

The man's face dropped, "sir, do you live at number eight?"

"Oh my god," I whispered, feeling like the breath had been knocked out of me. No matter how deeply I inhaled, I couldn't get enough air into my lungs. It couldn't be number eight. He must have got it wrong. Ash couldn't be dead. Please god, let him be wrong.

"Sir?"

"No, it can't be," I muttered in a daze, "it can't be eight."

"I'm sorry sir," I heard him say before the ringing in my ears took hold. I could see his mouth moving, but I had no idea what he was saying. All I knew was that I had to get in there. I had to see it for myself. I pushed past the cop and sprinted through the door. I could hear him shouting behind me, but I kept running, dodging artfully past another loitering cop, before scaling the stairs two at a time. My hips hurt and my knee was protesting, but I didn't care.

"Ash!" I shouted frantically, as I stormed up the hallway and flung myself through the open door. "Oh fuck," I breathed as time suddenly ground to a halt.

Life blurred into slow motion, and I was hit with an eerie wave of calm, as if my brain was unable to process the intensity of my fear. I was staring into my own personal horror movie. The lounge room was all smashed up, and there was blood splattered everywhere. I took a dazed step into the lounge room and two guys emerged from the kitchen, hoisting an occupied body-bag on a stretcher. My head began to spin. Oh god, it was a body. Was that Ashley?

"No, no, no, no, no," I collapsed against the wall with tears streaming from my eyes, and then proceeded to vomit everywhere. How could I have let this happen? I should never have left her on her own. How could I have been so stupid? Geoff was going to kill me, which would be a welcome reprieve, because I didn't want to live if Ash was dead.

I leaned against the wall and vomited until I had nothing left in my stomach. The cop who had tried to stop me at the front door, grabbed my arm gently and patted my back. I looked at his face and saw his mouth moving but I couldn't make sense of his words. He seemed to be more sympathetic than angry, but it was hard to hear what he was saying over the deafening ringing in my ears.

"Fuck," I spluttered through the upchuck and the tears. My undignified behaviour was only adding to the mess and chaos, but I had lost control over my faculties. Losing Ash was too much to bear. What an unglamorous end to our love story. I had so many questions, but the one thing I did know for sure, was that my life wasn't worth living if Ash wasn't in it.

– Epilogue –

I know what you're thinking, "that can't be right. Surely the book must be missing some pages, because the story can't end there."

Am I right?

Well, let me save you some trouble... this is most definitely not the end of the story, it is, however, the end of this book. Sorry to leave you high and dry, but I'm afraid our hero needs some space and time to process his own personal nightmare.

We'll pick it up again in Book Two, and I can promise you it will be worth the wait.

See you again soon, in Between City & Sea.

R.C. x

Between City & Sea

After the night from hell, the Artemis crew are now picking up the pieces of their shattered lives, and figuring out how to move forward with, and without, each other.

NATHAN STONE's world was turned upside down with the arrival of Ashley Granger. For the first time in his life he'd fallen in love, but now his new life has been violently shattered into pieces at the hands of a drug-dealing psychopath. In his girlfriends blood-spattered apartment, Nathan is facing the reality of life without Ashley Granger.

RITCHIE CARLTON is a lovable rogue. Under his mischievous facade, the Aussie larrikin is madly in love with his non-girlfriend, Amy Vaughn. All he really wants is to to is get married, settle down and raise a family, but Amy is resistant to his proposals and refuses to commit to him. It's time for Ritchie to make a choice, it's either stay or go.

RYAN MCPHERSON no longer recognises himself or his life. Full of rage and unable to cope with the discovery that his pregnant wife had cheated on him, Ryan veered off the rails and found himself in rehab. After the arrival of his daughter, Ryan is more determined than ever to pull himself back together so he can return to life with his new family.

KAT MCPHERSON made a huge mistake and has spent many months dealing with the fall-out. After spending time with her family in Framlingham, Kat decides to move back home so she can be near Ryan while he finishes his stint in rehab, but some unexpected news may change her plans. Will the McPherson's marriage survive this latest trial?

Out Now!
Buy your copy today.

- RITCHIE CARLTON -

Much like humans have defined time in accordance with the appearance and death of Jesus Christ, life at Artemis Advertising could be broken down into two distinct time periods: Before Granger (B.G.) and A.D. The only difference with our timeline being that we had a third phase in between those two, which we could refer to as C.G. or Cyclone Granger.

It might've been by sheer coincidence that Ashley Granger's arrival at our company marked a dead-set turning point for our small group of misfits but, co-inky-dink or not, life was definitely not the same from the moment she stepped foot in the Artemis building. It wasn't that Ash directly caused all of the drama, but her presence undoubtedly created stratospheric chaos in our little world.

I mean, don't get me wrong, I always thought she was a ripper chick, but there was no doubt that trouble had a way of following her around. She was Cyclone Granger. Spectacular and awe inspiring to witness, but if you got too close you risked getting sucked into the vortex.

Maybe that was part of her allure? Perhaps it was an adrenaline rush, like storm chasing. We could put my best mate, Nathan Stone, into the 'storm chaser' category. Stoner was a man who had run from relationships his entire life. Before Granger, he had made a conscious effort to avoid any sort of emotional connection with women, but when Ashley arrived, he was instantly smitten by the tall, blonde, force of nature. Everything I'd known to be true in relation to Stoner and relationships, was no longer applicable.

To be fair to Ashley, Nathan Stone was a force of nature himself. The obvious metaphor here would be something to do with 'blowing', but I'd hate to be predictable, so I'll just say that Nathan was a whirlwind of female destruction. He had the uncanny ability to whip women into a frenzy and, prior to Ashley, wherever Stoner went, he would leave a trail of broken hearts shattered behind him. Not only that, but Nathan had never failed to disappoint in the inappropriate entertainment arena.

Case in point… the week before Granger's arrival, he had been held captive as a sex slave by our French client and her stripper friend in Paris. Needless to say, controversy was hardly a new concept to Nathan Stone. Falling in love however, that was seriously out of character. Something changed in Stoner from the first moment he saw Ashley sitting in our office cafeteria. It was as if her mere presence had caused some sort of transformation in his DNA.

The first weekend after Ashley arrived at Artemis, it was prolifically clear that Whirlwind Nathan was on a direct collision course with Cyclone Granger. We could see the typhonic winds on the horizon, but there really was no stopping them.

- RYAN McPHERSON -

Another fucking night in rehab. No matter how many weeks passed, being held captive in a clinic, didn't get any easier, and now that Mia had entered the world, every second away from her and Kat felt like torture. It almost made things worse knowing they were back home in our flat. They were so close, yet so far away and on top of that, I was worried about Kat having to care for a newborn on her own. It certainly wasn't what we'd envisaged parenthood to be at the beginning of her pregnancy. But then again, nothing had gone to plan lately. Our world had been turned upside down several times over so, by all rights, we should have been experts at rolling with the punches. I was deep into my brooding when there was a knock at my bedroom door.

"Come in," I called, and the door opened to reveal the night orderly. "Hey, what's up?" I asked curiously.

I didn't usually get room checks this late in the evening.

"Ryan, your lawyer is on the phone."

"What? Geoff? Why?"

"I don't know, but he says its important."

"Okay," I said, my stomach churning with concern. What could possibly be classed as important legal business at 10pm on a Monday night? Was it about my application to defer? Or perhaps I'd inadvertently broken the terms of my sentence when Mia was born? Maybe Peterson had contested the verdict and was fighting my deferral.

I took a deep breath and followed the orderly to the office, where I hesitantly picked up the phone.

"Geoff?" I asked down the line, "is everything okay? I'm not going to prison, am I?"

"Ryan, calm down, it's got nothing to do with your case," he said calmly. "As far as I've heard you're doing really well, and I haven't heard back about the deferral yet."

"Oh, thank god," I breathed a loud and long sigh of relief.

"I just played the lawyer card, so they'd let me talk to you." He was calm and controlled but his tone was solemn.

"Very cunning," I said as my panic began to subside, "so what's actually going on then?"

"I wanted to let you know… since you've always been a good friend to Ash… that there was an incident tonight."

"An incident?" I asked, with renewed anxiety, "Is she okay?"

A note from Nikki

Thanks for reading my book! It means a lot to have your support now that this series is finally out in the real world. The Stories from the City series was a project long in the making!

It began as nothing more than a creative outlet way back in 2009, when I started to play with some characters and develop the beginnings of a plot. Instead of watching crap TV, I spent my evenings getting inside the minds of my main characters, Bobbi Granger and Jason Stone. Nope, I didn't get their names wrong, that's where our two protagonists began.

In the beginning, I was writing purely for myself - a guilty pleasure if you will - and I never dreamt that all the random scenes I was writing would become a completed book, let alone a whole series!

Over the following years, the fictional world that I had created, became an escape for me. Writing was my haven and, if I'm brutally honest, a therapy of sorts. When my world crashed down around me and real life grew more difficult to bear, I retreated further down the rabbit hole. It was me and my characters against the world. I'm not saying it was healthy, but it was my way of coping!

It was my productive rebellion. Creation amidst destruction. Love against rage. A sense of order in a world of chaos.

Soon enough, my own personal experiences infiltrated my beautiful imaginary world and, ever-so-politely, reality hijacked the entire plot and tormented my previously happy characters. I resisted it at first. My lovely story was all fairy floss and rainbows, so why would I want to upset utopia with the harshness of real life?

Then came an interesting revelation: Manure allows a garden to grow. Or in bookish terms, trauma makes characters more interesting. Pain creates strength. Struggle leads to triumph. In short, the problems that characters overcome is what makes them more, well, human.

So I embraced it. Not only in my story, but in my life. I faced the storm, I owned my shit, and I decided that I would turn my traumatic experiences into a positive.

Before long, the story had evolved into something else entirely. It had taken on a life and a personality of its own, as had my beloved main characters. They were now tarnished and weathered but so much stronger for it, and after the trials and tribulations they had overcome, neither of their names suited them anymore. Thus Ashley Granger and Nathan Stone were officially born. Also Kirsty became Kat; Ryan, well... he was still Ryan; and one story became three. It was now a series.

Stories from the City may not be (aka: isn't) perfect; it probably won't win a Pulitzer Prize; and it may never get turned into a film series but... it's mine and I couldn't be prouder.

When I look back at the original manuscripts, I can't help but be proud of how far we've all come: the books, the characters and me. We've all been riding this crazy, painful, dramatic, beautiful, lesson-filled ride together, and for that I am thankful.

About N.J. Ewing

Born and raised on the West Coast of Australia, N.J. completed a Bachelor of Arts with a double major in Communications and Media Studies at Murdoch University in 2002.

Although writing was part of her degree, she never expected to write a book (let alone three!) when she left Uni and embarked upon a marketing career. Her professional ambition led her to London for a large part of her twenties, which was where the idea for Stories from the City was born.

With the first three parts of the story now complete, N.J. is excited to get the series out into the world a decade after its inception.

With one of their best friends gone forever, the Artemis crew are no more. As they scatter to different corners of the globe, they must learn how to move forward without each other.

RITCHIE CARLTON has just moved back home to Perth to start a new life, but can he leave the past behind him? He secures a job with local entrepreneur Kane Thompson, and although Ritchie doesn't realise it, Kane is about to make all his dreams a reality.

NATHAN STONE has everything he never knew he always wanted. With his party days a thing of the past, and his previous dramas behind him, the only thing that would make life better would be to have his mum around. Would she ever be well enough to leave the hospital?

KANE THOMPSON is known as Perth's Golden Child, but his outstanding life isn't all it's cracked up to be. On the outside, things look perfect, but on the inside, he's cripplingly unhappy. Will Kane's new friendship with Ritchie pull him out of his funk?

A LONDON AFFAIR

by MONICA RITZ

This debut novel from Australian Author, Monica Ritz is just the first in a series that's set to take the romance genre by storm.

Combining romance with mystery, and some corporate espionage thrown in for good measure, this story will captivate readers of both genres.

Two jobs, two men, two lives all waiting to collide.

This world is tough, but exciting as Cari learns to live with the fact that she has become a passenger in her own life.

This is an epic roller-coaster ride of relationships and emotions, trust and betrayals, never knowing who really knows what, but Cari has to survive as there is no way out!

Genre: Fiction - Romance; Mystery; Corporate Crime

Why Would Ya?

"Why would ya?" is what you said,
That was all – messing with my head.
For you, a weekend of drinking and mate time,
For me, worrying and waiting for the tell-tale sign.

For years it's lasted, this sham we call marriage,
There's been no silver slipper or glass covered carriage.
Instead it's been tears, and beers, and rows, and sadness,
My dream of happiness and laughter are just complete madness.

Nothing I do is good enough, doesn't matter what,
Every time you drink and smoke – you are stuck in this nasty rut.
I can't do it anymore, carry on smiling,
You're breaking my heart, destroying me, I'm drained from all the crying.

Why do you hate me and treat me so bad,
The names you call me, the tone you take, believe me it hurts, and I'm so sad.
How many times do we give this a go?
Or is it now time to stop this show?

I've tried so hard to keep us together, to forgive and forget,
But my heart hurts now, it's done, too much regret.
I've begged, I've pleaded, I've cried, I've screamed,
But my being, my soul has no self-esteem.

You've lied, you've cheated, and your words are so cruel,
Yet 9 years on I'm still here, a fool.
But I've got to the end now, I'm drained and I'm broken,
I have nothing left in me because its beer, smoke and mates you have chosen.

- Anonymous

BRAND *Artisans*
AUSTRALIA

brandartisans.com.au

www.ingramcontent.com/pod-product-compliance
Lightning Source LLC
Chambersburg PA
CBHW020002120726
47903CB00004B/1101